Coming Home
and
A Good Catch

Fern Britton is the No.1 *Sunday Times* bestselling author of nine novels. Her books are cherished for their warmth, wit and wisdom, and have won Fern legions of loyal readers. Fern has been a judge for the Costa Book of the Year Award and is a supporter of the Reading Agency, promoting literacy and reading.

A hugely popular household name through iconic shows such as *This Morning* and *Fern Britton Meets…* Fern is also a much sought-after presenter and radio host. She has also turned her hand to theatre and toured with Gary Barlow and Tim Firth's *Calendar Girls*.

Fern lives with her four children in Buckinghamshire and Cornwall.

 /officialfernbritton

 @Fern_Britton

www.fern-britton.com

D0317799

By the same author:

Fern: My Story

New Beginnings
Hidden Treasures
The Holiday Home
A Seaside Affair
A Good Catch
The Postcard
Coming Home
The Newcomer
Daughters of Cornwall

Short stories

The Stolen Weekend
A Cornish Carol
The Beach Cabin
Published in one collection as

A Cornish Gift

Fern Britton

Coming Home
and
A Good Catch

HarperCollins*Publishers*

HarperCollins*Publishers*
1 London Bridge Street,
London SE1 9GF

www.harpercollins.co.uk

This edition published by HarperCollins*Publishers* 2020
1

First published by HarperCollins*Publishers* 2018, 2015

A catalogue record for this book is available from the British Library

ISBN: 978-0-00-846059-4

Set in Birka by Palimpsest Book Production Limited, Falkirk, Stirlingshire

Printed and bound in the UK by CPI Group (UK) Ltd, Croydon CR0 4YY

MIX
Paper from
responsible sources
FSC™ C007454

This book is produced from independently certified FSC™ paper
to ensure responsible forest management.

For more information visit: www.harpercollins.co.uk/green

Coming Home

PROLOGUE

Trevay, 1993

The house was still.

Her heart was hammering – she could hear it in her ears, hear her breath whistle in her nostrils.

She tried to quieten both.

In the dark of her bedroom, she strained her ears to listen for any noise in the house.

The church bell rang the half hour. Half past eleven.

She'd gone up to bed early, her mother asking her if she was feeling all right.

'Yeah. I'm fine.' She'd shrugged off the caring hand her mother had placed in the small of her back.

'If you're sure?' Her mother let her hand rest by her hip. 'Is it your period?'

She had hunched her shoulders and scowled at that. 'I'm just tired.'

'Ella and Henry had a lovely day with you on the beach,'

said her mother, bending her head to look up into her daughter's downcast eyes. 'You're doing so well.'

Sennen shrugged and turned to head for the stairs. Her father came out of the kitchen. 'Those little 'uns of yours asleep, are they?'

'She's tired, Bill,' replied her mother.

'An early night.' Her father smiled. 'Good for you.' She could feel her father's loving gaze on her back, as she ascended the stairs. She wouldn't turn around.

'Goodnight, Sennen,' chirped her mother. 'Sleep tight.'

Her parents had finally gone to bed almost an hour ago and now she picked up the heavy rucksack she'd got for her fifteenth birthday. It had been used once, on a disastrous first weekend of camping for the Duke of Edinburgh Bronze award. Even now the bone-numbing cold of one night in a tent and the penetrating rain of the twenty-mile hike the following day made her stomach clench. Back home she refused to complete any more challenges and dropped out. She used Henry as an excuse. He had just started to walk and her mother expected her to come home from school every weekend and do the things a mother should do for her child. On top of that she was expected to work hard for her exams. Why the hell would she want to learn how to read a map and cook a chicken over a campfire as well?

And then Ella came along.

Sennen had sat in the summer heat of the exam hall, six weeks from her due date, hating the kicks of her unborn child, hating being pitied by her teachers.

She rubbed a hand across her eyes and tightened the straps on the rucksack. What a model daughter she had been. Two babies by a father unknown and now she was leaving. Leaving them, her A levels, her over-indulgent liberal leftie parents who had supported her through it all – and leaving Cornwall.

She hovered on the landing outside Henry and Ella's room. She didn't go in. She knew she would never leave if she saw them, smelt them . . . She kissed her hand and placed it on their nameplates on the door. Downstairs, she tiptoed through the hall. Bertie the cat ran from under the hall table with a mew. She put her hand to her mouth to stop her startled cry then bent down to tickle him. 'Bye, Bert. Have a nice life.'

Slowly she turned the handle of the downstairs loo and edged in carefully, making sure that the rucksack didn't knock over the earthenware plant pot with its flourishing spider plant. Bert came with her and she had to nudge him out with her boot before closing the door behind him. The front door was too noisy to leave by.

The loo window always stuck a little and the trick was to give it a little thump with your palm. She held her breath, listened for any noise from upstairs. Nothing. She wound the small linen hand towel around her fist. It took three good pushes, each stronger than the last before the window swung open, noiselessly.

She threw the rucksack out first and then carefully climbed out after it.

She pushed the window shut and stood in the moonlit, tiled courtyard. In a corner was Henry's little trike and in another, Ella's beach pushchair. She had meant to take both in in case of rain, but had forgotten. She looked up to the night sky. Cloudless. It would be a dry night.

She picked her way over the sandpit, held in a wooden box that her father had made for her when she was little and now given fresh life to with a coat of scarlet paint, and made her way to the gate. The hinge creaked a little, but before it had shut itself she was already gone. Around the corner, down the lane and out to the bus stop by the harbour.

PART ONE
Adela's Only Love

1

Pendruggan, 2018

Kit Beauchamp stirred the tomato soup in front of him. 'When will your brother get here?'

Ella put her bowl down on the kitchen table and sat opposite him. 'Why? Nervous?'

Kit looked up into Ella's golden eyes. 'Should I be?'

'He'll adore you,' she reassured him. 'And if he doesn't, you'll know about it pretty quickly.'

'Oh blimey.' Kit really was nervous.

Ella loved that her boyfriend was taking this meeting seriously. Her brother was the only family she had left. His opinion counted for everything. She picked up her spoon and replied, 'Tomorrow lunchtime. He's getting the early train down from Paddington. Should be at Bodmin by about one.' Ella pushed curls the same colour as her soup behind her ears and dipped her spoon into the steaming bowl. She sipped and burnt her top lip. 'Ow.'

'Careful,' Kit said, blowing on his own spoon.

Freckles bounced across her face as she opened her mouth to fan cool air onto her burning tongue.

Kit tore at the centre of his crusty French roll and handed her some. 'It'll cool you down.' She took it gratefully.

For a couple of minutes neither spoke, quietly enjoying their simple lunch.

'I suppose,' frowned Kit, 'I don't want to make a bad impression.'

Ella giggled. 'I think Henry is the one who needs to be more worried. He can be a total arse.' She pulled Kit's hand over the table and rubbed it against her cheek. 'You'll be the brother he never had.'

Kit let his hand trail her cheek and chin. 'He's very important to you, isn't he?'

She blew on another spoonful of soup and nodded. 'We are the last of the Tallons.'

Kit wiped the final crust of bread around his bowl. 'Why do you think the solicitor wants to see you both?'

'The usual, I expect. Mum has either hidden herself so well that she doesn't want to be found, or she's dead.' Ella put her spoon down. Kit saw the lost child in the woman in front of him.

'He'll find her,' he said with a certainty he didn't feel.

'I don't know.' Ella sighed. 'Pass me your bowl.'

'I'll wash up,' he said glancing out of the window and looking at the sky. 'Fancy a walk? The dogs could do with one. Or are you too tired after all that vacuuming for your brother?'

Ella looked over at Terry and Celia who were lounging in their separate beds looking as disdainful as only Afghan hounds can.

'Well, Doggies? Fancy a walk?'

Terry managed a discreet waft of his feathery tail while

Celia sighed and raised an eyebrow. 'What a pair of lazy gits,' laughed Ella. She put her arm out to Kit as he passed on his way to the sink. 'But can it be to Trevay? I need to pick up some steak to make pasties for Henry tomorrow.'

Henry couldn't wait to get out of London. When the most recent solicitor's letter had arrived last week he had managed to wangle a decent chunk of leave in Cornwall. He wasn't too bothered about the letter. Another routine meeting. He and Ella had had so many since their grandmother had died. The problem lay with his unreliable, irresponsible mother who had left him and Ella when they were just tiny. He had been about two and Ella just over one. She'd disappeared to God knew where for God knew what whim and never come back. It had left Granny and Poppa heartbroken. Not to mention Henry, who still had vague memories of his mother. Sitting on her lap, being folded into her arms . . . *Stop it*, he told himself. *Hopefully the solicitor would tell him and Ella that his mother was lost forever, or dead. Either would be fine with him. Then at last they could sort out Granny's estate and move on with their lives.*

He returned his attention to the work on his desk. Two reports to finish, three phone calls to make and a handover to his colleague on how to deal with any issues that might arise in his absence and then – he rubbed his hands gleefully – Cornwall here he came.

Ella and Kit closed the door of Marguerite Cottage and waved at their nearest neighbour, Simon Canter, the vicar of Holy Trinity Church.

'Good afternoon,' Simon greeted them as he walked through the churchyard. 'Beautiful day. Enjoy it.'

'We will,' Ella called back.

He was right. It was a lovely day and as she waited for Kit to open up the car and load the dogs, Ella took time to absorb the moment. The Pendruggan village green with its cluster of old and new homes around it. Above her, tiny white cloud puffs floated in the bluest of skies. The smell of gorse on the wind, bringing with it the light rumble of surf on Shellsand Beach.

'Come on. Jump in,' said Kit, jangling the keys of his slightly aged car.

She climbed in. 'It's a day to be happy.'

'It's always a day to be happy for me,' he replied reversing out of the short drive.

She laughed. 'You're always so bloody happy. It's exhausting.'

'I'm a glass half-full man.'

'Don't I know it. My healthy scepticism, hoping for the best expecting the worst, balances us perfectly.' She waved and smiled as she spotted Queenie, owner of the village store and harbinger of all news, taking a quick fag break outside her shop. 'Queenie, however, is on permanent standby for disaster. Like Henry.'

Kit shoved the car into first gear and set off around the village green towards Trevay. 'So your brother's a miserable sod, then?'

'Yep. But he cheers up when he has beer inside him.'

'I'm the man for that job.'

They drove in friendly silence up the dappled lane that took them past their local, the Dolphin Pub and out to the top road headed towards Trevay.

Ella had always loved this road, even as a child living in Trevay with her brother and grandparents. She unwound the window and watched as the trees and small cottages gave way to high hedges with gateways offering tantalising vistas of the sea beyond. As the road reached its highest point the trees and farms opened to acres of green fields, with the glittering Atlantic below, crashing onto the rocks of the headland that sheltered her childhood village.

The final descent into Trevay revealed the busy harbour with its working fishing fleet tied up on the low tide. How she loved this place. How she had missed it when her old family home had been sold as a bed and breakfast business.

'Which way?' asked Kit as they got out of the car.

'Over to the headland?' Ella was opening the hatchback boot and putting Celia and Terry on their leads. 'These two can run around safely over there.'

The walk took them up the steep hill to the left of the harbour, past the Pavilions Theatre and onto the coastal path. The view from here was breathtaking. Jagged, slate-layered cliffs fell to the rolling boil of a gentle sea. Celia and Terry were unleashed and ran like cheetahs through the gold and purple of gorse and heather, forcing the shy skylarks to take to the wing and sing their beautiful song.

Kit pulled Ella towards him by the collar of her jacket and kissed her. 'Happy anniversary,' he said.

'Happy anniversary, my love.' She kissed him back. 'How many months is it now?'

'Five.'

She sighed. 'Five months. The best five months of my life.'

'And mine, sweetheart.' He kissed her nose and they walked on hand in hand. 'Fancy dinner out tonight? I mean five months is a hell of an anniversary, isn't it?'

'I've got to make the pasties for tomorrow. Henry will be disappointed if I don't.'

'Okay. How about coffee and a cake when we get back to Trevay?'

'Done.'

They walked and talked and threw Celia and Terry their balls until all four of them were ready to go back to the car.

'They'll sleep well tonight,' said Kit, shutting them in the boot.

'We all will.' Ella took off her jacket. 'I'm ready for that cake too.'

The Foc's'le was an old-fashioned teashop on the quay, two doors down from the Golden Hind pub.

'We could have a quick pint if you want?' said Ella.

'Much rather have a pot of tea.' Kit perused the slightly sticky, laminated menu. 'How about a cream tea? You need fattening up.'

'Do I?' She fluttered her eyelashes winsomely.

'Yes, indeed,' he said seriously. 'Being as lovely as you takes up many more calories than the average person. Fact. All that smiling and thinking kind thoughts is almost aerobic.'

'Well, in that case . . .' She nudged his knee under the table with her own. 'I can always do some exercise . . . at bedtime. You could join me if you wanted.'

'Oh, Miss Tallon,' he shrieked, pretending to be shocked, 'Just because you are a blazing firework of a woman with marmalade curls, you think you can do what you want with me?'

Ella giggled, 'Yes.'

'Then I am helpless, pulled by a current so strong I can't resist. Do what you will, but . . .'

She raised an eyebrow and in a deep voice said, 'Yes?'

'Be gentle with me.'

'Can I help you?' asked the middle-aged waitress with a name badge saying Sheree, who was standing over them.

Without missing a beat, Kit said, 'Two cream teas, please.'

The pasties didn't get made that night after all. When Ella came down in the morning the remnants of a chicken salad and a bottle and a half of wine were winking at her from the coffee table in the sitting room, reminding her of the evening they had spent curled up together, talking about everything and anything.

As she collected up the plates and stubs of candles she thought back to what they had talked about last night.

Ella wanted to talk about her plan to offer short painting courses for locals and holidaymakers. 'The cliffs, the harbour, the church. There's so much here for little children. We could go to the beach and find shells to paint or pebbles to paint on. That would be fun.'

'Like your granny did for you? Revisiting your childhood?'

'Oh.' Ella was anxious. 'Is that a bad thing?'

'Not at all,' Kit reassured her. 'It's lovely, and I think taking the little darlings from their parents for a couple of hours is a wonderful thing – for the parents.'

She flapped her hand and took another sip of wine. 'What about you? When are you going to get on the cliffs and paint?'

'I've got that portrait of Lindsay Cowan to finish, with her cat, dog and horse.' He rubbed his eyes. 'She's lovely, but what she sees as handsome, intelligent companions, I see as bloody pains in the arse. The cat is a toothless bag of bones, the dog stinks and growls at me and the horse farts and tries to bite me. But,' he topped up his glass, 'she pays well.'

'When you're done with her,' Ella lifted her hands and began to draw in the air, 'I want you to paint a huge canvas of a darkly rolling sea with stars twinkling and a lighthouse flashing across the waves. It'll be perfect above the fireplace.'

'One day,' he put his glass down and kissed her knee, 'that's exactly what I shall paint for you.'

Ella's hand was around his shoulders as he lay his head in her lap. The candlelight flickered warmly creating a cosy cocoon. 'This is nice,' she said sleepily.

'We won't be able to do this tomorrow. Your brother will be here and Adam will be back.'

'Oh yes.'

'And the day after, you might find out what happened to your mum.'

'Yes.'

'What do you think happened to her?

'A million things. I have spent my whole life thinking about her and why she left. Sometimes I want her to come back and other times I hope she's dead. It would be easier. I could build a picture of a mum I want. Not a phantom built from questions.'

Ella wondered if what she had said last night was true. She felt no anger towards her missing mother. Just a need to know why. She took the dirty plates and glasses from last night and stacked them into the dishwasher before putting the kettle on for a pot of morning tea. As she waited for it to boil, she tidied the rest of the sitting room, plumping cushions, opening the curtains to the early sun and picking up a chewed slipper and a rubber chicken, both toys left by Celia and Terry.

She heard both dogs yawning from their room next to the kitchen and went to let them out. Terry came out, then sat scratching like any human man under his armpits and Celia strode out as if she was wearing thigh-high boots.

14

'Good morning,' said Ella.

The Afghan hounds ignored her and, pushing through her legs towards the kitchen door, took themselves into the garden.

Leaving the back door open, knowing there were no escape routes from the garden, she took a tray of tea up to Kit.

He was propped up against his pillows, waiting for her.

'And how is the mistress of the house today?'

Ella gave a little bob of a curtsey, and as she put the tray down and went to climb into bed, the phone rang.

'Leave it,' said Kit.

Ella picked it up. 'Hello? Henry, where are you? Okay. Lovely. Can't wait to see you.' She smiled at a scowling Kit. 'And Kit can't wait, either! Bye. Love you.'

Kit watched her as she put the phone down. 'I suppose this means I'm not going to see your ankles, Ruby?'

She grinned at him. 'There's always time for ankles, m'lord.'

'Ow!' Ella squeaked, putting the hot baking tray down quickly.

Kit, coming downstairs freshly shaved and smelling delicious, popped his head into the kitchen. 'You okay?'

'The tea towel was a bit thin and I burnt myself on the pasty tin.' She ran her fingers under the cold tap. 'I'm fine.'

'They smell good,' said Kit checking his watch. 'Anything I can do?'

She looked at him over her shoulder. 'I just want you and my brother to get on well. It would mean so much to me.'

She looked so anxious, cheeks pink from cooking, hair caught up in a bun with a pencil allowing curls to escape over her ears, and her singed fingers under the tap. Kit got a clean tea towel and went to her. 'Here, let me dry your

15

hand.' He turned the tap off and gently wrapped her hand, kissing the tips of her fingers as he did so. 'Of course I'll like your brother. But will he like me?'

Ella began to laugh. 'Well, he will if you take him to the pub!'

'I think I can manage that.'

The rattle of a taxi in the drive heralded Henry's arrival.

'He's here!' Ella ran to the front door and opened it. 'Henry!' She charged out of the house and ran at him, smothering him in a hug and kisses. 'I've missed my bro.'

'Whoa, let me pay the driver,' he said, disentangling himself as best he could.

As he got his bag from the back seat and handed the driver his fare, he saw a man he assumed must be Kit. He gave him a quick scan. Thirtyish. Checked shirt and shorts. Nice tan. Looked okay.

He put his bag into his left hand and extended his right. 'You must be Kit. Henry.'

'Henry. Good to meet you.' It was Kit's turn to run a discerning assessment of Henry.

Long legs. Expensive jeans and jacket. White open-necked shirt. Flash watch. But he looked okay.

Ella looped her arms through each of the boys' and dragged them into the house. 'Welcome to Marguerite Cottage.'

Inside the hall, Henry dropped his bag on the flagstones and looked around him. 'Very nice, Ell's Bell's.'

'Come into the garden. Tea? Coffee? I could make a jug of Pimm's?'

Henry followed her through the lounge with Kit, and out through the double doors into the pretty garden. 'You have landed with your bum in butter, haven't you, Ellie? Very nice.'

'Yes, I have.' Ella replied, squeezing her shoulders to her

ears and grinning in delight. 'And I've got pasties for you. Homemade.'

'Fancy a pint?' asked Kit.

'Do I?' Henry smiled. 'With an offer like that, if Ella doesn't marry you, I will.'

Ella was mortified and dug Henry in the ribs. 'Shut up.'

'Just saying,' he said, clutching his side. 'Will the pasties keep for an hour?'

'Yes. Go on. They'll keep. I'll take your bag up to your room. You're in Kit's studio. For now.'

'I'll take it up later. It's heavy.' He opened it and hauled a bulging carrier bag out. 'Here, take this bag – it's got a huge pile of post for you. When you left me in London I didn't think you'd be falling in love and not coming back.'

Ella couldn't keep a blush from her cheeks. 'God, you are so embarrassing.'

Kit saved her. 'Neither of us expected to fall in love, but we did. I love your sister very much.'

Henry half closed his eyes and weighed up this open declaration. 'Good on you. Don't muck her about or I'll flatten you.'

'Fair enough.' Kit smiled. 'Now, how about that pint? Ella, do you want to come?"

'No thanks. You two go and get to know each other. I'll make myself a Pimm's and have a look through the post Henry's brought.'

She waved the boys off with their promise to be only an hour, or so, and took the Waitrose bag of post to the garden.

Getting a glass of Pimm's, she settled herself at the garden table and sifted through the mail.

The piles in front of her grew tediously. Catalogues. Charity requests. Bank statements. A postcard from an old school friend now living in Peru. Pension firms. Insurance firms. Funeral savings plan. And, a letter from a publisher. Months before she had written and illustrated a children's book called *Hedgerow Adventures*. She had hoped that her departed granny would guide her to a fruitful contract. She opened the envelope.

Dear Miss Tallon,
Re Hedgerow Adventures
    Thank you for your submission. Unfortunately this is not the sort of book we would publish. We will return the manuscript under separate cover,
    Yours etc . . .

She sat back and blew out a long breath of frustration.

'Granny,' she said, 'you got me excited for a moment. Ah well. C'est la vie.' She picked up her Pimm's and took a long, cool, self-commiserating mouthful.

Her phone buzzed. It was Henry.

'Hi, Henry, is everything okay?'

'Have you looked at your emails?'

'No, I've been going through the post. So much crap . . .'

'Check them now,' he said urgently.

'Okay, hang on.' She put her phone on speaker and looked at the screen. There was an email waiting to be opened. 'I've got it. It's from Granny's solicitor.'

'Open it.'

She did so and as she read it her heartbeat began to accelerate 'Oh. My. God,' she whispered. 'It can't be true.'

'It *is* true.' Henry's voice was gruff with anger.

Ella's hand was shaking as she gripped the phone. Swallowing hard to stop any tears she said, 'Our mother is alive?'

'Yes,' said Henry. 'And she wants to see us.' He was having

difficulty keeping the shock from his voice. As soon as he had read the message, relaxing with a pint on the Dolphin's oak bar and chatting to Kit, he'd excused himself and gone to the relative privacy of the pub car park to phone Ella.

He was scuffing the gravel with his shoes. 'I can't believe she's got the nerve.' He bit his lip, his face the definition of rage and pain. 'After all these years.' He pushed his free hand into his floppy fringe and pulled his hair. 'She's bloody alive. Well, I can tell you now, we are not seeing her.'

Ella sat down. 'But she's our mother.'

'Ha! She lost the right to call herself that years ago.'

'Henry, this is shock talking, we need time to think about it.'

'No, we don't. There's only one reason she'd come back. Because Granny's solicitor has told her that Granny is dead and that she is in for an inheritance. That's all there is to it.'

Ella loved her brother very much, but she didn't always agree with him. 'It must have been a shock for her to hear that. Her mother dead, her father too.'

Henry snorted and ran his hands through his floppy blond hair. 'Well, it was a bit of a shock for me too, you know, when I heard that my mum had run away. I was only two.'

'I know.' Ella looked at the garden she and Kit had started to plant. 'I can't imagine how she could leave you. She knew you. It was easier for me. I was just a baby. She didn't have time to know me. I don't have a clue what she was like . . . and that's why I'd like to see her.'

Henry sat on the wall of the pub's entrance, all the adrenalin leaving him. 'I don't know what to think. I was hoping they wouldn't find her. Or if they did, that she had died.'

'Don't say that!' Ella flopped into her squashy sofa. 'Is Kit still with you?'

'He's inside. I saw the email and came out to tell you first. He doesn't know.'

'Come home. The pair of you. Come home now.'

Ella had been hugging herself with joy just ten minutes ago. How quickly everything can change for the worse.

Ella took Henry's bag up to Kit's small studio and put it next to the single bed. It was getting on for late afternoon and through the open window a blackbird was singing in the magnolia tree. Instantly anger rose in her. How dare the bloody birds be so happy while her world was turned upside down? She shut the window with a bang, making the bird fly off. Good riddance, she thought to herself.

Downstairs she heard Kit's car pull up. She ran down and opened the front door.

Kit was looking serious, as if there had been a terrible accident and he now had the responsibility of the fallout. Which he had, she supposed.

Henry was pale and blowing out his cheeks in a childhood mannerism that always signalled upset.

'Hi,' she said softly.

Kit came to her immediately and put his arms around her. He felt the softness and sweetness of her incredible red curls then stood arm's length from her, his hands on her shoulders. 'You okay?'

She shook her head and at last felt hot tears springing to her eyes. 'Not really.'

Kit shepherded brother and sister into the kitchen and made them sit down. 'You both need a drink. Tea or alcohol?'

Ella settled for a cup of tea while Henry and Kit had large gin and tonics.

'Right,' said Kit, pulling out a chair from the table and sitting down. 'Tell me exactly what has happened.'

Ella looked at Henry. 'Do you want to tell him?' she asked.

Henry shrugged in reply and looked at his hands clenching the icy glass.

She looked at Kit. 'The solicitor has found our mother and she wants to see us.'

Kit was looking at her attentively. 'What do you think she wants after all this time?'

'Granny's money,' said Henry, flatly.

'Or,' said Kit trying to sound positive, 'she might be coming because she wants to see you two, after all she hasn't seen you for . . .'

'Almost twenty-five years.' Henry picked up his glass and drank.

Ella swallowed hard. 'The thing is, Henry has memories of her. Nice ones, I think.'

Henry grunted.

'They had had time to get to know each other. It was much more painful for him.' She looked at her brother. 'I should think.'

Henry said nothing but looked at the floor.

'Whereas I don't remember anything about her. I mean she left when I was only just over a year old,' said Ella, still watching Henry. 'That's why I want to see her.'

Henry glared at her. 'Really?'

Ella twiddled her fingers anxiously. 'I want to know what she looks like. Do we look alike? What she's been doing? Why did she leave us?' She wiped her nose as a tear ran down her cheek. 'Everything, really.'

Henry was angry. 'She's one selfish cow who doesn't deserve

to be listened to. I wouldn't be surprised if she's lied through her teeth anyway. She might not even *be* our mother. Just some strange woman who thinks she could get lucky. I wouldn't believe a word she said.'

'But, Henry, we must try. Then decide whether we want to be friends or not.'

'Friends? What are you talking about? She's a madwoman. We don't know anything about her. Correction, we know that she had two children by the time she was seventeen and she never told her own parents who the father – or fathers – were, and despite Granny and Grandad being kind and supportive to her, she ran away in the night and never looked back. What kind of person does that?'

'A sad person?' Ella said quietly. 'A person who finds them-selves in a really hard place at the start of their adult life and can't cope. People run away all the time. Every day. She was not in her right mind.'

'Why didn't she come back?' demanded Henry.

'She was scared,' Ella said. 'Once you've done something like that, maybe there is no coming back.'

Henry gave a short laugh. 'Really? Not to have any curiosity about how your children turned out? Not even to see your own parents? Who, in case you had forgotten, never recovered from the worry of what might have happened to her?'

Ella drained her cup of tea, gripped by a sudden anger at his unkindness. She scraped her chair back and took her cup to the sink. She kept her back to her brother. 'Have you no empathy?' There was a tea bag in the sink. She fished it out and put it into the food bin. 'She was just a young girl, Henry. One who had got herself in a mess and she wanted to change that.'

'By walking out and leaving her shit to be cleared up by her parents?' sneered Henry. 'Brilliant.'

Kit, who had been listening to all this quietly, now intervened. 'You two getting angry with each other isn't going to help.'

'Oh, shut up. You know nothing about it,' said Henry, waving his hand dismissively.

'I know Ella,' Kit replied calmly, 'and I agree with her. You both need to meet this woman and find out who she really is. If you don't like her after that, then fine. It's over. You can all move on.'

Ella softened and, walking to Henry's chair, put her arms around his neck and hugged him. 'Kit's right.'

Henry clasped his sister's hands and pulled her closer to him. 'It hurts . . .' He spoke quietly.

'I know,' she said.

'Was it me?' His voice caught. 'Was it my fault?'

Ella took her arms from his neck and knelt by his side. 'How could it be your fault. You were only two. It might have been my fault. I was the final straw. A second mistake.'

Henry's tears began to fall. He angrily wiped them away. 'I hate her, Ellie. I don't want to see her and I don't want you to see her either.' He took her upturned face in his hands. 'Promise me you won't see her? I couldn't bear it.'

Ella saw the pain in her brother's eyes and made her decision. 'I promise I won't see her for as long as you don't want me too. But I can't promise that I'll never want to see her.'

He nodded and let his hands drop. 'Thank you,' he answered simply.

2

Agra, India, 2018

Sennen was nervous. More than nervous. What was going on in Cornwall? Her solicitor had promised to phone as soon as he had heard back from Ella and Henry and she'd been restless all morning. She walked to the shuttered windows of her hotel room and looked down on to the bustle of the street market. She could almost feel the heat and smell the dust through the glass. It was monsoon season, and although the clouds had now cleared, the last downpour had left deep puddles on the muddy street and in the awnings of the market stalls. She watched as a young woman in a rose-pink sari stepped out into the busy road and neatly sidestepped a couple of hungry dogs who took a sniff at her shopping, a plastic bag filled with colourful vegetables and herbs. A passing tuk-tuk beeped his horn and she waved at the driver in recognition, rows of golden bangles slipping up her arm and glinting in the hot sun.

Sennen watched as the woman continued her journey until

she was no longer in view. How jealous she was of that woman.

She began pacing her hotel room once again.

What had she done?. She twisted her wedding ring and stared at the phone by the bed, willing it to ring.

The letter that had started this turmoil was next to the phone.

A letter postmarked 'Cornwall'.

Cornwall. She'd walked away a long time ago. She thought of a quote from *The Go-Between*: 'The past is a foreign country; they do things differently there.' Who wrote that? If Kafir were here he would know. Kafir . . . one of the most erudite men she knew. Not that she knew many men. Her life hadn't all been roses, and right now it was just the thorns.

She sat on the bed, closed her eyes and began her private ritual of summoning Trevay in her mind's eye and walking its narrow streets and lanes. What were the little boats in the harbour doing now? Would any of the ones she remembered still be working or were they left in the silt, their hulks rotting down to skeletons? Or perhaps they'd been dragged up to The Sheds where all boats rested, used and unused.

She could smell the seaweed and the salt.

Hear the gulls laughing.

The splash of water as children launched their crab lines into the deep harbour.

Her mother painting at her easel on the beach. Her washed-out linen shirts and faded trousers glowing in the sun.

Poppa sitting at his pottery wheel. The shiny slip of water and clay covering his hands to his elbows.

She dared, for a moment, to think about Henry but, as always, the electric nerve pain of the thought stopped her. She couldn't even summon his face now. Or Ella's. She had been a wicked woman. And now, with the letter from Cornwall, they had found her and would make her pay.

It had come like a ghost summoning her to her grave.

There were several old addresses written on the envelope as it had chased her around the globe, before finding her here, in India.

When she had read it, locked in her bathroom, away from any inquisition, the sense of fear had almost compelled her to run again.

The letter told her that her father had died some years ago, her mother three years ago. They had died intestate, had made no will, so she was the sole heir to the estate. The house had been sold for a good price when the solicitor, acting as trustee, had rightly thought the market was at its highest. That money was now in a high interest account and it was hers. She or her solicitor should come to Cornwall. All that needed to be done was to prove her identity and sign some forms. She didn't even have to come to Cornwall, she could send a solicitor as her representative.

There was nothing about her children.

It took several days before she could formulate her reply. In it she expressed a desire to meet Henry and Ella and would only return to Cornwall if they wanted to see her.

The solicitor agreed to phone her when he had their answer.

She lay on the bed and allowed memories of her childhood to fill her thoughts.

She was on the beach at Shellsand Bay. Her father, nut-brown and strongly muscled, was swinging her round and round. He was smiling. His bright blue eyes twinkling in his tanned face and his deep laugh making her giggle. 'Daddeeeee.'

'Bill, darling, she might be sick,' said her mother.

'Are you going to be sick?' he asked Sennen.

'Noooooo,' she giggled.

'Would you like to come swimming with me and Mum?'

'Yeeessssss.'

He put her down on the warm sand. 'Get your rubber ring and we'll look for the mermaids, shall we?'

Sennen ran to her mother. 'Mummy, Daddy's taking us swimming.' She'd pulled at the slender, elegant hand of her mother. 'Come on.'

Her father stood ready in his dark-blue swimming shorts.

Her mother smiled, 'Of course. Let me just sort myself out.' Adela had been painting in the small sketchbook she always carried with her, capturing the likeness of fishermen mending their nets or lobster pots piled high on the harbour or the holidaymakers napping in the sun.

'I like that,' said Bill peering over her shoulder at her water-colour of the beach scene in front of them. 'Good colours.'

Adela stood up and put her hands on her husband's bare chest. She kissed him. 'Thank you.'

He kissed her back then held her slim body in his arms. She pressed her cheek against him and smelt the warmth of his skin.

'I do love you,' she said.

'And I love you.'

Sennen bashed her mother on the back of the knees with her sand spade. 'Come! On!'

Bill and Adela laughed and, taking Sennen in a hand each, they ran to the waves, swinging her between them. She had grown up surrounded by so much love and kindness. How could she have turned her back on them?

3

Cornwall, 1972

Adela was Cornish to the heart. Her parents had been wealthy landowners from Bodmin, her father the quintessential country squire and her mother a beauty of her day. Adela had wanted for nothing. The only awkward thing being that they were none of the things she actually wanted. Money, comfort, beauty, beaus – all were hers for the taking. But it wasn't what she longed for. She dreamt of being a great artist, living a rackety bohemian life in London, preferably Pimlico, which she had heard about and liked the sound of.

When she finally told them, it had caused much consternation for her parents, who had planned a husband, Anthony, handsome and untroubled by intellect with a rather lovely medieval manor house on the banks of the Tamar.

But it was not to be. At the age of eighteen she won a place at the Slade School of Art on Gower Street, Bloomsbury.

She refused her parents' offer of a nice little flat in Baker Street and, instead, put her name down for a flat-share with any of the new, female, students she would be joining up with. She would find out who when she arrived for her first term.

Her mother, a woman with a great capacity for organisation, decided her talents would be best spent taking her only child to Truro for the day and kitting her out with a new wardrobe of fashionable dresses and accessories and, as an afterthought, paints.

Come early September her father ordered his cherished Morris 6 to be serviced, polished and refuelled and drove her up to London in what he noted was record time. Nine and a half hours. It would have been even quicker if it hadn't been for the thick fog that had rolled over Dartmoor and a puncture on the A38.

Adela had waved him off to his club, where he would spend the night before the return journey the following day, and set about her new life with enthusiasm.

Her new flat, off Marylebone High Street, was small but clean and her flatmates were fun. There was Elsie, who was Irish and smoked, and Kina, who tied her hair with bright cotton scarves and wore boy's jeans. She was from Jamaica and was the most exotic person Adela had ever met.

Together they shared everything, including Kina's fashion sense. Within days Adela's pretty dresses and gloves, were taken off their hangers and bundled into Adela's suitcase under her single bed. Now Adela hunted the jumble sales and bric-a-brac stalls for overgrown jumpers and men's shirts which she knotted at the waist and loose canvas trousers. For a brief moment she tried smoking too but she really couldn't get on with it so took, instead, to drinking halves of bitter when she met fellow students in the pub.

The first year flew by and, returning to Cornwall the

following summer, she was surprised by how much she had missed it.

Her mother wanted to know all the London gossip. She had none. Had she been to Harrods? No. At which restaurants had she dined? Again, none.

Had she met any nice boys as she would be delighted to invite them to tea? No, but if I do I shall let them know.

Why did she wear such shabby clothes? I like them.

Wouldn't she like to get her hair styled? It's fine as it is.

It was towards the end of August that Adela took herself up to the golden fields of swaying corn in order to paint the local men who were getting her father's harvest in.

Her mother had hung string bags of bread, cheese and pasties on her handlebars and in her panniers she had placed bottles of cider to give the men a snack. When Adela had arrived, the men, stripped to their vests, had cheered and stopped work to enjoy their break. She knew most of them by sight, if not by name, as they had been getting the harvest in for as many years as she could remember.

Perching on whatever they could find, the bolder amongst them asked about her new life in London. She told them about the London pubs she visited and the life-drawing classes where the models were naked.

There was one boy, wide-shouldered and sunburnt with very blue eyes and very white teeth who lay on his shirt and listened but didn't look at her or join in.

She had never seen him before.

When the snack was done and both thirsts and appetites quenched, Old John, her father's stockman, called the men back to their labours.

The new boy thanked her for the food and drink and introduced himself as Bill. His hand was rough and strong in hers as she shook it. 'Will you be here tomorrow?' he had asked. 'I'm not sure,' she replied.

He smiled as he put his cap on and picked up his pitch fork. 'Nice to meet you,' he said and strode back up the field.

'Who's that new boy helping with the harvest?' she asked her father over dinner that night.

'Aha,' smiled her father. 'No need to ask you which one. All the girls are after him.'

Adela looked at the asparagus on her plate and stabbed it. 'I was just wondering.'

Her father gave a sly look to her mother and said innocently, 'He's a good chap, actually. I know his father. Nice man but awfully worried for the boy. He doesn't want to join the family firm. He's down in St Ives, working with some pottery chap. Pity.'

Adela couldn't help but bristle. 'Pity? Because he prefers art to business?'

Her mother leant over and touched Adela's hand. 'No dear, your father is mischief-making. The boy – William, I think his name is?' She looked at her husband who nodded. 'William, is a super chap, although a bit of a leftie.'

Adela couldn't help but laugh. 'We are all a bit "leftie" now, you know.'

'We are not!' Her father banged the table.

'Well, I am,' said Adela calmly.

Her mother gasped and clutched her throat. 'Oh darling, is that why you dress like a man?'

Adela shook her head smiling. 'No, Mother, I dress like this because it's comfortable and practical and all my friends do the same.'

Her father took a mouthful of pork pie and mumbled, 'I told you we shouldn't have let her go to London.'

Her mother ignored him. 'But, Adela, dear, if you want a husband you must at least try to look pretty.'

'I'm not sure I want a husband.'

'But, dear . . .' Her mother was putting two and two together and making six. 'Do you not like men?'

Adela put her knife and fork neatly on her plate and said nothing.

'I mean,' her mother continued, 'it could be just a phase you're going through. I remember at boarding school there were girls who got quite friendly but they got over it in the end.'

'Mother, stop, you are embarrassing Father, me and yourself.'

'Your father's a farmer, he knows all about these things.' She turned to her husband. 'Don't you, dear?'

Her father finished his wine and stood up. 'I'm going to let the dogs out.'

'Mother, you are terrible,' said Adela watching her father go. 'Now let's clear the table.'

The next day, Adela went back to the fields and was pleased when William waved at her and was one of the first to get a glass of lemonade and slice of cheese. 'Hello again,' he said. 'Are you painting today?'

Adela was putting out the bread and cheese and a few apples on to a linen cloth for the lads. 'It's so lovely up here, I thought I would.'

'May I see it when you're done?'

'It depends.' She smiled. 'I hear you're a potter?'

He took an apple and rubbed it on his trousers. 'My father has been talking to yours, I suppose?'

Adela smiled wryly.

'I'm an apprentice,' said Bill, 'down in St Ives?'

'Ah, Bernard Leach country.'

'I'm impressed.' He took a chunk out of his apple. 'Nobody here seems to have heard of him.'

'I'm studying art at the Slade.'

'Yes, I heard. Your father has been talking to mine.'

Adela laughed and Bill looked at her closely. 'That explains it.'

'Explains what?'

'The way you look.'

She looked down at her crumpled linen smock and rolled up trousers, and said defiantly, 'What's wrong with the way I look?'

'Nothing.' He grinned. 'I like it. You look like the type of girl who wouldn't mind getting caught in rainstorm, or pushing a car out of a ditch.'

'Oh,' she said disconsolately.

'It's a compliment, believe me.'

'Didn't sound like one.'

She looked down at her scruffy sandals and brown, unshaved ankles. Self-consciously she tucked them under herself.

From the top of the field she heard Old John calling the lads back to work.

'Tell you what,' said Bill standing up and tossing his apple core into a hedge, 'what are you doing tonight?'

She looked at him suspiciously. 'Why?'

'I'm taking you out. I'll pick you up at seven.'

She had nothing to wear. The bed was littered with half a dozen garments which she'd had for years. Amongst which was an old dress she'd had since she was fourteen that was too short and much too tight; a pretty cotton skirt with a broken zip – and a horrible taffeta bridesmaid dress she'd had to wear for her cousin's wedding. Red faced from her bath and the putting on and taking off of so many things, she sat on the edge of the bed in despair. There was a soft knock at the door.

'It's Mother. Can I help?'

Adela sighed and flopped backwards on to the bed in despair. 'Come in.'

Her mother put her head around the door. 'I thought so. I found this. Any good?'

She was holding a Liberty-print cotton summer dress. 'I bought it ages ago. In a sale. It's too young for me. Too small, too. Try it.'

In the mirror, even Adela was pleased with her reflection. The dress was simple and hung a little loose on her but it was perfect. Her mother had brushed her hair into a neat ponytail and had attempted a little rouge and lipstick but Adela had been firm about saying no. Finally, her mother had stepped back. 'You'll do,' she said.

From downstairs they heard the bang of the old door-knocker and her father calling up the stairs, 'Prince Charming has arrived, Cinders.'

Bill had borrowed his father's car and drove Adela through the lanes and down to the pretty fishing village of Trevay. His shirtsleeved arm leaning on the open window, he chatted about this and that and gradually the knot in Adela's stomach began to loosen. As they came down the hill towards the harbour, Adela saw that the fishing boats were coming in on the tide, ready to land their catches on the quay. The sun was bouncing on the surface of the rippling sea making the light sparkle and flash.

'I love it here,' she said. 'I haven't been for ages. I could paint that sea every day.'

Bill parked the car outside the Golden Hind, picked up his jacket from the back seat and helped Adela inside.

'What will you drink?' he asked.

'Half a bitter, please.' She didn't see his amused smile as she looked around the dark and cosy bar. 'It's nice in here.'

Paying the barman, he carried his pint and her half towards the door. 'Let's take our drinks outside.'

The sun was beginning to set and the day was losing its warmth. She shivered a little as they sat on the harbour wall across form the pub and watched the fishing boats unload.

'Would you like my jacket?' he asked. 'Or I have a jumper in the car?'

'You'll need your jacket but the jumper would be lovely thank you.'

'Don't go away.' He set off for the car, Adela watching him. He was undeniably handsome, tall and muscular with an easy smile, the sort of man, she thought, one could fall in love with. She checked herself and looked back at the boat. She was only eighteen and she and Elsie and Kina had sworn to each other that they would play the field as men did, would never settle down with the first man they met. She looked over to him again. He was leaning into the car and reaching for something on the back seat. When he reappeared, he had the jumper in his hand and looked over at her with such a look that her heart jumped a little. She quickly returned her gaze to the boats, as if the unloading of their catches was of the utmost interest. She decided that, when he came back, she would be polite and cool. She would give no indication that she might find him attractive.

Adela waited a few seconds longer then glanced in his direction to see what was keeping him.

She saw at once.

Two girls were talking to him. Two *pretty* girls. One had her hand on his chest as she was talking to him, the other was pulling at his hand.

Adela's hand was shaking so much that she had to put her drink down. She looked over again. He was pointing at her and all three of them were laughing. At her? She felt her breath quicken and her cheeks redden. How could she escape?

Too late, he was coming towards her. 'Adela, meet a couple of old friends. Barbara . . .'

'Hello,' pouted Barbara, still holding Bill's hand.

'And Jill.'

'Hi,' said Jill, giving Adela a full top to toe scope.

'Bill . . .' Adela stood. 'I'm so sorry, I'm not feeling very well. I'll get the bus back.'

Bill frowned. 'Don't be silly, I'll drive you.'

'No, it's no trouble. I'll get the bus or ring my father. I don't want to spoil your evening.'

'Spoil my . . .' Bill was confused and exasperated. 'We've only just got here.'

Jill butted in. 'She'll be fine on the bus. Stay with us. We'll have a laugh.'

Adela stood fixed to the spot. Was she to be so easily shaken off?

Bill shook out his jumper and placed it around Adela's shoulders.

'Adela needs to go home and I shall take her.'

*

In the car, Adela said nothing. Her emotions were running high. She was elated that he had brushed those girls off but angry that he even knew them. Who were they? How well did he know them? Her father had said that all the girls were after him. Well, she wasn't. This would be the first and last time she would accept a date from him.

Her eyes slid over to look at him. His profile in the dark of the car was strong but his lips were tensed as he ran his hand through his hair. He felt her gaze and looked over at her. 'How are you feeling?'

'Okay.'

'Are you sure it wasn't something else?' She wondered if he was teasing her.

'Too much sun maybe,' she said.

'You don't get sun in London?' He was teasing her.

She turned to look out of her window and didn't give him the courtesy of an answer.

'I was looking forward to tonight,' he said. 'What did I do wrong?'

'Nothing.'

'Was it the girls?'

She shook her head, refusing to look at him.

'I grew up with them. They're fun.'

'Good for them.'

He slowed the car in the lane leading down to her family farm. The headlights picked out an owl on a gatepost as he brought the car to a halt and turned the engine and headlights off, then they sat without speaking. Only the gentle ticking of the engine cooling broke the silence.

'Adela,' he said gently.

'Why have we stopped?' she asked.

'I wanted a chance to talk to you. Without interruption.

We've got at least two hours before your parents will be expecting you back.' He settled in his seat, his back to the driver's door. 'What's the matter?'

'Nothing.'

'Feeling better?'

'Yes.'

'Good. So talk to me.'

'About what?'

'Tell me about who you are and what you want out of life.'

'I'm Adela Trip. I'm eighteen. I'm an artist and I want to make a living from my work. Is that enough?'

'Uh huh. Do you have a boyfriend?'

She shook her head, then dared to look into his eyes. 'Do you have a girlfriend?'

'No. Not at the moment.'

'Oh.' She smiled. 'And so who are you and what do you want to do with your life?'

'Right now I'd like a pint and some fish and chips. That was how I had planned tonight.'

'Sorry I messed it up,' she said shyly.

'I forgive you.' He was teasing again. 'Shall we start afresh?'

She bit her lip but managed a smile. 'Yes please.'

'Good.' He turned the engine on and reversed the car. 'We'll go over to Pendruggan village. There's a great pub there called the Dolphin. Proper beer, good food and quiet. Fancy it?'

From then on the evening went smoothly. Bill was an easy person to be around and Adela made him laugh with her stories of her flatmates and her tutors, two of whom were Graham Sutherland and Lucien Freud. He told her about his work with the pottery and the great Bernard Leach who was teaching him. 'He's a genius, Adela. I'd like you to come down and meet him.'

'That would be lovely.'

'Good. By the way, can you play darts? The board has just come free.'

She surprised him with her skill at darts and took a game off him straight away.

'Have you been having lessons?'

'Beginner's luck,' she laughed. 'Or maybe I've spent the last year in London learning to play in our local?'

'Right, if that's the case,' he picked up his darts, 'no more Mr Nice Guy.'

The drive back to the house was very different to either of the previous drives that evening. Now they were comfortable together, the small silences between them serene and pleasant.

At the front door, she thanked him.

'Will you be up at the harvest tomorrow?' he asked.

'It's my job to bring you all your snack, isn't it?'

'Ah yes. That'll be the reason you come up.'

'Nothing else.' She chewed her lip, hoping and fearing that he might kiss her. She tipped her head up to his and in a low voice said, 'So. See you tomorrow?'

She half-closed her eyes and waited. He hesitated, then stepped off the front step and walked backwards towards his car.

'Yes. See you tomorrow.' He opened the driver's door and bent to get in. She watched the way he folded his long legs into the seat and sat down. Being so tall, his head touched the roof. As he started the engine and the car began to pull away he leant out of the window and said, 'Did I mention how lovely you look in that dress?'

She stood for a long time, watching his taillights grow smaller until they disappeared from sight.

4

Pendruggan, 2018

Once Ella had promised not to meet their mother, Henry, Ella and Kit had a reasonably happy weekend. After a gin-fuelled sleep on the first night, Henry had quite a hangover. He lay in bed, hoping the throbbing of his head would subside enough to allow him to get up and go to the bathroom. There was a knock at his door. It was Ella carrying a mug and a foil pack of pills. She pushed the door open with her foot. 'Are you feeling as bad as Kit?'

'Worse,' he groaned.

'Gin head. Big time.' Henry was aware of his sister approaching the bed and placing the mug and tablets on the table next to him. 'There's coffee and paracetamol.'

'Thank you,' he said, waiting for a wave of nausea to pass.

'Full Cornish breakfast will fix you. I'll call you when it's ready.'

After a few minutes he managed to raise himself from the pillow and attempt the coffee. It was good. Hot and very strong. He threw the tablets into his mouth and washed them down.

There was another knock at the door. It was Kit, bleary-eyed and wearing a scruffy, short, towelling dressing gown and stubble. 'Showed the gin who's boss, didn't we?' he said, sitting on the edge of Henry's bed, his head in his hands.

'How much did we have?' murmured Henry.

'I remember opening a new bottle and then throwing it away once it was empty.'

'Oh.'

'Yeah.'

'Boys,' Ella called up the stairs, 'breakfast is served.'

A young man's powers of recuperation are not to be underestimated, and with the coffee and painkillers, plus Ella's enormous fry-up, by lunchtime they were almost functioning human beings once more.

They were sitting in the garden of Marguerite Cottage, warming themselves like cats in the drowsy sunshine. 'What shall we do this afternoon?' Ella drawled from her deckchair. 'Anyone fancy lunch out?'

'Love some,' said Kit reaching for her hand. 'Only you had better drive as I think Henry and I would never pass a breath test.'

'Pizza is what you need.' Ella gathered herself and got out of the deckchair as best she could. 'You need carbs, rehydration and some fresh air. We'll get all that in Trevay.'

'The old place looks very gentrified,' Henry remarked as he watched the little town of his childhood slide past his back-seat window.

'Would you like to see what they've done to Granny's house?' Ella asked over her shoulder.

'Sure.'

Ella pulled the car up on the corner of their old road and the three of them got out and walked up the short but steep lane to White Water. Henry stuck his head over the garden wall. 'They've kept Poppa's palm trees going,' he said.

'I know. I stayed here for a few weeks in the summer, remember? Our old courtyard for the sandpit and bikes has gone, though. They've put in a conservatory with a pond and a fountain.'

'Oh yes,' said Henry,' I can just about see. There are a couple of people having a coffee in there.'

'They'll be the B & B guests.'

'Double glazing and plantation shutters. Granny would think that *very* bourgeois,' Henry chuckled.

'Do you think so?' asked Ella, standing on tiptoes to get a view. 'I think she'd approve.'

Henry stepped back and rubbed the grit of the granite wall from his hands. 'Memories, eh?'

'Yep,' said Ella.

'I like the big window in the attic,' said Kit. 'Is that where your grandmother had her studio?'

Ella poked him in the ribs. 'You painters. All the same. Where's the best light? Can I get a tall canvas in there? Is there enough space for my paints?'

'So it *was* her studio?' asked Kit, fending off any more pokes by catching Ella's wrists.

'Yeah,' said Henry. 'Poppa had his space downstairs for his wheel and stuff, and the kiln was in the garden. That'll be long gone now.'

'Yeah, it is,' said Ella. 'Do you remember the excitement when we were allowed to open it up after a firing and find our pots?'

'Rubbish every one of them. But Poppa always told us they were great.' Henry smiled then rubbed his temples.

'I think your hangover needs feeding,' said Ella and she took Henry and Kit's hands in her own. 'Pizza time, boys.'

After a decent lunch, they went for a walk up to the headland and down to a small beach known only by locals and the odd inquisitive holidaymaker.

Henry picked up a slate pebble and sent it skimming across the smooth sea.

Ella counted the bounces. 'Six. My go now.'

They watched as Ella's stone bounced nine times before sinking beneath the water. Kit came up behind her and hugged her. 'Not fair. You've been getting practice in.'

'Poppa taught us. I think his record was twenty or something mad like that,' she said.

Henry sat on a damp rock and looked out to the horizon. 'We had some good summers here, didn't we, Ells?'

She sat next to him and put her head on his shoulder. 'Remember how good Granny was at French cricket?'

'When she wasn't painting,' said Henry. 'We've still got her painting books and sketchpads somewhere, haven't we?'

'Yeah, they're in Clapham. The loft, I think.' She tapped her brother's knee with her knuckles. 'How is Mandalay Road?'

'Nice and quiet without you.'

She gave him a pinch. 'I didn't expect to be staying here in Cornwall.' She looked over to Kit who was staring into rock pools. 'You do like him, don't you?'

'I've known him less than a day, but I've managed to spill all the family secrets and get blind drunk with him. What is there not to like?'

'He's a nice person,' she said thoughtfully. 'I really like him.'

Kit turned from the rock pools and looked up. 'My ears are burning.'

'They should be,' laughed Henry. 'Are your intentions towards my sister honourable?'

'Not altogether,' smiled Kit, walking towards them.

Henry turned to his sister. 'And is that all right with you?'

'Very,' she said, catching Kit's hand.

That evening the three of them lay sprawled around the lounge watching a movie on Netflix, full of Ella's cottage pie that she'd had ready in the fridge. Henry was on an armchair, Kit and Ella snuggled on the sofa, when they heard a key in the lock and the familiar sound of eight dog feet, tapping on the hall floor as they rushed to the door, then a voice calling, 'The bloody roads are full of idiots! Terrible road-works on the A38 and I'm absolutely starving.' A tall handsome man appeared at the door followed by two Afghan hounds that strolled in and flopped on the nearest rug. He surveyed the empty plates on the coffee table. 'Bugger. Have you already eaten?'

Kit and Ella jumped up. 'There's plenty left. I'll warm some up,' Ella said as Kit made the introductions. 'Adam, may I introduce you to Ella's brother Henry? Henry, this is my cousin, Adam. He's the landlord.'

Henry and Adam shook hands and Ella returned from the kitchen with a steaming bowl of cottage pie. 'Darling, sit down and eat while I give Celia and Terry their supper.'

'You're an angel.' He kissed Ella's hand as she passed him, taking the dogs with her.

'So,' said Adam, settling into his chair and blowing on a forkful of food, 'I've heard a lot about you, Henry. At last we are able to give you the once-over.'

'I rather thought I was here to give Kit the once-over, actually,' Henry laughed.

'And the verdict?' asked Adam, munching.

'Not bad at all.'

'We have bonded over gin and pizza,' smiled Kit. 'Anyone fancy a beer?'

Henry rubbed his chin. 'My liver is feeling a lot better, so yes please.'

'That's the spirit.' Kit went to the kitchen.

'What happened last night?' asked Adam, wiping a drop of gravy from his chin.

Henry sat back in his chair and wondered how to explain. 'I don't know if Ella has told you that we were brought up by our grandparents?'

Adam, concentrating on his food, nodded. 'Yep. Your disappearing mother has featured large over the last few months. The business of tracking her down for your grandmother's will?'

'Well, they've found her,' sighed Henry.

Adam swallowed his mouthful. 'Is that why you got hammered last night? Well, that's great.'

Henry stayed silent.

'Or is it?' asked Adam.

'Ella thinks it's great but I really want nothing to do with our mother, our grandmother's money or . . . anything.'

Kit came back with Ella, each carrying two cold bottles of beer. Celia and Terry loafed behind them.

Adam took his beer from Ella. 'Henry's just told me about your mum.'

Ella looked anxious. 'Her turning up? It's early days and quite difficult to get our heads round, isn't it, Henry.'

'Not yours.'

'Let's not start all that again,' said Kit.

Adam scooped up the last mouthful of cottage pie and put his plate down on the floor, pushing Terry's inquisitive nose out of it. 'So, Henry, you're staying here, are you?'

'If that's okay with you?'

'Oh, fine. I'm off again tomorrow, got a couple of weeks training in St Thomas's A & E. Serious trauma stuff in case of terror attacks. You can use my room.'

Ella saw Henry's puzzlement. 'Adam is a doctor, Henry. A very good one.'

'You can trust me,' laughed Adam.

Kit grabbed the television remote and unfroze the film they had been watching. 'Let's forget about all that tonight.' He picked up his beer and put his feet on Celia to tickle her tummy. 'Tonight we relax. Cheers.'

Henry left for London after breakfast the next morning. Ella had packed a pasty and a coffee flask in a cardboard and put it on the back seat of the taxi.

'That should keep you going.' She leant through the front window and kissed him. 'I love you, bro. Come back soon.'

'As soon as I can, but the office is really busy at the moment.'

'But the profit is good?' Ella raised her eyebrows, mocking him.

'Recession? What recession?' He tweaked her nose the way he knew annoyed her. 'The old Ruskies are still buying lumps of prime London real estate, lucky for me.'

Ella rubbed her nose crossly. 'Drive carefully.'

'I will, and Ella, thank you for saying you won't see that woman.'

'Mum.'

'Whatever. She can come, take the money and go. She doesn't deserve to see us.'

'It'll be okay.'

Kit came forward and leant on the car roof. 'Come and see us again soon.'

'And you look after my sister.' Henry said. 'She's had enough crap in her life. She doesn't need more.'

On the train from Bodmin, Henry's head was full of his mother. He couldn't forget the hurt that his grandparents had endured for all those years. He laid the responsibility of their unhappiness squarely at her door. What kind of mother would just piss off, dumping her children with parents who had only ever given her every helping hand they could? They had loved and supported her and she repaid them by running away without a backward glance. Not a note, not a phone call.

What a cow.

He had no desire to see her or listen to any pathetic excuses or apologies.

And who the bloody hell was his father? Was he the same man who fathered Ella?

Poor Ella. A girl needed her mum. Granny did her best, but even so . . .

On and on his thoughts went until he had exhausted his brain. Putting on his headphones he got out his laptop to watch a film he'd downloaded but he couldn't concentrate and eventually returned to looking at the world racing past his window while he brooded.

'So, do you like my brother?' Ella asked, nestling in to Kit as they walked on the beach that afternoon.

'He's got a bee in his bonnet about your mum, hasn't he?' he said, putting his arm around her.

'He remembers bits about her. Vague stuff, but I think it was nice things – and then suddenly she was gone. So, like a bereavement, he still grieves unconsciously.'

'And what about you? Do you want to see her?'

'I've promised Henry now.'

'That doesn't answer the question.'

'I'm curious.' They walked together in silence for a while before she said, 'Yes, I'd really like to see her. I'd like to know why. What happened. Who my dad is. I've always wanted to know, but Granny and Poppa had a sort of unspoken thing so that we didn't talk about her. Poppa was brokenhearted when she left and Granny bore the brunt of his grief whilst grieving herself.'

'Must have been hard for them.' Kit pulled her closer and kissed the top of her head. 'How old were you again?'

'Thirteen months. Henry was two. Not so bad for me – I have no memories, not even impressions. But Henry knew her. I mean really knew her. Had cuddles and bedtime stories and walking on the beach and playing. Somewhere in his head he must have those feelings. No wonder he's so angry.'

Henry arrived at Mandalay Road, Clapham at the same time Kit and Ella were talking. His taxi drew up, double parked, and he paid the cabbie before hauling his weekend bag over his shoulder. He stood motionless before suddenly throwing up Ella's pasty and coffee on the kerb outside his front door.

There were several letters on the mat as he pushed the door open. Bills and a catalogue. He picked them up and chucked them on the hall table, went into the kitchen to switch the kettle on before making himself a cup of tea. While the kettle was boiling he went up and dumped his bag on his bed and had a quick pee.

Downstairs, sitting on the sofa with his mug of tea, he looked around his home. Above the fireplace was one of his grandfather's paintings: a small girl with red hair sitting on the quay at Trevay with a crab line in her hand. It was unusual in that this was one of the very few canvases Poppa had painted. Poppa was the Potter – Granny was the painter.

In front of him was an Indian carved coffee table. His grandfather had brought it back from a trip to Rajasthan and Henry and Ella had always had their Friday night supper of fish and chips on it, rather than at the big kitchen table. It was their treat and marked the start of their weekends.

'Argh,' he said angrily to the empty room. 'I am *not* going to see that woman.' The sofa sagged as he leant back into it. His grandmother's again. She and Poppa had bought it when they first married and moved into Pencil House. A ridiculously tall, thin house that was one of the landmarks of Trevay. A place where visitors still stood and had photos taken of themselves. His own mother, born in that house, had grown up with this sofa, just as he and Ella had. He tried to imagine his mother as a child, sitting where he was sitting, having a bedtime story read to her. Being hugged by Granny or Poppa just as he and Ella had been. Well, she was not coming back to take this from him. Or the paintings. Or the table. Or the bloody wine glasses. They were his. His and Ella's, as was every stick of furniture or cutlery in this house.

5

Bill and Adela waited for two years before they married. Adela wanted to finish her degree and Bill wanted to make sure he had enough savings to begin married life in a home of their own.

Tucked up in the chill of Adela's Marylebone bedroom they talked of their future.

'Do you think we can afford to start a family straight away?' Adela had asked hopefully, her face pressed into the warmth of Bill's chest.

'How much do babies cost?' he had asked.

'Not much. I'll ask around the family for the essentials. I'm sure my old pram is stuck in the attic somewhere. We can use the kitchen sink as a bath and I'll feed the little mite myself so . . .'

She heard his laugh rumbling in his chest as he tightened his arm around her.

'What are you laughing at?'

'Your practicality and frugality. Most women would want brand-new everything.'

'Well, I don't. And I have a few books of Green Shield stamps that I'm sure would get us a cot.'

He kissed the top of her head. 'And where would we live? This garret of yours is fine for us but it would be a squeeze for three of us. And I don't fancy carrying the pram up and down three flights of stairs.'

'I always imagined us going back to Cornwall,' she said quietly. 'My parents have spotted a tiny place in Trevay, on the harbour.'

As she lifted her head to check his reaction to this piece of news, he saw the longing in her.

'I'm not having handouts from your parents.'

'No, no. Nor me. And I hadn't said anything to them about looking for something. Honestly.'

'Then how do they know about it?'

'My mother sent me something.' Adela shifted herself from her arms and slipped out of bed. She tiptoed across the icy lino and reached for a newspaper stuffed into her handbag and got back to the warmth of her bed as fast as she could. 'Here, look.' She turned to the properties page and handed it to him. 'There.' She pointed.

He scanned the small advert and blurry picture.

'What do you think?' she asked, tucking herself around him again.

'It's a derelict shop.'

'An old chandler's, actually.'

'But not a residential home.'

'That's why it's such a good price.'

'No indoor bathroom? No bedrooms? No kitchen and no heating? And it'll be freezing.'

'But, stuck between those two houses as it is, it will keep itself warm.'

He said nothing.

She pressed on. 'Bill, it's so pretty, and I don't mind living in a building site and I can do lots of labouring for you. Between us we could build the home we really want.'

He held her anxious gaze. 'You really like it?' he said.

She nodded, her fingers crossed under the eiderdown. 'Don't you?'

'Hmm,' he said, wanting to keep her in suspense. 'We could go down this weekend and take a look at it?'

She sat up clutching her hands to her chest. 'Could we?'

'Why not?'

To their delight, the second-class train compartment was empty. Bill put their small, shared suitcase up in the netted luggage rack while Adela opened up their packed lunch. 'It's only egg sandwiches and ginger nuts, I'm afraid,' she said, fussing over the greaseproof-wrapped packages and passing him one. 'Oh, and I've put the last of my chicken soup in the flask.'

Sitting together, watching as the smoky London scene beyond the glass began to morph into suburbia then farm-land, they munched and chatted and did the *Guardian* crossword until, leaning their heads together, they fell asleep to the rhythm of the train.

Newton Abbot, Exeter and Plymouth sped by in a drowsy haze until the guard, in a comforting West Country voice called along the corridors, 'Bodmin Parkway next stop. Next stop, Bodmin.'

As the bus rattled onto Trevay Harbour and came to a stop, Adela and Bill collected up their bits and jumped off.

'There it is,' Adela said with renewed energy, pointing at a very tall, thin building, 'I can see the estate agent waiting.'

They hurried across the road, past the Golden Hind pub and turned left into the narrow lane where the building stood, squeezed in between its neighbours.

It was at least a hundred and fifty years old. Dressed in clapboard, its white paint peeling, it carried two floors above the front door. The estate agent greeted them.

'Mr and Mrs Tallon, I presume? Tim Baynon.'

They all shook hands.

'Welcome to the Old Chandlery . . .' Mr Baynon began his spiel. 'There's been a lot of interest in the property, I can tell you.'

'Really?' asked Bill incredulous.

Adela glared at him and addressed the agent: 'I'm sure. It's absolutely gorgeous.'

Bill shot her a murderous look. And as Mr Baynon took a set of keys from his pocket and put them in the rusted lock of the warped front door, Bill pulled his wife aside and whispered, 'Don't act too keen. He'll bump the price up.'

Adela tutted, and whispered back, 'I want him to know we are serious buyers.'

She pushed past him and followed the agent, who had given the door a couple of kicks to open it, leaving a lump of damp and rotting wood on the mat, into what had been the shop.

'As you see,' Mr Baynon was all pomposity, 'all the original fixtures and fittings are still intact.'

Bill looked at the empty shelves lining the walls and the shop counter covered in dust. 'Seen better days,' he said.

'So much character,' countered Adela.

Mr Baynon continued his tour into the room behind the shop which housed an old Raeburn range and a large butler's sink. 'And beyond is the garden.' Grandly he lifted the latch of the old back door and showed them a patch of wasteland no bigger than a couple of wheelbarrows. 'Sun all day.'

Adela could see that Bill was losing interest. 'Can we see upstairs?'

A steep and narrow staircase took them up to the first floor which housed two small rooms back and front. The second floor was the same.

Adela felt certain that Bill would never agree to live here. As he and Mr Baynon chatted on the tiny landing, she walked towards the window of the uppermost front room, her heels knocking on the bare floorboards. She rubbed the dust and grime from one of the small square panes and looked out. Trevay and its harbour were laid out before her like a drawing from a child's picture book. She tried the rusty latch and after a couple of thumps with the heel of her hand it opened. Sunlight, sea air and the call of gulls flooded the room. She almost laughed at the simple joyousness of it all.

She heard footsteps behind her, followed by Bill's hand on her waist as he stood next to her.

She laid her head against his shoulder. 'Someone will make this into a lovely home,' she sighed.

'Yes, we will,' he answered.

She looked up at him, all alert. 'What?'

'I've put an offer in. My Baynon is going to let us know in a couple of days.'

She hugged him, then pulled away and pummelled him. 'You bugger! I thought you hated it.'

'Just my poker face.'

'Oh, darling.' She kissed him, then a horrible thought crossed her mind. 'You didn't offer him a stupidly low price, did you? We'll definitely lose it if you have.'

'I've offered what it's worth to us. Which is more than it's worth to anyone else.'

'I love it.' She hopped from one foot to another.

'I love it too. It's mad. It's too much work. It's totally imprac- tical. Who buys a building that's as tall and thin as a pencil?'

Adela laughed and leant on the filthy window sill to look out at the amazing view.

'That's what we'll call it. Pencil House.'

They got the keys and moved in within three weeks. The Raeburn only needed a good service and soon warmed the house through. Bill, always good with his hands, made the old shop counter into a kitchen unit, and built a sturdy kitchen table top out of the shop's shelves. Adela started upstairs. She swept, she washed and she painted everywhere and everything. Slowly, Pencil House was becoming a home.

At weekends they would take themselves off on bus rides, discovering seaside towns and hidden coves and simply immersing themselves in each other and life they were building.

It was about four months into their arrival that Adela began to feel sick in the mornings. The doctor confirmed her pregnancy and the following spring their daughter arrived.

Bill and Adela were as besotted with her as they were with themselves.

'What shall we call her?' asked Bill holding her for the first time by Adela's hospital bed.

Adela smiled. 'I would like to call her Sennen,' she said.

'Sennen?' asked Bill, puzzled. 'Why?'

She grinned. 'Remember that evening on Sennen Cove last summer?'

'Oh.' Bill remembered. 'When I . . . when we . . .'

She nodded. 'Yes, darling. Your daughter was conceived on Sennen Cove.'

A few days later Bill went to collect Adela and Sennen from the hospital. He'd bought himself an ancient red Ford Anglia for the occasion. 'Oh, Bill, it's wonderful,' exclaimed Adela when she saw it. 'Can we afford it?'

'For my wife and daughter, nothing is too much.' He opened the door for her and got her settled with Adela wrapped in her arms.'

When they got to Pencil House he told her to stay in the car while he opened up and took the bags in, then, when he was ready, he scooped Adela, who was still cradling Sennen, into his arms and carried them both over the threshold with Adela laughing and protesting until he placed her on the sofa.

'Welcome home.' He bent and kissed her. 'I am so proud of you.'

'What on earth for?'

'For making Sennen for us.'

'Well, it took both of us.'

'But you did the hard work.' He knelt by Adela's knee and lifted the shawl his mother had knitted from Sennen's face. 'Hello, my darling. We are three – and nothing and nobody will ever tear us apart.'

6

Pendruggan, 2018

At Marguerite Cottage, the day that Henry had left Pendruggan, making Ella promise not to meet their mother when or if she came back, Adam and Kit were cooking supper. Although they were cousins they were more like brothers. Adam, the elder, making suggestions as to how to dice an onion correctly and Kit arguing that the kitchen was a shared domain and if he was cooking, he'd do it his way.

Adam shrugged and started to lay the table. 'More wine, Ella? Supper will be a while.'

He poured a good slug of rosé into her glass and she excused herself. 'I'll take this into the lounge, if you don't mind?'

The boys barely looked up as they had started a ridiculous debate about whether to put chives on the new potatoes or mint.

Ella sat on the rug next to Celia and Terry and rubbed their ears. 'Don't tell Henry,' she whispered, 'but I would really like to meet my mum. I wonder what she's like? Do you think she'd like me?' Terry rolled over so that she could tickle his tummy. 'You don't have a care in the world, do you, Terry.' She turned to Celia who was in ear-tickle ecstasy, her eyes half-shut in bliss. 'Celia, you're a girl. What do you think my mum is like? Is she all bad? Selfish? Feeling guilty at what she did? Or is she funny and beautiful and clever and desperate for us to forgive her? Hmm? Do you think we could be friends? I'd like that. I really, really want to know. I want to see her. Is that too bad of me?'

In Clapham, Henry had ditched his tea and started on the wine. The anger inside him was building. If that woman was thinking of coming back and playing happy families, she had another think coming. But if she did come back, at least he would have the satisfaction of her seeing that, despite the pain and the chaos she had created, he and Ella had survived and done very well without her. Who needed her? She needed to be told some home truths. She needed to face up to the carnage, the wrecked lives of her parents, God bless them. Let her come and take the money and piss off back to wherever she'd come from. *He* didn't need her. *Ella* didn't need her. And he'd like to say that to her face. She deserved to see what she left behind and know what it's like to be rejected. He took another mouthful of wine and swilled it down as he picked up his phone and, in an impulse of fury, dialled Ella's number.

Ella stopped tickling the dogs and reached around for her phone. She checked the caller ID. 'Hi, Henry.'

'We *are* going to see her.' Henry emptied the bottle into his glass.

Ella felt her heart jump. 'Really?'

'Yes.'

'I'm so glad . . .'

'And I am going to tell her exactly what she's done. I am going to look her in the face and really tell her what I think of her.'

7

Trevay, 1995

Adela and Bill had taken the children to the beach. Adela loved her grandchildren dearly but she was exhausted looking after two little ones. They were growing up so quickly, she wished with all her heart that Sennen could see them. As the sun beat down on Shellsand Bay, Adela rested her eyes, just for a moment, listening to Henry's squeals of laughter above the crashing of the waves.

'Mama!' shouted Henry stamping his little feet in the shallow ripples of the sea. 'Mama!'

Sennen crouched as well as she could with her burgeoning pregnancy, and said, 'Smile, Henry. Smile for Mummy.' She pressed the shutter on her Kodak disposable camera just as her one-year-old son scrunched his eyes and gave her the broadest of grins. 'That'll be a good one,' she said, winding the film on.

Adela and Bill were sitting a little way up the beach, using the cliff face as a windbreak. Bill was asleep, Adela was watching her daughter and grandson.

'Darling?' She shook Bill gently. 'Darling?'

Bill woke up. 'Was I dozing?' He stretched, then put a hand to his eyes to check on Sennen and Henry. 'Are they okay?'

'I think so,' said Adela. 'She's being rather good with him today.'

'I think you're being very good with both of them.' He looked at her affectionately over the top of his Ray-Bans.

'I do worry. She's only just coping with Henry and now another baby on the way.'

'It's not quite what we were thinking of, is it?'

'No.' Adela steepled her fingers under her chin. 'Every child brings joy, we know that, but . . .' She shook her head. 'I do worry.'

'What are you worried about, Granny?'

Adela knew she'd been dreaming, but it was so real, so tangible, as she opened her eyes to see a smiling Henry standing in front of her with a crab net.

'Did I fall asleep?' She smiled at him.

'Grandad wants to take me and Ella swimming but you have to come too, to help Ella because she's not big like me.'

She reached out and stroked her grandson's soft cheeks. 'No, she's not as big as you, yet. Your swimming is coming on nicely. But you will teach Ella when she's big.'

Henry grabbed her arm and pulled her out of the nest of towels she'd created for herself against the cliffs where she and Bill always made camp.

'Quick, Granny, or Ella and Poppa will be finished before we get there.'

Henry pulled Adela down the damp and rippled sand to the water's edge where Bill was bouncing Ella's toes in and out of the shallow ripples.

'Hello, old thing.' He smiled at her. 'The water's not too bad.'

'Granny was asleep.' Henry told Bill.

'Was she snoring?' asked Bill conspiratorially.

'She was more sort of blowing air through her lips. Like Bert when he purrs.'

'Ah yes,' said Bill nodding his head as if Henry had given him the most important piece of information. 'She does that.'

Adela wasn't embarrassed. 'Well, Poppa farts when he's asleep.'

Henry burst into laughter. 'Poppa Farts! Poppa Farts!'

Ella, catching the fun and laughter, stuck her bottom out and began blowing raspberries through her teeth.

'That's quite enough, thank you,' said Bill, lifting Ella on to his shoulders. 'Who wants to find the seahorses?'

'Meeee!' shrilled Ella holding tight to her Poppa's ears.

'And meeeee!' shouted Henry running through the waves.

'And meeeee,' sang Adela as she skipped after them all, putting aside her post-dream sadness.

That night, after Adela had bathed Henry and Ella and dressed them in sweet-smelling pyjamas, Bill came upstairs to read the nightly story. Adela kissed the children and sat on the floor between their beds as Bill settled down with Enid Blyton's *The Magic Faraway Tree*. He read one chapter and then, after much pleading, read another.

'One more?' asked Henry sleepily.

'Ella is asleep. She'll be cross if we read on without her,' whispered Bill.

Adela stood up and gently tucked Ella and her teddy a little more cosily. Then she dropped a kiss on Ella's sleeping forehead. 'Night-night darling.'

Bill was settling Henry down. 'Did you read Mummy that story?' Henry asked, his bright blue eyes sharp with a need to know.

'Yes,' said Bill. 'I did.'

'Did she like Moon-Face best?' Henry settled himself more deeply into his duvet.

'Of course.'

'Good.'

'Sleep tight now. See you in the morning.' Bill ran his hands through Henry's soft hair.

'I will.'

'Night-night, Hen,' said Adela kissing his head. 'Love you.'

'Love you too.' Henry managed, before accepting sleep's kidnap.

Downstairs Adela watched as Bill mixed two gin and tonics. 'I dreamt about Sennen today. On the beach. She was being so good with Henry . . . so good.'

Bill clinked two cubes of ice into each glass and handed her one. 'But she couldn't keep it up.'

'She tried so hard, we expected too much of her.'

Bill sat in his favourite armchair and sipped his drink. 'Are you hungry?'

Adela swallowed the threatening tears no. 'No.'

'Oh, for God's sake,' he said impatiently.

A tear slipped down Adela's cheek. She raised her hand to wipe it away.

Bill shifted in his chair and after a while said, 'Cheese and biscuits? I've got some nice Yarg.'

'Okay.'

'I'll bring it in on a tray.'

'Thank you.'

He left for the kitchen.

Adela looked out onto the small courtyard beyond. On the washing line hung their swimsuits and trunks and beach towels. They'd be dry by morning if it didn't rain tonight, and another day would take her further away from her daughter.

Where was Sennen?

What was she doing?

Was she well?

Was she thinking of them?

Did she miss her children?

Adela put her hand in one of the deep pockets of her cotton, sun-bleached trousers and pulled out a handkerchief. She rubbed away the drying, salty track of her tear and wiped her nose.

It was more than five years since Sennen had gone, leaving Henry and Ella in her and Bill's care. Her heart had begun to grow a thicker tissue around the damage that had been caused, but now and again the pain caught her unawares.

Bill suffered too, although he couldn't admit it. Or perhaps, she wondered, he didn't have the words. There were no words big enough.

Friends had tried to empathise, well-meaning and kind.

Some of them had said harsh things about Sennen. Selfish. Cruel. Better off gone.

But the gravitational pull of the hole that was left drew Adela and Bill deeper until their fingers were clinging by the tips.

Bill arrived with two plates.

'Here you are.' He handed her one. Cheese, two digestive biscuits, a few slices of apple and celery. 'Enough?'

She nodded.

'So,' he said, easing himself back into his chair, 'what's the plan for tomorrow?'

'I thought I'd paint the courtyard walls with Ella. She wants a mermaid. She wants to glue some shells to it.'

'Good.' Bill carefully cut into his cheese and balanced it on his biscuit. 'Henry and I are going to work in the studio. He's getting very good on the wheel. We might try a jug tomorrow. Good practice.'

At bedtime that night, as Adela waited for the milk to boil for their Horlicks, she saw a spattering of rain on the window. She called out to Bill who was at the top of the stairs. 'I'm just going to bring Sennen's bathing costume in. It's started to rain. I'll bring the Horlicks up in a minute.'

Bill hesitated a moment on the stairs. Should he correct her? Remind her that the costume was Ella's not Sennen's? He closed his eyes and shook his head. No. He would say nothing. Remembering one of his mother's old sayings, he murmured to himself, 'Least said soonest mended, Bill. Least said.' And walked slowly to the bathroom.

8

1993: The Night Sennen Ran Away

Down the narrow lane she ran. Down to the bus shelter. It was empty. Her pulse was thumping at the base of her throat. She looked at her watch – eleven forty-five – and checked all around her again.

'Hiya,' said a voice in the shadows.

Sennen jumped. 'You scared me.'

'My dad took ages going to bed!'

Sennen shrugged. 'Are you nervous?'

'A bit.' Rosemary was Sennen's oldest school friend. She was shivering. 'A bit cold, too.'

Sennen checked to see if anyone had spotted them. The coast was clear.

'Let's do it,' she said. 'Come on.'

They walked up the hill and out of the village, leaving Trevay and its sleeping inhabitants behind.

At the top of the hill the two girls stopped and looked around. The moon was streaked across the low tide and the black silhouettes of the roofs and church spire were geometric and inky against the horizon.

Sennen blew out a long stream of breath.

'You sure you're cool about this?' asked Rosemary.

'Yeah.'

'Henry and Ella will be all right?'

'Yeah.'

The main road out of Cornwall was ahead of them. 'Listen,' said Sennen. 'Car.'

A set of headlights came into view and Sennen stuck her thumb out. 'It's now or never.'

The car slowed and stopped. 'Where are you going?' asked the lone, middle-aged woman driver.

'Plymouth, please,' said Sennen.

'Both of you?' asked the woman, clocking their appearance and their rucksacks. 'Running away?'

'No,' said Sennen, 'it's my parents. They're in France, on holiday. Our dad's been taken ill so we're catching the overnight ferry to see him. Mum said to hitch. We haven't got much money, you see.'

'Roscoff?' asked the woman.

Rosemary couldn't speak but Sennen said, 'Yeah.'

'You're lucky it was me who stopped, then,' said the woman, reaching round to unlock the door to the back seat. 'There are a lot of funny people about. Hop in.'

Sennen got into the front seat, leaving Rosemary to get in the back.

'Thank you very much,' said Sennen. 'My sister and I are ever so grateful, aren't we, Sally?'

Sennen looked around at 'Sally' with a cheeky grin. 'Aren't we?'

'Yes. V-very,' stammered Rosemary. 'Thank you.'

'Hello, Sally and . . .?' said the woman looking in her wing mirror and pulling away.

'Oh, I'm Carrie,' said Sennen with conviction. 'What are you doing out so late tonight?'

'I'm a midwife. Just delivered twins. Two little boys. Identical. I'm on my way home now.'

'That's nice,' said Sennen. 'Sally and I are twins too. Not identical though.'

The journey was remarkable only for the number of stories Sennen could weave about her bond with her twin, their father's weak heart and their mother's enormous worry about them all. Finally, the illuminated gates of the ferry terminal were in front of them.

'We'll jump out here, please,' said Sennen, feeling a fresh thrust of nerves and adrenalin.

'Sure? I can take you to the ticket office if you like?'

Sennen and Rosemary were already climbing out of the car. 'No, this is fine. We've got our tickets. Bye.' They shut the doors and waved at the woman who was doubtful about leaving them but she was tired and ready for bed and the girls seemed nice and sensible so she waved to them and headed for home.

The girls shouldered their rucksacks and headed off to the ticket office. 'Two tickets for Spain, please,' said Sennen as she delved into her bag for her wallet and passport.

'Santander return?' asked the tired man behind the glass.

'We're not sure when we're coming back,' said Rosemary, finding her courage.

'Two singles, then.' The man didn't look up as he printed out the tickets and took the cash. 'Follow the signs to the ferry. Sails in twenty-five minutes.'

The two girls spotted the signs and ran to the boat. They

clattered onto the gangway, laughing and breathless. Stepping on to the deck, Sennen dropped her rucksack and hugged Rosemary. 'We've only bloody done it! We're on our way to Spain.'

In Trevay, Ella woke and began screaming from her cot. Adela woke too. She listened. Would Sennen get up and see to her? After a couple of minutes, with Ella's crying becoming more agitated, the answer was clearly, no.

Adela didn't want Bill to be disturbed. He would stop her from helping, so she got out of bed as quietly as she could and padded onto the landing. Sennen's door was closed. Sighing with frustration and irritation at her daughter's lack of commitment to her children, she crept into the children's room.

Ella had managed to pull herself up by the cot rails, her tear-streaked face scarlet with the effort of crying.

The crying stopped when she saw her grandmother, to be replaced with shuddering gulps.

'Come on, you,' said Adela, lifting Ella into her arms. She put her hand under Ella's bottom and felt the damp creeping through her baby-gro. 'Got a wet bum, have you? Let's get you comfortable.'

Adela changed Ella's nappy and Baby-gro then walked around the small room with her granddaughter on her shoulder, cooing soft words until the precious baby rubbed her eyes and grew limp. Back in her cot with teddy close by, Adela left Ella sleeping. On her way back to her own bed she glanced at her daughter's closed door and forgave her her selfishness. What seventeen-year-old, with A levels looming, wouldn't be asleep?

*

At six fifty the next morning, Henry shook Bill awake. 'Poppa?'

'Yes?' rumbled Bill, emerging from deep sleep.

'Where's Mummy?'

Bill stretched his arms above his head. 'If she's not in her bed she's maybe downstairs.'

He turned over and put an arm around the sleeping form of Adela.

Henry shook him again. 'She's not, and Ella done poo.'

Bill lay still for a moment reluctantly allowing the realisation that he had to get up seep into his muscles. He turned round to face Henry.

'All right, old chap. Tell you what, you wake Granny and I'll make tea.'

Bill stood on the landing and glowered at Sennen's closed door. She really hadn't been pulling her weight recently. Yes, she had exams, but he and Adela were bending over backwards to help her through school while doing all they could to support her and Ella and Henry. He tucked his cotton sarong a little more tightly around his waist and headed downstairs. He would have words with Sennen later. She had to stop leaning on her mother so much.

Adela, woken by Henry, changed Ella's nappy. 'Shall we wake Mummy up now? She might give you a nice cuddle in bed.'

Henry said crossly, 'Mummy not in room.'

'Well, let's go and look for her,' said Adela smiling at both children.

'Where the bloody hell is she?' demanded Bill, having searched the house and garden.

'Shh. You'll frighten the children,' said Adela, full of fear herself. She closed the door to the lounge where Henry and Ella were watching *Bananas in Pyjamas*.

'Maybe she's gone over to Rosemary's for breakfast. Or to do revision,' she said, trying to keep the wobble from her voice.

They called Rosemary's family who told them that Sennen was not with them and that Rosemary was still asleep.

Five minutes later they called back.

Bill rang the police.

The church bells were ringing five in the afternoon when Sennen and Rosemary disembarked in Spain.

The sun still warmed the day and the girls were hungry.

They found a small pavement café and ordered coffee and eggs. Cheerfully, they raised their cups to freedom.

Adela and Bill ushered the uniformed officers into the kitchen, and offered coffee and biscuits as a way of making things appear normal. The disembodied crackle of speech from their radios was unsettling and the gleam of the badges on their hats, which now lay on the table, were alien and officious.

The officers sat on one side of the table, Bill and Adela on the other. One was broad-chested and ruddy-faced. The other reminded Adela of a vole, long-nosed with prominent teeth and sandy hair.

Adela told them all she knew since she'd last seen Sennen the night before.

Officer Vole was hovering his sharp pencil above his notebook.

'So, the last time you saw or spoke to her was when she went up to bed?

Adela squeezed the tissue in her hand. 'Yes.'

'Did she seem upset at all? Last night or in the past few days?'

'No.'

The sharp pencil scratched a note.

'Did she take any money with her?'

'Oh,' Adela looked at Bill puzzled, 'I don't know. She didn't have much.'

Bill was glad to be able to do something. 'I'll go and look.' He stood up, scraping the kitchen chair on the floor.

'I'll come too,' said the other policeman, cramming the rest of a digestive biscuit into his mouth and followed Bill out of the kitchen.

Adela swallowed the rising lump in her throat. Left alone with Vole she said, 'She's never done anything like this before.'

'A lot of youngsters do this sort of thing. They usually come home when the money runs out.'

He looked up as Bill and his colleague returned.

'Darling,' asked Bill, putting his hand on Adela's shoulder, 'do you still keep the housekeeping in your dressing-table drawer?'

'Yes?' answered Adela with fresh anxiety.

'How much?' Bill asked gently.

'Almost three hundred pounds.'

Bill sat down heavily. 'It's gone.'

Adela let her tears flow.

The broad-chested constable coughed uncomfortably. 'How was she coping with the children?' he asked, reaching for another biscuit. 'To have two kids before you're seventeen is pretty tough.'

Bill raised his voice. 'My daughter is a very good mother and, as a family, we have pulled together. My wife and I have given her every support. She loves Ella and Henry. There's no way she would abandon them.'

The police officers gave each other a sceptical glance.

The vole said, 'But she has.'

Bill felt his anger rising. 'No.'

'Can you give us the name and address of the children's father?' asked his colleague.

'No,' Bill spat.

Adela put a cool hand on his arm and said, 'We never knew who the father was. Sennen wouldn't tell us.'

'I see,' said Vole, jotting this down in his notebook. 'So it's possible there could be two different fathers?'

'Look,' said Bill, 'my daughter—' Adela looked at him sharply and he corrected himself, '*Our* daughter . . .' He took Adela's hand. 'Is missing. We want you to find her.'

The policemen left, promising to keep them in touch with any developments but repeated that most runaways turned up pretty quickly.

The next three days passed in a turmoil of worry, grief, anger and disbelief. Rosemary's parents came round and the four of them tried to think if there had been any clues to their daughters' disappearances.

Henry and Ella were fractious and naughty. More than once either Adela or Bill would raise their voices at them which only brought more tears and tantrums.

At the end of the week, the police began to take the idea that the girls may have come to harm, seriously.

Photos of Sennen and Rosemary were given to the newspapers and the local television station.

Witnesses came forward.

A psychic said she had spoken to them in the spirit world

and their bodies would be found in a disused tin mine.

A taxi driver said he'd given them a lift to a party out in Newquay until the genuine passengers came forward.

A midwife turned up at Plymouth police station to say she had given two girls answering the description, but not the names, a lift to the Plymouth Ferry Terminal. They were going to Roscoff, France to see their sick father.

A man who had been working in the ticket office that night thought he might have seen them and that they had bought two tickets to Santander, Spain.

Slowly the police put the runaways journey together and got in touch with the Spanish police.

'They'll be back before you know it,' Tracey, the family liaison officer, told Bill and Adela. 'With their tails between their legs.'

Sennen woke up cold and stiff and with a hangover. Next to her Rosemary twitched in her sleep and murmured something unintelligible. 'Hey,' said Sennen shaking her. 'What's the time?'

Rosemary turned away irritably. 'Dunno.'

Sennen gave up and crawled out of the makeshift bed in the basement apartment. She rubbed her face and gave herself a scratch. Last night the room had looked okay, but this morning she saw it for what it was. A shaft of sunshine from a narrow window illuminated the mattress on the floor and the worn blankets on top of it. She needed a pee. Stepping over her abandoned shoes she opened the bedroom door onto a corridor. She smelt coffee coming from a room at the end. '*Ola!*' a cheery female voice with a Mancunian accent called from what Sennen assumed was the kitchen.

'Hi. Which door is the loo?' asked Sennen.

'The one with Che Guevara on it,' the voice replied.

The mouldy smelling bathroom housed a shower, a loo with a wobbly seat, and a small basin with a dripping tap.

She had her pee then swilled her mouth with cold water and splashed her face. A speckled mirror told her she had a spot on her chin. 'Shit.' She gave it a squeeze, rinsed her face again, retreated and followed the smell of coffee.

'Surprised to see you up so early.' The girl was in her early twenties. She wore short dungarees, with a bright cotton scarf tied round her head. She handed Sennen a cup. 'Get this down you.'

'Thank you,' said Sennen.

'I remember my first night here,' the girl said. 'I'd got the train from Manchester to Portsmouth, then hitched a ride with a long-distance lorry driver all the way through France and Spain. Decent bloke. Had a daughter my age. Want a bread roll?' She picked up a brown paper bag and pulled out a small baguette. 'Got no marmalade or owt, though.'

Sennen took it gratefully, breaking it into small pieces, hoping she could keep them down. Her hangover was pretty fierce.

There was the sound of the bedroom door opening. Rosemary wandered out wearing a Snoopy T-shirt and tiny knickers. She sat down on a vinyl-covered stool. 'I feel shit,' she said bleakly. 'Morning.'

'Morning. Bread roll?' said her hostess brightly.

Rosemary reached for one and started eating.

'So,' said the girl putting her tanned legs on the table and sipping her coffee, 'what's the real reason you're here? Tell your Auntie Rachel.'

Rosemary looked at Sennen who was thoughtfully chewing her bread.

'Our parents chucked us out,' Sennen said.

Rachel's eyes narrowed. 'Really?'

Sennen pulled her lips down at the corners and nodded. 'Yeah. Apparently, I am a bad influence on Rosemary.'

'Well, I know you two can drink.' Rachel got up and opened a kitchen drawer. She rooted around then grabbed a brown pill bottle. 'This should help your hangovers.'

Rosemary, round-eyed, shot a frightened look at Sennen.

Rachel laughed. 'I'm not a dealer. It's aspirin.'

Twisting the lid off, Sennen downed two tablets. 'Thanks, Rachel. For last night. I don't know what we'd have done.'

'Yeah well,' Rachel shrugged, 'I know those people who were buying you drinks and you looked as if you needed rescuing, so . . .'

Sennen's hazy memories of last night were of a group of three handsome young Spaniards who'd found them wandering from the docks into the town and offered them dinner.

'They seemed nice,' said Rosemary. 'I liked them.'

'Yeah, they're okay, but you need your wits about you. Mateo is a player.'

Sennen thought back. 'Mateo in the white jeans?'

'The one and only. Not the type to take home to your mother.' Rachel sighed. 'I know from personal experience.' She retied the scarf in her hair. 'Moving on, what's next for you two? You need a job. Somewhere to live.'

Rosemary, who was feeling rather homesick and would have done anything to catch the next ferry home, looked pleadingly at Sennnen – who ignored her.

'We were thinking of bar work or chambermaiding, perhaps,' Sennen shrugged. 'Anything.'

Rachel got to her feet and put her mug in the sink. 'You can stay here for a week or two. After that you're on your own. I've got to go to work in an hour, so get dressed and I'll take you into town with me. We'll ask around.'

Rachel's apartment was underneath an old and ugly residential building which had many windows broken. As the three girls climbed the dark and smelly concrete stairs to ground level, Rachel explained that the building was due to be demolished. 'I've been here for three months now. One of the better squats I've known.' She pushed a heavy door and they found themselves on the street.

Sennen and Rosemary squinted at the sudden sharp light. Rachel found some sunglasses and perched them on her nose, sniffing. 'Gonna be hot today.'

As they walked, they passed small parks with ladies walking dogs and men sitting in the shade watching the ladies walking the dogs.

Café tables and umbrellas spilt out on to the pavement, the smell of the lunchtime tapas reminding Sennen that she could do with some breakfast.

They walked for about fifteen minutes, turned a corner, and saw the sea sparkling ahead of them with a long stretch of beach running to their left and right.

Sennen caught her breath. 'Wow.' She put her arm around Rosemary's shoulder. 'Fancy a swim?'

Rachel pulled them along. 'You can have a swim once we've found you a job.'

They walked for another mile or so, the heat building all the time. Sennen was hot and uncomfortable, Rosemary was thirsty and tired. 'Where are we going?' she bleated.

'Right here,' said Rachel.

They had stopped outside a busy café bar sitting in the shade of several trees opposite the beach.

'Come and meet my boss.' She shouted to a small man with a big belly who was working at a coffee machine. 'Ola, Tomas!'

He looked over at her and lifted his chin in greeting. He glanced at Sennen and Rosemary.

'Not more of your street urchins, Rachel?.'

'Tomas, these are friends of mine, just arrived from England. I was at school with them.'

Tomas turned away from her and shot a jet of hot steam through a pipe. 'You think I was born yesterday. You have been at school with all the girls in the UK?'

'I am very popular.' Rachel laughed, then putting her head on one side and blinking coquettishly said, 'Please, Tomas? Sennen and Rosemary just need a little tiny job.'

He gave a guttural throaty snort. 'Experience?'

Rachel nudged Sennen.

'Oh yes,' Sennen answered convincingly, 'I've worked in lots of cafés and pubs at home. I love it. Meeting so many interesting people.'

'Don't overdo it,' Tomas replied, smiling, 'I can tell bullshit when I hear it.'

'And I'm *very* good at that too,' said Sennen.

Tomas laughed. A deep laugh that wobbled his belly. 'Okay. I give you girls aprons and Rachel will show you what to do. By tonight I will see if you are good.'

It was a long day. The café was popular with tourists and locals and whatever language barrier there may have been the girls got over with sign language and a smatter of O-level Spanish.

Tomas watched them all day, shouting disapproval and orders or nodding silently.

It was gone midnight before the last customer left.

'Clear the tables and I will tell you my decision,' he told them.

At last the place was tidy, bar and glasses cleaned, chairs upturned on all the tables except one, where Tomas sat reading a newspaper.

He gestured for them to join him.

Rosemary sat down yawning. 'Tired, eh?' Tomas asked.

'Yes.'

'You work hard today. You were good with the customers.' He looked at Sennen. 'You are cheeky. Too much chat, but I think they liked you.'

Rachel clapped her hands. 'Told you they were good.'

He slid a sideways look at her. 'I tell you before, I was not born yesterday. These two have no experience. All bullshit.'

He put his newspaper on the table. 'No more lies. I will give you the job but bring me no trouble. No boyfriends, no police. Understood?'

Rosemary nodded. 'Thank you.' She looked at Sennen who was looking at Tomas's newspaper. 'Sennen,' she said. 'What do you say?'

Sennen tore her eyes from the paper. 'What?'

'We've got a job. Tomas has given us the job.'

'Oh . . . right. That's great.' She turned to Tomas. 'May I have your paper?'

In bed that night, Sennen looked at the newspaper again, at the photo of a young man in a sequined black biker jacket, swirling a magician's wand and a wolfish smile. He was here. He had told her he would be. He had laughed when she said she would follow him. She couldn't wait to surprise him. She read the article. Amongst the Spanish words she managed to translate were 'Senor A'Mayze seria en el Teatro Arriaga hasta el 30 do Septiembre.' So now she knew he was at Arriaga Theatre until 30th September. She had six days in which to surprise him.

The work at Tomas's Café was hard but as the days passed her feet got less sore and the heat more bearable. They were earning good tips and Tomas was pleased with them. On the night of 29 September, Sennen asked Tomas if she could have the next night off.

'Por qué?' he asked suspiciously.

'I have to go to the dentist.'

He laughed. 'No, you don't. You are meeting someone? A boy, perhaps? Not the dentist, anyway.'

She decided to tell – almost – the truth. 'Tomas, I want to see the magic show at the theatre in town. I have always loved magic and one of my favourite magicians from England is in the show and . . . Don't tell Rachel or Rosemary. They will laugh at me.'

Tomas looked right into her eyes. 'I smell the bullshit,' he said. 'But, I will give you one night off . . . to see the dentist . . . and then you will be back. Si?'

She flung her arms around him. 'Si, si. Gracias, Tomas.'

He peeled her off him. 'But you still have to work tonight and tomorrow.'

'Of course.' She hesitated before asking, 'May I have my wages?'

He shook his head. 'Not until the day after tomorrow.'

With no money she couldn't buy a ticket, but it didn't matter. She left work early and went back to the squat to shower and change. Looking in the small, speckled mirror she saw a slightly thinner, now-freckled, face. Her sun-lightened hair gleamed as it hung over her tanned shoulders. She looked really pretty. What a surprise he was going to get.

She walked into town, soaking up the evening sun. People were promenading, hand in hand, or sitting on the pavements under coloured umbrellas sipping cold wine or beer. A tapas bar was playing a pop song. Sennen relaxed. The music put a bounce in her step and confidence in her heart. Tonight was going to be the best night of her life.

Outside the theatre, an excited crowd was milling around, laughing and calling to each other. Sennen looked closely at the photographs of the performers hanging in the glass cases of the outer walls of the building.

There were names and faces of famous magicians from all over the world but she couldn't find Ali's. At last the crowd thinned as they went inside to find their seats and she could get a closer look. In a group photo of the cast, she saw him. Fourth from the end, next to the cabaret dancers in rhinestoned leotards with feathers in their hair and fake eyelashes. He was looking straight out to the camera, his dazzling smile lighting his face, his eyes looking right at her. She put her hand to the glass and touched him. It suddenly all seemed worth it. 'Ali. I'm here to surprise you. Not long now. I have missed you.'

She had two hours to wait. She sat in a side-street café next to the stage door and ordered a coke, her eyes glued to the theatre's exit. She could hear the band through the back wall and the applause from the audience as the last curtain call was taken.

She finished the coke and, leaving the money by the empty glass, she walked to the stage door. She was the first person there. Soon the fans would have escaped the theatre and be here, jostling with their programmes for autographs. She stood her ground as they started to arrive.

The stage door opened and a gaggle of the girl dancers appeared in leggings and warm cardigans, still with their showgirl make-up on. Their boyfriends swiftly escorted them away. Next came some men carrying musical instruments, then two glamorous women, a double act, Sennen supposed, who signed a few autographs and then . . . there he was.

Her heart missed a beat. His dark hair was even longer, hanging sexily in his eyes and tumbling over his shoulders. He beamed at the autograph hunters as they pressed forward.

She held back, wanting to freeze this moment for as long as she could. He signed a woman's ticket and, giving her pen back, looked around for the next person who wanted his attention. And saw her. At least, she thought he did. He reached for another pen, signed another programme, posed for another photograph then reached his hand out to her. She took it. 'Hello,' she said smiling at him. 'Surprise.'

He smiled back in confused recognition, then froze. He dropped her hand.

'Ali. It's me,' she said, suddenly fearful.

Another woman's hand reached to grasp his. He smiled now, but not at Sennen. He was looking at someone behind her. 'Darling,' he said.

Sennen turned. A pretty blonde with long legs was pulling him from the crowd. 'Ali, come on. I promised the babysitter we'd be back.'

Sennen stood between them. 'Ali? It's me, Sennen.'

He knew who she was. His eyes told her that. For a second he stared back at her with what, fear? Panic? The woman pushed Sennen out of the way. 'Excuse me, love. He needs to get out of here.'

Sennen fell back as Ali swept past, looking anywhere but at her.

When Rosemary and Rachel got home later that evening, Sennen was already packed.

'What are you doing?' asked Rosemary, puzzled.

'You're going back,' she said, struggling with the straps of her rucksack.

'What?' asked Rosemary.

Sennen looked at her, as though she were a halfwit. 'It's what you want isn't it?

'Well, yes, but . . . not right now. I'm sort of enjoying it now.'

Rachel, leaning against the bedroom door, held her hands up. 'I know Spanish dentists can be bad, but this is ridiculous.'

Sennen turned on her. 'It's nothing to do with a dentist, I just . . . I just want to go. Okay?'

Rachel shrugged. 'No skin off my nose. I'm going to make a cuppa if anyone's interested.'

Alone in their room, Rosemary sat on the bed and watched as Sennen gathered up her passport and make-up.

'What's happened?' she asked gently. 'Is it Henry and Ella? Are they okay? Are you missing them?'

Sennen sat down and burst into tears. 'I don't know. I just . . . It's me.'

'What's you?'

'I just want to leave here, okay?'

'Henry and Ella will be pleased to see you.'

'Stop talking about them!' Sennen rubbed her tears away ferociously.

'But you're their mum.'

'Shut up! I don't want Rachel to hear. Forget about them. I have.'

'Have you?'

Sennen dissolved into tears again. 'No,' she sobbed. 'But I want freedom. I don't want to be judged any more. I don't want my *sainted* parents looking at me in their disappointed way any more. I don't want to be woken up at all hours of the night. I want to sleep, and lie in – and be *me* again.'

'I'd love to have a baby,' said Rosemary quietly.

Sennen pulled herself together and wiped her nose. 'That's what I thought, too.'

'But I'll have their dad to help me,' said Rosemary.

'Ha,' Sennen scoffed, stuffing a pair of socks from the floor into her rucksack, 'assuming he'll want to hang around.'

'I'm sorry.' Rosemary passed Sennen a clean tissue. 'I shouldn't have said that.' She watched as Sennen rubbed the smeared mascara from her face. 'Any chance that their dad would help you?'

Sennen laughed bitterly. 'Oh no. Absolutely not.'

Through the long night Sennen and Rosemary talked. Eventually Rosemary persuaded Sennen to return to Cornwall with her in the morning. 'We'll get the earliest ferry. We'll go to your parents first and explain. I'll be with you. By tomorrow night you will be in your own bed and Ella and Henry will be so happy to have their mummy home.'

They got up and left the squat before Rachel woke up. Sennen left a note saying thank you and to tell Tomas that they were sorry, and Rosemary left half of her tip money next to it.

The sun was coming up as they walked towards the docks. The first boat from England had just come in and the cars with their shiny GB stickers were disembarking. The girls had to cross the road to the ferry terminal to buy their tickets and waited as the cars went by. A man driving an estate car full to the gunnels with luggage, two children in the back and his wife in the front, slowed to wave them over.

Rosemary lifted her hand in a wave of thanks. The wife stared at them. She nudged her husband, then lifted a newspaper from her lap. Sennen saw the photos of herself and Rosemary on the front page.

'Run!' she said sharply to Rosemary. 'Hide your face and run.'

In the terminal they dashed into the ladies loo, out of breath and panicking. 'They saw us,' gulped Sennen. 'Shit. We're in the papers.'

Rosemary went white. 'We must be in so much trouble!'

Sennen searched for her purse. 'Here.' She shoved what money she had into Rosemary's hand. 'Take it and go. I'm not coming with you.'

'But you must! You said you would,' Rosemary pleaded. 'We'll go together. It'll be okay.'

'Go and buy a ticket and get on that boat,' ordered Sennen.

'I'm not going without you,' Rosemary sobbed.

Sennen rubbed her forehead with the back of her hand. A bad headache was setting in. 'Okay, okay.'

Sennen checked around her. The building was quiet. A handful of foot passengers were waiting to buy their tickets but the cars were already embarking. Sennen could hear the metallic thump and rattle as each vehicle drove over the gang-plank into the bowels of the ship.

There were no police and nobody waving copies of British

newspapers about. 'You get your ticket. I'll just get a drink from the shop over there. Do you want anything?'

'No, I'll be fine.' Rosemary had calmed down and was looking much happier. 'See you at the ticket office.'

In the small shop Sennen went to a display of cuddly toys. She picked up a pink pony with a white fluffy tail and a green dragon with silvery wings. She stuffed them in her pockets while the lady shopkeeper had her back turned then marched to where Rosemary was waiting. She took the toys from her pocket and handed them over. 'Give these to the kids, will you? Tell them they're from me.'

Rosemary giggled. 'No, you give them to them.'

Sennen said nothing but looked at her feet.

Rosemary's face fell. 'You're not coming, are you.'

'I can't.' Sennen began walking backwards, increasing the distance between herself and her friend. 'Go. Be happy. I'm fine. Thank you.' Sennen turned and began running.

Rosemary shouted, 'Sennnen! Sennnnnneeeeeen.'

But Sennen didn't stop.

It was cold when the ferry docked in Plymouth. Rosemary stood on deck, watching the coast grow closer until she could see the red and white stripes of Smeaton's Tower sitting on the Hoe. She was shivering.

As soon as she disembarked she went to the first phone box she could see. She rang the operator and asked to reverse the charges to a number in Trevay. She heard her mother's worried voice accept the call and cried with sheer relief. She promised to stay right where she was until the police arrived to take her home.

They were kind and gentle to her, offering tea and a bacon roll in a Happy Eater, en route.

She said no, but would they please take her to Sennen's parents first, as she had a special present and a message to give them.

Adela opened the door and gave a shocked shriek. Her hand flew to her mouth, eyes wide.

'I'm so sorry, Mrs Tallon. I'm so sorry,' said Rosemary stepping forward.

'Where's Sennen?' Adela came out of the front door and looked around to see if Sennen was hiding. Ready to jump out.

'She's not here. She's not coming back.'

Henry and Ella came to the door, Bill behind them. 'Rosemary? Where's Sennen?'

Rosemary pulled the toys from her pocket. 'She gave me these to give to the children.'

'But she couldn't bring them herself?' said Bill, stiffly.

'She wants you to know she's okay,' Rosemary told him.

'Thank you,' said Bill to the police officers standing behind Rosemary. 'Please take Rosemary home.'

Rosemary held the toys out to Ella and Henry. 'These are from your mummy.'

The children came forward shyly and took them.

'What do you say?' whispered Adela automatically.

Henry said, 'Thank you. Where Mummy?'

Before Rosemary could answer, Bill took her elbow and turned her towards the gate.

'I think you'd better get home to your family. They've been worried. I'm glad you are home.'

'I'm so sorry, Mrs Tallon, I really am,' Rosemary tried to say, but she was crying with fear now. 'I tried to get her to come back.'

One of the two police officers took Rosemary's arm and led her to the car. His colleague hung back and said, 'I'm sorry we are not bringing your daughter to you this time. We will be questioning Rosemary and will tell you all we know as soon as we can.'

'Understood,' said Bill formally. 'Thank you.'

And he closed the door on them.

9

Bill was struggling to keep the anger and grief that burned in him from destroying the careful balance of the fragile reality that he and Adela had fought to create for Henry and Ella.

Adela was fussing with the children. Henry was questioning her.

'Where Mummy? She come home?'

'Not yet, darling, but she sent you these lovely toys.' She heard the front door close and watched as Bill's familiar shape walked away from the house.

'Not like dragons.' Henry bent down to Ella who was swinging her pink horse by the tail. 'You like your horsey, Ella? It from Mummy.'

Adela's tears flowed and she hurriedly looked away so that the children didn't witness them. 'Well, I think I'll get us all a nice drink. Who wants a biscuit?'

Rosemary's parents came over the next day, but their happiness at having their daughter home and their guilt that Bill and Adela didn't made the meeting uncomfortable to the point of being unbearable.

The police passed on the little information Rosemary had given them and the Santander police could only confirm that Sennen had left the area, leaving her job and her accommodation.

Adela kept a watchful eye on the effect all this was having on Henry and Ella. Ella seemed fine but Henry's sadness at his mother not being there had become an anger in him. The easy-going toddler was replaced with a child who shouted when crossed and slammed doors with fury.

Adela buried herself in caring for her grandchildren, while Bill spent more time walking by himself or immersing himself in his work.

A month or so later, Adela came home from a walk with the children and caught him searching in the cupboard under the stairs.

Stepping over the vacuum cleaner, a box of old jigsaws and all the general detritus of many households, she asked him, 'Darling, what are you up to? Can I help?'

He backed out of the awkward space, his back bent and a cobweb in his hair.

'Where are the photo albums?'

Henry charged past them and disappeared into the back of the cupboard. Ella toddled in after him and a row started immediately.

'Out, Ella. This my camp.'

Adela was glad of the interruption. She knew exactly where the photo albums were and they were not in the cupboard. She had been so agitated about Sennen running away that she'd hidden them in the loft. Some instinct told her that they would be too distressing for Bill to look through while his grief was so raw.

'Henry, can't Ella join you in there? There's plenty of room.'

'No!' Henry shouted from the darkness. Ella began a high-pitched wailing.

'Oh, for God's sake!' Bill went back into the cupboard and pulled Ella out, kicking.

'Don't kick Poppa, please.' Adela held her arms out to Ella and Bill passed her to him.

'Just like her mother. Always wanting her own way.' He was getting angrier.

Adela decided to do the right thing. 'The albums are in the attic. Behind the suitcases.'

'Well, who the bloody hell put them up there?' Adela didn't need to answer. He had already stomped off to get the step-ladder.

Left with Ella crying in her arms and Henry making monster noises from the back of the cupboard, she felt like screaming herself.

But she didn't.

She took a deep breath, coaxed Henry from his camp, and gave both children some milk in their sippy cups and fairy cakes.

Later, with the children ensconced in front of *Top Cat* on the television, she found Bill sitting on an old suitcase in the attic, going through all the photo albums. She sat with him and looked as he turned each page.

Sennen as a baby in her cot bought with Green Shield stamps.

Sennen learning to swim, rubber ring around her, Bill holding her up.

Sennen on her first day at school standing grimly next to her satchel.

Sennen looking so young and yet so tired holding a newborn Henry.

Sennen pushing the old pram. 'Is that Henry or Ella in there?' Adela asked over Bill's shoulder.

'Henry,' said Bill softly. 'Look at that mop of hair.' He turned another page.

Sennen pregnant, with Henry on her hip.

Sennen with a tiny Ella on her lap and Henry leaning in to say hello to his baby sister.

'Why are we looking at these now?' asked Adela, sensing Bill's rising anger and his deep, deep sadness.

'I wanted one more look before I burned them,' he said.

'What? No!'

'Yes. If Ella and Henry are to have a good life, a full life without this gaping hole where their mother should be, I am going to have to fill it in.'

'Bill, don't. They should know what she looked like. You already took down all the photos we had of her. Please . . . Let's just keep these in the attic. Forget about them that way.'

'She's broken my heart.' He bent his head to his chest. 'I miss her too much. I can't bear having her here, but not here, any longer.'

Adela put her arm around him and pulled his head onto her shoulder. He started to cry. More tears than she had ever seen him cry before.

'She'll be back one day, I'm sure of it,' she said softly.

But Bill built a fire in his kiln and put each album on to it and watched as they burned to ashes.

Sennen was gone.

10

Pendruggan, 2018

Ella jumped off the sofa with excitement and threw her arms around Kit. 'That was Henry on the phone. He wants to meet our mum after all.'

'Careful!' Kit balanced the two mugs of coffee in his hands. 'What changed his mind?'

Ella took the cup he offered her and got herself comfy on the sofa, her feet under her. 'I'm not sure, but he said he wanted to meet her to show her exactly what she'd missed all these years.'

Kit sipped his coffee. 'Good. I thought he'd be harsher than that.'

'Well, and to tell her to her face what he thinks of her.'

'Oh.'

Ella wasn't bothered. 'I don't care! We are going to see our mum and I won't feel like an orphan any longer.'

'Is that how you've felt?'

'Yes, now I come to think about it. All those times at school:

concerts, plays, art shows. No mum or dad like my mates.' She picked at the buttons on her cardigan. 'Granny and Poppa were amazing, but they were Granny and Poppa. Not Mum and Dad.' She stopped fiddling with the buttons and looked at Kit. 'Do you think she'll tell us who our dad is?'

'Do you want to know?'

'Yes.'

'Well, ask her.'

'I'll wait and see. Test the water. I can't just spring it on her.' She laughed. 'One parent at a time is best, don't you think?'

Henry, with a rather thick head, rang the solicitor's office the next morning. He asked to speak to the senior partner, Mr Penhaligon, an elderly man who had been his grandparents lawyer for decades.

'I'm sorry, but Mr Penhaligon is not in the office today. He hasn't been well and has handed all his clients to Miss Palmer. Would you like to speak to her?'

Henry waited while she connected him. A young, efficient female voice came on the line.

'Mr Tallon?'

'Yes, good morning. I don't know how much you know about my family history but . . .'

'Mr Penhaligon has passed me your files and I am as up to speed as I can be. I am aware your mother wishes to meet you and you are reluctant to do so?'

'Well, I was, but having thought about it, I would like to meet her. Yes.'

'Excellent. I shall let her know. Where would you like to meet? Here? In our Trevay office? Or do you have somewhere else in mind?'

'Your office would be a good neutral place I think.'

'Exactly so.'

'And my sister only lives in Pendruggan, so it'll be easy for her to get there too.'

'Good. Well, I shall phone your mother today and ask her to make her travel arrangements.'

'As soon as possible, please.' Henry chewed his lip. 'Has she far to travel?'

'I am not at liberty to tell you where she is located.'

'Oh. Is she in the UK?'

'No, she is not.'

Sennen felt sick with anxiety. Who was she doing this for? Her parents? Her children? Or was the reason more selfish? For herself?

Why would Henry and Ella want to meet her after all this time? She had proved herself to be unreliable, feckless and worthless. She paced around her simple hotel room, the whirring breeze of the ceiling fan neither doing anything to cut through the heat, nor helping her thoughts speed around more quickly. Why did she want to see them so much? To ingratiate herself? To show them that she was a decent person? The sort of person who wouldn't walk out on her two children unless she had very good reason?

And what had been her reason? Really, there was none. She couldn't cope. That was the bottom line. She couldn't cope and didn't want to cope. The truth was as basic as that.

Her mobile phone rang. She scrambled in her handbag.

'Kafir?' Her husband.

He was brief. 'Have you heard anything?'

'Not yet.' She hugged the phone to her ear, imagining the feel of his beard on her face. Softly she asked, 'How are you?'

'How do you think?' he said tersely.

She shrank into herself, hungry for his forgiveness. 'I'm sorry. I know I should have told you.'

He paused, then murmured, 'Yes, you should.'

'Please, Kafir. Please don't.' She lay flat on her hotel bed wretchedly pressing the phone ever harder to her ear, the pain of it stopping her tears. 'I know I have hurt you, but please, please don't push me away.' Her voice faltered.

Kafir was silent. She imagined him pulling at his beard the way he did when he was angry. Eventually he said, 'Go and find your English family. You have much work to do.'

'Yes.' The enormity of her mistake crushed her.

'But . . .' said Kafir.

'Yes?'

'Let me know how it goes.'

'Thank you, Kafir. That means so much . . . Kafir?'

But he was gone.

She rolled her face into the pillow and gave way to helpless tears. She had to atone for her past, face who she had been when she walked away from her parents and two helpless babies. Had the girl she had been gone? What scared her most was, that in trying to finally to face her past, she could end up destroying another family. Was she now turning her back on *them*?

The phone by her bed rang. Wiping her eyes, she picked up and croaked, 'Hello?'

'Mrs Tallon-Singh? It's Deborah Palmer. Your solicitor in Trevay?'

Sennen sat up, alert. 'Yes?'

'I have good news. I have just heard from your son and daughter – and they have both agreed to meet you here in Cornwall. When shall I say you will arrive?

11

Ella was literally singing with happiness. She couldn't sit still and bounced up the stairs to find Kit. He was in his small painting studio, working on a canvas of a grumpy cat for its besotted owner. The skylights above poured bright sunshine onto the cat's ginger pelt and whiskers.

'Very handsome,' Ella said.

He looked up, brush between his teeth, turps rag in his hands.

'Hiya,' he said, speaking like a ventriloquist. 'What do you think?'

'Lovely.' She ruffled his hair and kissed his cheek. 'Today, everything is lovely.'

Kit took the brush from his mouth. 'Is this anything to do with your mother?' he smiled.

'I'm so excited.' She squeezed him. 'Can you imagine what this is like for me? For all these years I've wondered about her. Where was she? Did she think about me? Was she dead? Was she happy? Was she in a nunnery? And now I know she'll be here. Soon. And I shall be able to see her face. Hear her voice.' She sat down on the little stool next to Kit. 'Do you think she'll like me?'

Kit pulled a face. 'Seriously? Darling, she's going to love you.'

'God, I hope so. And I hope Henry isn't too hard on her. He's so angry.'

'He'll come around.'

Ella frowned. 'He'd better. I don't want him messing this up.' She jumped up and skipped around the room. 'I am so bloody happy! And a bit scared and . . . Oh, I don't know. A bit of everything.'

'Do we know when she's coming?'

'Not yet. The solicitor is sorting it.' She stood behind Kit with her arms around his waist and began to nibble his ear.

'Are you trying to distract me?' he said.

'Yes.'

'It's working.' He closed his eyes enjoying her light kisses. 'We do have the house to ourselves,' he breathed softly.

'What are you suggesting?' she murmured, her warm breath tickling his neck.

'I was thinking . . .'

'Hmm?'

'We could take the dogs for a walk?' He twisted in his seat and took her face in both hands and kissed her. 'Or, they can wait a bit . . .'

When they finally came downstairs, Celia and Terry were waiting for them. Terry's long feathery tail wagged as excitedly as an aloof Afghan hound allows itself to get, and Celia got to her feet languidly and strolled to the back door.

Out on the cliffs the dogs pulled at their leads, eager to investigate any fresh new smells and unleash the energy in their legs. 'Off you go, then,' said Kit to them, 'and don't forget to come back.'

They took off like rockets, leaping over the gorse bushes and tamarisk, full of the sheer joy of being alive.

Ella laughed into the wind as it hit her face and blew her hair into her eyes. 'They are as happy as I feel.' She held her arms out and twirled and jumped across the soft grass path.

Kit was happy for her: she so deserved to be happy. She knew nothing about her parents or what they looked like, she might never know who her father was, but now she was on the brink of finding out who *she* really was.

A stab of anxiety made his stomach knot. There was every chance that this longed-for meeting may turn out painfully.

He caught her hand and pulled her to him. 'I'll always be there for you. You know that, don't you?'

She stopped dancing and looked at him. 'Will you really?'

He nodded.

She kissed him, and they walked along watching the waving flags of the dogs' tails as they explored every bush.

'I've been thinking,' said Kit. 'Maybe the solicitor's office would be too formal a place to meet your mother, and Marguerite Cottage a bit too emotional.'

Ella scooped her hair out of her eyes. 'In case it goes badly?'

Kit scratched his cheek and looked at his feet. 'I'm not saying it will go wrong, but maybe neutral ground?'

Ella saw the truth of what he was saying. 'But where?'

'Let's have a think. Something will come to mind.'

'We'll talk to Henry,' said Ella, 'We need to agree together.'

They began to walk on again. Ella rather solemn and thoughtful.

'I'd like to be there too,' said Kit. 'If you would like me to?'

Ella stopped again. 'Would you?'

'Of course.'

'I'd like that.'

'Good. Then I'll be there.' He pulled her close to him and she warmed her hands under his fleece. 'I want to look after you, Ella.' He kissed her nose. 'Always.' He was nervous. This wasn't exactly planned and yet it seemed the perfect moment.

'I do mean always. Ella, I know we haven't known each other long. Just a few months, really, but I love you and I wonder if we could get engaged? It would be some good news to tell your mother.'

Ella stared at him, her mouth slightly open. 'You want to marry me?'

'Yes.' He hesitated. 'If you want to marry me?'

She took a deep breath. 'Oh blimey!' She felt her heart beginning to speed up. 'This has to be the best day of my life. Yes, I'll marry you, you lovely boy. But you've got to get down on one knee.'

Kit laughed and looked around to see if they were alone on the cliff. In the distance he could see a couple coming towards them. If he was quick they wouldn't catch him. He fell to his knees and took Ella's hand. 'Ella Tallon, will you do me the honour of being my wife?'

'Let me think about it. It's all so sudden.' She grinned from ear to ear. 'Oh, all right then. YES!'

'Can I get up now?'

'Yes. I love you, I love you, I love you!' She pulled him to his feet as the two walkers got closer.

Kit hurriedly brushed the grass from his knees as the walkers arrived.

'Congratulations,' they both said. 'Couldn't help but see it all. Did she say yes?'

As Ella and Kit walked back home, Celia and Terry loping beside them, worn out after their exercise, Ella took Kit's hand. 'Can we get married in church?'

'Oh, definitely. You're not going to do me out of seeing you walk down the aisle, all eyes on you.'

'You're so soppy.'

'Soppy is my middle name.'

'Shall we keep this to ourselves for a bit?' She asked, 'Until we get used to the idea? I think, with all that's going on, this happiness might get lost.'

'Whatever you want . . . Mrs Beauchamp.'

12

Truro, 1989

Sennen had been a happy child, until she was eleven, when she was sent away to school.

'It's only Truro, and you'll be home every weekend. You'll love it,' said her mother, packing a case with starchy new shirts and scratchy skirts, every sock and vest with her name sewn inside.

Almost overnight, she hated her unusual name, hated her parents, hated all the friendly, hippy student artists who lived in her house and got to spend every day under the tuition of her mother and father while she was sent away, but most of all she hated the other girls in the new school.

They were the sort of girls who had cool, Liberal/Tory parents. The mothers wore designer outfits and make-up. Their fathers drove flash cars. Holidays were spent skiing in Klosters or sailing in Nassau. They were called Sara, Claire, Emma, Lisa.

No one was called Sennen.

'What's your name again?' asked a particularly appalling girl called Samantha, as Sennen was unpacking her case in their small dormitory.

'Sennen.'

'Why?'

'It's after the cove. Sennen cove.'

Samantha smirked. 'I think nanny took us paddling there when we were small. My little brother had diarrhoea. He shat all over the beach.'

Two other girls, the remaining roommates, were listening as they also unpacked.

Samantha turned to them. 'What are your names?'

'Katie,' one said. 'Hi.'

'Em,' said the other.

Samantha swung back to Sennen. 'This is Sennen. Sounds a bit like senna, doesn't it. I'm going to call you Senna Pod from now on.'

Sennen hid her flaming cheeks by stuffing her empty case under her bed as she'd been told. 'Why?'

'Because,' Samantha paused waiting for Katie and Em to join in with her joke, 'they give you the shits.'

There are many ways to deal with bullies. You can either stand up to them, or tell someone, or hide your pain and go off the rails.

Sennen chose the latter. If there was a wall to be climbed, a rule to be broken, or a boundary to cross, she did it. She grew a small gang of acolytes around her and by the age of fourteen was a dab hand at smuggling booze and cigarettes into her shared study. Her detentions were many but her academic marks held up. Teachers either loved her free spirit and creativity or loathed her for her insubordination and sharp wit.

Adela and Bill would always apologise when a major misdemeanour meant they were called to a meeting with the headmistress, but to them, Sennen was merely a creative soul who meant no harm. They were secretly rather proud of their bold daughter and when she came home she was a ray of sunshine.

It was the Christmas before her fifteenth birthday that Sennen got a holiday job backstage at the Pavilions Theatre in Trevay. She was to be one of two assistant floor managers for the pantomime season.

It was *Cinderella* and Buttons was to be played by the latest winner of the TV talent show, *New Talent*. He was a brilliant young magician, offsetting the corniness of his profession with a rock and roll image.

His real name was Alan Chisolm.

His stage name was Ali A'Mayze, and from the first time Sennen clapped eyes on him, she was in love . . .

During rehearsals she was given the job of being his runner. Anything he wanted she got, willingly.

On the final tech run rehearsal, there was a crisis. Alan had developed a sore throat. His singing voice was in danger. A doctor was called and, after examination diagnosed mild laryngitis. Sennen sprinted to the chemist with the given prescription and brought it back, beaming. 'Shall I take this to Mr A'Mayze's dressing room?' she asked the company manager who should have delivered it himself but was distracted by a problem on stage.

'Okay, but knock first and don't stay too long. He's got to rest his voice.'

She had never been allowed into the star dressing room before. She knocked tentatively. A whispery voice answered, 'Come in.'

He was lying on the cushioned sofa which acted as a day bed. The room was warm and he was wearing a tight T-shirt over boxer shorts. 'Is that my prescription?' he mouthed inaudibly.

'Yes.'

He beckoned her to him and took the small bag from her. 'Water?' he managed.

Sennen quickly filled a tumbler from the sink in the corner of the room and returned. 'Here you are.'

He smiled and popped one of the tablets between his wickedly sensuous lips. 'Thanks.'

She stood for a moment in case he needed anything else.

'It's okay,' he croaked. 'I'll be fine. What's your name again?'

'Sennen.'

He nodded again and held his hand out to her. She took it and he pulled her down to him, his strength sending her off balance so that she half fell onto his chest whilst banging her knee on the wood of the sofa.

'You're nice.' He smiled, then pulled her mouth down to his lips and kissed her in a way that the boys in Truro never had. Not knowing quite what the protocol here was, she kissed him back until he let her go.

'Good girl. That's the best medicine.'

She stood up and rubbed her bruised knee. Was she dismissed? He smiled and, closing his eyes, waved her out.

She left the room and closed the door gently behind her. Shit. He fancied her. Wow. She might be his girlfriend.

The rest of the day she was in a state of suspended bliss but she had no further meaningful contact with him for the next couple of days as they ran through the dress rehearsals. She jealously watched as he chatted to the dancers and cosied up to the actress playing Cinderella. Once or twice she took him a coffee as requested, but that was it. She understood that he had to concentrate on the work so she bided her time.

First night was a huge success. To a full house, the curtain rang umpteen calls. As he finally came off stage she was waiting for him in the wings. He saw her and hugged her, then picked her up off her feet and spun her round. 'I was good, wasn't I?' he panted. She could feel the sweat through his shirt.

'Yes. You were wonderful.'

He put her down. 'Didn't they love the levitation scene with the Ugly Sisters at the ball? I do it so well, even I'm amazed!' He was chuckling with the buzz of his own success.

Sennen was excited for him. 'They did,' she agreed. 'It's brilliant and you are so funny when you do it.'

'Yeah.' He grinned not so modestly and winked. 'Between you and me, I am bloody good.'

One of the Ugly Sisters, a man called Graham, walked past and pinched Ali's bum. 'You can run your magic wand over me anytime, young man.'

'I'm spoken for,' Ali grinned.

'Lucky fella,' sighed Graham, taking Ali's arm. 'Come on, love, get changed, I want the first dance at the party.'

The two men sauntered off to their dressing rooms.

The stage manager walked past her, 'Stop mooning over the boy wonder and reset for tomorrow. Two shows a day from now till mid-January, no time for slacking.'

The first-night party was in full swing by the time Sennen

arrived. She hadn't had time to change out of her working black trousers and T-shirt and was rather dusty and grimy, but she'd managed a spritz of Calvin Klein's Eternity – well, a rip-off market stall version, pinched from the wardrobe mistress – and she was good to go. Hell, this was Show Business and she was part of it.

The venue for the party was the stalls bar. She grabbed a glass of coke and wandered through the sea of people in search of Ali.

She didn't get far. Adela and Bill found her first. 'Darling, that was so much fun,' Adela said kissing her daughter's cheek. 'Did you hear Dad laughing?'

Sennen shook her head, eyes searching over Adela's shoulder. 'Can't hear much backstage.'

Her father grabbed her in a bear hug. 'So proud of you. My daughter in the theatre.'

She hugged him briefly still scanning the crowd. 'I'm only the assistant stage manager. ASM's are lowest of the low.'

'It's the oily rag that keeps the engine turning,' insisted Bill.

An elderly couple approached Bill and Adela, greeting them warmly. Sennen took advantage of the distraction and melted away.

Ali was in a dark corner at the back of the bar. He was sitting on a claret velvet banquette, on his own, with several empty glasses in front of him. 'Hi,' said Sennen shyly. 'What are you doing on your own?'

'I'm bloody annoyed.' He looked at his empty glass. 'Get me a drink, will you?'

'They won't serve me. I'm not old enough.' She sat next to him. 'Why are you annoyed?'

He stood up. 'I'll get them. What do you want?'

'Oh. Coke, please. Thank you.'

She noticed how he steadied himself against the wall as he got up and wondered how much he'd had already. 'Don't go away,' he instructed her.

'I won't.' She hugged herself. He really did like her. And she had him all to herself.

After a short queue at the bar he returned with a large gin and tonic for himself and a coke for her. He sat down heavily before raising his glass to her. 'Cheers, Sally.'

'Sennen,' she giggled.

'I knew that. Just kidding. Drink up.'

She raised her glass and sipped. It wasn't just coke. 'What's in this?' she asked.

He winked at her and put his finger to his lips. 'A little bit of what you fancy.'

'Lovely.' She smiled at him and took a big swallow, feeling a mystery warmth meander down to her tummy. 'So why are you so annoyed?'

He leant back and reached across the velvet to hold her hand. 'That stupid cow playing Cinderella keeps making passes at me and I'm just not into her. She's pissed me off.'

Sennen thrilled to this. 'Stupid cow,' she agreed.

'I like you, though.' He squeezed her hand.

'Do you?'

Adela and Bill arrived. 'There you are,' said Bill, pink from too much wine. 'Mum and I are off now. So come on and we'll get you home.'

Before Sennen could think, Ali, who had let go of Sennen's hand as if it were hot metal, said, 'Your daughter is a gem. I don't know what any of the company would do without her. A little star, she is. Would you let her stay a bit longer? I'll look after her and bring her home. You have my word.'

Adela looked at Sennen and back at Ali. He seemed nice enough and was, anyway, at least ten years older than Sennen if not more, and Sennen was a sensible girl. 'What do you say, Bill?'

'Fine, but not too late,' shrugged Bill.

'Bye, Mum. Bye, Dad.' She waved at them. Ali waved too. As soon as they were out of sight he took her hand again and kissed it. 'Fancy getting out of here? Somewhere we can talk?'

His shabby hotel was in the shabbiest back street of Trevay. His room was up three flights of crooked stairs and had a sloping floor so that she felt she was walking up hill to the bed. The room was decorated with thoughtless design, the carpet brown with beige swirls, the curtains pink and unlined, hanging limply from the plastic rail, the sagging bed covered with a threadbare lilac-coloured candlewick spread. Sennen, feeling warm and relaxed from whatever had been in her coke, flopped down on to the bed and laughed. 'I thought my dormitory at school was bad.'

He was rustling about in his suitcase and produced a bottle of vodka with a flourish. 'Ta-da! And for my next trick I shall magic up a couple of plastic toothmugs from the bathroom.'

'I like vodka,' said Sennen, seriously. 'One of my mates smuggles it in to school. Her dad likes the good stuff, buys a case at a time. He never notices a bottle missing.'

Ali came back with the mugs and poured some vodka into each. He rolled a spliff and lit it, then bounced onto the bed next to her. 'Ever smoked a joint?'

'Yes,' she lied.

'Good girl.' Lying back on the bed he took a lungful then passed it to her.

She took a small puff. 'Nice.' She smiled at him and passed it back.

He put it to his lips and inhaled slowly. She watched as he held the breath deeply and then let the smoke curl slowly from his nose and lips. 'That and the Bacardi I put in your coke will relax you nicely,' he said.

She did feel pretty good, now he mentioned it. She took another sip of her vodka.

He propped himself up on one elbow and looked down on her. 'So . . . Sally, Susie, whoever you are.'

Sennen giggled. 'Sennen.'

'Sennen. Do you know how attractive you are?'

'Er, no,' she giggled again.

'Well, you are.' He leant over and kissed her. She responded warmly.

'Hang on,' he said, 'I just need to get something. You can never be too sure, can you?'

'I suppose you can't,' she said, not getting his meaning.

'Let me just nip to the bathroom. I need a slash anyway.'

Sennen put her drink on the bedside table and stretched her arms above her head. He obviously really fancied her and she liked the way he kissed. She ran the fingers of her right hand over her lips, then reached for her glass again and drank it all down.

She waited for him.

Five minutes later he still hadn't appeared.

'Ali?' she called quietly. 'You okay in there?'

Getting no answer, she got off the bed and knocked on the cheap plywood door. 'Ali?'

She heard something like a snore. 'Ali?'

She turned the handle and the door opened.

He was sitting on the loo, trousers round his ankles, head resting on the wall next to him. 'Ali! Wake up.'

She put her arm around him and got him to stand up. 'I must have had a little too much of my voddy friend,' he slurred.

'Come on. I need to get you on the bed.'

Sennen managed to shuffle him – difficult with his trousers round his ankles – to the bed and get him lying down, albeit at an uncomfortable angle. She took his trousers off, trying hard not to look at his nudity.

'Ali? I'm going to go home now. I'll have to walk. Don't worry, I'll be all right.' She picked up her small canvas bag and tied her trainers. 'Thank you for a lovely night.' She bent down and kissed him, but he was dead to the world. 'See you tomorrow then. Bye.'

Downstairs, behind the studded leatherette reception, sat the night porter. He stared at her. 'All right?'

She blushed and stammered, 'Yes, thank you.' She pushed the glass front door open and stepped outside. A wind was whipping up from the harbour and racing up the narrow street. She felt the rawness of it stinging her cheeks and nose and pulled her duffle coat closer.

As she walked the quiet, deserted road and turned the corner at the bottom heading for home, she saw the first snowflakes of winter falling from the inky sky. She stuck her tongue out and caught one. This must be the perfect end to the most romantic night of her life, she thought.

The next morning the snow was slush but she was up early, energised, ready for work and brimming with the excitement of seeing Ali again. The daily matinees were scheduled for

2.30 and the evening shows were at 7.00. She got all her jobs done swiftly: fresh water in the wings, props laid out, stage checked, costumes distributed to the dressing rooms, coffee and tea ready in the green room. Ali and all the cast were expected to be in the theatre by 1.55. At 1.45 she positioned herself artlessly in the stage doorkeeper's office, to make sure she was the first person he saw when he came in.

Everyone had arrived with a couple of minutes to spare, except Ali.

The company manager, doing his rounds, was not amused.

'Mr A'Mayze will be getting a warning unless he's here in five minutes,' he huffed, checking his watch. 'Let me know the moment he's here. In the meantime, I'd better get the understudy ready. And you'd better tell everyone that all the magic stuff will be cut this afternoon.'

Ali strolled in with ten minutes to go, black sunglasses on, the fringes on the sleeves of his black leather jacket swinging.

'Where have you been? You've got ten minutes,' whispered Sennen as she dragged him to his dressing room. 'You're in trouble.'

He stopped dead in the middle of the narrow corridor and pulled his arm from her grip. 'I'm the star of the show. It won't start without me.'

Sennen wrung her hands, her stomach churning. 'Please, please get ready or your understudy will be on.'

Ali pushed his shoulders back and his sunglasses into his hair like an Alice band. His eyes were bloodshot and had dark circles beneath. 'We'll see about that.' And he strode off to his dressing room.

Somehow, he did get ready, leaving the audience to wait fifteen minutes. When he finally bounded on to the stage, shouting, 'Hello, boys and girls, mums and dads, my name's

Buttons. What's yours?' he got a huge round of excitable applause, mostly from the mums.

Between shows Sennen fetched him a sandwich from the café next door and a large, strong black coffee. He barely acknowledged her. 'How's your throat?' she asked, leaving a KitKat on his dressing table.

'Sore.' He made great show of swallowing with painful effort.

'You don't look very well,' she ventured.

'I'm fine. Bit of a headache, that's all.'

She went to the door. 'See you later?'

'Maybe.'

'If you need me, just call.'

After the second show, as she was making her way to his dressing room, she saw him with an older woman in a fur coat heading for the stage door. If he saw her, he didn't acknowledge her.

'Who was that with Ali?' she asked the stage doorkeeper, trying to keep her voice light and disinterested.

'His agent, I think.' He looked astutely at Sennen. 'Don't you go falling for him. He's nothing but trouble. I caught him trying to corner our Cinderella last night. Poor girl, he was like an octopus. All over her.'

Sennen was outraged. 'Actually, it was she who was after him. He's not interested in her.'

'Really? Too old for him, I expect. He likes 'em young. So don't you go near him.'

Her walk home was cold in more ways than one. The stars were clear and bright and the cold wind nipped her fingers and nose but there was no snow and no Ali by her side. She went over what had happened the night before. He had told her he liked her, he'd invited her back to his room and been sweet. He was working so hard – no wonder he'd fallen asleep. She was glad she'd been there to get him safely into bed. She would have to be very supportive of Ali. He was carrying the success of the show and he wasn't feeling well. She wouldn't put him under any pressure. She would simply be there for him and help him in any way she could.

All theatres shut their doors on Christmas Day. Actors and crew either spend the day with their loved ones or sleep the clock round. Sennen was tired. She had worked hard looking after her own job, as well as Ali, and it hadn't gone unnoticed. The company manager, her boss, had praised her and suggested that if she wanted a career in stage management he would be happy to employ her. She dreamt of working with Ali always.

Her mother woke her on Christmas morning with a cup of tea. 'Happy Christmas, darling.'

Sennen turned over without opening her eyes. 'I'm tired.'

'It's ten o'clock.'

'So?'

'It's Christmas morning and Father Christmas has been.'

'Let me sleep.'

'Just another ten minutes. Don't let your tea go cold. We are all waiting downstairs to open the presents.'

'I'll be down later.'

'Your tea is right there.'

'Mum! Go. Away.'

Time ran like quicksilver. Christmas came and went; New Year was celebrated and Sennen became a slave to Ali. He mostly ignored her, but threw her the odd crumb of a compliment which she savoured and took home to replay in her endless fantasies. Finally, in the middle of January, the panto run was up.

Sennen always stood in the wings to watch Ali's audience participation scene before the finale. She absorbed every joke, every glance, every move.

Ali would pick three children from the audience and bring them up onto the stage. Kneeling down to their height he would ask them silly questions and make eggs appear from behind their ears and pound coins from under their tongues.

When they were finished, she was the person who handed over a marvellous and always huge teddy bear as a prize so that every child in the audience was instantly jealous.

When the children had been safely delivered back to their proud parents, Ali would shout, 'Ladies and gentlemen, boys and girls, Cinderella, my best friend, is marrying Prince Charming and we are all invited to the wedding! See you in a minute!'

Running off stage his dresser would wrench off his costume and speedily Velcro him into his sparkly wedding outfit.

Sennen always had a small towel ready for him to mop the sweat running from his scalp. Usually he took it from her without a word, but that night, the last night of the run, he said, 'In my dressing room there are some gifts. They're labelled. Bung them round to the right people, would you?' He winked as he said it and gave her hand a squeeze then ran back on stage for the wedding finale and curtain calls.

She dashed to his room and found a pile of seven identically shaped parcels. She read the labels. One each for the principal members of the cast and one for her. She held it in her hands and pressed it against her chest. He had thought of her. Now he was acknowledging their relationship. She

opened the parcel. A book. *Ali A'Mayze's Simple Magic Tricks.*
It sold in the foyer for £4.99.

She felt a little let down.

She flicked through the pages back to front and then saw
his handwriting on the first page. He had dedicated it to her.

> *Dear Sally,*
> *Thanks, Doll,*
> *Ali A'Mayze*

And he'd drawn a little heart with a magic wand waving
above it.

The dressing-room door opened and he walked in. 'Jesus,
that was something. God, they couldn't get enough of me.
Eight curtain calls. Love it. Get me a drink, would you?' He
sat down at his dressing table and looked at himself in the
mirror, checking his hair and teeth.

'What would you like?' she asked.

'There's some champagne in the fridge.' He pointed to the
small fridge by the daybed. 'Pour yourself one, doll.'

'Thank you.' She smiled. She knew he really *did* remember
her name. 'And thank you for my book.'

He was creaming the make-up from his face. 'They'll be
worth a lot of money when I'm in Vegas.'

She went to the fridge and found the champagne, already
open, and poured it into two tumblers. 'Why did you write
Sally inside it?'

'Did I?' He took the tumbler from her. 'Just a little joke.
You are my mystery girlfriend, aren't you?' He patted his
knees, inviting her to sit on them. She did and immediately
thought back to when her father used to do the same.

'This is nice,' he said, jiggling his knees up and down to

make her giggle. 'Drink your champagne up and we can have another.'

He was so gentle as he stared into her eyes. Whispering loving words as his hand crept up inside her T-shirt and gently stroked her breast. His kisses were lingering, soft but passionate. He carried her to the daybed and took off her jeans and knickers before caressing her stomach and inner thighs. He was still dressed in his costume. The lace and taffeta of his knickerbockers scratched against her thighs as he told her how much he loved her.

When he had finished, he rolled off her and patted her arm. 'Well, that was very nice.'

Sennen's head was swimming with a mix of happiness and alarm. She understood what had just happened and she was proud of it. She had lost her virginity. To a man. Not a boy. A man who had told her he loved her.

He got up and kicked off what remained of his costume. 'Right, I'm off to the party.' He saw the undelivered presents. 'Haven't you done those yet? Hurry up.'

She didn't make the party. Being part of the backstage crew she had to pack props and costumes into the huge wicker travelling skips and load them onto the pantechnicon that had reversed into the scene dock ready to take it all back into store for next year. By the time she had done everything and made a final check that every dressing room was empty and the stage clear, it was almost 3 a.m.

When she got to the stalls bar, it was dark. She saw the shadows of empty glasses and beer bottles and could smell the thickness of tobacco'd air, but there was not a soul to be seen.

She called out, 'Ali?' She ran to the silent auditorium. 'Ali?' she called again. She heard footsteps on the stage and turned quickly in relief. 'Ali! I'm here. I thought you had gone.'

He was holding a torch and she couldn't see him behind it.

'Come on, whoever you are,' a gruff voice said. 'You got no home to go to?'

It was the stage doorkeeper on his rounds. He shone the light on her face. 'Is that young Sennen? If you're looking for young fella-me-lad, he's long gone. Come on, let me see you off the premises.

13

It was three weeks short of her fifteenth birthday, when she had already missed two periods and was regularly sick after breakfast, that Adela, who had hovered on the landing listening at the loo door, asked her if she was bulimic.

'Darling, I know that there is a lot of peer pressure to be slim nowadays, but you are lovely just the way you are.'

Sennen scowled and pushed past her mother to get to the sanctuary of her room. As she went to shut the door behind her, Adela put her hand out stopped her. 'Sennen, I'm worried for you. Don't shut me out. Would you like to see the doctor?'

Sennen flounced to her bed and fell face first into the pillow. 'No,' she mumbled.

'Darling, talk to me.' Adela sat on the bed and stroked Sennen's hair. She was feeling out of her depth. She tried again. 'You can tell me anything.'

She waited patiently for an answer, then shook her daughter's shoulder. 'Tell me. Please. Is it school? I know you didn't like it at first, but it's okay now, isn't it?'

She felt Sennen breathe deeply, then expel the air loudly. 'I'm pregnant,' she mumbled.

'What?' asked Adela gently. 'I couldn't hear you.'

'I'm pregnant.'

If asked, Sennen wouldn't have been able to say what she thought would happen next, but what she hadn't expected was the calm acceptance of her parents and their incredible support.

The doctor confirmed the pregnancy and then offered her solutions. A termination, an adoption, or keep the child. When he said this, in the clinical serenity of his consulting room, Adela and Bill were sitting either side of her. They said nothing, allowing Sennen to make her decision. Eventually she murmured, 'I want the baby.'

Adela beamed and clasped Sennen's hand. 'Good,' she said.

The doctor watched her over the frames of his half-moon glasses and asked the question her parents hadn't felt able to ask. 'And the father? Will he have any part in the baby's life?'

Sennen shook her head.

'May I ask who the father is?'

Again, Sennen shook her head.

'I see. Does he know that he has a child on the way?'

Bill gripped Sennen's hand tightly.

'No,' she said.

The doctor looked down at her notes on his desk and thought for a moment. 'You are very young. Your life will never be the same again.'

'She has us,' said Adela firmly.

The doctor frowned. 'That is true, but Sennen is a minor and the boy who did this to her was breaking the law.' He looked at Sennen and in a serious voice asked, 'Tell me, were you forced into having sex? Or did you know what you were doing? And did you do it willingly?'

Sennen closed her eyes and thought of that night and how Ali had made her feel. She nodded.

'You weren't forced into doing something you didn't want to do?'

She shook her head.

'Are you still seeing the boy?'

She shook her head again.

'Because if you are, I shall prescribe you some contraception. You do know what that is, don't you.'

'Of course she does,' Bill said. 'She won't be needing it.'

'Well, then.' The doctor sat straight and clasped his hands. 'I will write to your school and explain your circumstances. There is no need for you to give up your studies – indeed, your child will need a mother who is well-educated. Look after yourself: no smoking or drinking, be kind to your parents and I'll see you in four weeks.'

Henry Alan William Tallon was born at the end of September, 1991, with both his grandparents in attendance.

It was decided that Sennen would stay at her school in Truro to finish her exams and come home at weekends to be with Henry. In the meantime, Adela and Bill would care for him.

Back at school she was ostracised. Girls whispered about her as she walked the corridors or queued for lunch. Even her small coterie of daredevil friends shrank from her. No one asked her, and she told no one about Ali.

Thinking back, she realised that this was the time when she had begun to feel something that made her more than different. Of course she was different; which other of her friends had a baby? But a new and dangerous pit of teenage melancholy opened up in front of her. Who was she? She was neither child or parent. Her own parents had taken control with ease and efficiency. Henry was more theirs than hers. All her waking thoughts and sleeping dreams were filled with the desperate anxiety of trying to find Ali. If only she could contact him, he would come and sort all this mess out. He loved her. He had told her so, hadn't he? She longed to confide in Adela. To tell her about Ali. To have her help her find him. But she didn't know where to begin. And she had an uncomfortable suspicion that they would turn against him. They would accuse him of . . . well, she wasn't quite sure. He had not taken advantage of her. That was a fact. She had wanted him. But why hadn't he tried to contact her?

As soon as she knew about the baby she had asked for the address of his London agent from the Pavilions Theatre and written to him, asking if he could phone her as she had some news. After a few weeks she received a letter from his agent's secretary, thanking her for 'her interest' and enclosing an unsigned cheesy postcard photo of him.

When Henry was born, she wrote again, and this time received a leaflet with the dates of the *Ali A'Mayze On The Road* tour. She scoured the schedule and her heart sang when she saw that, for one Sunday night in November only, he was coming to the Pavilions.

She planned how she would tell him about Henry. He would be so happy. He would hold her and promise to take care of her. He would be so sorry that he hadn't been there for her, but now, everything would be all right.

She took fresh interest in Henry and whispered her secret

to him when she bathed him or took him for walks on the harbour.

Adela and Bill noticed how much happier she was. 'She's doing so well, isn't she?' said Adela, watching from the kitchen window as Sennen showed Henry the late butterflies on the buddleia.

Bill slipped his arm around Adela's shoulder. 'She is. And so are you.'

Sennen counted the days to seeing Ali again. She'd asked at the theatre if they needed any backstage help for the show. They didn't, but she could work front of house as an usherette.

At last the day arrived. The dress code was black trousers or skirt with a white blouse. She had a stretchy mini skirt that was a little too tight over her baby tum and borrowed a white shirt from her mother. She bought some sheer black tights and wore her old knee-high black leather boots. By the time she'd wound her hair into a bun and put on a little eye make-up and lip gloss, she looked very presentable.

'My word, you do look smart,' said Bill when she came into the sitting room. 'I'm very proud of you. Not many girls with a baby and exams would want to go out and earn a little money. Very proud indeed.'

'Thanks, Dad. Would you give me a lift down?'

'Yep. Let me just find my keys.' He wandered off into the hall.

Her mother came in from the kitchen with Henry on her hip. 'Let's have look at you.'

Henry blinked and burped.

Adela patted his padded bottom. 'Very high praise for your mummy indeed, Henry. Now say goodnight to her and say "See you later, Mummy".'

Sennen kissed them both, told them she loved them, and with a happy, hammering heart, left the house.

Standing at the back of the stalls as the house lights dimmed, leaving just a single spotlight on the crimson velvet curtains, Sennen's breathing was shallow and ragged with anticipation.

Prerecorded rock music blasted through the auditorium and a deep, slow voice announced 'Ladies and Gentlemen, you are about to witness incredible things. Things that will shock you, and fill you with awe. Tonight is a night you will speak of in hushed tones as your children, grandchildren and great-grandchildren beg you to tell them the story. The story of the night you witnessed real magic.' The audience gasped and giggled as the single spotlight snapped out and they were left in a silent blackness . 'Ladies and gentlemen, for one night only I give you: Mr Ali A'Mayze.' The voice dragged out the last syllables as a deafening peal of church bells rang through the audience. From the roof above them a spotlight revealed a coffin, lowering itself towards the stage.

Sennen had her heart in her mouth. Any moment now she'd see him.

The coffin stopped about a metre from the stage floor and floated free of any wires that she could see. A female undertaker walked slowly from the wings to the spotlit box. She drew a glinting silver sword from a scabbard beneath her cloak and proceeded to wave it all over the box to prove it was merely hanging there in space. A curdled scream came from the back of the stalls and made Sennen jump out of her skin. She and the entire audience turned to see what it was and, in that split second, the coffin crashed to the ground and from it leapt a powerful scarlet motorbike with Ali sitting astride it, revving the engine.

Sennen couldn't breathe. The audience began to cheer and applaud. Ali spun the back wheel until smoke poured from it. The crowd were in the palm of his hand. His eyes, outlined in black, stared at them until they felt he was looking into their souls. Sennen shivered with anticipation. He smiled, baring his teeth and in a white flash both he and the machine were gone.

Another gasp.

A man in an overcoat and cloth cap got out of his seat and ran down to the stage shouting, 'Where is he? Where is he?'

The audience didn't know who he was.

The man ran to the spot where the bike had been. He stopped, bent down and examined it. His back to the audience. Then slowly he took off his cap and then his coat and spun round with his arms wide open. 'You didn't think I'd leave you without a show, did you?'

It was him. Ali.

Sennen clutched her hands to her chest and yelled his name and was drowned out by eight hundred people doing the same.

She stood in a dream as she watched the show. This was the father of her baby. Her future. She couldn't wait to see him and tell him about Henry.

The show finished. She stood at the back of the stalls until the place had emptied, then made her way backstage and headed for the star dressing room. Her hands were shaking as she knocked on the door.

'Who is it?' asked a male voice. Not Ali's.

'Sennen.'

The door opened a crack and a small round man looked her up and down. 'Mr A'Mayze is not having visitors.'

'Who is it, Keith?' Ali's disembodied voice asked.

Keith curled his lip and said to Sennen, 'What's your name?'

'Sennen. I worked with Ali in the pantomime. Last Christmas.'

Keith relayed the message. Ali answered.

'Yeah? Okay, let her in.'

Keith opened the door wide and there he was. Naked but for his jeans, his long curls damp with sweat, his eyes looking her up and down. 'Yes?'

'Hi. You were great tonight. Truly. I can't believe you are actually here.'

He narrowed his eyes and looked at her more closely. 'I know you . . .'

'Yes,' she smiled.

'Sally? Susie?'

She laughed at his old joke. 'Sennen.'

'Of course.' He stood up. 'I'm fine now, Keith. I'll meet you back at the hotel.'

Keith was put out and his bottom lip jutted sullenly. 'I haven't sorted your laundry yet.'

'Out. Now. Sennen's an old friend of mine.' Ali looked at Sennen and gave her the kind of smile that made her whole body flush.

Keith was not happy and took his time, gathering up his coat and felt beret. 'Don't be late,' he said as he left the room.

'Want a drink, gorgeous?' Ali asked as soon as he'd left. 'I've got some wine in the fridge. Sit down.'

She sat on the same daybed where he had made love to her almost a year ago. He watched as her mini skirt slid up her thighs. 'I like your boots.'

'Thanks. How are you?'

'Right now I couldn't be better.' He poured the wine and,

handing her a glass, sat down next to her. 'How are you? Busy year?'

She giggled. 'You could say that.'

He was looking at the buttons of her shirt. 'You really do have lovely breasts.'

She melted. 'I have missed you so much, Ali.'

He put his wine down and kissed her, pushing her down on the bed.

'I love you, Ali,' she said.

'I love you, babe.' His face was hot as he opened her shirt and squeezed her breasts from her bra. 'And I really love these.'

It was a bit more comfortable than the first time and he took a little longer than before. He lay next to her panting. 'Pass my glass, would you?'

As she sat up her tummy rounded in her skirt which was pushed up to her hips. He took the glass. 'You've put a bit of weight on, haven't you? I remember you being a bit skinnier. Mind you, I don't mind a bit of curvy flesh.'

'Don't you?' She took a sip of her wine and lay back, looking into his eyes.

'Not on a young girl. It's like puppy fat. Don't want it on an old bird, though.'

She was so happy. 'Did you get my letters?'

'Where did you write?'

'Your agent.'

'No. They answer them.'

'I thought so. Otherwise I'd have heard from you, wouldn't I?'

'Maybe. I've been touring all year. It's hard for things to find me.'

She put her hand to his cheek. 'I understand.'

'I love a girl who understands.' He smiled down at her.

'I love you, Ali,' she whispered as he began kissing her again.

'I love you, baby.'

Keith, listening at the door, knew exactly the right moment to knock and get Ali out of there.

'Sorry to disturb, but there's an important call for you at the hotel, Ali. You must come now.'

'Oh, right.' Ali stood up and zipped his jeans. 'Babe, I've got to split. It'll be to arrange a meeting about my European tour – going to happen over the next two years. Scandinavia, Holland, Belgium, Italy, Portugal, then the final gig in Spain, lovely Spain in September '93. You must come when I'm there.'

Sennen was bewildered at this sudden departure. 'Which hotel are you in tonight? I could come over in the morning. I've got someone I want you to meet.'

'Great. It's the, erm . . .'

'Starfish,' said Keith handing Ali his T-shirt and coat.

'See you, babe. Bye.' He went over and kissed her. 'Thanks for everything.'

14

The next morning, she bundled Henry into his pushchair, escaping her mother's questions on the pretext of a need to get nappies, and set out for the Starfish Hotel.

She couldn't wait to see Ali's face when she told him that Henry was his son.

His family.

Her family.

In her shoulder-bag she had her little camera ready for the photo she had been longing for.

The well-groomed receptionist looked up from her desk and smiled warily.

'Can I help you?'

'Yes. I've come to see Mr Ali A'mayze. He's expecting me.'

The receptionist gave a patronising smile. 'I'm afraid he's already left.'

'Oh.' A distant alarm bell began to ring in Sennen's heart. 'Did he say where he's gone? Is he at the theatre?'

The receptionist revealed a set of perfect teeth behind her lacquered lips. 'No. He checked out before breakfast. He had to catch a train.' She remembered her flirty conversation with him very clearly.

Panic flooded, Sennen. 'Are you sure?' she asked. 'Maybe he's booked under his real name? Alan Chisolm?'

'Yes, I'm sure. Mr A'Mayze has definitely left.'

Sennen felt her heart actually crack with pain. Henry began to cry. 'Did he leave a message for me? Sennen Tallon?'

'I'll check, but I'm sure he didn't leave any messages.' The receptionist made a show of checking the cubbyholes behind her. 'No, I'm sorry.' She gave Sennen a professional beam and turned her attention to a couple who were next in line.

They were staring at Sennen and tutting as Henry's cries grew louder.

'Okay. Thanks,' she said, and pulling Henry's little jacket around him she hurried away in confusion and shame.

A few weeks later, she told Adela and Bill that she was pregnant . . .

When she came, Ella was a beautiful baby with a mass of red curls and a happy nature. Bill and Adela idolised her from the start. Henry was not so keen – like many a firstborn he didn't like sharing his mother with an interloper.

Sennen was cornered. Her loving, generous, caring parents watched her every move, were there for Henry and Ella's every cry. They were stifling her. Why didn't they confront her? Demand to know who this boy was who had fathered their grandchildren?

Sennen overheard them one morning in the kitchen as she was coming down the stairs for breakfast. She paused and quietly listened.

Bill was talking. 'If I ever find out who that lout is, I'll knock him from here to the middle of next week.'

'And what good would that do? What's done is done and it is our duty to protect Sennen and give her all the security and time she needs. She will tell us one day, I'm certain.'

'We aren't protecting her, though. She's not seventeen and she's just had her second child. We somehow let that happen.' Sennen heard Bill stirring his coffee loudly. 'I'm going to ask her outright.'

'You are not.' Adela sounded adamant. 'She is a woman and a mother. This is her body and her life and I want to make this transition for her as easy as possible. Family show-downs are not going to help. I want her to look back on all this with happy memories, not rows.'

Sennen wanted to run into the kitchen then, tell them all about Ali and ask for their help in finding him, but instinct told her that once that lid was off there would be only hell to pay. No, she told herself, one day, when Ali came back, they could explain together, when the time was right. For now, they asked no questions, gave her no pressure, wrapped her and their two grandchildren in unending love – and she hated them for it.

She dropped her friends, the ones that were left, before they dropped her. Only Rosemary, a girl who Sennen had never known well, came over because she loved playing with children.

Adela and Bill encouraged the friendship. 'Rosemary's a nice girl. We like her and she's good for you, Sennen. Why not go to the pictures at the weekend? We'll babysit.'

Sennen wanted nothing less, but Rosemary could be a means to an end. Instead of going to the cinema, Sennen took Rosemary to the pub and introduced her to Bacardi and Cokes and, over time, planted the idea of holiday in Spain.

They were walking on the harbour wall, eating chips. 'Don't

you ever feel like running away?' Sennen asked, chucking her chip paper into a bin, and missing, then passing Rosemary a Consulate menthol cigarette.

'No,' said Rosemary.

'I've got a friend in Spain. Fancy coming with me?'

Rosemary shook her head. 'Who is it?'

'A guy.'

'I don't think my parents would let me.'

'They don't need to know.' Sennen smiled slyly. 'We could just hitch to Plymouth, catch the ferry and be gone. Back before they knew it.'

'Really?'

'Have you got a passport?'

'Yes. I had for when we went to Oberammergau, in the Alps, on a school trip.'

'Money?'

'Some in the post office.'

'Okay. Leave it with me and I'll make a plan. Don't tell anyone.'

'What about Henry and Ella?'

'In a kind of a way, I'm doing this for them.'

'Oh, I see,' said Rosemary, clearly not seeing at all.

And now here she was, seventeen, on a ferry to Spain, abandoning her children to look for their father.

15

Trevay without Sennen

The black void left by Sennen was impossible to avoid, yet too painful to explore.

'How could she leave Ella and Henry?' Bill, staring out of their bedroom window, looking out over the roofs of Trevay and down to the sea.

He was like a wounded bear. He could neither sit down nor stand up without doing the opposite in moments.

'Please, Bill . . .' Adela tried to soothe him. 'We need to stay calm, for Henry and Ella. They are missing her terribly. Henry woke up at two this morning, sobbing his little heart out.'

'How could she do it, Adela? We have never judged her. Always loved her.' He wiped his broken eyes. 'Is she even still alive?'

Adela came towards him and put her arm around his shoulder. 'She's a young woman breaking free from her life. She needs to find herself.' He dropped his head onto her shoulder and sobbed. She stroked his head in the same way she had stroked Henry's just a few hours before. 'She'll come back.'

He broke away from her, angry. 'We were too soft on her. Should have been tougher. When she first told us about Henry, I should have shaken sense into her. How can a teenager deal with a baby? We should have demanded to know who the father is. Some little toerag out there is running around Trevay laughing at us, at her, at Henry.' His voice was rising, the words almost choking him.

'Darling, please – don't let the children hear you.' Adela put a hand on his arm but he shrugged her off.

'Just scraped her O Levels. Will miss her A levels. She's cruel and stupid.' He sat on the bed, his head in his hands. 'Where did we go wrong? I honestly thought I knew her, but I don't. She was laughing at us. Using us all along. She's ruined her life and the lives of Henry and Ella.' He stood up and walked to the window, banging his hands down on the sill. 'I never want to see her again. I will never let her back into this house. Never. It's Henry and Ella we must focus on now.'

Adela clutched him. 'Stop it, Bill. Stop it. You're hurting. You don't mean those things. She's Sennen. Our daughter. You love her. We all love her. She'll come back to us.'

Bill looked at her with sneering pity, 'Not while I'm alive.'

'Bill!' Adela was frightened. 'That's a terrible thing to say and untrue. She will come back and you will be alive and we will be a family again.'

He crumpled then. Adela watched the man she loved break down in front of her. She put her arms out to him and he came to her like a child. He clung to her, his whole body shuddering with every sob.

*

When Rosemary returned from Spain, without Sennen, and came knocking at their door with the presents for the children, Adela was even more worried for Bill. He took the toys and put them in the dustbin. He sat for hours in Sennen's room crying and finally burnt all the photos they had of her.

The doctor arranged for grief counselling, which Bill refused to attend, and it fell to Adela to care for him. She quietly carried the burden of the children, her husband, the house and her own desolation, never allowing the internal scream that deafened her to escape her lips.

At Christmas Sennen sent a postcard from Madrid. The message read,

> *Dear Mum, Poppa, Henry and Ella,*
>   *Happy Christmas. I'm okay. Don't worry.*
>   *Lots of love*
>   *Sennen*

Adela, always the first up in the house, picked it off the mat and read it. She never told Bill. It would upset him too much. She didn't have the strength to face that. Greedily, she kept it for herself.

Sennen never forgot their birthdays. Each year, from somewhere in Europe, cards would arrive. All with the briefest of messages and always ending with 'I'm okay. Don't worry.'

Adela kept them all for herself, and the years passed. Henry and Ella got through primary school well enough and were happy popular children. Ella had a real talent for art, which

Bill delighted in. She was the apple of his eye and wherever he was Adela would usually find her with him, chatting and laughing.

Henry was a good boy, but quieter, with a quick temper. He was good at maths and accumulating money. At school he ran an illicit tuck shop, selling penny sweets he'd bought from the newsagents for twice as much in the playground. The head teacher, whilst acknowledging his entrepreneurship, had to ban him, but it didn't stop Henry: he simply sold the sweets outside the school gate, and therefore outside the school's jurisdiction, instead.

Adela had always run a small ad hoc painting school for young artists, providing bed and board as well as classes. Sennen had hated having to share her parents with them and after she left, Adela stopped doing it.

It was Henry who suggested she should start it up again. 'How much would you pay me to help?' he asked.

'It depends,' she said, thinking about what needed to be done. 'I shall have to give the spare bedrooms a lick of paint and maybe make some new curtains.'

'I will paint. You and Ella can do the curtains,' said Henry. 'I'll do it for twenty pounds a room.'

'Ten pounds and you have a deal,' laughed Adela.

'Ten pounds for the small rooms. Fifteen for the big ones. Including Mum's.' He held his hand out to seal the deal.

'No. No, not Sennen's,' Adela replied.

'Granny, Mum's room has been a shrine for too long.'

'It is not a shrine.' Adela was firm.

'It is a shrine, Granny. If Mum ever came back, she'd think she'd never been away. And anyway, Ella would like that bedroom.'

'Would she?'

136

Henry nodded. 'Yep. She's almost thirteen and her room is tiny. She needs the space to grow up in.'

Adela sighed. 'Do you want a cup of tea? I'm going to put the kettle on for Poppa.'

'Don't change the subject,' Henry said gently. 'I was allowed a bigger room when I was twelve. Don't baby her.'

'I'll ask your grandfather.'

Bill was accepting of the idea. 'She's been gone over a decade. It's time to move on, Adela.'

'It's the last bit of her we have. It feels so final,' Adela said sadly.

'No, Adela. We have Henry and Ella to think of.'

Ella was delighted. 'Can I choose the curtains, Granny?'

'We'll go into Wadebridge and have a look.'

'Can I have Cath Kidston roses and matching wallpaper?'

'We'll see.'

It didn't take long to erase Sennen. Her posters, books, old make-up and dusty shoes were sorted into rubbish or charity piles and Bill filled his car and drove them away for good.

Adela felt winded, dizzy and teary but she kept a cheery face and only twice had to go to the end of the small garden to cry silent tears.

A week later and the room was transformed. Ella had kept her mother's old patchwork bed quilt, stitched by Adela's mother when Sennen was a toddler, and her old teddy, Buster, but apart from those two things, no trace of Sennen remained.

Bill and Adela took in four art students and set up a new daily routine. Adela began to enjoy cooking the 8 a.m. breakfasts for seven and Bill started to shake off the malaise which had dogged him since Sennen's disappearance. He began to lead stimulating conversations about art, politics and religion around their old kitchen table.

On wet days the students would have lessons in painting and drawing with Adela, or working clay by hand or on the wheel with Bill.

Once or twice a week there would be outings to Bodmin Moor, the cliffs around Trevay, or the beach of Shellsand Bay.

Laughter was again spontaneous in the house.

Henry did well in his GCSEs and was opting for Economics, Maths and Business Studies for his A Levels. In contrast, Ella excelled in English and her short stories were achieving some acclaim in the school magazine, but it was her painting that was her strength. From canvases of wild seas whipped by fierce winds, to small and delicate watercolours of field mice and wild flowers.

Lying in bed one night, Adela with Bill's arm around her and her head on his chest, said, 'I hope we've been good parents to Ella and Henry.'

Bill stroked her hair. 'Better than with Sennen, you mean?'

'I hope so.'

'Perhaps we were too good to Sennen.'

'I think of her every day.'

'I know.'

'I hope she's happy.'

'That's all we can hope for.'

'I've never stopped loving her.'

'There was a time I thought I hated her, but now I can remember her with love.'

'Do you think we'll ever see her again?'

Bill inhaled deeply and Adela felt her head move against his ribs. 'I really don't know. But we have each other, Adela.

And Henry and Ella. You've been so selfless with them. I was no help, was I.'

She pulled herself up and looked into his loving, familiar eyes. 'Do you regret burning her photos?'

He nodded. 'I was not in my right mind.'

'I know. But we pulled together.'

'Little did I know that the girl I fell in love with at harvest time would be so strong. It's been hard for you.'

Adela kissed him softly. 'Love at first sight for me.'

'Foolish girl.' He smiled at her.

'That's me.'

'Don't ever leave me, will you?'

'No.'

He hugged her. 'I love you Adela.'

'I love you, Bill.'

Adela woke early. Bill was still sleeping so quietly she left him to make herself a cup of tea. She loved mornings like this. It was late September and the house was slumbering around her. She opened the back door and went out into the small courtyard to sit and drink her tea. The air was warm and fresh. She filled her lungs with it and leant back in her seat to feel the early sunshine on her face.

She thought about Bill. He had been so badly hurt when Sennen had left, and suffered so deeply. But now the Bill of old was coming back. She could see a future for them both now. Not the one they had imagined, but there was a future. They were still young, only in their fifties. Henry would be leaving home in a few years and then r oyster. She'd always been keen on taking middle class of you,

But she knew that if she asked him to join her, he'd come like a shot.

Bill wanted to keep chickens. She had always said no, but, why not? Life was for grabbing with both hands. Sennen had done it. Why not them?

She finished her tea and went back into the kitchen to get breakfast started. The smell of coffee and sausages was always enough to get everyone out of bed and around her table. Bill was the only one absent.

'Ella, darling,' said Adela, 'go and get Poppa, would you?'

'I'll go,' said Henry, 'I've forgotten my phone anyway.'

When he returned a few minutes later, ashen and alone, Adela knew.

She put the milk jug she was carrying down and flew past Henry and up the stairs.

Bill was lying on his side as he always did. He was pale, but still warm to her touch. She stroked his forehead and kissed his lips before lovingly closing his sightless eyes.

PART TWO
Sennen Comes Home

16

Pendruggan, 2018

Ella was a cat on hot bricks. She needed to spend the day cleaning Marguerite Cottage so she shooed the dogs out into the garden and sent Adam and Kit out to collect Henry from Bodmin Parkway station.

'Don't come back too early. Go for a pint or something. Supper will be ready at eight.'

Kit pulled her to him. 'Darling, the house looks great. *You* look great. Your mother will love all of it – and if she doesn't, she's not worth a jot.'

Ella swatted him away. 'Go.'

When they had gone, Ella started on the bathroom. She had no idea whether her mother would want to stay the night, but she would probably need the loo in any event, and she'd better have the spare bed made up in case. In the end they had decided that Marguerite Cottage would be the best place for the meeting.

When upstairs was as she wanted it, she went downstairs.

The lounge was dusted and vacuumed, the small cloakroom scrubbed, and the kitchen floor, sink and cupboards wiped and polished.

The last job was to empty the bin. She gave it a quick spritz of air freshener before putting a new liner inside it.

Done.

'Right, Ella,' she said pulling off her apron, 'you can have a coffee.' She opened the cupboard above the kettle and pulled out a jar of instant. It was empty. She swore under her breath and took a quick inventory of anything else she might need to buy. Loo paper, tissues (there were bound to be tears) butter, milk, tea bags and bread (in case her mum stayed for breakfast).

She had made a quiche and a chilli con carne that were awaiting in the fridge, and she had plenty of beer and wine.

'Right, if I've forgotten anything, it's tough,' she said to Terry and Celia who had been allowed back into the house and were lolling in their beds, and set off for the village shop.

Queenie was behind the counter as always, reading the words on a packet of nicotine gum with an unlit cigarette in her mouth. She looked up as Ella came through the door, ringing the little bell above it.

'Ella, duck.' She coughed. 'Do you think this is any good? It says chewing it will help me cope with the withdrawal of not having me cigarettes.'

'Do you want to stop smoking?'

'No. I love me fags.' Queenie waved her cigarette as proof.

'So why are you looking at the gum?'

'I dunno. Maybe I should think about me health in the long term.'

'How old are you, Queenie?'

'Oh, you cheeky mare.' Queenie pushed her smeary, pebble-thick glasses up her nose. 'I'm as old as me tongue and a little bit older than my teeth.'

Ella smiled. 'How long have you been smoking?'

'About a hundred years.' Queenie's wheezy laugh brought on a coughing fit.

'Well,' said Ella, 'it's up to you, but after a hundred years it's not going to make any difference now.'

Queenie took her hanky from her sleeve and wiped her eyes. 'That's what I thought. Now, how can I help you, duck?'

Ella passed her scribbled list to Queenie who squinted at it and began collecting the bits together. ''ave a look at them magazines while I do this. That celeb, the one with the big bum, 'as got a lovely new 'airdo. It would suit you with all them lovely red curls you got.'

'I haven't got time at the moment. My mum is coming to see Henry and me tomorrow.'

Queenie, searching the grocery shelf, snapped her head round, on the alert for gossip. 'Oh yes?' she said. 'Your mum that left you and Henry when you was nippers? The local papers had her picture on the front pages for weeks.'

'Yes,' Ella replied, feeling uncomfortable.

'Oh my gawd, you'll be feeling a bit mixed, I expect?'

'Yes.' Ella scratched her cheek and tried to swallow down the sudden lump in her throat. 'Mixed is the right word.'

The bell on the shop door rang again. It was Simon, the vicar.

'Hello, Ella, Queenie,' he said jovially. 'Lovely day today.'

'Hmm,' said Queenie putting her head to her shoulder and nudging it towards Ella in a secret signal to Simon. 'Ella's got quite a lot on her mind, though.'

'Oh really?' asked Simon, not being able to fathom Queenie's coded signals. 'Why's that?'

'My long-lost mum is coming to see Henry and me tomorrow for the first time in more than twenty-five years.'

Simon looked at her thoughtfully. 'Is there anything I can do?'

Ella shook her head slowly and tried to smile, but the waiting tears beat her to it. Simon took a clean cotton handkerchief from his pocket and, as he passed it to her, pulled up one of the old armchairs that Queenie had scattered around for just this sort of emergency. 'Sit down,' he said.

Ella sat and apologised. 'I'm so sorry. I'm fine. I'm just being silly.'

'I'll make you a cuppa. You stay there,' ordered Queenie.

Simon dragged another chair over and sat down next to Ella. 'I remember how Penny was when her mother – well, her stepmother – died. It was something she couldn't possibly prepare for.'

'I'm so nervous.'

'Of course you are.'

'Will she like me?'

'She jolly well should do. You are a daughter to be proud of.'

'But Henry is so angry with her and I'm worried he's going say something awful that will make her go away again.'

'Where are you meeting her?'

'At Marguerite Cottage.'

Simon thought for a moment. 'Why not use the vicarage? Penny and I can be there, not to interfere, but to be on hand if things get a bit . . . emotional?'

Ella wiped her eyes. 'Oh, Simon, you are so kind.' Fresh tears rolled down her cheeks. 'But I couldn't do that to you.'

'But wouldn't you like to? It would mean a neutral space.'

She nodded. 'Yes. It would be lovely.'

He patted her hand. 'Consider it done. What time is she arriving?'

'We don't know yet. Her solicitor is ringing in the morning.'

'Well, the vicarage will be ready for you at any time. It is yours for the day and Penny and I will be right there for you.'

Sennen's flight from India had arrived at Heathrow at the same time as Ella left Queenie's shop, feeling a lot better than she had and excited to tell Henry that the meeting would be at the vicarage.

Sennen unbuckled her belt and looked out into grey drizzle. Nervousness gripped her. Why was she doing this? She should be back home in India with Kafir, her husband. But he'd been so angry with her when she had had to tell him about Henry and Ella.

'How could you deny the existence of your own children? To me? You are someone I don't know any more. What else do you have in your box of lies?'

He had told her to leave their home. To go back to Cornwall. To apologise and make peace with her children. Only then would he consider the future of their marriage.

He had frightened her with his appraisal of her. He was a good man. A moral man. What sort of woman was she? For years she had managed to bury the past. She had never forgotten a birthday or Christmas, always sending a card, but she had given neither her parents or Ella and Henry an address with which to find her. And now her parents were dead and her children had agreed to see her. But they must hate her.

In the terminal she handed her passport to the Border Control guard. 'Welcome home at long last, Mrs Tallon-Singh,' he said, smiling.

Guiltily, she held her hand out for the passport. 'Thank you.

Yes. It's been a long time.' And scurried through to baggage reclaim and customs before exiting the building and taking her first breaths of British air for so many years. After a moment or two she steadied herself and found the car hire office.

The M4 was wide and clean and well-organised, nothing like the madness of India's roads. The rental car smelt new and was easy to drive. She had never driven on the left before, but after a few miles her confidence grew. At Bristol she stopped for a coffee and the loo, then pressed on to Cornwall and arrived in Trevay in the late afternoon and drove to her solicitors, Penhaligon and Palmer. Deborah Palmer, young and new to the family firm, welcomed her into the office with a handshake. 'We meet at last,' she said, smiling.

'Yes. At last.'

Sennen estimated Deborah to be in her late twenties, petite in her smart suit and with an air of complete professionalism.

Sennen looked around her. The offices were old and crooked, smelling of dry rot. Built at the top of Trevay, the building was surrounded by new-build homes and a large supermarket with a petrol station. Sennen remembered when it had all been open fields where ponies had been kept. She would often walk up to feed them hay and Polos during the school holidays.

Deborah was opening a file on her desk. 'How long is it since you've been back?'

'A very long time,' Sennen said wistfully. 'A lifetime. It's changed a bit.'

Deborah looked up and smiled. 'I'm sure it has, but I think the old town is recognisable. I've booked you into the Starfish hotel, near the harbour. Do you know it?'

Sennen's mind went straight to the horrible morning that

she had walked into that hotel with Henry in her arms, ready to be with Ali for the rest of her life. The look of dismissal on the receptionist's face, the humiliation. She squeezed her eyes tight, the shame burning her.

'Yes. I know it.'

'The best on this coast.' Deborah flicked through the file. 'I've just had a phone call from your daughter, Ella.'

'Yes?' Sennen was anxious. Had Ella decided not to see her after all?

'They have chosen the vicarage in Pendruggan as your meeting place.'

'Why?'

'I think that she and Henry – and I rather agree with them – believe that neutral ground, No-man's land, if you like, would be sensible.'

'Are they very religious?'

Deborah smiled. 'The vicar, Simon Canter, and his wife Penny are friends of theirs. In fact, Ella was nanny to their daughter, Jenna. I think she does still do the occasional day for them.'

'That's nice.' Sennen's mind was racing. There was so much she didn't know. 'And Henry?'

'He works in London, something to do with property. A commercial surveyor as I recall.'

'Golly. That sounds grand. He must work very hard.'

'He has come down on the train today. Ella suggests that tomorrow's meeting is at eleven o'clock. How does that suit? You may be tired after your journey and want to start later?'

'No, that will be very good. Thank you.'

'Right, I shall pick you up from the Starfish at about ten thirty.' Deborah closed the folder and stood up. 'Here's some reading for you.' She handed the folder over. 'Just to get you up to speed. Nothing too difficult. Just some background and legal stuff that I shall be asking you to sign.'

Sennen took it. 'Thank you.' She collected her coat from the back of her chair and then said, 'I'd rather not stay at the Starfish if that's okay?'

'Of course. Would you like me to book somewhere else?'

'I'll find a B and B. I'd like to find my feet a bit. I'll phone you to let you know where I am.'

She followed her nose to the main road into Trevay. It was all so familiar and yet so dreamlike. Had she really lived here? Left here?

She turned onto the hill that would take her down to the pretty little fishing town and almost gasped as the beauty of the harbour and the houses that lay spread out beneath her. Her memories had faded the sheer beauty of the place. How could she have forgotten?

Her hands shook as she changed gear, slowing down to take it all in. Instinct took over and she guided the car to White Water, her parents' home. Which was just the same although much smarter. It had a conservatory, now, and pretty shutters at the windows. She inched past slowly. The front door was a different colour but there was the downstairs loo window she'd climbed out of and the gate she'd walked through as she made her escape. There was a sign on the wall. *White Water Bed and Breakfast. Vacancies.*

It took a split second for her to make her mind up. She was coming home.

The landlady came to the door, wiping her mouth of crumbs. 'Do excuse me. I'm just making a batch of scones for tea tomorrow and I can never resist one while they're warm! Can I help you?'

'Hello,' said Sennen shakily, 'I see you have a vacancy.'

'For tonight?'

'Yes.'

The landlady, a slender woman in her forties, wearing a simple dress and with her hair piled on the top of her head with tendrils escaping attractively, opened the door wide. 'Come in.'

Sennen stepped over the threshold and looked around. In her parents' day the house had been full of Bill's pots, large and small, some gathering dust, others filled with dried grasses or teasels.

The walls had been filled with Adela's large canvases of nudes or swimmers or both, which burst with exuberant colour and movement.

In their place now were subtle grey painted walls and stark window sills. It was lovely. But it wasn't her home.

'I'm Amy and my husband, John, is usually here, but he's out on the boat. Come into the lounge and I'll get you settled. Would you like a drink? Glass of wine?'

'That would be lovely,' said Sennen, following her into the room where her parents had sat in their old armchairs discussing art, or politics or listening to the radio. Adela had painted the walls sunset orange and on the old table there had always been bowls of fat chrysanthemum, daffodils or sweet peas depending on the season.

The room was now a shrine to grey in all its hues. The floor tiles were graphite, the walls a light slate, the ceiling a shade of mist and the linen curtains . . . well, Sennen could only describe them as Drizzle.

Amy invited her to sit on the taupe sofa.

'Isn't this room lovely?' Amy sighed. 'So peaceful. An artist and his wife used to live here and it was sold to a couple who started it up as a B and B a few years ago, and then John and I took it over at the beginning of the season. We've made some changes in the décor. It was very dated.'

'It was a potter who owned this,' said Sennen. It seemed important to correct the woman. 'His wife was the artist.'

'Did you know them?' smiled Amy, interested. 'I'd love to know more about the place.'

Before Sennen could think of a suitable answer, a ping came from the kitchen.

'That's the next batch of scones. I'll get you your wine and then take you up to your room. Sea view with en suite? Or garden view, which is quieter but no en suite.'

Sennen smiled, thinking how chichi Adela would have thought the phrase en suite.

'Garden view, please,' she replied.

Sitting in her parents' house for the first time in all these years, she closed her eyes and allowed memories to flood her mind.

In this room, she had told her mum and Poppa that she was pregnant.

In this room, the Christmas tree had always stood in front of the big window and she and Adela had covered it in a handmade myriad of shells and driftwood. And on the top, they had always put a mermaid with wings rather than an angel.

Where were those bits now? Had Henry and Ella kept them in the old cardboard box? Or were they rotting under some municipal rubbish tip.

So long ago, and so far away.

'Mrs Tallon.' Amy jolted her back to the present. 'You're tired after your trip, aren't you? John often has a doze in that chair. Most comfortable in the house, he thinks. Here,' she passed Sennen a glass of wine, 'take this and I'll show you to your room.'

As they climbed the stairs Sennen felt an odd sensation. Not regret. Not fear. She turned it over in her mind before she got it.

It felt like the first steps to coming home.

17

Ella hadn't slept well.

The night before, in the pub, Henry had had too much to drink and had been moody and tetchy.

Ella had tried hard to soothe him. 'It's a good idea to meet Mum at the vicarage, don't you think.'

Henry had barked a bitter laugh. 'I suppose so. At least we'll have an expert on hand if she needs to be exorcised.'

Ella had tightened her lips and glared at Kit, blaming him for the fact that Henry was drunk.

Henry put his pint down. 'I need a leak.'

When he'd gone, Ella had a go at Kit. 'How many pints has he had?'

'I think this is his fourth.'

'Four? Four? For God's sake, Kit.' She glared at him. Ella was furious and turned to leave the bar but walked smack into a returning Henry.

'Whoops, Sis. You need to look where you are going.' He was laughing, 'Or learn to handle your drink better.'

Ella, incandescent, turned on both of them. '*I* am not drunk. I'm going home.'

Kit watched her walk away and, draining his pint, set out after her with Henry following. In the car park he went to her. 'I'm sorry. Sorry. It's just this thing with your mum coming. We are all jumpy. Come here.' He held his arms out to her and she went to him.

'That was our first row,' she said.

He held her a little tighter. 'At least we've got it over with.'

Sennen woke up in what had been her parent's bedroom. The window was where it had always been, but everything else had changed. The far side of the room had been filled with two new walls to contain the en suite and the sleek Scandinavian bed, dressed with a linen throw and cushions, was a far cry from the heavily carved one she had leapt into each birthday and Christmas morning.

But she had slept very well in this one. Better than she had hoped.

Considering the day ahead.

The day she had longed for and dreaded in equal measure.

There was no going back now . . .

There was a gentle knock at the door.

She sat up, giving her hair a quick comb with her fingers before calling, 'Come in.'

Amy appeared with a tray of coffee and a newspaper. 'Good morning, Mrs Tallon-Singh. It's a lovely day out there.'

'Thank you so much.'

Amy placed the tray on the bedside table. 'How did you sleep?'

'Very well, thank you.'

'Good.' She pushed the plunger on the cafetière. 'Busy day planned?'

'I hope so.'

'Well, enjoy your coffee, and we'll see you for breakfast at eight thirty. Okay?'

'Lovely.'

When Amy had gone, Sennen got out of bed and went to the window. Opening the plantation blinds she looked down on her old garden. She flattened her nose against the cold glass and tried to see around the corner of the house, down to the harbour. The tide was out and she imagined she could smell the salty dankness of the weed in its bed; seagulls strutting to peck at amputated crab claws, the sand sucking at their feet.

A wave of sorrow slapped her in the stomach. Why had she waited so long? She drew back from the window and sat on the bed, sipping her coffee. She closed her eyes and tried to picture the faces of her parents. It was difficult after such a long time. She concentrated hard, but each time she thought she had found their likeness the images slipped from her brain. Silently she said, 'Mum? Poppa? Can you see me? Do you know I am here?' When there was no answer she opened her eyes and said to no one, 'I have come back.'

In Pendruggan, Ella was making two huge plates of sandwiches: cucumber with the crusts off and cheese with a good dollop of pickle.

Henry, bleary-eyed, slopped into the kitchen wearing baggy shorts. 'Who are they for?' He took a crust, put it in his mouth, and began to fill the kettle.

'For the meeting. A distraction.'

'Oh.' He rubbed his head. 'Got any aspirin?'

She pointed with her bread knife.

'Left-hand drawer next to the sink.'

He opened the drawer and pushed things around until he found the packet and threw two tablets into his mouth, swallowing without water.

He leant back against the counter, waiting for the kettle to boil. He scratched his chest and yawned.

Ella pushed past him. 'You stink.'

'You're welcome.'

'You need to be ready by ten thirty.'

'What time is the old bitch getting to the vicar's?'

'If you mean our mother, I've told you, eleven.'

'If she bothers to show up.'

Ella turned on him. 'Stop it! It's going to be a hard enough day as it is without you being so horrible. Today means a lot to me – and if you can't or won't see that, then I'll see Mum by myself and you can get the hell back to London and your money-mad chums.'

He held his hands up in mock surrender. 'Okay, okay. I was only saying: just don't expect it to be all kisses and white doves.'

'Shut up.'

The skittering of dog claws in the hall announced Kit's arrival.

'Morning. I do hope I am not hearing the snarling of siblings. What's going on?'

'Nothing,' said Ella through gritted teeth.

'Good. Let's keep it that way.' He kissed Ella. 'Fancy a walk on the beach?'

'Bless you, yes,' said Ella thankfully.

'My pleasure – and Henry,' Kit added, 'you had better get shaved and showered. Don't let yourself or your sister down.'

*

Bang on ten thirty the little party from Marguerite, clean and smart, pale and nervy, left for the vicarage, carrying two plates of sandwiches, a Victoria sponge, an extra litre of milk and some tea bags.

Penny opened the door. 'What's all this?'

'I couldn't expect you to feed us as well as give us your home,' said Ella, putting the cake box into Penny's outstretched hands. 'You've done so much for us.'

'Come into the kitchen and let's get our strategy right before your mum and the solicitor arrive.'

Simon was putting his car keys into the dish by the back door. 'Hello, Ella. How are you doing?' He came forward and hugged her.

'Okay. A bit nervous. Is Jenna at playgroup?'

'Yes, just dropped her.'

'Is she enjoying it?'

'Taken to it like a duck to water. Miss Davis said she was the most confident child she had this year.'

'That's my girl,' laughed Penny.

Ella hugged the Aga. 'We went for a walk on the beach this morning. There's a cold wind getting up.'

'Oh, for God's sake,' Henry grumbled, 'can we stop talking about the weather? Our mother is about to arrive and I don't even know if I'll recognise her.'

Simon passed Henry a cup of coffee and sat next to him. 'During difficult times like this, the power of small talk is often underestimated.'

Ella gave Simon a grateful smile across the table.

'Mum must be pretty nervous too,' she said.

Henry shifted in his chair. 'She bloody well ought to be.'

Simon took a gentle steer on the conversation. 'What do you hope for from this meeting, Ella?'

'Erm, I think . . . I think I want us to all get on with each other and trust that maybe we have a future. As a family.'

Henry was exasperated. 'Really? You think this might be one big happy ending? I believe she's come for one thing and one thing only, and it's not her darling children. It's Granny and Poppa's money. End of.'

'That's a very strong point of view, Henry,' said Simon softly. 'She may have come to atone for the past.'

Henry crossed his arms defensively.

Penny spoke. 'Tell me what the pros and cons of meeting your mother are for you, Henry.'

'The only pro is hers. She takes the money, tells us she's very sorry she dumped us, and buggers off back to the hole she crawled out of.'

'Put like that, I wonder why you are here at all.'

'To hear how she tries to justify herself.' And he added quietly. 'For my sister. For Ella.'

'I see.' Penny turned to Ella. 'How about you?'

'I want to know why she left us. To try to understand. To find out who she really is. If we share likes and dislikes. To see who we look like. All that stuff, really.'

Henry folded his arms and grunted.

Kit looked up at the kitchen clock. 'Five to eleven. Anyone needing a pee, go now.'

As they left the kitchen, Penny took Ella's hand. 'You'll be okay,' she whispered. 'She's your mum and anyone who could have such a lovely girl like you can't be all bad.'

Ella's butterflies were churning. 'You will stay in the house, won't you? In case?' she pleaded.

'I'll be in the kitchen all the time.'

Penny led Ella into the vicarage drawing room. She had lit

the fire and put a huge jug of roses on the piano. Ella's throat tightened with emotion. 'It looks lovely. Thank you, Penny.'

'It's the least I could do.'

Ella's eyes were shining with unshed tears. 'I'm scared.'

'Only natural.' Penny patted her hand and let her go. 'Simon and I will bring the tea and sandwiches in at about half eleven. You might need a bit of light relief by then.'

The heavy knocker sounded on the front door. Ella jumped. 'This is it.'

She went into the hall where Kit and Henry stood uneasily. Simon took over. 'You three go into the drawing room, I'll let them in. Close the door behind you.'

They did as they were told and listened as Simon went to the front door.

'Hello. Good morning. I'm Simon. How do you do.'

A woman's voice replied. 'Simon. Good to meet you. I'm Deborah Palmer, Mrs Tallon-Singh's solicitor. We spoke on the phone?'

'Indeed we did,' said Simon.

'And this is Mrs Tallon-Singh.'

'You are very welcome,' Simon's voice said. 'Come along in. Henry and Ella are in the drawing room.'

In the drawing room, Henry and Ella looked at each other, then at the door.

'Go on in,' they heard Simon say.

The door opened; Ella stretched her mouth into a welcoming grin while her eyes were round with apprehension.

Henry looked at his feet and then at a photo in a silver frame of Penny and Simon's wedding day, anywhere but at the door.

A woman's voice, strong and smoky, said, 'Hello, Henry. Ella.'

Both children looked up.

She was tall. Ella judged her to be almost six feet, wide-shouldered, slender and rangy. Her long hair, once fiery red, was now hennaed with silver strands glinting at the roots.

Ella recognised it as her own Titian curls.

Henry's chest had constricted to the point where he couldn't take a breath deep enough without panting. God, how he hoped this woman couldn't hear it. This woman who had his face, his nose, eyes, mouth, brow . . . She was staring at him. What did she want? If she thought he was going to rush into her arms and call her Mummy she had another think coming. He walked to an armchair and sat down, his arms folded.

'Well, then,' said Simon hovering by the door, 'I'll leave you to get to know each other. Penny and I will bring refreshments shortly.' He walked out into the hall, closing the door behind him. Why the hell did he say that? Get to know each other? Refreshments? He pulled his handkerchief from his pocket and rubbed the sheen of perspiration from his head.

Sennen smiled and sat on the sofa.

She was wearing a calf-length, billowing dress in jewel colours with a soft, midnight-blue scarf, mirrored and beaded, around her neck. On each wrist she wore rows of golden bangles. Her eyes were heavily lined with kohl and her skin was very tanned.

Henry was thinking, 'Of course. A bloody hippy.'

Ella thought, 'This is my mother.'

Kit thought, 'Oh, shit.'

Simon tiptoed to the kitchen where Penny's eyes were out on stalks.

'And?' she asked desperately.

'Tall. Very tall for a woman.'

'But does she look like a nice person?'

'I couldn't tell.'

'Oh, you are *hopeless*.' Penny looked at the clock. 'Roll on tea and sandwiches.'

In the drawing room Ella stood in a quandary. Where should she sit? Next to her mother on the sofa and risk looking needy? Or take an empty armchair and risk looking judgemental.

The solicitor solved the dilemma by taking the sofa. Kit loyally sat on the arm of Ella's chair.

The solicitor began. 'So I'm Deborah. Debbie. And you know I have just joined the practice because your grandparents original lawyer and senior partner of the firm has finally retired due to ill-health. But I am well acquainted with your family's history and I am honoured to be here on this important day.'

Henry made a noise in the back of his throat, somewhere between a growl and a groan. Ella flicked her head towards him and gave him daggers.

Sennen said nothing. She felt sick. The open fire was making the room overly hot and she could feel the sweat prickle her top lip.

Henry hated her. He was making that quite clear. She raised her kohl-rimmed eyes to look at him, to drink him in. Her little boy was now a man, a man who looked so like Poppa, well-muscled and tall, with a mouth, which while scowling now, had clear laughter lines around it.

She dropped her gaze. Of course he hated her. Once he had loved her. Hung onto her legs, climbed on her lap, kissed her with his sticky lips. And she had left.

She turned her head and looked at Ella. So like Ali. Neat, clever hands. Perfectly straight nose. Indigo eyes. But she had Sennen's wild red curls.

She couldn't blame either of them for their silence. Saying their names aloud as she had entered the room had been involuntary. A reaction, more like a prayer than anything else.

It had set the room on edge.

She decided to remain still and silent and wait for what might come.

18

Deborah took a file from her bag and began sifting through it. 'I have here copies of the valuation of Mr and Mrs Tallon's estate.' She passed one to Sennen, then stretched her arm out to Henry and handed him the remaining sheets. He took one and passed it on to Kit who gave it to Ella. Debbie continued, 'When Mr Tallon died nine years ago, he left everything to Mrs Tallon. When Mrs Tallon died, she left no will. However, in our role as executors we took advice from you, Henry and Ella, and due to the fact that you were both now living in London, you agreed that we should sell White Water, your family home. The monies from the sale of the property were invested by us. They remained so as we searched for your mother as she would be the sole beneficiary, if alive, or if proven to be deceased, her descendants, you, would become the beneficiaries.'

She turned to Sennen and smiled. 'Thankfully, we tracked you down.'

Sennen wasn't listening. She was reading the page in her hand.

Henry, white-faced, was reading his copy.

Ella's hands were shaking as she scanned hers. 'Golly. It's a lot of money,' she said.

Henry screwed his sheet into a ball stood up and walked to the fireplace. He tossed it into the flames. 'Well, that's all our darling mother's now.' He turned to look at her. 'You've got what you came for, now off you trot.'

Sennen stood up. 'Henry – I know you are angry . . .'

Henry laughed cruelly. 'Angry doesn't cover it.' He looked at his sister. 'Come on, Ella. She's got what she wants. You and I have coped this far without her. We don't need her or her money.'

Sennen reached for his arm but he swerved from her touch. She pulled back, stung. 'Henry, please.'

Fury suffused him. 'Do you know how old Poppa was when he died? Hm?'

Sennen gripped her hands, twisting her fingers.

'Well?' he shouted. 'No? You haven't a clue have you. Have you?' He stared at his mother and raked his hand through his hair. 'Selfish bitch. He was fifty-nine, that's all. He should be here now. He should be here to walk Ella down the aisle, if and when she gets married. He should be enjoying a comfortable retirement. But he's dead.' The last words were filled with pain and venom.

Sennen hung her head and Henry took a step closer. 'And do you know what killed him?'

Sennen shook her head and whispered, 'Don't. Please stop.'

He continued. 'You. You broke his heart.'

Ella put her hands to her face in horror. 'Henry, stop. Don't say such things.'

'Why not? It's true.' He glowered at the room. 'And because he died, Granny died too. The two people she had loved most in the world had gone. Her beloved husband and her feckless tart of a daughter who wasn't worth her love.' Henry saw the pain in his mother's face but couldn't help sticking the knife in deeper. 'Do you know that they removed every bit of you from our home? You hurt them so much that every trace of you was taken from the house. No belongings, no letters, no photos. You were deleted. It was as if you didn't exist.'

The room hung in stillness, the bitterness of Henry's outburst ricocheting through the air.

There was a knock at the door and Penny came in with a tea tray followed by Simon with sandwiches and cake.

'Thought you could all do with a cup of tea,' Penny smiled.

Deborah, remaining seated, managed, 'Lovely.'

Kit came from Ella's side towards Penny. 'Let me help you.'

Henry had thrown himself back into his chair and was biting his nails, staring into the fire.

Ella held back tears, her anger directed at Henry.

Sennen smoothed her multi-coloured dress and rearranged her scarf. 'That's very kind of you, but I have to leave.'

'So soon?' asked Simon anxiously.

'Yes,' Sennen replied and looked at Debbie. 'Would you take me back to Trevay, please?'

Deborah took the cue seamlessly and collected her bits together. 'Of course. Thank you so much for hosting this initial meeting, Simon. Penny.' She looked at Henry and Ella and held out her hand. 'Call me when you are ready.'

Ella got up and shook her hand. 'Thank you. We need time to . . . You understand?'

'Of course.' She looked over at Henry who was still chewing his fingers. 'Goodbye, Henry.'

The room emptied, leaving Ella and Henry with Kit, holding the teapot, in shocked silence.

'Well,' said Henry dryly, 'that went well.'

Ella let rip. 'You stupid idiot. You couldn't have made it worse, could you? That was our mother. You may not want to know her but I bloody well do. Granny and Poppa would be ashamed of you. They loved her. They loved us. They would want this to be a happy ending, but oh no, not you, you want to play life's victim and smash anything good that might come to us.'

'Who's playing the victim now?' Sneered Henry. 'I'm protecting you, Ella. Can't you see that? The minute you got close to her she'd kick you in the teeth and leave again. She'll break your heart and I'm not going to let that happen. Leopards do not change their spots.'

Ella began to cry with frustration and shock. 'She came out of love. Love for us.'

'Nope. It's love of money. That's why she's here.'

'You don't know that. People change. You haven't given her a chance. I want to know why she left and where she's been. Then I can make up my own mind and not have you doing it for me.'

Henry looked at his watch. 'Kit, would you be kind enough to take me to the station. I need to be back in London.'

He looked at Ella, sitting tear streaked and shaky in her chair. 'I'm sorry, Ells, but it's better you face reality.'

19

Sennen hadn't looked back as Deborah drove her out of Pendruggan village and down to Trevay. Neither woman spoke until Deborah drew up outside White Water's gate.

'I'll call you tomorrow?' she asked.

'Maybe the day after,' said Sennen. 'I need time to process what's just happened.'

'Understood. Get some rest.'

Sennen got out of the car.

'And Mrs Tallon-Singh,' said Deborah, 'these things are never easy at the start, but don't lose hope.'

Sennen let herself in through the newly familiar front door and climbed the stairs. The house appeared to be empty. She was glad; she could do without Amy coming out of the shadows bringing tea and questions.

On the landing she hesitated. A memory of bringing Henry home from the hospital suddenly assaulted her, his tiny hands and sweet lips, the fear that she wouldn't cope without Ali, the overbearing kindness of her parents choking her to the point where she didn't know who she was any more.

The hours she spent fantasising about finding Ali and becoming a family . . .

Across the landing was the door of her old bedroom. She held her breath, listening for any sound in the house indicating that she wasn't the only person in it. She had done this before, on the night she had left.

Black spots were forming in front of her and she felt weak and desolate. Her brain was foggy. A primitive reflex forced her to breathe again and she steadied herself on the smooth banister.

She looked at her hand on the wood. So like her mother's. Freckle-skinned and slender, long fingers. 'An artist's hand,' Poppa had always told her.

She closed her eyes and crumpled to the carpet.

'I am so sorry,' she whispered. 'I didn't mean to hurt anyone. I meant to come back. I didn't know you had died. I should have been here. For you and Henry and Ella. I've been so selfish and unkind. I would do anything to turn the clock back. Forgive me . . . Forgive me. Please.'

A ping of an incoming text sounded from her bag. Kafir. It must be Kafir. He hadn't contacted her since she had left India, although she had sent him several texts telling him she had arrived and asking after the children.

She scrabbled for the phone and checked the screen. It was from Deborah, checking that she was okay. She let the phone drop back.

Lying on the simple Swedish bed in her parent's old room, she closed her eyes.

Too tired to cry.

She felt leaden, almost relaxed.

The tumult of the meeting had drained her.

What had she expected?

After all these years.

She had left Santander on a train heading to Madrid.

For a few months she picked up casual bar work. She kept herself free of friendships and men, her only goal to eat, sleep and work. She ruthlessly scythed thoughts of home from her memory.

That first Christmas her postcard home was a picture of a female flamenco dancer. Her skirt was made of real fabric and lace and was sewn onto the card. She imagined Henry and Ella's little fingers stroking it. She had written something like 'Happy Christmas, don't worry.' She thought now how she'd feel if she received something similar from her children.

She had yearned to go home, but the shame of what she had done and fear of how she would be met, the trouble she'd be in, the punishment she'd face, kept her away.

She grew up fast.

From Madrid she travelled to Barcelona, learning the language, and how to survive. Bar work, shop work – anything that would pay for a little rent and food – she took.

But she never forgot the birthdays of Henry and Ella and would send cards, minus any hint as to her whereabouts, to the children and her parents on their special days.

Ali, she refused to think about.

One weekend a workmate suggested a trip to Sitges, a seaside town not far from Barcelona and renowned for its party atmosphere. She turned it down. 'Not my kind of thing,' she had said. But the girl wouldn't take no for an answer. 'You need some fun. A dance. A snog. A boyfriend.'

Sennen finally gave in. What else would she be doing on her day off? Her washing?

When they got there, the girl dumped her almost immediately for a handsome lifeguard and she was left to fend for herself.

It was almost lunchtime and she didn't want to sit on the beach feeling exposed and alone, so she found a café, with shaded awnings and scarlet geraniums and ordered a coke and a menu from the handsome waiter who began to chat her up.

'We have good tapas. Let me choose the best for you and maybe a glass of wine?'

She handed the menu back to him. 'Okay, but not the expensive stuff.'

He smiled. 'What are you doing on your own?'

'Having lunch.'

'Of course, I know that, but no friends meeting you?'

'Nope.'

'I can be your friend.'

'I'm fine.'

'Okay, I'll get your lunch.' He walked lightly through the tables and customers but was soon back with her food. He put it down with reverence and started chatting her up again.

'You're English?'

She nodded and began to eat to put him off.

'Your Spanish is very good.'

'Thank you.'

'My name is Emmanuel.'

She stopped eating. 'Please . . . I like to be on my own. Thank you.'

He put his hands up in surrender. 'Okay, okay, but I don't like to see sad girls eating in my bar. It is bad for business.'

He turned his attention to a group of four young men who had arrived noisily at a table behind Sennen's.

'You call me if you want anything,' he said to her as he went to welcome them warmly. Emmanuel clearly knew them well.

Sennen watched the four new arrivals as she ate. They spoke French and were very camp, flirting with Emmanuel outrageously.

Emmanuel played up to it, throwing his eyes to the heavens and saying, 'Ooh la la,' every time they said something a bit saucy.

Sennen caught his eye and ordered another glass of wine.

'My friends are very funny, no? You are not so sad now.' Emmanuel smiled as he poured the wine. 'Would you like to meet them?'

She shook her head.

'Please. They won't bite. Not you, anyway.' He smiled and held out his hand to her. Reluctantly she took it and he pulled her from her chair and introduced her to the boys.

'May I introduce Miss English?' He pulled out a chair for her. 'She won't tell me her real name and she is sad and has no friends.'

The boys sighed and pulled tragic faces, putting their right hands against their hearts as one. She tried not to laugh. 'My name is Sennen.'

The four men stood up and introduced themselves, one by one 'Serge.' 'Antoine.' 'Noa.' 'Clement.'

'The four musketeers?'

'Of course,' said the one called Serge. He was very tall and thin, with a large nose. 'Only we are much more fun.' He winked.

'They are here working in the Pigalle club,' explained Emmanuel.

'As what?' asked Sennen.

Serge pointed to the smallest of the troupe. 'Noa. Please.'

172

Noa instantly washed a hand over his twinkling face and revealed a frightened one behind it. He leapt onto his chair and began to search four invisible walls for a way out.

Sennen watched, enchanted.

He bent over from straight hips and began to feel for a trapdoor. As he bent over he pretended to fart and popped up straight again to mime an apology. He bent over again; the same thing happened and he wafted a hand under his nose. He did it a third time and fainted.

'You're mime artists!' said Sennen, clapping.

'Oui, mademoiselle,' said Serge. 'You win the star prize – which is to have another glass of wine and join us.'

The warm afternoon sun slowly dropped and the stars and lights of the café's canopy soon twinkled over the balmy evening.

Sennen had had enough wine to feel safe with these kind and funny strangers. When Serge put his arm around her she put her head on his shoulder without fear – the first time since Ali.

'You are very sad, Mademoiselle Sennen. Who has done this to you?'

'Too long a story.'

'I am all ears.'

She told him her miserable tale, leaving nothing out.

'C'est tristesse,' he said. 'You need to find another boy to erase the memory.'

'That's the last thing I want.' She picked up her wine glass and drank. 'I'm happy just as I am.'

'How old are you?'

'Almost twenty.'

'Oh well, you are very old.' He patted her hand and smiled.

'Tell me about you,' she asked.

'Of course. Well, I met Noa in Paris and we fell in love. He made me laugh and here we are. We were a little duo, writing and performing on the streets. One day we see Clement and Antoine busking outside Notre Dame. They are very good robots,' he said with great pride. 'So we convinced them to join us.'

'Was that hard?'

'Not really. They were hungry, we fed them pizza – et voila!' He laughed at the memory. 'You will see our show. We are very good. We have been in Spain all summer in the night clubs, doing our show, and now we are ready to go back to France.'

'Paris?' she asked.

'Paris, of course.' He gave a Gallic shrug. 'Want to come with us?'

'I can't.'

'Why not? You have told me you have no boyfriend, no family. We will look after you. Come and work for us.'

'I'm not an actor or anything.'

'Can you use a washing machine?'

'Yes.'

'That's it. Tous nos félicitations! You are the new Head of Wardrobe for Pour Le Silence.'

'Pour Le Silence?'

'Oui. That is what we are called.' He raised his eyebrows and asked in mock surprise, 'Do you know them?'

She played along. 'I've heard of them.'

'Parfait. They will love you. Okay, we go to Paris on Thursday.'

She spent almost seven years with the troupe. They travelled across Europe entertaining crowds of sometimes more than a thousand, sometimes only twenty.

Sennen graduated from laundering and mending their costumes to designing costumes for them. The more elaborate and outrageous, the more the group loved them.

One afternoon, as she was stitching feathers to a codpiece, Serge came looking for her. 'I have exciting news.'

'Tell me then.' She broke a bit of thread off with her teeth.

'We are going to England,' he announced.

Her heart lurched. 'Oh?' She avoided his eye.

'Yes. How long is it since you have been home?'

'What do you mean?' She stayed fixed on her stitching. Her hands were trembling.

He clicked his tongue. 'Home. To England.'

'It's no longer my home.'

'But we will need you to show us around.'

'Whereabouts in England?'

'Edinburgh, for the carnival.'

She was relieved. Just about as far from Cornwall as you could get. 'It's the festival, not carnival, and it's Scotland, not England.'

'Scotland? Will it be cold?'

'Not in August.'

'Good.' He pretended to shiver and warm his hands on her face. 'I don't like snow.'

'You'll need to wear some tartan,' she said already drawing sequined kilts and sporrans in her mind's eye.

'Like Jean-Paul Gaultier?' he said with excitement.

'Yessiree.'

He got up and did a little jig. 'The boys will be soooo happy.'

The boys were a huge success in Edinburgh and appeared on as many British talk shows and entertainment programmes as they could until they were found smoking hash in a BBC dressing room, so the work dried up and they returned to Paris.

Bickering broke out amongst them and eventually Noa walked out on Serge and ran towards an Italian waiter. Serge, heartbroken, left for his parents' home in Provence.

Pour Le Silence were no more.

Sennen was heartbroken, but she needed to find another job.

Through the grapevine she heard that a respected German ballet company were looking for a costume design assistant for an all-male production of *The Jungle Book*.

She got the job and within two weeks was in Berlin.

The production toured the world for five long years and she went with it. Europe. Scandinavia. South America. West Coast America. Australia. New Zealand. The Far East and finally, India.

20

Henry got off the tube at Clapham Common and headed towards 47 Mandalay Road, just as the London commuters were arriving home and the nightlife lovers were coming out.

The pavements smelt of a recent shower, and the restaurants and cafés were enticing people in with promises of smiling waiters, warm lights and fun.

He felt anything but fun. He knew he'd hurt his mother and Ella, that he'd said some terrible things – but what did they expect?

On the long train journey up from Bodmin, he'd turned the whole scene over and over in his mind. The woman he'd met today was not the mother he thought he remembered. He had thought he would know her. But the vague memories of sitting on his mother's lap, pointing at the pictures in a children's book were no more. All he now had in his mind's eye was redheaded bohemian who *couldn't* be his mother.

The phone in his pocket vibrated. He pulled it out and looked at it. 'Bugger off, Ella.' He terminated the call.

It was the sixth call he'd had from her since he'd left Cornwall. She must have phoned every half an hour and, in between, left texts ranging from kind and pleading, to tears and anger. Meeting his mother had turned his world upside down. The way she had said so little and been so unmoved by the whole experience . . . She hadn't explained or apologised for the past. She hadn't asked him, or Ella, anything about themselves.

Selfish. Cold. Cruel. Disinterested.

And what was this *Mrs* Tallon-Singh about? So she'd married and given herself a fancy double-barrelled name. Well hoo-bloody-rah for her.

A thought struck him.

She was young enough to have had a second family.

Now it all came clear to him. Yes, that was it. She had a new family and could do with some money. The old family, him and Ella, could go to hell. She done it before so it would be so easy for her to do it again.

His gut was seething. He could murder a pint. At the top of Mandalay road was his local, the Kings Head. The doors opened and a young woman in a leather biker jacket stepped out with her arms around a young man. They brought with them the waft of beer on the breeze, a waft he allowed to surf him to the bar.

'He's not answering his phone,' said Ella, banging hers down on the table. 'What a pig-headed, rude man he can be. Can you believe how awful he was today?'

Kit, rather more on Henry's side than Ella's, was noncommittal. 'I think he was just being honest. It was how he feels and he told her.'

Ella was horrified. 'Our *mother* was there, in front of us

after all these years, and instead of making her feel welcome, he was horrible. No wonder she felt she had to leave. I'm impressed she didn't give him a piece of her mind.'

They were in the lounge of Marguerite Cottage, sitting on opposing chairs rather than their usual position on the sofa together.

'I'm just saying that I could see his point of view.' He watched as Ella's face grew darker and quickly added, 'Just as I see yours.'

'Do you?' she asked angrily.

'Darling, of course I do. You know I do. But I'm a bloke; maybe I'm not so good at expressing it.'

She pulled one corner of her mouth up sullenly while defensively reaching for a cushion and holding it against her chest. 'Huh.'

'What does *huh* mean?'

'Just huh.'

He changed tack. 'Hungry?'

'No.'

'G and T?'

'No.'

'Okay.' He thought of something to say that wouldn't be too contentious. '*Coronation Street* is on in a minute. That always cheers you up.'

Ella burst into tears and left the room.

Henry was on the outside of two pints and feeling just a little bit better, when a hand caressed his shoulder. 'Hi, Henry.' Soft, heavily lipsticked lips kissed his cheek. He looked over his shoulder to see who it was and his spirits rose.

'Oh, hi, Ashley.' Glossy brunette hair, thick eyelashes, and great fun. When he had first come to London, he had rented a room in a flat she shared with two other girls. For Henry, Ashley was the one that had got away. Maybe tonight was his lucky night.

'Long time no see,' she said and smiled.

'Yeah. Sorry. Work. Stuff. You know how it is.' His eyes scanned her braless breasts, suspended inside a tiny, strappy crop top. 'Want a drink?'

'Sure. A Cosmo, please.'

Henry caught the eye of the barman and shouted Ashley's order plus another pint for himself. 'So,' he said, adopting his best pulling voice, 'what's new?'

She flicked her hair. 'I'm modelling, now.'

He tried to make himself more comfortable on his bar-stool 'Yeah? Given up the old temping lark, eh?'

The barman delivered their drinks. 'Cheers.'

'Cheers.' They raised their glasses and drank.

'What sort of modelling?' asked Henry, casually.

'You wouldn't be interested?'

'Wouldn't I?'

'It's rather . . . adult.'

He felt his pulse quicken. 'I think I could handle that.'

Her very white teeth bit her bottom lip charmingly. 'Well, it's for . . .'

'Tell me.'

'Underwear.'

'Oh yes?'

She laughed, then sexily revealed. 'Thermal underwear.'

He blinked twice as what she said sank in. She was laughing. 'Long johns and vests.'

He started to giggle and the more she laughed, the more he laughed, until he was wiping tears away. 'Ashley,' he

managed, 'You have no idea how much I needed to laugh tonight. Another Cosmo?'

Ella, in bed, lay on her side as far from Kit as she could manage. She felt more lonely than she had felt since Granny had died.

Her mother was back, the woman who had deserted her before she could even remember, had come back. Ella couldn't believe it was just for the money. No, she had come out of love – or, if not love, at least curiosity, just as Ella was curious about her. And Henry, her stupid brother, had behaved like an absolute child.

Anger infused her grief and brewed a painful stew of emotions. Why were men such idiots? How could Kit sympathise with Henry? How was her mum feeling right now after Henry's appalling outburst?

Ella imagined how disappointed Sennen must have been in them both today. No affection. No kindness. No attempt at reconciliation. God, how awful Sennen must be feeling now. Well, she, Ella, was going to meet her mother and make amends. In the morning she'd phone the solicitors and fix another meeting. Just her and her mum. Sod Henry.

Henry was very, very drunk by chucking out time.

Ashley was surprisingly sober and realised she was responsible for getting him home. 'Come on, time for us to get out of here,' she said grabbing an arm and put it across her shoulder. 'Good job I do kettle bells in the gym. Knew it would come in handy.'

'I love you, Ashley,' Henry slobbered. 'How come you and I have never got it on, eh?'

'You know why. Our house rule, remember? Never sleep with a flatmate.'

'But I'm not your flatmate now, am I?'

'That's true, but,' she sighed, 'my fiancé really wouldn't like it.'

'What's he got that I haven't?'

She laughed. 'You always were a trier. Come on, let's get you home.'

She managed to get him to his front door and find his keys in his trouser pocket. 'Here you are. Home sweet home.' She got him over the threshold and propped him against a radiator while she closed the door. He slid to the floor. She stepped over him and went to find the kitchen and coffee.

Henry crawled on all fours along the narrow hallway towards the lounge.

'Are you all right in there?' Ashley called, spooning sugar into a mug. 'Caffeine, mega dose, on its way.'

She found him on the sofa trying to turn the television on. 'This bloody clicker doesn't work. Bloody batteries I 'spect.'

Ashley took it and had a good look. 'Batteries are fine. It's just that this is a calculator. Now settle back and drink this.'

'Are you mothering me?' he slurred plaintively.

'No.'

'I need mothering, though. You see, my mum left me when I was little. I saw her today and I was very mean to her. My sister is cross with me.'

Ashley forced a mouthful of coffee between his lips. 'Drink.'

He took a mouthful then pushed the mug away. 'I'd like a whisky.'

'You're not having one.' She gave him the mug. 'Hold this and drink.'

'Okay.' He used his free hand to brush his fringe out of his eyes. 'I think I have to apologise.'

'No, you don't. We all get a bit pissed sometimes.'

'Not to you, no, to my mum. I was a horrid . . .' He began to sniff. 'I think that's why she left me. Maybe it was my fault. Something I did? And now I've been awful again and she'll go away again and my sister will never speak to me.' He broke down into wretched sobs. 'I missed her so much. Granny and Poppa tried their best but I felt their sadness. Why did she leave us all so miserable?'

Ashley sighed and put her arms around him. 'Come on, then. Let it all out. I'm here.'

When he'd cried himself to sleep on the sofa, Ashley removed herself gently so as not to disturb him and went in search of a blanket. Once she was sure he was settled and safe, she wrote him a note telling him not to waste any more precious time and to apologise to his sister and mother and go back to see them as soon as possible.

Then she let herself out of the house and disappeared into the night.

21

Sennen was lying in her room at White Water, channel hopping. So many channels. So much rubbish. Eventually she settled on a biopic of Audrey Hepburn but her mind refused to concentrate and she turned it off. What was she even doing here? Why come back and disrupt the lives of the two people she had abandoned? She had denied their existence, had never been there for them, when they scraped a knee or needed her. She'd been running. Scared. She knew her parents had turned their back on her as she had turned her back on them. She was an outcast who had had to reinvent herself, her heart under lock and key, lying deep in an impenetrable carapace of loss and self-hatred.

But then, Kafir had found her. Loved her and believed all she had told him, the made-up stories of her childhood and loving parents. At the beginning of their relationship she couldn't tell him about Henry and Ella. And later, when she knew he loved her and she lived within their safe and secure marriage, and she had wanted to tell him the truth, it was too late. She tricked herself into believing the past was in the past. Dead, buried and unable to rise up and bite her. Kafir would never find out.

And that was the second terrible mistake of her life.

She rubbed her hands over her eyes and tried to remember why she had thought running away, leaving Henry and Ella to her parents, had been in any way a good idea. Who had she been all those years ago? What had she imagined her future would be? She groaned into the empty air of her parents' old room. This time she had nowhere to run to.

She picked her phone up for the umpteenth time to see if Kafir had messaged her. He hadn't.

She argued with herself. If she sent him another text, would she seem desperate? If she didn't, would she seem uncaring? Should she send a message telling him how selfish he was and that he couldn't stop her from seeing the children? She would take him to court. They would divorce. He could visit for two weeks in the summer holidays.

Would he fight her? Yes, he would. He was a proud man with high morals and innate kindness and he hated injustice.

Had she lost another family? She was sure that Henry would never want to see her again. Ella might, but she couldn't be certain of that, either. She bashed the pillows behind her head into submission and picked up the phone again. She'd throw herself on Kafir's mercy. She had already gambled one family for another and possibly lost both. She had nothing left but her dignity.

The text she sent was an honest account of her day and how awful it had been. She asked after Aali and Sabu and told Kafir she loved him. She finished with her wish for him to speak with her – and added that she needed him more than even she had known.

*

Kafir. Even his name made her happy.

When she had arrived in India, all those years ago, she was no longer the girl who had left Cornwall. The ballet had toured Kerala, Goa and Delhi before its final end in Agra, Rajasthan. She wasn't sorry. Five years of touring was enough for anybody and she wanted to unpack her suitcase and call somewhere home. On the last night, cast and crew made their quiet farewells and took flights back to wherever they called home. They would never be together in the same group, sharing the same adventures, dancing the same dances again.

Sennen was envious that they had somewhere to return to. Partners, parents, families. She had no one. She wasn't welcome back in Cornwall any more. She told herself that this was what she wanted, that she was lucky to have her freedom, to be liberated from the bother of other people. So she stayed in Agra and looked for lodgings.

This was the city of the Taj Mahal. The mausoleum built of ivory white marble; the world's greatest monument a man has ever built to his dead wife.

Sennen had to see it. She went in the early morning – the best time to visit, according to the friendly concierge at her cheap hotel. And he was right. The day was still cool and the queues of air-conditioned coaches, spilling out tourists from around the globe, had not yet arrived.

Outside the famous walled grounds, trinket vendors and small children called out to her, holding Taj Mahal snow-domes, pens, postcards, mugs and all manner of delightful tourist tat. She couldn't resist a snowdome and paid too much for it but the small girl with a pink frilly dress and crutches pulled her heart strings.

Putting the treasure into her cotton shoulder bag, she walked to the great archway for her first glimpse of the shrine.

Shimmering in the early light, a bright blue sky behind it and a grassed garden with many still water channels in front of it, stood the Taj Mahal.

This was what the love of one man could do for one woman. She walked forward into the garden and saw a group of Canadian tourists gathered round a white marble bench, one of many set symmetrically around the garden. She stopped and eavesdropped, listening to what the Indian guide was saying.

'The late Princess of Wales sat right here on this very bench. You remember the photo?' he asked them. They nodded, wryly.

'Diana, the girl who married a future king but one who did not love her as Shah Jahan, the Moghul Emperor, loved his favourite wife, whom he called Mumtaz Mahal, which means Jewel of the Palace. Taj is the Indian word for Crown and that is why this building is called Taj Mahal. You understand?' His audience nodded. 'And now you would like pictures taken on Diana's bench, yes?'

Sennen moved away, not wanting to witness the scramble for mawkish photos. She was glad that she was single, with no chance of having her heart broken again.

The teenage girl she had been was gone. Replaced by this quiet woman who asked little of anybody.

There had been no boyfriend after Ali. She withdrew from relationships and told herself she was entirely happy being self-contained and free of complication. It wasn't that she didn't attract male attention: she was a very striking young woman. Her mane of glorious Titian curls fell around her shoulders, framing her pale-skinned, lightly freckled, face; her eyes were wide and lively, her long legs carried her tall, willowy frame with elegance. To herself, however, she was almost invisible. An invisible woman with too much height, too much hair.

Agra was a busy city, colourful and noisy. She enjoyed finding herself a room in a large house full of 'waifs and strays' as she thought of them, herself included.

She joined early morning yoga class and became friendly with the women there. They took her to the markets and introduced her to the exotic produce on sale and taught her how to cook with them.

Sometimes she held small dinner parties, trying out her new skills, and was gratified when her dahl was approved of. She lived simply and inexpensively, expecting nothing. If this was to be her life until the end, she was content. She lived like that, taking in mending and alterations, while residents came and went, some more pleasant than others, growing truly close to none of them. Then Tanvi arrived one afternoon, a childless widow who took the room across the hall from Sennen's, on the second floor of the house. Sennen liked her and their friendship grew. Soon they took it in turns to invite each other over to their rooms to take chai each Wednesday at four o'clock.

On one particular Wednesday it was Sennen's turn to invite Tanvi for tea, and when Tanvi knocked, Sennen was finishing off a pair of curtains that she had made from a bolt of glorious saffron-coloured cotton from the market.

'Come in,' called Sennen, snipping the last thread from the final drape. Tanvi appeared with her usual offering of sweetmeats. Today it was gulab jamum, an Indian version of sticky doughnuts.

She put them down on the small tea table and admired the curtains. 'So colourful.' She clapped and went to feel the fabric between her fingers. 'And good quality. Who are they for?'

'Me. I need something to cheer the room up,' smiled Sennen. 'I just need to press them and then I'll put them up.'

Tanvi looked at the high curtain rail surrounding the French windows leading onto Sennen's balcony. The existing curtains drooped exhaustedly.

'You have a ladder?' asked Tanvi.

'I'm tall, I'm sure I can reach standing on a chair.'

'And risk hurting yourself? No, no, you need a man to do this.'

Sennen smiled ruefully. 'And where would I find one?'

'My nephew. He is tall, and,' she gave Sennen a sly look, 'handsome and single.'

Sennen shook her head. 'Not him again! If I didn't know you better I'd think you were matchmaking.'

'I am,' laughed Tanvi.

'I'm sure your nephew is marvellous, but I am happy as I am. You know that. I'll make the chai.'

She walked to a corner of her room where a small kitchen, basic but perfectly practical, was set up. She lit the gas and put the kettle on the hob.

Tanvi was still sizing up the height of the curtain rail over windows. 'I cannot allow you to hang your glorious curtains without assistance.'

Sennen took the boiling kettle and poured it into her dented, chased-silver teapot. 'You make the rules for me, do you?'

Tanvi tutted. 'I care for you. I was joking about you liking my nephew, but I could come and get him to hang them – you give him chai and that's that. Nothing more.'

Sennen brought the tea tray to the table. 'Well,' she admitted reluctantly, 'it would be helpful. I tried to get the old ones down last night but I couldn't reach far enough. Does your nephew have a ladder?'

'If he doesn't, he can borrow one.'

Sennen weighed up the inconvenience of having a stranger in her room, versus the difficulty of doing the job. 'Okay. You can ask him. But I'll pay him for his trouble.'

'He'll come tomorrow afternoon.'

'You haven't asked him yet.'

'He will come. What time? I'll make sure he won't be late.'

It was arranged for five thirty the following evening and Sennen spent the following morning tidying her bedsitting room. No man had been here since she had arrived and her bed looked too intimate. She disguised it with a scarlet piece of beaded cotton, found in the general store across the road, and put two large, green, silk bolsters at either end. She hoped it looked more like a sofa.

She baked a few samosas in case the nephew might expect some food and then she waited.

At five thirty came Tanvi's recognisable knock. 'Come in,' called Sennen from the kitchen. Tanvi came in with a twinkle in her eye and a tall, very handsome, man in a pink turban behind her.

'Hello.' Sennen walked towards him, her hand outstretched. 'Thank you so much for coming to help me. It was your auntie's idea.'

He had the smoothest skin she had ever seen on a man. The whites of his eyes were like mother of pearl, his pupils like liquid chocolate.

He smiled broadly, showing perfect teeth. He put down the small stepladder he was carrying, took her hand and shook it. 'I am Kafir. What my aunt orders, I do.'

Tanvi touched his arm and looked at Sennen. 'Didn't I tell you she was very pretty? And almost as tall as you.'

He had the grace to look embarrassed.

'What have I said?' asked Tanvi. 'I only say what I see.'

Sennen waved a hand towards her kitchen, 'Would you like something to drink?' she asked.

'That would be kind,' he said, 'After I have put up the curtains, maybe?'

He set up his stepladder and Sennen held them still at the bottom, acutely aware of his long, strong legs so close to her face. She found herself noticing how nicely his jeans fitted.

'Here . . .' He handed down to her an end of the first curtain. His hands were beautiful. 'Now if I can just . . .' He reached over and unhooked the other end. 'Can you take this? It is a bit dusty.'

'Goodness knows how long they have been there,' said Sennen.

'I will go and get a duster,' said Tanvi, 'I have one in my room.'

Alone together, Kafir, still on the ladder, looked out at the view. 'You have a better view than Auntie and a bigger balcony.'

'Tanvi says that her view is better. She likes the garden, but I like the noise coming up from the street. I sit and watch life go by.'

'So you are nosey?' he said, looking down at her, smiling. He really did have lovely teeth.

'A bit,' she laughed.

'Here we are, here we are.' Tanvi came back waving a long-handled feather duster. She passed it up to Kafir.

'Better stand back down there,' he told the two women, 'I may disturb a few spiders.'

Within ten minutes, the three of them were standing back

and admiring their work. 'Very nice,' said Tanvi. 'Your sewing skills are excellent.' She looked at Kafir. 'The curtains in your house need updating. Sennen could do them for you.'

Kafir politely shook his head, 'My curtains will do as they are, and why would Sennen wish to make me new ones.'

'It would be something to keep her busy.'

Sennen was loading a tray with samosas and lemonade and heard what Tanvi had said. 'It's true. I could do with small jobs to keep me occupied.' She picked the tray up. 'Shall we have this on the balcony?'

There was a short flurry for the moving of the tea table outside and shaking the yellow bougainvillea blossoms from her outdoor chairs.

Sennen handed around the plate of samosas and poured glasses of fresh lemonade.

'May I ask what do you do?' asked Kafir, munching a samosa.

Tanvi interrupted and told Kafir all that she knew about Sennen's work.

He listened attentively. 'So that is how you have come to be in Agra?'

'Yes. More lemonade?'

'Thank you.' Kafir lifted his glass towards her and she poured some more. 'These samosas are very good,' he said taking another.

'She is a very good cook too,' Tanvi said. 'And she's still young.'

Kafir quietly rebuked her. 'Auntie, you must know you are embarrassing Sennen and me. Please.' He drew his finger over his lip. 'Stop talking.' He turned once more to Sennen. 'What did you study at university?'

Sennen laughed ruefully. 'I left school at sixteen and started to travel. I am qualified for nothing.'

'But you are a seamstress?'

'Well, yes, by default.'

'Do not talk yourself down. You have a creative skill that we are losing in schools. Too many parents want their children to be doctors or solicitors.'

Sennen put her glass down. 'So may I ask what you do?'

'I teach.'

She smiled. 'Medicine or law?'

'Neither. Economics.'

'He got his degree at the London School of Economics in London,' Tanvi pitched in proudly.

He scratched his ear self-effacingly. 'Auntie, I'm sure Sennen knows many people who went to the LSE.'

'I don't,' said Sennen. 'In fact, I've never been to London.'

She told him about her early years in Cornwall, painting a rather exaggerated picture of herself that was less than true and entirely missing out the existence of Henry and Ella.

'How wonderful that your parents let you go,' he said.

'Yes, well, they are artists and rather bohemian. They encouraged me to experience the artist colonies of Europe,' she lied.

'When did they last see you?' asked Tanvi.

And before she really knew what she was saying, Sennen said, 'Oh, I'm sorry to say they are no longer with us. I don't really like to talk to about it but they were very loving, kind parents.'

Tanvi leant forward and gently took Sennen's hand. 'Well, now you have me and our weekly chai afternoons.'

'Oh yes. My mother would have loved your recipe for the gulab jamum. Now tell me all about you, Kafir.' And, as simply as that, Sennen had rewritten her past and made her parents ghosts.

'Well,' said Kafir standing up some time later and collecting his stepladder, 'I have taken too much of your time.'

Sennen stood too. 'You have been very kind. Let me give you something for your time.' She went to her purse on the disguised bed.

'To see you happy with my work is enough.' He smiled and went to the door. 'Come along, Auntie. Let us leave Miss Sennen.'

As she closed the door on her visitors, thanking them both again profusely, she looked at her room and its new curtains. The colour was just right.

The evening had been just right.

Something inside her had shifted a little.

As if someone had poured a little oil on to a rusted bolt.

22

It was the cramp in Henry's calf that woke him. His face was squashed up against the arm of Granny's old sofa and he was dribbling on one of Ella's hand-embroidered cushions. His unsquashed eye felt sore and he rubbed a hand over it. It was gritty with the dried salt of last night's tears.

It all came back to him. His awful behaviour at the vicarage. Drowning his sorrows. He had cried. He was an idiot.

He tried to stand on his cramped leg and limped painfully to the kitchen. He needed some paracetamol.

He poured a glass of water, necked the painkillers and went back to the sofa.

How was he going to make amends to Ella after he said all those terrible things yesterday?

Ella woke up very chirpy. She had slept well, having made the decision to meet her mother without Henry. What was stopping her? She rolled over and spooned Kit, stroking his tummy to wake him up.

'Morning, Kit,' she whispered into his ear.

'Morning,' he said guardedly. He wasn't certain where this was leading.

'Sorry about last night.' She nibbled his neck.

'Okay . . .' he replied slowly.

'I'm going to forget about Henry and see Mum by myself.'

'Riight.'

'Would you come with me?'

'I don't know. Do you want me to?'

'Of course. She's going to be your mother-in-law.' Ella shifted her weight and sat on top of him.

'Oof,' he said, 'you're heavy.'

'Tell me you'll come to see Mum or I won't get off you.'

'Get me a cup of tea and we'll talk about it.'

She kissed him and jumped off the bed. 'Thank you.'

'I haven't said I will yet.'

'You will.'

Snuggled back in bed and drinking tea, Ella talked about her childhood. 'It was good, really. Better than if Mum had been around, probably. She was so young. I can't imagine what it was like for her. Seventeen and with two children. I sort of don't blame her for running away.'

Kit, wisely, said nothing. He drank his tea and listened.

'When Henry and I got chickenpox, he started crying for Mum. I think that's when I realised I didn't have one. Granny and Poppa were so good to us, though. They took in all these funny art students and taught them everything they knew about art and pottery. Those students really loved Granny and Poppa. Henry and I would get a bit jealous sometimes.' She twisted her red curls round her fingers as she talked. Kit watched her.

'You got your mum's hair.'

'I know. That was a shock. Having never seen even a photo of her, I had no idea. Do you think she's attractive?'

'Yeah. She's all right.'

'I wonder if I will look like her at her age,' she mused.

'How old is she?'

'I'm not sure. About . . .' She did some mental arithmetic. 'I'd say about forty-one or two.' She stopped. 'I don't even know when her birthday is. Or what sign she is.'

'Weird.'

'Yeah. She's missed all my growing up. Henry's growing up too. She won't know how well he did at business school or how well he's doing now. Or about the time he fell off his skateboard and broke my arm.'

'Really?' asked Kit.

'Yeah. I just happened to be in the way. Poppa was so good. Whizzed me off to the cottage hospital in Bodmin and got me fixed. I milked it like anything. Henry had his pocket money stopped for a month.'

'Poor Henry.'

'Poor me, actually. It bloody hurt.'

'Come here,' said Kit, lifting his arm so that she could nestle against his shoulder. 'It must have been very hard for your grandparents, but they did a fantastic job. I really like Henry.'

Ella looked up into his eyes. 'What about me?'

'You're not so bad.'

Ella's phone rang. 'Hello?'

'Hi, Ells, it's me.'

Ella rolled her eyes and mouthed to Kit, Henry, then said aloud, 'Hi.'

'I'm really sorry about yesterday.'

'You should be.'

'I'd like to come back to Trevay?'

'Why?' Ella didn't want to make this easy for him.

'Because . . .' She heard him sigh with frustration. 'Because I want to apologise to Mum in person. And get to know her. Like a civilised man should do.'

'Hmm,' said Ella.

'Don't make this difficult. Ells, please.'

'When are you thinking of coming?'

'Tomorrow? Can I stay with you?'

'I'll have to ask Kit.'

'Well, could you let me know? Then I'll arrange it with work. I'm due a bit of extenuating circumstances.'

'I was thinking I might see Mum on my own first,' Ella said airily.

'Oh. I see. Of course. I understand.'

'I'm going to phone Deborah today and sort a meeting out.'

'Will you let me know what's decided? I really do want to make amends.'

'Yeah, well. I'll bell you later.'

Sennen still hadn't heard from Kafir. She'd woken, very early, after a dream that he was on the next flight to Cornwall, bringing Aali and Sabu with him.

She checked the time on her phone – 5.45. The start of her day, but Kafir would be well into his. He would have given the children breakfast, taken Aali to school and Sabu to the nursery he loved. She imagined Kafir planning what he would cook them for dinner. Aali liked everything, but Sabu was picky. He liked rice and flatbreads and chicken, but most vegetables he shunned. Sennen smiled to herself, thinking how Kafir would get so cross after making a special cauliflower curry or vegetable bhaji. Sennen always had a supply of tarka

dal in the freezer for Sabu. She hoped now that there was still some left. She had better put lentils on the list. She checked herself. What was she thinking? She was not there, in India, not able to feed her own children. The thought inevitably took her onto the hamster wheel of anxiety that turned towards Henry and Ella. She hadn't been there to feed them, either. She had no idea of their likes and dislikes. The wheel turned another circle and took her to a place of self-flagellation. How could she have done what she'd done to all four of her children? Who was she? *What* was she? The emotional pain in her gut speared through her, made her restless.

Getting out of bed, she got up, got dressed and let herself out of the sleeping house as quietly as she could.

The harbour was as still as a millpond, the reflections of the fishing boats and pleasure boats shining in its glassiness.

A couple of gulls cackled above her and flew out over the water.

She stood against the harbour wall and listened. She heard another seagull, high among the slate roofs and chimney pots, skittering on the tiles, the gentle lapping of the sea against the hulls of the boats, the whistle of man walking his dog.

She closed her eyes and breathed in. Immediately, she was twelve. Poppa was looking over her shoulder and guiding her hand as she drew the line of a fishing boat in pencil, on her sketchpad.

'Remember what you know about perspective. That boat is face on to you. Think how big it is in comparison to the back . . . That's it.' He stood back and watched her childish work, her tongue between her teeth as she concentrated. 'You'll be giving your mum a run for her money,' he had said.

She screwed her closed eyes up tightly and shook herself. It was too late for regrets.

She walked around the harbour and down the narrow lane that connected with a network of smaller lanes crouching behind the sea. The old butchers, that had had the greengrocers next door, now knocked into one big 'holiday clothes' shop. The windows displayed jolly blue and white striped T-shirts, shorts, summer dresses and warm jumpers. She saw her reflection in the glass and realised how odd and foreign she must look in her long Indian skirt and scarf. Perhaps she should treat herself to a little shopping? Become a person of Trevay again. Yes, after breakfast when the shops were open, that's what she would do.

She crept back into the house and checked her phone. Nothing.

She switched on the radio, ran a bath and thought about what her new wardrobe of clothes should look like.

Breakfast was quick, just a coffee and cereal. Amy wanted to engage her in a discussion about sausages versus chipolatas for breakfast but Sennen made an excuse and escaped to the shops.

She needed some jeans. She went into the first shop that had clothes in the window and spoke to the young male assistant. 'How do people wear jeans nowadays? I mean, of my age. I want to look as if I understand fashion without looking laughable.'

He was a nice-looking boy with a cheeky face and wispy beard. His hair was shaven around the sides with a long top bit caught in a ponytail. 'What do you mean laughable? You look great. I love the Indian vibe you've got going on.'

'I have lived in India for a long time. But I'd like to look a little more local. Less foreign.'

'Cool. Whereabouts in India?'

'Agra. Do you know it?'

'Nah. I've been to Goa, though. Really cool place.'

'Yes. I have been there too. Very hot.'

'Yeah. It was. So what size are you?'

'A medium I'd say.'

He gave her a funny, mocking look. 'I mean jean size.'

'I have no idea.'

He ran his eyes over her. 'You look like a 28-29 waist and you've good long legs so . . .' He riffled through a pile of jeans and pulled a pair out. 'These are straight legs, but I'll see if I've got some boyfriends or skinnies. Do you like high or low rise?'

'I have no idea what you're saying,' she laughed.

'Go in the changing room and try these first.' He chucked her the jeans and obediently she took them to the changing room. She pulled up the zip, straightened the legs and gave herself a good hard stare. She was so used to seeing herself in the loose Indian trousers and tops that she loved, she was amazed to see that her stomach was, if not exactly taut, flatter than she had thought. She turned to the side and observed her profile. Her bottom looked smaller, her hips too.

She heard the assistant outside the curtain. 'How are they?' he asked.

Nervously, she drew the curtain back; her dress, that she hadn't bothered to take off, was hoiked up around her waist.

'What do you think?'

'Too big. I'll get the size down. Length's good and I like the low rise on you.' He handed her another two pairs. 'Try these. One's boyfriend, the other's skinny.'

'Okay.' She pulled the curtain back, stared at herself again. She felt a change. Maybe there was a glimmer of the person she had been or could be?

The young man came back and slipped the new, smaller jeans through the curtain.

She tried the boyfriends first.

He didn't like them. 'No. Hand them back. With your figure, I think the skinnies are best for you.'

Obediently, and thrilled by his compliment, she wriggled into the skinnies.

'Proper rock chick,' he said when she revealed herself. 'All you need is some flats or a pair of ankle boots – preferably with spiky heels – and you're good to go. Now just try the smaller straight ones.'

In the end she had the skinny's, the straights, a pair of Superga trainers, a couple of lovely soft cotton tops that fell, very fetchingly, off one shoulder, and a cream, cable-knitted sloppy joe pullover.

At the till, clutching her bag of goodies, she said, 'Thank you so much. You have been very kind.'

He handed her the receipt. 'Enjoy. You know where I am if you want anything else.'

She left the shop feeling ten feet tall. Her mind was on getting herself a pair of ankle boots when she heard her name being called. She looked in the direction of the voice and saw a woman, her own age, waving at her across the road. 'Sennen? It's Rosemary!' the woman shouted.

Sennen stared, open-mouthed, 'Rosemary!'

Rosemary crossed the road and hugged her. 'My God, what are you doing back here? I was only thinking about you the other day. Have you time for a coffee?'

Sennen, completely taken aback by this sudden encounter, said, 'Erm, well . . . I was . . .'

Rosemary cut her off. 'Just half an hour. I'm buying.'

*

The coffee shop was busy and the two women took a little while to reach an empty table, in a far corner near the loos, stepping across pushchairs and toddlers.

'You get settled and I'll go and order. Latte? Cappu?'

'Just a tea, please. Black, no sugar,' said Sennen. She was still reeling from the second collision of her past hitting her present in two days.

'So,' said Rosemary, 'what are you doing here? Visiting the children? I thought they had gone to London after your mum died?'

Sennen felt an anxiety headache creeping into the back of her eyes. 'It's all rather complicated, actually. Yes, I have come to see the children but the meeting didn't go very well.'

Rosemary eye's shone with compassion. 'Do you want to talk about it?'

Sennen surprised herself with how much she wanted to tell Rosemary everything that had happened since putting her on the boat at Santander, and it all came out.

The telling of the story in the cramped Cornish coffee shop, transported her back to the moment, standing in her bright, Indian kitchen, pans and herbs hanging from the ceiling, when she had told Kafir her secret.

At first his face, his glorious beautiful face, was clouded with confusion, followed by heartbreak and then pure, white hot anger, that the woman she had told him she was had never existed. He was married to a liar and a cheat. Sennen relived the moment as she told Rosemary.

'I had to tell you, Kafir,' she had wept. 'They have found me and I must go back.'

'You wouldn't have told me otherwise? You would have kept up the pretence forever?' he had shouted.

'It's not like that. I have been shamed by my lies. You have no idea how much I have wanted to tell you.'

'Then why didn't you? Did you think so little of me that you couldn't be honest with me?'

'No, no.' Her words came in sobs. 'I thought you wouldn't want me, that I was used goods, that you couldn't marry me because I have two illegitimate children.'

'You really think that I am that unsophisticated? You don't know me at all, do you?' He looked at her coldly. 'And I surely don't know you. What other lies have you told me?'

'Nothing. Nothing else.'

'Other than you told me that your kind and loving parents died long before they actually did die? You conveniently killed them off?'

'Well, yes. And I am so ashamed. But, it seemed easier and . . .'

'Sennen, I am sorry for you, but I am even sorrier that our marriage was based on your lies.'

She crumpled then, her shoulders hunched, her face in her hands.

Kafir watched her. 'So what are you going to do?'

'I must go home. I must sort it out,' she snivelled.

'And if I told you that I won't allow you to go?'

She stared at him in surprise. 'You wouldn't do that, would you?'

'Why not? You are my wife and it is your duty to stay with me and the children.'

'Yes, but . . .' She was confused; he had never been such a person. 'I *have* to go. You understand why, don't you?'

He folded his arms and looked at his feet.

'Kafir? Come with me. We can take the children.'

Still he said nothing.

'Please, come with me? I need you.'

'No. I shall stay here. Someone has to look after Sabu and Aali. If they haven't got their mother they will need their father. But I will get you a ticket to go home and you will face your first children and you will beg their forgiveness.'

'What will you tell Sabu and Aali?'

'The truth. It is better they know while they are young.'

'And us? Our marriage?'

'I can't promise anything. You have turned my world and the world of our children upside down. We will need to pray and think. Now, I shall pick the children up from school and you must pack. Do not be here when I get back.' He turned his back and walked out of the house.

Rosemary listened, occasionally offering a paper napkin in lieu of a tissue, and reaching over to rub Sennen's hand.

'You've been to hell and back,' she told Sennen simply.

Sennen wiped her nose and sighed. 'My own making.'

'Surely Kafir will come around.'

'I don't know. He can't understand how I could have lied to him. I am not the person he thought he'd married. I've hurt him.'

'Yes, but your two little ones . . .' Rosemary struggled to remember their names.

'Aali and Sabu,' said Sennen.

'You're are not turning your back on them, are you?'

Sennen pressed the heels of her hands into her eyes and rubbed at them. 'No. But I feel, oh, just . . . shit right now. I've let everyone down. My parents, my four children and my husband. And all because I made a huge mistake when I was so very young.'

Rosemary leaned in. 'I've always wondered, who is Henry's father? Did he hurt you? I mean were you . . . ?'

'It doesn't matter who he was. He was even more selfish and stupid than I was, and no, he didn't make me do anything I didn't want.'

'And Ella's father?'

'The same person.'

'I see. Do they know who he is?'

'No. I am the only person.'

'Even he doesn't know?'

Sennen shook her head, her mouth drawing a tight line.

Rosemary looked at her old friend with kindness. 'I think we need another tea and coffee.'

When Rosemary came back, she brought biscuits and a round of cheese and pickle sandwiches. Sennen forced herself to cheer up. 'So, I've bored myself and bored you too, so come on. Your turn. What has happened to you over the last twenty-five years?'

'Well, I'm a quarter of a century older,' laughed Rosemary.

'What happened when you got back from Spain. Were your parents furious? Did they hate me?' asked Sennen.

'No. They were happy that I was okay. I felt guilty because they were so nice about it.' Rosemary paused. 'And I felt so sorry for your parents.'

Sennen's throat tightened. 'You saw them? Took the toys for Henry and Ella?'

'Yes. I asked the police to take me to your house before they took me home. I gave them the toys but your father was very angry. He shut the door on me and I was too scared to see them again.'

'Angry?' Sennen felt tears pricking her eyes.

'Yes. But polite. You know what I mean? I think he was angry because I was on his doorstep and not you.'

Sennen dropped her head to hide her tears. 'And now my children are angry because I am on their doorstep, and not their granny or poppa.'

'Two wrongs don't make a right.' Rosemary said quietly. 'You can understand how they feel. You just have to show them, tell them what you feel about them and how much you've missed them.'

'Maybe.'

Sennen's phone rang. She snatched it up. 'Hello?'

'Mrs Tallon-Singh, Deborah Palmer here. I have news. Your daughter wants to see you. Just the two of you.'

Sennen sat up and looked at Rosemary. 'No Henry?'

'No Henry.'

'When?'

'Tomorrow. Afternoon. I've suggested tea at the Starfish hotel. Three thirty.'

'Oh, yes, yes. Thank you.'

'Perfect. See you tomorrow.'

Sennen put the phone down. 'Rosemary, you've brought me luck. Ella wants to see me tomorrow. For tea at the Starfish.'

'I could come with you, moral support and all that, if you'd like?'

'Oh, Rosemary, would you?'

'What are old friends for?'

The two women parted with a plan to meet in the Starfish reception the following afternoon and Sennen began shopping again. She needed to get ankle boots for tomorrow's tea with Ella. What a difference a cup of tea and an hour with an old friend made. She determined to take Rosemary out for dinner in the next couple of days and find out how the last twenty-five years had treated her. Rosemary had shown her such kindness today, more kindness than Sennen had shown her when they were young.

Her spirits lifted. Maybe she wasn't such a bad person after all. She had made mistakes, huge ones, but now fate was offering her a chance to atone.

With a fresh bounce in her step, she put her shoulders back and forged on. On the corner, where the pet shop used to be, was a hairdresser's. She hadn't had her hair cut for years. If it got too much she would simply lop at it herself. In the window there were model shots of young women wearing the latest styles. She compared them, unfavourably, to herself. She put her hand to the glass and screwed her eyes up to ascertain how busy the salon was.

She could make out six chairs with six mirrors, a short row of backwash sinks and a reception desk. Only two of the chairs were occupied by clients. One, an older man, was being given a trim by a young woman, the other was occupied by a woman with red curly hair like her own. A man in his thirties was combing it through and bending to hear what she had to say.

Sennen gasped and pulled herself around the corner and out of sight. Ella. Had she seen her? Would she think she was stalking her? Sennen held her hands to her burning cheeks and told herself to calm down. The worst thing to do would be to run away, up the street, in case Ella was even now leaving her chair to catch her. She held her position and painted an unnatural smile on her face while pretending to find the parking permit sign fascinating. After a few moments she knew Ella would not appear. Phew. Sennen headed for the lane that would take her back to White Water, where she sat on the edge of her bed and thought about Ella. Bless her, she was obviously getting her hair done to look her best for meeting her mum tomorrow.

Sennen quickly dismissed the idea. 'Don't make it all about you,' she told herself.

She lay on the bed and tried to sleep but the welcoming arms of oblivion were not playing her game. She got up, did some yoga poses to relax herself, then hopelessly tried to meditate. Finally, she gave up. Her mother had always suggested a good walk to get tired. 'Ozone in the lungs. Always done the trick for me.'

Sennen smiled at the memory. She picked up her scarf and phone and tucked a twenty-pound note in her pocket in case of emergency and went for a walk.

She intended to walk down to the harbour, turn left past the Golden Hind and follow the path up over the cliffs towards Sundown Beach, which would take her to Tide Cove and on to Shellsand Bay. But intention and action are very different things. Once out of the front door she didn't turn right to the harbour. She turned left up towards the back of Trevay and its church, St Peter's.

The doors were locked. She rattled them in annoyance. She was hot and could have done with having a quiet moment of reflection in the cool of the building.

She reprimanded herself again. 'You're a very selfish woman today. Stop it.'

She found some shade and a bench under an ancient yew and sat down gratefully.

'What the hell am I doing here?' she asked herself. 'I want the beach and the wild ocean, not this mournful garden.' She looked around at the ancient, lichened gravestones. But still she did not move.

She knew why she had come.

She began searching for her parents' graves. She was methodical, walking up and down the lines, wonky though they were, searching for the Tallon name. She didn't even know if they had been buried. It would be like Poppa to want to be cremated and scattered in the ground to feed the crops and trees. And Mum would have done whatever Poppa thought was right. And if they were buried, would they even be in this churchyard?

She stopped and caught her breath. An emotion, she couldn't identify, possibly shame, certainly fear, was sending a tremor through her. She felt them. They could see her, she was certain.

Looking around to make certain she was on her own, she said quietly, 'Mum? Poppa? Where are you?'

A blackbird fluttered from a nearby bush and startled her. He flew to the top of a gravestone some twenty paces from her and cocked his head. She challenged his beady eye. 'You're tricking me Mr Blackbird. And I'm not falling for it.'

He flew to another stone and another. Reluctantly, she followed him, glancing at the names on the memorials he had landed on. All strangers.

Ignoring the bird, she began her methodical search again. Some headstones were so interesting she stopped and read them, enjoying the history and mystery of each.

Eventually she reached the furthest corner and the boundary of the garden. The drystone wall had a seat set into it and she sat, feeling the warmth of the slate seeping through her skirt. It was peaceful up here and, beyond the roofs of the town and its harbour, she could just make out the sea.

Would she be buried here? Would she be welcomed as a

child of Trevay? Or had she lost the right to be thought of as a local? Closing her eyes and tilting her face to the sun she pictured the mourners who would have sat here over the centuries, wiping their eyes, glad to rest their grieving limbs, imagined the gravediggers sharing a Thermos of tea as they took a break from their sweaty work.

Something light landed on her shoulder, making her start. It was the blackbird.

'You again?'

He hopped off her shoulder and on to the wall, then flew to two gravestones a row ahead of where she was sitting.

Curiosity hooked her. 'This is your last chance, Cheeky.' She got up and read the inscription.

> *William 'Bill' Tallon*
> *Husband to Adela,*
> *Father to Sennen*
> *Poppa to Henry and Ella*
> *So loved and so missed*

Then she read the one next to it.

> *Adela Tallon*
> *Wife to Bill*
> *Mother to Sennen*
> *Henry and Ella's Beloved Granny*
> *No words will tell how much we miss you*

The blackbird had gone.

She was alone.

She fell to her knees between the graves and spread her arms over both of them, weeping.

23

Eventually her tears ended and she sat, legs crossed like a schoolgirl, looking at both headstones.

The plots were edged with granite and covered in small, pinkish, marble-like stones. She picked one up and tossed it from hand to hand.

'Did you ever think you'd see me again. Mum? After the last time? I never thought I'd be back, that's for sure. The prodigal daughter?' She laughed. 'No fatted calf for me, though, is there, Mum? You made that very clear.'

A butterfly, possibly a cabbage white, she thought, rose from a patch of white clover and flew around her hand before settling on her father's headstone. Opening and closing its wings, it basked in the warmth of the day.

'Poppa, did Mum ever tell you about me coming back?'

Sennen shut her eyes against the daylight that was suddenly too sharp, too bright.

In her darkness, she saw her mother again, opening the front door to her. Adela had stiffened the moment she had seen Sennen. Her smile had dropped, her knuckles clenching the door as she stepped out onto the front step, pulling the door closed behind her.

'What do you want?' Her eyes searched Sennen's face. 'What have you come back for?'

Sennen felt awkward and small. This was not what she had pictured, but then again, what *had* she pictured? Her parents enfolding her with love and forgiveness? Her children hugging her, burying their faces in her skirt?

'I don't want them to see you,' Adela had hissed.

Sennen knew who she meant.

'I just wanted to see if you were okay? You and Poppa and Henry and Ella.'

'We are fine.' Adela was terse. 'Now.'

'Please, Mum, please, I've come back to explain. I've missed you all so much. Things have been so difficult.'

'Difficult?' Adela almost spat. 'I'll tell you what difficult is. Having a daughter disappear, that's difficult. Difficult is nursing your father through a breakdown.' Her face was twisting in strain at the memory. 'Losing you almost killed him. Both of us. And Henry and Ella.'

Sennen had taken a step forward to her mother, her hands reaching out to her. 'But I'm here now and I want so much to explain.'

Adela stepped back. 'There is nothing to explain and nothing of you left here.'

'But Mum . . .'

Sennen forced herself to come back to the present. 'That was not good, Mum. If you hoped to hurt me back, you succeeded. I'm so sorry for everything.' She turned her face to her father's headstone. 'I bet she didn't tell you about that, did she, Poppa? I was longing to see you. I needed your love and forgiveness. I honestly didn't realise I had hurt you so much.'

She lifted a strand of hair from her cheek and tucked it behind her ear. On the horizon, she could make out the blurred shape of a tanker heading east. For a moment she pictured herself on its bridge, twirling the ship's wheel and heading out to wherever the wind blew her. Then, with a rueful shake of her head, she addressed her father's headstone.

'I ran away. I ran and ran until I couldn't come back. God, I was frightened. But I so wanted, needed, to see you and Henry and Ella. In my heart I thought that maybe you'd welcome me back. That we could get over the terrible thing I had done and I could be Henry and Ella's mum again.' Sennen threw the stone she was playing with high in the air. She watched as it turned and sparkled then fell into the grass beside her. 'It was pretty horrible.' She turned to the grave of her mother. 'Mum made sure she told me how you had burnt my school reports, Christmas cards, photographs. She told me you had wiped me out of your lives. She called me selfish, hot-headed, too independent for my own good. She said that Ella and Henry had no memory of me and that you, Poppa, had told them I had disappeared and would never come back to them.' Sennen bowed her head in shame. 'Mum said I was dirty.' Her tears flowed again but there was no sobbing. 'I know I did wrong. But when I went to Spain it felt right. I was trying to make it right. Give the children their father. Be married. Live happily as you both had.' She sniffed and shook her hair back from her face. 'But . . . Mum told me that I was no good. That the shock of seeing me would kill you, Poppa. That the sight of me would give the children nightmares again, that you'd only just got them on an even keel . . . But all I wanted was . . . I was only twenty!' Her tears were bitter now. 'I screwed it all up. I lost him. I lost you. I lost the children . . . it's not too dramatic to say

I lost myself. Until a few years ago when I met Kafir.' She wiped her eyes on her sleeve. 'You would both love him. Kind, gentle, knows right from wrong, and he's a Sikh. Imagine. I married a glorious, handsome Sikh and we live in India. In Agra. Yes, the Taj Mahal is there and yes, it's beautiful. Kafir has given me two wonderful children. A girl first and then a boy. Aali, my daughter, is so wilful. She takes after me, you'd say. Strong. Defiant. Funny. She's coming up for six now. And then there's Sabu. He's three. So loving. He likes stories and colouring and cuddles.' Her legs were getting stiff in their crossed position so she stretched them out in front of her and lay down between her parents and looked at the sky. 'The sky's very blue. I think you'd call it heliotrope, Mum.' She shifted her head. 'And the clouds are blooming in the west. Big, smoky puffs. But I don't think it'll rain. I've seen Henry and Ella, you know. I've been summoned by your solicitor as sole beneficiary of your will. Typical of you, Mum, not to have made a will. Henry is very angry about it all and Ella is trying to compensate for him. I'm meeting her tomorrow. I saw her today but she didn't see me. She was getting her hair done. What a girl you've brought up. She's very beautiful, I think. Henry is handsome, but he was so cross with me he hid it well.' She smiled at the thought. 'So here we all are. You two, me, Henry and Ella. Back in Trevay. I'm not sure what will happen next, to be honest.' She rolled onto her stomach and plucked a long, seeded grass head. 'I threw the pebble in the pond all those years ago and the ripples are still hitting the shore. I may have lost Kafir and Aali and Sabu too.' She suddenly remembered meeting Rosemary. 'Oh, I forgot to tell you. You remember Rosemary? The girl I made run away with me? The one you liked? I bumped into her today. She was very kind. I told her everything . . . almost. She's coming to my meeting with Ella tomorrow. I'm going to explain to her what happened and ask her forgiveness. Would you wish me well? Please? No matter how old a child gets, we still want our parents' approval. I know I lost yours a long time ago, but . . .' Her voice broke and the tears came again like a sudden cloudburst in summer. 'Please. I love you both so much. Forgive me. Help me.'

24

Ella woke up to a showery day. The billowing clouds Sennen had seen the day before had poured their heaviest rain in the night and were almost spent.

Kit slumbered quietly next to her, giving her time to think about the day ahead. At least her hair was done.

She ran through her wardrobe rail in her mind. Not trousers, maybe a skirt – but what would she wear on top? Perhaps a dress would be better? Not too formal or too casual, something that was just her. In that case, it was a choice between the pale cream shift dress with lily-of-the-valley print or the black linen.

Black? Too funereal. She went for the sprigged shift. Demure but strangely sexy and very daughter-like – whatever that was. With her denim jacket over the top and heeled boots she should look just right.

She slipped out of bed and went to the kitchen to make a tray of tea.

*

'Kit?' She put the tray down on the blanket box at the end of the bed. 'Tea?'

'What time is it?'

'Six thirty.'

He groaned. 'Why so early?'

'I couldn't sleep and I've been thinking about meeting my mum today.'

'Oh,' he said without opening his eyes.

She went to the wardrobe and pulled out the chosen dress. 'How about this? With my denim jacket? I thought the black suede ankle boots would be good or do you prefer the nude strappy sandals?'

'I like them both.' Eyes still closed.

'But with this dress?'

'Boots.'

'I was thinking the sandals might be better.'

'Maybe you're right.'

'Kit, this is important to me.'

He surfaced from the duvet and opened his eyes. 'Babe, you look great in both.'

'Hopeless,' sighed Ella, 'but thank you for trying. Ready for tea yet?'

They had both drifted off back to sleep, wrapped around each other, when the doorbell rang.

'Who the bloody hell is that?' Kit groaned.

Ella got up and went to the window. 'There's a taxi driving away, without a passenger.'

The doorbell rang again. 'Okay, I'm coming.' Ella reached for her silky dressing gown and went downstairs.

'Hi,' said Henry from the doorstep.

'What are you doing here?' asked Ella suspiciously.

'Can I come in?'

'It's half past seven in the morning.' She stood back to let him in.

'I got the sleeper from Paddington.'

She smiled. 'Granny's favourite.' She closed the door. 'Want some tea?'

'I'll make it.' Henry put his bag down and looked up the stairs. 'Kit here?'

'Yeah, but Adam's at some conference. It's just us.'

Terry and Celia came from the kitchen, stretching their legs and yawning. 'Hello,' said Henry bending down to give them a friendly pat. Terry stuck his nose straight into Henry's crotch and Celia went round the back and did the same to his bum. 'Charming. Thank you.' He extricated himself as Ella went to put the kettle on.

'So why are you here?' she asked him again, reaching for the tea bags.

'I told you I wanted to come.'

'I also said that I would call you.'

'But you didn't.'

Ella stopped finding mugs and faced him. 'I want to see Mum on my own.'

'But why? We should be a united front.'

'But we are not united, are we? You don't want to hear what she has to say and I do.'

Henry rubbed his stubbled chin to think of an answer, but there was no answer. 'True.'

'So, I'm going to see her by myself. With Kit.'

'Well, that's not by yourself, is it?'

'No, but at least he's not emotionally involved.'

She poured hot water onto the tea bag and squidged it around in his mug. She hooked the bag out with the spoon and poured some milk in.

'Here you are.'

'Thank you.' He took a sip. 'That's bloody hot.'

'It's just come out of the kettle, hasn't it?'

'Don't be sarcastic.' She raised an eyebrow then went to the larder and took out a box of cereal. 'Want some?'

He shook his head. 'So where are you meeting her?'

'If you mean our mother . . . at the Starfish. For afternoon tea.'

He blew on his mug. 'Nice.'

'Yes.'

'What time?'

'Teatime.'

'You really don't want me there, do you?'

'After the other day when you were so rude? No.'

'I promise I'll be nicer.'

'No.'

'Please?'

'No. Let me build some bridges, then maybe.'

They heard Kit's tread on the stair. 'Hey, Henry, what you doing here so early?' he walked in to the kitchen and hugged his future brother-in-law. 'Hey, buddy. Come to give your sister support today?'

Henry looked at Ella pleadingly. 'I'd like to.'

She turned away and began to unload the dishwasher.

'Well, that's great,' smiled Kit, sensing the atmosphere.

'He's not coming,' responded Ella, her back to them. 'And that's that.'

Henry sensibly backed off the subject and the morning was spent walking the dogs on the beach. There were a handful of surfers out catching the waves, their sleek wet suits gleaming in the water.

'I haven't surfed for years,' said Henry wistfully.

'Are you any good?' asked Kit.

'Used to be, but,' he patted his slight belly, 'not as fit as I was.'

Ella scoffed, 'Soft Londoner.'

'Oh yeah, and when were you last in the water?' Henry bridled.

'Ah. Good point. I honestly can't remember.' She pushed her red curls out of her eyes. 'Tell you what, I've got a deal for you. You can see Mum with me today if – and it's a big if – you stay calm and are nice. If you can do that, we'll swim at the weekend. If not, no swim.'

'I'm not six.' Henry gave her a disgusted look. 'I can swim when I bloody well want.'

'Okay,' Ella said airily, 'in that case you can't see Mum today.'

He glared at her for a moment, weighing the situation up. 'Okay. It's a deal. I'll button my lip.'

Sennen was trying on her new jeans. She was going for the straight-legged pair, with a white cotton shirt she'd got in a market in India years before. In front of the mirror she turned from her right side to her left. For years, the climate – and the modesty required of being Kafir's wife – had meant she had always shrouded herself in loose clothing. She picked up the hand mirror on the dressing table and looked at her rear view, and was more than pleased with the power of Lycra. Her hips were slim, her bottom lifted and her long legs looked longer than ever. She slipped on the new white sneakers. She'd do.

She walked from White Water to the old hotel that stood

tall just above the harbour. In her youth, she had gone there for the occasional Sunday lunch with her parents and remembered how high the ceilings were and the great sea view from the dining room windows. Then it had been past its Victorian heyday, when holidaymakers would make the tiring train journey from London to Cornwall and spill out on to the platform of the long-gone Trevay station.

Now, with the harbour behind her, she looked up at it. The beige pebble dash she remembered had been given a sparkling coat of white paint. Every one of the myriad of windows was gleaming and the steps, once chipped and dirty, were now smooth granite. Twenty-five years ago she had stood here with Henry in her arms to find Ali. And now she was here with her heart in her mouth to get her children back.

St Peter's clock struck the half hour. It was time.

The young woman at the reception desk looked up from her computer terminal. 'Good afternoon. Welcome to the Starfish. Can I help you?'

'Yes, I'm having tea, a family tea.'

'That will be in the bar. Can I have the name?'

'Oh, I think it'll be booked under . . .' She didn't know. Would it be Tallon? Or Deborah's name. She was saved by a hand on her shoulder.

'Sennen, have I kept you waiting?' It was Deborah.

Relief flooded Sennen. 'I've only just got here.'

Deborah spoke to the receptionist. 'I've booked tea for three of us. The name is Palmer. Have the other guests arrived yet?'

'Not yet. Perhaps you'd like to wait here?'

Sennen was embarrassed. 'I've invited an old friend, a bit of moral support, so there will be four of us. Is that okay?'

'No problem,' said the girl behind the desk.

Sennen checked with Deborah. 'Do you think it's okay to have my friend with me? Do you think Ella will mind?'

Deborah took Sennen's arm, which she noticed was trembling, and led her to one of the enormous white sofas in the reception hall. 'We could check with her first?'

'Okay, yes.' Sennen bit her lip nervously. 'Or Rosemary could always wait for me here.'

'Indeed,' smiled Deborah taking a seat. 'You look very nice,' she remarked.

'Thank you,' Sennen said, looking down and reminding herself of what she was wearing. 'I haven't worn jeans for over twenty years. Are you sure they look okay?'

'Absolutely.'

Sennen smiled gratefully and began to absorb her surroundings. The squashy sofas, colourful rugs, tall candles in huge bell jars, the assortment of beach shoes, buckets and spades for anyone who wanted to use them by the front door. 'Gosh, this has changed.'

'I believe it's been a very recent thing. It was becoming almost derelict, but a businesswoman from up country saved it. Apparently, she used to come here with her family in the sixties.'

'She's done a good job.' Sennen had her own final memory of the hotel. She looked at her hands, damp with perspiration.

Deborah spoke. 'How are you feeling?'

'Nervous.'

'It won't be as bad as the other day. Ella on her own will be a different Ella to the one with Henry.'

'I hope so.'

There was activity at the door. Sennen looked up as Ella came in. Kit was by her side and Sennen automatically got to her feet. 'Ella.'

Ella spotted her and smiled warmly. 'Mum, hello. I've brought a surprise with me.' She stood aside and Henry came in, looking anxious and, Sennen was astounded to see, a little sheepish. 'Hi,' he said.

Sennen was thrilled. 'Henry, I am so glad.'

There was a moment's unease as to what should happen next before Ella stepped forward and kissed Sennen with a hug.

Henry, after a short hesitation, followed suit.

Kit thought he'd better do the same.

Sennen felt dizzy. The closeness of her children, the smell and feel of them, was overwhelming.

'Are you all right?' asked Ella taking her mother's hand. 'You look a bit shaky.'

'I'm fine. So lovely to see you.'

Rosemary arrived. 'Sorry, am I late?'

'Rosemary, perfect timing.' Sennen introduced her: 'This is my oldest friend, Rosemary. Would you mind if she joined us for tea?'

Ella and Henry exchanged glances. 'This is *family* business,' Henry said.

'Of course it is.' Rosemary's easy smile was charming. 'I shall wait out here. I can make myself cosy with a glass of wine and people-watching.'

Sennen shot her a thankful look. Rosemary responded with a supportive wink.

The bar was quiet; only two other tables were taken which meant the waiters were able to be very attentive. Deborah had booked the best table overlooking the sun terrace and the harbour.

The business and flurry of getting everyone seated and

the ordering of the tea was a welcome respite from the over-powering sense of occasion.

As usual, Deborah set the ball rolling. 'After our initial meeting a few days ago, may I thank you for taking the time to proceed with the matter at hand?' She reached for her bag on the floor and began to pull out an A4 wallet of paperwork. Sennen stopped her.

'Maybe we should start with just talking to each other?' She directed her attention to the children. 'I'm sure you have lots of questions to ask me?'

Ella and Henry exchanged glances, then Ella plunged in, 'Well, the one thing we really want to know is, who is our father?'

'If he's the same person,' Henry muttered under his breath.

Deborah sat back and started to click the top of her pen.

Kit gripped Ella's trembling hand.

Sennen took a deep breath. 'Yes, Henry, you have the same father.'

'I knew it,' said Ella with satisfaction. 'Who is he?'

'I have never told anyone until now. I think I always knew you had to be the first I told.'

The table held its collective breath, all eyes on Sennen.

A waiter sashayed past, holding his pen and pad to his chest. 'Is everything okay?'

'Bugger off,' growled Henry. He did.

Sennen gathered herself. 'He was much older than me, in his late twenties. He worked at the Pavilions Theatre where I had a holiday job. I fell in love with him, but when the holidays ended he had to leave. I was very upset.'

'Where did he go?' asked Ella.

'He had to go back to London. We lost touch.'

Henry had his arms folded tightly across his chest. 'But he'd got you up the duff by then?'

'Yes.'

'Did he know you were fourteen?'

'No.'

'I don't suppose you wanted to keep me?'

Henry's words were like a slap in the face. 'Of course I wanted you.'

'Until you didn't and walked out on us.'

Ella glared at him. 'Henry!'

'It's okay.' Sennen gave Ella a gentle smile. 'Really. It's okay.'

'What did Granny and Poppa say?' Ella asked.

'After the initial shock they couldn't have been kinder. Granny was with me when you were born, Henry. Poppa was out in the waiting room and she called him in to see you.' Sennen's memories flooded back: 'He – he held you and t-told you that you were very welcome.' She gave a small laugh. 'He wanted to call you Mabwyn.'

Henry glowered at her.

'It's Cornish,' Sennen went on. 'It means child of a child, I think.' She looked at Deborah for back-up.

'I'm afraid I don't know,' Deborah said, 'but I can check Google.' She turned to her phone.

'So why Henry?' asked Henry, feigning boredom.

'It's a king's name,' she told him.

Henry rolled his eyes, 'Oh please. I was hardly your little longed-for prince, was I? What was the bloke's name?'

'Your father's name was . . .' She coughed, her throat suddenly dry. '*Is*, I suppose, Alan.'

Henry leant back and looked at the ceiling. 'Thank God for small mercies. I've never liked that name. Did you tell him about me?'

'I tried to. I came here, to this hotel, with you in my arms. He was staying here. But he'd already gone on to another job.'

'What work did he do?'

'He was a young magician,' she told them.

'Wow. Was he handsome?' asked Ella.

'I thought so.'

'Describe him to me. Or do you have a picture of him?'

Sennen could see the dreams in Ella's eyes. 'No, I don't have a picture, but he had long curly hair and always wore a leather jacket and jeans. He rode a motorbike.'

'Sounds very romantic,' said Ella.

'Oh, puh-leeze,' scoffed Henry. 'Sounds a complete tosser.'

Ella turned on him. 'Maybe that's where you get it from.'

'Stop it,' Sennen said loudly, exerting some maternal authority. 'This isn't easy for any of us.'

Deborah put down her teacup. 'I think it's time for a break. Sennen, would you like to get some fresh air?'

Sennen fidgeted with her hands then picked up her bag, 'Yes. That's a good idea.'

When they'd gone, Ella began to chew her hair and Henry anxiously jiggled his legs.

Kit was thinking. 'Is she telling the truth, do you think?'

'Of course she is,' Ella said swiftly.

Henry stretched across the table and crammed a small cucumber sandwich into his mouth. 'It's all very Mills and Boon. Long hair, leather jacket, motorbike. What a knob. I'm not sure I believe her.'

Kit frowned. 'Actually, I believe I do.'

Ella clutched his hand and kissed him. 'Thank you! Oh, thank you, Kit.'

*

Sennen and Rosemary were sitting outside the hotel on a comfortable swing chair. Deborah had made for the loo and Rosemary had brought a glass of wine and a cigarette out with her. She shook the packet towards Sennen. 'They're not the menthol we used to smoke, but would you like one?'

Sennen almost laughed. 'Yes, but I haven't smoked in decades and I'm worried I'll be sick.'

'How is it going?' asked Rosemary inhaling deeply.

'Henry hates me,' said Sennen.

'He's a little boy lost, that's all. He has memories, however deep, of you and him together.'

'I don't know.' Sennen picked at the chair cushion. 'He doesn't want me here.'

'Oh, he does. If you were to pick him up in your arms now and hold him tight, he'd burst into tears for missing you.'

'If I thought that was true, I'd do it.'

'Don't fight him. Stay calm. Be honest. You are the parent here. And don't you forget it.'

'I think it's too late for that.'

Deborah came back with freshly powdered nose and lipstick. Shall we go back?'

Sennen nodded. 'Yep.'

As Sennen stood, Rosemary said cheerfully, 'I'll have a large margarita for you as soon as it's over. Tequila is a cure-all.'

'I'll need it.'

Rosemary patted her arm. 'Once more into the fray, old friend. Once more.'

Back at the table, Sennen saw how depleted the sandwiches and scones had become. 'I'm glad you've had something to eat.'

'I saved you a scone.' Ella pushed a plate towards Sennen.

'Thank you.' Sennen was touched. 'I will in a minute, after I've told you more about your father.' She sighed, a deep slow sigh and began again. 'After you were born, Henry, I had no idea where . . .' She stumbled over the name. 'Where Alan was. I went back to school to do my exams and Granny and Poppa looked after you. The doctor had said that I needed to be able to get a good job after school so that I could look after you properly and they agreed with him. But,' her throat was again tight with tears, 'then, Alan came back to Trevay. To the theatre. It was only for one night. I was working as an usherette and saw him afterwards.'

'And you couldn't keep your knickers on?' sneered Henry.

Sennen ignored him. 'And I was so pleased to see him. We met after the show and yes, he and I made love. He asked me to come to the Starfish the next morning and that's when I brought you to meet him, Henry, but he had already—'

'Pissed off,' Henry said with less antagonism than before. 'What a charmer.'

'Yes,' Sennen rubbed her forehead, 'and I decided, very naively I admit, that I would go and find him and tell him about you, but I didn't know that you, Ella, were already on the way. When I did, I waited until you were born and safe with Mum and Poppa and then, knowing that he was in Spain . . . I went to find him.'

Ella burst into tears.

25

Deborah discreetly left the table and went to fetch Rosemary. 'I think you may be needed.'

Rosemary did the only sensible thing anyone could do in the circumstances and ordered two margaritas, one for herself and one for Sennen, and a bottle of wine with four glasses for the others. 'Send them to the party in the bar, would you?' she told the waiter and went to see for herself what was happening.

Sennen was comforting Ella. 'I was so happy to know you were coming. I was.' She rocked her daughter gently in her arms. 'It was a wonderful feeling, and when you were born, Poppa and I had the idea to give you Granny's name. But two Adela's would be confusing so we called you simply Ella instead.'

'He always told me that,' sniffed Ella.

'Here,' Sennen gave her her own crumpled tissue, 'wipe your nose.'

'So that's why you went? To find Alan and tell him about us?'

'Yes. And I regret it. Leaving you was the most terrible thing I have ever done.'

'Did you find him?' Henry asked.

Sennen shook her head. 'No.'

'Oh, Mum. How awful for you.' Ella was holding Sennen. 'Did you ever find out where he was?'

'No, darling,' Sennen said gently, 'I never spoke to him again.'

Rosemary and the drinks arrived. 'Somewhere in the world the sun is over the yardarm and you all look as if you need a drink.'

Henry looked at her darkly. 'Who actually are you?'

'I am the girl who ran away with your mother to look for your father. Here, have a glass of wine.'

Henry took the glass she offered him, dumbstruck.

'It takes a lot of guts to do what Sennen did,' said Rosemary 'And a lot of guts to come back and tell you both about it. She has thought about you every day of her life. Can you say the same?'

'What do you know about it?' Henry jeered. 'You've appeared from nowhere and now you're telling us you know all about it.' Henry took another large mouthful of wine and reached again for the bottle.

'We went to Spain, got jobs, found a place to live, a revolting little squat but it was safe enough. Your mum was determined to find your father and bring him home to you. All she wanted was to make you into one happy family.'

'Where did you look?' Ella asked Sennen.

'The theatres. I knew he was touring in Spain. I thought I had found him but . . .' The image of Ali's cold face refusing to acknowledge her at the stage door, the woman calling him, telling him to hurry up and get back for the babysitter, flashed jaggedly in her brain. She swallowed hard, wanting to tell the truth but still protect her children. 'I thought I had found him but it was not him. The man I found was married with his own children.'

'Why didn't you come home then?' asked Henry.

Sennen had no answer. 'I don't know. I wasn't thinking straight.'

'But Rosemary came home,' said Ella. 'Why didn't you come home with her?'

'I was too afraid . . .' offered Sennen.

'No,' said Rosemary, 'you were brave. Braver than me. I was homesick, desperate to come home.' Rosemary looked at Henry and Ella. 'Sennen took me to the ferry. I thought she was coming home with me, but she decided not to and I left her. I never should have come back without her, but I did, and it's something I have regretted always.'

She turned to Sennen. 'I am so sorry I left you.'

'This is all very touching,' Henry refilled his wine glass, and pointed it at Rosemary, 'but after you'd dumped your best mate and come back why didn't you tell anyone where she was? The police could have picked her up.'

'I did tell them, Henry,' Rosemary said. 'And I brought back the news that she was okay, presents for you two and a message about how much she loved you.'

Ella, hands in her lap, was leaning forward on her knees, hungry for more. 'Did you bring the presents back?'

'Oh yes. As soon as I got off the boat in Plymouth, I rang the police to tell them where I was and they took me straight to your house so that I could tell your grandparents that Sennen was safe and deliver the presents. You were very little, only just walking. I don't suppose you'd remember.'

'I do,' said Henry his eyebrows wrinkling in his effort to

recall. 'Ella got something pink and fluffy, and I got a dragon, with silvery wings.'

'Yes,' said Sennen, remembering. 'Did you like them?'

Henry's face was a mixture of confused emotions, then his face crumpled. 'I did – but Poppa put them in the bin.'

A fresh pain of parental abandonment skewered Sennen.

Rosemary passed her a glass. 'Drink your margarita,' she advised.

Sennen took a sip and said, 'Ella, Henry – did you get my postcards? Birthday and Christmas cards?'

They looked at her blankly. 'No.'

Deborah cleared her throat. 'I may be able to help. During Mrs Tallon's last illness, she asked her previous solicitor, old Mr Penhaligon, to collect several items from the house and take them to the office for safe-keeping. They remain in my care. One is a shoebox which holds many items of correspondence.'

Sennen put her hand to her chest, tears springing into her eyes. 'So she kept them?'

'It would appear so.'

'But she couldn't show them to the children or to Poppa because he couldn't bear anything about me to be in the house?'

Deborah nodded. 'It sounds harsh, but is a likely scenario, yes.'

'Can I see them?' Sennen's voice was shaky.

'Yes. They are among her personal affects which are now, legally yours.'

Sennen was now weeping soundlessly. Fat, glistening tears slid over her bottom lashes and made their way over her cheeks and into the creases around her mouth, then down to her chin where they hung like crystals before falling to her lap. 'I'm so sorry I wasn't here when they died.' Her voice was small and pleading. 'I wish I had known. I could have told them how much I loved them, thanked them for looking after all the mess I left them in.'

Henry crossed his arms tight over his chest and looked at the floor. Ella didn't know what to do. Her instinct was to go to her mother and hold her, but Sennen looked so vulnerable and withdrawn that she daren't touch her.

Eventually Sennen looked up and asked Deborah, 'Did your office try to find me?'

Deborah nodded. 'Of course.'

'I see.' Sennen wiped her nose on the back of her hand. 'I see.'

'We wouldn't have wanted you there anyway,' Henry said.

'No,' Sennen replied quietly.

Ella shifted. 'I would have loved you to come but you had managed to hide yourself so well.'

'Yes.'

'I could take you to their graves if you'd like?' Ella offered softly.

Sennen reached for her bag and, taking out a tissue, blew her nose. 'That's kind of you, but I have been to see them. I went yesterday. They are in a beautiful part of the churchyard.'

'Poppa chose the plots long before he was ill,' said Ella. 'He said it would be quiet up there.'

'It is,' smiled Sennen sadly, 'and the inscriptions on their stones are lovely. I was surprised to see that I was included. Whoever did that was very kind.'

Ella glanced at Henry, who had stuffed his head deep into the neck of his sweater. 'That was Henry's idea.'

Henry shifted in his chair. 'And now we come to the reason you are finally here. To collect your money and go.'

'No,' Sennen said clearly, 'No. I came to find you and Ella.'

Henry snorted. 'Not too hard a job. We were here all the

time. Unlike you. Ever since Granny died solicitors' letters have been chasing you around the world. What did you do? Every time one found you did you run again? Why turn up now if it's not because you need the money?'

Ella reached out to her mother with longing. 'Tell us about your life. Where you live. What you do.'

Sennen inhaled deeply and closed her eyes. This was the moment that she had dreaded. She opened her eyes and spoke. 'Well, I am married. To a lovely man. He's Indian. A Sikh, actually. We've been married for six years. His name is Kafir.'

'How wonderful,' Ella said with kindness.

Sennen looked at her gratefully. 'Yes. I am lucky. We live in a small house in Agra, just the four of us.'

Henry leapt at this. 'Four of you?'

Sennen's stomach twisted. 'Yes. We have a daughter, Aali, and a son, Sabu. Your half-sister and -brother.'

Henry sat back in his chair, his glass of wine on his chest. 'I knew there was something,' he said slowly. 'So Granny's windfall is for them, is it?'

Sennen again shook her head. 'No. I am here to heal the damage I did.'

'Ha!' Henry had a cruel smile on his face. 'Too late for that, Mother.'

Ella was still taking in the news that she had a brother and a sister. 'How old are they? The children?'

'Aali is five and Sabu three.'

'Are they here? Did they all come with you?' asked Ella.

'No.' But before Sennen could say more, Henry jumped in.

'So that's why you're here.' Henry sat forward in his chair, his hands gripping the sides. 'He's not here because he doesn't know about us.'

Sennen licked her lips nervously now. 'Not until a couple of weeks ago.'

Henry narrowed his eyes like a mongoose spying a snake. 'How did he take the news?'

'He, erm, he was angry that I hadn't told him before.'

'I'll bet he was,' drawled Henry. His eyes gleamed. 'He'd married a liar, hadn't he? A woman with a very chequered past.' He drained his wine glass. 'Poor sucker. I bet he chucked you out – and with nowhere else to go you came back to us.'

'It's not like that.'

Deborah put her hand up. 'Maybe we should stop there.'

Ella was shaken. She clutched Kit's arm. 'You all right?' he asked.

'Yes.' She looked at Sennen. 'Are you okay, Mum?'

Sennen was getting a tissue from her bag. 'Sure. Yes. I'm fine. I'm just so sorry to have hurt you and Henry. So sorry.'

Henry got to his feet and hissed, 'God, this is such a joke. This woman,' he pointed at Sennen, 'left me when I was a toddler and now, what a surprise, she's walked out on her next two as well. History repeating itself.' He picked up his jacket. 'Come on, Ells, we're going. Leave her to her own mess.'

'No,' said Ella.

Henry shrugged. 'Fine by me but don't expect me to offer sympathy when she hurts you again, and she will. I promise.' He threw two twenty-pound notes on the table. 'That's for the wine.'

Without looking back, he walked out of the hotel to find the nearest bar.

Sennen remained in her chair, drained and exhausted and shut her eyes. Pandora's box was open.

Rosemary called the waiter over and ordered two large margaritas.

Ella looked at Kit, not knowing what to do.

Deborah packed her bag and addressed them all. 'In my experience, family matters can and do improve. But it takes time.' She stopped and looked at Sennen. 'Mrs Tallon-Singh, don't take this as a final outcome. With gentle support we will get there. There will be a satisfactory, if imperfect, conclusion, I am certain. Try to get some sleep. Goodbye.'

She went to the ladies' loo and looked at herself in the mirror. She was glad that her professional face remained intact. She liked Sennen, for all her mistakes, and Ella was demonstrably kind and loving. Henry, however, was less than congenial. Behind his handsome face lay a spoiled child. But she vowed that she would do everything in her professional power to make things bearable for them all.

Outside the hotel she set off for the small house she had rented while she looked for one to buy. On the way, she passed the small and lively wine bar where she was becoming a regular. She had refused any of the drink offered at the meeting, but now seriously felt she deserved a drink. At the bar she was welcomed. 'Hello, Debs. Bit early for you, ain't it?' said the chirpy barmaid.

'Never have I needed a glass of Pinot more, Lily.' She climbed onto a bar-stool.

Lily opened the glass-fronted wine fridge and reached for a bottle. 'Small or large?'

'A pint glass wouldn't be too big.'

'You earned your money today, then?'

'I hope so.' The large wine glass, frosted with condensation, was begging her to take a sip of its contents. It was cold and fruity, with just the right amount of acid. She licked her lips.

'God, that's good. I'll have a bag of crisps too, please, Lil. Haven't had a chance to eat today.' She looked around the bar. 'Anyone interesting in?'

'A bit early yet,' said Lily passing her the crisps. 'But there is one good-looking bloke here. Never seen him before.' Lily looked around her. 'I think he must be in the gents. I hope so. He hasn't paid yet.'

Henry finished his pee, washed his hands and looked at himself in the mirror. 'Come on, buddy. You're a big boy now. Who needs this shit? Get on with your life. *She* has.'

He dried his hands and walked unsteadily back to his bar-stool.

A petite woman in a business suit had her back to him, talking to the barmaid. He clocked her slim legs in their sensible court shoes and thought he might have a crack at her. He walked towards her as the barmaid nodded in his direction, saying something to the woman, who turned. Deborah, the legal tart. He almost doubled back to the gents but she had seen him. 'Henry.' She patted the bar-stool next to her. 'Join me for a drink?'

'I've already got one, thanks.'

'Okay. Shall we drink together? Or alone like a couple of saddos?'

He looked at his pint sitting all by itself on the bar just a few feet away. 'Okay. We'll drink together, on the promise that we don't mention my mother.'

'Done deal.' She smiled.

He got his pint and hauled himself up onto the stool beside hers. 'So, where shall we start?'

'Tricky opener,' she teased. 'How about you first. Tell me about your work in London.'

He eyed her up. Without her legal face on, she was really quite pretty, in a girl-next-doorsy kind of way. 'I am in an office with a lot of other guys – and some women, you'll be pleased to know . . .'

'Why pleased?'

'Well, you're probably a feminist so I don't want you to think I live in an altogether male world.'

'I'm not *probably* a feminist. I *am* a feminist. So as long as I treat you as an equal, you may treat me as an equal.'

'Oh, right, that's me told.'

'Carry on. Large office. Mixed sex and . . . ?'

'Yeah, I'm a corporate surveyor for an expanding company and I check out plots of valuable land for people who want to make squillions.'

'Are you good at it?'

'Yes. I got a good bonus at the end of last year.'

'So you're doing all right?'

'Aha, now, you're trying to get me to say I don't need Granny's money. Leading the witness?'

'Would I do that?' She curled her lips up into one of the prettiest smiles Henry could remember. 'But you have a house in London?'

'Clapham, and before you ask, yes, old Mr Penhaligon, Granny's solicitor, gave me a little money for the deposit, on the understanding that if my mother was ever found, then I would pay it back.'

'Could you?'

'No. After the mortgage and the bills there's not much left at the end of the month.'

'But your bonus?'

'I helped Ella a bit and . . .' He stopped, realising he'd told her too much. 'Bugger.' He said and drank his beer.

Deborah laughed. 'Sorry. It's force of habit. Getting people to confess.'

He was mildly impressed. 'So, you do criminal stuff as well as probate, do you?'

'Yes, but when Old Mr Penhaligon retired the offer to come down here was too good to miss. I decided I loved the sea and Cornwall more than the workings of the criminal mind.'

'I'll drink to that.' He emptied his glass. 'Another?'

'I think I need to eat more than crisps first.'

'I'll get the menu.'

He ordered the drinks and two plates of whitebait with chips. Lily took his money and winked at Deborah. 'Why don't you two find a table and I'll bring it to you? There's one round the corner in the snug. It's a bit dark but it's private.'

She wasn't kidding. Two wall lights with red lampshades cast a boudoir effect over the small space filled by a table and two armchairs. They made themselves comfortable.

'Your turn,' Henry said. 'Tell me about you. Ever been married?'

'Close. I broke off an engagement when I came down here.'

'Why?'

'He had a daughter from a previous relationship and didn't want to live three hundred miles away from her.'

'Fair enough. Although,' he smiled, 'she's going to miss out on some cracking holidays.'

'Yes, and I'm missing out on marrying a nice man.'

Henry didn't know how to reply to that.

'What about you?' Deborah asked. 'Anyone special in your life?'

'Lots of girls, obviously, but I have no plan to settle down anytime soon.'

'Love 'em and leave 'em eh?'

'I've told you too much again! How do you do this, Deborah?'

'Debs, please.'

The whitebait and chips arrived and they tucked in.

Debs had a good look at him from under her eyelashes. A slick City Boy hair cut; a body that suggested regular trips to the gym and clean hands with well-shaped nails. His face was slightly irregular, but attractively so, with a tiny scar below his bottom lip and a crooked nose. 'Were you ever a rugby player?' she asked, picking up a whitebait and scooping it into a pile of tartare sauce. A glob of it dropped on the lapel of her jacket which she failed to notice and Henry was much too gentlemanly too mention.

'Yeah. Why?'

'I saw the scar.'

He rubbed at it. 'Teeth went through. Broke my bloody nose at the same time.'

'Do you still play?'

'No. I like to run. Do a few weights still. Swim.' He thought about Ella. 'I was supposed to be swimming with Ella and Kit this weekend but I think I've blown it now.'

He told her about the deal they had made.

'You can come swimming with me instead.' Debs surprised herself for saying it. The wine was having too much of an effect on her.

'Sure. Love to,' he said, touchingly pleased.

She looked at her watch. 'Well, that was lovely.' She pushed her empty plate away and finished her wine.

'You're not going, are you?'

'I must. I have an early office meeting tomorrow.'

'Do you have far to go tonight?'

'No, I'm just around the corner.'

'Let me walk you back.'

She was on her feet now, looking for her purse in order to pay the bill. 'Not at all. It's been a nice evening after a difficult day and I promise that all we have spoken about tonight will remain confidential.'

He stood up too. 'I insist on walking you.'

She relented. 'Okay, but I'm paying this bill. My treat.'

He held his hands up in submission. 'My treat next time.'

Lily said goodnight to them both as they left the bar and smiled to herself.

Debs and Henry began walking towards the lights of the harbour.

'Hasn't changed much since I was a child,' mused Henry. 'We used to crab off the wall here. Poppa had a little boat that he'd take out mackerel fishing. I didn't like it much. Hated the poor things gasping before he knocked them on the noggin.'

Debs laughed. 'Noggin?'

Henry put her arm through his. 'Don't laugh at me.'

'It's such a great word.'

'Lots of good words Poppa had. He was a lovely man, even after his breakdown. Granny was so strong. God knows what would have happened to Ella and me without them.'

They walked on, past the lane leading to Debs' house, and down to the water. The small town was quiet. Their footsteps echoing off the ancient cobbles. He led her to a wooden bench at the end of the harbour wall where they could hear the sea quietly lapping in the darkness.

There was a cold breeze and Debs pulled the lapels of her jacket up to stop the draught running down her neck.

'Cold? Here.' He put his arm around her and hugged her to his side. 'Better.'

'Thank you.'

She closed her eyes and noticed the warmth of his body and then the scent of his cologne, musky and masculine. 'What aftershave are you wearing?'

'Creed.'

'It's lovely.'

'Sitting here, with you, is lovely.'

She lifted her head and gave him a puzzled look. 'Really?' He had to kiss her, so he did.

'That was unexpected,' she whispered as they broke apart.

'It was.' He smiled. 'Shall we do it again just to make sure it wasn't a fluke?'

This new and surprising closeness flowed over them with ease. Finally, Debs broke away. 'I know this is boring, but I really do have to get up early.'

'I know. And I must get home to Ella and apologise.'

'You can't drive. You've had too much. I can give you a coffee at home. Sober you up?'

He kissed the tip of her nose lightly. 'Thank you.'

They walked back up to her little house that sat in the middle of a terrace of old fishing houses. It began to drizzle as she put the key in the lock.

The door opened into her unlit tiny lounge.

She closed the door behind them, took Henry's hand and led him upstairs.

26

Ella and Kit left the Starfish shortly after Deborah. Ella had given her mother a warm hug. 'I'm sorry about Henry. I'll talk to him.'

'I'm sorry I have caused such friction,' Sennen said ruefully. 'I honestly hadn't meant to. But I don't regret coming home and seeing you both.'

'Would you like my mobile number?' asked Ella.

Mother and daughter swapped numbers and said their farewells, promising to be in touch soon.

Now, only Sennen and Rosemary were left.

'Another margarita?' asked Rosemary.

'Oh God, yes.' Sennen slumped in her chair and exhaled loudly. 'What a day.'

The margaritas arrived and the two women sipped on them peacefully and thankfully.

'Ella's a good girl, and so like you,' said Rosemary.

'I like the look of Kit,' smiled Sennen, relaxing further into her chair. 'They seem comfortable together.'

Rosemary stretched her legs out and kicked her shoes off. 'Henry's hard work though.'

'Yes.'

'Anything from Kafir?'

'No.' Sennen felt suddenly wretched. 'What have I done?'

'The right thing.'

'But have I? Why do I keep making a mess? Ella and Henry don't need or want me and I've thrown away my marriage. I'm going to lose Aali and Sabu, my parents rubbed me out of their life . . .'

Rosemary shook her head. 'Oh, hello. Nora Negative has arrived!'

'Shut up.'

'If Posy Positive were here she'd be congratulating herself. She's come home, her kids are at least willing to meet her, she has a family in India who love her very much—'

'They don't,' Sennen groaned. 'They'd be here now if they did.'

'The reason Kafir is not here is because he's hurting, and he wouldn't be hurting if he didn't love you to bits. After all, it's not as if you've been unfaithful to him, is it?' Rosemary had a terrible thought. 'Is it?'

Sennen gave a short laugh. 'Absolutely not. Alan was my first and Kafir the last, with no one in between.'

'Really?' asked Rosemary, more interested than she should be.

'Really.'

'Even I managed more than that.'

Sennen looked at her friend. 'Tell me. Tell me about all that has happened to you since I put you on the ferry.'

27

Henry woke up in Deborah's bedroom – and immediately regretted it. What the hell had he been thinking? Without moving any part of his body, other than his eyes, he took in his surroundings. Everything was very white. Ceiling, walls, duvet cover, wafting curtains against the open window where daylight was creeping. He swivelled his eyeballs with some discomfort to the right. There was Debs, lying on her back and gently snoring.

He needed to leave.

Feeling like James Bond avoiding the hidden laser alarms, he inched himself out of bed and quietly picked up his clothes which were scattered on the floor, tangled with Debs'. She coughed. He ducked. She was quiet and then the snoring started up again.

He felt a heel but he really had to get out of here. Ella would be furious. He mustn't tell her. Under no circumstances. But would Debs spill the beans? He wondered whether he should wake her up and tell her this had to be a secret between them, but, coward that he was, he crept downstairs and left a note by her kettle. *Morning. Had to go. X*

He let himself out of the front door and ran as quickly as his hangover would allow him.

In the glove box of his car he found a roll of extra-strong mints and put four in his mouth to kill any telltale aromas of alcohol. Ella had the nose of a bloodhound.

As he drove out of Trevay, his mouth open to cool his burning tongue, he tried to come up with a feasible story as to why he hadn't come home last night but as Henry coasted towards Marguerite Cottage, the engine switched off, he noted, with joy, that all the curtains were still closed.

He put his head on the steering wheel in relief and to ease the pain.

Once inside the cottage, he tiptoed up the stairs, across the landing and towards his bedroom door. He congratulated himself as he placed his hand on the handle.

'I've been so worried.' Ella had appeared from the bathroom and was tying up her dressing-gown belt. 'Where have you been?'

Henry leapt with fear and screamed, 'Fuuck!' whilst clutching his chest.

'Shh,' said Ella crossly. 'No need to wake Kit up.' She stepped towards him and sniffed. 'That old trick.' She put her hands on her hips. 'Extra-strong mints will never cover the amount of booze you've sunk. Come downstairs. I want to talk to you.'

Meekly, he followed her.

Debs woke up and stretched from top to toe. She smiled, remembering last night. She rolled over to see Henry's adorable little face but he wasn't there. He must be downstairs making a coffee. She would help him. She got out of bed and walked naked down the stairs, hoping to seduce him again. 'Henry?' she called seductively. He was not in her tiny front room. She padded into the galley kitchen. Not there either. Then she realised, he must be in the bathroom which was just beyond the kitchen. 'Henry?' she called. 'I'm making coffee. Hot, strong and sweet. Want some?' She arranged herself in what she hoped was an attractive nude stance outside the bathroom door but she couldn't hear any movement. She put her ear to the door and then tapped. 'Henry? I'm putting the kettle on now. Coffee, tea or me?'

She chuckled as she went to the kettle and then she saw his note.

She ran to the empty bathroom and was sick.

She heard her phone ping as she walked gingerly from the loo, feeling better but weak.

She looked at the message and swore. Sennen wanted to know if she'd be free for another family meeting, this time in Deborah's office. *I need to make my position clear to Ella and Henry about my parents' legacy. Would you be free at 10? And arrange for them to be there?*

Debs rubbed her temples, poured herself a coffee and then replied. *What a marvellous idea. I am free at . . .* She stopped and looked at the clock on her radio – 09.00. She swore. Hastily she typed, *Yep 10 is perfect. Will text them.*

Ella poured boiling water into the two mugs and stirred in milk and sugar. She passed one to Henry. 'Get this down you.'

'Thanks,' he said obediently, trying to remember his fictitious backstory.

'So,' Ella pulled out a chair and sat at the table, 'where were you last night?'

'I found a pub and had a few drinks. To be honest, I wasn't thinking straight. The shock of discovering an Indian family and all that was too much.'

'Uh huh,' Ella said patiently, crossing her legs and waggling a slippered foot. 'And then where did you go?'

'Nowhere.'

'Where did you sleep?'

'In the car.'

She looked at him. 'I will ask you again: where did you sleep?'

'I told you, in the car.'

'I don't believe you.'

'It's true.' He flopped back in his chair like a teenager denying he cheated at his exams.

'So why, when I asked Kit to go and look for you, did he find your car empty?'

Henry's brain was not functioning as fast as he'd like, 'When was that?'

'Just before midnight.'

'I went for a walk to sober up and woke up on that bench down by the harbour wall. Poppa's crabbing bench?' He was rather pleased to have added a touch of truth, but was clutching at straws and he knew it. However, it was bang on target. Ella's natural empathy kicked in.

'Oh no,' she wailed, 'it was so cold last night. You must have been freezing.'

He nodded pathetically.

She stood up and kissed the top of his head. 'I'll run you a nice hot bath.' As she got to the stairs her mobile phone, sitting next to Henry on the kitchen table, trilled a text. She called over her shoulder, 'Would you check that for me?

'Sure.' His hangover was pounding but he valiantly focused his eyes on the name of the text. He blenched and swallowed hard. It was from Deborah.

'Read it to me, then,' said Ella, hanging on to the bannister.

'It's from, er, Debs.' He cleared his throat. 'Deborah.'

'Oh? What does she want?'

'She says, Mrs Tallon-Singh would like to meet you and your brother at 10 this morning in my office. Would you mind passing this message to Henry and letting me know if you will both be attending?'

'Great. Tell her we'll both be there.' Ella took a couple of stairs two at a time.

Henry wavered. 'Wait, let's think about it. Isn't it too soon after last night? I mean, yesterday afternoon.'

'Not at all. Strike while the iron's hot.'

'But the last two meetings have ended up in rows.'

Ella returned from the stairs and entered the kitchen. 'Which is why we need to move on. The money Granny left is hers. End of. When that's sorted we can begin to build bridges. I was saying to Kit last night how lovely it would be to go to India and meet our little brother and sister.'

Henry rubbed the back of his neck. 'Do we have to do this today?'

'Yes.' She took his hand. 'Now come and be a good boy and have a bath.'

Sennen read Deborah's text and smiled. Here was another chance to prove to her children that she was not thinking of herself where her parent's money was concerned. She contemplated getting up and having a shower.

Rosemary popped her head around the bedroom door.

'Morning. Sleep well?'

'Wonderfully well. The margaritas did their job.'

'Good. I bring caffeine in case you need a lift.'

Sennen stretched out in the pretty little bed in Rosemary's spare room.

'Thank you for last night.' She sat up and took her coffee cup from Rosemary. 'You've been such a friend. I can't believe how much you've helped me . . . when really, you should have steered well clear. I was awful to you when we were young and I am truly sorry.'

'Forgiven. We all learn from other's mistakes.' Rosemary sat on the end of the bed, tucking her feet under her.

'But anything could have happened to us in Spain. I bet your parents hated me. '

'Well, let's just say you weren't exactly top of their pops,' said Rosemary with a wry smile. 'After the initial anger and interrogations – have you taken drugs, had sex? – they calmed down but kept me on a pretty short lead. When I met Ray, the man I married, they were relieved. Dad knew his father from the Rotary club, so he already had the stamp of approval. I wanted to make up for my teenage misdemeanour and make my parents happy, so Ray and I married very quickly.'

Sennen sat up and pulled her pillows behind her to get more comfortable. This was going to be a long conversation. 'I'm assuming you aren't with him now?'

Rosemary looked in to her coffee. 'No.'

'Tell me about him.'

'Oh, he looked great, on paper. Tall, dark, handsome, attentive, generous. Everyone told me I had made a terrific catch and I managed to convince myself that I was in love.' At this she plastered on a huge smile, a brave smile. She didn't fool Sennen.

'But?' asked Sennen.

'He was . . . a bit jealous.'

'Difficult?'

'Understatement, my dear,' Rosemary said bluntly. 'I had a little job in the chemist on the harbour. Remember Miss Tangye, the pharmacist?'

'Oh yes.' Sennen smiled at a memory. 'She sold me my first box of tampons. So discreet and kind. She took me to one side and explained how they worked.'

'Bless her. Yes, she was lovely and I loved working there. I was right in the hub of village life – which is what Ray didn't like.'

'Why?'

'He would come home with a couple of beers inside him and accuse me of fancying the men who came in for ordinary things like razors or shaving foam, but he said they came in because I was flirting with them. I wasn't.'

'What happened?'

'My dad got ill and Miss Tangye gave me as long as I needed off to give me time to help Mum nurse him.'

'Oh dear, that must have been very hard. How old were you?'

'Mid-twenties, I suppose. Anyway, when he died, Mum still needed me and Ray encouraged me to stay at home. There were certainly less rows then, but, when Mum started to feel herself again and I was ready to go back to work, Miss Tangye told me that Ray had already told her I wasn't coming back and she had employed someone else.'

'He what?'

'Yeah. But anyway, I was so tired after Dad died, with the worry of looking after Mum and everything, I accepted it and was actually glad to have time to myself for a bit. But the more time I had, the more time he had to control me. He hated me seeing friends, phoned me all the time to find out where I was. I had to give him details of my plan for each day and he would check up on me.' Rosemary's eternally upbeat persona began to slip. 'Then the drinking began. And he began to hit me.'

'Whaat?' Putting her coffee cup down, Sennen leant forward and threw her arms around her friend.

'Yeah. Shameful eh?'

'For him yes,' said Sennen stoutly.

'No. You'd think so, but I was the one who was shamed. When I finally told the family I was leaving him, they turned on me. Apparently, it was my duty to stand by him. He was going through a rough patch. He was family. Huh. Some family. Even when it came out that he'd been having an affair with a woman I had been close to, they blamed me for being a boring wife. God, it was awful.' She wiped her eyes on her pyjama sleeve. 'Anyway, I divorced him – or rather, he divorced me, for unreasonable behaviour.'

'No! How come?'

'I don't know, really. Anyway, I simply couldn't fight any longer, I was just so tired with it all.'

'Typical small town mentality,' said Sennen angrily. 'And all the time I was running away, I envied you. I imagined you in a cosy home with a couple of children and Sunday lunches in the pub.

'I envied *you*,' said Rosemary quietly. 'You got away and I could have gone with you.'

Sennen moved up the bed and hugged her old friend. 'In lots of ways I wish I had got on that bloody ferry in Spain and come back with you. What a pair we are.'

'What a pair we *were*! But here we are, older, not much wiser but together again.'

Rosemary sat back. 'And you have so much to look forward to. Having Henry and Ella back in your life and starting afresh, no lies, with Kafir and your little ones.'

Sennen rubbed her hands over her face and through her hair. 'God, I hope so. And what about you? Do you have anyone special?'

'Yes.' Rosemary's eyes lit up. 'Someone very special.'

'And?' Sennen's romance radar pinged into life.

'And I am sure you will meet very soon.' Rosemary looked at her watch. 'If you're going to get to Deborah's for the meeting you'd better get in the shower.'

28

Deborah downed her coffee, sped upstairs, then sped down them, remembering she had to clean her teeth. She gave herself a cursory cat lick then added deodorant and perfume. She told herself she could come back after the meeting for a full shower.

Back upstairs she found clean underwear but no tights. It was much too cold and her legs were too white to go bare-legged so she unhooked her tights from last night's knickers and yanked them on.

She opened her wardrobe door and immediately cursed herself. She'd forgotten to collect her second-best business suit from the cleaners. She stared at yesterday's suit. It was in a sorry heap on the floor. Bugger! She scooped it up and ran down to the kitchen and threw it into the tumble dryer with a shot of Febreze.

Back upstairs, she sat at her dressing table and looked in the mirror. A bit of touché éclat, blusher and lipstick should sort her out. In her make-up drawer she came across a couple of Nurofen and tossed those down as insurance, then fixed her face. Her shaking hand made a bit of a mess of her flicky eyeliner but an extra coat of mascara camouflaged that.

She ran downstairs, pulled the refreshed suit from the tumble drier, ran back upstairs for a neat white T-shirt and shoes, and made it to the door by 9.27. Taking a deep breath, and raking a hand through her unwashed but passable hair, she stepped out of the house and walked to the office.

Miss France had been the secretary for Penhaligon and Palmer Solicitors for as long as anyone could remember, but when Old Mr Penhaligon retired, so did she. Her replacement was a young law graduate called Grace who was far too qualified for the job but was happy to take on any conveyancing work as well as general office work.

'Morning, Debs.' Grace scanned her boss from head to toe. 'Want me to go out for a coffee?'

'Thank you, how kind.'

'Rough meeting yesterday, was it?'

'You could say that.'

'Looks like you haven't slept a wink. Up all night, were you?'

'Why do you ask?'

'Your suit has a stain on the jacket and there's a hole in your tights.'

Deborah looked down in despair at the dried blob of tartare sauce and said the first thing that came into her head. 'It was a dog – it jumped up at me on the walk in.'

'Tall dog.' Grace raised her eyebrows in disbelief. 'I'll pick up a pack of wet wipes and some new tights while I'm out. Latte? Large?'

'Anything other than American tan.' Deborah was already heading for her office.

Grace shook her head and laughed. 'I mean the coffee, not the colour of your tights.'

As soon as Grace left, Deborah went to her office and began setting it up. First, she opened the only one of the large casement windows that actually did open, the other being long stuck with paint, to let the underlying pong of dry rot out, then she tidied away a pile of case files sitting on the floor next to her desk, and finally assembled a selection of chairs for her three clients.

On the wall above her desk was a foreboding portrait of Mr Penhaligon, the founder of these chambers. She surveyed him.

'Well, Mr P, it's Debs here. Goodness knows how it has happened, but I'll try to look after your old practice as best I can. I went to Oxford, you know. Got a 2:1. Sorry it wasn't better.' She hitched her skirt up. 'Sorry about this; I had a bit of a situation this morning. Don't look.' She pulled off her torn tights and threw them in the bin. 'You probably know that I broke the cardinal rule last night and slept with a client's son. Not very smart, I admit. And I have a hangover. So, I'd like all the help you can give me, please.'

The outer door slammed and Grace walked in. 'Large latte, extra shot and nearly nude.'

'Thanks.' Deborah grabbed at the packet of tights. 'How much do I owe you?'

'Nothing. You'd do the same for me.'

Deborah thanked her, then looked at the clock. 'Mrs Tallon-Singh is due in seven minutes. Would you hold her until I'm ready?'

'You're the boss.'

*

Deborah pulled on her new tights, settled into the chair behind her desk and took a mouthful of the lifesaving coffee.

Sitting back in her chair she closed her eyes, lowered her shoulders and took a few deep breaths.

Her headache was almost bearable.

Opening her eyes, she opened the file in front of her.

The legacy due to Sennen was quite substantial. Certainly enough to help Henry with his mortgage. She banged her hand on the desk. She must not think about Henry Tallon.

She sipped some more coffee and concentrated.

Yes, the money could help both Sennen's older children and there would still be enough to help her second family too.

If she were asked, that is what she would advise.

Then maybe Henry would come down to live in Trevay and they would fall in love and . . . She banged the desk again. Stop it.

Her door opened. It was Grace. 'Mrs Tallon-Singh is here.'

Deborah laid her head on the desk for just a moment then sat up, as bright-eyed as she could. 'Please show her in.'

She got up and met Sennen at the door.

Today Sennen smelt of patchouli and was wearing her new jeans with an Indian kaftan.

Deborah was always surprised by Sennen's height and had to resist standing on tiptoe as Sennen bent down to shake her hand.

Sennen looked at the chairs and asked hopefully, 'Three chairs? Ella and Henry are coming?'

'They're certainly invited.'

'Oh, that's good. I have made some decisions and it would be better if they were both here when I say them.'

'It's always useful,' smiled Deborah. 'Has Grace offered you a coffee?'

'Yes. She is taking the orders as we all arrive.'

There was the sound of someone else arriving. Grace knocked at the door and announced Ella, who was holding tightly to Kit's hand, and Henry. Deborah was pleased to notice he looked worse than she felt. He kept his eyes firmly on the carpet.

Ella bent to kiss her mother on both cheeks. 'Hello, Mum, you look nice.'

Sennen could have wept for this kindness. 'Thank you, Ella. So do you.'

Suddenly the room felt a little cramped and over warm. Deborah started to feel flustered and faint. The room slid under her feet. She sat down.

Grace noticed. 'Do you need more chairs, Miss Palmer?' she asked with professional calm. 'And before I get the coffees, perhaps I'll open another window?'

'Chairs, yes thank you but the window is a bit . . .' She swallowed rising nausea. 'A bit erm . . .' Deborah gripped her desk.

Henry leapt up and, Deborah could tell, he almost immediately regretted it. He steadied himself on the back of his chair. 'Let me help you.' He crossed to the window and, after a few goes, managed to thump it open. 'There.' He took the opportunity of a gulp of fresh air. 'Now chairs, where are they?'

Grace pointed out a heavy chair in the outer office. 'Maybe that one?'

'Of course.' He made an effort to produce his winning Tallon smile. 'Could you direct me to the gents first?'

'On the landing. First left.' She looked at the beads of sweat on his forehead and shaking hands. 'Are you all right?'

'This family stuff is very emotional.' He wiped a hand across his brow. 'Do you have any aspirin?'

Grace knew a hangover when she saw one. 'I'll get some when I go on the coffee run. It might be a bug.' Grace narrowed her eyes. 'Miss Palmer isn't looking too good today either.'

'Really? I must just . . . on the left?' She watched as Henry scurried to the loo.

'Will that be everything, Miss Palmer?' asked Grace, fifteen minutes later, coffee and aspirin distributed and everyone seated.

Deborah gave her a thankful smile. 'Yes, thank you.'

Grace closed the door silently behind her.

Deborah sipped some coffee, quelled her mild nausea and began. 'You all now know the extent of Mrs Adela Tallon's estate. As her nearest living relative, everything now passes to Mrs Sennen Tallon-Singh. That is the law.' She looked at Sennen, who held her hands to her mouth as if in prayer. Deborah continued, 'All that needs to be done is to sign the relevant documentation and the money will be placed into Mrs Tallon-Singh's bank account.'

'Thank you,' breathed Sennen, 'it's almost too much to take in.'

Deborah stood up and offered her hand to Sennen. 'Congratulations.'

'You don't know what this means to me.' Sennen held out her trembling hand. 'It's a miracle.'

Henry shifted loudly in his seat. 'So that's it, is it?'

Deborah chanced a quick glance at him. 'Yes.'

'What about Ella and me?'

Ella put her hand on his arm. 'Henry, the money is not ours.'

'It shouldn't be hers.' He looked at the faces around him. 'Just saying. I'm allowed to say what I think, am I not?'

Deborah opened her mouth to speak but Sennen beat her

to it. 'I have something to say. To you all. I have been thinking about what to do for the best with this windfall. What my parents would want me to do with it. So here it is.'

Ella looked at both Kit and Henry and smiled. 'You see?' she said. 'I knew Mum would be fair.'

Henry frowned and gave Deborah a filthy glare as if it were her fault.

Sennen went on, 'I hope you will all approve.'

Henry put his elbows on his knees and his head in his hands and groaned. 'Please don't let it be the local cats' home.'

Sennen ignored him and turned her attention to Ellla and Kit. 'I'm thinking of starting a painting school, here in Trevay, in memory of Mum and Poppa. The Tallon School of Art.'

Ella's eyes lit up and her mouth opened in joy. 'Brilliant. That's a wonderful idea.' Sennen held her hand up in front of her to stop her. 'And, I should like it if you ran the school. You and Henry between you.'

Ella sat still, pink-faced with happiness, clutching at Kit's hand. 'Oh, my goodness. Oh. Oh. It's perfect. Mum, thank you. Granny and Poppa would be thrilled.' She turned to Henry. 'Isn't it wonderful, Henry?'

Henry scratched his elbow and pursed his lips. 'I have a job in London. A good one. Why the hell would I want to run an art school?'

Kit had promised himself that he would say nothing in this meeting, he was only there to support Ella, but he couldn't allow Henry to pour cold water on her happiness. 'You could be a sleeping partner.'

'Oh, fuck off,' said Henry, appallingly, 'this is nothing to do with you. You're just my sister's boyfriend.' He stood up, almost knocking his chair over. 'I've had enough of this fairy la la land crap.'

Ella was horrified. 'Henry! Please. Sit down. Just listen. Please.'

Henry looked over at Sennen who was sitting with her eyes firmly on him. He stared back. 'And how long will you be around to help with this school?' he asked. 'Because Ella hasn't the faintest idea of how to run a business.'

Ella bridled. 'I can learn.'

Henry ignored her and directed his anger towards Sennen. 'As soon as things go wrong, when bills aren't paid and the bailiffs come knocking, you'll run away again, won't you?'

Sennen kept calm. 'I never meant to leave you forever.'

He splayed his hands out in front of him and looked bewildered. 'And yet you did.'

'I'm back now,' she answered patiently.

'For how long?' asked Ella, gently.

'I'm not sure.' She twisted her wedding ring.

Henry said quietly, 'And how much will you be taking home to your other family?'

Sennen shrugged. 'Nothing.'

'I don't believe you,' Henry said coldly.

'Please, Henry, I am just trying to do a good thing, the right thing.'

'Why start now?'

'Stop it,' pleaded Ella. 'If it's going to make you so beastly, let Mum have all the money. We have everything we have ever needed: Granny and Poppa's love, their memories and keepsakes, their art. We don't need anything else, least of all their money.'

Henry shouted, 'What about my mortgage? What about you?'

'Stuff it,' said Ella peacefully. 'Mum can do what she wants with it all. She never had what we had.'

Sennen blinked back a torrent of grief. 'And that is the sorrow I carry with me forever. I lost them. I lost you.'

'Oh, this again!' Henry waved her words away.

Ella spoke. 'It's a kind and generous thought, but if it's going to cause this much trouble, no thank you.'

Henry began to laugh. A rumbling laugh that swelled in his diaphragm and soared from his lips. He wiped his eyes. 'This is ridiculous.'

Sennen's mind was whirling. 'But I want to help you.'

Henry scowled at her. 'We'd rather go without, thank you.'

Deflated and confused, Sennen shook her head. 'This is not how I hoped it would turn out. I'm sorry. I've come in all guns blazing and not thought things through at all. Maybe . . . maybe we could let this lie for a bit. Sit on it. Have a think. But I want you to know that this is something I would really like to do for you.'

'Thank you,' said Ella, 'but perhaps it's all just a bit too sudden.'

'Yes. Sorry.' Sennen picked up her bag and took Deborah's hand. 'Thank you. For everything.'

'My pleasure. The money will be in your account by this afternoon.'

Sennen looked at her children. 'May I take you out to lunch?'

'You must be joking,' mumbled Henry, looking at the floor.

Ella glared at him then turned to her mother. 'Yes, please. I would love to have lunch.'

Sennen was grateful. 'And you too of course, Kit?'

Deborah saw them all out as Henry fumed silently.

Deborah walked quietly back to her desk and sat down. 'That was the worst meeting I have ever had.' She kicked her shoes off and drained her coffee. 'Well done.'

'What is she thinking?' Henry was biting his thumb. 'She may as well give it all to the cats' home.'

'Instead of you?'

Henry gave a shamefaced grimace. 'I'm sorry I left you this morning. Without saying goodbye.'

'I didn't notice,' she said coldly.

'Ah. So last night didn't happen?'

'No, it didn't.'

He looked at her lapel. 'Although you do have a tartare sauce stain on your jacket, evidence that it did.'

Deborah placed her hand defensively on the stain.

He looked at the rubbish bin by her desk. 'And a pair of torn tights in your bin.'

'I don't have time for you, Henry. Last night was a mistake.'

'Oh dear. I rather enjoyed it.'

She shot a look at his smugly handsome face and put her head on her desk in shame. 'I have a terrible hangover,' she mumbled.

'Me too.' He stretched his arms above his head. 'If you're not too busy, how about we take the afternoon off and blow away the cobwebs?'

Sennen walked Ella and Kit down to a small fish restaurant on the corner of the harbour. Rosemary had suggested it and she was waiting outside. She greeted Sennen with a kiss. 'How did it go? No Henry with you?'

'No,' said Sennen,

'But you're okay?'

Ella put her arm around Sennen's shoulders and replied, 'Yes. We are okay but ready for a glass of something cold and white.'

The cheery waitress put them at a window table. The day

was warming up and she had opened the sliding windows onto the view of passers-by and the harbour. Sennen took in a lungful of the salty air curling around them.

'I shall miss this when I go back home.'

Ella was dismayed. 'You're not going soon, are you?'

'I have to go back eventually.'

The waitress arrived, causing a distraction as she handed them menus. 'Fish of the day is on the marble counter.' She pointed to a counter in the centre of the room, heaped with ice and an abundance of seafood including lobster and crab.

'Anything to drink?'

Rosemary chose a bottle of Sancerre for the table, then took Sennen to choose her fish.

The restaurant was filling up with more lunch customers.

Voices bounced off the white ceramic tiled walls and their chair legs scraped the ceramic floor.

While they were alone, Kit took Ella's hand, 'Ella, why don't we announce our engagement to Sennen today? It'll be some good news for her.'

Ella bit her lip. 'I don't know. I don't want her to think I'm trying to keep her from going back to India . . . although . . .'

Rosemary and Sennen returned. 'We've chosen the monkfish,' Rosemary told them, 'How about you two?'

'Dover sole, I think,' said Ella, closing the menu.

'Me too,' smiled Kit. He squeezed Ella's hand conspiratorially and readied himself to break their news but the waitress arrived to take their order.

When she had gone, Rosemary wanted to know how the meeting had gone. 'An art school? That's marvellous and would do so much for Trevay,' she exclaimed.

'It feels right,' agreed Sennen, 'only Henry thinks it's a waste of money.'

'I'm sure he'll come round,' said Ella loyally. 'He doesn't like things changing too quickly. It took him a long time to settle in London after leaving here and he had a lot of grief counselling when Granny died.'

'Did he?' asked Sennen. 'Oh, poor boy.' She put her head in her hands. 'I hadn't thought of how Mum's death would affect him. Affect both of you.'

'It was very hard.' Ella thought back. 'Losing Poppa was awful, but we stuck together and Henry helped Granny get through. They were very, very close. When you left, Granny became everything to him. He remembered you, you see. It was easier for me because I didn't.'

A weight of guilt and regret lowered itself onto Sennen's shoulders, pressing down on her neck, pushing her into her chair so that she physically slumped. 'Of course, yes.'

The waitress arrived with the monkfish. 'Roasted monk-fish for two with crushed potato and watercress sauce.'

Kit prepared again to announce the news of their engagement, but, with ineffable timing, the waitress reappeared.

'Two Dover soles with buttered leeks and shrimps.'

She placed them in front of Kit and Ella and standing back, clasped her hands. 'Is there anything more I can get you? Some bread? More water?' She looked at them. 'No? Well, call me if you need anything.'

Sennen had lost interest in her food. 'Ella, I can never explain how sorry I am to have made such a mess and taken so many wrong turnings. If I could turn back time I would never have left you. Sorry is just not a big enough word. All I can say is that I am here for both of you now, for as long as either of you need me or want me.'

Ella's eyes began to brim with tears. 'Don't, Mum. What's done is done and I want to get to know you now. Properly. Henry will come around.'

'But I have missed so much. Birthdays, Christmases. Mum and Poppa.'

Kit took his moment. 'Sennen, you haven't missed it all. Ella and I are engaged to be married . . . if you don't mind?'

29

Agra, 2010

Every time Sennen admired her curtains she couldn't help but remember Kafir. He was very handsome and his courteous nature and charm were very attractive. If she wanted a man, he was certainly the type she would go for but a man was the last thing she wanted. She was happy as she was.

This morning she was going down to the market to buy some trims and tape for a set of curtains she was making for a new client. She picked up her cotton shoulder-bag, threw a shawl over her shoulder and let herself out of her room.

She wondered if she should knock to see if Tanvi needed anything brought in, then decided against it. It was early and Tanvi liked a lie-in.

Sennen stepped out into the heat of the morning sun. The market was already set up and looked fresh and inviting in the shimmering haze. She stepped off the uneven kerb and walked into the heart of the stalls. A couple of blond dogs with curly tails trotted behind her. They walked as if doing dressage; slightly sideways, crossing their back paws with each step. She addressed them. 'Good morning, girls, and how are your puppies today?' The smaller dog with long nipples looked at her with expressive eyes. 'Hungry? Shall I get you something? Come on, then.'

The dogs followed Sennen, as they did most mornings, to a busy stall selling pouches of pet food.

'Namaste,' the young man behind the wooden crates greeted her. 'More food for the dogs? Every day you feed them. You are their mother.' He smiled his toothy grin.

'Namaste.' She put her hands together and nodded her head in respect. 'I can't let them go hungry. Not with their puppies.' She reached for her purse as he handed her the usual four pouches of food.

'Chicken chunks in gravy. Very delicious.' He laughed and licked his lips.

'Their favourite. Thank you.' The dogs scampered off behind the stall into the shade and she followed. There was a sheet of tattered canvas hanging from a wall by two nails. The two dogs immediately wriggled inside their shabby home where Sennen could hear the puppies whining. She knelt down and lifted the canvas.

'Here you are, then.' She opened the pouches and the dogs waited patiently as she emptied the food into two plastic bowls that she had put down weeks ago. 'There now. Dinner is served.' She ruffled their ears as they tucked in, and counted the bundle of puppies mewling in the dark recess of their home. All six were still there. 'See you tomorrow, girls.'

She replaced the canvas flap and stood up. First job of the day accomplished.

She walked back into the market and on through the teeming tide of shoppers who were pushing each other along or swerving to avoid those who had stopped to inspect a display of green beans, ripe tomatoes, mangoes or herbs.

Women in jewel-coloured saris, men in white shirts, ill-fitting trousers and dusty sandals, children laughing and twisting amongst familiar legs. This was her place.

Turning left, leaving the human river behind, she entered a more shaded, cooler part of the market. It was less busy and all the nicer for it. Here there were proper shops with solid walls and shuttered fronts. It was the haberdashery quarter of Agra.

Several of the shopkeepers greeted her by name. She stopped to swap pleasantries but headed on, knowing exactly where she wanted to be. And there it was.

'Namaste, Mr Kuranam.'

The proprietor, rotund and serious, looked up, smiled and clasped his hands to his belly. 'Namaste. You have come. I am keeping some very special fabric for you.'

'Did it arrive?' she asked excitedly.

He wobbled his head. 'From Jaipur. It is the very best. Let me show you.'

He walked into the murky depths of the shop, past the shelves bulging with bolts of exotic fabrics. She followed him.

He pulled out a large roll and thumped it down on his cutting table. The noise was muted, absorbed by the density of material around them. He unrolled it with pride. 'Look.' He rubbed the end between his fingers. 'Pure cotton and linen.'

She did the same, but knew not to look too impressed. 'How much?'

'I give you very good price.' He wobbled his head and smiled. 'Very good.'

'Mr Kuranam, you know I am a poor woman.'

He laughed. 'But the lady you are making these curtains for is a rich woman.'

'But if I charge her too much, she won't use me any more and I will be poorer still.' She grinned. 'And I won't be able to be your best customer.'

'Oh, Miss Sennen, you are naughty lady. Let me think.' He took a pencil from the pocket of his immaculately ironed shirt. 'How many metres?'

An enjoyable amount of bartering ensued, during which he tried to persuade her to buy several metres of Black Watch tartan – 'Queen Victoria's favourite' – but Sennen stuck with her original purchase and got him to throw in thread, lining and tape.

Mr Kuranam made a huge show of flapping open a large carrier bag and putting everything inside. 'You will never make me rich, Miss Sennen.'

'I don't believe you,' she laughed, momentarily losing concentration as she backed out of the shop. 'See you soon.' She fell, catching her foot awkwardly and falling hard on her left hip and elbow.

Mr Kuranam moved to comfort her. 'Come. Sit in my shop. A glass of water? Are you hurt?'

Sennen took his helping arm and checked herself over. 'I'm fine. A bit bruised, probably, but I'm fine. Thank you.'

'Would you like a chai? There is the café on the corner.'

She recollected seeing it. 'Yes, I think that would be a good idea.'

He insisted on helping her cross the road and finding her a seat in the shade. In rapid Indian he ordered and paid for a chai.

'You will be okay now. Just the ticket?'

Sennen gave a small laugh. She loved the way many Indians still used British idioms. 'Yes. Just the ticket. Thank you, Mr Kuranam.'

When he was satisfied that she was absolutely fine, and distracted because there were two potential customers hovering by his shop, he left her to her chai.

Her hip was rather sore but undamaged, she was certain. She lifted her sleeve and checked her elbow. The skin was scuffed and a small bruise was blooming, but otherwise there was nothing to write home about. She pulled her sleeve down and picked up her drink.

'Good morning,' said a vaguely familiar voice.

She looked up. Standing with the sun against his back, forming a golden halo around his head, was Kafir.

'Hello,' she said.

'Are you okay? I saw you looking at your elbow.'

'Oh, it's nothing – I fell out of a shop. Literally. But I'm fine.'

'Would you like to have it checked with the doctor?'

'Absolutely not. Chai is the best medicine.' She held her cup up to show him.

'May I join you?' he asked. 'I was wondering if I would see you today – I am on my way to visit Auntie.'

'What a coincidence.' She smiled, moving her large carrier bag from the empty chair beside her. He shouted an order for lemonade and sat down.

'You are up early,' he said.

'It's a habit now. I can't sleep in. It gives me a headache.'

'Me too. But it means I go to bed too early. I am not much of a night owl.'

'Me neither.'

Kafir's lemonade arrived and, as he took a sip, she took a

sly glance at him. Today he was wearing a pale blue turban, navy polo shirt and chinos. His dark beard framed his lips and accentuated their fullness. He was lovely. 'So, what have you been buying?' he asked, putting his glass back into its china saucer with a clatter.

'Buying more curtain fabric, but for a client this time.'

'May I see?'

Sennen opened the bag and he peered in. 'Not my cup of tea,' he said.

'Nor mine. A bit too overpowering.'

'You know that Auntie says I need new curtains?'

'But you don't think so?'

'I didn't, until I saw how nice yours looked the other evening.'

'Well, if ever you need some, I'd be happy to do them for you. Mates rates.'

'Mates rates? Lovely jubbly. That's funny. Do you like that comedy programme?'

'*Only Fools and Horses*? Gosh, I haven't seen it for years but my father adored it.'

'Do you remember the one where the man falls through the bar? It is very funny.'

She laughed 'Oh yes! David Jason. He's a Sir now.'

'The Queen knighted him? She must like the programme too.'

'I can imagine her and the corgis sitting down to watch it, can't you, gin and tonic in one hand.'

'Crown in the other.' Kafir laughed louder.

'Are you a royalist?' Sennen asked.

'Not really, but there is something very charming and old-fashioned about them, don't you think?'

'They aren't my thing.' Sennen stirred her chai.

'Auntie loves them.'

Sennen exhaled loudly. 'Don't I know it. I've seen her commemorative plates.'

'You are honoured.'

'So you are on your way to see her now?'

He looked surprised, as if he had forgotten, 'Ah yes! I shall walk you there, if you would like the company.'

She had never walked through the market with a man before. Handsome or otherwise. Maybe it was her imagination, but it seemed as if, walking together, they drew respectful glances from the passers-by. Women certainly noticed him and she wondered if, when they slid their eyes to her, it was in admiration, envy or surprise that she could walk with such a man.

As he talked by her side, she felt different. Taller. Prettier. She listened to his stories of growing up on this street and the history behind some of the older buildings. She hung on to all that he said and tucked them carefully away in a new box in her brain, to bring out and lovingly examine later.

Finally, they got to her building and they walked up the stairs to her landing. 'Let me put your bag in your room, and then I shall take up no more of your time.'

She fumbled for her key in her bag and he gently took it from her and unlocked her door. 'Where would you like your shopping?'

'Just there. On the floor. Thanks.'

He gave her her key and they said goodbye.

She watched him cross the wooden floor to Tanvi's room opposite.

His long, lean, elegant body bewitched her.

'Bye,' she said.

He turned and smiled at her. 'Bye.' Then he knocked at Tanvi's door and Sennen closed hers.

She couldn't wait for chai at Tanvi's the following Wednesday, but Tanvi didn't mention him and Sennen's natural reticence made it impossible to ask.

She found herself not leaving the house too often or for too long, in case he came calling. At least, it meant that she finished making the new curtains quickly, much to her client's happiness.

She thought about Kafir most of the time and was irritated that she knew so little about him. He was an economics graduate and a teacher, but where did he live? And, the stomach-churning question, did he have a girlfriend?

A month passed. She continued her weekly routine of chai with Tanvi, cooked a small dinner party for a few of the house residents and fed the stray dogs and growing puppies who were almost weaned. Of Kafir, though, there was nothing.

It was Tanvi who eventually brought him up. 'Kafir has been asking after you.'

Sennen's grip on the kettle almost slipped. 'Oh yes?' she said carefully.

'I have been telling him for weeks to ask you about his curtains but he is too shy.'

'Oh.' Sennen couldn't hide her disappointment.

Tanvi looked very put out. 'Don't you want the work?'

'I do.'

'Are you too busy?'

'No.'

'Then I shall tell him we are coming over to measure up.'

Sennen was nervous. 'When?'

'This afternoon. It's perfect. Wednesday's are his afternoon off.'

Sennen was again alert, 'Oh. I didn't know teachers have half-days.'

'Not normally. He's a part-time teacher.' Tanvi shook her head. 'He also works with children who have suffered emotional trauma.'

'Oh.' Sennen was surprised. 'Like a therapist?'

'A very good one,' Tanvi said with pride.

'Yes, I would think so,' said Sennen, her brain reordering and shifting all the mental files she had on him. She pictured him surrounded by smiling children, so grateful for his ministry. She smoothed her hair and smiled to herself.

Tanvi's hawk eyes caught her. 'Does that make him attractive to you?'

Sennen's cheeks burned and she answered primly, 'No. Not that he's not handsome, I mean, but it's an attractive quality in a man . . . to like children.'

'Ah yes.' Tanvi gave Sennen a knowing look. 'He would make an excellent husband and father.'

Sennen tutted. 'Don't start that again.'

'Start what?' Tanvi was all innocence.

'You know.'

They took a tuk-tuk to Kafir's home, which was a little out of the city on the road to Mangaleshwar Temple. Sennen didn't take tuk-tuks very often due to the cost and also because she enjoyed walking, but this trip with Tanvi was a treat. Sitting on the narrow back seat, pressed against her friend, with the breeze whipping her hair, she delighted in the exhilaration. The driver, she hoped highly skilled, sped through narrow gaps in the traffic that made her hold her breath and squeeze her eyes shut. He stopped for nothing, his thumb firmly pressed on the horn.

Hanging from his rear-view mirror and across the sun visor he had secured bright pink tinsel and golden tassels. Sennen remembered the fairs in the green fields of Trevay, the spinning lights and gaily painted carousel horses. All she needed to complete the picture was to have the driver shout, 'Hold on tight, here we go!'

'I'm loving this,' she shouted to Tanvi. 'So much fun.'

Tanvi patted Sennen's knee. 'You are too easily pleased.'

At last they pulled up in a quiet street dotted with small bungalows.

'This is Kafir's. Ignore his décor. You can work on that later,' said Tanvi climbing the two shallow steps to the verandah.

Sennen had butterflies waking in her stomach. What was she doing? Would he think her a stalker?

Tanvi knocked loudly, her tiny fist belying its power.

Sennen was ready to turn and flee when Kafir opened the door.

'Auntie.' He opened his arms, his face wreathed in smiles and hugged her. 'What a surprise.' He looked over Tanvi's shoulder and saw Sennen. She thought she saw his smile drop just for a split second, then he said, 'And Sennen. Welcome to my humble home.'

But it was humble only in so much as it was uncluttered. He led them through a small hall and into a simple sitting room with shuttered windows, two inviting rattan chairs, a table and a door opening onto a courtyard which was filled with pots of exotic fruit trees, flowering plants and herbs. In the sunshine there was a wicker lounger, with an open book lying beside it, and an empty glass.

'We've interrupted you,' said Sennen apologetically.

'Not at all. Let me make you a drink. I have Coca Cola which Auntie does not approve of but I love. Would you like one?'

'I would love one.' She smiled.

'And you, Auntie?' he said.

'Do you have 7 Up?'

'I do.'

'Then I shall have that.'

'It is as bad as Coca-Cola. Tut tut,' he said, as a parent might to a toddler. 'Are you sure?'

'It is less trouble for you than to find teacups.'

'That is very thoughtful.' He looked at Sennen, bringing her in on the joke. 'Make yourselves comfortable and I will bring the drinks and then you can tell me why you are here.'

He was an easy host, making his guests feel comfortable and important. He asked after Sennen's sore hip and elbow and Tanvi berated them both for not telling her about the fall and their meeting. He talked a little about his work and how few resources or desires there were to help children with their mental health. 'The point is,' he concluded, 'none of us is perfect. We are all a little mad. And we all need a little help at times.' He looked at Tanvi. 'Except my auntie. She is perfect and is right about everything, isn't that so, Auntie?'

'I'm glad you see that.' She nodded. 'Which is why I have brought Sennen to your home. She will make you new curtains.'

'I have shutters,' he said.

'They don't keep the heat in when it's cold.'

'Hello, this is India,' he said.

'You need curtains.' She folded her arms and stared at him.

He looked at Sennen. 'Apparently, I need curtains. What would you suggest?'

'I like your shutters.'

'He needs curtains,' said Tanvi obstinately.

'Well . . .' Sennen thought, then, 'A light muslin perhaps? To diffuse the light?'

'Perfect,' agreed Tanvi. 'And what about chair covers?'

'I don't do upholstery.'

'Cushions, then?' Tanvi insisted.

'Erm . . .' Sennen glanced at Kafir for help. 'Do you want cushions?'

'No, but I would like a rug.'

'I'm not an interior designer.' Sennen was embarrassed. 'I just make curtains.'

'But your flat is so lovely,' Tanvi interjected. 'Isn't it, Kafir.'

'I remember it being very charming and welcoming.' He thought back. 'The curtains were good and your balcony very pretty.'

'Thank you,' said Sennen.

'So, Saturday morning early you will go shopping for curtains and a rug,' Tanvi declared. 'I'm glad that is settled.'

'Is it?' laughed Kafir. 'Sennen may have plans of her own.'

Tanvi sniffed. 'Believe me, she has nothing else to do.'

'Excuse me,' said Sennen, 'I do have a life.'

'So tell me?' Tanvi challenged her. 'What are you doing on Saturday?'

'As it happens,' Sennen said, 'I am free this Saturday.'

Tanvi looked at Kafir in triumph. 'You see? Auntie is always right.'

At dawn the next day, Sennen watched as the sun crept over the wall of her balcony. She had lain in bed for hours, thinking about Kafir and how happy she was to be spending the morning with him. Of course, she told herself, he wouldn't be thinking the same. He was doing what his auntie expected of him and he was too kind to refuse her. He was not interested in her romantically. Why would he be? A thirty-four-year-old spinster who could sew curtains was hardly a great catch. But he had smiled at her while he'd been teasing Tanvi and been so attentive when he had walked her home through the market that time.

She threw back her sheet angrily. 'I am just the person who is making him curtains he doesn't want, and helping him choose a rug I know nothing about.' She swung her legs onto the floor. 'Now get up and shut up.'

She went to the bathroom on the landing that she shared with Tanvi. She showered and washed her hair, pinching some of Tanvi's excellent conditioning hair oil.

Back in her room she sat on her balcony, with tea, bread and jam, brushing her hair dry until it gleamed. It was past her shoulder blades now with flecks of grey at the temples, just as her mother's had been when she was a child. She stopped brushing and caught her breath. What were her parents doing right now? She looked over at her clock. They were about four and a half hours behind so it would be the middle of the night for them. They'd be in bed, slumbering peacefully next to each other. Then she thought of her children.

Henry would be almost nineteen, now. Probably at university. Maybe studying art. As a toddler he had always loved painting with her and Adela. She wondered if she would recognise the loving little boy who was now a man.

And Ella? She was seventeen, the age when Sennen had already run away. What had her parents told them about her?

Had they heard all the little stories of her as young girl? Did they think of her fondly? She closed her eyes and sent fervent waves of love to them all. 'Stay safe. Please stay safe.'

She heard a dog bark below. There were her two little canine friends promenading with their puppies, teaching them where best to scavenge for food. She called to them and they looked up. She dropped several pieces of her breakfast bread down and watched as they tussled for them before sauntering off, tails up and curly.

30

Kafir arrived on time, with Tanvi standing across the landing, checking that the plan was going as she wished.

'You both look very nice,' she said approvingly.

'Auntie, we are going to buy a rug, not go to a wedding,' he told her firmly.

Tanvi raised her eyebrows. 'That is a funny analogy to use. Don't you think, Sennen?'

'I think you need to stop being naughty,' Sennen said.

Kafir laughed his deep laugh and held his arm out for her. 'Take my arm and let us leave the naughty Auntie to meddle with someone else's life.'

Sennen tucked her arm through his and Tanvi watched them go and called after them, 'Be sure to show me the rug when you get back!'

The market on Saturday, even this early, was already packed. Sennen allowed herself to be guided by Kafir as he kept her arm close to his chest. It took longer than usual to get to the haberdashery quarter but when they did, the cool shade revived them.

Mr Kuranam welcomed her warmly. 'And who is this gentleman?' he asked, studying Kafir from top to toe.

'Namaste, Mr Kuranam,' Kafir replied, very formal. 'I am Miss Sennen's client, Kafir Singh.'

Mr Kuranam held a hand up in apology. 'A client! I am so sorry to embarrass. Miss Sennen is a good friend. Please, come in and tell me what you are looking for.'

Kafir chose quickly with Sennen's guidance. A linen voile that would drape well. 'Perfect choice, Mr Singh,' smiled Mr Kuranam, clearly not convinced that the relationship was solely a business one. 'I am certain Miss Sennen will make a good home for you.'

Kafir hesitated slightly but thanked him.

Sennen hurried them out of the shop. 'I'm so sorry, Kafir.'

'What for?'

'Mr Kuranam's presumptions.'

Kafir shrugged, 'It seems that a lot of people are making presumptions for us.'

Sennen giggled nervously, kept her head down, and, taking his arm, allowed him again to guide her to the rug shop.

They were invited in by a young man who offered them a seat before asking exactly what they were looking for. Kafir was stumped. 'I don't exactly know.'

The young man turned to Sennen for help.

'Well, let's start with colour,' she said. 'What is your favourite colour, Kafir?'

'Blue.'

'Dark? Light? Aqua?'

He thought. 'Dark?'

The young assistant sprang into action. 'I have good dark-blue rugs. Let me show you.'

Within minutes at least six beautiful rugs were unrolled in front of them.

Kafir was lost. 'Maybe they are too dark?'

'Let me get lighter ones.' The boy scampered off and returned with more rugs, this time in light blue. He unfurled them with pride before Kafir.

Kafir inclined his head in a suggestion that he liked them. 'What do you think, Sennen?' he asked.

'I think I prefer these, but with new drapes and your rattan furniture, maybe a cream or gold design would be nice?'

He stroked his beard. 'Maybe.'

'I get them,' said the eager young man.

Eventually Kafir chose a dusty pink pattern with a rich cream-coloured background.

'Very good choice,' said the boy. 'Taj Design. Agra knotted. Very nice rug.'

He and Kafir haggled over the price and, when both were happy, the deal was struck. The rug would be delivered that afternoon.

Kafir checked his watch. 'Time for a coffee?'

They walked to a small park where a café was set up in the shade of a grove of Banyan trees. Kafir ordered two coffees from the slender teenaged girl who was serving the tables.

'I have enjoyed this morning. Thank you,' Kafir said, stretching his legs out in the dust.

'Me too,' said Sennen, draping her shawl over her hair. 'The rug is very beautiful.'

They drank their coffee in comfortable silence, neither feeling the need to talk. Sennen watched the sparrows hopping under the tables, pecking for crumbs.

'In Cornwall, where I grew up, we have lots of sparrows. My mother has a bird table outside the kitchen window. My father calls them Spadgers, I don't know why.'

'Do you know we have robins in India?'

'Really? I didn't think robins migrated.'

'Not your robins. Ours are called Indian Robins but they don't have red breasts. They are dark all over but quite tame.'

'Poppa, my father, had a tame robin in our garden. He would come to my father and take crumbs of cheese from his hand.'

'That's nice. We had a tame tiger who would take steak from my father's hand.'

'Really?'

'No. I am joking.'

She laughed. 'For a moment there . . .'

'Tell me about your home,' he asked.

She described Trevay and its harbour, the fishing boats and the hard life of the fishermen. She told him about her days of sun and rain on the beach, and the childhood of paddling, then swimming and eventually graduating to surfing. She made him laugh, telling him about the terrible things she did at school and the punishments that she received. And, finally, she described her house, her parents and their work with the art students.

'I would like to see Cornwall.' Kafir said. 'When I was in London, studying, there were students who talked about it, had holidays there, but we Sikhs get a little hydrophobic around the sea, or even the rain.'

'Why?'

He pointed at his head. 'The turban is not waterproof.'

She laughed. 'Do you never swim?'

'Yes, but maybe with something on that doesn't mind getting wet.'

'I never thought about that. But you take it off to sleep? And shower?'

'Of course.'

'I like your turban. It suits you.'

He inclined his head self-deprecatingly. 'Well, thank you. And may I say I have noticed you have very shiny hair?'

She reached up and felt it. 'I have something to confess. I sometimes pinch a little of Tanvi's conditioning oil from the bathroom.'

'I shall have to call the police immediately . . . or I can take you to the shop that sells all sorts of hair products. You can buy some for yourself and some for Auntie too.'

When they got to the shop, Sennen was enchanted by the toiletries. She bought two new bars of sandalwood soap, some body moisturiser and the hair conditioner for herself and Tanvi. At the till the assistant carefully wrapped and tied each purchase and asked Sennen if she'd like to buy some cologne for her husband.

Sennen flushed and was relieved that Kafir was on the other side of the shop. She whispered, 'We are not married. He is my friend.'

But the assistant was not to be put off. 'Can you not buy a friend a small gift? I have very special gentlemen's cologne on offer. See?' She squirted a tester onto Sennen's hand. 'Smell.'

Sennen put her nose to her hand and inhaled. It was lovely. The freshness of lime with a base of sandalwood and musk. She bought it.

*

The walk home was quite long but Sennen's senses were alive to everything she saw and heard. The birds in the trees, the warmth of the sun, the sound and feel of Kafir walking next to her.

Back at her house, Tanvi's door flew open as they reached the top of the stairs. 'Successful shopping?'

'Very,' smiled Kafir. 'Have you been waiting to catch us?'

Tanvi was all innocence. 'Not at all, but I was thinking you might be hungry?'

'Not at all,' said Sennen as Kafir said, simultaneously, 'Starving.'

That was all the encouragement Tanvi needed to produce plates of tasty food with fresh fruit juice.

Eventually, Kafir said he had to leave or he would miss the delivery of the rug. Taking their leave of Tanvi, he walked Sennen across the landing to her door. 'Thank you.'

'I haven't done anything.'

'But you will make my beautiful curtains and you have given me a happy day.'

'You have given me a happy day too.' She rummaged in her bag. 'I have a small, very small, gift for you.' She handed him the wrapped bottle of cologne. 'I hope you like it.'

'May I open it now?'

'Yes.'

His slender brown fingers with their well-shaped nails undid the string and unfolded the paper. He took the bottle out and read the label. 'But this is too nice.'

'Smell it. If you don't like it I won't be upset.'

He twisted the top open and put his nose to the glass. 'It's very nice.'

'Really? It was the woman in the shop; it was on offer and it might be like loo cleaner . . .'

He put his hand to her cheek. 'Stop talking. It is beautiful and it is kind of you.'

He looked into her eyes and she felt his gaze deep inside her. She closed her eyes and turned her cheek further into his hand.

'Now I must go.' He dropped his hand.

'Of course. The rug.'

'Well, goodbye – and thank you.' He made a small bow then turned and walked down the stairs.

She stood rooted to the floor. The skin of her cheek that he had so gently held felt cool. She ran her fingers over it with happiness and hope.

The following morning Tanvi knocked on her door. 'I have had a phone call from Kafir. He wants us both to go to see his new rug and he will be cooking us lunch. I have said yes, so hurry. We will get a tuk-tuk in half an hour.'

Sennen was filled with energy and excitement and was pacing the landing impatiently before Tanvi was ready.

'You look very pretty,' Tanvi said. 'What have you done to yourself?'

'Nothing.'

'Hm. Something has happened. You are changed.' She screwed up her eyes and peered at Sennen. 'Yes, there is a change in you.'

Kafir opened his door looking a little frazzled. 'I have moved the rug this way and that and I still don't know if it is right. Come and see.'

Under her bare feet, Sennen felt the softness of the wool. 'It's gorgeous – and perfectly placed. Tanvi, what do you think of the colour?'

Tanvi was pushing her toes, with sensual delight, into the deep pile of the rug. 'I was sure he would go for blue. He always liked blue since he was a little boy. But this I like.'

Kafir blew his cheeks out in relief. 'That is good. Now all you have to do is like my lunch. Are you ready?'

He had made a beautiful vegetable curry with fluffy rice and chapatti.

'My auntie's recipe,' he admitted, smiling at Tanvi. 'I have never cooked it before.'

'He has never cooked for a girl before,' said Tanvi.

'Yes, I have,' he protested.

'When?'

'In London.'

'Ha!' said Tanvi. 'When you were a student. That doesn't count.'

'Well, it's delicious,' Sennen said dipping her chapatti in the sauce. 'And thank you for having me.'

'You should invite him round for supper in return,' nudged Tanvi. 'She cooks well, Kafir.'

'I would like that very much,' said Kafir looking at Sennen. 'If you would invite me?'

And that was the true start of their courtship. He would finish work and come to her at least three times a week, always leaving by ten o'clock. It was two months before he kissed her and a year before they gently made love. Sennen had never known the true tenderness that a man could show a woman.

On her birthday he promised her a mystery tuk-tuk tour. She had to meet him, just before dawn, outside her house where he would be waiting.

It was cold as she stepped outside, wrapped in a large shawl, and the birds were starting to wake up. He was there, as promised, and helped her into the tuk-tuk.

As the little motorbike engine started, he put her hand in his, his warmth spreading into her. 'Happy birthday.'

She guessed where they were going when the driver turned in to the road leading up to the Taj Mahal.

Kafir paid the driver then helped Sennen out. Leading her under the gated arch and into the perfect peace of the gardens, he pointed to the horizon and the glow of the promised sunrise. Turning her to face him he said, 'This sun brings with it the day when it is in your power to make me the happiest of men.'

She could hardly believe what he was saying. She put both hands to her mouth.

He knelt down. 'You know I am in love with you, and you have told me that you love me in return. I would be most honoured if you would say yes to allowing me to be your husband.'

Sennen could not speak. This man, this wonderful, gentle, loving man wanted to marry her? She swallowed hard and looked deep into his upturned, honest eyes. 'Yes. Yes, please.'

He stood up and took her in his arms. 'Thank you. Thank you.'

'No,' she laughed, 'thank you.'

Tanvi came with them to Jaipur to ease the meeting between Sennen and Kafir's parents. There was some disappointment that he was marrying a non-Sikh, but when they saw how happy he was, and how charming Sennen was, they took her to their hearts.

Her new in-laws could not have been happier with their beloved son's choice. Kafir, at thirty-seven, had had few serious girlfriends and Sennen, now thirty-six, was unusual in that she had not been married before and, according to Tanvi, led a modest and boyfriend-free life.

The wedding was to be a quiet one, a civil ceremony to be followed by a more traditional wedding in the Gurdwara or place of worship.

A few days before the ceremony, Sennen was invited to meet with the Granthi, a woman who would officiate at the wedding. She was a handsome, devout woman with kohl-rimmed eyes and a darkly glossy plait.

'Do I have to become a Sikh?' Sennen asked anxiously.

'Only God can decide if we are true Sikhs, so no. Do you believe in God?' The Granthis asked.

'I think so. My family were not very churchy, though. I suppose I believe that God is within us all.'

The Granthi smiled. 'Sikhs do not show other religions in a bad light. We believe that there is one God and we see no racial or gender bias. We stay humble and honest. As Guru Nanak himself said, "I am not good, but nobody is bad."' She held her hands together as if in prayer and blessed Sennen. 'May you and your husband walk the rest of your lives together on one path. May there be openness and truthfulness, with no secrets to come between you.'

When the Granthi had finished, Sennen bowed her head in deference and the woman showed her out.

Kafir, waiting outside for her, waved. She waved back trying not to think what the Granthis had said about no secrets coming between them. Gradually, a dark stone of dread, so long and deeply hidden, began to glow white hot within her.

The memory, even now, scorched her as she watched Ella and Kit's glowing faces in the Cornish café.

'Engaged? That's wonderful,' she said.

Rosemary was calling for a bottle of celebratory champagne.

Sennen felt the wet tears on her cheeks. She was crying for herself.

'Oh, Mum,' said Ella pushing her chin up and her lips down, 'you sentimental old thing. Here.' Ella brushed Sennen's tears away with her fingers. 'You are happy for us, aren't you? I know this is all going very fast for you but Kit and I have been together for over six months now and I love him so much.'

'It's wonderful, darling.' She gulped. 'I wish you every happiness. Both of you.'

Somewhere a phone began to ring. It was coming from Sennen's bag down by her feet. 'Just a moment.' She retrieved the phone and checked who was calling. Kafir. Had she willed him to ring her. 'Hello? Kafir?'

'Yes. How are you?' he asked, the line so clear he might have been in the room next door.

'Where are you?' she asked, surging with the hope that he may actually be next door.

'At home. Just giving Aali and Sabu their dinner.'

Ella gave her mother a questioning look, mouthing at her, 'You okay?' Sennen nodded and pointed towards the front door before, getting up and leaving the noisy room. 'Are the children okay?' she asked, hoping that one of them hadn't been taken ill.

'Fine. They are fine.'

'That's good.' She stepped out on to the narrow pavement and leant against the old bowed wall. 'Have they asked about me?'

'A little. But no trouble. What is happening with you?'

'I've met Ella and Henry.'

'And?'

'Ella has just told me she's getting married. To a very nice boy called Kit.'

'I wish them well. What about Henry?'

Sennen burst into tears. 'I've mucked everything up. I should never have opened that bloody letter. I should never have told you. Never have come here. Henry hates me. And *you* hate me.' She was crying loudly.

'I don't hate you,' Kafir said softly. 'I think maybe you hate yourself.'

'Yes, I do. I've made a mess of my whole life even when I've tried to do the right thing. And I miss you and I miss the children.' She wiped her running nose on the back of her hand.

'When is the wedding?' he asked.

'I don't know. I think they've only just decided to get married.'

'Would you like me to come?'

Sennen was aware of two women on the opposite pavement watching her, wondering whether they ought to see if she was okay. She gave them a small thumbs up and a watery smile before turning her face to the wall, 'I . . . I don't know. It may be too soon. Ella would be fine, I think, but it might be too much for Henry.'

'I see.'

'It's not that I don't want you here . . .' She heard the bleat in her voice. 'I miss you. I love you so much.'

'And we miss you.'

'And I would love you all to be here, Kafir. I need you. I need to see you. All three of you. Please, please, you are my husband, I don't want this to break us.'

'I think you should work out the situation you are in with Henry and Ella first, before we begin thinking of our marriage.' She heard a child's voice calling him. 'I must go, Sabu is calling me. I will send him and Aali your love. Now I must go. Goodbye, Sennen.'

'Kafir?' she said weakly, but he had already ended the call.

31

Pendruggan, 2018

'Way-hay,' shouted Rosemary as the bottle of house champagne went off with a loud pop. 'You're just in time!'

Sennen, arriving back at the table having tried to repair her face, put her shoulders back and decided to be the happiest of mums, for Ella's' sake.

'Get me a glass,' she ordered.

The other diners, couples old and young, families the same, watched and couldn't help but be cheered by the obvious happiness emerging in front of them. Sennen took her filled glass and raised it to the room. 'Please celebrate the engagement of my elder daughter, Ella Tallon to the handsome Kit . . .' She realised she didn't know his surname.

'Beauchamp,' Kit said helpfully.

Sennen inclined her head towards him in thanks. 'Yes, Kit Beauchamp. He is to marry my daughter, and I couldn't be more pleased. Would you be kind enough to raise your glasses . . .' She acknowledged the beer and wine drinkers. 'Your beakers . . .' She smiled at the younger children. 'And your cups . . .' She winked at the older customers. 'And now – to Ella and Kit!'

The room responded with a cheering, 'Ella and Kit!'

'Thank you.' Sennen sat down. 'Well, that's got you two off to a good start I should say.'

Gradually the champagne bottle emptied and Sennen insisted on settling the bill. Finally, Kit and Ella said their grateful goodbyes, leaving Rosemary and Sennen among the debris of the table.

'Cocktail?' asked Rosemary after Sennen's credit card had been returned.

'Why not? I have had more to drink on my return to Trevay than I've had in sixteen years in India, and I like it.'

She couldn't have told you what time she got back to White Water that night, other than that it was very late.

She peeled off her clothes and dropped them on the floor, then in the bathroom, held the sink unsteadily with one hand as she cleaned her teeth with the other. Her make-up she ignored. In bed, she pulled the duvet up to her chin and fell asleep immediately.

She dreamt of the day she had told Kafir the truth about herself.

She had got home after collecting Aali and Sabu from school, to find the multi-addressed envelope in the hall. Her heart plummeted when she saw the postmark: Cornwall.

It could only be bad news, she knew. Mum or Poppa must be ill?

In the dream, she relived the moment she had taken the

letter into her bathroom and locked the door to read it. The torment of grief that overwhelmed her, reading of her parent's deaths, hit her again. She saw Kafir's beautiful face switch from love to betrayal as she told him the truth.

He had shaken his head, disbelieving her.

'How could you deny the existence of your own children? To me?'

He had stood tall over her as she knelt at his feet in supplication.

'I thought I knew you,' he said, barely believing. 'What else do you have in your box of lies?'

She grabbed his knees. 'Nothing. I promise. Please, Kafir.' But he had swiped her away as if she were nothing more than a fly. 'Go home. To Cornwall. Make your peace. Apologise to your children and hope that they forgive you. But know that to find your past you may have lost your future.' His words were like ice and he chilled her blood as he continued, 'I must protect Aali and Sabu. I will tell them you have returned to England and we don't know when you will return. Tonight you will leave this house. Stay in a hotel, if you must, but you must go.'

She had woken sweating and shouting, 'No Kafir. No.'

She sat up in bed, alarmed, and tried to steady her breathing. She took a gulp of the water from the glass on her nightstand.

She knew what she had to do, and by God she would do it.

She was up early and made sure she was looking her best. Downstairs, she had the briefest of breakfasts before dialling Ella's number.

'Hello,' answered Ella, sleepily.

'Hi, darling. It's Sennen – Mum.'

'Hi. You're up early.'

'Early bird catches the worm and all that, so I wondered, if you were doing nothing else today . . .' She took a deep breath to keep her resolve strong. 'If you might like to go wedding dress shopping. With me?'

'Oh.' Ella sounded unsure.

'If you're busy, I quite understand,' said Sennen, backing off.

'No, that would be great. I haven't even thought about it to be honest. We haven't even set a date.'

Sennen heard Kit's voice, drowsy and mumbling, 'Who is it?'

Then Ella, speaking off the microphone, 'It's Mum.'

'Is she okay?'

'Yes, she wants to take me wedding dress shopping.'

'Nice.'

Ella came back louder again. 'I'd love to, Mum.'

'Any shops you can recommend?'

'There's a shop in Truro that someone told me about.'

'Well then, let's go to Truro. I can pick you up from your house?'

'Okay.' Ella reeled off the address. 'Marguerite Cottage to the right of the church, down a little drive. Can you give me an hour to get ready?'

The next hour was sixty minutes of impatient agitation for Sennen. She walked to the newsagents, bought herself a paper, sat in a coffee shop, ordered a cappuccino and attempted the crossword. She checked her phone, strummed her fingers, paid the bill and was finally on her way to Pendruggan.

As she drove into the heart of the village she could see why Ella loved it. The village green was like something out of a children's picture book. There was the large farmhouse with its barns and milking parlour, the village stores next to the church and a row of attractive cottages, maybe two hundred years old, with slate roofs, well-tended gardens and pastel-coloured front doors.

She found Marguerite Cottage and, as she parked, Ella came bounding out of the front door, her red curls streaming behind her. She jumped into the passenger seat. 'This is so unexpected and all the more exciting for it,' she exclaimed. 'Thank you, Mum. I never thought this would happen. Me and you. Wedding dress shopping!'

Sennen began to reverse the car. She had butterflies in her stomach. This was something she had never allowed herself to imagine. She glanced at her beautiful, loving, kind and forgiving daughter as she shifted the car into first gear and set off.

'Thank you, Ella, for allowing me this,' she said softly.

Ella was putting her bag by her feet. 'Who else would I do it with?'

'If I hadn't have come back, you could have asked anyone.'

Ella turned to Sennen. 'But anyone wouldn't have been you.'

'You know what I mean. I am a stranger to you really. We hardly know each other, so, thank you.'

'Mum?'

Sennen slowed the car as she approached the junction to the main Truro Road. 'Yes?'

'We may not have spent my childhood together, but I do know you, even though I don't, if you know what I mean?'

Sennen stopped the car, waiting for a break in the fast traffic. She put her left hand out to Ella who held it tight. 'I do love you,' she said, her throat tightening with emotion, 'and this is so special.'

A car arriving behind her beeped loudly. She waved into the rear-view mirror and mouthed 'Sorry,' to the agitated driver, then, kissing Ella's hand, let it go and got on the road to Truro.

Parking in Truro took a little time, but once they'd got a space Ella quickly marched her to Truro Bridal Boutique. A petite young woman greeted them. 'Do you have an appointment?'

Ella's face dropped. 'Should I have made one?'

'It is recommended, but let me just check the book.'

Sennen held her crossed fingers in front of her face and Ella giggled. The assistant came back. 'Yes, we have a spare hour right now. What sort of style are you looking for?'

Ella gave a little jump of joy. 'It's just like *Say Yes to the Dress*.'

'What's that?' asked Sennen, catching her daughter's joy but not understanding.

Ella explained.

'Well, let's do it!'

The assistant, who was called Erin, took them through the initial questions.

'What sort of wedding are you having? Register's office or church?'

'Church,' said Ella definitely.

'And your budget for the dress?'

'Oh. Erm . . . about . . .' She hesitated, waiting for her mother to be shocked. 'Seven hundred pounds?'

'How much?' said Sennen on cue. 'I can make you one for a fraction of that.'

Ella went quiet. How could she tell her mother that she didn't want a homemade dress?

Erin said diplomatically, 'I think we can find something very beautiful for the bride within that budget.'

Sennen took the tacit rejection in her stride. She had lost the right, a long time ago, to give orders where Ella's needs were concerned.

Erin whisked Ella away into a fitting room while Sennen found a tasselled and buttoned velvet chair and sat on it gingerly, testing its sturdiness under her weight. Gradually her confidence in its strength grew and she tried to make herself comfortable. She glanced around, taking in the ruffles and drapes, the deep pile carpet and the scented candle on the payment desk. There was a huge mirror on one wall with a circular platform in front of it. Presumably for the bride to stand on and admire herself in full rig.

In the mirror, she saw herself. Her father used to describe her as 'rangy'. Tall, broad shoulders, narrow waist and hips, long legs. She stared into her own face and wondered where the young Sennen had gone. When had the smooth skin and unhooded eyes been lost among her sun-exposed skin? What would her mother have said to her right now? If things had been different Adela would have enjoyed this shopping trip. She would have loudly complained about expense and the over-commercialisation of two people getting married, but she would have been determined to share the fun. Sennen closed her eyes. Mum? Poppa? Look at me. I'm being Ella's mum. Helping her to choose her wedding dress. I can hardly believe it and I expect you can't either. So thank you. Thank you both for looking after her. She is perfect, and I know that that is down to you. Oh, I miss you. And I so wish you were here to see her . . .

The swish of the fitting room curtain interrupted her. She opened her eyes and gasped as Ella walked out in a confection of tulle, twinkles and hoops that swamped her perfect figure.

Sennen smiled nervously. 'Wow!' she managed.

'It's not me, is it?' said Ella.

'Um . . . I think you should try a few more before you decide.' It was as honest as Sennen was prepared to go.

Ella was whisked away again and modelled three more dresses, each more disastrous than the first.

Ella's spirits were sagging. 'Mum, maybe this isn't the shop.'

Erin, never known to lose a customer, sprang into action and tapped something into her iPad. 'Hang on, there may be just the thing, in the stockroom. We occasionally get sample dresses from the big designers for a very affordable sum. We should have some that have just arrived in stock. She swiped her screen several times then picked up the phone on the desk. 'I'll check the stockroom . . . Hi, Moira, it's me – has the Wang 2016 come in yet? Yes, I'll hold.' She covered the mouthpiece and said, 'She's just looking.' There was a long and silent wait until, 'Yes, I'm still here . . . a ten? Terrific!' She winked at Ella whose eyes were wide and desperate. 'Okay, thanks, Moira. Bring it up.' She put the phone down. 'Right, I've got a size ten Vera Wang 2016 – ticket price was two thousand pounds but we have it for seven hundred and fifty.'

Of course it fitted like a glove. A romantic, narrow fall of tulle which briefly hung on Ella's shoulders then slid over her waist, hips and ankles before puddling at her feet. She stood nervously in front of her mother for the final verdict.

Sennen viewed her as she might an Old Master in the Tate. Her eyes narrowed, her head first on one side then the other. Finally, she said, 'You look spectacular.' She stood and put her arms around her elder daughter and held her tight. 'So, so beautiful. And this is my treat.'

Ella flatly refused. 'No, Mum. The gift you have given me is you being here.'

'But I want to give you something special for your wedding day.'

Erin, starting to get tissue paper and dress bags from under the desk was listening and suggested, 'Will you be wanting a veil?'

Ella looked at Sennen. 'I would love a veil. But aren't they very expensive?'

Sennen laughed. 'Just like your Granny. But in this case I think she would tell you that it is never your extravagances you regret, it's your economies.' Then Sennen had an idea. 'I could make you one. A proper gift from me to you. What do you think?'

'Would you? Could you?'

'I've earned my living as a seamstress all these years – why not?'

'And so,' Ella finished off, 'I got the most gorgeous dress and then Mum bought the finest chiffon for my veil and that's all I'm going to tell you.' She put her hands around Kit's neck and kissed him. 'I am so, so, so lucky to have you, and Mum and Henry all here.'

Kit kissed her back. 'Talking of Henry, I haven't seen him since the meeting with Deborah.'

Ella smiled naughtily at him. 'Don't worry about him. He knows tons of people here who have a sofa to lend him. He'll come back when he's ready. But in the meantime, we do have the house to ourselves . . .'

Henry was spread across Deborah's sofa, wearing one of her T-shirts and little else. In front of him lay the remains of a cheese and pickle sandwich and two empty cans of lager. He was watching the cricket on Sky. He didn't take his eyes from the television as his phone rang. 'Yes?'

'Nice telephone manner,' Ella said. 'You're alive, then?'

'Yeah . . . Ooooh . . . Howzat!'

She sighed. 'You're watching the cricket.'

Sarcasm took over. 'Oh, hello, Ella, and how can I help you?'

'You can stop sulking for one thing.'

'I am not sulking, I'm getting on with my life.'

'Where? Are you back in London?'

'Not at the moment.'

Ella was getting irritated. 'I am not going to play twenty questions with you, just tell me: where the hell are you.'

'In Trevay, with a friend.'

'A lady friend?'

'Not right at this moment, but she will be back later.'

'I don't need to know the details. When are you going to come back and face all this stuff with Mum? You have got to let all these feelings of entitlement go. We have Granny and Poppa's furniture and art, and all our memories of them. She will *never* have those.'

Henry turned the sound down. He knew that Ella was right, but every time he thought of how his heartbroken grandparents were let down by his mother he was overwhelmed by a sense of injustice.

'It's just . . . oh, I don't know. It's just seeing her, here in Trevay. Trying to take over and make everything all right. Well, it isn't all right. It never will be all right. She doesn't know them better than us and Granny and Poppa would be spinning in their graves if they knew we were making it easy for her.'

'No, they wouldn't,' Ella said patiently. 'They loved her and would be glad that we have got her back.'

'I don't want her here. She can hop off back to her new lot, never to be seen again as far as I'm concerned.'

'Actually, she's staying on for a bit.'

'Why?'

'Kit and I are getting married.'

Henry couldn't help but be happy. 'Really? That's great, Ells. Does the poor bloke know what he's letting himself in for?'

'Oh, ha ha ha. But Mum is staying for the wedding. She's making my veil for me and she helped me to choose the dress.'

'Mommie dearest doing her bit to get you on side?'

Ella sighed. 'Please, Henry. She's our mother, and the idea of the art school and everything is a good one and I hate it when you distance yourself from me. Please, could you just try to be a bit more accepting? See things from her point of view?'

'You mean forgive her?'

'Eventually.'

'I'm not as nice as you.'

'But could you just try? For me? Just until she goes back to India?'

Henry ran a hand over his stubbled chin. 'For you, Ells Bells, I'll try.'

32

Sennen was having trouble sleeping. Her dreams were vivid and full of panic. She would find herself running from an unrevealed horror, but her legs wouldn't work, dragging behind her as if stuck in treacle or cement. Sometimes she'd be drowning in Trevay Harbour, other times she was lost in an Indian town she didn't know. The sun was beating down bringing the warm scent of the spices to her nose and she was walking in the busy market with her children, Kafir by her side. Then, abruptly, they were gone and she was lost and scared. She knew her family were in danger but her voice didn't work, and even though she screamed for help, no sound came and no one heard her. She would wake distressed and crying.

That morning, she woke breathlessly trying to quell the panic in her body.

Outside it was still dark and she could hear the patter of soft rain falling on the eaves.

She lay still for a while and tried to will sleep back to her but it was a fruitless effort. She checked the time. Six fifteen.

A walk, that's what she needed, to feel the earth under her feet and the elements on her face.

In the silent streets of Trevay she felt like the only person in the world. Down the cobbled lane, right onto Fore Street and then left onto the harbour. Here, there was a sign of human life. She could see the baker and her assistant working away in the kitchen behind the Old Bakery shop. The smell of fresh bread and pasties took her senses straight back to Saturday mornings with Adela, buying long French sticks and doughnuts for the students. On the way back from her walk she promised herself a treat.

On she went, down to the boats drifting on a high tide, the light drizzle cool on her face. She went past the Golden Hind pub, past the lane that led to Pencil House, until she found the start of the footpath that would take her over the cliffs towards the lighthouse and Tide Beach.

The cliff path was steeper than she remembered, but the view, when she finally reached the top, was as spectacular as it had always been. 'Million-dollar view for nothing,' her father had always said. Until now, she had never appreciated his words, but standing looking out over a horizon that stretched more than 180 degrees around her, she felt tiny yet huge. Alone but not lonely. Neither happy nor sad. She simply accepted her existence. The rising sun lit a golden path on the ocean below her and behind her a skylark began to sing.

She continued walking, thinking about how she had got to this junction in her life. She wasn't a bad person, but she had done bad things. Or . . . were they bad or just wrong? It hadn't been wrong to have Henry and Ella, but her decision to run away and look for Alan had been. She had hurt her parents, who hadn't deserved to be hurt, and now she was hurting Kafir, Aali and Sabu.

Henry was rightly angry with her. She had had no idea that her parents were leaving her so much: she had not come for the money, she had come to apologise, reclaim her children and explain why she had left them. Was that selfish too?

But it was the money that was causing so much trouble. Ella didn't want it. Sennen didn't want it. Perhaps she should just give it all to Henry? But that didn't feel right either.

She kept walking and thinking. She passed the lighthouse, crossed Tide Beach and found herself on Shellsand Bay.

The sand dunes glowed gold and the rain had stopped and she spotted a small lobster boat cutting bravely through the waves.

She sat on a barnacled rock and told herself she needed to make a plan.

She must have sat there for over half an hour, cloaked in regret and the desire to make amends.

She heard voices chatting breathlessly before she heard the regular thud of runners' feet upon the sand.

She looked up. 'Rosemary!'

Rosemary, red-faced and wearing a neon yellow running jacket and headband, puffed to a halt. 'Darling, what are you doing up this early?'

'I might ask the same of you.' Sennen looked from Rosemary to her companion.

'This is Jools. My partner,' Rosemary said. 'Jools, this is Sennen.'

Jools shook Sennen's hand. 'I've heard a lot about you.' She smiled. She was in her late forties, Sennen judged, with blond hair tucked behind her ears and an open friendly face.

'What are you partners in?' asked Sennen.

Rosemary gave her a mischievous smile. 'Jools is my girl-friend. She was away on business when you spent the night.'

Sennen's eyes widened. 'Oh.' She tried hard to keep her voice level. 'Gosh. Fantastic.'

Jools laughed. 'I think so.'

'How did you meet?' Sennen was aware she was gabbling.

'Very romantically.' Rosemary took Jools' hand. 'She took me to hospital one night after Ray had had a drink too many.'

'I'm a police officer. Rosemary's husband had attempted to strangle her.'

'Oh my God.' Sennen was horrified. 'You didn't tell me about that.'

Jools put her arm around Rosemary. 'She's been through a lot, this one.'

Sennen nodded. 'Including the time I made her run away to Spain with me.'

'Oh, that was fun,' Rosemary insisted. 'Well, it wasn't then, but it's a good story now.'

'Come on,' said Jools, readying herself to run again, 'we've got another two miles and then it's coffee.'

'See you later, Sennen? Coffee in Trevay? Ten-ish?' shouted Rosemary as she set off.

'Great. See you then.' Sennen watched as they jogged off down the beach. 'Well,' she said to herself. 'Life is full of surprises. I never saw Rosemary as a runner.'

From the opposite end of the beach, Kit and Ella, with Terry and Celia chasing a ball, appeared.

'Is that Mum?' Ella put her hand up to shield her eyes from the brightness of the rising sun, 'Look, skimming stones?'

Ella cupped her hands to her mouth and called, 'Muuum! Mum!'

Somehow the words reached Sennen's ears on the ragged wind and seeing Ella and Kit she waved.

'Hi, Mum. You're up early.'

'Well, I've got lots to think about, haven't I?' Sennen hugged them both. 'Veils, weddings . . .' She bent down and tickled the dogs.

'That's Celia and this one is Terry,' said Kit. 'They are both drama queens but love chasing a ball. Watch.' He threw the tennis ball into the waves and both dogs sped after it.

'I have missed the sea,' said Sennen watching them. 'Really missed it. Agra is about as far from the sea as you can imagine. I've been trying my hand at skimming but I'm so out of practice. Watch.' She picked up a smooth sliver of slate and, with a flick of her wrist, loosed it at the sea. After two skips it sank. 'See. Rubbish. Poppa was good but Mum had the talent. Sometimes seventeen or eighteen bounces.'

'I remember that,' said Ella. 'I would usually have my birthday parties on the beach and she would always set up a skimming competition.'

'She did the same for me too, when I was little.' Sennen was surprised at how clear the memory was. 'Shall we have a go, now? Six stones each?'

Celia and Terry thoroughly enjoyed the game and, refusing to chase their tennis ball, began to swim out for the stones.

'Woohoo!' shouted Ella, her arms in the air as her last stone reached fourteen bounces. 'I win.'

'Oh, that was fun,' said Sennen breathlessly. 'I am going to miss you both so much when I go back.'

'No, you won't. As soon as we can we'll come out to see you and meet our new family,' said Ella stoutly. 'If you don't mind.'

'I want that more than anything. I'll show you both the Taj and we'll eat wonderful food and you'll love the market. I would love Henry to come too.'

'I'm sure he will,' smiled Ella. 'He can never bear to be left out of anything.'

Eventually, Sennen left them to return to Trevay, and Kit and Ella headed back towards home.

'I've been wondering,' Kit said, 'now that you've got your wedding dress, and before it goes out of fashion, or you get too fat for it . . .' He dodged a thump from Ella. 'That maybe, if you're free over the next couple of weeks, you would consider getting married to me?'

Ella jumped on the spot. 'You mean, book the church and cake and guests and . . . ?'

'That's the idea.'

'But don't we have to get a licence and read banns and get blood tests and stuff?'

'I don't think we need blood tests, but we can ask Simon about the rest.'

Ella hugged herself. 'Oh yes! We can just walk next door and into the church. How romantic is that? Hope it doesn't rain.'

'You look lovely in the rain.' He kissed her soft lips then buried his face in her perfumed hair. 'I have loved you from the first moment I saw you.'

She leant into him and closed her eyes. His arms felt so right as they held her. Six months ago she had no job, no boyfriend and no mother. Happiness had been sent to her by whatever transient passing fate had decided to drop on her shoulders. She held Kit tighter. 'I love you more than I can say, Kit. I promise to be a good wife. Faithful. Loyal. I will always be by your side, no matter what.'

'And I, Kit Beauchamp, promise that I will take care of you always. I will never let you down.'

*

Sennen walked back along the cliffs to Trevay alone. Her mind was splitting off in so many directions. How long could she feasibly stay? Until Ella was married? She didn't want to rush Ella and Henry but she also had two little ones.

Should she stay and help to build the art school?

But she wasn't sure if that was what Ella really wanted, not with Henry's negative response.

Should she run back to India and never come home again? But what was left in India? Did she have a marriage? Wouldn't Sabu and Aali be better off without her?

Or should she just run away to another life altogether. Leave both the mess here and in India and build a life somewhere else. She had done it before. She could do it again.

That was the simple solution. Simple for everyone. Clean. Done.

The cliff path was narrow now, the edge very close to the steep drop and the sea. She took a step closer and viewed the broiling waves below, crashing on to the mussel- and limpet-encrusted rocks; sharp and deadly.

She thought back to the stones she had been skimming just a short while ago. One stone could make many ripples. One person could create a storm that drowned others' lives.

She stepped back from the edge and sat on the grass tufted edge of the path. 'Where do I belong?' Her question was ripped away on the wind.

Closing her eyes, she lay back on the soft sward and allowed her senses to take in the thump of the thundering waves, the call of a gull, the chug of a boat's engine, the fingers of the wind brushing her cheeks and the tangy smell of salt and nature.

She couldn't tell when it started but she became aware of something, somebody, at her side. A presence.

She didn't dare open her eyes for fear of what she might

see. She knew who it was. She heard her. Not through her ears, but through her body. It was her mother. 'I am with you,' she was saying. 'All is well.' The words were repeated like a chant, a mantra, many times, until Sennen saw, in her mind's eye, her mother place a hand on her forehead. The touch filled her with peace just as the vision of Adela began to fade.

When the dream or mirage or apparition had left, Sennen lay still, allowing her conscious mind to absorb the knowledge she had been given. She opened her eyes and sat up. 'Thank you, Mum. Thank you for the answer.'

Simon Canter, vicar of Pendruggan, sat at the desk in his study and beamed at the happy couple in front of him.

'Congratulations. This is happy news,' he said. 'When were you thinking of having the wedding?'

Kit jumped in. 'As soon as possible because we don't know how long Ella's mum will be here for and we want her to be there, obviously.'

Simon looked at the large diary in front of him and turned the pages. 'There's a space two Saturdays from now but that would be too soon. We couldn't get the banns read in time, or . . .' He riffled through some more pages. 'There's an empty Saturday in six weeks.' He looked up and saw the disappointment in their faces. 'I mean, there are ways of doing this very quickly if you get a common licence. I can help you with that. It costs a bit but there will be no need for any banns to be read, so off we go.'

Ella sat forward to the edge of her seat. 'How soon could that be fixed?'

'As long as there are no hitches, I should think you'll be married in two weeks. Midday is a good time.' He blinked kindly behind his glasses.

Ella grinned at Kit. 'Shall we?'

'Why not?'

They left the vicarage, bouncing with happiness. 'I've got to tell Mum,' said Ella, beaming.

'Now?'

'Yes, before she does something stupid like book a flight back to India.'

'What about Henry?'

'I'll call him after I've spoken to Mum. He's going to have to give me away, after all.' Thinking of something she stopped. 'You'd better phone Adam – he will be your best man, won't he?'

'Yes. I suppose so.'

'And Jenna will be my flower girl.' Ella was zinging with happiness. 'She'll be perfect, carrying a little basket of petals to spread before me.'

Kit shook his head in bemusement. 'Really? Do we need all this?'

'I am only getting married once, Mr Beauchamp, so it had better be bloody perfect.'

Kit grabbed her and kissed her. 'Remind me, did I buy you an engagement ring?'

She squealed. 'NO! Well, not yet anyway.'

'We'll go shopping tomorrow.'

She hugged him, 'Thank you. This is all so exciting. When shall we send the invitations out?'

'Tomorrow?'

'Yes. Maybe Queenie has some in the shop.'

'They'll be from 1956 if she has.'

Laughing, they headed up to the Village Stores.

*

Queenie was sitting on one of her old but comfortable armchairs by the counter of the shop, her feet up on a plastic bottle crate, made more comfortable with a cushion on the top. As the bell tinkled on the door she struggled to her feet.

''Ello, me ducks. What brings you 'ere so cheerful?'

'Can you keep a secret?' breathed Ella.

Queenie's canny old eyes lit up behind her pebble-thick specs that were the size of re-entry shields. 'I'm known for me discretion, me.'

Ella put her arm through Kit's. 'Kit and I are getting married!'

'Never! Well, bless me. Ain't that lovely. When's this, then?'

'Two weeks tomorrow.'

'Oh, my good Gawd. Come and give me a kiss.'

She bestowed her whiskered kisses on both of them, then asked them what they had come in for.

'Wedding invitations.'

'Oh now, I've got some somewhere – 'ang about and I'll find them.'

Kit and Ella passed knowing smiles to each other as Queenie rummaged in the huge bottom drawer of an old haberdashery dresser. 'Ere, Kit. Give me a hand.'

Kit obediently went behind the counter and helped her lift a faded cardboard box onto the counter.

'Have a look in there, while I put me legs up again.' She went back to her chair and put her feet on the crate. 'They may be a bit out of date but that's cos they're vintage.'

Ella lifted the lid and put her hand over her mouth to stop herself from laughing. 'Queenie, these have got photos of Prince Charles and Lady Diana on them.'

'Dig a bit deeper, dear.'

'Oh, these are nice.' Ella held out a handful of cards that

had prettily painted forget-me-nots, primroses and larkspur on them. In silver writing they had either *The Happiest of Days is Here*, *Marriage Joy* or, rather more jocularly, *Aisle be Seeing You* written upon them.

'Let me look, dear.' Queenie held out her hand and looked closely at them. 'Oh yes, these are definitely vintage. Seventies, I should say. Do they have envelopes?'

Ella felt about in the box. 'No.'

'I'll find you some, but they might not fit. How many people you inviting? It's a pity your mum isn't here.'

'But she is!' Ella smiled excitedly. 'She came back!'

Queenie was dumbstruck. 'And no one told me?' she gasped.

'It's not a secret, but we've had a lot to talk about and we had to get to know each other without distractions.'

'I had the newspaper, here on me counter, with that poor girl's face looking out. I can still see it clearly. We thought she'd gone for good. Her poor parents were heartbroken.'

'Yes, it wasn't an easy time.' Ella wanted to change the subject, 'Anyway, I shall be needing about twenty invitations.' She counted in her head. 'No more than twenty.'

'Does that include me?' asked Queenie, pointedly brushing cigarette ash off her bosom.

'Of course it does.'

'Oh, good. I could do the catering if you like? Twenty of me famous pasties is easy for me to do.'

Kit said a little too quickly, 'We haven't talked about the reception yet.'

Queenie cackled naughtily. 'Got you there, boy. You have what you want, only I don't like prawns so don't have any of them, or vol au vents. Pastry gets stuck in my dentures.'

'Understood,' said Kit.

Queenie looked over at Ella. ''Ave you found enough cards, duck?'

'Yes, just about. I like that they are a bit mixed up and not the same.'

Kit paid for them and the extra envelopes and before he left with Ella he reminded Queenie, 'Please don't say anything to anyone just yet. About the wedding or Ella's mum. We don't want any more attention than necessary.'

Queenie held her hand up. 'Don't you worry about that. Me lips are sealed. Careless talk costs lives and all that.'

She waved them off from her armchair and watched as they walked back towards Marguerite Cottage. In her cardigan pocket, next to her smoking tackle, was her mobile phone. She pulled it out and punched a number into it.

''Ello? Beryl, is that you? I've got some news for you. But you mustn't tell anyone . . .'

PART THREE
Ella's Wedding Day

33

Pendruggan, 2018

'Mum, I've got some news,' Ella said down the phone. Sennen, in bed, sat up, the thrill of hearing her daughter call her Mum always filling her with joy. 'Is it good?'

'Definitely. *Very* exciting. What are you doing two weeks today?'

'Tell me.'

'Kit and I have set the date for our wedding.' The end of the sentence went up at least an octave and with added volume.

Sennen held her receiver from her ear until the shrieking finished, then said, 'Darling, that is so wonderful! Where?'

'You remember the church next to our cottage? Holy Trinity? There.'

'And this is in two weeks?'

'Yes. At midday. I'm going to ask Henry to walk me down the aisle and Kit's cousin, Adam, he's a doctor, is going to be the best man.'

Sennen bit her lip. 'How does Henry feel about me being there?'

'Mum, *you* will be there, Henry will be there – and it will be the happiest day of my life. Okay?'

Sennen loved Ella's optimism. 'I might need some help with an outfit. What do mothers of the bride wear? Do you want me to wear a hat?'

'Yes, hats, confetti, silly little kitten heels – and everything, please.'

'I can't promise kitten heels.'

'Mum, you will look gorgeous no matter what. I'm going to ring Henry now and let him know he's walking me down the aisle. Bye.'

Ella ticked Sennen's name off the top of her 'who to phone list' and dialled the next name down.

'Henry, it's me.'

'Hello, you.'

'What are you doing two weeks today?' And she poured out the good news before he'd taken a breath.

'And Mum is coming too.'

Henry said nothing.

'Henry? Are you still there?'

'Why do you want her there?'

'You know why.'

'I can't help how I feel, Ells.'

'She's your mum.'

'Well, we all have a cross to bear.'

'Henry, I'm not going to beg. Will you give me away and behave like a brother should? Or are you really prepared to break your sister's heart?'

'Resorting to emotional blackmail won't help.'

'How about wheedling?' She coughed and pitched her voice

girly high. 'Pleeeeeese, Henry. You're my brother and I love you. And you love me, don't you?'

'You know I do.'

'So you'll do it? It should be Poppa, I know, but it would make him so proud of you if you took his place. Please don't let me down.'

Henry softened. 'I would never let you down, Ells.' He took a moment to absorb how much it meant to her. 'Of course I'll do it. I'd be honoured to.'

'Thank you, thank you, thank you. You are the best.' She blew a kiss down the phone. 'When are you coming home by the way? Are you still holed up with some poor misled female?'

Henry looked over at Deborah who was looking gorgeous, wrapped in her sheets and licking Marmite off her fingers. 'At a mate's. Actually, Ella, I think we should invite Deborah Palmer – you know, the solicitor? She can keep Mum in order.'

'Good idea,' said Sennen, writing Deborah's name on the list. 'I'm posting invitations today so that people get them on Monday. Have a good weekend and see you soon? I'm cooking leg of lamb for Sunday lunch if you are about.'

'I'm not sure if I'll be back in time for that, but I will come over later. Need to find my suit and get it to the cleaners.'

Sennen, still sitting in her bed at White Water, was chasing all sorts of thoughts around in her head. The wedding was going to be tricky but she would do everything in her power to make her children happy and to make good memories of it. The one person she wanted to be there, standing next to her, though, was Kafir. She couldn't bear to allow her mind to go near the thought that her marriage may be ended. No, she must hope that he would love her enough to get over this painful bridge and put it behind them. She had texted him twice over the last couple of days, telling him her news as she got it, but he hadn't replied. She picked her phone up. Should she text again or take the plunge and ring him?

Several times she put the phone down, only to pick it up again, but finally she picked it up and, with determined, shaking fingers, dialled his number.

It went to voicemail.

'Kafir, it's me. I know this sounds mad, but the other day, I had a vision of my mother. A sort of visitation I suppose. Anyway, she was saying she was with me and all is well. Kept saying it over and over. And since then a lot has happened. Ella is getting married, two weeks today in Pendruggan church at Midday. Henry is giving her away, and I need you by my side. Please come. Bring Aali and Sabu . . . We'll be doing it together. You and I. I want Henry and Ella to meet you and know how good you are. Why I love you. It's so hard here without you. I know it's all my own fault, but I feel as if Mum is with us and all will be well, as she told me. Mad. Mad, but please come. It's the only way we can find out what the future holds for all of us. I will fight hard for you. The pain of losing you is actually physical. It's real. It hurts. I miss you. Please, please come. I love you, Kafir. And I am so very sorry for my lies. I am not lying now. I need you. Please, please . . . call me.'

Kit was on the phone to Adam, talking about best man duties, while Ella finished writing the invitations. Addressing the last envelope and gathering them all together into a neat pile, she signalled to Kit that she was nipping up to Queenie's to get them posted and, pulling on her waterproof, headed off through the rain that had been falling all day to the village store.

Queenie was ensconced again in her chair in front of an electric fire. 'That rain's brought some cold,' she said.

Ella closed the shop door against the downpour. 'I hope the weather will be all right for the wedding. My dress isn't exactly thermal or waterproof.'

'Never rains on the bride,' wheezed Queenie, hoisting herself up. 'You'll be okay. What do you want? Stamps?'

'Yes. Thank you.'

Queenie got out her antique stamp book with its well-thumbed tabs. 'First or second?'

'Twenty first-class.'

'Righty ho.' Queenie pushed her enormous glasses up her nose and began searching. 'So, where's the hen do?' she asked.

'I hadn't thought of having one,' said Ella.

'You have to have an 'en do. Tradition. Your last chance of a proper knees-up as a single girl.'

'I don't know.' Ella looked doubtful. 'I shouldn't think Kit will have a stag party.'

'Well, he should.'

'Should he?'

'Oh dear, yes. Bad luck for you both not to be given a proper send off.'

'I'll talk to Kit. How much do I owe you for the stamps?'

Queenie was not to be fobbed off. 'A nice Chinese meal is what you want. The Chinese are experts at bringing good luck.'

'Are they?'

'You don't want to risk bad luck do you. That'll be £13, please.'

Ella handed over the money. 'I suppose a meal is better

than getting drunk in a nightclub with an L plate tied round my head.'

'I wouldn't be able to come if it was a nightclub do.' Queenie shook her head. 'It's me legs.'

'Would you want to come for a Chinese supper?'

'Oh, that is kind of you. Yes please. When are you having it?'

Ella laughed at how easily the wily old lady had manipulated her. 'What day suits you?'

'The wedding is on a Saturday so you don't want to go out on the Friday night – how about the Thursday before?'

'Okay, Thursday week it is. Do you have a favourite restaurant?'

'The Fighting Duck, the back of Fore Street in Trevay. They do a lovely sweet-and-sour pork there.'

'I'll book it. And I'll organise a taxi to pick us both up. Say seven o'clock?'

Queenie made her way back to her chair. 'That'd be fine dear. I don't want to be home too late, neither.'

'A stag night?' Kit scratched his chin, 'I hadn't thought about it. Who would I invite?'

'Adam, Simon, Piran and Henry to start with. It's part of Adam's duties as best man to organise it, isn't it?'

'Good point. So, who's going to your hen party? Apart from Queenie?'

'Mum, Penny, Helen. I think Mum would like her friend Rosemary too.'

'Nice.'

'It's all so unreal, isn't it. Can you believe this is happening?'

'It definitely is happening.' He rattled his car keys. 'Shall I tell you how I know?'

'Tell me.'

'I am going to drive the woman I love to the jeweller's and buy her the best engagement ring I can afford.'

Ella caught her breath. 'OMG! I'd almost forgotten!'

'And wedding rings.'

'Oh yes! Oh gosh.' She put her arms around him and smooched. 'I am so lucky to have you. I can't wait to be Mrs Beauchamp. Could things get any better?'

34

The Hen Party

The Chinese restaurant was pleasantly busy, enough for the waiting staff to give Ella's party plenty of attention. The food was excellent and kept on coming, as did the drinks. Queenie was on her fourth Tia Maria and lemonade when she decided to make a speech. Penny and Helen, on either side of her, helped her up and readjusted the veiled hat she had insisted on wearing.

'I just want to wish young Ella 'ere, all the best for her big day and also a big welcome home to her mum, Sennen.' Queenie turned to Sennen, who was plucking at her napkin, 'Sennen scarpered many years ago leaving two little 'uns with her parents. We all thought she was dead, but here she is, right as rain. Sadly, her parents died before she got home to see them.'

Ella's toes were curling and could see that Sennen was screwing her napkin into a tight ball.

Penny saw all this and shot to her feet to save Queenie

from embarrassing herself further. 'That's enough, you can sit down now, Queenie.'

'I need to make the toast.' Queenie was adamant.

'Okay then, just a short one, wishing Ella well.'

'I know what I'm doing. I'm not doolally.' Queenie pushed her hat to the back of her head whilst pulling her arm from Penny's crossly. She returned her attention to the table, 'So please raise your glasses to those no longer with us, to absent friends.'

Penny shouted over her quickly, 'To Ella.'

'To Ella,' repeated everyone.

Queenie sat down and knocked her hat into the remains of her banana fritter syrup. 'Now look what you made me do,' she said to Penny. 'That's me best 'at. I'm going to wear that at the wedding.'

Penny removed the hat from the pudding, and put Queenie's Tia Maria to one side. 'Coffees, anyone?'

When the coffees and After Eights arrived, Rosemary tapped her cup with a teaspoon. 'Ladies, what a wonderful evening this has been and I am honoured to have been invited. Thank you, Ella.'

Ella smiled. 'Thank you for looking after Mum.'

'As you know, Sennen and I met as teenagers. She looked just like you, Ella, and I see in you the funny, kind, adventurous girl who loved you and Henry very much. To come back and face the music now is brave, particularly having to leave her family in India to do so. So my toast tonight is to: the Mother of the Bride, Sennen.'

Sennen was overcome and however hard she tried, the tears flowed.

She mouthed to Rosemary, 'Thank you.' Then Ella came next to her and hugged her. 'Thank you, Mum. For coming back. Everything will be all right now.'

Penny and Helen raised their glasses again, all except Queenie who was talking to a tall pot plant. 'Who's in India, then? Nobody bloody tells me anything.'

Coffees finished, chocolate mints eaten, the evening began to wind up. Rosemary was looking at her watch. 'Jools is just coming off shift. Anyone want to come back to mine for a nightcap?'

Ella shook her head. 'I'm up early tomorrow. Kit and I are making quiches for the reception.'

Sennen, who had quietly paid the bill, tucked her arm through Ella's. 'Thank you for including me tonight. You had every right not to.'

Ella looked into her mother's face and said in all sincerity, 'Mum, I love you.'

Everyone was up now and finding coats and bags, all except Queenie who was licking the banana syrup off her hat and still talking to the plant. 'Lovely food tonight. Did you have the pudding? Try some.' She offered her hat to the plant. 'Go on. Have a lick. Delicious, innit.'

Penny leant down and said, 'Queenie. You're hammered. I think it's time for bed.'

'Let me just say goodbye to this gentleman first.'

'Queenie, it's a plastic pot plant.'

'Oh Gawd. Is it?' Queenie peered at the plant and laughed wheezily. 'Bloody hell, it is an all. Lovely fella though.'

Penny called to Helen, 'Help me with Queenie, would you? She's off her head.'

'I'm perfectly sober, if you don't mind.'

Helen and Penny pulled her to her feet. 'You need to get home.'

'I tell you what I need.'

'What's that?' asked Helen, plonking Queenie's hat back on her head.

'I need a pint to sort me out or else I'll have an 'eadache in the morning.'

'I think you would have a worse one if you had a pint,' said Penny, hauling Queenie out onto the pavement.

A collection of wolf whistles sounded behind them. Penny refused to look back but was nonetheless absurdly gratified, until running footsteps came towards her and someone pinched her bottom. She spun around, ready to confront her attacker.

It was her husband, Simon, who was swaying slightly and had a dozy grin on his face. 'It's me,' he said.

Behind him were Kit, Adam, Henry and a couple of local lads, all sniggering.

Helen saw her partner Piran amongst them. 'Hello.' He smiled, fidgeting with the gold hoop in his ear. 'Spotted your arse a mile off.'

Queenie took advantage of the distraction and broke free. ''Ello fellas. Who wants a pint?'

She tottered towards them and before she knew what had happened she was hoisted up in a fireman's lift across Piran's shoulder.

She cackled loudly. 'Oh, Piran, I 'aven't been slung over a bloke's shoulder for a long time.'

Penny and Helen rolled their eyes and watched as Queenie was carried off with her skirt over her head and her bloomers on show.

'She's going to feel so ill in the morning,' giggled Penny.

'Oh, leave her to it. The boys will look after her. Actually, I feel almost jealous,' smiled Helen. 'Almost.'

35

Bill died just a couple of months short of his sixtieth birthday. He and Adela had been sharing a peaceful life.

Occasionally they still took in students who sat rapt as Bill told them about his apprenticeship with the great potter Bernard Leach, teaching them all he knew, and Adela cooked enormous breakfasts and suppers for them, as she always had, and took them to interesting spots around Trevay where they would set up their easels and paint, with her looking over their shoulders and offering generous advice.

Adela was worried about Bill's health. It was hard to put a finger on it but he was lacking the vitality he'd once had.

'Darling,' she said gently, knowing his suspicion of the medical profession, 'I think we should both go to the doctor for an MOT. Blood pressure, cholesterol, that sort of thing.'

'Why?' he asked gruffly. 'What's wrong with you?'

She hadn't been prepared for that and said rather lamely, 'I think it's sensible, that's all.'

They didn't go.

Adela told herself that it was natural for a man of his age

to enjoy long naps in the afternoon – she often did so herself – and, although he was losing weight, he still enjoyed her cooking.

Ella and Henry would visit when they could and the last time they had come Bill seemed rejuvenated.

However, Adela confided in Ella. 'How does Poppa look to you?'

'Really good,' Ella said breezily. 'He's lost a bit of weight and I think it suits him.'

When the children had returned to London, Bill was full of Henry's success in his new job. 'Where did he get such a good business brain? Not from us that's for sure.'

Adela thinking about their father's identity said. 'We'll never know now will we.'

Bill sipped his tea. 'Ella is definitely a chip off the old block, though. Did she show you her illustrations for the book she's writing?'

'Yes. Her line drawings in particular are very good.'

Bill smiled. 'I think we did okay with Henry and Ella.'

'Better than with Sennen?' They rarely talked about their daughter, and to hear her name spoken out loud created a crackling tension in the air.

Bill looked at Adela steadily. 'Yes.'

'Maybe we did too much for her?'

'Possibly.'

'She was so bright. Doing well enough at school. And funny and kind. She'll be thirty-seven now.'

'Well, wherever she is I hope she's happy.' He tapped his fingers on the arm of his chair. 'How the hell could she not come back and see the children?'

'She did,' said Adela simply.

'*What*? When?'

'When you were feeling so wretched and upset.'

Anger flared. 'Why didn't you tell me?'

'I'm sorry. I should have. But she just turned up and you were so ill and Henry and Ella were just getting settled. I couldn't face having her back and creating all that turmoil again. I told her to go away.'

'How – how was she?'

'Grown up. She was only twenty but she seemed, I don't know, a seasoned adult. She had been working in Spain and France and had come here with some actors, to Edinburgh, I think, and decided to come and see us and Henry and Ella.'

'Why the hell didn't you tell me?'

'I was so angry. She was standing there, right as rain, while I had picked up her mess and I was so worried about you. You had burnt all her photos, eradicated her from our lives, and I honestly thought that seeing her would make you ill again. So I told her to go away. My decision. I made the choice for *you*, not for her. I couldn't bear to see you so unhappy and ill again.'

'Did you let her see the children?'

Adela shook her head in regret. 'No. I asked if she was going to stay. And she couldn't promise, so I didn't let her see them.'

Bill softened. 'It must have killed you.'

'Yes. I said some very unkind things to her.'

'We all say and do unkind things in anger. Can you imagine how I felt as soon as I burnt her photographs?'

'I know how I felt.'

'She hurt us, we hurt her. Not very clever.'

'She hates me because I told her to go away.'

'She'll hate herself more.' He smiled. 'Do you remember when she tipped my birthday cake onto the floor because she was so cross that it was my birthday and not hers?'

'It had taken me all morning to make. I wonder if she married and has a new family.'

'Possibly. But she would be so proud of Henry and Ella. We must pity her for not knowing them.'

'I'm so relieved to have told you.'

'That she came back?'

Adela nodded.

'Come on, old girl. No one's life is a piece of cake. We have both done things we regret but we have each other and we have Henry and Ella.'

'I love you, William Tallon.'

'I know – and I love you very much, Mrs Tallon.'

Bill died just a few weeks later. Leukaemia. It had been too late to offer treatment. Adela thanked God that they had no more secrets between them.

36

It was Friday afternoon. The wedding was less than twenty-four hours away, and Ella was getting fractious.

'Kit, I asked you *not* to put anything on top of the trifles.'

'I haven't.'

'Then what are the salmon pinwheels doing?'

'Oh that. Well, the trifles are clingfilmed and there was no other room in the fridge, so I put the salmon things on top.'

Ella noisily banged about in the fridge, moving salads and quiches and cheese before admitting to herself, but not to him, that Kit had been right. There was nowhere else to put the bloody salmon.

'How about a cup of tea?' asked Kit helpfully.

'The dishwasher needs emptying first.'

'Right. Well, I'll pop the kettle on, empty the dishwasher, and then we'll have a cuppa. Yes?'

Ella reversed out of the fridge and closed the door carefully. 'What time is Adam due.'

'About seven, if the traffic isn't too bad.'

Ella was irritated. 'He'll expect me to cook for him, I suppose.'

'No. I'll take him to the pub, with Henry,' Kit said patiently. 'How about a biscuit with your tea? A nice digestive?'

'I don't want to look fat in my wedding dress,' she snapped.

He took her in his arms and kissed her passionately.

'What was that for?' she asked, slightly more mellowed.

'To shut you up. Now sit down because you and I are going to have a cup of tea and a biscuit.'

A couple of hours later Ella finally sat down and went through her check list. Food? Tick. Cutlery, crockery and glasses? Tick. Flowers? Tick. Sheets changed, loos cleaned, toenails painted? Tick.

Kit was upstairs gathering his suit and toiletries ready to take over to the vicarage where he was going to spend the night. He came downstairs and put the suit bag and a smaller bag on the hall floor.

'Ready?' asked Ella coming out of the kitchen.

'I think so.'

'Rings?'

'Yes.'

'Sorry I got a bit Bridezilla earlier.'

'Forgiven.'

The doorbell rang, making them both jump.

'Hi,' said Henry on the doorstep. 'Here I am and I have got something for you. My present to you both.'

Ella was excited. 'What, what?'

'I need to get it from the car. Hang on.'

They watched as he opened the boot and pulled out a large picture frame. All they could see was the back of the canvas, but Ella gasped and whispered to Kit, 'I think I know what this is.'

Henry carried it down the short path and into the house. 'No peeking. Close your eyes and let me take this through to the lounge to set it up properly.'

Ella and Kit stayed where they were until Henry called, 'Okay. Come on in.'

Ella couldn't believe her eyes. 'It's me,' she shrilled, delighted. 'The one Poppa painted of me. Kit, look it's me when I was about five, paddling at Shellsand.'

The painting was large and beautiful. Against the golden pinks of a sandy beach, and the wild blue of the sea beyond, a small girl in an old-fashioned scarlet swimsuit was paddling. Her back was to the viewer, but the long red ringlets rippling down her shoulders were definitely Ella's.

Kit stood for a while, admiring it. 'It's amazing. But I thought it was your granny who painted.'

'Poppa was a very good painter, but he knew that Granny was better so he usually left it up to her. I haven't seen this for a long time. Where was it, Henry?'

'I had it on the wall at Mandalay Road. When Granny died I found it in Poppa's studio. It was behind all sorts of things, hidden really well. I snaffled it hoping that when some idiot married you, not you obviously, Kit, you are the opposite of idiot, I could give it to you on your wedding eve.'

Ella's eyes shone, 'Oh, Henry, you are the best brother.'

'I am your only brother.' He stopped and frowned. 'Actually, I'm not, am I?'

Kit was keen to steer off the subject of the half-brother and sister in India and said, 'Ella, do you remember him painting this?'

'No. I don't. But then I was only little.'

'Well, it's lovely.' Kit gave Henry a man hug. 'Thanks, mate.' They heard a car draw up. 'That'll be Adam,' said Kit walking into the hall to let his cousin and best man in and was surprised to find Sennen on the doorstep.

'Hello, Kit.' She kissed him, her warm Indian fragrance enveloping him. 'Everything ready for tomorrow?'

'Yep. Henry's here. Come into the lounge.'

Walking into the room Sennen immediately saw the painting. She shivered as if someone had walked over her grave. 'I haven't seen that for years,' she almost whispered.

Ella bounced on her toes. 'Henry gave it to me and Kit. Wedding present. Isn't it lovely? The only picture that Poppa painted of me.'

Sennen was quiet. 'Of you?'

'Yes.'

Sennen walked towards the picture and read her father's neat signature. 'Is there a date on it?'

'I haven't looked,' said Henry.

'I had a red costume like that,' said Sennen.

Realisation hit Ella. 'It's you?'

'I think so.'

Henry began to work it out. 'When Granny died, we didn't find any pictures of you. No photographs or school reports or anything. Which I thought was odd because they took photos of Ella and me all the time. I have rows of photo albums in London, as well as our school books and art and stuff.'

'I would like to see those, one day,' Sennen said.

'Yes, okay. But there are no pictures of you. Ella and I never knew what you looked like.

'But he kept this?' asked Sennen, getting closer to the picture.

'Yes, he did.'

Henry picked the picture and turned it over. He scanned the canvas carefully then found something. 'Let's get a light on this.'

Ella angled a table lamp on to it and they crowded round. On the bottom right-hand corner, in faded pencil, Poppa's hand had written. S. Shellsand summer '81.' He looked sharply at Sennen. 'How old were you in 1981?'

'About five. The same age as that little girl in the picture.'.

'You must have it,' Ella said immediately, pushing it to Sennen.

Sennen smiled but waved it away. 'No, my love. If you give it to me I will give it straight back to you. It's yours.' She looked at Henry. 'I'm so glad you had it. It makes me feel that Poppa did still want to keep a bit of me.'

Henry was appalled to find his throat tightening against tears. He grabbed his glass and drank.

'By the way,' said Sennen, 'I've not properly thanked you for the headstones, Henry.'

Her words were sincere.

'But mostly, thank you for adding my name. When I saw it, it made me feel a bit less invisible.'

Henry coughed, embarrassed. 'Yes, well . . . Got to get the facts right. Good. Drink anyone?'

Much later, when Sennen had gone back to Trevay and Kit and Adam had retreated to the vicarage, Henry poured Ella one last gin and tonic. 'To you, my lovely little sister.'

'Aw, thanks. And thank you again for the painting. Did you have any idea?'

'No. If I believed in the occult I'd say Granny and Poppa had a hand in all that tonight.'

'Maybe. It was nice of Mum to let me have it.'

'It was never hers to have. I kept it for you.'

'I know. But still . . . And you did the right thing when you added her to the gravestones.'

'Yeah, well, you know . . .'

'Be honest with me, aren't you glad Mum's back?'

Henry was surprised by the question. 'Blimey. Why do you ask that? I don't know.'

'I think that you *are* glad. You wouldn't be so emotional if you didn't care.'

'Emotional? What are you talking about?'

'You were pleased when she thanked you for the inscription, and you sounded funny when she thanked you for keeping the painting of her.'

'I didn't know it was her though, did I?'

'No, but when you did, I saw your face. You were glad it was her and that we'd had that picture up on the wall when we were little, that Poppa had kept one thing of her to watch over us.'

Henry stood up. 'Come on. It's my duty to make sure you arrive in a fit state at your wedding tomorrow. You need your beauty sleep.'

She took his hand and he hauled her to her feet. 'Henry, beneath your bad-tempered façade, you really have a good heart, don't you?'

He turned off the lights so that she couldn't see his face. 'Bed,' he said. 'Now.'

37

The Wedding Day, White Water

The drill of rain on her bedroom window woke Sennen, like the sound of gravel being thrown onto to the glass.

She got up and looked out at the lowering clouds, blossoming dense and grey. A strong wind was bending the palm trees in the garden below and beyond the wet rooftops she saw the plumes of spray crash onto the harbour wall. Poor Ella. What a terrible day for a wedding.

She thought about sending her an uplifting text on the lines of 'It never rains on the bride, trust me'. But she thought better of it.

There was a knock on the door. It was Amy, the landlady, carrying an unordered tray of coffee and unwanted concern. 'Morning. What a terrible day. I thought you'd like an early coffee, what with getting ready for the wedding and everything.' She went to the window and looked out. 'Terrible, isn't it. Your poor daughter.'

Sennen couldn't help but think the woman was revelling

in the awfulness and was unstoppable. 'The photographs will look terrible. Everyone under umbrellas. The bride's dress will be ruined with the mud. And her hair. Shame.' She turned from the window and shone a pitying smile over Sennen. 'Have you got a raincoat?'

Sennen refused to be martyred. 'It's going to clear up in an hour or two.'

'Is it?' asked Amy, frowning. 'I checked my App and it said it was set for the day.'

'It's an Indian thing. We can smell weather changes,' lied Sennen.

'Really?'

Sennen nodded and drank some coffee. 'Thank you so much for this. Just what I needed. Now, I must get ready.'

Once Amy had gone, Sennen turned her television on in time to catch the weather forecast. 'This belt of rain, coming in from the Atlantic, is producing heavy downpours across the south west and will continue throughout the day . . .' Sennen switched it off and then turned on the main bedroom light.

She opened her wardrobe door and took out her wedding outfit. She had known exactly what she would wear. She had packed very little when she had left India, but she had brought something that had been lying in a drawer for many years. Something she had bought for her mother. Always she had expected to meet her mother again and give her this one thing that she knew the bohemian in Adela would love. Now it was too late but she would wear it for her daughter's wedding. She would wear it so Adela could be there on the day.

It was carefully wrapped in two tissue packets. She opened the smaller one first and shook it onto the bed. The navy-blue silk bodice gleamed under the overhead light. The second packet was heavier. She ran her fingers around the taped edges of the tissue and gently revealed the rich claret and gold silk of the skirt. She rubbed the finely woven fabric between her thumb and forefinger.

She was anxious not to embarrass Ella on her wedding day, but, if by a miracle Kafir did come, she, Sennen Tallon-Singh would be seen as her true self: an Indian wife in a traditional sari.

Marguerite Cottage

Henry barged into Ella's room and farted. Ella stuck her head under her duvet. 'You're disgusting. Go away.'

'I have tea for you. And Jammie Dodgers. Oh, and it's raining.'

Ella's head popped up, her hair tousled, freckles scattered perfectly across her lovely face. '*What?*'

'You look really very pretty. I can almost see why Kit wants to marry you. Budge up.' He settled himself on Kit's side of the bed.

'Is it really raining?' she asked.

'Yep.'

'Have you seen the forecast?'

'Yep.'

'Stop being so irritating. Is it going to stop?'

'Doesn't look good, I'm afraid.'

Ella ran her hand through her hair in despair. 'My shoes.'

'I'll carry you.'

'You'll drop me.'

'If you want.'

'Oh, shut up.'

'Eat a Jammie Dodger – you'll feel better.'

The Vicarage

In the vicarage, Penny was boiling an egg with toast soldiers for Jenna. 'Put fower dress on, Mummy?'

'After breakfast, and then we'll have a bath and then you can put your dress on.'

'Want put it on now!'

'I know, but you don't want tappy egg all down it, do you?'

'Ella put her dress on now?'

'No. She'll be having her tappy egg, then she'll get ready.'

'She like tappy eggs?'

'They are her favourites, and it's lucky for the bride and her flower girl to have the same breakfast as each other, so eat up.' Penny popped the egg into an egg cup and the toast next to it. 'There you are.'

Simon came in, fresh from the shower. He kissed the top of Jenna's head and then smooched Penny. 'Good morning to my favourite girls. I hear that there's a flower girl in the house today.'

Jenna bounced up and down. 'Me is!'

'You? And what do you have to do?'

'Walk front of Ella, not stop till get to Daddy.'

'And what else mustn't you do?'

'Be naughty.'

'Good girl. And what will you do with the petals in your basket?'

'Frow on floor for Jenna walk on.'

'Perfect.' Simon kissed his daughter again.

Penny got up to rinse her cup and looked over the sink into the garden. 'Do you think it'll stop raining?'

'I have faith,' smiled Simon.

'Well, have a word with The Boss.'

'I already have.'

White Water

After a quick breakfast downstairs, Sennen escaped Amy and retreated back to her room. She checked her phone. Kafir had not responded to her voicemail or bothered to text. She sat on the edge of her bed, feeling lonelier than she had ever felt. The want for him was vast and tormenting. She took a deep breath and told herself that today was not about her or her unhappiness, it was about Ella and her happiness.

Her phone buzzed with a text. Her heart bounced. But it wasn't Kafir, it was Ella.

Morning Mum, are you as excited as I am? Can't wait to see you. I'm back from the hairdressers at about 11.30 if you want to come over. I need help getting my dress on. What would I do without you? Love you, Ella xx

Sennen reread the message and her sorry heart soared again.

She typed back,

See you at 11.30. So excited and happy for you. Can't wait. I love you too, Mum xx

She checked it to make sure it wasn't too much too soon, then pressed send.

Three seconds later a line of heart emojis were her answer.

The Vicarage

Kit wrapped a bath towel round his waist and crossed the vicarage landing to Adam's room. 'Morning, best man. Sleep well?'

'Very.' Adam stretched and sat up. 'How's the groom?'

'Worryingly fine and looking forward to getting married to the future Mrs Beauchamp.'

'I thought I had to give you the obligatory speech about it not being too late to back out and to only do this if you were absolutely certain?'

'I *am* absolutely certain.'

'Well, that's that done. Is it raining?'

Ocean View Hotel

Kafir had no idea if he was doing the right thing or not, but instinct told him that he had to get on a flight to Heathrow and be with Sennen. He was her husband still and a husband supports his wife where family is involved. And curiosity had got the better of him. He needed to see what she had left behind, had denied and lied about, to truly be able to make the right choice about his marriage. That, and Aali and Sabu who were missing their mother and begging everyday to know why they couldn't see her or speak to her. When he told them that they were coming to England to see her they started packing their little bags straight away.

They had arrived at Heathrow on Thursday. Standing in the long immigration queue, Kafir pulled out his phone and switched it on. Sabu snatched it from him and started playing with it. 'Give it back Sabu, please,' he said impatiently.

Sabu was jumping up and down just out of his father's reach. 'I want it.'

'Give it to me, I need it back now, Sabu.'

'No.'

The phone began to ring and Sabu dropped it in surprise. Aali rescued it and dutifully handed it to her father.

'Who is it, Daddy?'

'A message. Shh.' He dialled into his voicemail and listened to Sennen's voice.

'WHO IS IT,' shouted Sabu, spinning around in a circle.

'Shh, it's Mummy.'

Aali caught hold of Sabu and held his hand. 'Shh, Sabu, Daddy is talking to Mummy.'

'Mummy?'

'Yes.'

'I'm going to see her.'

'We all are,' she whispered.

Kafir put the phone back in his pocket. 'That was Mummy. We are going to give her a big surprise because she really is missing us.'

The journey from the airport to Cornwall was long but the train was comfortable with enough space for Kafir to lie the children across the seats to sleep.

He couldn't sleep. What was he doing coming over on the spur of the moment? Arriving in time for an English family wedding had not been on his agenda at all. He had hoped that he would be able to assess his wife's situation and be able to decide what he needed to do. But now he was on the back foot. What on earth was he walking into?

At last the train pulled into Truro station and the weary three caught a cab to their hotel, the Ocean View, just two miles down the coast from Trevay.

It was evening, and after a simple supper, Kafir got them washed and ready for bed, but blighted with over excitement and jetlag, they barely slept until it was morning when they fell into deep sleeps.

Letting them rest, Kafir made some tea from the array of

hot drink choices set out on a little tray. He didn't like the taste of the milk from the tiny plastic tubs much, but he enjoyed the biscuits and munched steadily through the two tiny packets. He could have done with some proper breakfast but was too afraid to leave Aali and Sabu on their own. Instead, he lay on his bed and watched the television news until he too fell asleep.

At lunchtime, Aali and Sabu woke up grizzly, thirsty and hungry. Kafir had the solution. 'Who wants to see the sea?'

'Me me me,' sang Aali. 'I've never seen the sea.'

'Have I seen the sea?' Sabu asked. 'What does it look like?'

'Look out of the window.' Kafir pulled the curtains open.

'Are there fishes in it?'

'Yes.'

'Can we see them?'

'I don't know, but we can eat fish and chips. Mummy told me all about them. They are her favourite.'

The day became a very jolly one: fish and chips sitting in a shelter on the beach, a little paddling but not for too long as none of them had experienced water as cold, and then an ice cream.

'When will we see Mummy?' asked Aali later, yawning as she cleaned her teeth.

'Tomorrow,' said Kafir, helping Sabu with his pyjamas.

'Good,' shouted Sabu, jumping up onto his bed. 'I have missed her.'

Kafir tucked them both in. 'We all have.'

White Water

Sennen looked at herself in the wardrobe mirror. Tanvi had taught her how to wear a sari years ago and Sennen hoped she had done a good enough job. She had kohled her eyes heavily and added a red bindi between her brows. On her wrists she wore many rows of golden sparkly bracelets and on her feet she wore her favourite Indian sandals. Outside, the rain was still coming down so she put the only warm jacket she had on, and her scarf over her head. She would do.

Ella

The hairdresser had dressed Ella's hair simply and beautifully. She had allowed her natural curls to do their own thing while adding shine and extra bounce.

'You scrub up all right,' said Henry, who had waited at the salon to drive her back to Marguerite Cottage.

'You're so funny, not.' Ella watched the windscreen wipers as they valiantly cleared the persistent rain. 'How much time do we have before we need to leave the house?'

Henry looked at his watch and calculated. 'I reckon about an hour and a half?'

'That's perfect. Mum's coming over to help me into my dress.' She saw, out of the corner of her eye, Henry's lips tighten. 'Don't be like that.'

'Like what?'

'You know like what.'

He changed the subject. 'Do you mind that the painting is her and not you?'

'No. Would you?'

'Probably.'

'Oh, Henry. Get over yourself. We thought we were the last of the Tallons but it turns out we're not and that's exciting, isn't it?' She closed her hand on Henry's knee.

'I suppose.'

'That's a start.'

The Vicarage

'Jenna, would you please put your crayons down and come and get dressed,' said Penny impatiently.

'Not want to.'

'Yes, you do.' Penny was gritting her teeth. 'Come along.'

'Daddy do. Mummy nails scratchy.'

Penny looked at her freshly gelled nails and could only agree with her. 'I think it's the glitter,' she said.

'Did I hear my name?' asked Simon coming in to Jenna's bedroom wearing his full clerical garb.

'Daddy dess me?'

Penny flashed him a look that screamed *help me.*

'Okay. Righto. Now, shall we put the felt-tips away and find your tights and then we'll put your lovely new dress on . . .' Penny slunk out of the room and took sanctuary in her bathroom. She touched up her powder and lipstick and gave herself a last squirt of Tom Ford's perfume Mandorino Di Amalfi. Hellishly expensive, she knew, but so worth it.

Adam, dressed and ready in the hall, called up the vicarage stairs, 'Penny? Simon? Kit and I are going over to the church. See you there?'

'Yes . . .' Simon sounded a little distracted. 'I won't be long. See you there. Jenna, I think we've got this on back to front.'

Ocean View

Kafir had been watching for the taxi through the rain-streaked windows of the hotel reception, tapping the tip of his borrowed umbrella nervously on the floor. As it drew up he called to the children who were swinging on the impressive banister of the wide Victorian staircase. 'Aali, Sabu, Mummy is waiting. Come on.'

He had been thinking a lot about how he would greet Sennen. She had turned their marriage upside down with the revelation of her true story, and he had been angry. Which he now regretted. He had missed her. They had a long road ahead of them, and much to discuss, but he missed her. Could he trust her again, though?

He shepherded the children into the back of the cab and settled himself in the front.

The taxi driver was a chatty one.

'Fancy-dress party, is it?'

'We are going to a wedding,' said Kafir with dignity.

'Is that what you lot wear to weddings?'

'No, in India I would normally wear something more elaborate.'

'Must be hot over there.'

'It can be.'

'I love a curry, me.'

'As do I.'

The driver looked in his mirror at Aali and Sabu on the back seat. 'Do the little'uns eat curry an' all?'

'They do.'

'Not the really hot ones? The vindaloos?'

'If they like it, yes.'

'God love 'em. Have your nippers tried a pasty yet?'

'Yes, my wife has made them before.'

'Not proper Cornish, though.'

'My wife is Cornish.'

'Is she? Where did you meet?'

Kafir told him the story briefly.

'I met *my* wife in Magaluf. She's Spanish. Lovely girl,' the taxi driver chipped in.

'And do you eat paella?'

'No. Can't stand fish.'

'But you are a Cornish man?'

'Funny, isn't it? By the way, have you got any confetti? For the nippers? All kids like confetti to throw over the bride.' He thought for a minute. 'Or do you throw rice?'

Kafir's good manners prevented him from saying anything unpleasant. 'Perhaps you would stop at a shop that sells confetti?'

'There's a shop in the village where I'm taking you. She sells everything in there. Not too far now.'

The taxi drove them to Queenie's shop and the driver pointed out the church just a couple of hundred yards away. Kafir thanked him and handed him the fare with a generous tip.

As the children hopped out of the car, Kafir steered them around the puddles and then realised the rain had stopped.

Queenie's Village Store

Queenie was behind her counter applying dark purple lipstick to her spidery mouth. When the bell on the door jangled she looked up, expecting it to be the postman for parcel collection. But it wasn't. The person who walked in was dressed as a Bollywood film star and twice as handsome.

Tall, strong and wearing a pink turban, he smiled at her. 'Good morning. My children would like to buy some confetti.'

Queenie looked down at the two adorable faces looking up at her in happy anticipation.

'Oh my good Gawd. You're the bloke what's married to Ella's mum.'

'I am Kafir Singh. Pleased to meet you.'

'I'm Queenie. Pleased to meet you too. Oh, you do look a treat. I love your jacket. Is it what you'd call brocade?'

'I believe so.'

'And the kiddies! Pretty as a picture.'

'Thank you. I hope their mother will agree.'

'Oh yes, Sennen Tallon. I remember when she went missing you know. Poor girl. What with having her babies so young, and all them tongues wagging, it was no wonder she ran away. It was hard on her mum and dad but they were always a bit hippyish, if you know what I mean. They never talked about her after she went. I felt sorry for Ella and Henry. Not that I knew them then, only what I read in the paper, but they're lovely now. And Ella's marrying a smashing young man, Kit. They're both artists. But I expect you know all about it.'

Kafir was absorbing all this fresh information. 'Not all of it. Now, the confetti?'

Queenie dug out several packets and showed them to the children. 'There's some with bells and doves, some what's coloured pink and blue – and hang on . . .' She dug about in another box. 'These 'ere, they're rose petals. I think the vicar prefers these because they biodissolvable.'

Aali grabbed a packet. 'Can we have these please, Daddy?'

Queenie clutched her bosom, 'Lovely manners. Don't see so much of that these days. Would the little boy want some too?'

Sabu nodded shyly and took the packet she offered him.

'That's three pounds twenty-five please. And would you like a sweetie from old Queenie because you've been so good?'

Aali and Sabu's eyes were saucers as she showed them the rows of sweet jars on her shelves. 'You point at what you fancy and I'll get it out for you.'

Aali chose a jelly snake and Sabu a lollipop.

''Ere look at that,' said Queenie looking out of the shop's windows, 'that's sunshine, that is. Looks like the rain has blown through. Now, I'll just get me 'at and me fur coat and then I'll close the shop. Would you mind escorting me over to the church?'

The Churchyard

Upstairs in Marguerite Cottage, Ella was staring at her reflection. She had to start on her eye make-up but her hands were shaking too much. She pulled nervously at the opening of her old dressing gown and saw her engagement ring catch the light. She had fallen for it the moment the jeweller had pulled the tray of antique rings out from under the counter. A circle of alternating tiny aquamarine and diamond stones. When Kit had put it on her finger it had fitted perfectly.

'Aquamarines are said to be lucky for couples and travellers,' the jeweller had said brightly. 'This one is dated from the 1920s and is very special.'

'I love it,' said Ella running her fingers over it gently and letting it twinkle.

'How much is it?' enquired Kit crossing his fingers.

When he was told the price, Ella swiftly took it off. 'It's lovely but too much.'

Kit stopped her. 'Do you like it?'

'It's beautiful.'

'Then it's yours.'

There was a gentle knock at the bedroom door. 'Come in,' called Ella.

It was Sennen still in her coat and carrying the box which

she put gently on the bed. 'Hello, darling, Henry said you were up here.'

'Oh, Mum. I'm so glad to see you.'

Sennen heard the catch in Ella's throat, 'Darling? Are you okay?'

Ella nodded her eyes filling with tears. 'Yes.'

'Then why the tears? Are you having doubts?'

'No . . . but, it's all so overwhelming.' Ella got up and went to Sennen who put her arms around her.

'Of course it is. I felt the same on my wedding day.'

'Did you?' Ella snuffled.

'Yes. It wasn't that I didn't want to marry him, it was just such a huge thing to do.'

'That's how I feel. I love Kit. He's kind and gentle and funny and I don't want anyone else but . . .'

Sennen stood back and held her daughter at arm's length. 'I think this is all perfectly normal. He's probably got the jitters too. Right now he's wondering how someone as wonderful as you would want to marry him.'

'Do you think so?'

'I know so. Now, let's get you ready.' Sennen unbuttoned her coat and chucked it onto the bed.

'Mum!'

'What?' Sennen turned and saw her reflection in the dressing table mirror.

Ella was beaming, 'You're wearing a sari!'

Henry popped his head round the door, 'Mother, how do you take your tea?' He eyed her sari, 'Blimey. You won't have to worry about anyone else wearing the same as you today, will you?'

'It's fabulous!' exclaimed Ella, wide-eyed. 'I love it! Granny always said she wanted to wear a sari. Now here you are in one.'

'This was meant for Granny,' said Sennen. 'I bought it years ago. Too late now.'

'God, she would have loved it. Can I try it on later?'

'Let's get you ready for this wedding first.'

'Tell you what,' said Henry, still loitering, 'forget the tea, I've got a bottle of Krug downstairs.'

Getting Ella dressed was the gift Sennen had given up hope of ever earning. But here she was helping with shoes and blusher, hairspray and buttons.

'Let me look at you.' Sennen drank in the vision in front of her. 'You are lovely.'

'Thanks, Mum.'

'Just one more thing.' Sennen collected the small box from the bed and gave it to her daughter. 'For you, from me,' she said simply.

Ella opened it and gently lifted the gossamer veil from its safe keeping.

'Oh, Mum. It's perfect. Help me put it on?'

As light as thistledown, its crystal dewdrops spinning rainbows around the room, Sennen placed it carefully on Ella's hair.

'There.'

Henry was waiting for them at the bottom of the stairs, three glasses of Krug on a tray, and his phone ready to take photos.

'Ells, you look really beautiful,' he said, taking her hand to help her down the last two stairs. 'We'd better do a selfie of the three of us.'

Putting his free arm around Sennen's waist he crammed the three of them into half a dozen laughing selfies.

'Now let me take one of Mum and daughter. Smile . . . gorgeous.'

'Let me take one of you and the bride,' said Sennen. Henry took Ella's hand proudly and smiled broadly as Sennen took the shots.

'Let me see them,' asked Ella. They all crowded around the small screen and for the first time saw photographs of them all together.

'My children and me.' Sennen wiped her eyes. 'It's a miracle.'

Henry pulled his mother to him and kissed her hair. 'Don't go wobbly now, Mother, we've got a whole day to get through.'

He solemnly handed out the glasses of champagne. 'This is a very special day. Not just for Ella but for all of us. It's a day to enjoy ourselves as a family. The Three Tallons.' He lifted his glass: 'To us.'

'Thank you, Henry,' Sennen said softly. 'Thank you.'

Sennen knew she wouldn't be able to keep her emotions at bay much longer so she swallowed some champagne and said briskly, 'Right, I'm off. Henry, don't forget to help Ella pull the veil over her face before you leave the house.'

'Yes, Mother.'

'Good. Right. Let me have a last look at you both. Oh, I love you so much.' She stepped towards her children to give them one last hug, but Henry stopped her.

'Now, no more crying, and no more hugging. We can't get all creased up at this stage!'

'Love you, Mum,' said Ella.

'See you in church.'

She blew a final kiss and left.

Now, with a deep breath, shoulders down, head up, she walked towards the church.

She heard the squeak of children's voices and saw two

young children running at her across the churchyard. She stopped dead in her tracks, unbelieving as Aali and Sabu ran gleefully towards her.

'Mummy! Mummy!' they shouted.

She felt her stomach lurch and her pulse quicken as she tried to take in what was happening. They were with her now, clinging on to her legs, Aali kissing her hand, Sabu with his arms up, pleading to be carried. She bent down and drew them to her, kissing them and saying their names over and over again.

Then she heard Kafir's voice and looked up.

He was coming towards her, controlled and calm and so very handsome.

'Hello, Sennen.'

She stood up quickly and black dots swam in front of her eyes. Her breath came in short pants. She knew she was going to faint but as she faltered he caught her. 'Are you okay?'

'Yes. Yes. It's you. You came. You got my message?'

'Only when I got to London. I was already on my way. Here, you need to sit down.' He led her to a long bench next to an ancient yew tree.

'Sit,' he ordered.

She sat, Aali and Sabu climbing up next to her. 'We've come to surprise you.' Aali said.

'Well, y-you have,' Sennen managed. She looked up at Kafir. 'You all look so lovely.'

'I like your sari,' Kafir said.

'Thank you. I thought I'd be the only one in Indian dress but now . . .'

'We look like a family,' Kafir finished for her.

'Yes.' Sennen held her hand out to him. 'Oh, I have missed you. Thank you for being here.'

'Can we open the carfetti now?' asked Sabu.

'Not yet.' Sennen kissed him. 'We have to wait until the bride and groom are married.'

Queenie came breathlessly to join them. 'I've asked the vicar to save some seats for us. Front row.'

The church was filling up but as the splendidly dressed Kafir Singh walked down the aisle with his wife and children the chatter muted as all eyes turned to them. Kit and Adam were waiting nervously by the pulpit, eyes front, but sensing something unusual was happening, turned and saw them.

Kit beamed at Sennen. She looked so exotic and so happy and he came to greet her with a kiss and then shook hands with Kafir. 'Hello, sir,' he said respectfully, 'Kit Beauchamp. I'm the groom and this is Adam, my cousin and best man.'

Kafir bowed his head. 'It is a pleasure to meet you. I hope you don't mind me joining you without notice?'

'Not at all. You are very welcome.'

The congregation watched the drama unfold in front of them, and as this new and exotic family took their seats, the babble of conversation rose higher than before.

The organist had been playing a medley of classical background themes but on a hidden signal struck up Mendelsohn's 'Wedding March' and the congregation stood as one, their heads swivelled to the main door.

Ella, proudly supported by Henry, began the long walk down the aisle.

Jenna toddled ahead, chucking handfuls of petals at everyone she knew, shouting, 'Hello, hello, hello.'

38

The 'Wedding March' finished on a flourish, its final notes ricocheting around the church's vaulted roof.

Kit felt Ella come to his side and dared to glance at her. Her red curls were muted by her veil, but he could see the light in her eyes.

Jenna turned her flower basket upside down and banged it on the bottom to make sure it was empty before Ella gently nudged her and reminded her to take her bridal bouquet to Penny, who would look after it. Ella watched her go and then looked for her mother. There she was, surrounded by Kafir, Aali and Sabu.

Sennen gave her a look of, 'I know, I know!' and a shaky thumbs up. Ella almost giggled but returned the thumbs up. And whispered to Kit, 'You see who is here?'

'Yes. I met them earlier. Really nice. And by the way, you look amazing.'

Simon, dignified in collar and stole, coughed. 'Please be seated. We are gathered here today in the sight of God . . .'

The wedding was simple and all the more emotional for it.

As Simon pronounced them man and wife and said, 'You may kiss the bride . . .' the congregation applauded loudly. If euphoria is contagious it would explain why Ella and Kit floated down the aisle on a raft of joy.

The sun was shining brightly as they stood for pictures of every permutation. Ella, being drowned in confetti by Aali, Sabu and Jenna, had only the briefest of moments to say hello to Kafir and welcome him.

When the pictures were eventually done, the guests trooped after the bride and groom and into the garden of Marguerite Cottage where trestle tables sagged under the weight of food.

A local lad, who ran a mobile disco, played 'Isn't She Lovely' and the prosecco began to flow.

Henry introduced himself to Kafir. 'I'm Henry – Sennen's first son,' he said rather pointedly, if not a little proprietorially.

Kafir inclined his head in respect. 'I am very happy to meet you. I am Kafir Singh, Sennen's first husband.'

Sennen disengaged herself from Queenie and hurried to Kafir's side. 'You have made your own introductions?'

'We have,' said Henry. 'But I should like to meet my half-brother and -sister too.'

'Oh, they are with Ella. Sabu has fallen in love with her. He thinks she is a Royal Princess and Aali won't let go of her hand.'

'You didn't tell us they were coming,' Henry said to Sennen, pointedly.

'I didn't know. It's a wonderful surprise and a bit of a shock too.' Sennen began to feel anxious. 'It's okay, isn't it?'

Henry ignored her and addressed himself to Kafir. 'But

how did you know there was a wedding today? You got to the church at just the right time. Someone must have told you? Or was it an extraordinarily lucky coincidence.'

Kafir replied calmly, 'Sennen asked me to come.'

Henry looked at his mother in false surprise. 'Did you? But you said you didn't?'

Sennen said awkwardly, 'I didn't think he would come.'

Henry turned back to Kafir. 'To quote Mrs Merton, when were you first attracted to the soon to be wealthy Sennen Tallon?'

'Stop it!' hissed Sennen.

Kafir stood between mother and son. 'That is enough. This is the wedding of your sister. Do not speak to your mother in that way.'

Henry smirked. 'Mother, didn't it even cross your mind? Is he here for you or the money he thinks you've been left?'

Kafir was thunderous and took a step closer to Henry.

'Okay, okay!' Henry backed off. 'Keep your turban on. I'm was going to find another drink anyway.'

'I am so sorry,' Sennen said, watching Henry retreating, 'I-I don't know what to say.'

'Maybe I shouldn't have come after all.'

She put her hand on Kafir's arm. 'Thank God you're here. I can never thank you enough for coming. I have missed you so much.'

He placed his hand over hers.

'Can you forgive me?' asked Sennen. 'Am I still your wife?'

'Let us talk later. For now, I would like you to introduce me to everybody.'

Henry had topped up his glass and was now searching for Deborah amongst the familiar faces. He found her being chatted up by Adam and, walking up behind her, pinched her bottom.

'Ow.' She spun round. 'Oh, it's you. Henry, this is Adam, he's Kit's cousin.'

'I know. He's also the best man.' Henry glowered at Adam. 'Debs is my girlfriend,' he said.

'Am I?' asked Deborah. 'News to me. Since when?'

'Now.'

She held her hand to her throat. 'This is all so sudden. And so romantic buuut . . .'

'What?'

She turned to Adam. 'Would you care to dance?'

'I'd love to.' Adam took Deborah's hand and guided her to the patch of lawn designated as the dance floor, while throwing a wink over his shoulder to Henry.

Henry seethed and went in search of another bottle of prosecco. Rosemary found him sitting in a heap under a tree as the sun started to go down.

'You all right?'

'Tip top,' he said acidly.

'Then why aren't you dancing with Deborah? I know you're seeing her.'

'How?' he sneered. 'Private detective, are you?'

'No, but my partner is in the police force and . . . well, let's say that you have been seen coming and going from Miss Palmer's house.'

'It's a free country, isn't it?'

'Of course, but Trevay likes a gossip.'

Henry crumpled. 'She's dancing with the bloody best man.'

'And you're jealous.'

'Pah. Not a jealous bone in my body.'

Rosemary raised her eyebrows. 'Really? Then why were you so rude to your mother's husband?'

He frowned. 'I don't know what you're talking about.'

'No need to lie to me. Sennen told me what you said.'

Henry looked small. 'I worry about her, you know? Who is this bloke and why is he here?'

'He's her husband and he's come to support her and, I think to confront their marriage problems head on. Like adults.'

'I don't want her going back to India with him.'

'Why not?'

'Because,' his voice trembled, 'because she'll go again, like before.'

'When you were young?'

Henry dashed a tear away with his fist. 'Uh huh.'

'Did you know she came back to see you, when you were little?'

'No she didn't.'

'Your grandmother sent her away. Wouldn't let her see you or Ella or your grandfather.'

'Granny would never have done that,' Henry said, picking at a knuckle.

'But she did. For good reasons, I think. Your grandmother had been left with two tiny children and a husband who had a nervous breakdown. She was angry. I think she must have regretted rejecting her only daughter every day after.'

'I don't believe you.'

'Maybe you should ask your mother.'

Henry stood up. 'That's exactly what I'm going to do.'

'Not now.' Rosemary stood up too. 'Tomorrow.' She tried to stop him but he threw her arm off him and strode off to find Sennen.

Deborah saw him and stopped him. 'Henry, where have you been? I've been looking for you.'

'Really?'

'Yes, really.'

'I thought you were having a lovely time dancing with dreamboat Adam.'

Deborah laughed. 'He's very nice but too smarmy for me.' She stepped closer to Henry and pouted. 'I wanted my caveman Henry to come back to me.' She slid her arms around his waist and spanked one of his buttocks. 'Or is naughty Henry sulking?'

'No.' He felt his resistance lowering.

'I think he is and I think I will have to punish him.'

He pushed himself closer to her. 'You are a naughty girl.'

Their passionate kiss was interrupted by Adam with a microphone, ready to deliver his best man's speech.

Henry took Debs' hand and dragged her off into the bushes.

It had got a lot darker when they returned and the fairy lights in the trees transformed the garden into something magical.

Brushing off their clothes they arrived just as Adam and Kit had finished their speeches and the applause was dying down.

A small section of the crowd started calling, 'We want the bride, we want the bride.'

Ella blushed and waved her hands to say no, but eventually she gave in and took the mic.

'Hello, everyone.' She was clearly a bit tiddly. 'I just want to say how happy I am to be married to Kit and to be Mrs Ella Beauchamp.' She gave a small, breathy laugh that bounced from the sound system. 'Mrs Beauchamp. Who'd have thought it? And I know the wedding was a bit quick, but it's not because I'm expecting or anything . . . No, It's because my mum is here and I wanted her to be here when I got married, so she is here and it's FANTASTIC. Stand up, Mum.'

Sennen cringed, but stood up anyway and waved, then sat down quickly.

'And she's brought a new step-dad for me and Henry. Woo yeah. He's the tall handsome one in the turban.' She waved at Kafir who bowed his head and acknowledged the other guests. 'And, she's brought us a half-brother and sister who are adorable, so cheers to them.' Jenna and Sabu tried to get up to wave and show off but Aali pulled them down and did a little dance instead.

Ella laughed and continued, 'But, I just want to ask you all now, to stand up and make a toast to Granny and Poppa who can't be here tonight because . . . because they are in heaven. Granny and Poppa!' She spilt most of her prosecco down the front of her dress as she missed her mouth but she was incapable of noticing and took her bow to whistles and cheers.

Henry raised his glass and watched as Ella sat down with some help from Kit. He dipped his head and said to Deborah, 'Excuse me. I just need a word with someone.'

He had seen Sennen and Kafir sitting under a garland of bunting, but now Sennen was on her own. Henry walked over and joined her.

'Hello, Henry.' She smiled at him. 'Are you okay?'

'Not really. Rosemary has just told me that you came back to see Ella and me years ago and that Granny told you to go away. Is that true?'

Sennen looked at her hands. 'Yes.'

'So you left us twice?'

'Granny was very clear that she didn't want me here.'

'And you couldn't be arsed to fight and stay? For the sake of Ella and me?'

'It wasn't like that. She said that it would upset you both

too much and that I had made Poppa ill and that if I stayed it could kill him.'

'Granny would never say a thing like that.'

'I am afraid she did, and it hurt me deeply but I did as she said because I couldn't bear the thought of you and Ella being hurt and confused again.'

'You're saying that to cover your own back.'

Kafir, who had returned, was standing behind mother and son and had heard the exchange. He stepped into their vision. 'Your mother is telling the truth.'

'Oh, fuck off,' said Henry.

'I don't mind you using that language in front of me,' Kafir said firmly, 'but not in front of your mother, please.'

'What about me and Ella? What about us?' Henry was red with anger and drink. 'She left us. She's going to leave us again as soon as she can.'

'Look at it another way, Henry,' Kafir's voice was low and grave, 'your grandmother's actions were cruel. Yes. But what did that do to both of them? And how courageous is your mother in coming back to make amends?'

Henry's anger was fading and a small, lost boy emerged. 'Why did you go? Was it me? What did I do? Was it my fault you left us? Did I do something wrong? Did you go away because you didn't want me? Why did you stop loving us?'

Sennen took Henry in her arms and held him, whispering maternal words of comfort.

She led him into Marguerite Cottage and found a small study where son and mother could speak without being overheard.

'Henry, I was so stupid and so clueless, I didn't know what else to do. I was ashamed of who I was. Pointed and stared at. Held up as an example to other stupid young girls. I loved you and Ella so much. It was why I left. I went to find your father and to tell him about you both. I told you, I took you to see him when you were just a baby. But he had gone. I would have run away with you, and gone to find him, but it wasn't long before I found out I was expecting Ella so I had to stay. Then, as soon as I thought you were both able to be left with Granny and Poppa, I persuaded Rosemary to come with me. I was so cowardly. Running away has no valour attached to it. I even left Rosemary to face the music alone. I ran and ran from you, from myself, from Granny and Poppa.' She put her head in her hands. 'Not brave at all. And when I came back I was terrified. But I had no idea about the extent of the damage I had done. Granny stood on the doorstep, wouldn't let me in, and made me understand I was not welcome.'

'So why did you come back this time?' Henry asked.

'The letter that found me almost killed me. How could my parents be dead? Both not yet sixty. And I had felt nothing. No sign or premonition that they had died years ago. I thought I'd be able to *know* if anything bad happened and get home in time to be with them, but the threads had been burnt and I had noticed nothing.'

Her voice was breaking. 'I had pictured them hale and hearty and enjoying life. Proud of their two grandchildren, taking time to paint and potter. While I . . .' She laughed bitterly. 'I was gratefully living my new life, selfishly happy with my second chance.'

Henry rubbed his eyes. 'And what about my father?'

Sennen didn't know what to say. 'Do you mind if we leave that to another time? I don't know what that would bring up. I didn't really know him. I was a fool really. I can't honestly tell if he was a bad man or just the wrong man. And I want to protect you from that.'

Henry shuffled his feet and cleared his throat. 'What are you going to do with Granny and Grandad's money?'

'I promise you I did not come back for that. God's truth. I came back only for you and Ella. I thought, naively, that I could explain what happened and rebuild the family I have dreamed about these past twenty-five years. But I see it's not that easy. There's a lot of work to do on my part, if you'd let me.'

'We have come this far without you.'

'Of course.' Sennen was quiet. Thinking. 'Ella's an amazing young woman. And you, you are brave. You always were. When you fell over or banged your knee you never made a fuss.'

Henry swallowed hard. 'I remember being on the beach,

and I think it was you, but, do you remember me getting stung by a bee?'

She nodded. 'Oh yes. Horrible. It had got in the crook of your knee and as you bent down it was crushed and stung you. You screamed so loudly.'

'It *was* you then. I remember you holding me close to you while Poppa sucked the sting out.'

Sennen leant forward and rubbed his head. 'That was me. I feel your hugs even now. You won't make the same mistakes I made. I have been so lucky to be given a child who is the opposite of me. If you were like me I wouldn't like you at all.' She smiled.

'So it wasn't my fault?'

'None of it was your fault. It was me all the time.'

They stood at the same time and faced each other. 'May I hold you again?' asked Sennen.

Henry didn't wait to give his answer. They embraced with mutual affection and a new trust.

Breaking apart, Sennen hitched the scarf from her sari, back onto her shoulder and said, 'Now, do you want to come back to the party? Meet Kafir properly?'

'Maybe tomorrow? Go out for a coffee?'

'That sounds good.' She stroked his cheek. 'See you tomorrow.'

In the garden the wedding party was in full swing. The DJ had pumped up the volume and the disco lights were flashing their colours all over the dark garden. Sennen couldn't find Ella or Kit but she spotted Kafir sitting on a garden bench with two sleepy children leaning against him.

'I'm sorry I disappeared,' she began.

But Kafir understood. 'How did it go?'

371

She sat down and stroked Aali's hair. 'He'd like to meet you all properly tomorrow.'

'I should be delighted,' said Kafir.

'Always the gentleman.' She looked into Kafir's eyes. 'Would you all come home with me tonight? I need to be with my family.'

Kafir kissed her gently, on the cheek. 'I think we would like that very much.'

Back at White Water, Kafir and Sennen each carried a sleeping child up into her bedroom.

'This was my parents' room when I was little,' Sennen whispered.

'Do you think they would be shocked to see a man in a turban here?'

Sennen giggled softly. 'Not at all. Very egalitarian, my parents.'

'But not always kind?'

'Not always. No.' She shrugged. 'But I did push them beyond their limits.' She smothered a little laugh. 'In fact, seeing you wouldn't surprise them at all!'

They laid Aali and Sabu in her big bed and pulled the covers over them. Sennen stood nervously in front of Kafir, alone, with him for the first time since she had told him the truth about her past.

'Well. Here we are,' he said.

'Indeed.'

He looked around. 'I shall take the little sofa.'

'No. You are six foot two, you can't do that. Have the bed.'

'But you are five foot eleven.' He smiled at her and put his hand to her hair, stroking it. 'You can't do that either.'

'So what shall we do?' she asked.

'We shall sleep on the floor. Together.'

40

Kafir found two blankets on the top shelf of the wardrobe and spread those on the carpeted floor.

Sennen took the top cover from her big bed and two pillows and laid those down too.

In the bathroom they cleaned their teeth, padding around each other softly so as not to disturb the children.

Kafir unwound his turban and let his slightly greying but still glossy hair fall to below his shoulders. Sennen ran her hands through it and then hugged him.

'I love you so. I need to explain so much to you.'

He pulled her chin towards him and kissed her slowly. 'We have the rest of our lives to talk. If you want to stay?'

'Yes,' she said. 'Yes. I'd like to stay.'

He took her hand and led her back into the bedroom.

Lying in just their underwear on the makeshift bed on the floor, they held each other, warm and loving. They slept better than either of them had slept since they had been apart.

*

Kafir woke to the sound of an American cartoon on the television and his children laughing. He twisted his head and saw Sennen coming out of the bathroom, dressed and ready for the day.

'Morning, sleepyhead.' She knelt down to kiss him. 'I'll tell Amy, the landlady, that you are all here, and to bring breakfast up for you. I have to nip out. I'll be back in the hour.'

He caught her arm as she rose. 'You're not leaving me again?'

'Never.' She smiled at him. 'Never ever. But I do have something I need to do.'

'What? No secrets please.'

Sennen looked at the children to check they weren't listening then whispered her plan.

'That is good.' Kafir said, when she finished telling him. 'That is right.'

It took only ten minutes to drive from Trevay to Pendruggan and Marguerite Cottage.

Ella opened the door with a hangover. 'I know I look awful. I couldn't be bothered to take my make-up off last night.'

Sennen gazed at her daughter. Her mascara still looked fresh and her cheeks had the bloom of a happy woman. She was wearing an oversized shirt of Kit's which exaggerated her long, slim legs. 'You look like the front cover of a glossy magazine.'

Ella threw her arms around her mother. 'Ohh, Muuuum. Come in.'

Sennen stepped over several pairs of shoes, discarded jackets, a plastic box full of empty prosecco bottles, and a pile of wedding presents on the hall table. ''Scuse the mess.' Ella flapped a hand airily.

'How are you feeling, darling?' Sennen asked, following Ella into the kitchen.

'Fine. Well. No, not totally fine but . . .' She twirled with her arms out wide. 'I'm soooo happy.'

'Shall I make you a coffee?'

'I've had one. I'm thinking of going back to bed. My husband – that sounds funny, doesn't it? – my husband is still sparko. Sit down. I'll make you a coffee.'

'I've only just popped in to make sure you're all right, but I will be back later and I'll cook breakfast and clear up for you. Is Henry here?'

'Yes, he's here somewhere, maybe the sofa? With Deborah. Did you know they had got it together?'

'Yes, Rosemary mentioned it.'

'Oh, Mum, I have something for you.' Ella opened the back door, and disappeared into the garden. Sennen saw her from the window, skipping across the wet grass. She returned clutching her bridal bouquet. 'I left it in the garden overnight to stay cool. I didn't want to throw it to anyone. I want you to have it.'

Sennen was speechless. 'I'm going to cry again.'

'That's all right.' Ella gave the flowers to her mum and cuddled her.

'What have I done to deserve you and Henry?'

'You've come back. That's enough.'

'We still have lots to say to each other,' said Sennen, cradling the precious flowers.

'I think it would be too much to take it all in in one hit,' laughed Ella. 'There's no hurry. Are you sure I can't make you coffee?'

'No thank you. I have something to do but I will be back later, if that's okay with you?'

'Bloody hell, yes!'

As the two women walked to the front door, Ella popped

her head through the lounge door to check if Henry was there. Momentarily unchecked, Sennen achieved her reason for being there and slipped two white envelopes from her pocket amidst the pile of wedding presents. One addressed to Ella, the other to Henry.

Ella came back. 'Yep, Henry is in there, snoring like a little pig.'

Sennen smiled. 'Bless him. Now you go back and get some sleep.'

'I will. Thanks, Mum.'

Sennen was soon back in Trevay and walking up the hill towards St Peter's Church carrying Ella's bouquet. The sun was bright that morning but an onshore breeze ran a coolness through it. She opened the creaky gate, the rusty spring cata-pulting it back to its latch, and walked up the path that took her behind the church to the furthest corner of the graveyard.

She found her parents' graves and sat between them as she had done just a few weeks before.

'Hello, Mum. Hello, Poppa.' The wind was blowing her hair into her eyes, and she brushed it away. 'It's a bit blowy today, Poppa. Good for the drying though, eh Mum? Remember how you used to have to nag me to put the washing out? I hated that job. I love doing it now. In India, everything dries so quickly and smells of sunshine. Funny how we change, isn't it?'

The church bell began to clang, calling the early risers to the first service of the day.

Sennen lifted Ella's flowers to her nose and smelt the sweet freesias and roses. 'Ella got married yesterday and these are her flowers. She was a truly beautiful bride and I think she and Kit will be happy. He's a lovely boy. You have done a good job with her. She's so kind and full of life. What was she like as a teenager? Not as bad as me, I hope.

'I suspect Henry may have been a handful. He's been very tough on me, and rightly so, but underneath he's so gentle. I want to thank you properly for doing the job that I should have done. You have done it better than I ever could at the age I was. Aali and Sabu have a much better me than the one I was. I know I robbed you of the chance to see me grow up, but then again, you had had enough of me, hadn't you, Mum? I ask for your forgiveness – and I forgive you for turning me away when I so wanted to come home.'

She placed the flowers on her mother's grave. 'These are for you both, but I think Mum will appreciate them more than you, Poppa. And by the way, thank you for guiding me, Mum. I think everything will be okay now. Oh, and I've decided what to do with your legacy. I think you'll be pleased. I love you both very much.'

When Sennen had gone, Ella couldn't rest and so brewed a pot of coffee, the smell of which soon lured Kit, Henry and Debs into the kitchen.

'What a wonderful wedding.' Debs gave Ella a hug. 'And you were the most lovely bride I have ever seen. Don't you think, Henry?'

Henry put four mugs on the table and took the milk from the fridge, 'As sisters go, she looked all right.'

'Gee thanks,' said Ella sticking her tongue out.

Kit swung her into his arms and snuggled up to her. 'Morning Mrs Beauchamp.'

Ella raked her hands through his hair and kissed his neck. 'Good morning, Mr Beauchamp.'

'Yeuch,' said Henry. 'Not before breakfast!'

Ella and Kit giggled.

'How about a fry-up?' suggested Debs.

'Sausages, eggs, bacon in the fridge,' Ella said. 'If you don't mind doing that, Kit and I shall open our wedding presents.'

Kit and Henry carried in the exciting parcels and cards and Ella armed herself with notepad and pen to make a thank you list.

Much laughter and excitement was had as wrapping paper was eagerly ripped apart revealing presents that ranged from the good, the quirky and the ridiculous.

Ella was now sorting through the envelopes addressed to Mr and Mrs Beauchamp, her new name giving her little butterflies in her stomach every time she saw it. But then she saw two that were addressed differently. Simply, one said Henry, the other, Ella.

She passed Henry his and together they opened and read the contents.

Ella read hers.

Dear Ella,

I need nothing. I have everything I could ever want. I have found you and you are so precious to me.

I know Mum and Poppa will be happy knowing you are financially secure. Please do whatever you want with the enclosed cheque.

I shall be going back to India with Kafir soon. He is to me what Kit is to you. I do hope you will come and see us as often as you like. I'll teach you how to wrap a sari.

Thank you for letting me back into your lives.

Love

Mum x

Henry read his.

Dear Henry, my son.

I made such a big mistake years ago. Leaving you was so wrong, but I never stopped thinking about you and loving you. Seeing you walk your sister down the aisle yesterday was the proudest day of my life.

The enclosed cheque is for you. I realise now it's not my choice but yours.

I love you very much and always have.

Mum x

A Year Later

It was a stiflingly hot day in Agra. Sennen had the ceiling fans in the house doing their best to stir the turgid air, and outside she had set a small table under the shade of a Plumbago tree. She leant back in her chair and took a sip of the iced lemonade she had made that morning.

Kafir came out to join her. 'Post from Cornwall,' he said, handing her the letter.

She pulled her reading glasses from her head. 'Thank you. Have some lemonade?'

She opened the envelope as Kafir helped himself.

Her new reading glasses brought Ella's handwriting into sharp focus. 'It's an invitation.' She smiled. 'To Billie's Christening.'

Little Billie Beauchamp, named after her great-grandfather and just eight weeks old, blinked and gurgled as the Reverend Simon Canter sprinkled holy water from the font on to her head. He blessed her and kissed her and handed her back to her mother, Ella, who beamed. Her grin could not have stretched further.

Sennen took a photograph on her phone and then asked Simon anxiously, 'Sorry. Is it okay to take pictures in the church?'

'Of course. A joyous occasion such as this must be recorded. How about I take one of you and Grandfather Kafir with Billie and her parents?' Aali and Sabu barged in. 'Oh, yes, and you two. Goodness. Can't forget the uncles and aunts can we?' Simon took several pictures before turning his attention to Deborah and Henry. 'And what about the godparents! Come on, everyone, squeeze in.'

Henry put one arm around Ella and another around Deborah whose pregnant bump was clear.

With all the pictures done, Kit said, 'Right, time for tea. Simon, you and your wife are very welcome. Pencil House is tiny but we'll all squeeze in I'm sure.'

'That's very kind, I'll go and collect Penny and we'll follow on. I have always wanted to see inside Pencil House. It was Ella's grandparents' home, wasn't it?'

'Yes. Their first house. I think Sennen may even have been born there. When it went up for sale, Ella insisted we put an offer in.'

Ella, cradling Billie, touched Kit's arm, 'Your daughter will be hungry in a minute and your wife needs a cup of tea. Mum and Kafir are so looking forward to seeing the house.'

Debs was desperate to take her shoes off. 'Henry, I need to sit down, your son is kicking the hell out of me.'

'Oh, darling. Sorry. I just want a word with the vicar before he goes. Sit on the pew here.'

Henry caught Simon as he was on his way to the vestry. 'Excuse me,' he said.

'Yes, Henry?' Simon replied, smiling.

'I'm not much of a churchgoer, but would you – would we be able to ask you to baptise our baby?'

'Of course. I'd be delighted. May I ask, have you been baptised?'

Henry hung his head, 'No, if that means we can't . . .'

'Not at all, in fact, I could always do a double baptism? Father and child?'

'I don't think that's really . . .'

'Well, maybe a wedding and a baptism?'

Henry chewed his lip. 'Ah well, I haven't asked Debs . . .'

Simon patted him on the shoulder. 'Then I suggest you do.'

The little front garden of Pencil House was bright with pots of dahlias and hydrangeas. Kit had hung pink bunting around the windows and front door and outside was a hand-painted sign saying:

BILLIE BEACHAMP'S CHRISTENING GUESTS WELCOME

The tall thin house gathered the day's joy within its walls and passed that happiness to the people within. Guests left full of sandwiches cake and tea, safe in the certainty that Billie would grow up loved and secure.

The star of the show herself, had not let anyone down and was now sleeping blissfully in her upstairs cot.

Sennen and Ella crept in to look at her. 'She's been a good girl, hasn't she,' doted Sennen. 'And she looks so like you.'

'Does she?' Ella asked, surprised that Sennen would remember.

'Oh yes. And I think she will have your temperament too.'

Sennen stroked the sleeping face with the back of her hand.

'So wonderful. Three generations in the same room. The room where I suppose my cot was and where Mum and Poppa would stand like this looking at me.'

'Four generations if they were here,' sighed Ella.

'I believe they are here,' said Sennen, 'in our hearts and minds.'

Much later, they heard a noise on the stairs and Kafir appeared at the door.

Sennen put her finger to her lips, 'Shh.'

'I've come to tell you that Sabu and Aali are very tired so if it's okay, I shall take them back to the hotel,' he whispered.

'I won't be long,' she whispered back.

Ella hugged him. 'Thank you for coming, Kafir. Billie is lucky to have an Indian grandfather. Think of all those summer holidays.'

'I am proud to have a granddaughter. In India, I would be called Nannaa I believe.'

'Nannaa?'

'Nani, I think.'

Ella looked from Kafir to Sennen, 'Well, from now on, you are Nannaa and Nanni.'

'Thank you.' Kafir bent to kiss Sennen. 'See you later.'

When Ella and Sennen got downstairs, Kit was setting off the dishwasher and Debs was on the sofa, her swollen legs on Henry's knee. He was rubbing her ankles.

'Drink anyone?' called Kit from the kitchen. 'I have a bottle of good red that I have hidden away. And an orange juice for pregnant and breastfeeding women.'

Debs groaned. 'I could murder a glass of Pinot Grigio.'

'Patience my love, patience,' smiled Henry.

Kit came from the kitchen with a corkscrew and three glasses.

Sennen fetched the orange juice. When she came back Ella, Kit, Henry and Debs were all looking at her. 'What?' she said, handing over the orange juice.

Ella looked at Henry. 'Go on Henry. You first.'

Henry stopped massaging Debs' ankles and cleared his throat. 'Over the last few months we've all been talking and, well, I have decided to leave my job in London, sell the house in Clapham and . . .'

'Not Mandalay Road? I thought you loved it?' interjected Sennen.

'Yes, well it seems I love Debs and our baby enough to leave all that behind and buy something here, in Trevay.'

Sennen was amazed. 'Really?'

'Yes, and to erm . . .'

Ella was fidgety with excitement, 'You know the old Chandlers shop up by the boat sheds?'

'Yes.' Sennen was puzzled.

'We've bought it.'

Sennen clapped her hands. 'Whatever for?'

'For Granny and Poppa's art school.'

Sennen's jaw dropped. 'Really?'

'Really.' Henry nodded. He continued. 'It'll give us all a job. Debs has done the conveyancing. Kit and Ella will run the courses and teach, and I'll mop up everything else.'

'But, this is wonderful.' Sennen's tears came suddenly. 'Wonderful. A dream come true. I don't know want to say.'

Henry put his hand in his pocket and threw her a freshly laundered handkerchief, 'Sorry I can't stand up. I'm pinned by these galumphing fat ankles.'

Sennen began to laugh, 'Are you sure about him, Deborah?'

'As sure as I'll ever be,' she sighed.

'So,' said Ella, picking up her glass of wine, 'Let's raise our glasses to the Adela and William Tallon School of Art.'

'To Granny and Poppa,' cheered Henry.

'And,' said Sennen, 'to coming home.'

A Good Catch

To my darling Goose.
Thank you for making me laugh so much.
Love you, Mum.

PROLOGUE

Greer Behenna had never felt so drained. Relieved to be alone at last, she closed her front door and leant her head on its cool, solid wood.

The inquest had been conducted with meticulous precision. The courtroom, even with its lights on, couldn't pierce the gloom of the winter's day hanging outside its windows. The warmth from the old-fashioned radiators filled the air, right up to the high and corniced ceiling, with a density of heat that had left Greer drowsy and with the beginnings of a headache. She had listened to all that the witnesses had said and heard none of it. When called to the stand she gave her own evidence, but remembered little of it now.

So separated were her mind and body she almost floated up the stairs and into her room, where she pulled off her black Armani dress and carefully hung it up in the wardrobe. She found her jeans and a warm jumper and put them on. In the kitchen she filled the kettle. Tom was outside, sitting on the windowsill and mewing crossly. As soon as he saw her he jumped down and clattered in through the cat flap. She fed him. The kettle boiled and she wondered what she'd put it on for. She couldn't face another cup of tea that day. She went to the fridge but there was no wine. She'd drunk the last of it the previous night. She drifted through into the drawing room and then the dining room, where they'd had so many family celebrations. Back in the drawing room, she reached for the remote control. The television came to life with a rather camp man talking about antiques; she switched the TV off again. Restlessly she got her coat and warm boots from the boot room, picked up her keys from the console table in the hall and left Tide House for the only place that felt right: the cove.

Greer had found herself seeking the solace of the cove more and more of late. The tide was out and she walked down to the water's edge. She found a patch of smooth rock to sit on that was otherwise covered in mussels. She closed her eyes and breathed in the scent of ocean and seaweed. She saw him in her mind's eye. He was standing in the surf, casting his line to catch the sea bass that were lurking beneath the waves. His back was to her but she knew that he'd be frowning slightly, concentrating on the fish, his fingers feeling for a bite on the line. She watched him turn round and, when she saw his face, it wasn't the man that she saw, but the boy. His blond hair, almost white from the heat of summer, plastered around his face, his eyes the colour of the sea, looking at her coolly with that familiar mix of curiosity and indifference. Remembering his face as it was then, Greer was suddenly taken back to the long hot summer of 1975, when she was almost five, and she first saw Jesse Behenna . . .

*

He was sitting on Trevay quay, loading a crab line with a mackerel head. His tousled blond head was bent closely to the task and, when he was happy that the bait was secure on the hook, he swung the line to and fro before dropping it into the deep, oily water.

He drummed his dangling feet over the slimy sea wall in concentration. For a few seconds he watched the line sink to the bottom. Satisfied that it had, he shifted his face to the horizon and screwed up his eyes, as if hoping to bring into focus something that he couldn't see. He rubbed the back of his hand across his nostrils and then turned his attention to a bucket by his side.

''Ere you go, lads,' he said, putting a hand into the bag of chips by his side before dropping one into the bucket. Greer saw the quick scuttle of pincers through the opaque of the plastic.

'Move up, Greer.' Her mother, Elizabeth, sat down next to her on the sun-warmed, sea-roughened wooden bench, checking for seagull mess. 'Your dad's just bringing the ice creams. Don't get any on your dress.'

'Can I do some crabbing?'

Greer's mother looked almost offended. 'Whatever for?'

'It looks fun.'

Her father sauntered up, carrying three dripping 99s. ''Ere you go, my beauties.'

'Can I have a go at crabbing, Daddy?'

He looked at her sideways. 'What does your mother say?'

'I say she's in her best dress and I have quite enough laundry to do,' said her mother.

'She can take it off,' replied her father, Bryn, winking at Greer. 'Lovely day like today.' He ignored his wife's horrified stare. 'Eat up your ice cream and we'll nip to the shop and get you a crab line.'

'And a fish head.'

'Yeah, and a fish head.'

'And a bucket.'

'Of course, can't go crabbing without a bucket.'

The sun was warm on her bare shoulders as she sat, in just her vest and pants, on the gritty, granite sea wall, just a few feet from the boy. She dangled her legs, thrillingly and dangerously, over the sea wall, just as the boy was doing.

She had seen him pull in several crabs and drop them in his bucket and was desperate for the same success.

'Right. There you go. Mind that hook, it's sharp.' Her father passed her the baited line.

She looked at the lump of fish stabbed through with the large hook and nodded solemnly. 'I will, Daddy.'

'Do you want me to show you how to feed the line out?'

'I can do it.'

'Well, keep it close to the wall. The crabs like it in the dark. The tides comin' in so they'll be washed in with it. 'Tis no good crabbing on an outgoing tide.'

Greer was getting impatient. All the crabs would be in that boy's bucket if she didn't hurry up.

'Let me do it, Daddy.'

She took the square plastic reel from her father and slowly let the line out. She leant her head as far forward over the edge of the wall as she dared.

'It's landed, Daddy.'

'Good girl. Now sit on the reel and it won't fall in. If you lose it, I ain't buying you another.'

She lifted her thigh, already growing pink from the sun, and wedged the sharp plastic of the reel firmly under her buttock.

'Can I pull it up now?'

'Give it a couple of minutes.'

She looked over at the boy who was again wrinkling his eyes and staring at the horizon. Her father surprised her by talking to him. ''Ello. You're young Jesse Behenna, aren't you?'

The boy reluctantly turned his gaze to the man talking to him. 'Yeah.'

'Watching for your dad's boat, are you?'

'Yeah. 'E's been out three days.'

'Has he? That'll be a good catch he's bringing in then.'

'Yeah. As long as the bastard at the market gives them a good price.'

Greer's father laughed. 'Is that right?'

'Yeah.'

'I've got one!' Greer was pulling up her line and, as it broke water, her father and the boy could see that she had three fat, black, glittering crabs clinging greedily to the bait.

'Bring 'em in slow, Greer.'

'Get the bucket, Daddy!' she called excitedly.

'That's it. Nice and slow. Now drop 'em in.'

Greer watched as the three crabs plopped into her bucket.

'Mummy! I got three in one go!'

'Did you?' responded her mother from the safety of the bench; she was still not looking up from her magazine. 'Well done, darling.'

'Do you want to feed them a chip?' The boy passed over the bag.

She picked up the fattest chip she could see and dropped it into her bucket.

'Thank you.'

The crabs, which had been scrapping with each other, now started scrapping with the chip.

'Want one yerself?' asked Jesse.

Greer darted a glance at her mother, who shook her head. 'You've already had an ice cream, Greer. You don't want to get fat.'

Greer looked back at Jesse. 'No, thank you.'

'Suit yourself,' he said, shovelling a handful into his mouth.

'What bait you using?' he mumbled, standing up and wiping his hands on his cotton shorts. He ambled over, with his hands in his pockets, to look at her catch.

'Fish,' said Greer.

'What sort of fish?'

Greer's father replied, 'Mackerel, boy. But I reckon 'tis bacon that's the best. When I were a nipper, I always used bacon.'

The boy looked at him, nodding his head slowly, weighing up the pros and cons of mackerel versus bacon. 'I prefer mackerel. It's what Dad says is best and he's the best fisherman in Trevay.'

'Then he must be right,' smiled Greer's father.

The emptying of the crabs back into the water was a serious business. One by one they were counted and Greer had a pleasing sixty-four to Jesse's eighty-one.

'Not bad. For a beginner,' he told her.

'Bryn,' called Greer's mother, impatient to get home to a cooling shower. 'It's time to get Greer back.'

'Stop your nagging, woman. We'm 'aving a good time.'

'I've got to get tea on and it's getting late.'

'I told you to stop nagging,' he said, and silenced her with a look.

The children said their goodbyes and Greer's father said, 'Send my regards to your dad.'

'What's your name?' asked Jesse.

'I'm the bastard at the market who never gives him a good price.'

*

Greer snapped her eyes open, remembering Jesse's straight talking as being so typical of him, even as a young boy. He always seemed so sure of himself; he didn't ever seem to care what anyone thought. But had she ever really known him? Had any of them? She continued staring out into the churning, dark sea and pulled her coat closer around her, though she knew that it wasn't the winter chill that was making her shiver.

The sea in front of her was devoid of boats, reflecting the emptiness she felt inside.

*

Loveday Chandler knocked and waited for several minutes. She pulled her mobile phone from the pocket of her fleece and dialled Greer's number. She heard it ring out behind the closed front door. Snapping her phone shut and putting it back into her pocket, she turned away from the house and headed towards the only other place where her friend could be.

'Greer,' Loveday called as she jogged breathlessly down the beach. 'Greer!'

Greer hung her head and blew out a stream of warm breath into the cold wind. Why would no one leave her alone?

Loveday reached her, panting. 'Greer, darlin', you OK?'

Greer dragged her eyes from the horizon and focused on her oldest friend. 'I'm fine,' she said flatly.

'Only we was worried. You left so quickly.'

'I wanted to be home.'

Loveday sat down on a bunch of mussels next to Greer. ''Twas a tough day.'

Greer nodded, grim faced.

'Brings it all back again,' said Loveday, picking up a small pebble and throwing it into the lapping water.

Greer turned her gaze back to the horizon and again nodded. 'I can't believe he isn't coming back,' she said quietly.

Loveday put an arm around her friend's shoulder. 'I know.'

Greer turned her white and stricken face towards her friend. 'And I can't believe that you'll soon be gone too. My oldest friends are leaving me.'

Loveday felt the tightening belt of guilt around her chest. 'You've got lots of friends . . . And as soon as we're settled, I want you to come out to New Zealand and spend long holidays with us.'

'I haven't got lots of friends. I have clients, I have acquaintances, but there's no one who knows me like you do.'

Greer found an old tissue in the pocket of her coat, blew her nose and took a deep breath, trying to calm herself. 'I'm sorry. It's just self-pity.' It took a supreme effort for her to plaster a tight smile on to her face. 'I'm happy for you. I really am. And, anyway, I can't leave. Not yet. I must be here . . . in case . . .'

Loveday pushed a strand of her corkscrew hair behind her ear. Once such a brilliant copper red, it was now faded to a rust colour and flecked with white. She thought how lucky she was to have this opportunity of a fresh start. Looking at Greer she felt lucky that she had made the right decision all those years ago.

Awkwardly, she fumbled for Greer's hand and gripped it hard.

Greer said softly, 'Do you think he ever really loved me?'

Loveday pulled Greer towards her and hugged her tightly, but couldn't answer.

The dice had been thrown a long time ago.

Part One

1

Autumn 1975

Greer's mother had planned on sending her daughter to a small private school in Truro but her husband had soon squashed another of her dreams. 'Trevay Infants' was good enough for you an' me, and it'll be good enough for Greer.' Which is how Greer was to meet Jesse again.

It was early September. Trevay had said goodbye to all the holiday-makers and could get on with being the small Cornish fishing port that it was.

Greer was in her uniform of grey pleated skirt and navy-blue blazer, with dazzling long white socks and shiny buckled shoes. She walked between her parents as they covered the five-minute stretch from home to school. She was nervous. She had never been left anywhere on her own before. As they got closer to the school, more and more children filled the narrow pavements around her. Some of them she recognised but barely knew. Her mother had few friends herself, having always put them off with an extreme shyness which was often interpreted as an unwarranted air of superiority.

In the playground, Bryn bent to kiss Greer. She might not be the son he had wanted, but she was everything to him. His sun and his moon. He would – and did – give her everything. 'You be a good girl, mind.'

'I will, Daddy.' She put her arms round his neck and hugged him tight. 'Will you come and get me when I'm finished?'

'Aye.'

Her mother kissed her too. 'Have a good day, darling. See you later.'

Greer watched as her parents walked out of the playground. Her father striding out and nodding at acquaintances, her mother trotting to keep up with him and turning to give one last wave to her only child.

Greer's legs started to move towards the school gate and her parents and away from the school building. She was picking up her pace and tears were pricking her eyes. I don't want to be at school. I want Mummy, she was saying to herself.

She was getting closer to the gate. She took a breath, ready to call out to her mother. She could see her father chatting to man in a fishing smock. Her mother was surreptitiously wiping her eyes while her father was laughing at something the man was telling him.

Greer's lungs were now full and ready to shout to them. She opened her mouth but, before she could get any sound out, a small but firm hand caught her round the waist.

'Where you going?'

The air in her lungs escaped soundlessly at the surprise pressure on her diaphragm. She struggled but was held even more tightly.

'Hey. You're going to get into trouble if you go through the school gates.'

Something in the voice made her stop and turn to see who her captor was. It was the crab fishing boy from the quay.

A woman carrying a handbell was walking through the playground. She began ringing it loudly.

'Come on,' Jesse said.

He took Greer's hand and ran with her into the school.

*

A male teacher was standing inside the building, at the door to the school hall, identifying the new children. 'New boys and girls, walk to the front of the hall, don't run, and sit on the floor, cross-legged, facing the stage, please.'

Greer was feeling anxious but grateful to have Jesse's hand in hers. Once they got to the front he let go of her and sat on the floor.

'Are you a new boy too?' she asked him, settling down next to him.

'Yeah, but I know everybody 'ere. My brother comes 'ere too.' He was looking over her head and smiling at someone. Greer followed his gaze and saw a fat, plain girl with her flame-red hair in pigtails, also sitting cross-legged, showing her knickers and waving at him.

'Who's that?' Greer asked, feeling sorry for this unattractive-looking girl.

'That's Loveday.'

The fat girl bum-shuffled her way towards them.

'All right, Jesse?' she smiled.

'Yeah.'

'What's your name?' the girl asked Greer.

'Greer. I am named after a famous film star who was very beautiful.' Greer couldn't help herself.

'Oh,' said Loveday, her smile pushing her fat freckled cheeks up towards her eyes. 'That's nice. I'm called Loveday after my dad's granny.'

Jesse's eyes were darting around the gathering faces. 'Seen Mickey?' he asked Loveday.

'He's there.' Loveday pointed at an open-faced, tall and very skinny boy standing on the other side of the hall.

'Mickey,' Jesse called. 'Mickey, come 'ere, you beggar.'

'Who's he?' Greer asked Loveday.

'Jesse's best friend. Do you want to be my best friend?'

Greer had never had a friend and thought that she might as well start with this poor fat girl. 'Yes.'

'Can I tell you a secret then?'

'Yes.'

'I'm goin' to marry Jesse.'

Greer frowned. 'Has he asked you?'

'No. But I am going to marry him.' Loveday smiled, then had a thought. 'You can marry Mickey! That way we'll all be best friends for ever.' Greer looked at Mickey, who winked at her. She frowned back. Loveday was tugging at her sleeve and saying something. 'Do you like Abba?'

It was a long day. The new children were introduced to their teacher, Mrs Bond, who took them to their classroom. Loveday grabbed two desks next to each other for her and Greer. Jesse and Mickey were a row in front. Mrs Bond called the register, explained a few school rules – spitting and swearing were not to be tolerated, hard work was to be rewarded – and lessons began.

Greer already knew her numbers and most of her letters. She wrote her name quite clearly on her new exercise book.

Loveday was impressed. 'What you written there?'

'My name.'

'Really?' She leant forward and poked Jesse in the back.

'Ow.' He turned round. 'What did you do that for?'

'Greer can write. Look.' She showed him Greer's book.

He looked at Greer, 'Did you write that?'

'Yes.'

'Clever.'

With that one word, Jesse's fate was sealed. Greer decided it was she who was going to marry Jesse. Not Loveday.

2

Spring 1987

'You'd do a lot worse than to marry that girl,' Edward Behenna told his son.

'Shuttup, Dad.' Jesse Behenna ducked out of reach of his father's hand as he tried to ruffle his son's hair.

'It would be a dream come true for your granddad,' continued Edward as he pulled out an ancient wooden chair, scraping its legs across the worn red tiles before seating himself at the kitchen table opposite his younger son.

'If he were still alive,' murmured Jesse.

Jesse's mother, Jan, slid the tray of pasties she'd been making into the top oven of the Aga; she banged the door shut and swung round. 'Edward, don't start all this again,' she warned him, irritated.

But Edward hardly seemed to hear her. 'I promised my dad, as he promised 'is father afore 'im, that I'd do all I could to build the business and make Behenna's Boats the biggest fleet in Trevay.'

'And you have, Dad,' Jesse assured him. 'Behenna's is the biggest fishing fleet on the north coast of Cornwall.'

Edward nodded, but a frown marred his lined face. The pressures of running the business were very different from those of his father's day. This year, the European

Union had really become involved and laws were being passed governing fishing quotas for member states. Cornwall and Devon MPs had tabled questions in the Commons about their impact on their fishing industry. How could they all hope to keep going in this climate, when the government was impounding vessels and fining their owners? This interference, along with upstarts like Bryn Clovelly screwing them for every penny down at the fish market, were driving some fishermen to the wall.

The old ways were dying. Small fleets were struggling to remain at sea and Edward knew that it was the likes of Clovelly who represented the future. Edward's father had fished these waters for fifty years, man and boy. Sometimes his fish would be bought by a fishmonger from somewhere as exotic as Plymouth, but Clovelly saw the swollen wallets of the flash London City boys as rich pickings; he was buying monkfish for restaurants in Chelsea and exporting scallops to New York.

'Aye, it is. I've been working the boats since I was fourteen and left school. I didn't have your education.'

Edward knew he was a good fisherman, one of the best, but being an entrepreneur, like Bryn Clovelly, was beyond him. Behenna's Boats had provided a good living for many families up to now, but carrying on as a lone operation was looking like an increasingly risky option. Clovelly would love nothing more than to add a big share in the Behenna fleet to his portfolio and Edward was finding his offer harder and harder to resist. He knew there were men with fewer scruples than he who would bite Clovelly's hand off for a deal such as the one he was offering.

'I'm only staying on to do O levels,' Jesse reminded Edward. 'Then I'm full time working at sea on the fleet.

But when I'm a bit older and I've saved up a bit, I'm off travelling.'

His father looked at him as if he'd just said he was off to buy a Ferrari. 'Go travelling? Travelling? There's more to find in your own home town than you'd ever find travelling.'

'Oh, that's right. I'd forgotten. There're the Hanging Gardens of Bodmin, The Pyramids of Porthleven, The Colossus of St Columb . . . Cleopatra's Needle up Wadebridge. Silly me.'

Edward scowled at his son. 'That's enough of yorn lip, boy. You're the next generation. Greer Clovelly is a lovely girl and the only child Bryn and his lah-di-dah wife ever managed. Poor sod, never 'ad a son. Poor me, I got two and neither of them any bleddy good.'

'Leave off mithering the poor lad. He's only sixteen. He's got ideas of his own,' Jan said.

'I knew by his age that you were the one for me,' Edward told her, and Jan groaned inwardly as Edward played his familiar riff. 'As soon as I saw you, twelve and lookin' like an angel, I said to my mate, "There's the girl I'm gonna marry".'

'Yeah and, more fool me, I did marry you.'

Edward caught Jan's hand as she walked from the Aga to the sink. 'No regrets though, maid? No regrets?'

Jan felt the warmth of her husband's rough and calloused hand on hers and wondered. She'd had plans to travel to the Greek Islands and sleep on the beach under the stars, like the character she'd read about in a book once. The last book she'd read. Must be more than twenty years ago. But Edward had wooed her into submission and she never did send off the passport application form that had sat on her mother's dresser for two years after she'd married. For their honeymoon, Edward had taken her to Exeter and they'd seen a rep production of *The Mousetrap*. Edward had promised her that the next show they'd see would be in Paris. Almost twenty years on and they still hadn't made that trip.

She stooped and dropped a kiss on her husband's weatherbeaten forehead, feeling the spikes of his overgrown eyebrows tickling her chin. Edward Behenna would now be more likely to see the surface of the moon than the insides of the Folies Bergère. She smiled. 'No regrets my 'andsome.' She straightened up. 'But that don't mean to say you can dictate what Jesse's future is going to be.'

Edward let go of her hand and turned his attention back to Jesse. 'Greer is a lovely girl. Clever, beautiful, and comes from a good family.'

Jesse gave his father a glare. 'I'm not marrying someone so that you can do a business deal.'

'What are you talking about? Business deal? Who said anything about business? I'm just saying she's a lovely girl.' Edward looked at his son with a patient, innocent smile. Bryn Clovelly was a sharp operator. For all of his talk about a merger, Edward knew that selling a share of the business to him was a risk. However, Bryn had no boys of his own. Like Edward himself, and most vain men, Bryn was desperate for his business not to die with him. If Jesse and Greer were married, it would ensure that Behenna's Boats was safe and Bryn would have himself a son-in-law from one of Trevay's oldest fishing families. They were building a dynasty. But Jesse seemed to have other ideas. Edward got a hot itch on the back of his thinning scalp when he thought about selling his son's future off to the highest bidder.

'She may be, but I'm not marrying her. If you want to

do business with old man Clovelly, do it yourself, but leave me out of it.'

'An' what's the matter with lookin' to the future?' Edward spread his hands, fingers splayed, on the old table, his extraordinary eyebrows raised in innocence.

'Plenty.' Jesse dropped his head and stared at his lap.

'Oh, now,' cajoled his father. 'You're not bleating about that other girl, whatshername . . .'

Jesse's mother took her hands out of the sink and wiped the suds on her apron.

'Edward, leave him alone. Loveday Carter is a really nice girl. Jesse would be happy with her. Let the boy fall in love with whoever he wants.'

'Her mother hasn't got a pot to piss in, and anyway, what's love got to do with it? He doesn't know what love is.' Edward was exasperated.

'But you did, or so you say,' Jan threw back. 'And stopped me from having a bit of life in the bargain.'

'Oh, you and your life.' Jesse recognised the brewing of a row and his father didn't disappoint him. 'You didn't have a life till I took you on. You've wanted for nothing since we married. I'm a good man. I'm not a drinker or a womaniser.'

'And I'm supposed to be grateful for the fact that life now starts and ends at Trevay harbour sheds, am I?'

Edward stood up. 'There's no talking to you when you get in one of your moods like this. You sound like your mother, and she was a miserable old cow. I'm going back to work.'

'But the pasties'll be ready in a minute.'

'I'm not hungry.'

In the simmering silence that remained after Edward had stomped out of the door and into the spring sunshine of Fish Lane, Jan stood for a moment in powerless frustration. Edward had set his mind on securing the future of the fishing fleet, and if that meant arranging a marriage between Jesse and Greer Clovelly, heiress to the Clovelly Fisheries Company, then that would be it, no matter what Jesse wanted.

She ran her thin hands through her short hair and bent to get the pasties out of the oven.

'They're hot,' she said needlessly, serving one to Jesse.

'Thanks, Mum.'

She put one onto a plate for herself and, wiping her hands on the tea towel that was perpetually tucked into her apron, sat opposite her son.

'Eat,' she told him. Jesse did so. After a couple of mouthfuls, she asked. 'So . . . is it Loveday?'

Jesse shuffled a bit in his seat. With a full mouth he said, 'I dunno.'

'But it's not Greer?'

'How do I know? I'm sixteen. I want to see the world before I decide on anything. I've got my own mind and my own life.'

Jan nodded in understanding. It was one thing encouraging Jesse in a particular direction, but quite another thing to put all this pressure on the poor lad.

'I'll ask your dad to back off.'

*

'Bloody ungrateful kids.' Edward was on his boat, *The Lobster Pot*, checking the trawl nets with his old friend and ship's mechanic, Spencer. 'He doesn't know his arse from his elbow. Does he think I wanted to take on the fleet from my dad? No I bloody didn't. But it was the best thing that ever happened to me.' He looked up from his work and surveyed the harbour around him. 'Look at this place.' He swept an arm dramatically across the view. 'Trevay is the most beautiful place on earth. What's he think he's going to find anywhere else? Answer me that.'

Spencer moved his stained and smouldering hand-rolled cigarette from one corner of his gnarled mouth to another and made a noise that sounded as if he was in agreement. Edward continued: 'Fifteen boats we've got in the fleet now. Fifteen! If my dad hadn't been so canny after the war and bought them first few cheap from those poor fishing widows whose husbands had never come home from the Navy, we'd still have the arses hanging out of our trousers.'

Spencer gave another grunt.

'You and me, Spencer, you and me, we know how the world works. Hard work brings good things. Not nancying around doing yer O levels and packing yer spotted handkerchief to go travelling. What's that about?'

As inscrutable as ever, Spencer peeled the damp cigarette from his lips and revealed a handful of tobacco-stained teeth. 'Want a brew, Skip?'

Edward stopped what he was doing and looked at his old friend as if for the first time.

'See. You've seen it all, haven't you, Spence? I'll have a cup of tea with you and then, when we've finished here, I'll take you for a pint. How does that sound?'

Spencer went below decks to the galley and Edward could hear the comforting sounds of the pop as the gas was lit and the rattle of the old kettle as Spencer banged it on the hob. Edward took another look at the fishing village that had been his home from birth. The gulls were cackling above him and the May sunshine made mirrors of the water on the mudflats. 'Bloody kids,' he muttered to himself. 'Bloody women.' He rubbed the thick gold wedding band on his finger. 'Bloody Jan.'

He took a deep breath of the salty Cornish air and thought about his boys. Grant a bloody liability, and Jesse a dreamer. What had he done to deserve them? He loved them. Of course he did, but why didn't they do what he told them? When his dad had told him to jump, he'd asked how high. When his dad got ill and Edward had had to take on the fleet aged only eighteen, he'd had no choice. Sink or swim. He'd chosen to swim. He'd shut the door on the dreams he'd had to go to America. He'd taken on his responsibilities. He'd swallowed his resentment and done the right thing. Why the hell wouldn't Jesse?

*

Jesse knew he should be in his room revising for the imminent O levels, but he couldn't see the point. He'd be leaving school in June and joining his dad at sea. He knew how lucky he was to have a job, and he loved the sea but . . . oh, there were so many buts. He took his Levi denim jacket off one of the pegs by the back door and kissed his mum, who was now setting up the ironing board.

'You going out, son?'

'Yeah.'

'Where are you going?'

'Up the sheds.'

'Shouldn't you be doing some school work?'

'What's the point, Mum?' He bent and kissed her cheek to stop her from asking any more. 'See ya.'

He was out of the back door leaving his mother to watch him, shrugging on his beloved denim jacket, slipping his Sony Walkman headphones on his ears and retreating down the short front garden path. She heard the little gate click shut for the nth time in her life; on her own, again. She worried about her boys and their future. Grant was in the Royal Marines now, stationed in Plymouth. Last time he called he said he was going for Commando Training at Lympstone. Ever since he was 16, fuelled by the nightly bulletins reporting the Falklands War, he'd wanted to wear the Green Beret of a commando. Now, at 21, this was his chance to earn it. Grant had been a handful from the off. His unpredictable mood swings had always marked him out. It could be like treading on eggshells living under the same roof as him, and school had been one long round of visits to successive heads. He'd left school with only one exam pass to his name, in metalwork. He was lucky that the army recruiting officer had seen something in him beyond the defensive, edgy character that he conveyed.

'We'll smooth the rough edges off him, Mrs Behenna,' he told her.

She was proud of him, of course, but fearful about the dangers he would face in any war, and of those dark moods which had got him into trouble with the police already. He was such a contrast to Jesse, who was calm and steady, but still waters ran deep with Jesse – Jan knew that there was much more to him than his father gave him credit for. At least Jesse would be safe at home, working with his dad and groomed to take over the business. But what if Edward's plans to marry him off to Greer Clovelly came about? Jesse would be stuck in a loveless marriage, burdened with the responsibility of a very big business and no chance to see the world and enjoy his freedom. Just like she'd been.

'Stop it, Jan,' she said into the silence. 'Just stop it.' She plugged in the old iron, turning on the radio for her daily infusion of *The Archers* as she waited for it to warm up.

Jesse was still just a boy. Let him have his dreams; there was time enough to be a man.

*

Jesse left the cool of the narrow lane of terraced fisherman's cottages, and was walking up the hill away from Trevay and towards St Peter's, the fishermen's church. The graveyard slumbered in the warm sun and delicate white cow parsley heads shuddered in the light breeze, making shadow patterns over the cushions of forget-me-nots growing beneath them. He always glanced at his grandfather's grave as he passed. Today its granite headstone glittered like a smile. Jesse touched his brow and saluted his grandfather before carrying on up the hill towards the sheds.

The sheds were a series of around thirty to forty homebuilt wooden structures, owned by the people of the town who had no garages attached to their houses, which, since most of the houses were built long before the motor car was invented, was the majority. The sheds had started as makeshift stables and boat-houses but now contained all the detritus of modern living. It was a kind of shanty town sited on a two-acre plot of flattened mud and sand. Opposite the sheds, some of which were now two storeys, stood a long line of boats of all kinds. Dinghies, clinker boats, fishing boats, rotting hulks, along with trailers of varying sizes on which the boats could be towed down the hill, through the town and down the harbour slipway into the water. At the entrance to the sheds was the second of only two public phone boxes in Trevay. The other box was down on the quay. Every resident knew the number of these boxes and regular calls were made between the two to give a shout to the lifeboat crew or call a man home for his tea.

Jesse walked past the phone box, kicking up a little sandy dust as he did so. He looked over to his father's shed, which had expanded over the years and was now a run of four sheds linked together. On the upper floor were the words Behenna Boat Yard est. 1936, painted in fading blue and white letters.

He saw Mickey before Mickey saw him. His best friend since nursery school, Mickey Chandler was the person Jesse shared everything with. Mickey was standing outside his own family's smaller shed, unlocked now with its doors wide open to the sun, and was polishing the chrome of his pride and joy: a two-year-old Honda moped, a present from his family and friends for his recent sixteenth birthday.

Jesse lengthened his stride, taking the headphones from his ears and calling, 'Hey.' Mickey stood up and shielded his eyes with the hand holding the stockinet duster; Jesse could smell the metal cleaner on it.

'Hey,' he replied.

Jesse was now close enough to give his best mate a punch on the arm, which was returned with equal force and affection.

'I thought you were revising,' Mickey said, returning to his polishing.

'I thought you were too.'

'Waste of fuckin' time, isn't it?'

'Yeah. Want a snout?'

'Please.'

Jesse pulled a crumpled packet of Player's No. 6 out of his pocket and offered one to Mickey.

'Ta.'

'You got a light?'

'No. Have you?'

'No.'

'Shit.'

Both boys pondered on the dilemma of having cigarettes but no means of smoking them. Mickey laughed first. 'You're bloody useless, Behenna.'

Jesse grabbed his friend in a headlock and they scuffled contentedly for several minutes.

Eventually they stopped

'Bike's looking good,' Jesse told him.

'Got my test next week.'

'Gonna pass?'

'Of course.'

'Can I come out with you?'

'Sure. I'm gonna ask Loveday out when I've got me licence.'

Jesse's heart flipped at the sound of Loveday's name. Mickey was in love with Loveday and had never made any secret of it. Jesse had never admitted to Mickey that the mention of her name, let alone the sight of her, was enough to shoot a flame of desire and longing coursing through his body.

'Her arse is too big for the seat,' he observed.

Mickey smiled. 'Yeah. And what an arse. Imagine having her arms around you, holding tight, pressing those big boobs against your shoulder blades.'

Jesse could imagine all too clearly, but said only, 'Fill your boots, boy.'

3

'How do I look in these?' Loveday had struggled into a pair of lime-green leggings, her face flushed and perspiring.

Greer, sitting neatly on the edge of Loveday's unmade bed, wondered what to say. Should she tell her friend that she looked embarrassing? That the hideous leggings were pulling at the seams and clearly revealing the revolting cellulite clinging to her thighs. Could she tell her that she needed to lose a lot of weight and learn how to dress properly? Though on the plus side – and Greer did feel slightly guilty about this – Loveday did make Greer look great by comparison.

'You look like Loveday Carter,' she managed.

Loveday turned back to her reflection in the mirror that hung off the back of her bedroom door. 'I like the colour. They didn't 'ave 'em in the next size, but I'm gonna lose a bit of weight before the summer comes.' She turned sideways and looked at herself from right and left. 'If I put on my orange T-shirt, that'll cover me bum.'

Greer looked down at her own slim legs in their perfectly fitting Pepe jeans. The orange T-shirt might cover Loveday's bottom, but it wasn't going to disguise the two rolls of fat wobbling between the bottom edge of her bra and the elastic waist of the leggings.

'There. What d'ya think?' Loveday asked a few moments later. Greer looked up.

She wanted to say, 'Loveday. You look ghastly. You couldn't be wearing a less flattering outfit. Your breasts are too big, your stomach is enormous and your derrière huge.'

Instead, she said, 'It's very you.' She stood up and smoothed her hands over her own trim derrière, brushing off imaginary flecks. Loveday was now at her dressing-table mirror. The dressing table itself was strewn with several used cotton wool balls and a large amount of ancient make-up; a cold, half-drunk cup of tea and an empty Diet Coke tin. Hanging from a glass hand with curved upright fingers were strings of gaudy beads and a worn pair of knickers.

Greer pulled the collar of her crisp white shirt up at the nape of her neck and checked that the cuffs of her sleeves were turned back as the models in her mother's monthly *Vogue* magazine did. She wanted to get out and see Jesse. 'Come on. The boys will be waiting for us.'

Loveday took one last look in the mirror and smacked her matte red lips together. Recently she'd been copying Madonna's make-up, even adding the beauty spot above her lip with an eye pencil. 'I can't find my black pencil so I've used the green one. I rather like it. What do you think?' she said, turning to Greer. 'It shows off me green eyes, don't it?'

Greer blew her cheeks out and thought for a moment. 'I think you look . . . unique.'

Loveday hugged her uptight friend. 'You are so sweet. Unique? Really?'

'Really.' Greer extricated herself from the miasma of

Giorgio Armani's Beverly Hills rip-off scent, bought in Truro's pannier market.

'And what does that mean? Sounds posh,' bounced back Loveday, reaching for her heavily fringed and studded, stone-washed denim jacket.

'It means you are a one-off.'

*

Jesse was first to spot the girls walking up towards the sheds. Loveday's marmalade hair with its wash-and-wear perm gleamed in the sunshine; her beautiful body was gently undulating towards him in skin-tight green leggings, her large breasts swinging to the rhythm of the fringes on her jacket. He thought often about those breasts. Sometimes, when she wore her white T-shirt, he could see the outline of her nipples. He turned his back on the girls, feigning disinterest, and called over to Mickey, who was checking his quiff in the wing mirror of the Honda moped. 'The girls are coming.'

Mickey smiled in the mirror at his own cheeky face. 'I'm going to give Loveday a night to remember.'

'Oh, yeah? When's that then?'

'Tonight.'

'Never. She won't touch you with a barge pole.'

'She won't need to. I've got me own barge pole to touch her with.' Mickey ducked swiftly out of reach of Jesse's punch and together they locked the precious motorbike in its shed.

'All right?' Mickey raced to get ahead of Jesse and be first to walk by Loveday's side.

'Yeah.' She smiled at him and, for him, the sun seemed suddenly to be shining extra bright. Then he frowned.

'You've got something on your lip.' He lifted a finger to wipe at the mark on her face. She grabbed his wrist before it got to her.

'It's me beauty spot. Like Madonna's. It's unique.'

'Oh. Looks like you've drawn on yourself.'

Loveday stopped and waited for Greer, who was a couple of steps behind with Jesse.

'How does my beauty spot look?'

Greer and Jesse both looked at the green blob on Loveday's sweating lip.

'Well, it's smeared a bit,' said Greer.

'Oh shit. Badly?'

'A bit.'

Jesse looked through his pockets and found an old, dried-up tissue. 'Shall I wipe it off for you?' he offered.

'Yes, please. Get it all off.'

He lifted the tissue to Loveday's mouth. 'Spit.'

She did so and, tenderly, he wiped all trace of the green pencil away. Standing so close to her, Jesse could sense the rise and fall of her chest, and smell the heady scent that emanated from her. Her dewy golden skin glistened in the sunlight and her emerald eyes were like those of an exotic cat. The combination was suddenly overwhelming.

'There. All done.'

'Thanks.' Loveday gave her rescuer a hug, leaving him breathless on many counts.

She turned to Greer. 'Has it all gone?'

'Yes.'

'Maybe I'll try an indelible ink next time.'

'Best not,' murmured Greer.

Mickey muscled in and grabbed Loveday's arm. 'Have you eaten your tea?'

423

'Only a bit. Mum did shepherd's pie earlier. But I could do with some chips.'

'Come on then.' And, taking her hand he ran down the hill, forcing Jesse and then Greer to run after them.

*

Edward Behenna had been in the Golden Hind since he and Spencer had finished on the boat. Edward was full of beer and the memory of the row with Jan was disappearing as fast as a sea mist on a warm morning. The beer had warmed his heart and his humour. 'Spence, you'll 'ave another before 'e go.'

Spencer removed a battered tin of tobacco from the front of his canvas smock and nodded. 'Aye.'

'Good man, Spence. Good man.' Edward lumbered heavily to his feet and clapped his friend on the back, dislodging the scanty twigs of tobacco from the near transparent cigarette paper that Spencer was balancing between thumb and grimy index finger. He hailed the landlord. 'Same again, Pete.'

Pete, a very tall man with a stomach straining against the buttons and belt of his shirt and trousers, bent down so that he could see through the forest of pint tankards hanging from hooks on a shelf above the bar. 'Skinner's?' he asked, reaching for the empties Edward had placed on the damp counter.

'Aye.'

Without anyone taking much notice, the door of the pub opened and a slim man in his early forties entered. His quick, bright blue eyes skimmed the familiar faces and he nodded at those who acknowledged his arrival. His prey was at the bar, delving into a handful of change to pay for the two waiting pints. He walked lightly and quickly towards him. 'I'll get those, Pete, and a Scotch for me, please.'

Edward turned to see who was buying his pint. 'Bryn Clovelly, you're a gentleman.' He turned his eyes to where Spencer was sitting. 'Spence, Mr Clovelly bought you a pint.'

Spencer had rolled his cigarette; its smoking fragrance drifted towards the bar. 'Thank 'ee, Mr Clovelly.'

Bryn ignored him and spoke to Edward. 'So, Edward, when are we going to do business?'

Edward looked down at his feet, uncomfortably aware that Clovelly was completely sober.

'Bryn, I've 'ad a drink. Me 'ead's not straight for talking business.'

Bryn pulled up an empty bar stool and indicated for Edward to do the same. 'It's not business as such, is it?' He unhooked the casual blue jumper he had knotted round his shoulders and draped it on the back of the stool. 'We've known each other a long time, haven't we, Edward?'

Edward rubbed a hand over his mouth and chin. 'You've gone up in the world since we were nippers though, ain't you, Bryn?' Edward looked at Bryn's clean hands. 'Look at you. Smart clothes, smart way of talkin', smart car outside. You're different now, Bryn.'

Bryn placed his right hand on his chest. 'Not 'ere. Not in my 'eart. I can still talk as Cornish as you, boy, and don't 'e forget it. There's nothin' wrong in doing well and earning a little cash, is there?'

'No,' Edward agreed reluctantly. He had given more thought to Bryn's continued insistence that their businesses were stronger together than he wanted to let on, but it didn't do to show your hand too early where Bryn was concerned. Besides, what Jan and Jesse had said also nagged at his thoughts. Now that Bryn was sitting here in front of him, in his flash clothes and with a conceited look on his face, Edward's doubts had once more risen to the surface.

'I don't know whether I want more. I'm happy with the boats and passing them on to Jesse.'

'Not Grant then?'

'No. 'E's happy in the Marines. Best place for him.'

'Is he settling well?'

'Think so. Better to get all that anger out of 'im in hard training than 'ere in Trevay.'

Bryn placed his hand on Edward's shoulder. He knew that Grant was a worry. A drinker with a short fuse and handy fists. 'Maybe the discipline is just what he needs,' he said.

'Aye.'

Bryn remained silent, watching as Edward took a long mouthful of beer. Then he asked, 'What does Jan think?'

'With women you've got to pick your moment.'

'So you haven't told her about the offer that I've put on the table?' Bryn leant closer to Edward. ''Tis a good offer, Edward. You know that these EU quotas could be the death of the Cornish fishing industry. We need to diversify and open up our markets if we're to survive. We're better together – you'll never get an offer like this one again. The future of Behenna and Clovelly will be settled.'

'But you getting fifty-one per cent: you'd have the controlling interest then. You might leave me high and dry.'

'Look, Edward,' Bryn leant in closer. Edward could smell the scent of cigars on his beautifully laundered Pierre Cardin shirt. 'I'm prepared to sell you a share in the fish market, if that would sweeten the deal. We'd both sit on the board of Behenna and Clovelly and each have a fair shout on how the business is managed.'

Edward frowned and rubbed his chin. Bryn looked appraisingly at him.

'When did you and Jan last have a holiday?'

'What do we need an 'oliday for?'

'You'll need a holiday from all the hard work we'll be putting in running the new business together. Imagine. You could go up country and see the sights of London. Catch a plane to Italy or Greece. Or maybe have a week in New York.'

'Who'll look after the boats while I'm away?'

'Me. And you'll look after the fish market and the refrigeration factory for me when I'm away with my missus.'

Edward shook his head. He'd been thinking about Bryn's 'business' plan since the idea had first been floated. It was all very well for Bryn to talk about them joining forces but, as the months had gone by and Bryn had kept on about Jesse and Greer getting married, it felt more and more like Bryn was leading them all down a road that led in one direction, where there was no turning back. As a reality, he knew where his moral compass was pointing.

'No, no. The boy has his own life to lead, and that's with me at Behenna's Boats. The fishing fleet was built up by my dad and I'm building it now for Jesse. 'Tis enough.'

'And I'm building the fish market business for Greer. But when she's married she won't want to work. She needs a man to run it all . . .'

Edward looked at Bryn sharply. 'I've told you before.

Jesse has to make his own decisions. I could no more make Jesse marry Greer than I could get Spencer over there to stick on a tutu and pirouette off Trevay harbour wall.'

Bryn laughed and picked up his Scotch to take a sip. 'I was going to say partner, not husband. Someone bright. Someone we can trust and – yes – Jesse would be ideal.' He took another deeper draught of his whisky. 'It ain't a case of forcing anyone. My Greer's going to grow up to be a fine wife and mother. She's refined; a good catch. Anyone can see that – your Jesse just needs a bit of encouragement.'

Bryn Clovelly reached into his pocket and took out a brown envelope and placed it on the table between them.

'You've been blessed with two strapping boys, Edward. Greer is a daughter to make any man proud but . . . she's not a man, with a man's head for business. Imagine, Clovelly Fisheries and Behenna's Boats becoming one big company. Your boats supply my market. We squeeze the opposition and supply the hotels and London restaurants at the best possible prices. Finally, when our rivals are no more, we call the shots and demand the best prices we can get whilst giving the best-quality fish and customer service. When you and I are retired, my Greer and your Jesse could run the business themselves. We will have created a really lasting legacy. The icing on the cake would be for them to marry and merge two great family businesses into one. A fairy-tale ending.' Bryn swallowed the final mouthful of Scotch, pushed the envelope towards Edward and stood up, retrieving his jumper from the back of the stool. 'Just think about it, Edward. A fairy tale. That's all.'

Edward eyed the brown envelope warily.

'Saw your Jan yesterday about Trevay. Looks like she

needs that break, Edward.' With this parting shot, Bryn slung his jumper over his shoulders and headed towards the exit. For a moment, Edward was filled with the urge to run after him and stuff the envelope into Bryn's self-satisfied, smug face.

But he didn't. Instead, he picked up the envelope and looked inside. A careful observer would have seen his eyes widen momentarily, then he opened his jacket and put it quickly in the inside pocket.

He nodded to the barman. 'Another pint for me and Spence, Pete.'

*

The pain in Greer's heart was real and tangible. She didn't know how to make Jesse see her. Want her. She was slim, spoke nicely, dressed with style and had impeccable manners. A miniature of her mother who lived in the fantasy film-star world of the 1950s and 1960s. 'Greer Garson was the most beautiful and gracious actress of her day. That's why you have her name. If you'd had a sister, I should have called her Audrey after Audrey Hepburn. But your father and I were not to be blessed.' Greer was happy to be an only child. Spoilt and petted and treated to anything she wanted. The one thing she wanted now, though, was Jesse, and not even her parents could fix that.

Jesse and Mickey were sitting either side of Loveday on the harbour wall. Greer glanced across at Loveday. They were best friends, of course, but Greer felt sorry for her, really. Loveday, with her ample frame, a face full of freckles and her yokelish ways. She was pretending to read Mickey's palm. 'Ooh, now, Mickey. You're going to 'ave three children and a long life.' With his hand in hers she traced a line across his palm. 'There may be some unhappiness in your thirties, but you'll travel to faraway places and live to be an old man.'

''Ow old will I be when I die?'

She held his hand up to her face and squinted. 'At least sixty-five.'

Jesse was getting impatient. 'Do me now, Loveday. What do you see?'

'Well now, let's 'ave a look.' She held his hand softly in hers and looked into his sea-green eyes. Without looking at his palm she said, 'I feel you 'ave met the woman you will marry. There'll be two beautiful boys and you'll have lots of money.'

Jesse looked down into Loveday's mischievous green eyes; it took all of his restraint not to reach out to her and kiss her like he longed to.

'Is that right?' They held each other's gaze steadily and, for a moment, Mickey and Greer faded out and it was as if they were alone on the quay.

'Aye.' Loveday wanted more than anything for Jesse to kiss her, but not here in front of Mickey. She adored Mickey and he made no bones about his feelings for her. She'd do anything not to break his heart, but Jesse was the boy she loved and he was looking at her now with such a look . . .

Greer stepped forward from the cold metal railing she'd been leaning against. 'Let me read yours, Loveday.'

The spell was broken and Jesse pulled away.

Loveday laughed good-naturedly, 'OK, Greer. What do you see?' and stretched her hand towards her friend.

Greer had no idea what she 'saw' but she said, 'Hmm. I see you married to a really nice man. I see the initials

C and M and . . .' She folded Loveday's hand into a fist and examined the creases that her palm made by her little finger. 'I see three children.'

Loveday was impressed. 'Really? I'd love three children. I wish I had brothers and sisters, but when Dad died . . . Mum would love to have lots of grandchildren.'

Mickey was thinking who they knew whose initials were CM. 'Who's this CM bloke?'

'Dunno,' said Loveday, thinking that Jesse's initials were JB.

Greer helped them to figure it out. 'Well, it might be MC, I suppose.'

Mickey's face lit up. 'Those are my initials!' He looked as pleased as punch and Greer felt, for the second time that evening, a pang of guilt.

'Read my palm, Greer.' Jesse opened his hand to her.

She took it happily, touching his warm, dry skin and smoothing her fingertips over the calluses caused from helping his father on the boats.

'Well, I see a very happy marriage for you and lots of children. Your wife will love you with all her heart.'

'Can you see any initials?' Jesse asked. Greer thought for a moment; she knew she couldn't say her own so she truthfully said, 'No. I can't see any letters this time.'

Mickey let out a big laugh and started to play-fight with Jesse. 'No letters for you! And French letters don't count.'

Across the harbour car park, the door of the Golden Hind opened and Bryn Clovelly stepped out. He looked across to see where the laughter was coming from.

'Greer? Is that you?'

'Yes, Dad.'

'Come on then. Time you were home. Your mother'll be mithering me else.'

The pain in Greer's heart seared again. The last thing she wanted to do was go home now. Why wasn't she allowed to stay out, like her friends were?

'I can walk up later.'

'Get in the car now.'

Greer was far too well behaved to either make a scene or to defy her father, no matter how crestfallen she felt at having to leave. 'OK, Dad,' she acquiesced.

She hugged Loveday, who clung onto her dramatically. 'Bye, Greer, and thanks for helping me get ready tonight.'

'Night, G,' said the boys.

'Night, Mickey, goodnight, Jesse.'

Greer lingered momentarily and cast a meaningful glance at Jesse, but he was looking beyond her and watching her father as he walked towards his new BMW, casually pointing the automatic key fob at it. Four orange lights flickered twice as the car made a beeping sound and the locks clunked open.

'That's frickin' awesome,' declared Mickey.

'Gonna get some on the Honda, are you, Mick?' laughed Jesse.

Greer walked towards the car and heard more laughter from her friends, knowing that they had already closed the gap that she had occupied. She climbed into the car.

Her father started the engine, steering the car away from the harbour towards home. From the depths of the leather front seat, Greer craned her neck to wave at her friends, but they weren't looking at her now. Loveday was walking on the sharp upturned stones of a low wall and flapping her arms to keep her balance. Jesse went to help her but, to Greer's satisfaction, Mickey beat him to it.

As both Mickey and Loveday lost their balance and

slipped off the wall, Greer couldn't help but notice Loveday's ample bum and bosom wobble as she clumsily tried to regain her balance. Greer looked down at her own slim thighs and taut stomach, feeling pleased with what she saw and vowing that she was never, ever going to let herself end up like poor Loveday. But as the three-some slipped out of view, Greer wondered again what it would take to capture Jesse's undivided attention once and for all.

4

June 1987

'Mickey, you want to come fishing with me tonight? Celebrate the last of the exams?'

Jesse was pulling off his school tie as he walked out of the school gates for the last time. It was a momentous day; along with many others he had finished his final O level, and the occasion was marked by the usual flour and egg fight, ended only when the deputy head raged at the rabble-rousers for covering her car in cake ingredients and escorted them off the school grounds. The long hot summer lay, full of promise, ahead of Jesse.

Mickey shook his head disappointedly. 'I've got to help my dad on the boat.'

Jesse put his arm round his friend. 'Tell you what, I'll help you and we'll go out later.'

'Would you?' Mickey said gratefully, picking bits of batter off his shirt.

'Yeah. Donna at the Spar shop fancies me. She might sell us some tins of cider with our pasties.'

Mickey smiled gratefully at his best and oldest friend. They'd navigated school life pretty well together. Football, detentions and girls. He was still hopelessly in love with Loveday, but she never seemed to take him

434

seriously. He'd found comfort with females who were more than willing.

And now school was over and out. He didn't have to worry himself with further education. He had no need. He'd been offered a job as deckhand on *Our Mermaid*, one of the newest boats on the Behenna fleet and skippered by his dad.

Meanwhile, Jesse was being groomed to take over the fleet when his own father eventually retired. He had to start at the bottom, though, and was to be deckhand on *The Lobster Pot*, the flagship of the fleet, skippered by Edward Behenna himself.

As the boys loped down the hill from school towards the harbour, they heard Loveday's voice calling to them breathlessly.

'Boys. Wait up!' Loveday was galloping towards them, her school skirt covered in flour and rolled up at the waistband to reveal wobbly thighs, her white shirt pulling at the buttons as her bosoms jiggled invitingly with every pace. A little way ahead of her, Greer was jogging effortlessly in her spotless school uniform.

'Where are you two off to?' panted Loveday.

Mickey put his arms out to catch the girl he adored. His hands caught her waist and he felt the warmth from under her breasts. She turned her smiling freckled face up to the two boys. Mickey could smell the sweetness of her breath as she asked again, 'Where are you two going?'

'Mickey and I have got stuff to do,' said Jesse, staring into the middle distance with feigned nonchalance.

'What sort of stuff?'

'The sort of stuff that don't need girls,' Jesse grunted.

Loveday looked crushed. 'Greer and me thought we

could do something together with you two. You know. Celebrate the end of school.'

Greer narrowed her eyes astutely. 'You're going fishing, aren't you?'

Jesse ignored her and said to Mickey over the top of both girls' heads, 'You bring the bait and I'll bring the food.'

'We can come with you,' Loveday told him, not prepared to brook any objections. 'Greer and I'll be good company for you.'

Jesse shook his head. 'No. Blokes only.'

Loveday pulled a face. 'Blokes only? You arrogant arse.'

Mickey laughed and turned to Jesse pleadingly. 'They can come, can't they?'

Jesse, who was trying to wean himself off his desirous want for Loveday, thought he might be in with a chance with Donna from the Spar shop later that night. Loveday was a no-go area while Mickey still had the hots for her. But maybe it would be nice to hang out with the girls – they hadn't all been together for a while.

Damnit, Donna could wait.

'OK. Seven o'clock at *Our Mermaid*,' he agreed reluctantly.

Loveday took Greer's arm and pulled her away excitedly. 'What are you going to wear?' she asked.

'Jeans, I think,' said Greer.

'Me too,' smiled Loveday.

*

Greer left Loveday at the cobbled corner where her mum had a tiny cottage. Then she walked on past the harbour and out onto the road that led towards the better end of Trevay.

When her father had sold the two trawlers his dad had left him, and bought the small fish market on the quay, he'd quickly turned the ailing business round. He'd taken a small selection of the best of his fresh catches up the M5 and the M4 to London's swankier restaurants and hotels, persuading the chefs that he could undercut any of their other suppliers and provide better fish. He had worked hard. As soon as the fishing boats unloaded at his market, he paid the skippers the least he could get away with and then jumped in his refrigerated van and personally drove the lobster, plaice, turbot and crab to the back door of the poshest kitchens in the United Kingdom. Gradually he could afford to pay better prices to the fishermen, and that enticed boats from around the Cornish coast to land their catches with him. As business grew he expanded the old fish market, taking up at least three times more quayside and landing space. Now he had three vans every night ploughing the motorways and bringing home the money.

Naturally, the cramped house in the back lanes of Trevay had given way to a modern and airy executive bungalow, and this was where Greer was headed now.

Greer's mother opened the front door as soon as she saw her turn into the drive.

'How did it go?' She took the proffered, and now redundant, blazer from Greer and hung it for the last time on a padded hanger in the coat cupboard, next to her husband's golf clubs.

'The English paper was fine and the history paper was everything I'd revised, so I think I'll have done OK.'

'You are a clever girl.' Elizabeth kissed her. 'I've got crab salad for tea.'

'Actually, I was hoping to go out.'

'Where?'

'Fishing with Loveday and Mickey.'

'Just Mickey and Loveday?'

'Erm, I think Jesse will be there too.'

'I see.' Elizabeth knew all about Bryn's plan for Greer and Jesse. There had never been any other children after Greer and no doctor could ever tell them why. Elizabeth was not really sorry. Childbirth was messy and dangerous, and once had been enough for her, but she knew how much it unsettled Bryn to think about what was going to happen to the company. Women were taking the reins in business more and more these days, but Greer had never shown the slightest interest – and quite right too, thought Elizabeth. Fishing was a man's world and women had no place in it. Part of her wanted Greer to marry someone outside Trevay, someone with a bit of breeding; but she supposed that Jesse Behenna was as close as it came to old money in Trevay. Besides, look at Bryn, he'd been just like all the other coarse Trevay fishermen when he'd courted her, but she could sense his ambition and together they had come far. All men could be moulded by a strong woman who knew what she wanted.

'Mum, there's nothing to worry about,' said Greer, interpreting her mother's interest as concern for her morals. 'He has tons of girlfriends and I'm not one of them.'

'But you'd like to be.'

'*Muuum*. Don't. You sound like Dad.'

Elizabeth turned and walked towards the kitchen. Greer followed her.

'Can I take the crab salad with me?' She tried to appease her mother. 'I don't want to waste it.'

Her mother nodded. 'Yes. I'll make a little picnic up. Don't want you getting hungry and eating chips or you'll get as fat as Loveday.' Mother and daughter exchanged knowing smirks.

*

Greer heard Loveday thumping down the stairs before she pulled the front door open. She had teased her hair into a big, orange, candy-floss ball and was wearing a low-cut, sleeveless, fashionably ripped T-shirt, her pink bra partly on show. She was pulling at a fringed ra-ra skirt that was at least two sizes too small for her.

'Ha!' she crowed, taking in Greer's tight white shorts, blue and white striped top and long, tanned legs. 'I knew you wouldn't wear jeans so I've pulled all the stops out. Hang on while I get my shoes.'

Greer watched as Loveday bounded back up the stairs, her ra-ra skirt lifting with every step and exposing tiny black knickers stretched over her generous bottom.

'Wait till you see these,' Loveday called from upstairs, 'They arrived from the catalogue this morning.'

A few seconds later and Loveday came down the stairs, with as much grace as a jolly pig in electric blue stilettos, gripping the banisters for balance.

'What do you think to these beauties?' She bounced off the last stair and posed like a stripper.

Greer couldn't help but smile. 'They are very eye-catching.'

Loveday looked at Greer's flat ballet pumps with sympathy. 'A word to the wise. You'll never pull Mickey in those.'

Down on the quay, the warm evening sunshine had

brought out the couples with pushchairs and people with dogs. The holiday-makers wouldn't be down in force for another six weeks so at the moment Trevay still belonged to its locals. The tide was out and the inner harbour was littered with boats lying on their keels, green fronds of seaweed hanging from their mooring ropes.

Greer couldn't help but always remember the first time she saw Jesse down here when they were both so young. His skinny brown legs hanging from his shorts and his blond hair falling over his eyes. Now he was a man. Six foot four, broad and muscular. Greer's feelings for him had intensified over the years. She dreamt about him, he lit up her life when she was with him, but he treated her like a sister. Greer his friend. Not Greer his girlfriend.

Sometimes she wondered whether he had feelings for Loveday. He certainly seemed to enjoy her company, and she knew that Loveday had a crush on him. But he always seemed careful not to encourage her, from what Greer could see. Anyway, how could he fancy someone as chaotic as Loveday? No. Jesse couldn't fancy Loveday, he probably just felt sorry for her. Mickey fancied Loveday and, one day, Greer hoped, he'd land her. Loveday would be a fool not to go for Mickey. And one day, Jesse would see that Greer was the woman for him.

Loveday jolted Greer from her musings. 'There they are!' She pointed at Jesse and Mickey, who were strolling about a hundred yards ahead with fishing rods over their shoulders. 'Jesse! Mickey!' she shouted. 'Come and give us a hand with this.' She hefted the weighty picnic basket, which Greer had asked her to carry, from one hand to the other, then waved extravagantly to the boys. Mickey, of course, came to help Loveday. His lanky frame, dark hair and sweet face with its slightly large nose and eyes that drooped at the corners a little, reminded Greer of a lovesick greyhound. As soon as Loveday had loaded him up with the picnic basket, she raced off to walk beside Jesse.

At that moment, Greer felt enormous compassion for Mickey. 'Here. Let me help.' She took his fishing rod and put it across her left shoulder, then looped her right arm through Mickey's free one and walked with him.

'Don't worry about Loveday. I know how you feel about her. She'll see sense one day,' she told him.

Mickey blushed and quickly brushed her off. 'Loveday's all right but I'm playing the field.'

Greer raised an eyebrow, unconvinced. 'Are you, Mickey?'

'Sure. I'm a fisherman and there's plenty more fish in the sea.'

'Oh, Mickey,' Greer laughed, 'you're fooling no one.' Mickey looked at her ruefully but then laughed too.

Loveday looked back over her shoulder and saw Greer and Mickey walking arm in arm. Heads together and laughing.

'Jesse, look, I knew it. Mickey and Greer are a match made in heaven.'

Jesse turned to look too, but said nothing. He was trying not to think about the lace bra that was showing through Loveday's T-shirt, which was only serving to accentuate her generous cleavage, while also trying to keep in check the dangerous sensations that threatened to overwhelm him whenever he was in close proximity to Loveday Carter.

*

Our Mermaid was a good-sized trawler painted in the traditional local colours of sky blue, chalk white and clotted cream yellow. The hull had streaks of rust coming from the holes where the anchor chain fed, but she was in good condition and well maintained. She was tied up alongside the deepest part of the harbour wall where the boys hoped to fish from.

'Hey, Dad,' called Mickey as they approached.

An older version of Mickey was standing on the fore-deck drinking a mug of tea. ''Ello, son! Where the 'ell 'ave you bin? You're too late to help me. I'm all finished.'

'Sorry, Dad.'

Mr Chandler put down his mug and helped Loveday onto the boat. 'Thank you, Mr Chandler.'

''Tis all right, maid.' Alfie Chandler was very fond of Loveday. She was warm, down to earth and undeniably sexy. A girl he'd be happy to call daughter-in-law. He hoped that Mickey would make his move before someone else came on the scene; there were many young lads who would bite their own arms off to get close to Loveday – he certainly would've done at Mickey's age.

'Hello, Mr Chandler.' Greer was holding out her hand to him. 'Would you help me aboard?'

'Certainly.' Alfie offered her his grimy and calloused hand. He couldn't deny that she was a looker, but she was too bony and prim for his taste. Poor Jesse Behenna. He was caught in a net, whether he knew it or not. Bryn Clovelly and Ed Behenna would make sure of that.

Alfie leant into the wheelhouse and put his mug on a wooden ledge. 'Right, you young 'uns. Tide's flooding in now and you should get some good mackerel off the side.'

'Cheers, Dad.' Mickey gave him a short embrace.

'Don't be home too late or your ma will be worried.'

'We won't.'

Alfie stepped off the boat. Without a backward glance he walked off along the harbour wall that led straight to the Golden Hind and its welcoming bar.

'What you got in the picnic basket, Loveday?' asked Mickey, rubbing his hands.

'You're always hungry!' Loveday swatted him away. 'How do you stay so skinny?'

Greer and Loveday unpacked a checked tablecloth that Elizabeth had thoughtfully put in, and placed the Tupperware boxes of crab, potato salad and tomatoes on the cloth.

Jesse pulled out of his fishing bag four pasties and six tins of cider; certain proof that Donna from the Spar shop might be two years older than Jesse but that she definitely fancied him rotten.

After they'd eaten (Greer had picked at the salad and declined her pasty so Loveday had had it instead), the boys set up their fishing rods. The sun slowly dropped towards the horizon and gave a final fiery blaze before sinking into the sea. Greer, who was watching Jesse bait the large hook on his line, shivered at the sudden chill. He looked up.

'You cold, Greer?'

'I am a bit.'

'Come here.' Amiably, he opened an arm up to her and she tentatively let him put it around her. She was enclosed between his arms as he held the fishing rod. She could feel his chest moving in and out as he breathed. Conversely, she held her breath, in fear of actually touching him more closely.

A tug on the line disturbed the moment and he lifted

an arm over her head, letting her out of the enclosure. 'Want to reel this one in?' he asked.

'Show me how.'

He handed her the rod and instructed her gently on how to wind in the reel. The flapping mackerel broke the surface. 'I don't like this bit,' she said.

'And you a fisherman's daughter!' He laughed kindly. 'You'd never make a fisherman's wife.'

5

The summer they left school was a good one. The sun shone, the sea remained calm and the beaches were inviting. The holiday-makers came down in their droves, so there was plenty of work for the school-leavers, waiting tables or taking money in dusty beach-side car parks.

Jesse worked on his father's flagship, *The Lobster Pot*. Being a Behenna and heir to the business made no difference: he was not given an easy ride. He had to learn the business from the bottom up.

Like most Cornish trawlers, *The Lobster Pot* had five crew members. Edward was the skipper, the toothless Spencer was his mate. In charge of the engines was the mechanic, Josh, a Kiwi of about 35 who'd landed in Cornwall as a student, years earlier, and never gone home. The cook was Hamish, a Scotsman with a surprisingly good palate, and the two deckhands were Jesse and another young school-leaver, Aaron.

The boat went out for up to seven days at a time, with two and a half days back on dry land before going to sea once more. It was a steep learning curve for Jesse, who'd not been allowed to join his father on these trips before, but he had the sea in his soul. Not only did he enjoy the work, he enjoyed the money that was divvied up at the end of each trip.

Once a catch was landed and sold at market, the money was used to pay for the diesel, food and other essentials, then the largest share of what was left over went to the owner – in this case Edward. The rest was split between the crew. The skipper Edward (again), Spencer, Josh, Hamish and then the deckies Jesse and Aaron.

It was not just a good summer for the visitors, the fish seemed to like it too; they were swimming in their droves to the Cornish fishing grounds.

The Lobster Pot would glide out of Trevay harbour with most of the Behenna fleet behind her, ready to make their fortunes. For Jesse, released from the classroom and still weighing up life's possibilities, these were halcyon days. He found he was loving life at sea: the sound of the engine chugging below his feet, the cry of the gulls performing stall turns above him, and the instinct he was starting to develop from his father as they sat poring over the charts, determining where the next good catch might be waiting for them.

On one particular warm August night, Edward and Jesse were in their usual seats in the galley, having had a supper of poached cod and bacon with new potatoes coated in bacon fat. Edward was drinking a large mug of powerfully strong tea.

'I'm reckoning we aim for Tring Fallows. Word is they'm the best fishing grounds just now.' He tapped the chart, then leant back to stretch tension out of his lower back.

Jesse remained hunched over the charts, studying the distance between where they were now and where they were going. 'How long will it take to get there?'

'Should be there in about four hours.'

Jesse glanced at the time. 'I'm on watch at midnight.'

'I recommend you get some shuteye now then,' his father said.

Jesse heaved himself a little off the leatherette bench seat and craned his head to see out of the starboard porthole. '*Our Mermaid* is still with us. She coming to Tring Fallows too?'

'Aye. We'll need both of us to haul the buggers in. This'll be a good catch if we get it right.'

The ship's radio came to life and the familiar voice of Alfie Chandler, Mickey's dad, spoke.

'*Lobster Pot, Lobster Pot, Lobster Pot.* This is *Mermaid*. Over.'

Edward unhooked the small receiver/mouthpiece from the radio set and put his thumb on the talk button.

'*Mermaid*. This is *Lobster Pot*. Wass on? Over.'

'*Mermaid, Lobster Pot*. We still headin' for Tring Fallows? Over.'

'*Lobster Pot, Mermaid*. Can you switch to channel nine? Over.'

Edward waited a minute for Alfie to swap to a channel that they could use just between themselves.

'*Lobster Pot, Mermaid*. Over.'

'Yeah, Alfie. Tring Fallows it is.'

Jesse, desperate to talk to his mate Mickey, held his hand out to his father, opening and closing his fingers in the universal code for 'hand it over.' Edward kept talking. 'Is your Mickey there, Alf? Only 'is mate wants to 'ave a word.'

'I'll get 'im.' They heard Alfie shout for his son as Edward passed the mouthpiece to Jesse.

Mickey's voice came over the airwaves. ''Ello?'

'Mickey, 'tis Jesse. You sleepin' before we get to the fishin' ground, or no?'

'Gonna have a snout up top then I'm going to grab some zeds. You?'

'Same. Give us a minute and I'll be out too.'

Edward reached forward and snatched the radio from Jesse. 'That's enough. It ain't for you two to make your social engagements on.' He pressed the talk button. 'Mickey, you still there, you great long streak of piss?'

'Yes, Mr Behenna,' came Mickey's nervous voice.

'Well fuck off and 'and me back to your dad.'

On deck the moon, although not full, was bright; its face looked down at the two trawlers as they slipped through the benign waves. Jesse, now standing in the stern of the boat, put his face to the cool wind and closed his eyes. He felt secure and peaceful. He was increasingly realising that the sea was his home; as long as he had it in his life, he knew all would be well.

Looking to starboard, and travelling at the same speed, was *Our Mermaid*. Jesse listened to the thrum of the engines together with the swish of the wash that they churned behind them. He could make out the tall, thin silhouette of Mickey appearing from a hatch and sparking up a cigarette.

'Hey, Mickey,' Jesse called over to him.

'Hey, Jess,' called back Mickey.

'Can you think of anywhere else you'd rather be?' Jesse asked his friend.

'Inside Loveday's knickers?' answered Mickey truthfully.

Jesse frowned at Mickey, knowing that – at this distance and in the dark – Mickey wouldn't be able to read his face. He didn't like Mickey talking about Loveday like that.

Loveday was under Jesse's skin. He'd known her since

. . . well, forever. And he hated to hear Mickey discuss her in such crude terms. He felt protective towards Loveday. He wanted to look after her and treat her well. He felt something that he couldn't describe; something, maybe, close to love? He pulled himself up. Love? No, not love. Not for Loveday. Loveday was Mickey's and he'd never hurt Mickey. He was like a brother to her. He just liked her. A lot. That was all. God, no, he didn't love her. He was going to see the world. Not settle down with the first girl he'd ever known, right here on his doorstep. Bugger that.

'Where would you rather be then, Jesse?' asked Mickey, sucking on his cigarette and exhaling a long plume of smoke to trail behind him.

'I told you. Nowhere other than here.' There was a splash behind him. He turned and shouted, 'Look, Mick. Dolphins!' And, sure enough, in the wake between the boats, two dolphins slipped out of the water in perfect arcs, the moonlight glistening on their skins.

'There's two more!' shouted Mickey. He bent down to the open hatch on the deck and shouted, 'Dad. Come up. Dolphins.'

Any crew member on both boats who wasn't already sleeping, or didn't have a drop of romance in his soul, came on deck to watch the display that the dolphins put on for them. They counted up to fifteen, although it was hard to tell if some had been counted twice. Both Alfie and Edward cut their engines and, for maybe five or ten minutes, fisherman and dolphin enjoyed each other's company. Finally the creatures slid beneath the waves and disappeared.

A thought dawned on Edward.

'The little fuckers'll have our catch if we don't get a

move on.' He moved quickly towards the wheelhouse. 'Full steam ahead, lads.'

Jesse was nudged awake at just before midnight. He'd been dreaming of swimming with the dolphins. One of them was swimming alongside him and he reached out to stroke its side. The dolphin turned to look at him and smiled. The smile grew wider and more familiar and Jesse became aware that this was not a dolphin but Loveday. Her red hair was streaming behind her as she swam above and below him, twisting and looping in the simple joy of being with him. Streams of air bubbles danced from her as she swam, always just a little bit faster and a little bit further out of reach. 'Come on, Jesse. Come on,' she spoke from beneath the waves, smiling up at him. 'Come on. Before you lose me.'

'Wake up, mate. It's your watch. Come on. Get up.' Jesse opened his eyes and slowly became aware of the familiar heat and smell of the *The Lobster Pot*'s cramped cabin. The tired face of Aaron, who'd just finished the first watch, loomed over Jesse's bunk. 'Wake up, you bugger. I need some kip before we start the trawl. Get out and let me in.' Jesse flipped back the blankets, lifted his head from the pillow and swung his legs onto the floor. Apart from taking off his boots, he hadn't bothered to get undressed before he slept so, apart from a quick rub of his eyes, there was no time wasted. Aaron was already crawling into the warm bunk and gave Jesse a shove as he reached for the blankets. 'Get out and let me 'ave me beauty sleep.'

'And what time would Sir like his wake-up call?' a yawning Jesse asked sarcastically.

'Bugger off.'

'As Sir wishes.' Jesse bent down and whispered in Aaron's ear, 'Would Sir like a goodnight kiss?' Aaron produced a two-fingered salute and turned over. He was already asleep by the time Jesse closed the door.

Jesse reported to his father in the wheelhouse. 'Any news?' he asked him.

'Aaron spotted some boats off to starboard about half a kilometre away. Spanish, by looks of it.'

'Shit.'

'Aye. Seeing more and more of 'em out here. Bastards are depleting our stocks and using up the quotas. Go and make us a brew, will you?'

Jesse gladly did; he was in need of one himself to wake him up. The next two hours went quietly and they saw no more foreign boats.

On the horizon he watched the occasional tanker as it headed off for who-knew-where with its lights shining in the gloom. The hypnotic throb of the engine and the rhythmic slosh of the sea water brought on an almost meditative state. He sipped his tea and thought about his future. The places he would go, the people he would meet, the money he would earn. Once he'd done all that, if Loveday were still free, he'd come back to her and marry her. Maybe Mickey would meet someone else; marry the first girl he got up the duff, like the soft bugger he was. Yes, that's what he'd do. He smiled, contented with his plan.

Gradually he grew aware of the engine note changing and the boat slowing. Edward leant out of the wheelhouse window and said, 'Get the lads up and prepare the trawl.'

*

Edward looked down from his vantage point in the wheelhouse and watched as the two derricks holding the beam trawls on either side of the boat swung out from the deck and over the water. He could hear the shackles and chain links of the trawl nets rattle as they went into the water. The rubber wheels at the bottom of the nets would allow the trawl to travel smoothly on the sea bed and gather their precious haul. He'd set the engine to a gentle towing pace of around two knots. He watched Jesse, in his yellow oilskin trousers and boots, working alongside the rest of the crew. He was a good lad. A born fisherman. He wished there was another way he could ensure the survival of Behenna's Boats, but these were dangerous times for the fishing industry – in Cornwall in particular – and no one could predict what was going to happen. The mood in the harbour was one of doom and gloom, and every week it seemed as if more boats were being decommissioned after desperate fishermen had taken the EU grant and allowed their boats to be broken up in the name of keeping the UK's quotas. It defied belief, and he knew that his own father would be turning in his grave to see the parlous state that things had reached.

But, if Behenna's Boats and Clovelly's Fisheries merged, his father's legacy would be secured, for now at least, and Jesse would have a future. But was he condemning Jesse to a life with that skinny Greer? He shook his head – it was the 1980s, for God's sake, not the 1580s and he had no power to make Jesse do anything. He felt a flash of anger at his own indecision. Damn it – why did all of this make him feel like he was selling Jesse to the bloody Clovellys?

'You'm a bleddy old fool,' he told himself. The envelope of cash was also preying on his mind. He could still give it back, couldn't he?

He'd get this haul home and tell Bryn Clovelly to get

stuffed, that's what he'd do. Relieved to have made a decision at last, he turned his concentration to the job in hand.

It was a good night. Each haul on both boats was teeming with good fish. Sole and Dover sole, mostly. These would sell like hot cakes to London chefs, who fed them to their overstuffed clients for a fortune.

Down in the hold, in the fish room, the crew were working in well-drilled harmony. The fish were sorted, gutted, washed and placed in boxes of ice ready to be landed for the market. The smell of fish guts was usurped by the gleam in every man's eye. This was a good haul, and they knew they would be well rewarded when they got it back to Trevay.

*

Bryn Clovelly caught the mooring rope that Edward threw over to him. 'I hear you had a good trip,' Bryn called, tying the rope to an ancient metal ring set into the harbour wall.

'Aye.'

'What have you got for me?'

'Some good Dover sole and plaice.'

'Not so much call for either at the moment,' shrugged Bryn, giving a hand to Edward as he stepped off the boat and onto the first dry land he'd seen for seven long days. Edward was not in the mood for haggling.

'Don't give me any of that old shit, Bryn. There's always call for Dover sole from those lah-di-bleddy-dah London types.'

Bryn shrugged again. 'I'll make my mind up when I see the catch.'

The crews of *The Lobster Pot* and *Our Mermaid* hoisted the fish boxes out of the hold and onto the quayside. There were plenty of them, and Edward could see Bryn's eyes darting over them and making calculations. He held out his hand to Edward and gave him a figure. 'Shake on it. You'll not get a better price.'

Bryn had not mentioned the sweetener and neither had Edward, but it hung there between the two men.

Edward was no fool and he held his nerve; he'd agreed to nothing as yet. Keeping his hands in his pockets, he started the negotiations.

At last a figure was agreed on and they shook hands, each man regarding the other steadily. 'I'd have given you more,' said Bryn wryly, 'if I knew that Clovelly and Behenna were destined to be one company.'

Edward pursed his lips and thought for a moment. 'If I knew that the deal was only between you and me and that it had nothing to do with your Greer and my Jesse, I might just say yes. Jesse is his own man, Bryn. He'll do as he likes.'

'You're a good negotiator, Edward, with strong powers of persuasion. You'll sway him.'

Edward said nothing, but he saw a glint in Bryn Clovelly's eyes – and it looked worryingly like victory.

'I need to know that Clovelly's has a future,' said Bryn. 'I need to know that I am passing it onto the next generation of my bloodline. I want my grandchildren to carry on the name of Clovelly. If Greer and Jesse were to marry, that would happen. But if you can't see your way to giving your son a helping hand in the world, then there are plenty of boat owners – with unmarried sons – on this coast who will.'

6

The postman, never knowingly uninterested in people's business, was enjoying his morning. It was that day in August when, around the country, exam results were dropping through letterboxes, anxious pupils waiting on the other side, braced for what news they might bring. The postman always took it upon himself to hand-deliver the envelopes in Trevay – whether he was conveying good news or bad, he wanted to pass it to the addressee personally.

Today he'd witnessed four people in tears (three of them mothers) and received two hugs of joy. No one had yet offered him a brew, and he could do with one. He was driving from the small modern housing estate at the top of Trevay, down the hill towards the old town and the sea. He pulled on the plastic sun visor to shield his eyes from the glare of the early morning light glinting off the water in the estuary. He turned right onto the posh road where the white stucco executive bungalows sat with their unfettered view of the river, the harbour and the open sea beyond. Each home was surrounded by a generous plot of land, either planted with palm trees, china-blue hydrangeas, large mounds of pampas grass or a selection of all three.

He stopped his van at Bryn and Elizabeth Clovelly's conspicuously expensive bungalow, unimaginatively named

Brybeth. He sorted through the bundles of post. He was looking for one with Greer Clovelly's name on it. He found an electricity bill, a Cellophaned edition of *Golfer's Monthly* and a letter from the DVLA (all addressed to Mr B. Clovelly), a postcard from Scotland (addressed to Mrs E. Clovelly) and finally a plain envelope addressed to Miss Greer Clovelly with a Truro postmark. He got out of his van and walked with dignified purpose towards their front door.

Greer was lying in bed listening to the radio. Kim Wilde was singing 'You Keep Me Hangin' On'. As usual Greer was thinking about Jesse. She didn't hear the doorbell ring or the bustle of her mother coming from the rear kitchen to the front door. But she did hear her mother calling her name.

'Greer. The postman has a delivery for you.'

'What is it?' she called back.

'Something you've been waiting for.' Her mother was using her singsong voice.

Greer sat up quickly. 'Is it my exam results?' She didn't listen for the answer as she leapt out of bed, grabbed her Snoopy dressing gown, a cherished Christmas present from Loveday, Mickey and more especially Jesse, and dashed down the hall to the open front door.

She thanked the postman and slid her thumb under the flap of the envelope. Her hands shook a little as she took out the letter inside and unfolded it.

The look on her face told the postman all he needed to know. He hung about briefly in case there was a congratulatory cup of coffee to be offered, but when it wasn't he set off, desperate to spread the news.

Bryn stood at the kitchen table and read the letter through again. 'You passed! Ten O levels. My God, Greer, I'm proud of you.'

'Thank you, Daddy.'

'Ten! That's ten more than you and me, eh, Elizabeth?'

'It certainly is. Oh, Greer, we are proud of you.'

'This means I can go to sixth-form college and do my art and design A level.'

Her father sat down opposite her and, pushing his reading glasses onto the top of his head, adopted a patient tone. 'How about getting a good secretarial qualification? Hmm? Secretaries are always needed. Good ones, anyway. They are the oil of the engine in any business. And when you get married, you won't need to work. You'll be looked after by your husband, while you look after your home and your family. Like Mum.'

Greer looked at her father in exasperation.

'I want to be an interior designer, and a wife and mum.'

'Well, I'd like to be a professional golfer, but we all have to be realistic.'

'I am being realistic. Lots of women have jobs these days and bring up a family.'

'You're talking about those lah-di-dah city types with posh nannies and banker husbands. It's different here.'

'And who says I can't be a lah-di-dah city type?' she countered mutinously.

Her father glowered at her. Greer chewed her lip and there was a strained silence. She knew it was pointless to provoke her father, but she consoled herself with the thought that he'd have to stop treating her like a child one day.

Her mother went to the bread bin and sliced two pieces of granary bread before popping them in the toaster. She was thinking of how best to back Greer without antagonising her dinosaur, chauvinist husband.

'I think she'd make a very good interior designer, Bryn,'

she said quietly. 'Look what she's done with her bedroom. And interior designers can charge the earth for their services. She has good taste, and people are prepared to pay for good taste.'

Bryn shook his head dismissively. 'A fool and his money are easily parted.'

*

'Mum!' Loveday was bouncing uncontrollably round the tiny stone-flagged hall of the cottage she shared with her mother. 'Mum! I got seven! And an A for maths!' She flung herself into her mother's arms and jigged them both up and down on the spot. 'Can you believe it, Mum?'

Beryl Carter managed to extricate herself from her daughter and, panting, said, 'Oh, my darlin' girl, you done so well! Your dad would be proud of you and no mistake. Seven! You'll be going to university at this rate.'

Loveday stopped jumping and pulled her mother into a giant bear hug. 'Mum, I'm not leaving you. I'm going to get a job and bring some good money into the house. I'm going to look after you properly. The way Dad would've.'

'No,' Beryl told her firmly, pulling herself out of Loveday's grip again. 'You'm not giving up your future for me. I can look after myself. You get out and see the world. You could be a doctor or . . . or . . . a professor or something.'

'Not with only seven O levels,' laughed Loveday. 'And what do I want to see the world for? I'm happy in Trevay with you and Greer and Jesse and Mickey.' A thought suddenly struck her. 'I'll ask if there's a job going at

Jesse's dad's or Greer's dad's. I'll work as hard as they like. Harder than anyone they know.'

*

Jan Behenna took the envelope from the odious postman and propped it against the teapot on the kitchen table. She prayed Jesse had done well. She wanted him to be happy and fulfil his dreams, whatever they were. If that meant emigrating to Australia, so be it. She'd barely left Cornwall herself, let alone the United Kingdom. If Jesse went to Australia, Jan could apply for a passport and fly on an aeroplane. She'd have the chance to see the Sydney Harbour Bridge. She sighed as she dreamt of Jesse's future. The one thing she didn't want for him was to be pushed into a marriage of convenience to Greer bloody Clovelly and her jumped-up family.

'Morning, Ma.' Grant came into the kitchen; he'd come home for the weekend and looked better than he had for ages. His hair was shaved close and neat and, despite being out last night drinking with his old Trevay mates, he was up bright and early this morning and looked none the worse for it. It was early days, but Jan hoped that life in the army was giving the boy the discipline he sorely needed. She fervently prayed that he'd turned a corner and was putting his old ways behind him.

Movement upstairs signalled that Jesse was awake. He and Edward had come home from a long fishing trip the night before and he was only now stirring, the smell of eggs and bacon wafting up from the kitchen as good as any alarm clock.

Jesse entered, naked except for his boxers. He hadn't known Grant was due a visit home, and the sight of his brother grinning at him from the breakfast table wasn't an entirely welcome one.

'All right, Grant.'

'Hello, little brother.' Grant ruffled Jesse's hair roughly and Jesse jerked his head away quickly.

'Get off.'

'Oo-er, someone's a bit touchy today. That Loveday Carter not let you 'ave a feel of 'er big tits yet?'

Jesse stiffened. Jan could sense the tension between them and tried to head it off at the pass.

'Grant, leave Jesse be, he doesn't need your teasing this morning. Here, Jesse.' She handed him the envelope.

Jesse could have done without Grant being there while he opened the letter. Whether the news was good or bad, his brother would find some way of goading or mocking him for it.

'Go on, son, open it,' his mother said encouragingly.

Jesse looked from her to the letter. Would any of the contents make the blindest bit of difference to his future? He doubted it. Behenna's Boats beckoned and there wasn't much in this letter could change that.

He ripped open the envelope and eyed the contents.

'Well?' Jan asked anxiously.

A grin spread across Jesse's face. Six O levels. He'd failed at geography and a couple of others, but all of the key subjects were there.

'I got six!'

'Oh, well done, son!' Jan embraced him warmly and Jesse tried not to squirm. 'Enough for college, are they?'

Grant sneered. 'College? What – our Jesse a college boy, with all those other little stuck-up snivellers.'

'Fuck off, Grant. Just because you were too busy getting in trouble and never got anything.'

'College is just for nancy boys too shit-scared to do a proper man's job.' He shovelled a mouthful of bacon and eggs into his mouth.

'Grant, stop winding Jesse up and, Jesse, mind your language at the table, please.'

'I'm going out on the boats with Dad,' Jesse announced, in a bid to put an end to both his mother and Grant's speculation.

'You don't have to decide now, Jesse,' his mother told him. 'Wait until after the summer and see how you feel then.'

'Anyway,' said Grant, talking through his mouthful of food, 'Dad's got Jesse's future all sewn up, ain't that right? You're going to be the family whore!' He let out a snort of laughter and continued to shovel in the last few forkfuls of his breakfast.

Jesse felt the urge to get as far and as fast away from Grant as possible. He stood and headed towards the kitchen door.

'But, Jesse, your breakfast?' his mother called after him.

'Not hungry, Mum.' Jesse leapt up the hallway stairs two at a time, still with Grant's spiteful laughter ringing in his ears.

*

Mickey wasn't surprised by his results. He sat up in bed as his mum brought the envelope to him with a mug of tea.

'B for technical drawing and physics, C for maths, English and history, and the rest I failed.'

His mum was thrilled, and said so. 'How many is that you got, then?'

'Five.'

'Five,' she said with relish. 'Five O levels. You'm bleddy Einstein, boy.'

The phone in the hall started to ring. Annie Chandler gave her son a last pat on the leg and went downstairs to answer it. Mickey listened, still looking at his results letter with satisfaction.

''Ello? . . .'Ello, Jesse. How did you do in your . . . Did you? Well done, boy . . . yes, Mickey's got his . . . five, yeah . . . shall I put 'im on? . . . Just a minute.' Mickey didn't need to be called; he was already coming down the stairs two at a time and took the phone receiver from his mother.

'What you got, Jesse?'

'Six. I can't believe it!'

'You bleddy swot.'

Jesse laughed. 'You did all right, didn't you? Five!'

'Yeah.' Mickey couldn't help smiling to himself. 'Yeah. Bleddy five O levels.'

*

'Mum. Please,' Greer was pleading. 'I know it's kind of Dad, but I don't want to go out to dinner tonight.'

'You're not going to the Golden Hind and that's an end to it.' Her mother's voice was muffled as she dragged the vacuum cleaner out of the understairs cupboard.

'But everyone's going and I want to be with my friends.'

'No.' Her mother unwound the cable from the back of the cleaner's handle. 'Your dad and I want to celebrate as a family.' She handed Greer the plug end. 'Put this in, would you?'

Greer did as she was told but wouldn't give up. 'Well, can we go out early? So that I can finish and get down to see everybody after we've eaten?'

But her mother had already drowned her out with the roar of the machine.

Greer went to her room seething with frustration. She'd been everything a daughter should be to her family. She was thoughtful, obedient, clever. She always looked her best and watched her figure. She never asked for anything. Well, she didn't need to; her parents gave her everything before she asked. And now, here she was, almost 17, and they wouldn't let her go out on the most important night of her life.

Loveday had phoned an hour ago and told her her results. Greer was pleased for her, but even happier that she had done better. Loveday had asked her to come down to Figgotty's – a locals' beach. No holiday-maker ventured there; it had such a steep descent that no buggy or grandma would be able to get down to it or, if they did, up from it again.

'We're taking some pasties,' Loveday had told her.

'Who's we?' Greer had asked.

'About eight of us.'

'Is Jesse going?' Greer had hated herself for asking, so she added hastily, 'And Mickey?'

'Course they are. It was Jesse's idea. He told me to call you.'

'Did he?' Greer hugged herself. 'Hang on, I'll just ask Mum.' A few moments later she was back on the line, almost in tears. 'My mum won't let me. She wants me to go into Truro with her.'

'Never mind.' Loveday had suddenly felt sorry for her friend. 'Maybe you can come tonight?' she'd suggested.

'The pub's doing an "exam result special" night. There's a hog roast in the beer garden and a DJ.'

But now Greer's mum had categorically said no.

*

'*Buona sera*, Signor Clovelly.' Antonio, chef proprietor of the eponymously named Italian restaurant greeted Bryn with his arms wide and a dusting of pizza flour on his cheek.

'Good to see you, Antonio. How's the golf?' Bryn and Antonio were cronies both at the golf club and in the local Masonic Lodge.

Antonio was taking Elizabeth's wrap from her shoulders and replied in his heavily accented English, 'I am playing offa sixteen.' He shrugged. 'But if I had more time, I could be closer to you. What you playing offa now?'

'Twelve.'

'Twelve? My God, you musta never be at work? *Sì?*'

The two men laughed and then Antonio saw Greer standing hunched and miserable in the doorway. He stepped towards her, holding his arms out wide again. 'Look at leetle Greer! All-a grown up.' He inclined his head to one side and brought his hands together as if in prayer. 'But you are a beautiful young woman now!'

Elizabeth beamed with pride and said, 'She got her exam results today. She did very well, so we're here to celebrate.'

'Why she not look so happy?' asked Antonio, staring at Greer as if it was he who had upset her.

'I am happy,' Greer said, trying to smile, but desperately wishing that Antonio would leave her alone.

'Thank God!' Antonio boomed. 'And now, Antonio make you even more happy with his food.' He walked them to a pretty table overlooking the inner harbour, where they could watch the visiting yachts bob on their hired moorings. The tide was high that night and Greer could see it lapping almost to the top of the wall. She heard laughter from the pavement and saw several schoolfriends walking towards the Golden Hind . . . and the party she wasn't allowed to go to.

'Well, this is nice,' Bryn smiled, once Antonio had lit the red candle in the centre of the table and left them to get drinks and menus.

'Isn't it?' smiled Elizabeth. Greer said nothing. Knowing that all of her friends were out enjoying themselves – and she was stuck here – was like a slow death.

'What's the matter with you?' asked her father.

Greer put on a bright, tight little smile. 'Nothing.'

Elizabeth turned to Bryn and explained. 'There's a do at the pub. Pete's doing a hog roast and a disco for the school-leavers. Her friends are celebrating over there.' Bryn turned his head and looked over at the Golden Hind. 'That sounds fun. Why aren't you invited, Greer?'

'I was, but Mum said I couldn't go as we're having a family dinner, so . . .' Greer shrugged and looked at her hands, trying not to cry.

Bryn winked at Elizabeth. 'You can go over after we've eaten.'

Greer immediately brightened. 'Can I?'

'Of course you can. I like a bit of a bop.'

Greer's face dropped. 'You're coming?' She couldn't think what was worse. Not being allowed to go, or going but being saddled with her parents, who were bound to embarrass her.

'Yeah. Me and your mum haven't had a night out for ages.' Bryn put his hand on top of Elizabeth's, which was resting on the table. He turned to her. 'We'll show the youngsters some of our jive moves.'

Elizabeth, who had been looking forward to an early night with her new Jackie Collins book, hid her dismay. 'What a lovely idea.'

'Yes,' murmured Greer. 'Lovely idea.' Really just wishing that the ground would open and swallow her parents up.

7

The air in the beer garden was heavy with the smoke of the hog roast. Long chains of coloured lights were swung in a zigzag from fence to wall and back again, above the dusty grass. The DJ Ricky and 'his Roadshow from Liskeard', was playing 'Walk Like an Egyptian' and blowing bubbles over a couple of girls who were vying for his attention. The centre of the garden was a heaving mass of dancing, sweating teens.

Greer arrived and stood on the periphery. She was on her own. Her mother had nipped to the Ladies and her father was at the bar chatting. Loveday spotted her and came bowling over, wreathed in smiles. 'You made it! How did you manage it?'

Greer briefly explained and Loveday handed her a glass of punch. 'My mum's here too, see.' Loveday pointed over to the bar area where her mum was laughing and joking loudly over a large vodka and orange with a group of fishermen and their women. Her cheeks were flushed, and when Loveday waved over to her, she blew her daughter an ostentatious kiss. Greer couldn't understand why Loveday wasn't more embarrassed by her mother. She dressed in clothes more appropriate for a girl half her age; her own mother would have said that she was mutton dressed as lamb.

'Here, try this. It's mostly fruit juice, with some sort of wine in it.'

Greer took a sip. It seemed innocuous enough. 'I Wanna Dance with Somebody' was playing now. 'I love Whitney!' Loveday shouted above the noise. 'Come on, Greer. Let's dance.' Greer was not the dancing type but she took another mouthful of punch and, looking around for Jesse, reluctantly followed Loveday into the throng.

Jesse was in the pub kitchen with Mickey, making another industrial-sized bowl of punch. The landlord, Pete, told them to help themselves to the cartons of fruit juice that he'd put into the huge fridge, and to add half a bottle of Lambrusco to each batch. 'No more, mind! I don't want to lose my licence.'

Mickey and Jesse had assured him they wouldn't overdo it but, as soon as they were on their own, Mickey stepped outside the kitchen door and fetched the bottle of vodka he'd hidden in the hedge and he and Jesse took a swig each from it before pouring a good slug into the punch. 'Well, Pete never said nothing about vodka, did he?'

'No,' agreed Jesse, assiduously measuring only half a bottle of Lambrusco into the deep container. The two boys took another mouthful of vodka each before hiding the bottle back under the hedge.

*

Loveday was hot. The music was getting faster and louder and she was getting thirsty. She spotted the boys lugging the punch tureen towards a trestle table. 'Want a drink, Greer?' she shouted.

Greer nodded and gently dabbed at her forehead with

the back of her hand. She was glad to stop, and gladder still to see Jesse.

Mickey saw the girls approaching and, emboldened by the vodka, nudged Jesse and slurred, 'I'm going to make sure I give Loveday a big one.'

Jesse giggled. 'You ain't got a big one.'

Mickey snorted with laughter, 'I don't mean give her my big one.' He creased over with hysteria.

'Well, I'll help you out and give her my big one if you like,' hooted Jesse.

Mickey stopped laughing and squared up to his friend. 'What did you say?'

Jesse was shocked that he'd said anything at all. The drink was muddling his thinking, but thoughts of Loveday were always bubbling just beneath the surface these days.

'It was a joke. Just a joke. That's all.' He put his hands up in surrender. 'Sorry, mate.'

Mickey looked stony faced. 'Loveday means the world to me and one day I'll marry her, so no more talking that way about her. She's my girl, you got that?'

For a brief moment, Jesse wanted to push back at Mickey, to ask him who said that Loveday was his girl. Why should he have her?

Mickey stood his ground, staring hard into Jesse's eyes. Jesse saw the fierce possession that burned there and instead of challenging Mickey, the words that came from his mouth were ones of appeasement.

'Of course, mate. I'm so sorry. I just . . . I don't know . . . must be the booze.'

Then suddenly Mickey began to giggle again. 'Yours is just a little chipolata anyway.' Jesse, relieved, started to laugh too.

'Oh, yeah?' said Loveday as she arrived at the table. 'What you two bollock-heads laughing at?'

The boys gave each other sidelong glances and started giggling again.

Loveday shook her head, dismissing their silliness. 'Honest, Greer, how these two ever managed to get any O levels is beyond me. Bleddy idiots.' She reached for the industrial catering ladle lying in a sticky pool on the paper tablecloth and dipped it into the punch.

'Give it a good stir, Loveday,' hiccuped Mickey, putting his arm round her fleshy waist and giving it a squeeze. 'All the good stuff is at the bottom.' She looked at him suspiciously. ''Ave you been drinking?'

'No.'

She turned to Jesse. 'Has he?'

Jesse attempted to focus his eyes on Loveday. 'No.'

Loveday shook Mickey's arm off her and leant forward to sniff his breath. 'I can smell alcohol.'

Mickey was affronted. 'You can't smell vodka, 'tis a well-known fact.'

She opened her eyes in disbelief. 'Yes you can, and where the bleddy hell did you get vodka?'

Jesse owned up. 'Grant got us two litre bottles to celebrate. He's home for the weekend.'

'Your Grant is trouble – and now he's going to get you into trouble.' She stood with her hands on her hips, frowning at both boys. 'Where is he now?'

Greer, who'd been listening to all of this, looked around the garden and pointed to Grant, who was dancing with a couple of girls. He was in a skintight T-shirt which enhanced his muscular shoulders and tattooed pecs. The girls looked very pleased with themselves for having netted the handsomest man at the party. DJ Ricky was not looking happy – it looked as if he'd be going home alone . . . again. 'He's over there,' Greer said.

Jesse was unimpressed. 'Janine and Heather? Is that the best he can do? Anyone can pull them.'

Grant was now bumping and grinding his hips, bum and crotch towards the girls as 'Le Freak' by Chic was blaring out over the speakers. The girls willingly followed his moves.

Loveday leaned towards Jesse's ear and – above the noise – managed to ask him to dance with her.

'No thanks,' he answered, pouring himself another glass of punch. 'Not in the mood.'

'What are you in the mood for?' she asked, putting her hand on his chest. She was wearing a low-cut baby-pink vest and the skimpiest of denim skirts. Her hair was tied in a side ponytail with a pink scrunchie, and her lips were parted seductively as she gazed up at Jesse.

He felt the warmth of her skin through his shirt and wanted more than anything to drop his mouth to hers and kiss her deeply. They were so close, with barely a hair's breadth between them; all he'd have to do would be to lean in . . . but all at once Jesse became aware of Mickey standing right next to them. He took a step back, knocking the table as he did so. Loveday let her hand drop back by her side.

'I'll dance with you, Loveday,' grinned Mickey. He grabbed her elbow, guiding her erratically onto the dance floor as she looked disappointedly over her shoulder at Jesse.

He and Greer were left to watch as Mickey and Loveday were swallowed by the crowd.

'Want another drink, Greer?' asked Jesse.

Greer drank very little, but the last glass of punch had

left her feeling a little woolly around the edges, and she was enjoying the sensation. 'Yes, please.' She handed her empty glass to him. Carefully he dipped the ladle into the bowl and filled their glasses to the brim.

'Cheers, Big Ears,' Greer surprised herself by saying; the punch was definitely kicking in.

'Cheers, Greers,' he replied solemnly.

They clinked and drank.

'Why aren't you dancing?' he asked.

'No one's asked me. Except Loveday, and she doesn't count.'

'Loveday's a good girl,' Jesse said quietly.

'Mickey thinks so.'

Jesse pulled his mouth down at the corners. 'Yeah.'

'They're well suited, don't you think?'

'I s'pose.'

Greer, powered by the warmth of vodka, elucidated. 'I mean they're two of a kind. Loveday has no ambition to leave Trevay. Mickey's future is mapped out for him on the boats. Whereas you and I . . .' She took a step closer to him. 'We're lucky. We come from families who have made something of themselves.'

Jesse was now feeling very drunk but also – and this surprised him – he suddenly felt attracted to Greer. She wasn't sexy and exuberant like Loveday, but her shiny, blunt-cut bob and neat, even teeth were fascinating him. He wasn't sure what she was saying exactly, but whatever it was, she was saying it very sweetly.

'You're all right really, aren't you, Greer?' he managed. 'I don't think you're a snob. Like some of them say. You're just a bit different. That's all. Want a top-up?'

Greer frowned slightly. 'Yes, please, and I'm not a snob. Who said that?'

'Janine and Heather.'

Greer drank some more punch and enjoyed its zing as it ran down her throat and hit her stomach. 'They are a pair of bitches.' She put her glass down. 'I'm going to sort them out.' She took a step forward but her knees sank a little. Jesse caught her. 'No you don't.' He pulled her closer to him. 'You're staying with me.' Her slender frame felt surprisingly good – firm, but there was a softness there too, not soft like Loveday, but . . . He felt a shot of desire stir in his groin.

She relaxed into his arms and raised her face to his. She giggled. 'You've got strong arms, Jesse Behenna.'

He demonstrated his strength by pulling her closer to him. 'You'd better believe it.'

She snuggled into his arms. She could feel his warm breath on her hair as he rested his cheek on the top of her head. She closed her eyes and allowed herself to melt into him, to feel the heat of his body against hers. Greer felt a heady thrill at being in Jesse's arms. This was it. This was their moment.

The pounding beat of Jackie Wilson giving his all to 'Reet Petite' broke through the moment as Greer heard a familiar voice.

'Scuse us, you two,' said her father. 'Your mum and I are going to show you young 'uns some real dancing.' Her parents pushed past them and cleared a space on the dance floor before going into an incredible jive routine.

Bryn spun Elizabeth under his arm and towards him, then spun her out and away from him. They were good. They rocked back on their heels at arms' length and pinged back together with their arms round each other. Pushing Elizabeth a little away from him, Bryn caught her by the waist and bounced her high above his head then swept her down and between his legs. Elizabeth had enjoyed two large gin and tonics and was unembarrassed as her skirt slid up her thighs to reveal comfy mum knickers.

Greer was mortified. The spell was broken and she extricated herself from the bliss of Jesse's embrace to take in the full horrific embarrassment of her parents. Couldn't they see how ridiculous they looked? How could they do this to her? In front of all her friends. On tonight of all nights. She turned and ran to the Ladies where the combination of alcohol, her yearning for Jesse and the grimness of her parents' behaviour made her vomit violently.

After a while, she felt a bit better. She closed the loo lid and flushed, then sat down on the seat and dabbed at her perspiring face with a wad of loo paper. She had never had so much to drink. She stayed put, with her head in her hands, praying that the room would just slow down for a moment.

A timid knock on the cubicle door made her jolt.

'Is anyone in there?' It was Loveday's mother.

Greer got to her feet and flushed the loo again to make it look as if she hadn't been sitting there trying to sober up. She opened the door and Mrs Carter smiled kindly at her.

'You all right?' she asked.

'Fine, Mrs Carter. Thank you.'

'I saw you run in here and wondered if you might like a glass of water or something, darling?'

Greer wondered how much Mrs Carter had seen and understood.

'No, thank you. I'm fine, really.'

'That's good.' Mrs Carter made no move to go into the cubicle. Instead she put her hand comfortingly on Greer's shoulder and leant in closer. She smelt of alcohol mixed with Dior Poison.

'Seeing your mam and dad dancing like that has taken me back.' She shifted unsteadily and her eyes seemed glazed over.

Greer wanted to sit down or go home or both, but this wretched woman wouldn't leave her alone. She made an attempt at good manners. 'Taken you back to when?'

'When we was all at school together. Your dad was so handsome. All we girls wanted to dance with him. He's still got it, hasn't he? I haven't seen him dance like that since he married your mum.' Mrs Carter had a faraway look in her eye that Greer didn't like.

'He used to dance like that with me, you know.'

Greer was feeling queasy again. 'What do you mean?'

'He and I went out with each other for a little while, but your mum took dancing lessons and before long they were a couple on the dance floor . . .' Mrs Carter sighed again. 'And in life.'

Beads of sweat popped out on Greer's top lip and forehead. She didn't want to hear any more. 'Excuse me, Mrs Carter, but I must get some fresh air.' She made a dash for the door and just heard Mrs Carter's imploring, 'Don't tell Loveday, will you? She thinks her dad was my one and only boyfriend.'

God, what was going on with these adults? What kind of role models were they? She slipped through the pub bar and out to the front where she found an empty bench tucked into the shadows. She breathed the cool night air. It was tinged with the familiar smell of salt, seaweed, diesel and fish and chips. She took stock of her evening.

Her parents were some kind of dancing nuts, and her best friend's mother had gone out with her dad. She didn't want to imagine how intimate they might or might not have been. Her world seemed to have turned upside down. Then she thought of Jesse and the way he had held her tonight. She was sure she'd seen a flicker of real emotion in his eye. Until her parents had shown themselves up. What would he think of her now? She buried her face in her hands for the second time that evening.

After a while she sensed that she wasn't alone. Someone sat on the bench next to her and the wooden slats gave way a little, making her bounce slightly.

'All right, are you, Greer?' asked Jesse.

She stayed hunched but took her hands from her face. 'Yes.'

'Loveday's mum's worried about you. She thought you might not be feeling well.'

'I'm fine.'

'Sure?'

'Sure.'

Jesse stretched his long legs out in front of him and stretched his arms over his head. She turned to look at him. He was staring at the stars. She drank in his wonderful profile. His always tousled blond hair was carelessly sticking out in all directions. His eyebrows framed his honest sea-green eyes. His lashes were fair but long and his nose straight and strong. His lips, slightly parted, were on the thin side but they framed his teeth perfectly.

He spoke. 'Satellite. Look.' She tilted her head up and followed his pointing finger. Sure enough, across the heavens a bright light was moving at speed. 'I wanted to be an astronaut when I was young.'

She smiled. 'You are young.'

Now he turned those sea-green eyes to her. 'Greer, I've got six O levels and I'm leaving school to work with my dad. I'm already old.'

'You're only sixteen. You can go to college, get some more qualifications.'

'That's for people like you. You want to go to college, don't you?'

'Art school. But my dad wants me to do a secretarial course.'

'Sensible.'

'I don't want sensible. I want to be an interior designer. To make beautiful houses for beautiful people, and . . .' She looked down at her feet in their pretty pink suede court shoes, 'and I want to be married and have children.'

Jesse lifted his arm and put it round her shoulders, aware of what he was doing, thinking again of her smooth skin and her firm thighs. He couldn't seem to stop himself: the mix of alcohol, the heat of the pub and his raging hormones had put his body and his mind at odds with each other. 'Do you now? And who have you got your eye on?'

It was now or never, under the starry night sky, and still slightly drunk she looked him full in the eye and breathed, 'You.'

His father's words – *you'd do a lot worse than to marry that girl* – drifted through Jesse's alcoholic haze.

Greer felt his arm lift a little away from her and he was silent for a moment before he started to laugh. Now his arm was back by his side, searching for his other arm to cross defensively over his chest, his heart.

'You're a funny one when you're drunk, aren't you?' He stood up. 'Let's go back. The others will be wondering where we are. We don't want to start any rumours, do we?'

She stayed where she was, horrified and ashamed that she'd played her hand so openly.

'I'll join you in a minute.'

He looked down at her and held out a large hand. 'Come on, you. We all say silly things when we're pissed. I promise not to tell. Now take my hand and let's go back.'

*

The party had degenerated into several couples clinging to each other in a slow dance. Around the edges sat groups of people chatting or snogging. The fire pit for the hog roast had died down to a mellow glow and the hog itself was just a charred carcass. Greer glanced around to find her parents. She saw them through a window sitting inside in the bar.

Her feeling of relief was swiftly abated when a breathless Loveday ran up to them in distress.

'Jesse, your brother's challenged Ricky the DJ to an arm-wrestling match. He's ever so drunk and I'm frightened he's going to hurt him.'

'Oh shit,' said Jesse, and he sprinted off into the pub.

A crowd had gathered around Grant and Ricky. Ricky was a big lad with strong arms and a beer belly, and he was holding his own. Grant's tattooed muscles, though, were as dense and hard as granite. He was staring into the DJ's pudgy face and through bared teeth said, 'Come on, fat boy. You can do better than this, can't you?'

Ricky dug deep and strengthened his grip. 'You don't scare me, soldier boy. I was in the Falklands. I've killed people.'

'Yeah?' grimaced Grant, pushing his muscles till they quivered. 'Well, you're a tub of lard now, aren't you?'

There was a sudden parting of the crowd as Mickey and Jesse pushed through. Their arrival momentarily broke Grant's concentration and Ricky, seeing his chance, slammed Grant's arm down. The crowd cheered but quickly quietened as they saw Grant smash his fist into Ricky's face. There was the sickening sound of crunching bone and a splatter of blood arced from the DJ's nose across the crowd.

Someone must have dialled 999 because within minutes two police cars and an ambulance had arrived, their sirens and blue lights strobing the peace of the harbour.

A few of the more drunken and troublesome teens lingered on the harbour, looking for trouble, before they were herded away by the police; the party quickly broke up, with only the hardened rubberneckers lingering. Ricky the DJ was put in the ambulance with a police officer and driven off to Truro and Treliske Hospital.

Grant was handcuffed after attempting to resist arrest and was being questioned in the bar. It wasn't long before a Royal Marines Police vehicle arrived and he was locked in the back for the return journey to his Plymouth barracks. Jesse could only watch helplessly as Grant was driven away. Thanks to him, the night had ended on a downer and all the excitement and expectation that had been flowing through the crowd had now drained away, just like the remains of the punch that Pete was pouring down the sink.

Jesse was left with the difficult of job of going home to tell his parents that Grant was, once again, in trouble.

8

1989

Greer stepped off the train at Bodmin and walked out to the pavement, where cars were parking ready to collect her fellow travellers. She shielded her eyes against the dazzling June sunshine and stood her suitcase and two canvas 'overspill' bags at her feet, face turned to the sun, inhaling the scent of clean Cornish air.

'Greer darling!' Her mother's voice carried on the breeze. Elizabeth was stepping half in and half out of the passenger seat of Bryn's latest car. Her left leg was still in the footwell, her right on the tarmac, and both hands holding onto the top of the open car door. She was beaming and waving frantically.

Greer could see her father pushing his sunglasses to the top of his head and then opening the heavy door of the big BMW. He got out and walked to the boot. He opened it and then strolled towards her, giving Greer a chance to admire how fit and tanned and successful he looked. 'Darling, welcome home.' He kissed her and picked up the suitcase and one of the canvas bags. 'You can manage that one, can't you?' He nodded his head to the remaining bag.

'I've managed all of them from London, Dad.'

'Hope you haven't gone all women's lib on us?' He laughed.

Greer was thinking that her dad was being as embarrassing as usual and was struggling to come up with a suitable retort when her mother bustled up. 'Darling Greer. You look so lovely! So slim in that dress. But what have you done with your hair?'

Greer's free hand flew to the back of her neck where perfect feathers of hair lay short. 'I got bored with the bob.'

'But it was a classic cut. You've had it since you were three.'

'Exactly. I'm eighteen years old. I needed a change.'

Her mother sniffed disapprovingly before saying, 'Never mind. It will grow.'

Her father loaded her bags into the boot and Greer stepped into the back seat. As with all her father's cars it was the best he could afford. Top of the range, walnut, soft leather and deep-pile carpet.

'I like your new car, Dad.'

'Only picked it up two days ago. Wanted to collect you in style.' He put the gearstick into drive mode and pulled away from the kerb. Her mother craned round to chat to her daughter.

'Congratulations on your typing speed and shorthand. And how you've mastered the word processor, I've no idea. Your father has two in the office. The girls were showing them to me but it's all so complicated.' Her mother turned back to face the road.

'Not when you know how, Mum.' Greer was looking out of the window, enjoying the sights she hadn't seen for two long years. The valley to her right held woodland and fields. To her left were the steep lanes leading to Lanhydrock House.

'There's a job for a secretary in the office at the

moment.' Her father caught her gaze in the rear-view mirror. 'Tessa's going off on maternity leave in a couple of weeks. She says she'll be back, but she won't. Women don't come back once they've started a family. But I have to pay her while she's away. It's a government con.'

Greer tried to let her father's misogynistic stream flow over her. She had got what she'd wanted. She'd done a two-year course in interior design at a smart private college in Surrey, and, to keep her father happy, studied for a secretarial course in London during the holidays. That had left her no time to return to Cornwall while she focused on gaining her qualifications, but it meant she'd achieved them as quickly as possible.

'I got a distinction in my design course.'

There was a tight silence from the front seats.

'Good,' her mother finally said.

Greer persevered. 'Actually, I have a surprise for you.'

Silence.

'I got Student of the Year.'

She saw her father raise his eyebrows in a look that said, 'What's the bloody use of that?' before her mother managed: 'That's nice.'

Greer said nothing more. She knew that she'd done extremely well, despite their dismissive attitude. They could ignore it if they liked, but Greer had worked hard for that distinction and it wouldn't go to waste, no matter what her father might think. She continued to look out of the window, content to watch the familiar landmarks slide by. Trelawney Garden Centre, the bridge over the river at Wadebridge, and the Royal Cornwall Showground. They continued along the dramatic and romantically named Atlantic Highway until the first sign to Trevay came into view.

'Nearly home now, Greer.' Her mum turned back to smile at her.

Greer's heart was starting to pound and butterflies were battering away inside her stomach. Nearly home. Nearly. She opened her mouth and asked the question she'd been burning to ask since she got off the train. 'How's Jesse?'

*

Loveday was forking a chip into her mouth and lapping up everything Greer was telling her about her two years up country. The girls had stayed in touch with occasional letters and postcards, but Greer hadn't come home for the entire two years that she'd been away at college. She had been determined to get her head down and finish the course as soon as she possibly could. She'd asked Loveday to come and see her, in the hope that Mickey and Jesse might tag along too, but Loveday never seemed to have enough money or time to make what she appeared to regard as an epic journey.

Greer had vaguely entertained the thought of staying on, but when she'd tried to find a position in one of the interior design companies up there, she never seemed to have the right connections. Despite the Clovelly name meaning something in Trevay, she had quickly become aware it stood for nothing in Guildford or Woking. The Surrey set she'd mixed with had all been very sophisticated and well-to-do; the girls who had found positions all had posh dads with serious connections. Greer realised she missed that feeling of being part of an influential and wealthy family, getting what she wanted when she wanted; being envied by people around her for her style and wealth. In short, she missed being in Trevay.

'I shared a flat with another girl, Laura, who was on the same design course. You should have seen how we did the place up! We painted the kitchen warm terracotta and hung garlands of fresh hops around the top of the wall units. Our landlord had never seen anything like it. He said he'd get twice the rent for it now. Laura taught me how to make curtains and we bought yards and yards of ticking fabric in the market and made the longest drapes you've ever seen. Really theatrical with swags and tie-backs.'

'What's a tie-back?'

Greer got out a little notebook which held her sketches for ideas and showed it to her friend. It was about time Trevay had its own interior designer and Greer knew her mother had lots of wealthy friends who would jump at the chance to have their houses improved by someone with her talents and training.

'Bleddy hell. No wonder you got Top Student,' Loveday said with real wonder. 'I bet the boys loved you.'

Greer put the notebook back in her bag. 'It was a virtually all-girl course and the boys we did have were gay.'

Loveday's eyes virtually popped out of her head. 'Gay? You mean like they had boyfriends?'

'Yes. Don't be so parochial.' Greer frowned, taking a sip of her coffee. There had been a few casual boyfriends and nights out, but nothing serious, and there was no one who could give her the same thrill of excitement as she felt when she thought about Jesse. 'Do you want my biscuit?' She pushed her saucer with its small round of shortbread on it towards Loveday.

Loveday had finished her fish and chips and shook her head. 'No, thank you, I'm on a diet.'

'Are you?' Greer said archly. 'I thought Mickey liked you just the way you are.'

'Mickey's just Mickey. There's never going to be anything between him and me.'

'Is he seeing someone else?'

Loveday absentmindedly picked up the shortbread biscuit and popped it in her mouth. 'I know he wants to go out with me but, as I keep saying no, Jesse and he are playing the field. Every spare minute they're in Newquay or St Ives, doing the clubs, picking up girls. We don't hang out like we used to.'

Greer clutched her coffee cup and hoped that Loveday didn't notice her hand shaking at the mention of Jesse.

'Is he seeing anyone special?'

'No, they're just being idiots.' Loveday hoped that Greer didn't see how much it hurt to know that Jesse had become a bit of a wanker, 'making hay while the sun shone', as he called it. That was one way of making it sound nicer than it was, she thought darkly.

Both girls stared out of the window of the little café in one of Trevay's side streets. Across the road, in the window of the dress shop, Doreen's, a woman was dressing a dummy, pulling up the elasticated waist of a pair of white trousers, and adding a short-sleeved nautical T-shirt.

'Talk of the bleddy devil.' Loveday banged on the glass café window. 'Jesse!' she shouted in a voice that carried around the restaurant, out of the open door and onto the pavement.

Greer saw him as he looked around, trying to work out who was calling him and from where.

'In here!' Loveday was banging and shouting until he

saw her. He gave a small wave but kept walking. 'Greer's home, look!' she shouted again, embarrassing Greer and eliciting tuts from customers who merely wanted to eat their lunch in peace. Loveday pushed her chair back with a screech and ran out onto the pavement, physically stopping Jesse. Greer couldn't bear to watch in case Jesse shrugged and walked on. She'd seen him only twice, briefly, since the night of the hog roast, and whenever she thought about how she'd virtually proposed to him a cold river of shame poured over her.

In spite of herself, she took a quick glance through the window and out to the scene on the pavement. Oh my God, he was walking towards the café with Loveday grinning and chatting by his side.

He came in and walked up to her table. He looked taller; his muscles had filled out and he was a ton more handsome, if that were possible. Suntanned, with a chiselled jaw and his unruly blond hair just a little longer, he stood over her, smiling, making her insides do funny things.

'Hello, Greer. It's been a long time. I wouldn't have recognised you with your short hair.'

Again her hand flew to her head. 'Do you like it?' Oh God, what kind of question was that?

He appraised her steadily before saying, 'It's all right. Do you girls want a cup of tea?'

'I'd like a milkshake,' Loveday announced, noisily pulling her chair back up to the table.

'Flavour?'

'Banana.'

'Right. You, Greer?'

'No, thank you.'

'You'm skin and bone, maid.'

Greer looked at her narrow thighs in their tight black jeans. 'Oh, OK. I'll have another coffee. Thanks.'

Jesse laughed and showed his good teeth. 'Black no sugar?'

Greer hated him laughing at her. 'White coffee with sugar,' she said defiantly, even though he'd been right in the first place.

The waitress brought the order to the table.

'So, how have you been?' Greer asked stiffly.

'Brilliant,' said Jesse. 'I'm on the boats full time now. Hard work, but the pay is good. I've bought a car.'

'Gosh. How grown-up.' Greer was seething with jealousy. A car meant he could pick up as many girls as he wanted. 'What sort?'

'Ford Capri. I'm doin' it up right now. Want to come and see it?'

'Maybe.'

'Well, don't if you don't want to.' He looked rather crestfallen. 'I expect you saw plenty of nice cars up country.'

'No, I would,' she said quickly, afraid of losing this chance to be with him. 'I'd love to. Where is it?'

'Up the sheds.' He spooned three sugars into his tan-coloured mug of tea. 'What's new with you then, Greer? Been a long time since we clapped eyes on you. How was it at college?'

'It was good. Quite fun.'

'Only got Student of the Decade and all her secretarial stuff too,' interjected Loveday, proudly.

Jesse raised a blond eyebrow appraisingly and nodded slowly. 'Right, well, when I get my house I might let you do it up for me, then.' He looked at her with a smile playing around his lips.

Greer felt he was trying to bait her. And was irritated by his attitude. 'I'm very expensive.'

He smirked. 'Oh, really? How much?'

'It would depend on what you wanted.'

Loveday jumped in. 'Tell him about the curtains.'

'Well, I could do a set of curtains at about three hundred a window.'

He roared with laughter. 'No. How much really?'

'Three hundred.'

'Straight up?' He looked amazed.

'Or flounced and tied back,' joked Loveday.

Her joke flew over his head and he looked at Greer with fresh interest. 'Three hundred? Fools and their money are easily parted!' He drained his tea, pushed his chair back and stood up. 'Anyway, I gotta go back to work. Dad wants me.' He walked to the door. Greer refused to turn and watch him. At the last moment he said, 'Mick and me will be up at the sheds about half six if you want to see my car.' And he left.

*

Mickey looked the same but even taller, if that were possible. He gave her a huge bear hug.

'Greer, you've gone all posh an' that, 'aven't you?'

Greer smiled. 'Have I?'

'Yeah, look at you. London clothes and haircut and that.'

Greer looked down at her jumpsuit with its padded shoulders and wide belt and supposed that she was rather more on trend than the rest of Trevay. 'Oh, it's only Chelsea Girl.'

Loveday had already quizzed her friend on her new

wardrobe and was planning a trip to Plymouth to update her own clothes. 'Don't she look good? And what about her hair?'

Mickey took in the urchin cut but said nothing other than: 'It's good to see you. I thought you'd dumped your old mates.'

The thing was, once Greer had left Trevay, she hadn't really missed her friends that much; there was too much going on and the thought of going back home and being treated as a kid by her father was unappealing. Besides, her mother loved the shopping in Guildford, and even at Christmas they'd been quite happy to come and have their Christmas lunch at a posh hotel in Surrey. She smiled. 'I know I haven't been home for two years but I was busy, and Mum came up to see me all the time. She kept me up to date with all the Trevay news, though.'

Jesse walked over to the Behenna's Boats shed and pulled at the big doors. ''Ave a look to this beauty.' The doors opened and behind them in the workshop was Jesse's Ford Capri. Bright blue with the Cornish flag painted on the roof.

'Wow!' Greer said sarcastically. 'Who did the paint-work?'

'Me and Dad.'

'It's lovely.'

'Want a ride?'

Greer caught her breath. The thought of sitting next to Jesse after two years of dreaming about him made her giddy. She managed to say, 'Sure.'

'Right,' said Jesse. 'You two girls hop in the back and we'll all go for a ride.'

The roar and rumble of the throaty engine bounced

off the shed walls. Greer and Loveday, squished into the back, were forced backwards as Jesse put his foot to the floor and shot the little car out of the shed and off down the lane towards the harbour.

*

'Cheers, Edward.'

'Cheers, Bryn.' The two men clinked their glasses of ale at the pub and supped contemplatively for a moment before Bryn spoke.

'My Greer's back from up country today. Got her exams and 'ome for good now.'

'She done well up there. I 'eard from Jan. What she planning on doing now?' Edward asked cautiously.

Edward knew what Bryn was likely to say, but there was still a part of him that hoped Greer Clovelly would decide that the bright lights of Surrey had more to offer her than her home town of Trevay.

Edward Behenna and Bryn Clovelly eyed each other along the bar of the pub.

'Like I said, she'll be 'ome for good now, be ready to settle down and start a family, I reckon.'

'What about her qualifications? She'll want to put them to good use, won't she?'

Bryn blew out a cloud of smoke dismissively and gave a firm shake of his head. 'That decorating course is just a Mickey Mouse qualification. Kept 'er happy for a couple of years and she got to see a bit of life, but it's kids and family that will be the making of her.'

Edward stroked his chin thoughtfully. 'She might 'ave ideas of her own.'

'All she wants is to marry your Jesse, and that's what

I want for her as well. Don't you think it's time you told 'im about our little arrangement?'

Edward had been dreading this moment. He and Bryn had put the final touches of their merger together and all the papers had been drawn up and signed in triplicate. It was a done deal. The Clovelly Fisheries Company now owned a controlling share in Behenna's Boats. The future of the company was secured and Edward Behenna had a seat on the board. But there was one clause that didn't appear in the reams of papers that he'd read through in the offices of his Trevay solicitors, Penrose and Trewin: what would happen to Jesse's inheritance – the one that both he and his father had spent their lives trying to ensure? One fail-safe way that Jesse could guarantee his share and carry the Behenna name into the future was by marrying into the Clovelly family.

He rubbed his chin and creased his brow, anxious about how he was going to break the news to Jesse.

'Come on, Edward. Your Jesse will see sense – he'll have money in his pocket and a beautiful girl for 'is wife. For God's sake, what's to decide? Come on, here's to our future and that of our grandkids!' He clanked his pint against Edward's again. But Edward found it hard to raise a smile, let alone his glass.

*

When Greer got home that evening her parents were waiting up for her.

'Can I get you anything before bed?' asked her mother.

'No, thank you, Mum.'

Bryn folded his paper and got out of his armchair. 'How was Jesse?'

Greer, already pinkened by two glasses of white wine, coloured a deeper shade. 'Fine,' she told him, before kissing her parents goodnight.

Bryn gave his wife a knowing look, which she returned as they watched their daughter retreat to the childhood bedroom she hadn't slept in for two whole years.

*

'How was Greer?' asked Jesse's father.

'Fine, I think.'

Jesse stepped over his father's outstretched legs in an attempt to get to the stairs and the safety of his bedroom before Edward could ask any more questions.

No luck.

'Hold on, boy. I want to talk to you.'

Jesse's shoulders dropped but he put on an innocent smile and said, 'What's that then, Dad?'

'Come and 'ave a seat, lad. Want a snifter?'

Jesse's father indicated the bottle of whisky from which he'd just poured himself a generous measure.

'Not really, Dad.' Jesse thought his dad had already had enough.

'I want to 'ave a proper talk with you, it's about your future.'

Jesse knew his father was about to launch into his usual sermon about the future of Behenna's Boats and him marrying Greer Clovelly. If he'd heard it once, he'd heard it a million times – especially when his dad was in his cups, like now.

'Dad, can we talk about this tomorrow? It's late and we've an early tide.'

Jesse made another attempt to get to the stairs but

his father was out of his seat and put his hand out to hold Jesse back.

'Dad?'

'Sit down, son,' his dad said firmly.

Jesse could see something in his father's eyes that he hadn't seen before. It stopped him short.

'What's happened, Dad?' Jesse asked, taking a seat opposite his father.

Edward steeled himself and took another mouthful of whisky. 'I've sold Clovelly Fisheries a share of Behenna's Boats. We're now one company.'

'What?' Jesse felt the news wash over him like a bucket of cold water. 'But what does that mean? Are we out of a job?'

'No!' Edward almost shouted. Then more calmly, for fear that he was losing control of the conversation, 'No, son, this is a good thing. I had to make sure you had a business to inherit. Things have been more of a struggle than you realise over the last few years. Bryn's paid a good price and we're out of the danger zone. Clovelly Fisheries will open up new markets for our fish and all of our jobs are safe. The company will carry on as we always have – for now, anyway.'

'What do you mean "for now"?' Jesse asked stiffly. He couldn't believe that his father had actually gone ahead and done this. He knew that his father and Bryn Clovelly had been cooking up some stupid plan between them, but for his father to actually sell some of their assets off . . . 'How much 'ave you sold him?' he asked coldly.

Edward paused. 'Fifty-one per cent.'

'Fifty-one per cent?' Jesse exploded out of his chair. 'But that means they own more than half – Behenna's

Boats isn't yours any more – isn't ours. They can do whatever they want with us.'

Edward held his hands out to Jesse in a placating gesture. 'Of course they can't. I'll sit on the board with the other members. And as part of the deal, I've acquired a small share in the Clovelly Fisheries. I'll have a say, like all the other members, and we can't be railroaded into anything.'

Jesse felt a well of emotion rise up in his throat. All his life he knew that his future lay with his dad on the boats. It had been his granddad's, then his dad's, and one day it was going to be his. Of course he wanted to see the world, but he always knew he'd come back for the boats one day. But now . . . now they belonged to the Clovellys.

'You've sold our birthright.'

This time, Edward was out of his chair again, his face almost purple with emotion. 'No, no! It's the opposite! I've *saved* your birthright. If things had carried on as before, there might have been precious little to leave you, and what would you have said about me then? I've done this for you, Jesse, for you and for your kids. I can't rely on Grant, can I? I have to do what I think is right for *you*.'

Father and son faced each other across the living room, their chests heaving with emotion. Edward rubbed his hands across his face.

'Listen, Jesse, this is the way to survive. We're bigger and better like this . . . believe me.'

Jesse slumped down in his chair, unable to look his father in the eye. 'What will happen to the business when you're gone?'

'Well, my share will go to you.' Edward hesitated. 'But

there is one way you can guarantee that the business will stay in the family . . .'

Jesse looked at his father, knowing exactly what he was going to say, but this time the words took on a whole new meaning.

9

December 1992

It was the Tuesday after Christmas and Truro was in the grip of the coldest winter in years.

'I'm gonna feel a right prat dressed up like a tailor's dummy.' Mickey was standing in the changing room of the gents' outfitters in just his boxer shorts and socks.

Jesse, in the cubicle next door, agreed. 'But it keeps the girls happy.'

'Aye,' sighed Mickey. 'You sure that's what you want, Jesse?' Jesse never talked of it, but anyone with an ear to listen and eyes to see couldn't but notice how much Edward Behenna had interfered in his son's life. Not for the first time, Mickey felt relief that his own father seemed to want only his son's happiness, rather than talk of dynasties and building the future.

Jesse didn't answer for a moment and Mickey heard only the rustling of clothing as Jesse undressed.

'I've got everything I've ever wanted,' Jesse replied flatly.

The dapper sales assistant returned with an armful of garments on hangers.

'Now then, sirs, here we are.' He passed over matching pinstriped trousers and tailcoats to the young men. 'If you'll just slip those on for size.'

After quite a lot of fitting and twirling, even Jesse and Mickey liked what they saw in the mirrors.

'Now have you thought about what collar you'll be wearing? Wing or regular? Of course it would depend on the neckwear – cravat or the traditional tie? Also, would you be wanting a handkerchief in the pocket or would that be too much if you are sporting a bloom in your buttonhole?'

What seemed like hours later, Jesse and Mickey emerged from the shop carrying their hired finery. 'Goodbye, gentlemen, and may I extend every good wish for the future.' The shop assistant smiled benignly and closed the door behind them, with a last admiring glance of their tightly muscled backs as he did so.

*

It was already dark outside and the Christmas lights swagged across the street were blinking merrily. Jesse and Mickey pushed open the door of the nearest pub. It smelled comfortingly of tobacco and beer, accumulated over many years. Large paper snowballs dangled from the ceiling, paper chains connecting them in a maze of loops. Only one other customer was in the bar and he was playing the fruit machine; a bored barmaid sat on a stool smoking. She stubbed out the cigarette and walked round behind the bar as Jesse and Mickey ordered two pints.

'I didn't know what to say when he asked if we were sporting a bloom in our buttonholes!' Jesse laughed as the two propped up the bar.

Mickey started sniggering. 'I didn't dare look at you. But 'e knows his stuff, though. You can't deny 'e's made a couple of silk purses out of our sow's ears.'

Jesse cupped his hands round his crotch. ''E's not touching my sow's ears.'

Mickey grinned, then started mincing up and down the bar, imitating the salesman's melodious voice. 'Would sirs prefer a stiff or soft one? Tie that is . . .' as Jesse brushed away tears of laughter.

'Stop it, Mickey, you idiot!'

Jesse grabbed his pint and turned to see that the salesman had entered the pub; his face made it clear that he'd seen Mickey's imitation. Jesse and Mickey stood stock-still, horrified.

'I saw that you sirs had come for refreshment. I had forgotten to give you the receipt you will require for returning the suits. This is proof of your hire agreement.' He handed over the receipt to Mickey with dignity.

Mickey didn't know what to say, so he blurted out, 'Thanks and . . . well, thanks.'

'It's been my pleasure.'

The assistant turned to leave but Jesse stepped towards him. 'Can we buy you a drink?' he said quietly.

The assistant thought for a moment then looked at his watch. 'I shut the shop in twenty minutes, after which time, if you gentlemen are still here, I should love a drink. A large gin and tonic should suffice. My name, by the way, is Bill.'

It was one of the funniest evenings Mickey and Jesse had ever spent. Bill told them stories of his life as a tailor, and of his brief marriage to a girl he had truly loved – but not in the way that either of them had wanted.

'I have a son who I dote on, and he and his mother and I have an excellent relationship. I even helped to choose her dress when she remarried. A lovely man. Just like you two young gentlemen. He laughed at me behind my back, too, but I won him round.' Mickey and Jesse felt ashamed.

'I'm really sorry . . .'

'No need to apologise. I have grown a very thick skin. Now, tell me all about the young lady you are to marry. New Year's Eve, did you say?'

*

Greer's mother was having trouble getting the zip over the gathers of the waistband. She gave it a tug.

'Ow. That's my skin.'

'It's not bleeding. Now breathe in.'

She worked the zip all the way to the top.

'There now. Turn round and let me look at you . . . oh, you look like a princess.'

'Really? It feels a bit tight.'

'Where?'

'The waist, under the arms, round my boobs.'

'That's because you've only just had lunch. No supper tonight and it'll be fine.'

'I don't know . . .'

'Once your hair's up and you've got the white silk poinsettia in, your neck will look longer and you'll look taller.'

'Really?'

'Yes.' Loveday's mother turned towards Greer, who was standing next to her. 'Greer, you've chosen her a beautiful dress for the wedding.'

Greer smiled warmly at Loveday in her bridesmaid's dress. 'You look amazing. Peach is so the right colour for you.'

Loveday lifted her arms as far as the dress would allow

and hugged her best friend. 'Thank you, Greer. I'm so proud to be your bridesmaid.'

'Loveday, who else would I ask? Now, the hairdresser is coming at nine thirty tomorrow morning. You're first, while I have my make-up done, and then we'll swap. You've got to be at the church for one forty-five and wait for me to get there at two. I've told Jesse to be there before one thirty. I don't want him hanging around the Golden Hind with Mickey getting him drunk.'

*

Jesse was at home with his mum. She was ironing her best dress.

'What you thinkin' about, young Jesse?' She turned the dress half a circle on the board and continued with a good jet of steam.

'Nothing.'

Her mouth made a firm line. 'You can tell me.'

'Nothing, honest.'

'You're getting married tomorrow. No one thinks of nothing the night before they get married.'

Jesse shifted in his chair. His mind was racing with the thought of marrying Greer tomorrow. He was 21 years old and he was getting married. He wanted to run away, or get drunk, or both.

'Nothing, Mum.'

'If you're marrying the wrong girl then it's not too late to back out,' she said, concentrating on a difficult pleat. She had decided that she wouldn't be able to sleep soundly again if she didn't speak up. Jesse kept his feelings to himself but, as his mother, she saw more than most.

Jesse shut his eyes tight for a moment. 'Greer and I

will be a good team. Dad's happy, 'er dad's happy. Greer's happy.'

'And you're not.'

Jesse didn't answer. His mum scratched her throat, then resumed her ironing as she told him quietly, 'There'll always be a bed for you here.'

The door swung open, bringing with it the chill of a frosty night and the stamping of two sets of feet.

'Bloody 'ell, it's as cold as a witch's tit out there. 'Ello, Ma.' Grant Behenna stood in the small kitchen in the full uniform of a Royal Marine, proudly wearing his green beret.

His mum put the iron down and gasped. 'You got it. The beret. You're a commando?'

'Yes, Ma. Proud of me?'

She went to him and put her hands on his shoulders. 'Yes.'

'Hello, little brother.' Grant looked at Jesse. 'Ready like a lamb for the slaughter?'

Ed Behenna finished hanging his coat up on the pegs by the door and went to the kettle.

'Don't start on him. Commando or no, you're not too old for me to give you a good hiding.'

Grant smirked, 'Wanna take me on, do you, Dad? I'm trained to kill a man with my bare hands.'

Jan let go of her elder son and gave him a stern look. 'We don't want any more trouble, Grant. Promise me.'

He laughed and hugged her. 'Why would I give my old mum any trouble? I'm a changed man. I'm one of the Queen's élite soldiers now. I fight only for her and my country. No one else.' He looked over at Jesse. 'The condemned man's allowed a last drink, isn't he? Why don't I take my little brother down to the pub?'

Jesse had known his brother would be coming back for his wedding and there had been precious little he could do about it. You could hardly *not* invite your brother to your wedding, though he had resisted pressure from his mother to ask Grant to be his best man. Grant hadn't ever been a brother he could rely on; Mickey was his best man and that was that.

'Cheer up, little brother.' He attempted to grab Jesse in a headlock, which Jesse deftly sidestepped.

'Watch it, Grant,' he warned.

Grant laughed, a little too loudly. 'Just messing, little brother. I know you didn't want me to be your best man, but I'm over it! Let me look after you tonight.'

Jesse couldn't think of a worse person to spend his last night of freedom with, but he was struggling to say no in a way that wouldn't offend his mother, his brother – or both.

Ed was pouring boiling water into an old brown teapot. 'You'll stay in and have a cup of tea and an early night if you know what's good for you.'

Grant turned towards his dad with a familiar air of menace. 'You got what you wanted when you sold the poor beggar down the Swanee. It's the night before he gets married, 'is last happy night and I'm taking him for a drink. Any objections?'

Ed took a step towards Grant but Jan stood between them. 'One drink won't do no harm. Let them go, Ed.'

*

The Golden Hind was as welcoming as it had always been for the centuries of fishermen it had served. Grant was greeted with respect, but no warmth, as he shouldered his way through in his uniform.

He nodded at the familiar faces. People he'd grown up with, gone to school with – and fought with.

He stopped to chat with a group of them, forcing Jesse to go to the bar and pay for the drinks. A pint of Skinner's for Grant and a St Clement's for himself. He'd promised Greer he wouldn't drink tonight. He saw Mickey and Loveday sitting in a corner by the Ladies and made his way over to them. Mickey shook his hand and Loveday kissed him on the cheek. 'Didn't think you were allowed out tonight,' she smiled.

'Grant's home.' Jesse looked over his shoulder as he pulled up a low stool. 'He kind of insisted.'

'He looks smart in his uniform, don't 'e?' said Mickey.

'S'pose so.' Jesse took a sip of his St Clement's. 'Don't do nothing for me.'

'Or me,' agreed Loveday. 'When's 'e going back?'

'Dunno. He said he had a forty-eight-hour pass or something. Dad picked him up off the Plymouth train just now.'

They all sipped their drinks thoughtfully. Grant was unpredictable, especially when he'd had a drink. Jesse, already nervous, had an extra strand of anxiety plugged straight into his stomach.

Mickey broke the tension. 'Loveday had 'er final dress fitting tonight.'

'Did you?' asked Jesse, glad to talk of anything but Grant. 'What's it like?'

'Well I can't tell you, can I? It's unlucky.'

'I thought it was only the wedding dress that I wasn't supposed to know about.'

'You're not supposed to know about anything.'

'Oh, right.'

'Wait till you see us in our suits,' Mickey grinned, taking Loveday's hand. 'You won't be able to keep your hands off me.'

Loveday looked down at her drink and gave what passed for a smile. 'You always look good to me, Mickey boy.'

Mickey put his arm round her and squeezed her awkwardly; her shoulder crunched up into her ear.

'Ow.'

'So,' said Jesse, putting down his drink and trying to squash his desperation for a proper drink and the chance to swap places with Mickey, 'when are you two gonna get hitched?'

Before they could answer, Grant loomed over the three-some, a pint in one hand and a large whisky chaser in the other. His eyes were brighter than they had been half an hour ago, his cheeks flushed.

'Well 'ere 'e is. The little shit my brother's chosen to be 'is best man. Better than 'is own brother. Let me buy you a drink.'

'We're all right, thanks,' Mickey told him in a flat tone. 'We were just going to make a move. Big day tomorrow, and all that. Want to be fresh.'

Grant's eyes wandered to Loveday's generous cleavage. 'There's only one person I want to get fresh with, and it isn't you, Mickey boy.' He sat down unsteadily next to Loveday. 'Got a boyfriend at the moment, Loveday?'

'Mickey,' she said quickly, taking Mickey's hand.

'Mickey? Mickey Mouse 'ere? You need a man not a mouse.' He swallowed the remains of his pint then downed the whisky chaser. He took her free hand and placed it under the table onto the front of his trousers. 'That's what a man feels like.' He held her hand against him; his grip was brutal and she couldn't pull away.

'Oi!' Mickey yelled, standing up and squaring up to Grant. 'Get your filthy hands off my girlfriend.'

'Oooh, little mousey's got a little squeak.' He leered over at Mickey.

'Let her go, Grant,' Jesse ordered, putting himself between Grant and Mickey.

'Get me another pint and a chaser and I'll let her go. But I think she likes it.' He squeezed Loveday's hand more tightly against him. 'Don't you, Loveday?'

Loveday's face was white with fear and disgust. She glanced up in mute distress at her friends. She was terrified of Grant, but petrified too at the thought of either of them getting into a fight with him.

Mickey lunged towards Grant, his face contorted in anger, while Grant threw his head back and laughed cruelly.

'Well, well, little mousey's gonna have a go with a commando? That's the funniest thing I've ever seen – little Mickey Mouse!'

With a momentous effort, Loveday managed to yank her hand away and hurl herself away from Grant. She moved quickly to Mickey's side, desperate to get him away. 'Come on, love,' she barely managed to whisper. Her voice was shaking. ''Bout time we was leaving.'

*

Jesse walked out of the pub with Mickey and Loveday, leaving his troublesome brother to tell anyone who would listen how hard it was to win a green beret. Jesse had rarely seen Mickey so fired up, but he gradually seemed to be calming down as they left the source of his fury behind.

Jesse couldn't face his parents' anxious faces if he went home without Grant, so he'd left Mickey and Loveday with promises of seeing them tomorrow, and now found himself walking towards St Peter's Church. It was the church where all the Behennas, going back three hundred years, had been married, baptised and buried.

He didn't give his usual salute to his granddad lying in the churchyard. His thoughts were absorbed by the life mapped out before him. Husband to Greer, a father, the boss of 'Behenna and Clovelly'. What had happened to his dreams? Had he ever been allowed to have any? That night when his father had told him about the merger with Clovelly, he had pushed him to marry Greer.

'She's a lovely girl. You'll want for nothing. You'll be the boss of the biggest fishing fleet and fishmongery business this side of Plymouth.'

Jesse had resisted, thinking of his feelings for Loveday and his dreams of travelling the world.

'Loveday's all right but she's got no prospects,' his father had reminded him. 'You're better than that.'

Jesse hated himself for being persuaded and, for a while, had been blinded by the riches that Greer's father had told him he would earn. And it had been easy to start a relationship with Greer. She was mad about him. She looked good. She was an heiress. The thing was, he did fancy Greer and she adored him. She was elegant and cultured; they looked good together and turned heads in Trevay. They'd become a couple.

It pained him to see Loveday. Jesse thought he had resigned himself to being with Greer and to pushing all thoughts of Loveday from his mind, but the more he tried, the more she intruded on his thoughts. Loveday would come to him in dreams, her tumbling red hair flowing over her milky-white breasts, asking Jesse, 'What are you in the mood for?' and Jesse would wake, remembering Greer and the expectations forced on him.

His engagement to Greer was a *fait accompli*. Once they'd become an item, whispers of weddings seemed to follow him everywhere. Greer dropped subtle hints, flicking through the pages of *Bride* magazine while his father urged him on. 'No time like the present, boy.'

On his twenty-first birthday, his father had handed him a wad of cash and told him he was promoted to second mate.

'Enough money there for a ring, boy,' he'd told Jesse, who had taken the money but felt like he'd sold his dreams.

The engagement had been the talk of the town. Both sets of parents had thrown a big party at the golf club, and Greer had revelled in the attention, wearing a stunning new outfit by Bruce Oldfield that she had bought in Debenhams on a special trip back to Guildford. Greer preened, showing off the diamond solitaire that Jesse could never have afforded before Behenna and Clovelly had merged. Jesse remembered little of the event, except for the strain of trying to avoid Loveday, and the sadness that he thought he saw reflected when they caught each other's eye.

Shortly after the engagement, Loveday and Mickey started to go out with each other. That had hurt Jesse, even though he had no reason to expect anything different, and he struggled to keep on top of his jealousy. To compensate he became ever more attentive to Greer, which only served to make Loveday ever more attentive towards Mickey.

He'd once asked Mickey, when they'd both been drinking,

what Loveday was like in bed. Mickey told him. That hurt too. Mickey asked what Greer was like. Jesse said that a gentleman never tells. The truth was that there was nothing to tell. Greer had never let him get further than a snog and a hand in her shirt. Her breasts felt small and pert. Nothing like the way he imagined Loveday's felt.

He'd left the church behind him and was now up at the sheds. A northerly wind was blowing and it rattled the tarpaulins tied to the boats lying against the far edge of the yard. Jesse turned his face from the wind and pulled up the collar of his parka. He wanted to be alone for a while. He fished in a pocket for his key ring and found his key to the Behenna's Boats shed.

Inside, whilst not exactly warm, it was at least wind-proof. He went into the small makeshift office made of plywood that he and his dad had built a few summers ago. He switched a light on and found his father's bottle of Scotch. He pulled the cork and took a sip. The burning in his throat felt good. He took another sip before hearing the creak of the outside door opening.

10

'Is that you, Mickey?' Jesse called out tentatively.
He peered round the office door and nearly choked on his whisky.

'Hello,' said Loveday in a quiet voice. 'I just wanted to see you, you know, make sure you were all right an' that.'

'I'm fine.' He stood and wiped his suddenly sweating hands on his jeans. 'Do you want a drink?' He watched her as she closed the main door. The sound of the flapping tarpaulins in the yard was instantly silenced.

''Tis windy outside,' she said. 'And ever so cold.'

'I can make you tea? No milk, though. That would warm you up.'

'What are you drinking?'

Jesse looked sheepish. 'Me dad's whisky.'

'I'll 'ave one of those then.'

'Right.' Jesse found a cleanish mug and poured her a decent measure. She had walked closer to him now. 'Come in and make yourself comfortable. My dad's chair is the best.' He pointed at an ageing armchair.

'Lovely. Thanks,' said Loveday, taking the drink he handed her and settling herself. 'I thought you might be up 'ere. Are you nervous about tomorrow? Mickey's like a flea on a trampoline about his speech.'

'Is he?' smiled Jesse, plonking himself on the only

509

other seat, the part-time accounts secretary's swivel chair. 'He won't tell me nothing about what he's going to say.'

'He's told me some of it. It's good. Nothing too embarrassing. He doesn't want to upset Greer's family, them being so proper an' all.' She raised her mug. 'So, cheers then. 'Ere's to you and Greer.'

'Cheers,' said Jesse, and they both drank.

'Is your dress all right then?' asked Jesse.

'No.'

'What's wrong with it?'

'Everything.' Loveday began to laugh. 'It's truly 'orrible. Greer calls it peach but it's more like orange – not my kind of colour at all. It makes me look like a really fat milkmaid and I can't move my arms in it.'

Jesse frowned. 'Have you told Greer?'

Loveday waved a hand airily. 'Oh, well, it's Greer's day and it's what she wants. I can't tell her I hate it, can I?'

'I bet you look lovely in it, really.'

'No, really I don't. I mean, my mum likes it and Mickey will like it because he likes whatever I wear but . . .' She looked down at her drink, the smile gone. 'I look awful in it and I feel awful in it and I know what people will be saying behind my back.' Jesse heard the catch in her voice.

'Hey.' He leant forward and looked up into her eyes. 'I'll punch anybody who says you don't look beautiful. You always look beautiful to me.'

She wiped a burgeoning tear away and tried a smile. 'Shut up, you idiot.'

Jesse tilted back into his chair. 'I'm a bit nervous too.'

'Whatever for?'

'Well, getting married is a big step.'

'But you and Greer are made for each other.' She looked at him carefully. 'Aren't you?'

'Oh, yes, of course we are. She's great you know, we're mates. Known each other for ever, almost as long as I've known Mickey, and you.'

'I used to have a crush on you when I was little.' The whisky had gone to her head.

Jesse laughed. 'I know.'

Loveday stuck her tongue out at him. 'Don't laugh! 'Twas awful. All you ever did was go off with Mickey and play football.'

'What did you want me to do?'

'Play with me.'

'And do what? Talk about Barbie and work on dance routines?'

'You're a shit dancer, Behenna.'

'So are you.'

She stuck her leg out and kicked his shin. ''Ow dare you! I was disco champion one Christmas at school.'

'The boys voted for you because your bottom wobbled so nicely in your costume.'

She gave him another kick in the shins. 'Got any more of that whisky?'

Jesse reached for the bottle and poured each of them a generous slug.

'D'you remember the school poetry competition?' said Loveday. 'The one when Greer wrote that soppy thing about the universe and the animals.'

Jesse started to giggle. 'I didn't understand a single bleddy word.'

'Her face when she was up there reading it.' Loveday

put on a holier-than-thou expression. 'All serious like and putting on a posh voice.'

'She won, though,' said Jesse loyally.

'Yeah, but only because the bleddy teachers didn't understand it either. They only gave her first prize 'cos they couldn't face her mother complaining.'

''Er mum's all right, really,' Jesse said.

'Yeah. Course she is,' Loveday added quickly. She hadn't meant to be so mean about her friend. She blamed it on the whisky and being made to wear a dress that looked horrid.

'No . . . it's just that, well, that's my new family we're laughing about.'

They sat in silence, absorbing this reality.

Loveday moved to stand up. 'Well, I only came to see if you were all right, that's all, and you look fine to me.'

Jesse put his hand up and stopped her. 'Don't go. I like you being here.'

Loveday touched his blond hair and stroked it. 'Do you?'

'Yes.'

Loveday sat down slowly. 'How nervous are you about tomorrow?'

Jesse stretched up, leaned back and blew a long breath out of his mouth. 'To be honest, I'm shit scared. Am I doing the right thing, Loveday?'

'Course you are, Jesse.' She gave him a reassuring smile. 'You're marrying Greer. How can that be wrong? You're going to be part of a new company. You'll make money and drive a flash car and have holidays in Spain. Of course you're doing the right thing.'

'Then why does it feel so wrong?'

'What are you talking about?'

'It feels wrong. I'm only twenty-one and I'm not sure if I want to marry anyone . . . not just Greer. It's not her fault.' He stuck the heels of his hands over his eyes and almost soundlessly said, 'The truth is I'm scared.'

Loveday came off her chair and knelt in front of Jesse. 'Scared of what, darlin'?'

'Just plain scared.'

She hesitated, then put her arms round him and rocked him soothingly. 'It's all right, darlin'. I'm here. What you're feeling is normal for a bloke. Getting married is a big day, but that's all it is. A big day, then everything gets back to normal. You'll go on your honeymoon and when you get back we'll all still be here. Just the same. Nothing changed.'

'That's what makes it so frightening. Nothing will have changed and nothing will change till the day I die. Trevay, the boats, my family, you and Mickey. All the same. I'm stuck.'

'What nonsense is this? You're not stuck. You'll have money to go anywhere in the world, do anything you want.'

'With Greer and her money.'

'With your wife and your money.'

He took his hands from his eyes and looked desperately at Loveday. 'I've made a mistake. I'm . . . I'm marrying the wrong person.'

Loveday let go of him and sat back on her heels. The wind had picked up again and the sound of the wires on the masts of the boats in the harbour travelled up the lane, past St Peter's, and now swirled through the crack in the door of the Behenna shed. 'What are you talking about?'

'I should never have let Dad persuade me.' He looked at her in desperation. 'It's you, Loveday.'

He had crossed the Rubicon. The words were spoken. The truth was told. Loveday's heart was hammering in her chest. She felt faint and a bit sick.

'Me?'

He nodded.

Outside the first flurry of snow twisted in the wind. Inside she leant forward and kissed him.

*

'What are we going to do?' Loveday was lying on the makeshift blanket of Jesse's parka.

'We could do it again.' He traced the soft dough of her stomach from her belly button to her breasts. She shut her eyes to enjoy the pleasure of him squeezing her nipples and taking each in turn into his mouth and sucking gently on them.

'I mean about Mickey and Greer.'

He took his lips from her sweet breast and moved up her body to look into her eyes.

'I don't know.'

'I don't want to hurt Mickey.'

'Kiss me.'

'I don't want to hurt Greer.'

'Kiss me.'

His kiss was gentle and she couldn't help but kiss him back. Gently they made love again.

Outside the wind caught hold of something and the bang woke Loveday.

'Oh my God. Look at the time.' Loveday was holding her watch. 'We've been here for ages.'

Jesse, curled round her hips and thighs, woke groggily. 'Shit.'

The almost empty bottle of whisky, regarding them from the top of the dusty metal desk, stood as the sole witness to their crime.

They dressed in near silence, passing each other a stray sock or lost shoe.

Together they left the shed. It had been snowing and a small drift had built along the bottom edge of the door. Jesse struggled to push the door shut, leaning his full weight against it to fit the padlock in the hasp and lock it.

Finally it was done and, putting their arms around each other, they walked out of the yard, down the lane, past the church and on to their homes and their beds.

Watching them go, bivouacked between the hulls of two clinker boats, was Grant. He'd followed Loveday when she had slipped out of her house after Mickey had dropped her off. He had had ideas of his own about what he and she could get up to that night. When she'd headed towards the sheds it had seemed to him almost as if she wanted him to follow her. Then he'd seen that the door was already unlocked and that his shitty little brother, the golden son, was already there. He'd watched them then and he watched them now. This was a little treasure hoard that had fallen into his lap. He'd spend it wisely.

11

'It's still snowing.' Jesse's mother clattered the wooden curtain rings into each other as she ruthlessly ripped open his curtains. 'Rise and shine, young man. You're getting married today.'

Jesse clenched his eyes tightly as the blistering daylight lasered its way around his childhood bedroom.

'There's a cup of tea by your bed. By the smell in here you'll need it. Your brother's fault, I suppose.'

The memory of Loveday's softly yielding body erupted in his mind. What had Grant got to do with last night?

'Why ever did you both stay out so late?' He could picture his mother standing with her hands on her hips, frowning down at him. He gingerly lifted one eyelid and saw that he was right. 'You're a bloody idiot, Jesse. You'll look terrible in the photos, and what's Greer and your new in-laws going to think about a groom stinking of booze?' Jan sat down on the edge of the bed and the bounce made him feel sick. She put a cool hand on his forehead. 'You need a fry-up and some aspirin and you'll be fine.' She stood up, and again the movement of the mattress brought on nausea. 'This is the most important day of your life, Jesse, and I'm not going to let you let yourself down. Get showered and I'll put some sausages on.'

*

Greer sat up in her four-poster bed and looked around her beautiful bedroom. This was the last morning she'd ever wake up as a single woman. She closed her eyes and imagined, for the millionth time, the look on Jesse's face as he turned from the altar and watched her walking up the aisle, towards him. She was going to be the most beautiful bride Cornwall had ever seen. She looked to her left, at the oyster satin bag draped on a softly padded and pearl-beaded hanger on the door of her French armoire. Inside was the perfect dress. Not the flouncy meringue so many of her friends had chosen for their weddings. Hers was a chic column of finest silk satin, cut on the bias so that it fell narrowly at her ankles and then puddled into the perfect train. She sighed with pleasure and wriggled back under her lavender-scented sheets. It was only seven thirty and she had plenty of time to enjoy the most special day of her life.

There was a soft knock at the door. 'Come in,' she called.

Her mother nudged the door open with an elbow and came in carrying a breakfast tray with orange juice, coffee and a croissant. She'd put confetti on the tray.

As soon as she saw Greer, tears sprang from her eyes. 'Oh, my darling daughter. I can't believe this is your wedding day.' She put the tray on the blanket box at the foot of the bed and helped Greer to sit up whilst plumping her pillows for her. 'Comfortable?'

'Thanks, Mum.'

With the tray settled securely on Greer's lap, her mother went to the window. 'There's a little bit of magic to add to the day, my darling.' She pulled the cord and the curtains swept open, like in an Odeon cinema, to reveal the scene behind. Greer was expecting to see the familiar view of

Trevay and its harbour, with maybe a wedding helicopter on the front lawn. But it was better than that. Trevay had transformed itself into a snow-covered fairy kingdom.

'I ordered it, just for you,' said her mother.

*

Mickey Chandler had been up with the lark and was polishing his best brown shoes on the kitchen table.

'How's your speech?' asked his mother. She skirted awkwardly round his pulled-out chair as she negotiated the small room from larder to oven.

'I think it's all right.' He spat on a toecap and rubbed vigorously with a balding yellow duster.

'What does Loveday think?'

'She laughed in all the right places.'

Mrs Chandler cracked an egg into her gnarled frying pan. 'Well, that's a good sign, innit? Two eggs or three?'

Mickey thought for a moment. 'Three. I'll need something to drink on later. Is there any bacon?'

'Of course. Can't 'ave egg without it.'

'Cheers, Ma.' He leant back in his chair and puckered his lips for a kiss. She wiped her eggy fingers on her apron and obliged. 'You're a good lad.'

Mr Chandler ducked his head as he came through the low doorway from upstairs. 'Mornin', son. 'Ow's the best man today?'

'Bit nervous,' said Mickey as he picked up his second shoe and spat on that one as well.

'Nervous? What the 'ell have you got to be nervous for? 'Tis bleddy Jesse who should be nervous. Marrying that girl and that family. His dad has sold him down the river.'

Mrs Chandler clunked two old blue and white china plates down in front of Mickey and her husband. 'Now stop saying stuff like that. Jesse ain't no fool and he knows which side his bread is buttered. He'll be a very wealthy man. Two eggs or three?'

'Three.' Mr Chandler gave Mickey an astute look. 'You got the better girl and no mistake, son. I'd have Loveday Carter over Greer Clovelly any day.'

*

Loveday looked in her dressing-table mirror and groaned. On the side of her face, in the dip between her nose and her cheeks, was the largest spot she'd ever had. There was no head yet but it was hot and hard and she knew that as soon as she entered the church it would force its way to the surface of her skin in all its pus and glory, ready to take centre stage in the photographs. Greer would be furious.

'Fuck.' She put her head in her hands. It was the least of her problems. Greer was going to be furious anyway. As soon as Jesse told her what happened last night, there would be no photographs.

The memory of Jesse's loving words washed away the horror of the spot and filled her with a dreadful happiness. Greer and Mickey would be hurt, that was only to be expected, but they'd come round in time, hopefully. They were old friends. They would understand that it would have been a big mistake for Jesse and Greer to marry. It was always going to be Jesse and Loveday.

She looked at her bedside clock. She wondered if Jesse was awake yet. Had he been able to sleep? She'd slept for no more than a couple of hours. The combination of whisky and wonderment had kept her thoughts racing. She hoped he'd still be sleeping. He needed all the sleep he could get. Today of all days. He'd have to go round to see Greer. Explain before it got too late to let the guests know there wasn't going to be a wedding. Then he'd phone her; or maybe come and see her. Either way, she couldn't wait to be with him again.

*

'Whatever did you get Jesse drunk for?' Jan looked at her elder son with frustration and latent anger. 'You knew he had to get home early and get some sleep. Where did you two go?'

Grant looked at Jesse sitting at the other end of the table. He didn't look good. Grant had heard him throwing up under the sound of the running shower. Jesse had thought no one would hear him if he kept the shower running, but Grant had heard him. Grant knew all Jesse's sordid little secrets.

'Don't know what you're talking about, Mum. Jesse left the Hind before I did.'

Jesse looked up from his dry toast and Grant was pleased to see panic in his eyes. 'Where did you get to, little brother?'

Jesse looked at his mother and then pleadingly back at Grant, who toyed with him like a cat with a vole. 'Shall I tell our mummy what you were up to last night?'

If it were possible, Jesse grew a shade paler. His mind was in overdrive. Grant couldn't know that he had been at the sheds with Loveday. *Could he?* No. It wasn't possible. His hungover brain tried to think of an answer that would satisfy his mother's curiosity. 'I . . . I was wi—'

'It's all right, little bro.' Grant spoke over him. 'I'll explain.' Grant turned to his mother. 'He was up the sheds, drinking Dad's whisky with . . .' Grant threw a glance at Jesse's petrified face. '. . . With me. I'm sorry. I led him astray. I confess.'

Jan folded her arms and looked at her two sons as if they were no more than eight year-olds. 'I knew it. You're a pair of idiots. Grant, I can understand, but you, Jesse, I thought you had more sense. Neither of you have the brains you were born with . . . Where're you off to, Jesse Behenna?' Jesse felt the room reeling, the rancid whisky making its way up his throat. He dashed for the bathroom and made it just in time.

*

What the hell was he going to do? He rinsed his face and cleaned his teeth, then began the arduous task of shaving. His hands weren't his own. They belonged to someone who had the shakes. He nicked the bit of skin under his nose and it started to bleed and sting. He tore off a bit of loo paper and, spitting on it, stuck it on the cut. Greer wouldn't like that. She wanted him tall and strong and handsome. No blemishes or shaving nicks. He'd have to tell her. He'd phone her now. He heard the front door open and his auntie Gwen's voice calling out to his mum. The phone was there. By the front door. Everyone would hear him tell Greer that he was very sorry but he wasn't marrying her after all. He couldn't ring her. He'd have to walk up the hill and tell her. Like a man. In front of her mum and dad. How do you say something like that? 'I'm so sorry, Mr and Mrs Clovelly, but I can't marry Greer. I slept with Loveday last night. Up at the sheds.'

That was the truth, but he couldn't put it like that. How about, 'Greer, you're a wonderful girl and I've always liked you, but I can't marry you because I don't love you.'

Her father would punch him. That would hurt. He rinsed the shaving foam from his face and patted his cheeks dry. Using the mirror, he peeled off the drying loo paper and found the cut had stopped bleeding. He splashed a good deal of Paco Rabanne aftershave on his palms and slapped it on his face. The stinging made his bloodshot eyes water even more.

In his pain he heard the front door open once more and his mother call up the stairs. 'Jesse. Your best man's here. I'm sending him up to get you ready.'

*

Loveday looked at the now-redundant but still horrible, orange bridesmaid dress hanging on the back of her bedroom door. Why had she told Greer she liked it? Why had Greer chosen it for her? It hid every good feature of hers; made Loveday feel utterly frumpy and unsexy. She still hadn't been allowed to see The Wedding Dress. That was Top Secret. Loveday had more than a suspicion that it was nothing like the marmalade horror. But, she realised suddenly, she wasn't going to have to wear it after all. When she married Jesse, she'd make Greer wear a horrible dress. She laughed at the thought, then checked her bedside clock again. She'd hear from Jesse soon. He'd come round to get her after he had explained everything to Greer and her family. Perhaps they would go away for a few days until the dust settled. That would probably be best.

She heard a heavy knock on the front door. This was

him, it was Jesse! She ran out of her room, taking the stairs on the narrow staircase two at a time. Her mother got there a split second ahead of her and opened the door, revealing Greer's father. She stood a little way behind her mother. Mr Clovelly had obviously come to tell them the wedding was off. But he looked quite relaxed about it. He was kissing Loveday's mum and smiling.

He saw Loveday, breathless and expectant and said, 'Morning, Loveday. You look as excited as Greer! She's so thrilled with this snow. Are you ready? I'll take you up the hill in the BMW. Apparently the hairdresser is stuck over at St Agnes, but her mother's boyfriend has a Land Rover so he'll get her over here as soon as he's done the milking.' Loveday stood stock-still, barely able to take all this in. Where was Jesse? Why was everything still going ahead? Surely he'd say something before it was too late?

'Come on then, Loveday,' chided her mother. 'Get your dress bag and shoes. And don't forget the silk poinsettia for your hair.'

*

Mickey was preening himself in the mirrored wardrobe door of Jesse's room. 'I look all right in this, don't I? Loveday won't be able to keep her hands off me.'

Jesse was fumbling with the buttons of his shirt. His heart was beating way too fast and his breathing was more like a pant. Mickey turned away from his own reflection to look at Jesse. 'You'm real nervous, eh, boy? You shouldn't have had a skinful with Grant last night. Bad move.'

'I'm not doing this right.' Jesse looked at Mickey, trying to find the words. 'I am not doing the right thing.'

'I tell 'e you're not. You're doing those buttons up all wrong. Let me do them for you.' Jesse stood shaky but compliant as Mickey did up his shirt buttons, fixed his collar, got him into his pinstriped trousers and pinned the cravat. 'We'll put our tailcoats on at the church. Don't want to crease them.'

Jan came in with two mugs of tea. 'Don't you boys look smart?' She gave each of them a once-over, straightening their cravats. 'You're as white as a ghost still, Jesse. Get this tea down you. Mickey, you look after him at the altar and make sure he don't faint.'

'I need to speak to Greer,' said Jesse. 'I must go and see her.'

His mother laughed. 'You'll be seeing plenty of her after the wedding. You'll see her every day for the rest of your life.'

Jesse was desperate, his voice catching. 'I have things I need to talk to her about. It'll be too late if I don't go now.'

'You're staying here, even if I have to get Grant to hold you down.' His mother took his hand. ''Tis nerves, that's all.' She turned to Mickey. 'Come on, Best Man. What does it say in the book about nervous grooms?'

Before Mickey could think of an answer, the bedroom door was thrown open and Grant stood in the doorway in full uniform. He saluted the groom and said: 'Escort Party for Mr Jesse Behenna ready and waiting. It is the brother of the groom's duty to get a hair of the dog down his neck before he bottles it. And a Marine always does his duty.'

The little party of Grant, Mickey and Jesse prepared to leave the house. Mickey and Jesse had their tailcoats safely in protective bags to put on at the last minute. A light flurry of snow danced through the air; Jesse reached for his parka. The scent of Loveday clung to it and he immediately visualised her lying on it as he made love to her. It took all his willpower not to bury his face in it and drink her in once more. Then he saw it. On the lining by the fishtail back was the unmistakable stain of their passion, and it was red with blood.

12

Greer looked wonderful. Her hair had grown in the last six months and was styled into a glossy 1920s bob. Her make-up was natural and glowing, her dress exquisite. Her high pert bust, nipped-in waist and slender bottom were celebrated and worshipped by it. Greer was a vision of serenity and fulfilment.

Loveday, on the other hand, was not. She was having her hair pulled and backcombed by the hairdresser's sister who had come to lend a hand, seeing as the snow had made them almost two hours late. The blowdry had left Loveday's face scarlet. Her make-up lay thick on her young skin and she could feel her spot fighting vigorously to break its way through the crowd of concealer, foundation and powder. She felt sick, hungover and horribly emotional. Where was Jesse? Tears threatened yet again and she reached forward to grab a tissue from the box in front her.

'Feeling sweaty, are you?' asked the hated hairdresser, yanking the hair on the back of her neck and pinning to her head, with unnecessary ferocity, the ghastly silk poinsettia.

A tear fled down Loveday's face and she mopped it quickly with the tissue. 'No.'

'You're feeling very hot. Crying always gets me hot too.'

'I'm not crying.'

'Are you crying, Loveday?' asked Greer, looking like a cool breeze in front of her French cheval mirror.

'No.'

'Ah, Loveday, you're such a softie. It is emotional watching your best friend get married to the boy of her dreams, but don't cry off all that make-up. You'll have that spot popping up again.'

'I'm not crying.' Loveday brushed the vestige of another tear away.

'I know what will make you smile. Look at this.'

Loveday watched in the mirror's reflection as Greer opened a satin drawstring bag and took out a delicate garter made of gauze and swan's-down with tiny glittering crystals. The two hairdressers gasped in wonder, their mouths forming perfect Os.

'That's beautiful, that is,' said the older one. 'Put it on.'

Loveday watched as Greer shucked off her bridal slippers and pointed one perfect ballerina foot inside the garter. Then her slender, manicured fingers teased it up over her calf and her knee. Finally it whispered to a halt and lay perfectly in the middle of her slender thigh. It clung just below the lacy top of her sheer ivory stockings.

'My God, that'll drive Jesse Behenna mad,' screeched the hairdresser, grinning.

Greer let the satin folds of her dress fall perfectly back to the floor and smiled a secretive smile.

Loveday was being given the last squirt of hairspray and looked at herself in the mirror. Her natural curls had been tortured into a regiment of ringlets. Her young, open face was now made hard with darkened eyebrows and peach lipstick. Her throat and chest were covered in nerve-induced red blotches and the hated dress was digging into her. Where on earth was Jesse? Why hadn't he come?

*

Jesse was being helped up the snowy lane towards St Peter's. The lads in the Golden Hind had given him more than a hair of the dog. He'd had the entire pelt.

'Come on, little bro,' said Grant, pulling him up the lane. 'Your destiny awaits.'

'I don't wanta get married today,' he slurred, trying to pull away from them both. 'I can't.'

'Don't be silly,' Mickey said firmly, taking Jesse's weight as he slid on an icy cobble. He looked over at Grant on the other side. 'You shouldn't have let 'im drink so much.'

Grant laughed unpleasantly. 'He'll be all right. He's only getting married. It's nothing serious, is it?'

'But Greer's going to kill me. I'm the best man. I'm supposed to be looking after him.'

'And I'm helping you, aren't I?'

*

The Reverend Rowena Davies was immensely under-standing and compassionate. She had been an army chaplain and knew the frailties of men. She sat Jesse down on a rickety wooden ladder-backed chair and unlocked the vestry cupboard that was used by the mothers' and toddlers' group, raiding their refreshments shelf.

'There's a biscuit tin,' she said in triumph. 'Please God, let it not be empty.' Her prayer was answered. 'Oh dear.

Ginger nuts. Still, needs must. Sit down here, Jesse, and eat these. We've got about twenty minutes to get you shipshape.'

From under a curtained shelf she then produced a kettle and a jar of instant coffee. 'Only black, I'm afraid. No milk but there's sugar. Make him a strong one, Mickey. Plenty of sugar. I'm going to nip out front and greet any early-comers.'

Mickey could have kissed her. 'Thanks, Vicar.'

'All in a day's work. See you shortly.'

*

Jesse drank the coffee, ate the biscuits and swallowed a couple of pills that Grant had in his pocket. 'They give us commandos these when we're on ops. Keeps us alert.'

'Speed?' asked Mickey, shocked.

Grant tapped the side of his nose. 'No name no pack drill.'

Whatever it was that Grant had given him, Jesse began to feel a little less drunk and a little more alert very quickly. Grant crouched over him, hands on his uniformed knees, and examined his brother's face. 'You're coming back to us, Jesse boy, you're coming back.'

'Grant, I . . .' Jesse started to speak.

'Now don't do nothing stupid. We're going to walk into the church now and you and Mickey are going to look happy and sober. Got it? You're taking one for the team, ain't you now, boy? Can't let Daddy down.'

Terror gripped Jesse's heart again, but he nodded. 'How long have we got?'

Mickey checked his watch. 'About five minutes if she's on time.'

Edward Behenna burst into the vestry. 'What the hell's going on?' He took one look at Jesse, who felt his resolve stiffen. He gulped back some more of the coffee and shook himself. He knew what he had to do.

*

Loveday had been brought to the church in one of Greer's cousin's cars. She was finding it hard to absorb what was actually going on around her. She found herself squashed into the back seat of an ancient Hillman Imp, with the cousin's husband driving gingerly over the compacted snow and the cousin twisting round in the front seat to talk nonstop at her. At least she left no space for replies. Loveday's brain was left to wonder how on earth Jesse was going to stop this wedding.

The Hillman Imp couldn't make it up the lane to the church, so Loveday struggled over the front tip-up seat and out into the snow. It was cold but at least it had stopped snowing. Her pinching satin slippers might as well have been made from blotting paper as she trudged on up the road, the sound of the bells pealing in her ears, the cousin yakking by her side.

*

'You look beautiful.' Bryn Clovelly stood in awe as his only daughter stepped from her bedroom and stood in front of him. 'Give us a twirl.'

Greer obliged. 'Will I do, Daddy?'

'My darling, you'd do for a prince, never mind Jesse Behenna.'

They were alone in the house. Greer's mother had

already left with her brother, Uncle Alan, and his wife, Auntie Lou, with a handbag stuffed full of tissues.

'You do like Jesse, don't you, Daddy? You do think he is going to be a good husband?' Greer felt suddenly nervous that maybe her father didn't want her to marry Jesse.

The truth was that Bryn was delighted at the thought of the merger with the Behenna fishing fleet, and about all the money they were going to make now that the two families were one. A small gust of guilt hit him. Was this really the right thing to do?

'I'll marmalise him if he hurts you.' Greer's innocent smile of relief made him pity her, so he added, 'But he won't.'

There was the honk of a car horn outside.

'Your carriage awaits, my lady.' Smiling, Bryn proffered his arm. Greer slipped her hand through the crook of his elbow and took a deep breath. 'Ready?'

*

The 1955 cream Bentley with its wedding ribbons drew lots of attention. Its slowly negotiating the snow on the road down to Trevay meant that the locals could get a good look at Greer Clovelly on her way to marry Jesse Behenna. Greer made the most of it, smiling and offering little waves to the children through the big glass windows. She felt like a princess. At the bottom of the lane to the church, the Bentley stopped. The driver in his dove-grey peaked cap turned and said to Bryn, 'I'll 'ave to let 'e out 'ere. She'll never make it up to the church.'

Greer looked horrified. 'I can't walk up. My dress will be ruined.'

'I thought this might happen, so I've organised a little help,' smiled Bryn. 'Look over there.' He pointed towards the harbour. Sitting on the wall were two of the Trevay lifeboat crew in yellow wellies and thick navy wool jumpers. One was the coxswain, the other a strapping younger crewman. They got off the wall and came towards the car.

Bryn stepped out and shook their hands. 'Morning, lads. This is very good of you.'

The coxswain of the lifeboat, a wily old seaman who'd seen just about anything there was to see in life said, 'Our pleasure, Mr Clovelly. Can't 'ave this beautiful maid getting 'er feet wet, can we?'

Bryn walked to the other side of the car and opened Greer's door. The young lifeboat man stepped forward and smiled an appreciative smile at Greer. 'You look lovely,' he said, before sliding one strong arm under her bottom and the other around her back. He lifted her easily out of the car and began the short climb up the lane towards St Peter's.

At the church door, a damp-footed and shivering Loveday watched Greer draped in the arms of the handsome Stevie (everyone at school had fancied him), looking for all the world like a bloody poster for *An Officer and a Gentleman*. Loveday felt trapped in a nightmare that she wasn't about to wake up from any time soon. She hadn't seen Jesse or Mickey, but the Reverend Rowena had whispered something about having to sober the groom up, which had sent Loveday's brain into meltdown. Was Jesse going to leave it right till the last moment to drunkenly jilt Greer in front of everyone? This was not how it should be. Loveday's feet grew colder and wetter.

Greer was now two paces away from Loveday and

smiling happily in the arms of the handsome Stevie. 'Isn't this romantic, Loveday?'

The wedding photographer took a couple of shots of Greer in Stevie's arms before Stevie put Greer down gently inside the church porch, which was more or less dry.

Loveday tried a bright smile, but inside her thoughts were tumbling around; a terrible confusion of guilt and fear and an over-riding yearning for Jesse to come and sort everything out. Knowing that this radiant bride was about to have her bubble burst tore at her insides. Still, better now than a few months down the line when a messy divorce would be on the cards. 'You look wonderful, Greer.'

'Would you sort my veil out for me?' Greer asked her.

'Sure.' With hands that were shaking from cold and apprehension, Loveday lifted the froth of soft tulle over Greer's face.

'Daddy,' called Greer.

'Just coming, my love.' Bryn replied, palming fifty pounds to the coxswain and saying *sotto voce*, 'Cheers, mate.'

'Come on, Loveday. Stand behind me and Daddy and let's go. I can't wait to see Jesse's face when he sees me.' Greer watched as Loveday got into position and then she took her father's arm. The church bells had stopped pealing and there was a moment's silence before the organ struck up Mendelssohn's 'Wedding March'.

*

Jesse's heart was hammering in his throat. He felt dizzy. Mickey touched his arm. 'You OK?'

The organ's swelling notes were increasing the panic he felt. He started breathing loudly through his mouth.

'Here she comes,' nudged Mickey. 'Look at 'er.'

Jesse held the back of his pew for support as he turned. Greer was coming towards him as if on a cloud. He wanted to shout 'stop', but instead his eyes slid to Loveday walking behind, her eyes glued desperately to Jesse's. His brain was telling his mouth to open and speak, but when he tried it would not obey. He turned quickly back to the altar. Behind him he could hear his mum sniffing into her hanky.

The Reverend Rowena had seen nervous grooms before, but never as stricken as Jesse. She smiled at him and offered a prayer to bring him peace.

Greer arrived at Jesse's side. She looked up at him adoringly. He couldn't move.

Greer turned to Loveday and handed her the bouquet. Loveday took it and stood rooted to the spot, staring at Jesse, who looked as if he might faint. Greer was whispering to her, 'My veil. Lift my veil.' Loveday looked at her hands, each holding a bouquet, her own and the bride's. 'Give them to my mother,' Greer hissed.

'Dearly beloved, we are gathered together here, in the sight of God, and in the face of this congregation, to join together this Man and this Woman in holy Matrimony, which is an honourable state . . .'

13

'I can't believe we've been married for almost three weeks already.' Greer stretched out her left hand and wiggled the fourth finger to allow the two shiny rings, one a diamond solitaire set in gold, the other a matching gold band, to twinkle in the sunshine.

'Are you happy, Jesse?'

Jesse, at that particular moment, was happy. He was lying on a comfortable sun lounger, by a sparkling azure pool with a cold glass of beer by his side, hundreds of miles away from the mess he'd left behind in Trevay. He was almost starting to believe he'd got away with the biggest mistake of his life. That's not to say that several times a day he didn't break out in a cold sweat thinking of his betrayal. Last night he'd dreamt of making love to Loveday in his parents' bed. Neither he nor Loveday had heard the footsteps coming up the stairs or the turn of the door handle. They hadn't seen the faces of his mother, his father, Mickey and Greer contorted in grief and horror until Mickey had pulled out a fish-gutting knife and had stabbed himself in the heart. His blood had pumped in a perfect arc over Loveday's face and into Jesse's eyes. His mother was screaming. Greer was shouting, 'Jesse, Jesse, stop it, stop it!' She was tapping at his face and shaking his shoulders. 'Jesse, wake up. Wake up! What's the matter?'

He'd opened his eyes, knowing that he would see Loveday's blood-covered face staring at him accusingly, Mickey's body lying across her. But all he saw was the concerned face of Greer gently shaking him. 'Jesse, it's OK. I'm here. It was a dream.'

His eyes slowly took in the hotel bedroom and its whitewashed walls. The early light was twinkling through the shutters and he heard the clatter of a woman in heels walk across the floor of the room above.

His heart was thudding more gently now and his breathing was returning to normal.

'You were shouting Mickey's name.' Greer's face was full of concern.

He hated himself. 'Was I?' Guilt swept through him. 'Did I say anything else?'

'You were mumbling and pushing your arms out in front of you, and you kept saying, "Mickey".'

He sat up and rubbed the sweat from his top lip. 'I must be missing the bugger.'

'Can you remember what the dream was about?' asked Greer.

'No. Funny how dreams just vanish like that.' He rubbed a hand over his bleary eyes.

Greer pushed the thin sheet off herself and padded over the marble-tiled floor towards the bathroom.

He heard her pee and wash her hands. When she came back there was just enough light in the room to penetrate her gauzy nightdress. He saw the flatness of her stomach and her small, high breasts. He hadn't been a virgin when he married Greer. There had been nights out in Newquay with Mickey and other mates where they'd all succumbed to sexual experiences of varying satisfaction and success.

He had been gentler with Greer on their wedding

night than he'd been with Loveday. He knew for sure that this was Greer's first time. He wished he'd known it had been Loveday's. He wished many things. The seething guilt rose in him again.

Greer moved gracefully to her side of the king-size bed and got under the sheet next to him. He was still getting used to the novelty of asking for sex at any time – and getting it. He rolled towards her and put his hand on her thigh, pushing the nightie over her hips and up to her stomach.

'Why do you wear this thing?'

'I always wear a nightie.' He felt the tension – or was it reluctance? – in her body.

'I like you naked.' He moved himself on top of her and eased his legs between hers.

She kept her eyes closed as he kissed her. As he pushed into her she tensed again but made no noise.

'Does it still hurt?' he asked, slowly pushing in and out of her.

'A bit.'

'You just need a bit more practice, that's all.'

Afterwards she got out of bed and had a long shower before getting dressed and organising her bag of poolside essentials. He watched her. He was fond of her. She had a good heart and loved him, he knew. She wasn't Loveday but she was his wife.

And now, here they were, lying in the January sun by a sparkling pool in Gran Canaria.

'I still can't believe how Mummy and Daddy managed to keep this whole honeymoon a secret from us,' sighed Greer. 'Hasn't it been dreamy?'

Jesse took a mouthful of the cold Spanish beer and nodded.

He still couldn't think with any clarity about his wedding day. He remembered Loveday's flow of silent tears as she stood behind them at the altar, Mickey's concern for her, and the congregation applauding when the vicar pronounced them man and wife.

In the vestry, as they had signed the register, he had tried to catch Loveday's eye, but she had kept as far away from him as she could. Then, once the signing and the photos were done and Greer had taken his arm possessively in order to walk triumphantly down the aisle, showing off her new husband, he had felt something being stuffed into his jacket pocket by Bryn, his new father-in-law. He was saying, 'It's your honeymoon, lad. Treat her well. The flight goes from Bristol in five hours. Four weeks of sun in the Grand Hotel Residencia, Gran Canaria.' Jesse had looked at him stupidly. 'And,' continued Bryn, 'when you get back, no need to worry about moving in with us. I've got a little place all set up for you.' He elbowed his new son-in-law in the ribs. 'After all, you don't want the "outlaws" breathing down your neck every time you want some privacy, do you?' He winked at Jesse as Jesse allowed himself to be dragged out of the vestry and down the aisle to the triumphant organ and hearty applause.

*

The reception, held at the golf club, had been noisy and boozy. Mickey's speech, nervously delivered, had gone down well, and Jesse managed the thank yous and the toasts he was obliged to give. 'And, finally,' he said, putting his crib notes down on the tablecloth, 'I'd like to thank my two best friends for sharing this day with me. Best man, Mickey Chandler, and bridesmaid . . .' He swallowed pushing down the terrible but wonderful thoughts of what had happened between them. '. . . Loveday Carter.' The crowd applauded and a few wolf-whistled as Loveday left her seat and took a mock bow. Smiling and waving, she smoothed down the hideous dress and walked sedately to the ladies to cry in the peace of a cubicle.

Jesse watched her go. With a cowardice that shocked him, he stayed put and continued, 'And, finally, my greatest thanks go to . . . Greer, who I've known since we were both five and who is now . . . my wife.' He raised his glass. 'Ladies and gentlemen. The bride.'

*

A few minutes later, Jesse had made his way to the lavatories. Instead of going into the Gents, he dived into the Ladies, praying no one would catch him. Instead of a row of urinals he was met with a dully lit lobby, a fulllength mirror and a dressing table with stool. On the dressing table was a tissue box festooned in lilac lace and a clothes brush. He couldn't face looking at his reflection as he found the second door leading to the inner sanctuary of the women's stalls. Five in a row and only one door closed.

'Loveday, I know you're in there. Let me in.'

Loveday, sitting on the closed seat, was crying as quietly as she could. She stopped and sat still.

'Loveday. I want to talk to you.'

'Go away.'

He heard the outer door – the one that led to the small lobby – opening, and two women talking. 'She looks lovely, don't she?' remarked one.

'Aye, she does that, but her mother was always a looker and 'er dad weren't so bad when 'e was a young 'un.' As they pushed the inner door, Jesse dived into the empty cubicle next to Loveday's.

To make things sound authentic he thought he might as well have a pee while he was there. Giving himself a shake as he finished, he listened as the two strangers peed like camels, keeping up a stream of gossip about their opinions on the various outfits on display. Finally he heard their flushes and the two women washed their hands, still talking, before the hand driers drowned them out and they finally left.

He felt a hand tickling the top of his head. It was Loveday, standing on the loo seat next door. He looked up at her and a smile flooded her face. He opened his mouth to say something but she put a finger to her lips.

'Loveday,' said Jesse. 'I love you.'

'Don't, please don't say that.' Loveday's eyes welled with unspent tears. 'You're Greer's husband now and I wish you all the happiness in the world.'

He reached up and took hold of her hand.

'I mean it, Loveday. I love you and I'll never regret what happened last night.'

'Nor me. I'll never forget it and I'll never tell anyone neither.' Loveday looked so pitiful.

'Come out of there and let me hold you,' he begged.

'Someone will see.'

'No they won't.'

'They will.'

They looked at each other in a tragic impasse over the partition wall. Tentatively he asked, 'Loveday, am I . . . was I the first to . . .? Have you ever done . . . that with Mickey . . . or anyone?'

She shook her head. 'I've never let Mickey touch me.'

Jesse was surprised. 'But he told me that you had.'

'Well, he would, wouldn't he? But I couldn't. Not with Mickey and not while I was waiting for you.'

They stood in their tragic tableau, neither knowing what to say.

'You've got to go,' said Loveday with finality. 'You've got a plane to catch, haven't you?'

They heard the outer door opening again and Loveday jumped down so that she wouldn't be seen. A familiar voice called out, 'Loveday? Are you in there? I'm going to change into my going-away outfit and I need my bridesmaid to help.'

Loveday flushed her loo and came out, smoothing down the hated dress over her curves.

'Here I am.'

*

It had started to snow heavily again. The taxi company had sent a big white Range Rover to make sure that it would get out of Trevay and up the hill towards the A30 safely. Jesse helped Greer into the back seat before climbing in next to the driver. Greer opened her electric window and immediately a flurry of snow and a handful of pink and blue confetti flew into her face, landing prettily on her eyelashes and the lace of her suit jacket.

'Catch!' she shouted, throwing her bouquet towards Loveday.

Loveday tried hard not to catch it. She closed her eyes tight as the beautiful flowers arced through the snow-filled air. But the fates had decreed that it land in the centre of Loveday's chest, scraping the skin, and she had no option but to let the flowers fall into her arms. Mickey slid his arm around her waist and gave her a beerily passionate kiss on the lips.

The crowd ooh'd and aah'd and someone shouted, 'Run Mickey, run!' to a burst of laughter.

*

Jesse, sitting on his sun bed, shivered with the dreadful memory and took another swig of his cold beer.

'Yeah. It all seems unreal.'

Greer leant over and kissed her husband. 'I can't wait to get home and show off this tan. A tan in January seems so luxurious. Loveday will be so jealous.'

Jesse shifted away from her. 'She's not like that.'

'Yes, she is. She'd love Mickey to bring her on a holiday like this.' Greer sniggered. 'Not that he'd know how to leave Cornwall. Has he ever crossed the Tamar?'

Jesse hated it when Greer ran Mickey down. 'Leave it, Greer. I couldn't afford to bring you here if your dad hadn't paid.'

Greer reached her hand to his face and stroked his cheek. 'Don't be angry. I was teasing. I know how lucky we are.' She sat up and pushed her sunglasses on to her head. 'Aren't you excited about our new house, though?'

'Yeah.'

'Well, don't sound too enthusiastic.' Greer looked down at her manicured toes. 'Are you cross that Mum and Dad have done it and we don't even know what it looks like?'

Jesse frowned. 'A bit.'

'Ah, my poor caveman. Did you want to go out with your club and bash the other troglodytes on the head to steal the best cave?' She ran her fingers down his chest and tickled his stomach. He pushed her hand away.

She was apologetic. 'I was just teasing.'

'Well, don't. Your parents have been very generous. The wedding, this holiday—'

'Honeymoon.'

'. . . honeymoon. Somewhere for us to live . . .'

'And an important new job.'

Jesse rubbed his hand over his face. 'Yes, and the new job.' Suddenly the latent anxiety lapped at the base of his throat. 'It's all too much. I . . . we . . . should be making our own lives. Our own decisions.'

Greer saw the anxiety in Jesse's face and misread its reason.

'It's a dream come true for me, Jesse, and I know you'll be wonderful. Don't ever think you could let me down. I know how hard you work and what the business means to your dad as well as mine. I'm so proud of you.' She took his hand in hers. 'And, one day, you'll pass it all on to our children. It's exciting.'

Jesse felt a tightening round his chest. He was like a mackerel, caught in one of his father's trawl nets.

14

Elizabeth Clovelly couldn't stop herself from turning the loo paper roll the 'right' way round on its holder. Jan Behenna watched her.

'What did you turn it round for?'

'The loose edge mustn't rest against the wall. It must hang out into the room.'

'Why?'

'Well, over time, a grease mark will appear on the new paint, from where people's hands have to touch the wall to pull at the roll.'

'Oh, I see,' said Jan, who didn't.

'It's something my mother did; once you know about it, you can't stop doing it.' Elizabeth smiled. 'Sometimes I do it when I'm out. At other people's houses. Or restaurants. Silly, I know, but it makes sense.'

Jan wondered if this woman had done it in her house. She'd have to check the bloody thing whenever she came round.

Elizabeth was straightening the towels now. 'Sweet bathroom,' she managed to say, whilst thinking the exact opposite.

Jan looked round with pride at the room she'd lovingly decorated. She couldn't wait for Jesse and Greer to see it. The bath, basin and toilet were in aqua blue and she'd chosen dear little tiles to put around the sink, each with a picture of a penguin at his ablutions. One cleaning his teeth, one having a shave and one – her favourite – lying in a bubble bath with a shower hat on his head.

'Isn't it?' She smiled with satisfaction. 'I never had an indoor bathroom when we first got married. Outdoor privy and a wash in the old Belfast sink in the kitchen. Used to put the boys in there too when they were babies.'

'That must have been . . . difficult.'

'Well, it was fun really. We'd all dry off in front of the fire and Edward would dry my hair by brushing it till it gleamed.' Jan reached up to her short crop. 'It used to be thick and had a wave but . . . 'Tis more practical to have it short, isn't it?'

Elizabeth thought of the monthly bill to have her expensively blond hair cut and coloured and said, 'Yes, it must be.'

Jan was on the tiny landing now and peeking into the master bedroom. ''Tis proper cosy. I love the colour. I'd never have thought of mushroom.'

'It's called Drizzle,' said Elizabeth, pushing past Jan and stepping into the small but light room.

'Drizzle!' Jan laughed. 'How they come up with these names! I'd have done something like blue. Edward says bedrooms need to be blue. Calm, see. And in a marriage you need to stay calm.'

Elizabeth was twitching the duvet and smoothing it straight for the umpteenth time. 'This has a warm feel, don't you think?'

'Oh, definitely.'

Elizabeth checked her slim gold watch. 'They'll be here soon. It's nearly time.'

*

Jesse and Greer were met at the airport by the same driver who'd dropped them off four weeks before. 'Welcome home, Mr and Mrs Behenna. How was the trip?' he asked as he stowed the suitcases into the large boot.

Greer clutched at Jesse's arm. 'Wonderful, thank you. I can't believe we've been away for such a long time.'

'The sun's come out for you,' he told them, jumping into the front seat and starting the engine. 'The snow has all gone.'

Jesse felt the need to take charge. 'Would you drop us off at my parents' house, please, Fish Lane at the top of Fore Street?'

'Ah, no, sir. I have another address I have been asked to take you to.'

Greer clapped her hands with glee. 'Is it our new home?'

'Can't possibly say, Mrs Behenna,' the driver said, looking at her in his rear-view mirror.

'It is! How exciting.' Greer took Jesse's arm and snuggled in. 'We're going to our new home.'

The yellow of the early February sun lit the moors as they drove west towards Trevay and the sea. Driving down the hill and into the village, past the peeling grandeur of the old Great Western Hotel, the newlyweds wondered whether the driver would turn left or right along the estuary road. He turned left towards the heart of Trevay. Greer clutched one hand to her chest and the other to Jesse's arm. 'I wonder where it is? Will it overlook the harbour, do you think?'

Jesse frowned. The creeping, suffocating certainty that his life was not his own any more was seeping into his psyche. He was in the control of others. He wanted to order the driver to stop the car and let him out so that he could run as fast as he could away from Trevay.

'Dunno,' he muttered.

The car went past Fore Street and followed the harbour road round towards the Golden Hind. The driver indicated left and turned into Cobb Lane. Greer leant forward and pointed saying, 'Look, look!' On the right Jesse saw a house with ribbons and balloons on the gate. Both sets of parents were waving.

Greer was bouncing on the seat with excitement. 'It's Pencil Cottage! I've wanted to live here since I was a little girl! Look, Jesse, isn't it wonderful?'

Jesse looked at the house he'd walked past, and never given a thought to, for almost twenty years. Pencil thin and squeezed between two regular-sized Trevay fishermen's cottages, this was his new home.

The car rolled to a halt and the faces of Elizabeth and Jan peered in through the back windows, grinning. The driver jumped out and opened Greer's door for her. She fell into her parents' arms, where she was showered with hugs and kisses and questions about the honeymoon.

Jesse climbed out and walked to the boot of the Range Rover to help with the bags. 'I'll do that, sir,' said the driver. 'I think you're needed to carry something else over the threshold.'

Jesse looked over his shoulder and saw Greer and both sets of parents waiting expectantly for him.

*

Standing in the front room, Bryn spoke first. 'Now then, young Jesse, please accept Pencil Cottage as a wedding present. It'll keep you both warm till you can afford your own place. The company has paid for it and it should be a nice little asset for us. When the time comes for you to need a bigger house, the company will sell this and I'll split the profit with you. That way you'll have a tidy deposit for a proper family home.'

Jesse experienced three emotions. One, gratitude that this should be happening to him; two, fury that this man had, in one fell swoop, totally emasculated him, and three, the feeling that his balls were being squeezed in an ever-tighter vice.

His father stepped towards him wearing a tight smile. 'Welcome home, son. Your mother and I couldn't be more proud of the both of you.'

*

The house might have been thin on the outside but, inside, it went a long way back and up. The front door opened immediately into the sitting room, which was traditional, warm and inviting. Elizabeth had kept it all white with simple furnishings, knowing that her daughter would want to customise the entire house. It led into a smart galley kitchen, which in turn led out to a tiny concreted yard with raised flower beds full of prettily nodding daffodils.

Greer wriggled with joy. 'I bet this is a suntrap. It feels warm right now!'

Back in the house she pointed out the dishwasher, television, the large framed wedding photo on the mantelpiece that Jan had had printed especially, and the view from the front window.

'Wait till you see upstairs,' Jan said, longing for Jesse to see her handiwork in the bathroom.

'Yes, you'll love the bedroom, Greer,' said Elizabeth, leading the way before Jan could get ahead of her.

Jesse's muscles were beginning to tire where he was

attempting to smile with genuine pleasure. Greer kissed his nose and galloped up the stairs ahead of him.

'Oh, Mummy!' gasped Greer as she saw the bedroom. 'It's so glamorous!' She called out to the landing: 'Jesse, quick. In here.' Jesse ducked his head under the low latched door and absorbed the pinky-brown walls, frilly bed linen and heavy Austrian blind at the window. Greer gripped his arm with eyes wide. 'Isn't it stylish?'

Jesse nodded slowly, mystified.

'He's overwhelmed, Mummy.' Greer went to her mother and hugged and kissed her.

Jan, desperate for Jesse to see the bathroom, pulled at his arm. 'I've got something to show you too.'

The bathroom was much more to Jesse's taste. 'Oh, Mum. 'Tis lovely.'

Jan beamed with happiness. 'Look at the penguins!'

Jesse smiled. 'I like them.'

'I knew you would, and come here.' Jan pushed the loo lid shut. 'Sit here and look at the view!'

He sat. Through the tiny square of the tiny window straight ahead of him, Jesse could just make out his father's flagship, *The Lobster Pot*, bobbing gently at anchor in the harbour. Jesse laughed then and shouted out to his father on the landing, 'Dad, I'll be able to make sure you're working hard from here.' Edward laughed too. 'Aye. But I've checked it out and I can see you doing your business on that toilet if I get my binoculars out.'

Everyone but Greer and Elizabeth laughed heartily.

'Well, now. I've got tea and sandwiches ready, if you want some,' said Elizabeth, heading back downstairs. 'There might even be a bottle of bubbly in the fridge.'

*

'What's that bleddy 'orrible paint Betty's put on your bedroom walls?'

Edward had taken his shoes off and was sitting in his favourite armchair back at the family home in Fish Lane. The three Behennas had left Pencil Cottage on the pretext of collecting Jesse's bits and pieces.

'Edward.' Jan looked at her husband sternly. 'That's the latest, most stylish colour. And don't call her Betty. She prefers to be called Elizabeth, as you well know.'

Edward made a grumbling noise. 'She was Betty when we was all at school together.'

Jan ignored him. 'So, son, we missed you. What was Gran Canaria like?'

'Hot. Nice.'

'Food good?'

'Not bad. Mind you, I could have murdered a pasty.'

Jan brightened up. 'I've got some ready to heat up if you want one.'

'Go on then.' Jesse smiled at his mum as she went to the kitchen.

Edward, making sure she'd left the room before he spoke, asked under his breath, 'So, everything all right in the bedroom department?'

Jesse squirmed a little. 'Fine.'

'Ah. Good. Only some women—'

'Dad. Please. It's fine. She's fine . . . and that's all.'

'Well, that's all right then.'

'Yes.'

*

At Pencil Cottage, Greer and her mother were unpacking her suitcases in the bedroom.

'How was the honeymoon, darling? Was he kind to you?' asked Elizabeth delicately and without making eye contact with her daughter.

Greer was embarrassed. 'Yes. He was lovely.'

'He . . . didn't make things uncomfortable for you?'

Greer folded a bikini and put it into one of the new drawers, then sat on the bed. 'A bit. I think I just have to . . . get used to it.'

Elizabeth moved a pile of underwear and sat next to her daughter. 'It's not easy at first, but it gets better. It makes men happy. And in time it'll make you happy too.'

Greer looked into her mother's eyes. 'I do love him.'

Elizabeth patted her hand. 'That's all you need.'

Downstairs the phone rang and they could hear Bryn answer. ''Ello, Mickey . . . yeah, they're home safe and sound . . . right, yeah, we'll meet you there. Ten minutes? Rightyo.' He called up the stairs. 'Get your coats on, that was Mickey. He and Loveday are going down the Hind. They want to welcome you home with a couple of drinks.'

*

The Golden Hind was thick with tobacco smoke and the heady scent of Cornish beer.

Loveday really hadn't wanted to come. 'Let them have their first night in their new home by themselves, Mick,' she'd pleaded.

Mickey was incredulous. 'They've just spent four weeks on their own. If I know Jesse, he'll be desperate for a beer or two and some male company.' He added as an afterthought, 'And Greer will want to see you as well. She'll want to tell you all about her posh hotel and that.'

'That's what I'm afraid of,' replied Loveday gloomily.

'That's my girl.' Mickey put his arm around her. 'We'll have a great night.'

*

Mickey and Loveday got to the pub before anyone else and Loveday stationed herself on one of the Dralon banquettes on the far wall. From there she could see who was coming in and out of the bar. As the place filled up, it would be harder for anyone coming in to spot her first.

Mickey got her a cider shandy and a bag of pork scratchings. 'There you are. I'm going to wait at the bar. I'll send Greer over as soon as she arrives.'

Gee, thanks, thought Loveday. Her heart was beating so fast that she could feel the pulse in her neck. Waves of perspiration hit her every few minutes. She felt sick. Had Jesse told Greer what had happened between them? Was he filled with the same longing to see her as she was to see him?

She jumped as the pub door opened, but it was a group of locals trooping in to fill the space with laughter and a blast of cool February air.

Her nerves were raw. What would she say to him? What would he say to her?

The pub door opened again, and again it wasn't Jesse or Greer. At least the bar was filling up and she'd be very hard to find when – if – he came in.

She pulled at the opening of the bag of pork scratchings. Her hands were slippery with sweat and she couldn't get a good grip. She put the bag to her mouth and ripped it open with her teeth. The entire bag split from top to bottom and its greasy contents spilt itself all down her good T-shirt. She almost cried. 'Shit shit shit,' she said under her breath as she tried to pick the larger lumps up and brush the powdery residue off her clothes and onto the floor.

'All right, Loveday?' Jesse was standing over her. Smiling his warm, familiar smile. His eyes shining in a very tanned face, his good looks were almost blinding.

'I've just tipped bloody pork scratchings all over me,' she said helplessly.

'Do you want me to lick 'em off for you?' Her eyes darted to his face to see if he was laughing at her. He wasn't, but there was a look in his eyes that she couldn't read. Something she had never seen there before. A hardness.

'Do you want a drink?'

'Yes, please, darling.' Greer appeared from behind Jesse and plonked herself neatly on the bench next to Loveday. 'White wine spritzer, please.'

15

'The house is just adorable. Mum and Jan worked so hard setting it up for us. Dad's bought all new carpets and appliances. I've got such plans for the interior. I think I'm going for modern with a twist of "olde worlde". We're going to save up for bits as we go along. You must come and see it.' Greer was on a roll. The boys had left the girls to it and were now standing at the bar with a group of male pals. How Loveday longed to be with them.

'I'd love to,' said Loveday, feeling horrible but trying to sound normal. 'How was the honeymoon? Was the hotel nice?'

'It was *sooo* luxurious. Our room was huge with a balcony overlooking the pool and our own table and chairs out on it. One day we had breakfast out there. Room service. Just a continental breakfast, croissants, black coffee, freshly squeezed orange juice. I loved it, but Jesse didn't want to do it again. You know what these boys are like. He wanted the full English in the dining room. Most nights we ate in the English bar in the marina, but once or twice I made him eat local stuff. He liked the paella . . . and the calamari, until I told him it was baby octopus.'

Loveday grimaced. 'Octopus?'

'Yes. He's a fishermen! I thought he ate anything that came out of the sea.'

Loveday had been around the fishing boats all her life, and enjoyed cod and chips as well as the next woman, but octopus was going too far. She kept smiling, but as Greer went on and on, about the weather and the pool and the waiters round the pool, and the one waiter that Jesse got really jealous about because he was paying so much attention to her, and how being married gave her such a feeling of enormous security, and on and on and bloody on, Loveday fought the desire to tell her best and oldest friend to shut up.

Here, with Greer sitting right in front of her, she was struggling with the conflicting and terrible feelings she felt crashing around within her: jealousy that Greer had been alone with Jesse for so long; overwhelming guilt about sleeping with Jesse; horror at how she'd betrayed her best friend, betrayed Mickey. The last four weeks had been hell for her. She'd been dreaming of Jesse coming home. Stealing away with him, up to the sheds, to talk and make love and disentangle themselves from the mistake he'd made in marrying Greer. In her most optimistic moments, she'd imagined him coming back and explaining to Mickey and Greer what had happened and, after a while, in due course, after the divorce, Jesse would marry Loveday and Mickey and Greer would be happy for them. Everyone would understand what a mistake it had been for Greer and Jesse to marry and they'd be glad that a mistake had been rectified. They'd see that, and they'd all be so much happier. In the meantime Greer was still chuntering on, and it was seeming increasingly unlikely that was going to happen.

'Perhaps you and Mickey would like to come over to Pencil Cottage tomorrow night? Just kitchen sups. Spaghetti Bolognese?'

Loveday flicked a glance over to Mickey at the bar and saw Jesse heave himself off a well-worn bar stool and begin to walk towards them. She answered Greer with a vague, 'Erm . . . yeah, I'll ask Mickey.' She was so alert to Jesse getting closer to them that every atom in her body started to shake. He reached their table and took a seat on a low stool opposite Greer, who immediately took his hand. 'Hello, husband!' She glowed. 'I've just been telling Loveday all about our honeymoon.'

'Not everything, I hope,' he said, looking at the floor, finding a beer mat to pick up.

Greer blushed a little. 'No. Stop it. What are men like?' She looked at Loveday and raised her eyebrows. 'Honestly! Boys have one-track minds, don't they?'

Loveday picked up her pint of shandy and tried to look world-weary. 'Gosh, don't they?'

Greer twittered on, 'I've just asked Loveday and Mickey round for tea tomorrow. Loveday wants to see the house.' Jesse looked sharply at Loveday, who gave her head the slightest of shakes. Greer cantered on oblivious, 'And I know you've missed Mickey. I thought I'd do spag bol.'

Jesse was still looking at Loveday, but with an expression she couldn't interpret. Why was he being so cold towards her?

She blurted hurriedly, 'I didn't say I wanted to see the house . . . well, not the day after you come home. You need to get settled.'

Jesse turned to Greer. 'Yeah, we've only just got home, love. Let's get ourselves sorted out first.'

Mickey ambled over and put his hand on Jesse's shoulder. 'Come on, big man. I've got a hot game of bar billiards to play with you.'

Jesse stood up and, putting his hand in his back pocket,

pulled out his wallet and took out a ten-pound note. 'You girls get yourselves a drink and maybe something to eat. Mickey and I have some serious cueing to do.'

Both young women were silenced. Greer felt slighted, abandoned by her husband on her first night home, and Loveday felt, without having the right to feel it, dumped.

Just before ten thirty, Pete the landlord rang the old ship's bell behind the bar. 'Last orders, ladies and gentlemen. Last orders, please.'

*

Greer and Loveday were sitting where the boys had left them almost two hours before. In front of them was a barely touched prawn sandwich (Greer's) and the last crumbs of scampi and chips in the basket (Loveday's). They were each nursing a drink and had run out of conversation. The bar was thinning out and, across the floor, they could see into the games room, where Mickey and Jesse, more than tipsy, were whooping with jeers and laughter after each cue shot.

Pete was calling out to the stragglers, 'Drink up now, ladies and gents. Time to get home.' He was moving between the bar and the tables, collecting up the dirty glasses and ashtrays. He stopped by Loveday and Greer. 'Welcome home, Mrs Behennna. 'Ow was the honeymoon?'

'Lovely, thank you,' said Greer with an automatic politeness.

'Glad to have your mate back, aren't you, Loveday?'

'Yes,' said Loveday dully. 'Yes. Very glad.'

'I'll round those two lads up for you,' Pete assured them. 'You'm ladies need your beauty sleep.'

Pete was as good as his word and within a couple of

minutes Jesse and Mickey appeared, still giggling with each other.

'Get my coat, would you, Jesse?' Greer was irritated and impatient to get back to Pencil Cottage.

Jesse took the long black coat off one of the row of pegs by the pub door and handed it to her. 'I mean, can you help me into it?' asked Greer with an edge to her voice.

'Since when couldn't you put your own coat on for yourself?' he asked her.

'It's what husbands do for wives,' she told him, handing the coat back to him.

Loveday zipped up her scarlet padded Puffa jacket and opened the pub door. A wall of now icy February air hit her and she was glad to breathe in the freshness of it after the fug of the Hind.

Mickey stepped out behind her and put his arm through hers. His eyes were glassy with beer and he smiled soppily at her. 'That was a nice evening. Did you have a good time catching up with Greer?'

'Hmm,' said Loveday tersely. 'I know all about bloody Gran Canaria anyway.'

The pub door opened again and a coated Greer and a sloshed Jesse appeared. 'Gosh, it's cold,' shivered Greer. 'But of course after a month of winter sun we'd feel it, wouldn't we, Jesse?'

'You would 'cos you ain't got enough meat on your bones. Not like Loveday. I bet she's warm as toast, eh, Loveday?' Loveday couldn't believe that Jesse could be so heartless towards her and felt tears stinging her eyes.

Mickey grabbed at Loveday's bum and gave it a good squeeze. 'Yeah. She's got enough flesh on her to keep her warm.' Jesse laughed with him, and Loveday, feeling like a heifer, turned towards home.

'By the way, Mickey,' she heard Greer saying, 'I've invited you and Loveday round for kitchen sups tomorrow. Spag bol. Six o'clock?'

Before Loveday could warn Mickey not to accept the invitation, he had, with great bonhomie, replied, 'Lovely. That'd be just the ticket, eh, Loveday?'

'That's sorted then,' smiled Greer, before taking Jesse's arm and looking up into his eyes in a way that made Loveday feel sick. 'My husband and I are to give our first dinner party to our best friends.' She stood on her tiptoes and gave Jesse a slow kiss. 'Excited?'

To Loveday's horror, Jesse returned the kiss with warmth. 'Let's get you home, Mrs Behenna.'

He wheeled Greer round and walked her off towards Pencil Cottage. Mickey pulled Loveday towards him. 'Must be nice to be married. Jesse was telling me they had a great honeymoon.'

'Did he?' Loveday felt empty.

They started walking towards Loveday's house. She said, 'My mum's not back till tomorrow. She's gone over to Auntie Sheila's.'

'Will you be all right on your own?' asked Mickey, not understanding what she was saying to him.

She spelt it out. 'I thought you might like to stay over and keep me company?'

'What? You mean like . . . ?'

'Yes, Mickey, that's exactly what I mean.'

'Loveday,' Mickey said thickly, and Loveday returned his overjoyed smile with one of her own. She may not have Jesse, but she had the power to make Mickey the happiest man in the world.

*

559

Jesse and Greer were lying in their new bed in their new bedroom in their new house. Greer was listening to the old place talking to itself as it settled its eaves onto its ancient rafters and cob walls. She couldn't have felt happier. Pencil Cottage was her home. Growing up, this had been the one house in the whole of Trevay that she had dreamt of owning. And now she did. Well, OK, her dad's company owned it, but it was hers to live in and love.

She turned and snuggled into her husband, who was recovering after a short, sharp, drunken but satisfying – for him – five minutes of lovemaking.

'Are you happy?' she asked.

He was getting fed up with her always asking if he was happy.

What would she do if he told her the truth? If he just opened his mouth right now and said:

'No, as a matter of fact I'm not particularly happy. I only agreed to marry you because my father and your father persuaded me that it would be good for me, for them and for the whole financial health of Trevay. Our boats would get a better deal with the fish market; we'd freeze out the boats from further up and down the coast. They told me that you were the best catch in Cornwall and I'd be a lucky man to have you as my wife. And I am so thick, and so greedy, that I went along with it and sold my soul to the devil.

'I am no longer my own man. I married you and received a house, a job and a honeymoon as payment. I am a whore; I don't want to be lying next to you tonight, I want to be with Loveday. Yes, fat Loveday with no prospects. She has been a loyal friend to you and you despise her.

'I made love to her once, the night before our wedding,

if you want to hear the gory details, but now I'm married to you. It was cruel of me to talk about her flesh keeping her warm and to kiss you in front of her, but I was cruel tonight because I wanted her to get the message that I cannot give her anything. She deserves to be with a good man like Mickey. And you don't deserve to be with a shit like me. I'll try to be the best husband I can to you and to make you happy, but am I happy? You're happy, your dad's happy, my dad's happy, so who cares if I'm happy or not? Only Loveday, and she's as miserable as I am.'

He shifted a little so that Greer could rest her head on his shoulder. 'Yes, I'm happy, maid,' he said, and lay still, staring into the unfamiliar darkness of his new home.

*

Mickey couldn't believe that, at last, Loveday was his. She had led him up her narrow stairs and taken him into her bedroom, which looked the same as it always had. The grey carpet with swags of spring flowers woven into it was the same one that the four friends had played endless games of Monopoly on. He remembered that he and Jesse had had a huge fight, one Christmas, over paying the bill for a Monopoly hotel he'd put on Park Lane. Jesse had refused to hand over the money and they'd ended up brawling on the floor. Loveday had ended the fight by getting in between them and forcing them apart. Greer had quietly and carefully simply folded the board and put all the pieces back in their little boxed compartments.

The wallpaper was the same too, but now the A-ha posters that had littered it had come down. He'd been so jealous that Loveday had fancied Morten Harket. 'He's a poof,' he'd told her, and got a whack for his trouble.

Her single bed with the old satin eiderdown was still pushed up against the wall, and her teddy, Annabel, was still sitting on the pillow.

Loveday didn't put the bedroom light on. Instead she let the light from the landing spill softly into the room. She took his hand and knew he was nervous. 'Come on. Sit on the bed with me.'

He sat next to her and watched as she put Annabel down on the carpet. Then he kissed her more deeply than he'd ever dared before.

She felt for the buttons of her denim shirt and began undoing them, before shrugging it off to expose a large black bra, straining against the flesh and weight of her breasts. Mickey stopped kissing her and looked in wonder at her. 'You're so beautiful,' he breathed.

She helped him with the tricky clasp of her bra and, after that, he needed no help in easing both of them out of their clothes and in between the cool sheets. As inexperienced as Loveday was, she knew that where Jesse had been a lover with passion and force, Mickey was altogether different. He was tender and careful. She closed her eyes and gave herself up to the pleasure he was giving her. He wasn't Jesse. He was Mickey, and she prayed he would never, ever find out about her and Jesse.

16

The 'Sunday night sups', as Greer insisted on calling their get-together (apparently because she'd read somewhere that that's what Princess Diana called her informal evening meals), was endured and enjoyed in equal measure.

On the way there, Loveday steeled herself, determined not to let the situation get to her, or to let her emotions show through. But it was so hard. It was Jesse who answered the doorbell; instantly those sea-green eyes locked with hers, sending her stomach into backflips of desire before she had even crossed the threshold. As Jesse went to take her coat, Loveday tried to shrug her way awkwardly out of it, but she was not fast enough, and she felt Jesse's strong hands close round her shoulders, seemed to feel them burning through the thick material. She shuddered, making her way quickly through to the kitchen to give Greer a hand, trying to put distance between them. Still, when Jesse handed her a drink, she saw that her hand was shaking.

Greer was a good cook, and Loveday wasn't sure if she tucked into her meal with such relish because of her discomfort or in spite of it. Once or twice she caught Jesse's eye, but when she did he would look quickly away, or disappear to the kitchen on the pretext of getting another couple of cans of beer. He must have noticed the way she'd been in the hallway, she decided, squirming inwardly: he was making certain that they were never on their own together, or sitting anywhere near each other. Well, OK, if that was how it was going to be, Loveday thought, bristling, she had her pride. As the wine flowed and her taut nerves finally began to relax, Loveday got her own back by cosying up to Mickey, who was very happy to bask in his sexy girlfriend's attention.

Inside, Loveday was finally processing the stark message that was being ruthlessly delivered to her: that their lives had settled into a new phase – and that nothing she could do or wish for was going to change that.

*

Jesse still spent long hours at sea hunting the best catches he could. He knew his father was pleased with his progress – not that he would ever hear him say so – and he was given more responsibility on the boat. At sea he could be the old Jesse. Laughing with the boys, working hard and always respecting the ocean.

Life at Pencil Cottage was surprisingly pleasant. Comfortable. Greer was a great homemaker and the little house soon took on a polished and stylish personality. Out went the colours chosen by her and Jesse's mother; in came buff and beige and cloud grey. Jesse liked coming home to a lovely home, a decent supper and clean laundry. It was like living with his parents, but with the added bonus of sex and the satisfaction of being the man of the house. The only bore was Greer's extreme standards of tidiness, and her insistence that he should remove all his smelly fishing clothes the moment he entered the house. She would place a large towel on the floor, exactly a one-metre stride from the front door, so that he could, simultaneously, step on it, close the door behind him and strip off. She would hold out the laundry basket for him to drop the ripe jeans and overalls into before putting them – rubber gloves on – into the washing machine on a boil wash. Jesse would go upstairs to find a hot scented bath waiting for him. He'd have a soak, then a shave and clean his teeth, before finding Greer and giving her the sex he thought she was as eager for as he was.

*

It was Valentine's Day when Greer met him off the boat – odd in itself – and, odder still, kissed him full on the lips, even though he stank to high heaven.

'What was that for?' he asked as they broke apart.

'I've got some news.' She put the back of her hand to her mouth, tasting the sourness of his breath and trying not to gag.

Jesse swung his kitbag over his shoulder and, taking her hand, walked quickly towards home. The surprise of her appearance and the passionate kiss was sending messages of the bedroom kind to his nether regions.

'Let's get home.'

Lying breathless by her side, his filthy overalls for once allowed upstairs and strewn on the spotless dove-grey carpet of their bedroom, Jesse smiled. 'That was nice.' He exhaled slowly and pulled her head to rest on his shoulder. 'Now, tell me your news.'

The odour from his armpits was strong and stale. Greer shifted a little in order to avoid the worst of the fumes. 'I think we're going to have a baby.'

The fingers that had been stroking her waist stopped

abruptly. The room grew a silence that became a little thicker with each second, and then so heavy that Greer felt panicky and thirsty for oxygen.

He spoke. 'You think? Have you taken a test?'

'Yes.'

'And?'

'The blue line appeared.'

'And that means?'

'I'm pregnant.'

Jesse turned to face her, moving her from his shoulder to the soft pillows. He looked down at her pale, worried face and felt a wave of fear and exultation.

'Really?'

She nodded. 'I need to see Dr Cosgrove to confirm it, but I think I am. I've been feeling really sick for about a week and this morning I actually was sick so . . .'

'Wow.' He put his hand on her flat tummy. 'Hello, you in there. It's your daddy.'

Greer giggled and the look of worry was replaced with relief and love for her husband.

*

Dr Cosgrove moved his strong brown hands over her tummy and pressed gently, feeling for a thickening of her womb. He had known Greer since her mother was pregnant with her. He stopped his probing and left Greer lying on the ancient wood and leather examination table to get a tape measure from his desk drawer. He found the yellow booklet of tide times and, checking his watch, slipped it into his pocket. He was due to have an afternoon fishing trip with his son and he didn't want to be late. He retrieved the tape measure and stepped back to

Greer, lying prone on the bed. 'Right. Let me just make some measurements and we can work out roughly when your baby is due.'

'So I am pregnant?' asked Greer, daring to hope.

'You certainly are.' He measured from her pubic bone to a point below her navel. 'You can pull your dress down now and come and sit down.' He walked to his desk and made a squiggle in pencil on her notes. 'When was your last period?'

*

Jesse hadn't been to the doctor since he was a baby and certainly didn't feel the need to sit in on the business between Dr Cosgrove and Greer. He'd made his excuses and had gone to a meeting with his father and father-in-law to discuss business.

Greer heard his key in the lock and said hurriedly into the phone, 'Mummy, Jesse's home. I've got to go . . . Granny!' She heard her mother laughing as she put the receiver down.

Jesse closed the front door and, walking past Greer, went to the kitchen to put the kettle on. Greer followed him. 'So, ask me.'

He threw a teabag into his favourite mug and wrinkled his brow. 'Ask you what?'

'Jesse!' Greer was standing looking at him in sheer disbelief. 'You've forgotten where I was today?'

He reached for the kettle and poured the steaming water into his mug. 'At your mum's?'

Her bottom lip trembled and she turned, but he caught her before she got away and spun her round. 'I'm sorry. I was teasing.'

'Not funny. I've been waiting to tell you.'

He pulled her to him. 'Is it a girl or a boy?'

She punched his chest. 'Whatever it is, it's due on October the seventeenth.' She smiled up at him dreamily, 'A honeymoon baby. That's what Mummy said.'

He let go of her and went to the fridge for some milk. 'So you've told your mother then?'

'Don't be cross. I couldn't *not* tell her.'

'So I can tell my mum and dad now, can I?' he asked, looking over his shoulder at her.

She went to him and put her arms round his waist, leaning against his back. 'Of course. Let's invite them for supper.'

Jesse knew how uncomfortable his parents felt in Pencil Cottage, and how hurt his mother had been when Greer had repainted the bathroom and chiselled off the penguin tiles in favour of plain white Italian ones. He decided that discretion was the better part of valour. 'You don't want to cook. You need to put your feet up a bit. Let's take them to the Hind.'

Greer quietly cheered inside. Her in-laws were nice, but she had very little in common with them, and Ed didn't seem to enjoy her cooking anyway. 'Good idea.'

*

It seemed the whole of Trevay were delighted with news of the baby. Greer thoroughly enjoyed the fuss that was being made of her and played it up to the hilt. On nights when Jesse was at sea, Elizabeth would come and stay in the small spare bedroom that was destined to become the nursery. She held Greer's hair from her face when she was being sick; she massaged her stick-thin ankles in case they got puffy, and she fed her exquisite morsels of goodness – but not too much, as neither of them wanted to let Greer gain more weight than was necessary.

Mickey was happiest of all. 'Jesse, mate.' He bear-hugged him when he'd got the news. 'I didn't know you had it in you!'

Jesse adopted a macho pose. 'Plenty of lead in my pencil.'

'Pencil? You mean that tiny little thing?' The young men wrestled affectionately for a moment, as they always had done. When they broke apart Mickey asked, 'Fancy a pint? Or have you got to get on home to the missus?'

'I don't have to ask her for permission, you know,' swaggered Jesse. 'Barefoot and pregnant and tied to the sink. That's the way it is in my house.'

Mickey grinned. 'Yeah, right. Just don't let Greer hear you say that!' They were walking back from a day's work on the harbour and heading towards the Golden Hind.

Settled in a favourite corner of the dim bar, they each took a sip of their pints and sighed with pleasure in unison.

'So when's Jesse Junior due?' asked Mickey, wiping the froth from his lips.

'Middle of October.'

'Were you trying for a baby this quick?'

'No. We hadn't really spoken about it. And I thought these things took a bit of trying for.'

'She wasn't on the pill?'

'With the wedding and everything, Greer said she hadn't had time to get to the doctor's and – you know – she hadn't needed anything like that before, so . . .'

'You were her first?'

'Yeah.'

Mickey took a mouthful of beer then said, 'I was Loveday's first, too.'

Jesse tried not to react to this, but he spilt his beer a little onto his jeans. 'Shit,' he said, rubbing the damp patch into the fabric. When he'd gathered himself, he looked straight into Mickey's eyes. 'Were you? When was this?'

'The night you came home from honeymoon.'

'But you always told me . . .'

Mickey looked embarrassed. 'Yeah, well, that was just talk. She never let me touch her until that night. I think seeing you two so happy tipped the balance for me, so I have a lot to thank you for, mate.'

Jesse felt shame and fear wash through him, but smiled warmly. 'Well done.'

'Yeah.' Mickey put his pint on the table and looked down at the floor as if deciding whether to say anything more. 'Truth is, Loveday thinks she might be pregnant too.'

Jesse stared hard at Mickey. 'What?'

*

Dr Cosgrove washed his hands in the small sink in his surgery and took a paper towel to dry them. 'Congratulations to you both. Now, let's work out when this baby is due. When did your last period start, Loveday?'

Loveday clutched Mickey's hand. She had two answers and fervently hoped it was the second one. She crossed her fingers and said, 'About the tenth of January.'

Dr Cosgrove consulted his diary. 'This baby is due roughly around . . . October the seventeenth.'

'That's the same day as Jesse's baby!' Mickey was thrilled and squeezed Loveday's hand tight. 'That's amazing!'

Dr Cosgrove was putting Loveday's notes back into the brown envelope to be filed. 'You feel a little bit bigger than your dates suggest.'

Loveday looked anxious.

'No need to worry, my dear.' Dr Cosgrove smiled reassuringly and turned to Mickey. 'There are twins on your side of the family, aren't there?'

Mickey and Loveday walked out of the surgery holding hands, each thinking their own thoughts. Loveday prayed she was having Mickey's baby, or babies, as the doctor had suggested. She didn't care if she was expecting quadruplets, just as long as they were Mickey's and not Jesse's.

Mickey's mind was in a whirl. He was twenty-one. The same age his dad had been when he'd had him. He had a good job and he loved Loveday so much it hurt. They could live with his mum and dad for a bit till he'd got some money together to rent a little place. He was going to be the best dad he could be to this little baby, and the best husband to Loveday.

He stopped abruptly in his tracks and Loveday with him. 'Darlin', will you marry me?'

17

Greer was lying on her bed and smoothing oil onto her flat stomach in the hope of preventing stretch marks. *The Giant Book of Babies – From conception to five years* was next to her.

'It says here that at six weeks the baby is the size of a lentil. Imagine.' She stopped her massaging and clasped both hands across her abdomen. 'A lentil.'

Jesse was cleaning his teeth in the newly painted bathroom (a nondescript colour called Pebble Putty, apparently). He stepped onto the landing and stuck his damp face round the bedroom door. 'I don't like lentils.'

Greer tutted silently and said more clearly, 'I'm saying that the baby is the size of a lentil right now. And please remember to fold the towel and hang it on the towel heater.'

Jesse, safely back in the bathroom, pulled a face and mimicked her with childlike satisfaction. However, he did as instructed and turned out the bathroom light.

'Did you put the loo seat down?' she asked as he got into bed.

'I think so.'

'Well, can you check, because I need to pee so much in the night and I can't stand the feeling of cold, probably wet, china to sit on.'

'Turn the light on if you need to go.'

'I don't like to disturb you.'

Jesse disturbed himself and got out of bed and went to the bathroom to check on the loo seat. It was up. He closed it as quietly as he could and returned to bed.

Greer had stopped massaging her tummy and was rubbing hand cream into her hands with vigour. 'Was the seat up?'

'No.'

'Well, thank you for checking.' Greer had finished emolliating herself and kissed Jesse before turning her light out.

'My pleasure.'

Jesse turned his light out and got himself comfortable.

Greer rolled towards him and snuggled in. 'By the way,' she said sleepily, 'wonderful news about Mickey and Loveday.'

Jesse was immediately on his guard. 'What news?'

'Oh, you boys! I know you know. Loveday told me.'

'Told you what?'

'That she's pregnant. It's so sweet. They've been destined for each other ever since that first day at school.'

'Oh, that. Yeah, Mickey told me.'

'And the baby's due at about the same time as this little one.' She reached for his hand and pressed it against her stomach.

Jesse was thinking about the babies arriving at the same time. 'So does that mean that she and Mickey were at it at the same time we were?'

'Yes, I suppose so.' Greer giggled. She felt Jesse's body relax against her and assumed he wanted sex. 'Now don't get any ideas. You know how worried I am about hurting the baby. Maybe we can resume games in the second trimester.'

Jesse's thoughts were far from sex, but he played along. 'When's that then?'

'About another six weeks.'

*

Jesse chose a day when he knew that Mickey was in Bodmin, on an errand to pick up an ignition coil for *Our Mermaid*, to see Loveday. She opened the door to him in a short dressing gown that was at least two sizes too small for her. She looked awful.

'Jesse,' she said anxiously. 'What are you doing here?'

'Can I come in?'

Jesse filled the space of the small front room. He didn't sit down but stood looking at her with such tenderness that it took all Loveday's strength not to reach out and hold him.

'How are you feeling?' he asked her.

'A bit shit. Sorry, I must look awful. I didn't sleep very well and I keep being sick.'

'Poor you.' He touched her arm with his hand.

She stepped away and towards the tiny kitchen. 'I was just about to put the kettle on. Want one?'

'Yeah. OK.'

'How's Greer feeling? She said she was a bit tired.'

'Yeah. She's OK. Yeah.'

Loveday busied herself with taking mugs from the old kitchen cabinet. It was the type that had a pull-down worktop and cupboard space for larder items and crockery. He saw that she'd been making toast.

'Had your breakfast then? That'll help with the sickness, my mum says.'

The blue enamel kettle was whistling on the gas stove.

Loveday poured water into her mother's ancient brown teapot. And kept her back to him. 'What are you doing here, Jesse?'

He moved towards her but she turned and stood with the hot kettle between them. 'This baby is Mickey's,' she said.

'Loveday, I'm not cross. I'd help you. If this baby is mine, no one need ever know, if that's what you want.'

He wasn't expecting her reaction to be so swift and angry. 'So you'd let Mickey think this baby was his – which it is – and you'd be the big man secretly helping me out?'

Jesse nodded, feeling scolded and confused. 'Yes. I would. Is that so bad?'

'It'd be worse than cheating on your best friend . . . which you did.'

'So did you.'

Loveday was angry. She slammed the kettle back on the metal stove. 'I know I did. Don't you think I regret it every minute? Every time I look at Mickey? Every time I look at Greer? Shit, Jesse, we did something terrible.' She looked up at him, the anger draining away to be replaced by sheer horror and sadness at what they had both done – sleeping with each other's best friend; sacrificing their own happiness. Tears started to spill from her eyes.

Jesse slowly stepped towards her and took her in his arms. 'Hey, baby. It's OK. It's over. No one will ever know. I'm here for you. Always.' She pushed him away and wiped her eyes furiously with the backs of her hands, and then tore off a sheet of kitchen roll to blow her nose.

'You're not the father,' she snuffled.

'Are you sure?'

'Yes.'

'How can you be so sure?'

'The dates.'

Jesse shoved his hands into the pockets of his yellow waterproof jacket. 'Well, in that case, congratulations . . . to you both.'

They heard the front door squeak open and Mickey's voice calling, 'Loveday, I've got a surprise for you! What are you doing on Wednesday the seventeenth?'

Mickey ducked through the doorway of the kitchen. 'Hello, Jesse. This is lucky: I can kill two birds with one stone. What are both of you doing on Wednesday the seventeenth of March?'

He looked from one to the other and back again. 'No? Can't answer? Well, I'll tell you what you are doing – you're going to a wedding! We've got an appointment at the Register Office on Monday, then we have to wait fifteen days, but then . . .' He bounced forward and squeezed Loveday into his arms. 'You're going to be Mrs Chandler, and Jesse – ' he smiled at his best friend over the top of his wife-to-be's head – 'you're going to be my best man!'

*

The Bodmin Register Office had a small and pretty marriage room. The walls were Doulton blue and the ceiling white. There was a large arrangement of silk flowers in a corner by the window, in front of which happy couples usually had their first photos taken as man and wife. There was room for only forty guests but, as neither bride nor groom could afford a large wedding, at least ten seats were empty.

Mickey and Jesse sat in front of the important-looking leather-topped table on which the registrar, a woman in her early forties with a chirpy smile and earrings to match, was laying out her various ledgers and pieces of paper.

Mickey had had a short back and sides and was wearing a new suit from Burton's.

He was nervous and couldn't keep his hands from checking his tie, his hair and eventually his pockets. The inside breast pocket yielded the washing instructions.

'Machine washable at 40°,' he read. 'That's handy.'

'Very,' said Jesse, and the two men grinned at each other, enjoying the momentary distraction.

'Do I look all right?' Mickey asked.

'You'll do.'

'Have you got the ring?'

'Yes.'

'At least I'm not pissed like you were.'

Jesse instantly flashed back to his wedding morning and the horrible secret he was keeping from Mickey. 'If I can be half the best man and best mate you've been to me, I'll be doing OK.'

Mickey shone his innocent smile at Jesse. 'I'm so happy. I can't believe that Loveday is actually going to marry me and that we have a baby on the way. This is the best day of my life.'

*

Outside, in the chilly anteroom, where brides could gather with their flotilla of bridesmaids and attendants, Loveday was taking deep breaths. Greer was rummaging in her bag for some Rescue Remedy.

'Here,' she said, holding up the small brown bottle and opening it to reveal the glass pipette. 'Three drops under the tongue. Open wide.'

Loveday did as she was told and Greer dripped in the recommended amount, with another couple of drops for luck.

Loveday grimaced. 'That's bleddy brandy!'

'It's needed to preserve the delicate flower essences.'

'We're not supposed to drink, with the babies and all.'

'This is medicinal. How are you feeling?'

'A bit better. How do I look?'

Greer gave Loveday an inspection from head to toe and back again. The charity shop wedding dress was in good condition, but clearly bought at the height of the mania to imitate Princess Diana. Oddly enough it suited Loveday, who had the bust to fill it.

'Have you lost weight?' asked Greer who, in spite of being careful with what she was eating, had put on four pounds.

'I have. I think it's all that sickness.'

'How much have you lost?'

'About ten pounds.'

'Well,' Greer smiled thinly, 'it suits you.' Then, knowing that had sounded mean she added, 'You look very nice. Very nice indeed.'

Loveday beamed. 'Thank you. You look amazing in that dress too.'

'Thank you. Can you see my bump? I feel huge.' Greer stood sideways to let Loveday get a proper view.

'No. But your bosoms are blossoming!' Loveday gave an earthy laugh.

Greer pulled at the top of her stylish shift dress. 'Oh God. I'm hoping they don't droop.'

Loveday hoiked up her own breasts with gusto. 'Mine were drooping when I was born.'

There was a knock at the door. The assistant registrar, a middle-aged man wearing glasses, popped his head round the door. 'We are ready for the bride.'

Greer collected up her tiny clutch bag and a box of confetti and held out her hand to Loveday.

'Are you ready to become Mrs Chandler, Miss Carter?' she said before adding, 'It's not too late to say no, you know. In my capacity as best woman, it's my duty to ask you.'

Loveday looked at her closest friend. So many people found Greer to be a bit cold, rather too pleased with herself and – to be frank – a snob, but Loveday knew Greer had a good heart and she felt such guilt that she could have betrayed her as she had. She had chosen Greer to give her away as a way of exorcising that night with Jesse and of consolidating their friendship again. She reached for Greer's hand. 'Bless you for taking my dad's place and giving me away. Mum's really chuffed too.' This wasn't true. Loveday's mother had wanted to give her daughter away herself, but had deferred to Loveday's wishes.

'My pleasure,' smiled Greer, swelling with importance. 'Now pick up that bouquet and go get your man.'

*

The two women walked hand in hand down the short aisle. There were oohs and aahs from the small congregation as they pulled unruly toddlers onto laps and fished for tissues in their pockets. Loveday was well loved in Trevay and they were thrilled that she was marrying the man who adored her. This was true romance. A budget shotgun wedding with heart and a guaranteed happy ending.

Mickey gulped with emotion as he saw his bride in all her lacy finery. Loveday's mother leant out into the aisle with a disposable camera and took two shots, winding each one on carefully, before starting to sniffle. Jesse stared straight ahead until Greer, who had delivered Loveday to Mickey's side, slipped in next to him. She reached for his hand. He took hers as a drowning man would grasp at a life raft.

The registrar started. 'Welcome, everybody, to the marriage of Michael and Loveday.'

Loveday took her vows and meant them. She was determined to do her best by Mickey and be the best wife to him that she could, no matter what had gone before.

*

The reception was a boozy, smoke-filled affair at the Golden Hind. As best man, Jesse had put plenty of money behind the bar as his wedding present to the couple. The buffet table was groaning under pasties and sausage rolls, and a good time was had by all.

Jesse's speech was well judged, if short, and everyone agreed the day couldn't have gone more smoothly. At least that was until the time for the reading of the telegrams.

Jesse had had a couple of pints and was relaxing. His best friend was married. Loveday was expecting her husband's baby, and Greer was expecting his. The sky was not going to fall in, after all.

There were four telegrams. One from Mickey's godmother, who now lived in New Zealand, and two from old friends of Loveday's mother. It was the final one that struck like a sniper's bullet. He started reading it before he'd checked who it was from. It was from his brother, Grant. 42 Commando had been deployed to Northern Iraq to ensure the security of Kurdish refugees. Somehow, Grant had managed to get a telegram out. It said: CONGRATULATIONS STOP HOPE THE BABY DOESN'T LOOK LIKE HIS DADDY STOP DRINKS WHEN I GET HOME STOP REGARDS BIG G STOP

Jesse couldn't help flicking his eyes towards Loveday, who looked as if she might faint. Did Grant know what they had done? Why had he put that?

Mickey was on his – unsteady – feet now and was clapping Jesse on the back. 'Typical of your fucking brother. What a wind-up merchant.' Mickey was laughing and so was the rest of the pub. Jesse laughed nervously and again looked over at Loveday, who had been collared by a tipsy auntie. Jesse did the only thing he could think of and hauled Mickey to the bar to get smashed.

18

The following months were kind to Mickey and Loveday. Her mum welcomed the newlyweds into her tiny cottage and Mickey got a pay rise on the boat. He'd also started an apprenticeship to be the ship's mechanic and was away at sea a lot, but the fishing was good and now that the Behenna and Clovelly Fish Company was established, the prices at market were steady.

Loveday worked shifts at the bakery where she'd been a Saturday girl since she was at school. She liked the work and the banter between her colleagues and customers. She also liked the fact that her pregnancy had driven her hunger for pasties and sausage rolls right out of the door. Her weight was dropping and her midwife was pleased.

'Good girl. That's another two pounds off.' Loveday was worried.

'Will the baby be OK?'

'Baby is fine. Growing well. Don't worry, just keep listening to your body and eating healthily.'

Loveday stepped back into her shoes. 'It's funny 'cos before I was pregnant I craved chips and chocolate; now I crave salad and fish.'

The midwife was writing in her records book and laughed. 'You'll make my other ladies jealous. Just promise me you're not going on any fad diets.'

'Oh, I promise. My mum and Mickey would never let me. Mickey worries more than I do.'

The midwife handed Loveday her records card and said, 'I wish all dads were the same. See you in four weeks.'

*

If everything was going well for Loveday, things were not as easy for Greer. Her first three months were marred by extreme exhaustion and a chest infection. The second three months by heartburn and headaches. Also, she was putting weight on; she'd noticed her wedding ring feeling tighter on her finger.

During a routine visit to the antenatal clinic, in her twenty-seventh week, the midwife looked concerned. 'Greer, your blood pressure is a bit too high for my liking. You need to rest more. In fact, I am telling you to get as much rest as you can.'

Greer shifted her bulk on the uncomfortable plastic chair and felt tears burning her eyes. 'I'm so huge. I need to take exercise, don't I?'

'It depends what sort of exercise.'

'A little walk.'

'How little is little?'

'I go up the hill to The Pavilions and along the cliffs to Shellsand Bay.'

'Absolutely not. That's a good forty-minute round trip!'

'But I'm getting so fat.'

'Let's weigh you.'

The scales registered a considerable weight gain since the last visit.

The midwife smiled a poker-face smile. 'Let's get a

urine sample done and I'll get Mr Cunningham in to see you. You're lucky he's got his clinic here this morning.'

Greer went to the Ladies and duly peed into the small plastic tube. Her arm was only just long enough to get round her bump and to the required position. Naturally the first try splashed on her hand and onto the outside of the pot. 'Oh shit shit shit,' she said to the cubicle walls. 'Just what I bloody well needed.' Eventually the pot was filled and the lid screwed down. She just about managed to get her knickers up with her one dry hand and then washed the pot and her hands under hot water with lots of soap.

In the mirror above the sink she hardly recognised the pale and bloated face staring back at her.

The midwife took the pot and said nothing about the damp label. 'Mr Cunningham will pop in in a moment. Would you like a cup of tea?'

Greer was grateful for the kindness and accepted the tea without any sense that she should have warning bells ringing.

She was quietly enjoying her hot drink when there was a sharp knock on the door.

'Hello, Mrs Behenna.' A tall handsome man of about fifty entered the room and closed the door quietly behind him. Mr Cunningham was a consultant gynaecologist of extreme experience and fame among the women of the area. He had a suntanned face and wore a well-tailored navy-blue suit, both of which said, 'I'm a professional. You are in good hands.' Greer felt safe. 'Hello, Mr Cunningham. I wasn't expecting to see you until nearer the delivery.'

'Ah, yes, but Midwife Yvonne is rather worried about you.' He pulled a chair out and sat opposite her, taking her hands into his. He carefully pressed her finger joints and gave a gentle tug of her wedding ring. 'Have you noticed your wedding band getting a little tight?'

'Yes. I'm getting so fat.'

He let go of her hands and asked to see her ankles. 'They look a bit swollen too.'

'Horrible, aren't they?' She felt deeply unattractive.

The midwife entered with the results of the urine test and handed them to Mr Cunningham. 'Thank you, Yvonne. Now let me see . . . Protein is present. Tell me, Mrs Behenna, how are you feeling generally? A bit grotty?'

'A bit. I'm just tired, I think.'

Mr Cunningham thought for a moment then said, 'Yvonne, help Mrs Behenna up onto the couch. I just want to check on baby.'

Mr Cunningham examined her thoroughly. He listened to the baby's heartbeat and measured the size of her bump. When he had finished, he offered a strong arm to help her sit up and step off the couch. 'Come and sit down and I'll explain what I think is going on.'

*

Greer was advised not to walk home, but to phone her mother to come and collect her. Elizabeth had arrived looking distraught; her car was left parked rather messily in a disabled bay.

She listened intently to what the midwife had to say and together they got a frightened-looking Greer to the car. An elderly man was pacing angrily, waiting for them.

'Are you entitled to park in a disabled bay?' He jabbed his finger at Elizabeth, who ignored him. He came closer and stuck his face into Elizabeth's, flecks of spittle flying through his dentures and onto her cheek. 'Are you deaf? Do you have a blue badge?'

Midwife Yvonne put an arm out to fend him off. 'Please. This lady is a patient of mine. She can't walk too far. Just a couple of minutes and you can have this space.'

'So she doesn't have a badge.' The man was triumphant. 'I'm taking your registration number and using it as evidence. You have parked unlawfully.'

The pugnacious little man had found a pen and a tatty envelope and was scribbling down the number plate. 'I want your name,' he snarled at Elizabeth as she walked round the car to get into the driver's seat. Still she ignored him.

'I said, I want your name,' he shrieked.

Elizabeth got into the driving seat and turned on the ignition. Putting the car into reverse she backed out of the space. From within the car she could see the man in the rear-view mirror; she reversed a little further until he was forced to step aside. He was still ranting. As he ran to the front of the car to check her tax disc, Elizabeth calmly opened her electric window and said, in her most polite voice: 'Piss off, you odious little berk.'

*

Greer was settled in their bed by the time Jesse got home. Elizabeth had phoned him as soon as they'd arrived, thanking God that he wasn't away at sea.

'Darlin',' he said, taking her hand. 'What the 'ell's going on?'

Greer looked pale and puffy but comfortable on the pillows that her mother had so lovingly arranged. Her swollen feet were raised on more cushions. 'I'm fine. It's all going to be fine. I just need to rest. They're worried I've got pre-eclampsia.'

'What the 'ell's that?'

'Something to do with my blood pressure being high and I've got protein in my wee, whatever that means. I just need to rest and get this puffiness down.'

'Is the baby all right?'

Greer looked at Jesse's face, full of concern for her and their child, and was overwhelmed with compassion and love for him. 'Yes. The baby's fine. As long as I rest and take things easy. The gynaecologist said that he'll keep an eye on me and as long as I don't get worse, everything will be fine.'

'And if it does get worse?'

Elizabeth elbowed the door open, carrying in a tray of tea with tiny cucumber sandwiches on a plate. She answered for Greer. 'She'll have to have the baby a bit earlier than planned, that's all.'

Jesse looked panicked. 'Have the baby early? That's not good, is it?'

Greer reached up and touched his cheek. 'Darling, it just means I'll have a Caesarean and the baby will be fine and I will be fine.'

'Sure?'

'Sure.'

Jesse watched as Greer sipped her cup of tea and nibbled a cucumber sandwich. Was this his fault? His punishment? He would rather die himself than let anything happen to the baby or Greer. In a sudden guilt-ridden moment he knew that he loved her. The sudden realisation of what he had to lose if anyone found out about how despicable he had been, the lie he was keeping, hit him like a sledgehammer. Oh God, he said to himself, if you exist, please *please* let everything be all right. I promise I'll be true to Greer for the rest of my living days.

*

Loveday was bouncing with energy and good health. The fat from her hips and arms had melted away and her tummy stood round and proud in front of her. Most days, after her shift at the bakery finished, she'd walk up to Pencil Cottage with a little posy of sweet peas or an individual apple crumble or a small but interesting piece of gossip to entertain her housebound friend.

Greer was always pleased to see her. 'Mummy is driving me mad! I can't have five minutes' peace without her checking on me. I managed to dig out my sketchbook and pencils without her noticing. I wanted to do work on some design ideas for the nursery, but in she came and took them away from me. Said I had to sleep. It's like being a toddler again. Can you root about downstairs and see if you can find where she put them?'

Loveday laughed. ''Tis only because she loves you. She's worried for you and the baby. Not long now,' she consoled her.

*

By the third week of September, Loveday was feeling ready to pop. At the antenatal clinic she was asked if she had got her dates wrong. The baby looked to be full term.

'I'm sure I'm right. End of January this one got started.' The midwife gave her an old-fashioned look and a card with the maternity ward's phone number on it in case the baby came sooner than she expected.

It was the morning of 3 October at 7.45 when Loveday's waters broke. Mickey had been given some shore leave so that he could be on hand if anything happened.

'Mickey,' called Loveday urgently from the bathroom. 'Mickey, help.'

Mickey had been dreaming of his old scooter and how he missed it, but the anguish in Loveday's voice soon roused him. Seeing she wasn't next to him, he leapt out of bed calling, 'Loveday, where are you?'

'I'm in bathroom, you div. I think the baby's coming.'

He ran to the bathroom to find her on all fours with a large puddle around her.

'Oh my good God. What do I do?'

'Call the maternity unit and tell them we're coming in. Pick up my bag – it's packed and under my dressing table – and get me to the bloody hospital.'

*

In twenty minutes she was sitting in a warm birthing pool and feeling a ton less scared than she had been on the floor of the bathroom – or, for that matter, in the front seat of Mickey's crappy Austin Allegro, whose suspension had clearly collapsed.

Two hours later, both mother and father were besotted with their wailing, nine-and-half-pound son, who they named Hal.

19

Mickey sat in the softly lit gloom of Loveday's curtained bay on the maternity ward, holding his son and watching with fascination the dear and oddly familiar face. Phantom dreams twitched Baby Hal's lips and wrinkled his nose. Mickey lifted the swaddled body to his face and nuzzled the soft red hair, sitting like a halo on the fragile head. Hal looked like Loveday but he smelled of his own unique perfume. Warm, new and precious.

He whispered in his son's ear: 'I love you, Hal. I'll always be here for you. You can come to me for anything, 'cos I'm your dad.'

Hal wriggled and stretched, a beatific smile spreading over his face. His eyelids fluttered and opened a little. Man and boy stared at each other. 'Hello. I'm your daddy,' said Mickey.

'And I'm the mummy,' said Loveday, rustling the water-proof mattress and cotton sheets as she hauled herself upright from her sleep.

'Hello, Mummy,' grinned Mickey. 'We were just having a little chat while you were grabbing a few zeds.' He held Hal up, in front of his own lips, and said in a squeaky voice, 'Hello, Mummy. Daddy and I were just thinking of going for a pint.'

'Lucky you. I could murder a cider,' Loveday smiled.

'No luck, love, but I can get a cup of tea if you want?'

Mickey carefully handed his precious bundle to Loveday then went in search of refreshment. Loveday held Hal and stared at him. Examining every inch looking for similarities. After a few moments, she grunted with satisfaction. He looked like her. Same hair colouring. Same chin . . . but whose eyes did he have? Mickey's. Definitely Mickey's. Yes, Mickey's.

She analysed again her beautiful son's face; she couldn't find a trace of Jesse.

But a voice in her head began to whisper insidious doubts.

He's a big boy for being two weeks early. But he's the right size for being ten days overdue. Are you sure that little bleed – spotting really – in January was an actual period?

She bent her face to her innocent child and drank in the scent of him. Her lips feeling the wrinkles of his neck as she mouthed softly, 'You're mine and that's the important thing.'

The curtains around her bed swished on their plastic track and Mickey appeared with two cups of tea on rattling saucers. 'Here you go, my bird. Just saw the nurse. She's asking about breast-feeding. I said yes please.'

Loveday laughed, in spite of herself. 'Daddy's a cheeky monkey, isn't he, Hal?'

As if on cue, Hal started to whimper. His little face screwing up in pink confusion as he thought about what he really wanted. Then came the full-blown cry of a hungry baby.

By the time the nurse, an efficient woman of about thirty with short blond hair, got to him, he was happily clamped onto Loveday and suckling drowsily.

'Well done, Mum!' congratulated the nurse. 'You're a

natural. Now then, I think we'll keep you in tonight and
. . .' She turned to look at Mickey. 'Daddy, if everything
is all right, you can come back in the morning and take
your lovely little family home.'

'Ideal,' smiled Mickey happily.

The nurse turned back to Loveday. 'I'll check on you
both later, but first I've got to check on a lady who's on
her way in as an emergency.'

They heard the sound of wheels on the rubber floor
and the noise of anxious voices approaching.

The nurse stopped and listened. 'That'll be them.' And
with another swish of the curtain, back and forward on
its rail, the nurse left.

'Have you phoned home yet and told the grandparents?' asked Loveday, who had happily lost track of
all time and all responsibility for the outside world. Her
focus had shrunk to her son.

'Yeah. Did that when you two were having a kip.
They're all delighted and your mum sends her love. She
wanted to come in tonight but I told her you were
knackered.'

'Thank you, darlin'.' Loveday did feel a bit knackered
now she thought about it. 'Do I look all right?'

'You look bleddy beautiful.' He got up from the
armchair and bent to kiss his wife. 'Who's a clever girl?'

'I am.'

'All right, big head!' he joked, ducking before she
cuffed him.

'I think I might make tracks. I want to tell Jesse all
about fatherhood. It'll be the first time I've ever had
anything before he has.'

Loveday felt the wound of her betrayal split open a
little.

'Bye, Hal.' Mickey was bending to kiss his son. 'Be a good boy for Mummy.'

*

Beyond the curtains, a man's voice started to shout, sounding panicked. 'Nurse. Nurse. My wife is unwell. Help. Nurse.'

Mickey and Loveday listened, stock-still, as at least two sets of footsteps walked quickly towards the man's voice.

'She's shaking. She's blue. What's happening, Nurse?' asked the man, his voice trembling with panic.

'She's having a seizure,' said a female voice, who they recognised as the nurse who had just left them. She was using a calm, professional voice, which became more urgent as she issued sharp instructions to her colleague. 'Call theatre. Tell them we're on the way down.'

'Will she be OK? Will my baby be OK?' The man was beyond anguished.

'Mr Behenna, we will do everything we can to safely deliver your child. Now please . . .' Mickey and Loveday heard the metal sides of a hospital bed clang. 'I must get your wife to theatre.'

'Can I come with her?'

'The best thing you can do is wait here and I'll bring news as soon as possible.'

They listened as the bed rattled from the ward and went down some unknown corridor.

They listened as the man tried to quieten his frightened sobs.

Mickey knew what he had to do. He stepped out of the cubicle and put his arms around his best friend.

Jesse started. 'Mickey! They've taken Greer to theatre. She was shaking and her eyes were rolling. I'm scared. They won't let me go down to be with her. I've got to wait here.' He looked at the empty bay that had just held Greer's bed. 'Will you wait with me?'

'Of course I will.'

'You haven't got to get home to Loveday?'

'No.'

'Did Mum tell you we were in the ambulance up here? Is that why you came?'

'No. I was here anyway.'

'What?'

'Loveday's had a little boy. We've called him Hal.'

Jesse looked demented. 'You have a son?' He clasped at Mickey's sleeve. 'Loveday has a son?'

Mickey nodded, and steered his bewildered friend to a chair. 'Let me get you a cup of tea.'

'Can I see them? The baby and Loveday?'

Loveday, behind the safety of her curtains, gripped her sleeping son a little tighter and held her breath, hoping fervently that Mickey would say no.

'Let's see them later,' she heard him say. 'When we know Greer is all OK. Then we can meet together. Babies, mums and all.'

Jesse was slumped onto his chair. 'Yes. Yes. Of course.'

'Right, let me get you that cup of tea.'

*

Greer's son, Freddie, was delivered at 9.38 that night, by Caesarean section. He weighed five pounds six ounces and, despite being two weeks early, was pronounced healthy. Greer, on the other hand, knew nothing of the birth, or that she had a son. The severe pre-eclampsia had developed very rapidly that afternoon. That morning she had woken with a painful headache, which she couldn't budge. By teatime she had blurred vision with flashing lights and her hands, feet and face were getting increasingly swollen. It was Elizabeth who had called the ambulance.

*

Jesse, pale and exhausted, was finally allowed to see her some time after midnight. She was asleep in a quiet side room. Drips and monitors surrounded her. 'How is she?' he asked the young nurse who was writing something on the clipboard that hooked onto the foot of the bed.

'She's stable but needs complete rest.'

'Can I sit with her?'

'Of course, but she needs to sleep. I'll be back in fifteen minutes to do her checks again.'

Jesse nodded his understanding and pulled up a small plastic chair that was nearest to the bed. He sat and took her hand. There was a cannula taped to the back of it with a tube leading to a stand with a bag of fluid on it. Like a metronome, it dripped its regular drip into her body.

'Greer?' he whispered. 'Can you hear me?' She gave no response. 'We have a little boy. Freddie has arrived! We did agree on Freddie, didn't we?' He wrinkled his eyebrows anxiously. 'If you want to change it when you wake up, that's no problem.' The quiet hiss of the oxygen tube under her nostrils was the only response. He carried on regardless, the sound of his voice in the silence reassuring him, soothing his frayed nerves.

'I've been to see him. Handsome boy. Ten fingers and ten toes. He's in special care at the moment. They're keeping an eye on him till you're able to.' He felt the prick of tears and bowed his head, resting it on her hand. 'Darlin', you'm gonna get better soon. The doctor says your liver, or did he say kidneys, I always get them mixed up; anyway, they might be affected, but you're in good hands. You've got to rest, take it easy.'

The nurse entered the room. 'I think you should go home now, Mr Behenna. We've given your wife a sedative that should keep her sleeping for the next few hours. Get some rest. Come back in the morning. Your wife is going to need you to be fit to take care of her and . . .' She raised her eyebrows questioningly.

'Freddie,' he said.

'Freddie. What a lovely name. So yes, you go home and we'll see you in the morning. Any change and we'll call you.'

*

Mr Cunningham sat reassuringly and handsomely at the desk in his consulting room. Greer's father was insistent that this should be a private appointment rather than NHS.

Greer and Jesse were shown in by the cool secretary, who looked like Miss Moneypenny and had clearly also been in love with her employer for years.

Mr Cunningham stood up and greeted the couple.

'Do take a seat.' He gestured to the comfortable uphol-stered chairs facing his desk.

'How are you, Greer?'

'A lot better, thank you.'

'And young Freddie? Not keeping you awake too much?'

'Oh, you know. He's not a great sleeper, but my mother is doing the night feeds and being back at my parents' house is nice.'

'All those home-cooked meals?' smiled Mr Cunningham. He turned to Jesse.

'And how's Dad doing – you've had quite a lot to deal with, haven't you.' It was a statement, not a question.

Jesse took his eyes off the silver-framed photos of Mrs Cunningham and offspring and tried to shake the tiredness from his brain. God, he was exhausted. Freddie was noisy, angry and impossible. Greer was fragile, and distanced from him, now that she was back at her parents' house.

'Sorry . . . what did you say?'

Mr Cunningham gave a benign professional smile. 'You've had a lot to deal with. Greer's illness. A new baby.'

'No, I'm fine. Just want to know how Greer is.'

'Ah, yes.' The consultant opened a leather folder on his desk and took out a more modest buff folder. Inside were several sheets of paper: Greer's medical notes. Mr Cunningham cleared his throat. 'Greer has had an episode of severe pre-eclampsia which developed into eclampsia. If we hadn't operated on her and delivered Freddie, you might have lost them both.'

The consultation took thirty minutes. Mr Cunningham explained that the condition was little understood, but that it needn't necessarily stop the majority of women from having normal pregnancies in the future. Mr Cunningham paused and arranged his features sombrely. 'Unfortunately, Greer falls into the minority group of women who I wouldn't recommend trying for another baby. It could be dangerous for her and the child. This is only my recommendation and you must do as you think best – but, truthfully, I do believe you shouldn't contemplate adding to your family. I'm sorry.'

20

Greer absorbed the news with a quiet acceptance. Jesse was devastated. But as neither of them was able to talk to each other with anything other than superficial stoicism, they didn't know how each of them truly felt.

When Freddie was almost six weeks old, Jesse made his regular nightly trip to his in-laws' house to see his wife and son.

Freddie was in the arms of his grandmother, drinking greedily from his bottle of formula.

Greer was taking a bath.

In the silence of the beige and cream sitting room, with its sateen sofas and Tiffany lamps, Jesse felt a stranger. Foreign. His presence neither understood nor recognised.

'How is Greer doing?' he asked Elizabeth. He wanted to ask his mother-in-law specifically when Greer could come home, but he felt awkward. He didn't want Elizabeth to accuse him of pushing Greer before she was ready.

Freddie released the teat from his mouth and Elizabeth expertly lifted him upright and forward so that she could rub his back. Freddie obliged with a deep burp.

'Good boy,' said his grandmother. 'Who's a good boy for Nanny? Want some more? Still hungry?' She stroked the teat against Freddie's lips until he took it in his mouth and closed his eyes, sucking sleepily.

Jesse asked again. 'Is she feeling better?'

Elizabeth didn't look at him as she answered. 'She's still very weak.'

Jesse tried again. 'You've been wonderful. Looking after her and Freddie. I can't wait to have them home.'

'Yes, well, Greer will know when she's well enough.' Freddie was now asleep. His head lolling in the crook of his grandmother's elbow. A small stream of creamy dribble was escaping from his lips. 'Now then, young man. It's the Moses basket for you,' said Elizabeth, putting the bottle on the table at her side and preparing to stand up.

Jesse jumped up from his chair, hoping that he might be able to help. He hadn't had many chances to hold Freddie in the last six weeks. He had not yet been allowed to give him his bottle. 'Can I hold him?'

Elizabeth hesitated before saying, 'I think he needs to sleep. He likes it. It's better that we keep his little routine going.'

Greer came in wearing her old Snoopy dressing gown and with her hair wound into a towelling turban. 'Hi, Jesse. You're earlier than usual.' Her face lit up. 'Mum, you didn't tell me Jesse was here.'

'I didn't want to disturb you when you were having a nice bath.'

Greer went to Jesse and hugged him. 'Have you had a cuddle with Freddie?'

Jesse saw his chance. 'I was just asking your mum.'

'He's asleep,' said Elizabeth, still holding Freddie. 'I'm just about to put him down.'

'Mum! Jesse and Freddie haven't seen each other since

yesterday. And Jesse didn't get a cuddle then because you'd put Freddie down. Hand him over.'

'It's important to have a routine,' Elizabeth protested, but couldn't stop Greer taking Freddie.

'I know, Mum, and you've done a wonderful job, but hand him over to his daddy.' Greer turned to her husband, who gave Elizabeth a triumphant smile. 'Now, Jesse, sit down in that armchair and get comfy.' Greer took Freddie from her mother's arms and passed him into her husband's.

Elizabeth sniffed huffily as she left the room. 'I'll be in the kitchen if you need me.'

Jesse took him gently.

'Hello, Fred. Daddy's going to bring you and Mummy home soon,' he said in a comforting soft voice.

'Let's take him to my room for a proper cuddle.'

In her room and surrounded by the paraphernalia of babyhood such as boxes of Pampers, sterilising kits and bottles, Jesse sat on the bed holding their son while Greer sat at his feet, resting her chin on his knee. 'Did you get the cot built?'

'All done.'

'And the little mobile up?'

'Yes.'

'And the changing table? Is there enough room? It's such a tiny little room.'

'It's perfect. Like an efficient galley. Everything in arm's reach.'

She sighed happily. 'I'm looking forward to coming home.'

'When do you think that'll be?'

'Another couple of weeks.'

'Another two weeks! Freddie's six weeks now.'

'I know. Doesn't time go fast?'

Jesse didn't think so. 'I want you home at the weekend.'

Greer stiffened. 'I don't think I'm ready.'

'I want you back home. In our bed. I miss you.'

'You know what the doctor said.'

'He said no more children. Not no more sex.'

Greer pulled away from him. 'I'm just not ready to be on my own with Freddie. I haven't got the confidence yet.'

'You never will have if you let your mum do everything for you.'

Greer bit her bottom lip and Jesse could see tears forming. 'What's the matter?' he asked gently. 'Don't you want to come home?'

'It's not that.'

'Well, what is it?'

'I'll be lonely when you're working.'

'Loveday's just down the road. She can't wait to see you.'

Greer brightened a little. 'How is she? How's Hal?'

'Mickey says they're both doing really well.'

'Have you seen them? Loveday and Hal? I hear he's huge!'

'I haven't actually seen her or the baby since they left hospital, but I've seen pictures.'

Jesse hadn't risked seeing Hal or Loveday. He felt blessed that Freddie had survived and swore to himself that he would never be on his own with Loveday again. Mickey was like a dog with two tails with his new family, and Jesse wasn't going to jeopardise that happiness.

Greer shifted her weight and stood up, stretching. Jesse admired the slenderness of her figure through her dressing gown and felt the stirrings of desire.

'You look good, Greer. You don't look as if you've just had a baby.'

She pulled her gown closer. 'Thanks.'

'I really miss you.'

'I miss you too.'

'I mean I miss making love to you. We haven't done it for months.'

Greer took the sleeping Freddie from Jesse's arms. 'Well, we had this little one to think of, didn't we?'

Jesse got up and stood by Greer. They both looked at the sleeping Freddie. Jesse put his hand on Greer's bottom and caressed her buttock. 'I want to take you home now and have you in our bed.'

She pulled away. 'Don't. Mum might hear us.'

'To hell with her. We're married, aren't we?' He leant in and nuzzled her neck, dropping light kisses on her until he reached her mouth and tried to kiss her deeply. Greer kept her mouth shut tight.

'What's the matter, Greer?' he whispered.

'We mustn't have any more babies.' He could feel the tension in her.

'I know, darling. That's what the doctors say now, but medical advances are happening every day. We're only young. It's terrible for us both but we can still have sex and be careful.'

'It's not that.'

'What is it then?'

'I just don't feel like it.'

'Well, you will. When I've warmed you up.' He opened the front of her dressing gown and lifted her small breast out. He bent to lick her nipple.

'Don't. Please don't.' He stopped and she pulled her robe closed.

'What's the matter? We need to talk about this properly. I'm in bits. Trying to be strong and all that, but it's breaking my heart. I want to fill you and the house up with children but, like my mum says, we have got Freddie and we can give him the very best love a boy could ever have.'

Greer looked at Jesse intently and said, 'It's not that. I'm glad Freddie will be our only one. I hated being pregnant and I hate what it's done to my body. I'm fat. I have stretch marks. My breasts aren't the same. I don't think I ever want to have sex again.'

Jesse had been told by his mum that women needed a bit of love and patience after they'd had a baby, so he wasn't surprised or worried by this little speech.

'You look bloody gorgeous to me. I fancy you like mad. A few days at home and we'll get back to normal. Don't worry.'

Greer looked so frail and vulnerable, with her baggy Snoopy gown hanging off her tiny frame, that Jesse was overcome with compassion and passion. 'You need to come home. I need to have you home. You and Freddie. You're coming home tomorrow. I'll pick you up after work. Tell your mother.'

*

The next day Jesse was down on the harbour checking the gear on the boat. Greer's father, Bryn, was walking, with some purpose, towards him.

'All right, Jesse,' he called.

Jesse saw him and knew Bryn was on a mission from Elizabeth.

'Can I have a word?' Bryn asked.

'Sure. You can have a bucketful if you want, but I'll not be dissuaded from having my wife and son home tonight.'

Bryn stepped onto *The Lobster Pot* and held his hands up in surrender. 'Am I that transparent?'

'You and Elizabeth have been wonderful, looking after Greer and Freddie. But it's six weeks now and time they came home,' said Jesse firmly.

'Well, of course you want your family home. Who wouldn't?' Bryn patted Jesse's shoulder. 'But it's a little too soon.'

'Who says?'

'We all do,' said Bryn smoothly. 'Maybe I should give you some time off. Paid leave. That way you could spend more time at our place.'

Jesse stuck his hands in the pockets of his overall and stood his ground. 'You've given me enough. Pencil Cottage, a say in the new business—'

'Yes, and you've given me a terrific grandson to carry the Clovelly name on in the business.'

'He's not a Clovelly. He's a Behenna.' Jesse was using a dangerously quiet voice.

'You know what I mean, son.' Bryn was smiling at Jesse as if he was the village idiot who needed appeasing. 'Greer is my first consideration. She needs looking after.'

Jesse had had enough. 'Bryn, with due respect, you've given Greer everything she's ever wanted. You even made sure you gave her me.'

Bryn sneered. 'Yes, and God knows why. You were happy to take the money that she came with, weren't you? The house, the pay rise, the promotion?'

Jesse felt anger burning in his gut. 'Greer is my wife. Freddie is my son, and they'm coming home tonight. I'll play the perfect son-in-law and I'll make this company a success, but you can't stop me bringing my family home. Oh, and by the way, your friendship with Monica at the golf club is common knowledge. Wouldn't take long for that to reach Elizabeth's ears.' This was a long shot. A piece of gossip that had been circulating for as long as Jesse could remember. He hadn't been sure it was true until this very moment.

Bryn went scarlet. 'What the hell are you talking about?'

'Oh, it's OK for me to tell Elizabeth about this stupid rumour, is it? If you're innocent, that's fine.'

Bryn's slick eyes were narrowed. 'You say one word of that filthy lie and I'll have your balls for shark bait.'

Jesse laughed. 'Mum's the word, then. Make sure Greer and Freddie are all packed when I get there.'

*

Jesse helped Greer and Freddie into Pencil Cottage. 'Welcome home,' he said, putting the sleeping Freddie and his car seat on the front-room carpet.

Greer looked around her. 'It looks so cosy.'

'Mum came round earlier. She's left flowers on the table for you. Look.'

A big bunch of Jan's late dahlias was sitting in a vase with a little envelope propped up next to it with Greer's name scrawled on it.

'That's sweet of her.' Greer hated blowsy dahlias and made a mental note to chuck them out the next day and get some white long-stemmed lilies which would be more in keeping with the house style. Then she sniffed. 'Can I smell cooking?'

'Oh, yeah,' grinned Jesse. 'She's popped a chicken pie to warm in the oven and she's brought some of her frozen runner beans over too. Are you hungry?'

'Not very.'

On cue a hungry Freddie woke up and started squalling. 'Shall I make up a bottle?' asked Jesse.

'I'll do it.' Greer began rummaging in one of the copious baby bags that Freddie seemed to need.

'Well, I'll watch how you do it, then I can do the next one,' Jesse said gently.

'It might be the middle of the night.'

'I want to share it with you. I need to learn. I'm used to being up in the night, remember?'

Greer unclipped Freddie from his chair and handed him to Jesse. 'Bloody hell, he pongs,' he laughed, pulling a face.

'Well,' said Greer on her way to the kitchen, 'this will be a night of firsts. I'll teach you how to change a nappy too.'

21

Being back at home felt better than she had expected, and seeing Freddie sleeping in his cot in the tiny nursery gave her deep satisfaction. Her days were full of washing and sterilising, feeding and winding, but she coped well. Some days she even managed to grab a shower and make a simple supper for Jesse when he came home.

If she'd had any worries about resuming their sex life, she needn't have bothered. Jesse, who insisted on doing the night feeds, was too knackered to ask.

*

It was the second week after she'd returned home that Mickey rang and invited her and Jesse round for supper.

'Bring littl'un, too. Loveday and I are dying to see him. Loveday wanted to come round the other day but Jesse said you weren't up to visitors yet.'

Greer was surprised. 'Did he? I'd love to see you. I've tried to phone Loveday a couple of times but either Hal was crying or I got no answer.' Greer had wondered if Loveday was avoiding her.

Mickey laughed. 'Yeah she's never in. If she's not out with her mum, she's walking the pram. Say you can come for your tea?'

'Yes,' said Greer decisively, 'we'd love to come.'

*

Loveday was not happy. 'What did you do that for? I haven't got time to make supper and look after Hal. And what's Mum going to do? I can't ask her to leave her own house because there's no space for her round the table.'

Mickey had already thought of that. 'I asked her if it was all right and she thought it's a great idea. She's going to her sister's for the night so that we can really let our hair down.' He slid his hands round Loveday's hips and pulled her to him. 'We 'aven't seen them in ages. We'll have fun.'

*

At Pencil Cottage, Jesse looked cross. 'I don't want to go round for tea.'

'Why not? Mickey's your best mate,' Greer sighed. 'And why did you tell him I wasn't up to visitors?'

''Cos you're not.'

'Yes I am. I think it's Loveday who's not coping. I want to see her but she's always making excuses. I feel all cooped up in here.' Greer swept her perfectly cut fringe across her face. 'I miss seeing people. You see Mickey every day at work.'

'Exactly.'

'Oh, you're being silly. We're going over there and that's that.'

*

Loveday was as nervous as kitten. She'd spent all day cleaning the house and cooking an enormous fish pie and was now laying up the small kitchen table. Hal, who had been grizzling and needy since the early hours, was strapped to her chest. 'Now then, Hal my lad,' she told him as she folded some paper napkins into triangles and popped them into the empty wine glasses, 'you'm going to meet your friend Freddie tonight, so I want you on your best behaviour. Understand?' She looked down at him, seeing his little face snuggled against her breasts. 'I don't want any trouble from you.' He looked up at her and gave a smile to melt her heart. 'That's my boy.' He caught her gaze and continued to hold it, his face gradually turning from shell pink to puce. 'Oh, no. Not now. I've only just changed you,' she beseeched, but it was too late. She felt the release as a magnificent poo hit his nappy and then the unmistakable liquid warmth as it escaped through the leg holes of his baby-grow. 'Oh, Hal.' She unclipped his harness and held him at arm's length. She looked down at her last clean shirt. 'Oh, no, you've done it all over me as well.'

She heard Mickey's key in the lock and called from the kitchen, 'Darling, Hal's just shat all over me. Do you mind helping me wi—' She stopped as she saw Mickey was not alone. Greer and Jesse were with him, and a perfectly sparkling clean, sleeping Freddie too.

Loveday wanted to cry but instead she said, 'Hello. Don't come too near, I stink. Mickey, get everyone a drink. I'll be back in a minute.'

Upstairs, feeling flustered, Loveday did let a few tears flow as she undressed Hal and quickly washed him in the sink. As soon as he was clean and dry, she popped him in his cot, where he promptly fell asleep. 'I'm not surprised you're tired. A big poo like that takes it out of you, doesn't it!'

She caught sight of her reflection in the long mirror on the landing. There were unpleasant marks on the shirt she'd just changed into and her hair could do with a trip to the hairdresser's, but so what, she told herself. She was a mum and proud to bear the battle scars.

Mickey called up the stairs, 'What you having to drink, Loveday?'

'Big mug of tea.' She laughed at the sight of herself. 'I'll be two minutes.'

*

When she got downstairs, Greer was giving Freddie his bottle.

'Sorry about that,' said Loveday. 'Now let's have a proper look at you both. I've missed you.'

She bent to kiss Greer's proffered cheek and sat down next to her. 'How are you? I'm so sorry that you had such a bad time.'

Greer looked fabulous, despite having been so ill. Her hair and make-up were understated but effective, her figure trim and her clothes unsullied. 'I'm a lot better. How about you?'

'Oh, as you can see . . .' Loveday held her hands out to show off the chaos of the cottage. 'Just the same.'

Greer smiled.

Mickey came in from the kitchen. 'Glass of wine for you, Greer, and a cup of tea for my darling wife.'

Loveday took her mug gratefully. 'I think this'll be the first hot cup of tea I've managed all day.'

'Would you like a hold of Freddie?' asked Greer,

putting his bottle aside and reaching for the glass Mickey was proffering.

Jesse put a hand to his mouth involuntarily. 'Loveday's got a hot drink in her hand,' he said.

'She can put it down,' smiled Greer reasonably.

Loveday felt caught under the expectant, innocent eyes of Greer and Mickey and the unmistakably hard eyes of Jesse.

'Here you are,' said Greer, handing Freddie over. 'This is your auntie Loveday.' Loveday took Freddie in her arms and looked quickly at Jesse, who was pulling at his upper lip, his eyes on the carpet. 'In actual fact,' Greer continued, 'I want her to be more than your auntie.' She beamed at Loveday. 'I want her to be your godmummy.'

Loveday didn't know what to say, but it didn't matter because Greer was still talking. 'And, I want you, Mickey, to be goddaddy.'

Mickey was shocked with happiness at this honour. 'Oh my! Well, that's just wonderful. I accept.' He pumped Jesse's arm and then hugged him for good measure. 'Ain't that marvellous, Loveday?'

Loveday was staring into little Freddie's face and saw a look, a fleeting look, of Hal. No, no it couldn't be. They were not brothers. They weren't. She'd been mistaken. She was feeling clammy and wanted to get Freddie out of her arms. Mickey obliged. 'Come and have a cuddle with your uncle Mickey.' He took Freddie, freeing Loveday to get to her feet. 'Excuse me, I must look at the fish pie.'

'Hang on,' said Mickey, stopping her. 'I want to ask something of you, Greer, and you, Jesse.'

Loveday knew instantly what was coming.

'I haven't had a chance to run this past Loveday yet.' He put his arm round her shoulder. 'But I know she will be wanting the same thing.' He left a small but dramatic pause. 'My wife and I would be honoured if you would both be godparents to our Hal.'

'It would be our pleasure,' smiled Greer. 'Wouldn't it, Jesse?' She looked over to where he sat, motionless.

Loveday could barely breathe.

Jesse looked at Mickey, still cradling Freddie; he looked at Greer, waiting expectantly. Finally he looked into Loveday's eyes. 'Yes. It would be an honour. I am proud to accept.'

Greer took her glass in her hand and raised it. 'To our sons, who will grow together like brothers.'

Upstairs, Hal opened his eyes and his lungs and screamed.

*

Apart from Hal screaming and Freddie sleeping like an angel, Greer drinking wine because she was bottle-feeding and Loveday having to stick to tea because she wasn't, the little supper party was more or less enjoyable.

Jesse dealt with his inner turmoil by drinking too much beer and Mickey matched him out of the sheer joy at their being all together again.

The fish pie was complimented and the pudding of arctic roll and tinned peaches was welcomed as an old favourite. Even Greer had a spoonful.

Loveday told Mickey to get everyone settled in the lounge while she brewed up a pot of coffee and cleared the table. The babies were finally sleeping. Hal in his cot upstairs and Freddie in his car seat on the rug.

Alone in the kitchen, Loveday took a moment to release the tension of the evening. She stood at the sink, clutching the cold enamel and staring out into the dark of the back garden. She could see the reflection of the room behind her in the glass. Mickey so happy and so unweighted by any of the guilt that burdened her. Greer so pretty and so bloody perfect.

Jesse, so . . . fucking annoyingly gorgeous. She knew Mickey was a much better person than Jesse; she knew she was so unbelievably lucky to have him, his unconditional love, and her beautiful Hal. But her mind and her body were saying different things; she just could not help that feeling of pure desire that surged through her whenever she saw Jesse bleddy Behenna.

She saw him bend his head to hear something Greer was saying, then he stood and came towards the kitchen, towards Loveday. She didn't turn round.

'Loveday?'

She turned the taps on and squeezed a healthy stream of washing-up liquid into the bowl. 'Yeah?'

'Do you have any sweeteners . . . for Greer's coffee.'

She turned and pointed to the shelf next to the cooker. 'If I've got any they'll be on there.'

She concentrated on picking up a wine glass and washing it carefully in the suds.

'Nope. Can't see any,' he said, stepping back to stand next to her.

'Sorry.' She rinsed the glass under the cold tap.

Still he stood next to her. 'You OK?' he asked quietly.

'Yeah.' She pulled a face. 'Why wouldn't I be?'

'I looked at Hal tonight and can see only you in him,' Jesse said.

'That's because he's mine,' Loveday said firmly.

'And Mickey's?' Jesse asked.

'And Mickey's.'

He still didn't move. She picked up another glass and began washing it with a little more vigour than last time.

'Good,' he said.

'Yeah. Good.' Her hands stopped in the soapy water and she looked at Jesse intently. 'Hal is Mickey's and Freddie is yours, and that's that.'

22

Spring 1996

In the light morning mist, Jesse could see the white brick of the day marker on the cliffs cupping the entrance to Trevay's harbour. For almost two centuries it had guided the fisherman to safety.

The engine of *The Lobster Pot* chugged reassuringly at just over ten knots. The sea was choppy and a cackle of seagulls followed the churning wake, hoping for a breakfast of fish gut and titbits.

Jesse was at the wheel. Over the last two years Edward had slowly handed the role of skipper to his son and now hardly ever came out on the boat. Not that he didn't want to. He was a victim of the success of the merger between the Behenna and the Clovelly families, and spent almost all his working hours office-bound.

Jesse knew his father and father-in-law would be pleased with the latest catch. The hold was brimming with the best the sea could offer. He counted his blessings.

His own boat.

Money coming in.

A son he adored.

A marriage that was happy enough.

A secret that was safe.

The longer time went on, the more he began to feel sure that the moment of madness that he and Loveday had shared would never be discovered. He and she had buried it deeply. They never spoke of it. Anyway, Hal was a dead ringer for Loveday. Reddish hair, still plump. While blond, wiry Freddie looked every inch a Behenna. Everyone commented on it.

Loveday and Mickey were happy and were now expecting twins. Jesse had cried when he'd heard. He covered it up as joy but really it was envy. He would love more children but he couldn't risk asking Greer. Risk her health. Risk the wrath of his father-in-law, who never let him forget that he would be nothing without Greer.

The only piece of grit in the oyster was Grant. Sometimes Jesse was certain Grant knew something. Snide comments. Quips with a sting.

Once, when he and Mickey had taken the boys down to the harbour to look at the boats and to give their mums a rest, they had run into Grant. He was on leave and was on his way back from the pub. He wasn't drunk, but he'd obviously had a couple, Jesse could tell from his swagger and the taunt in his voice.

'Well, well. What a stroke of luck running into you two, out with my two little nephews – oops, sorry, just one nephew, isn't it?'

Grant bent down and ticked the chins of the two boys in their respective buggies. He pulled a face and little Hal laughed.

'Funny thing is, if you didn't know better, you might think these two little 'uns were related,' Grant said, through narrowed eyes.

Jesse stiffened but Mickey interjected and said pointedly: 'They'll be like real blood brothers – who can rely on each other – like me and Jesse.'

Grant let out a guffaw. 'Bleddy blood brothers! Be careful what you wish for, Mickey boy.'

With a raised eyebrow he went on his way, but it was the same whenever he saw Freddie and Hal toddling together. Playing together. Thank God he wasn't home very often.

The next time he'd seen Grant, Jesse had challenged him.

'Why do you keep saying stupid stuff about Hal and Freddie?'

Grant smirked. 'You tell me.'

'If you've got something to say, just say it.'

'I think it's you who's got something to say.'

'I haven't got anything to say.'

'Well that's all right then, isn't it?' Grant gave him one of his trademark sly grins and Jesse had to fight down the urge not to wipe it off his face.

Grant had been away for a few months now, somewhere in the Middle East. Apparently he was doing well and had been involved in a successful raid on insurgents. Or at least that's what he'd told their mum in one of his infrequent phone calls home.

Jesse pulled his thoughts back to the present. Nothing had been said. Nothing was going to be said. His secret was safe. Dead and buried. He concentrated on heading *The Lobster Pot* safely into Trevay.

*

Our Mermaid, Mickey's dad's boat, was already tied up alongside, its catch unloaded.

Jesse expertly manoeuvred himself next to him.

'All right, Jesse?' called Alfie Chandler.

''Andsome!' replied Jesse. 'Mickey in yet?'

'He's about an hour away. Got a cracking catch, he told me.'

'Yeah. He was gloating on the radio last night.' Jesse laughed, throwing a rope up to his deckhand on the quay. 'Ever since he started skippering *Crabline*, he's turned into the Midas of the ocean!'

'It was good of your dad to let him have a boat.'

'Mickey's like family, isn't he?' bantered Jesse.

'Aye. Like those two boys of yorn. Might as well be brothers.' Alfie chuckled cheerfully.

A thread of fear dropped into Jesse's stomach. First Grant. And now Alfie.

'What do you mean?' he said a bit too sharply.

Alfie was surprised. 'Well, born on the same day and that, and you and Mickey growing up together. He's more a brother to you than Grant, ain't he?'

Jesse pulled himself together. 'Oh, yeah, yeah. I see what you mean.' He should be less sensitive. It was only his own jitters.

Alfie remembered something. 'Oh, nearly forgot, your dad's looking for you. He's in Mr Clovelly's office. He said if I saw you to tell you to go and see him straight away.'

*

Jesse strode through the busy fish market, full now of Alfie's iced and boxed catch, shouting greetings to the customers he knew. 'Don't touch Alfie's lot. Mine's unloaded in a minute. It's the best catch Trevay's ever seen.' Laughter followed him to the small office in the corner of the market. He knocked on the door and walked in without waiting for an answer. His father was sitting clutching a cup of coffee. His face was strained but he looked relieved when he saw Jesse.

Jesse was scared. 'What's the matter, Dad? Is it Mum?'

'No. Not Mum. It's Grant.'

Jesse's mind's eye flew to a scene in a hot desert where the bodies of British soldiers lay mutilated. Blood seeping into the dust and sand. He could see his brother lying wounded, lifeless . . . and he felt a surge of relief. Grant, the only person who might know something about him and Loveday, was dead.

'What's happened, Dad?'

'He's in trouble.'

Relief left Jesse, to be replaced by guilt that he could possibly have felt so good about his brother dying.

'Trouble for what?'

'We're not sure of the details. Someone from his base is coming to see us this morning. Your mum wants you there.'

'Of course. Can I unload the boat first?'

'No. Leave it. I'll get the lads to do it. Your mum's in bits.'

*

The officer from 42 Commando spared none of the details.

'It would appear that your son formed an attachment with a local girl whilst on deployment. Her family tried to stop her from seeing him and he went to the family home where he attacked her father. Her father is currently in a British field hospital and in a coma. The medical team are deciding whether to evacuate him to a hospital here in the UK.'

Jan pulled her crumpled tissue through her fingers, too shocked to weep. 'Are you sure Grant did it?'

'We have witnesses who would appear to be reliable.'

'But Grant has wanted to be a Marine since he was little. He worked so hard for his green beret. Why would he risk everything he loved?'

The officer, looking embarrassed, pulled at the sleeves of his immaculate uniform. 'His commanding officer has had previous cause to be concerned about Private Behenna's attitude. It was only a matter of time before he was facing a lot of trouble.'

Jan stared at him from her dry eyes. 'But he had been brave, hadn't he? He told us he'd been on a raid against the bad men – he always called them the bad men – and had saved his friend's life.'

The officer coughed and crossed his feet, his gleaming boots winking like mirrors.

'Ah.'

'That's what he told us.'

'Private Behenna has not been on active duty in the field. His unpredictable behaviour caused serious concern that he might be a danger to other men; he has been confined to base for some time. There seems little veracity to the story he has told you.'

'You mean it's not true?'

'I couldn't comment; I am sure his commanding officer will be able to give you more information.'

Jan's heartbroken face spoke clearly of her pain. 'He's always been a liar. Ever since he was a little boy.'

Edward, sitting next to her at the old kitchen table,

put his arm around her. 'Jan, let's get him home and then we'll know more.'

The officer shuffled his feet again. 'When he returns to the UK he'll be held at the barracks until his court martial.'

Jan stood up so fast that she knocked the chair over behind her. Her voice rose in an ascending scale. 'Court *martial?*'

'Yes. I know this must come as a terrible shock to you.'

Now Jan's tears came thick and fast, in a torrent that made her breathing difficult. Jesse went to her and held her as tightly as he could. She pressed her face into his dirty fishing smock and allowed Jesse to absorb the shock waves of her sobs.

The officer stood. 'I very much regret having to make this visit.' He took a card from an inside pocket of his jacket and handed it to Edward. 'Here are my details if you need any more information. I'll endeavour to be of assistance in any way I can.'

Edward took the card and placed it on the kitchen table, not knowing what to do next.

'I'll see myself out,' said the officer.

*

Edward went on a bender like no other. He sat in a dark corner of the Golden Hind, rebuffing all overtures from friends and colleagues, and drank solidly and efficiently until Pete, the landlord, refused to serve him any more.

'You've had enough, mate,' he said, taking the pint glass from his hand.

'Not yet,' Edward replied thickly. 'I don't think I'll ever have had enough.' He left the pub and, after deciding that he wasn't going home, he staggered up to the sheds and let himself into his old office. It was dusty from misuse, but he quickly laid his hands on the litre-bottle of Scotch he always kept hidden for emergencies. This was an emergency.

*

Jan had gone to bed, leaving Jesse not knowing quite what to do.

He needed to go home and get his head round what was happening. If Grant was found guilty, he could go away for a few years. If he knew anything about Jesse and Loveday, that secret would be locked up with him. Despite himself, and the evident distress all of this was causing his parents, Jesse felt a shot of elation.

'Mum?' He stuck his head round her bedroom door. 'Mum. You awake?'

His mother didn't answer. Shock had closed her down and she was in a deep sleep.

Jesse wrote a note and left it by her pillow. It said

Mum,
    You're sleeping and I need to get home. Give
me a call when you wake up.
    Love you
    Jesse.

The late afternoon sunshine surprised Jesse. He was expecting it to be much later. Had it been only this morning that all this had unfolded? He walked back to the harbour and hesitated outside the Golden Hind. Should he go in and join his father? He had no doubts he was in there already. He was tempted, but decided he needed a clear head to think over what had happened.

He passed the Hind and turned left into the lane where Pencil Cottage stood. The small front courtyard was merry with spring flowers, basking in the late sunshine. Greer had been doing a distance-learning certificate in garden design; she had planted up dozens of terracotta pots of differing sizes with daffodils, blue hyacinths and cherry blossom trees. Their scent, and the news of his brother's downfall, made Jesse almost cheerful.

*

'I'm sorry to say it, but your brother is a horrible person,' said Greer, swinging Freddie into his high chair and popping his pelican bib round his neck.

'Yeah, but can you believe he would hurt someone so badly that he'd put them in a coma?' asked Jesse, passing the bowl of freshly made broccoli gratin to her.

'Yes I can,' she retorted, before turning her attention to Freddie. 'Freddie, it's your favourite! Mummy's made you yummy broccoli.'

'No,' said Freddie, turning his head away. 'For Daddy.'

'Come on, Fred, it'll make you big and strong. Just like Daddy.'

Freddie pointed at Jesse. 'Daddy, for you.'

Greer pushed a spoonful of the supper into Freddie's mouth and watched as it came smoothly out again. 'Come on, Freddie. This is silly, and Mummy's not having any nonsense.'

Freddie put his pudgy hands over his eyes and blew a raspberry.

'Let me help,' said Jesse, trying not to laugh. 'You go and watch a bit of telly, or do your nails or whatever it is you'd like to do.'

'I do need to finish the last module on planting a fruit garden,' she said, looking defeated.

'Well, off you go then, and I'll look after Littl'un.'

As soon as Greer had gone, Jesse shut the kitchen door and smiled conspiratorially at Freddie. 'Want some ketchup on this?' Freddie nodded gleefully whilst putting a finger to his lips and saying, 'SShhh. Mummy no.'

'Our little secret, son. And with a bit of luck she'll never know.'

*

For the next few weeks, the local press were full of gossip about Grant, and all and sundry came out of the woodwork to sell their lurid stories about him. Local girls gave kiss-and-tells about his bedroom exploits, and so-called friends from school said how they'd always known he was a wrong 'un.

During that time, Jan was too ashamed to show her face outside of the house while Edward, by contrast, spent even more time in the pub.

One day at the Behenna and Clovelly offices, Bryn rounded on Jesse.

'When is that father of yours going to stop drowning his sorrows in the bottom of a pint glass and get back to work? We're running a business here.'

Jesse balked at the suggestion that the catches were suffering. He and Spencer had been holding the fort admirably; if anything, their yields had been up the last few weeks since Jesse had taken the helm.

'You've got no gripes with the catches, Bryn?'

Bryn looked patronisingly at his son-in-law. 'Ain't a case of gripes, but it don't look good, your dad not turning up to meetings. People are talking.'

'Then your job is to shut them up. He's your partner, ain't he?' Jesse said firmly.

Bryn pursed his lips tightly at this unwanted defiance from his son-in-law. 'Now look 'ere—'

'No, you listen to me, Bryn. You might think that you bought me and that you bought my dad too, but what you really bought is the Behenna family. And we're strong.' He took a step closer to his father-in-law. 'You're going to give my dad an official leave of absence and I'll take a seat on the board till he's better.'

'I'm not sure that the shareholders—'

Jesse lowered his voice dangerously. 'You'll tell the shareholders what I tell you to, Bryn. Otherwise, word might start getting around that not only are you knocking off Monica and Doreen from the club, but also that you've been passing off second-grade fish as premium to one of your big clients. Where would your precious shareholder confidence be then, Bryn?'

Bryn's face drained of colour and his voice was tremulous. 'Jesse, that's blackmail.'

'Come off it, Bryn, no need to be dramatic. Just call in the shareholders and we'll all get back to business. Catching and selling fish.' He gave Bryn a cocky grin and a friendly clap on the back.

The following week, Jesse was installed on the board by a unanimous vote.

Edward pulled himself together eventually, but Jesse never relinquished his seat on the board.

It took almost six months for Grant to be found guilty of assault. He was sentenced to eight years. His mother was never the same.

23

September 1998

Greer couldn't help the tears as she bent to straighten Freddie's school tie.

'You've got your lunch box?' she asked him, pointing at his school bag, which looked enormous hanging from his narrow shoulders.

'Yes,' he said.

'I'll be waiting here when you're finished.'

'Right here? By the gate?'

'Yes, right here by the gate.'

'Will Daddy come?'

'Yes, he should be back by then. You'll have lots to tell him.'

Freddie looked so smart in his new uniform. Exactly the way she remembered Jesse on their first day at school. Sturdy legs sticking out of his grey shorts and bruises all down his shins. 'Two peas in a pod,' her father-in-law was fond of saying.

Freddie fidgeted under her gaze then pointed behind her. 'There's Hal!' Then he shouted, 'Hal!'

Hal was walking fast, his hands holding the edge of the double buggy as Loveday had taught him. 'Can I see Freddie?' he asked his mum, who was looking ragged with the stress of getting all three children dressed in time to drop Hal for the school bell.

'Just wait till we cross the road,' she said, looking both ways and then heading towards Greer.

'Morning, Loveday,' Greer said as she kissed her friend's cheek. 'How are you?'

'Knackered. The girls got me up at half five and Hal insisted on making his own lunch box.' She turned to Freddie. 'Hiya, Fred. All ready for your first day?'

'I've got houmous and crudités in my lunch box.'

'Have you?' Loveday said. 'Hal's got Dairylea Dunkers.'

'What are they?' asked Freddie.

'I'm sure Hal will share them with you,' Loveday assured him.

Greer, who spent her life trying to keep Freddie away from preservatives, E numbers and unnecessary sugar, hurriedly changed the subject.

'Auntie Loveday, Uncle Mickey, Daddy and I all became friends on our first day at school, didn't we, Auntie Loveday?'

'Oh, we did,' laughed Loveday. 'I asked your mummy if she liked Abba. I don't think she knew who Abba were.'

Greer, hating being made fun of, said quickly, 'Yes I did.'

'Well, you did once you'd listened to my tapes.'

'What are tapes?' asked Hal.

'Things we had in the olden days . . . before CDs,' chuckled Loveday. 'Now say goodbye to your sisters.'

'Bye-bye, Becca.' He reached into the pram and gave his sister a sloppy kiss. 'Bye-bye, Bea.' He leant in to kiss her too but got a smack from a chubby hand instead. 'Ow. Bea hit me.'

'She didn't mean to. Now, off you two boys go and look after each other. Be good and do what the teacher tells you.' Loveday kissed the face of her dear son and he kissed her back.

'I love you, Mummy.' He blinked a watery smile.

'I love you too. Now off you go, you little monkey.'

Greer knelt to look into Freddie's eyes. 'Be a good boy and don't forget I love you. I want to hear all about it tonight. Now give us a kiss.'

Freddie put his arms around Greer's neck and squeezed tight. 'I'll be good and you be good too, Mummy.'

'I will,' she said solemnly, 'I promise.'

Finally disentangled from their mothers, the two boys ran towards a gathering group of small children who were being summoned by a smiley female teacher called Miss Woods. 'Good morning, children. Wave goodbye to your mummys and daddys. We've got lots of lovely things to do today, so get in a nice line and follow me to the classroom.'

*

Loveday and Greer watched as their precious boys disappeared into the familiar building.

'Where has the time gone? 'Twas only yesterday they were in nappies,' sighed Loveday.

'It was only yesterday since we were coming to school,' Greer said, wryly. She checked her watch. 'Got time for a coffee?'

'Yeah. Why not?'

*

The Cockle Café was situated just off the quay in a narrow back street. It had only been open since the start of the summer season, and had been very busy with the holidaying, trendy young parents who appreciated its organic menu.

As Loveday and Greer turned the corner towards the café, they struggled with the double buggy on the cobbles; it was cumbersome and awkward to manoeuvre. Three women in their sixties were sitting outside, enjoying the September sunshine, an Ordnance Survey map spread out in front of them. They were clearly discussing their walking route for the day, but there seemed to be quite a vigorous exchange of views going on.

As Loveday and Greer drew nearer, the leader of the pack pulled her glasses onto her head, where they were anchored securely by a fierce perm. Seeming suddenly to make a decision, she barked at them, asking: 'Excuse me, are you local?'

Loveday reversed the buggy and yanked it onto the smoother pavement. She looked in the direction of women and said, 'Yes, more's the pity. The roads round here are very bumpy.' She applied the buggy's brake and straightened up. 'Can I help you?'

The leader, Ena, outlined her ambitious plans. Her idea was to get a bus to Boscastle and the start of the Smuggler's Way, continue to Rough Tor and then finish at Looe, thirty-seven miles away. Her companions voiced their concerns about the length of the trek, wondering where they would stay if they didn't reach Looe.

'Well, it's a tricky walk,' Loveday agreed. 'And are you ladies familiar with using a compass? The way isn't marked too well.'

'My sense of direction is excellent. Never needed a compass,' preened Ena.

'It's going to be the Isle of Wight all over again,' one of her companions murmured, *sotto voce*, to the other.

'I heard that.' Ena turned back to Loveday. 'You see, I am a great fan of ancient neolithic monuments. I mean to see Rough Tor and push the legendary Logan Rock to see if it really does rock back and forth.' She jerked her head towards her companions. 'These two don't harbour the same love of the magic of Cornish landscape in their souls as I do.'

'Really,' said Loveday, somewhat bemused, but also already flatly disliking this woman. She turned away. 'Greer, would you order me a strong tea and the girls a juice each. I'll get us settled on the table over there.' She waved at a table as far away from Neolithic Woman as possible.

At this safe distance, Loveday unbuckled the harnesses of both Bea and Becca. The little girls struggled out of their confinement and into the freedom of the cobbled lane. A seagull was strutting in the gutter, cocking his beady-eyed gaze from left to right, searching for a snack. Bea and Becca toddled after him, laughing as he quickened his pace until, finally, he flew to the top of a lamp-post where he opened his beak and laughed.

'Now little girls,' called Ena. 'Don't encourage the seagulls. They're dirty and spread disease.'

Loveday stopped folding Becca's anorak and said, 'I beg your pardon? What did you say?'

Ena was unabashed. 'I was just telling the little girls not to encourage the seagulls.'

'And what business is it of yours?' asked Loveday stonily, the sequence of broken nights with the girls and the emotional rush of Hal's first day at school combining to produce a spectacular red mist. Loveday gave vent. 'My girls live here. They understand seagulls and they know more about bloody Cornwall and its magic than you'll ever know.'

'Well, *really*.' Ena flared her nostrils and stood up, busying herself with folding her map and packing it into her canvas knapsack. She gave rapid instructions to her companions. 'Sylvie, it's your turn to pay the coffee bill. Babs, come with me. Let's wait for Sylvie on the quay.'

Greer came out of the shop. She was laden with a tray of teacups, teapot and juice cartons, and was just in time to see the three women scuttling off to the harbour and Loveday yelling, 'And, by the way, 'tisn't pronounced Rough Tor, except by grockles like you. It's Row Tor. Row, to rhyme with cow.'

'Loveday!' Greer was horrified. 'Shush! What's happened?'

Loveday retold the story and had the grace to be embarrassed. 'I don't know why I saw red. Tired, I suppose, but I get so fed up with these visitors thinkin' we'm got straw in our ears.'

Greer smiled. 'You get very Cornish when you're cross, don't you? Why don't you go home and get a nap? It'll do you the world of good.'

'I can't. I've got the girls.'

'Well, I'm their godmother, aren't I? And today I'm your fairy godmother too. Let me take them and we'll have a lovely day. You and I will meet up at the school to pick the boys up. What do you say?'

'Are you sure?' Loveday was feeling exhausted. 'That would be wonderful.'

Greer shrugged her shoulders. 'Well, now my little man's gone to school, I've got all the time in the world.'

Loveday put her hand out to her friend. 'Are the doctors sure you can't have any more babies?'

Greer shrugged again. 'They're not always right, are they? And it's almost five years now . . .' She chewed the inside of her cheek. 'The thing is. I know it would make Jesse so happy to have another little one. He envies Mickey and you. Three children!'

Loveday felt the old twang of guilt deep within her breast. 'Yeah, well, they'm buggers too. Run me ragged.' She tried to make Greer smile, 'And they ruined my supermodel figure.'

Greer didn't laugh. She looked ashamed. 'That's what I hated about being pregnant. I told Jesse I never wanted to be pregnant again. It was an awful thing to say. I think I was scared. But I'd do it again for Jesse.' She hesitated. 'In fact, please don't say anything to anyone . . . Promise?'

Loveday frowned, not wanting to hear what Greer was about to say. 'I hope you haven't done anything silly?'

Greer started to chew her cheek again. 'Well I . . . I've stopped taking the pill. Jesse doesn't know, but I thought, why not? Give it a try. If it's meant to be . . . and all that.'

Loveday was shocked. 'My God, Greer. It could kill you and the baby.'

'Well, it didn't last time, did it?' Greer smiled tightly. 'Please don't tell Jesse. I just want one more chance. Promise you won't say anything.'

Against her better judgement, Loveday nodded. 'I promise.'

Bea ran up and helped herself to her carton of apple juice. 'Take Becca's too, would you, darlin'?' she said as her mind whirled. She turned her attention back to Greer. 'How long you been off the pill?'

'About five months.'

'But no luck?'

Greer's face told her all she needed to know. 'Oh my God,' Loveday breathed. 'You're pregnant.'

Loveday nodded. 'I think so. I'm late. About two weeks.'

'Have you seen the doctor?'

Greer shook her head. 'He'll be cross with me.'

'Cross?' Loveday said in a voice louder than she intended. 'Cross? That's a bleddy understatement. You've got to make an appointment now. Today. And tell Jesse.'

24

Louisa Caroline was stillborn at twenty weeks.

It was one of the most difficult funerals the Reverend Rowena had ever had to conduct. What can you say to grieving parents to heal their pain?

God was merciful and loving?

He never sent more than a person could bear?

He needed Louisa as an angel?

These trite but trusted platitudes just didn't match the enormity of the situation.

Would a loving God do this?

Rowena found herself struggling with her faith these days. Too many wars. Too many deaths. Too much sadness.

*

She was standing in the porch of St Peter's Church and watched as the small funeral cortège came up the hill. It was a bright but bitterly cold December day and she was grateful for the extra clothes that were hidden under her cassock.

Jesse insisted on carrying Louisa's coffin. He held it tenderly as he entered the church, his feet echoing on the red tiles of the aisle. He walked towards the flower-strewn dais that was to be Louisa's.

Behind him walked a Greer so pale and so thin that

she was almost translucent. She walked with Freddie, gripping his hand with a determination that frightened her. He was everything to her now. Nothing and nobody would ever take him from her. For his part, Freddie was scared. His mother had been ill and nearly died. His sister, who he'd never met, had died, and his father looked so ill that it was possible he was going to die too.

They reached the front pew and watched as Jesse laid the tiny white coffin on top of the sweet-smelling lilies and ivy.

*

Afterwards Freddie went to play with Hal, who always cheered him up. He'd packed a bag with his pyjamas in. He liked going to Auntie Loveday's and Uncle Mickey's. They let him and Hal eat crisps on the sofa and watch loads of television. Freddie felt that today he'd be allowed anything he wanted.

*

Greer was still frail. She had lost a lot of blood and needed to rest.

After the burial, next to Jesse's granddad, she and Jesse turned down all offers of lunch from their parents and returned home to Pencil Cottage.

'Would you like a cup of tea, darlin'?' asked Jesse, watching as Greer took off her coat.

'No, Thank you.' Greer ran her hands through her hair. 'Can I make you one?'

'No, thanks.' Jesse felt big and awkward and out of his depth. 'Can I get you anything at all?'

Greer shook her head and headed for the stairs.

'You going to have a lie-down?' he asked.

'Yes. I'm tired.'

He was tired, too. Weary to his bones. He'd been cross with Greer when she'd told him that Louisa was on the way. But when she had explained, so tenderly, that she wanted to give him another child, maybe a daughter, he hadn't stayed cross for long. The doctors had wheeled out all the usual warnings, but Greer said that she was feeling fine. She was only twenty-eight, and strong enough to have several more babies.

That is, until her blood pressure rose, her ankles swelled and Jesse found her unconscious in the kitchen having banged her head on the corner of the stove during a sudden seizure.

That was it. Game over.

He watched her tiny frame climb the staircase and head towards their bedroom. He fought the desperate need he had to follow her and cry in her arms.

The house was as quiet as the grave. No Freddie. No Greer singing to the radio in the kitchen or telling him off for leaving his shoes by the door rather than the specially designed shoe rack in the tiny entrance.

The phone rang and gave him a start. He went to it quickly before it disturbed Greer.

'Hello?'

'Jesse? It's Mick. I thought you might like a drink.'

*

The bar of the Golden Hind was weighted down with tinsel and paper lanterns. The jukebox was playing a medley of Christmas songs and the comforting smell of tobacco smoke and beer hit Jesse like a hug. Mickey was at the bar, foot on the brass footrail, tenner in hand and two frothy pints sitting on the bar towel in front of him.

'All right, mate?' He looked at Jesse with pure love and friendship. 'Want a pasty?'

They ate their pasties and drank their pints, talking about anything but the morning they had just endured.

'Two weeks to Christmas,' said Mickey, wiping the pastry crumbs from his lips with a red paper napkin.

'Not sure I feel very Christmassy,' sighed Jesse.

'Why not come over to us? Loveday and her mum always cook for a blessed army.'

'I think Greer's mum may have something arranged.'

'Oh shit. Poor you.'

Jesse managed a smile. 'Yeah. Not a barrel of laughs over there. Lunch at one on the dot. The queen at three. Presents at six.'

'What? You can't open your presents till six? You're definitely coming over to ours. If ours aren't open by six in the morning, there's something wrong.'

'We let Freddie open his early before we go over there. But he's still got to wait for his grandparents' presents at six like everyone else. And then we all sit in a circle on those bleddy uncomfortable sofas of Elizabeth's and have to go round in turn opening our gifts and bleddy oohing and aahing over them.'

'Fuck that,' said Mickey, finishing his pint. 'Want another?'

'I should be getting back.'

The thought of Jesse's return to the sadness of Pencil House brought their mood down again.

'I'm really sorry, Jesse,' Mick said, putting his arm round his best friend and squeezing him tight. 'For both of you.'

'It's pretty shit,' said Jesse.

'Yeah,' agreed Mickey. 'It is.'

*

Walking round the corner to Pencil Cottage, Jesse could see the twinkling of fairy lights through the window into the lounge. Was Greer putting up the Christmas decorations?

Taking his key from the lock and pushing open the door, he saw her, in her old Snoopy dressing gown, sorting through a large box of baubles. There was an open bottle of champagne on the coffee table by the gas-effect fire and a champagne flute next to it.

'Hello, darling,' he said gently. 'This is a nice surprise.'

She was a bit drunk. He could see that.

'Hello, Jesse.' She showed him two baubles, one green, one blue. 'Shall we go for a green theme or a blue theme? We had green last year, but blue doesn't seem quite right. What do you think?'

'I dunno. I like the green.'

'But is it Christmassy enough? You see . . .' She delved into the box and brought out three more baubles. 'Red, gold and silver. Now that's Christmassy, isn't it?'

'Definitely.'

She put the decorations down and poured herself another glass of champagne. 'The thing is, we've got to make the house nice for Freddie and Louisa.'

Jesse saw that the champagne bottle was more than half empty. 'For Freddie, you mean?'

'Yes, of course, and Louisa.'

Jesse went to Greer and held her. 'Louisa isn't here.'

She hugged him. 'I know. I'm a bit pissed but I'm not

mad. Or maybe you'll think I am.' She pulled back from their embrace and picked up her glass. 'I'm drinking champagne to toast Louisa's short life. I want to celebrate her. I never want people to feel they can't talk about her. I want to talk about her.' Greer's eyes filled with tears and her voice cracked as she continued, 'I was asleep earlier and I had such a dream. She was in bed with me and we talked about Christmas. She wants to see what a Christmas tree looks like, with all the lights and the sparkle, and I'm going to let her see it.' Greer held her glass towards the ceiling and raised her eyes. 'Louisa, this is for you, for ever and always.' She brought the glass to her lips and drank. She turned to Jesse. 'Would you like to toast your daughter?'

'OK,' he said guardedly. He'd never seen Greer like this before.

'I'll get you a glass.' She went to the cabinet where a row of Stuart crystal champagne flutes glistened. Untouched since they'd been imprisoned there as wedding presents six years ago.

She took one and filled it with the last of the champagne. She offered it to Jesse. 'Make a toast to our daughter Louisa.'

Jesse felt the prickle of tears at the back of his eyes and a constriction at the back of his throat. He held the glass out as Greer had done. 'Louisa. If you can see us and hear us, you know that we miss you. We will always miss you. And we're sorry.' The tears of both of them were flowing now. 'We're so sorry.'

*

'I'm going to open another bottle,' said Greer. 'We need to make this a night that we'll always want to remember.'

The champagne loosened them both so that they could talk freely of their grief. Sitting on the sofa with her head on Jesse's chest, Greer asked, 'We shall always remember her, won't we, Jesse? You'll never forget.'

'We'll never forget.' He kissed the top of her head. 'I'm so glad we saw her.'

'I'm going to put her photo up next to Freddie's. Our two children.'

'Our two children.'

'Poor Freddie. Did Mickey say he was all right?'

'Yes, he's fine. He and Hal were planning to watch *Toy Story*.'

'I love that film.'

'Yeah.'

Greer tilted her head so that she could see Jesse properly. 'Jesse. Do you love me even though I can't . . . I can't . . . give you any more children?'

'Don't be silly.'

'But do you love me? You don't say it very often.'

'Well, I'm a bloke, aren't I?'

'Mickey tells Loveday all the time . . .'

'Well that's just Mickey.'

'Do you love me?'

He kissed her nose. 'Of course.'

'Say it.'

'You know I do.'

'Say it.'

He took a beat, and in the silence Greer could hear the hiss of the flame-effect fire. She waited until he said, 'I love you.'

*

In the end, Christmas was spent at Pencil Cottage, just the three of them.

Greer used all her design skills to turn their little home into a cosy and inviting grotto.

The front door sported a wreath made of preserved apples and bundles of cinnamon sticks tied with gingham ribbon.

The Christmas tree was the biggest Jesse could fit into their tiny front room. It glistened with red, green, silver and gold baubles and countless strings of bright white lights.

The fireplace was cloaked in a fresh swag of fir, pine cones, holly, and heavily berried ivy.

Freddie was helping. 'What's in this box, Mummy?'

Greer watched as Freddie shook the box, then she knelt down next to him.

'Something special. One box for you, and . . . look, there's another box for Louisa.'

Freddie stretched across the pile of tissue paper and empty boxes of fairy lights. 'This one?'

'Yes.'

'I will open it for Louisa because she can't.'

Greer's heart contracted with love for her son. 'Good idea.'

Inside lay a small and glittery pink fairy carrying a wand.

'Ooh,' said Freddie. 'She'll like this.'

'There's a little button by her wand. Can you see?'

'Yes.'

'Press it.'

His warm little fingers found the button and pressed it. The wand lit up.

'Isn't that pretty?' smiled Greer.

'What's in my box?' asked Freddie, bored already with the fairy.

Greer laughed. 'Open it.'

He opened it and inside was a small cowboy wearing a T-shirt that read, 'Happy Christmas, Freddie Behenna.'

'Is this Woody from *Toy Story*?' asked Freddie, his eyes like saucers.

'Yep.'

'Has he brought Buzz?' Freddie, with Woody in one hand, was riffling through the tissue paper to see if there was another box.

'No. Buzz is on a mission. But he might come next year.'

'OK.' Freddie stopped looking for Buzz and picked up Louisa's fairy. 'Shall we put them on the tree? Woody on the top?'

'I think the fairy should go on the top.'

'No, Woody should. Then he can look for Buzz in the sky.'

'We'll be the only people in Trevay with a cowboy on the tree and not a fairy!' said Greer.

Freddie knitted his brows and thought for a moment. 'Don't tell Louisa, but I don't really like fairies.'

Greer took a moment before she could speak.

'I don't think she'll mind.'

Part Two

Part Two

25

July 2009

Jesse Behenna, managing director of Behenna and Clovelly Fish Company, surveyed the assembled faces of his staff as they lined up in the bar of the Golden Hind and waited for him to say a few words. Spencer was finally retiring after a lifetime spent working on the boats with three generations of Behenna men. There would be a retirement luncheon later on, which Jesse would be too busy to attend. But his father would be there, along with plenty of Trevay's salty old seadogs, who would regale each other with tales told a thousand times before. Scanning the expectant faces, Jesse noted that Bryn Clovelly wasn't there. Both he and Edward still held their seats on the board, in non-executive roles, but Bryn was more likely to be seen on the golf course these days, though he still enjoyed blustering pointlessly at the annual shareholder meetings.

Three years ago, Jesse had bought another stretch of the harbour, at least the length of a football pitch, and had demolished the ramshackle buildings that had been there for as long as anyone could remember. The old chandler's, the boat engine workshop, the damp and worm-riddled sail loft. All gone, to be replaced with a twenty-first-century, three-storey building made from glass and metal, with an atrium and balconies over-looking the estuary. The old fish market next door had been given a revamp and was still the money-making heart of the business, even more so now that it had its own adjoining restaurant, which had become a destination in itself and attracted wealthy holiday-makers and locals alike.

Jesse looked like the epitome of the relaxed modern executive. His open-necked shirt was Paul Smith and his tan leather brogues were Church's, but his full head of blond hair still fell in boyish waves and, even though he was often stuck behind his desk, driving deals stretching from London to Madrid, he still liked nothing better than going out with the boats and crewing with Mickey. Creeping crow's feet around his eyes were the only indicators of the stresses and strains that came with Behenna and Clovelly.

'And so, let's raise a toast to the man who has been the beating heart and soul of Behenna and Clovelly for longer than anyone else – Spence! It won't be the same without you, but luckily we'll still get a chance to see your ugly mug every lunchtime here at the Hind, which is where I imagine you'll be spending most of your retirement.'

There was a round of cheers as Jesse gave Spencer and his wife two all-expenses-paid tickets for dinner and a show in London. Spencer's wife wiped away a tear, and Spencer, embarrassed at all the attention, looked awkward.

As the group clapped and crowded around Spencer, oohing and aahing at his gift, Lauren, Jesse's assistant, touched him on the arm to get his attention.

'Houston, we have a problem.'

Jesse was on immediate alert. 'What's up?'

'Just got a call from Bob. A lorry jack-knifed on the A30 and there's been a pile-up. His van is totalled.'

'Is Bob all right?' Jesse's brow was creased with concern.

'He is totally fine, but he won't be able to get that consignment of John Dory and sea bass where it's supposed to be.'

'They were destined for the River Café and the Dorchester, weren't they?'

'Correct.'

Jesse thought quickly. 'Has Phil left with that order for Rick in Padstow yet?'

'I think he's just loading up.'

'Right.' Jesse fished in his trousers and pulled out a pile of notes. He quickly counted out £200 and pushed it into her hand. 'Tell him change of plan. He's to take his delivery to London instead. Give him a new manifest, and I'll give Rick a call and square things with him.'

'What will you do?'

'I'll find him something even better and drive it there myself.' He took his BlackBerry out of his pocket to make a call just as Greer's number popped up on his screen. He hesitated a moment before answering.

'Hi.'

'How's Spencer's send-off going?'

'Fine, but I've got a work crisis so won't be back until later . . .'

'Jesse – I was counting on you to take Freddie to his maths tutor tonight.'

'Can't you do it?'

'No! I told you, I'm visiting clients in St Just this afternoon – that new restaurant that looks out over the headland. It's a really important commission as they're

refurbishing the whole place. It needs my complete attention. I did tell you all of this already.'

'Well, it's tough, Greer. He'll just have to get on his
bike and take himself there. Where is he now, anyway?

'He's managed to twist my arm to let him out on the
boat with Hal, even though he should be revising.'

'You're too soft.'

'And you're not?'

'Listen, I've got to go. I'll text you later.' He sighed and
rang off, running his hands irritably through his hair
before heading back to his office.

*

Hal was feeding a mackerel line off the side of Freddie's
solid wooden rowing boat. His hair was flame red like
his mother's but, unlike her, he was as brown as a nut;
he always went a deep golden brown like his dad. Freddie
was pulling at the oars, his blond hair now almost
bleached white in the intense heat of the Cornish
summer.

The sun was hot and the sea smooth and both boys
were stripped to their waists. Hal was wearing a pair of
battered Converse and an old pair of cut-off jeans. Freddie,
by contrast, looked as if he was out of a Ralph Lauren
advert, in his tailored shorts and expensive deck shoes.

The only sound was that of the oars in the rowlocks
as Freddie pulled them in and out of the water, backwards and forwards.

'I've got another,' Hal said, pulling a flapping gleam of
mackerel out of the water and into a bucket that held two
others. 'I'm a mackerel magnet!' He thumped his chest,
Tarzan-style. 'Can't wait to get these babies over a fire.'

'Do you always think about your stomach?' Freddie laughed.

'Oh, yes,' said Hal, putting his baited line over the side again. 'That and the gorgeous Kelly Brook. Keeps me busy.'

'You're always busy, ain't yer!' and Freddie made the universal sign for wanker at his best mate.

'Oh, fuck off,' Hal replied genially. 'What you doing later?'

Freddie pulled a face. 'Mum's got me a maths tutor for the summer. Says I've got to buck up.'

'Bollocks. Can't you duck out? Dad's getting the barbecue out later and Mum will be doing some of her Chinese pork ribs.'

The idea sounded a lot more appealing to Freddie than swotting over his maths books. Didn't his mum know that it was summer?

'What's the point in maths anyway? Ain't you going out on the boats when school's finished?'

'Not if Mum has her way. Stick me in a suit and call me an accountant, she would.' Freddie frowned at the thought, but then something in the distance caught his attention. He stopped sculling and laid the oars inside the boat. 'What's that bloke doing up there?' He pointed to the headland above Tide Cove.

Hal followed his gaze and saw the outline of a man struggling to stand up straight. As the two boys watched, the man staggered, fell over, got up again and then tottered to the edge of the cliff. Trying to find his balance, he staggered forward again and then, missing his step completely, fell and slid over the side of the cliff onto a narrow shale ledge, which began to crumble at its edge.

'What the fuck's he doing?' said Freddie.

'Oh shit,' shouted Hal, and the two friends watched,

horrified, as the man tried to stand again but slipped, breaking the shale beneath him. They heard his scream as he fell the one hundred metres headfirst into the sea below.

The boys remained shocked for a split second, then Hal pulled out his mobile phone and started to dial 999.

'Shit. I haven't got a fucking signal.' He shook the phone violently, hoping that it would catch some radio waves, however small. Nothing.

Freddie had already turned the small boat round and was heading towards the spot where he thought the man had fallen.

'Can you see him?' he asked breathlessly.

'Nothing.' Hal was still waving his phone about. 'Got it. Got a signal.'

Freddie pulled with all his might on his oars as he heard Hal speaking down the phone. 'Hello? Yeah, there's a man just fallen off the cliff at Tide Cove . . . I'm in a boat . . . no, it's a rowing boat . . . about two minutes ago he fell. We're on our way to see if we can find him but I think we'll need the lifeboat . . . yeah, I'll hang on but I might lose the signal . . . Hello, hello?' He looked at the phone. 'Shit. Lost signal.'

'Are they coming?' asked Freddie breathlessly.

'She said she was going to put me through but—' His phone rang. 'Hello? Yes it was me who rang you . . . we need the lifeboat and an ambulance . . . I'm Hal Chandler . . . my dad's the mechanic on the Trevay lifeboat . . . hello ? Hello?'

Hal threw the handset into the bottom of the boat in frustration. 'The signal keeps going.'

'They'll get here,' said Freddie, his arms straining with effort. 'I know they will.'

For the next few minutes, neither boy spoke to the other.

Freddie was trying to ignore the pain in his shoulders in an effort to keep the boat moving forwards, and Hal was kneeling in the prow of the boat, scanning the rolling sea.

'I see him,' he shouted suddenly.

Freddie drew the boat alongside the man, not knowing whether he wanted to see what lay there. 'Is he breathing?' he asked Hal.

'He's face up, anyway,' said Hal.

Bravely he put his hand in the water and pulled at the man's jacket, bringing him closer to the boat. 'All right, mate?' he said fearfully. 'We got you.'

There was no response.

Freddie turned and looked over his shoulder at the man's face. It was pallid, the eyelids puffy and closed. A good week's worth of grey stubble covered his jowls and a frond of red seaweed had caught in it. 'Is he dead?'

'I don't know,' said Hal shakily.

'Keep his head out of the water until the lifeboat comes,' Freddie ordered.

'I'm trying.' But Hal didn't know how much longer he could hold on.

*

Jesse was just a minute away from the office when he felt his pager vibrate in his pocket just as he saw Mickey dashing towards him.

His face was etched with anxiety.

'We got a shout on the lifeboat, Jesse.'

'Not a boat in trouble, not in this weather – the water's as still as anything.'

'There's a body in the water. But, Jesse, it's the boys.'

Jesse's heart froze. 'What do you mean?'

'They made the call.'

All thoughts of lorries, John Dory and maths tutors fled his mind.

He and Mickey raced to the lifeboat station.

*

Freddie thought he could hear something. An engine coming fast from around the corner of the headland. He looked over his shoulder and, with a shout, said, 'It's them. They're here.' In crazy relief he stood up and started to wave and shout. 'We're over here! Dad, we're over here!'

'Sit down,' shouted Hal. 'You're tipping the boat, I can't keep hold of him.'

The Spirit of Trevay in its orange and blue livery, had never looked more wonderful as it approached the boys and the drowned man. At the helm was Jesse. 'There they are,' He slowed the powerful engines and expertly brought the boat alongside the small rowing boat.

Leaving the engines idling, and shouting orders to the crew, Jesse climbed up on deck and leant over the side. He saw the white faces of Freddie and Hal staring up from the little boat.

'Are you boys all right?' he called.

'We're fine, Dad,' said Freddie with a sob of relief. 'It's this bloke, he fell off the cliff.'

Hal was still hanging on to the man's jacket and valiantly keeping his head out of the water.

Jesse, thanking a God he wasn't sure existed that the two boys weren't harmed, took a look at the casualty. His heart skipped a beat and he involuntarily swore.

Mickey was up on deck now and scanning the rowing boat for Hal.

'Hal!' he called. 'You're OK?'

'Yes, Dad.'

'What you got there?'

'This man just fell off the cliff,' Hal called back, tears coming in shock and in the relief of seeing his father. 'I've been holding him. I don't know if he's dead.'

Mickey was first to clamber down into the wooden boat and take the weight of the man from Hal. 'It's all right. I've got 'im. You can let go now.'

When Mickey could see the man's face he frowned. 'Jesse,' he shouted. 'It's your'n brother. 'Tis Grant.'

Jesse was feeling an old sickness in his stomach, a sixth sense that the past was about to collide with the present. 'Are you sure?' he asked.

'Yeah, I'm sure.'

Mickey had a toughness that his wiry frame belied. Swinging Grant's body round in the water, he managed to get his hands under his arms and haul his dead weight into the bottom of the little boat.

'Is he dead?' asked Jesse, who as coxswain would never leave the lifeboat.

'Give me a minute,' said Mickey. He put his ear to the man's nose to see if he could hear or feel any breath. It was hard to tell with the soft breeze playing around the two boats. He put a hand inside the collar of Grant's camouflage jacket and felt the cold neck for a pulse.

Jesse and the boys waited.

'I've got it!' Mickey said. 'I've got a pulse, but it's faint. Radio for the ambulance to meet us on the harbour. Let's get him back quick.'

*

The side ward in the hospital looked over the car park and a sprawling cemetery.

Grant lay in the bed with a drip in his arm, an oxygen tube in his nostrils and a big bandage round his head. The young doctor was talking to Grant's parents and Jesse.

'He's had a pretty big bang to his head. He must have hit something when he fell. Not a rock but maybe a piece of flotsam. Piece of wood, maybe. There's not much of a cut but he has a lot of swelling. When he wakes up he's going to have quite a headache.'

'It's a miracle he didn't drown,' said Jan, his mother. She was sitting on a small chair at Grant's bedside and was holding his hand.

'Indeed,' agreed the doctor. 'He managed not to swallow much water but I think that the amount of alcohol he'd already consumed meant that he was very relaxed when he fell and therefore didn't panic when he hit the water.'

Edward was standing by the window, his back to the room. He was watching an elderly man wearing a tweed hat standing by a grave. A small girl of about twelve, maybe his granddaughter, guessed Edward, was hopping and skipping around him whilst swinging a Marks & Spencer plastic bag. The man said something to her and she stopped her skipping and opened the bag, taking out a potted plant with garish pink blooms. The old man took it and reverentially removed his tweed hat and bent to place the offering at the headstone. As he struggled to stand up, the young girl offered her arm and the two of them walked away. Edward turned his back on the comforting mundanity of the scene, and faced his own.

'It's Freddie and young Hal I'm proud of,' he said. 'Young lads. To do what they did. Bloody brave.'

Jesse nodded. 'Yeah. They'm did well.'

'What was Grant doing on those cliffs?' Edward asked. 'We haven't heard from him for years.'

'Two years,' said Jan. 'We had that letter from him. Remember? Telling us he was out of – ' she lowered her voice so that the doctor wouldn't hear – 'prison.'

Edward's mouth tightened to a thin line. 'Sorry, Doctor, but you may as well know. Grant has been a Heller all his life. Since he was a boy. If there was a fight he'd have started it, if there was trouble, he was in it.' Edward shook his head. 'When he joined the Marines we thought he was in the perfect job.'

'He got his green beret, Doctor,' said Jan, wanting the doctor not to think too badly of her son, but Edward ploughed on.

'Fat lot of good that was. He couldn't keep his fists to himself. Got court-martialled. Banged up in chokey for eight years.' Edward put his hands to his head and rubbed his temples. 'Dishonourably discharged four or five years ago. We haven't heard from him since. He couldn't even send me a note just to let me know he was all right. We had no idea he was back till today.'

Jan started to cry quietly and rummaged around in her handbag for a tissue.

Edward looked at her with pity. 'He broke his mother's heart and now look at him. I wish he'd never come back.'

Jan shouted through her tears. 'Don't say that.'

'I'll say what I like.' Edward raised his voice in return. 'He's brought us nothing but heartache and—'

Jesse stepped in. 'Dad. That's enough. We're all upset.' He turned to the doctor. 'I'm sorry, Doctor.'

*

Jesse had insisted that his parents go down to the hospital cafeteria to get something to eat and drink.

'Let me sit with him till you get back.'

On his own with Grant, Jesse wondered what his brother's dramatic reappearance would mean to the family. Did Grant know that Jesse was managing director of Behenna and Clovelly? Bryn and Edward were still nominally joint chief executives, but the day-to-day running of the company was in Jesse's control. Had Grant come back hoping to get a slice of the company? There was no way Jesse would give him one. He looked down at Grant, lying so still in the bed, so white against the pillow. How could he come back here after all this time? Jesse had seen the damage that Grant's behaviour had done to his parents, and he had worked his fingers to the bone doing fourteen-hour days to make Behenna and Clovelly the best in the business. He had clients across the globe, and a reputation that was the envy of his competitors. He was damned if Grant was going to come back and fuck it all up.

'What are you doing back here, Grant?' he asked.

Grant didn't open his eyes. But he answered, 'I missed my family.'

Jesse put his face close to his brother's. 'Well, we haven't missed you,' he said with menace.

'That's nice, little brother.' Grant slowly opened his eyes and winced. 'My head hurts.'

'It will.'

'I didn't mean to fall off the edge. I was just having a little drink when I saw the boys in the boat. Thought I'd get a better look at 'em.'

Jesse's heart started to pound. 'You're lucky we got you out.'

'You rescued me?' Grant coughed a little. 'Got any water? My throat's sore.'

Jesse looked and saw a plastic jug of water and a beaker on the bedside cabinet. He poured half a cup and handed it to Grant. 'Here. I ain't nursing you. Hold it yourself.'

'How lucky I am to have a brother so kind.' With difficulty, Grant took the cup and held it to his lips, taking a couple of mouthfuls. 'So you rescued me then.'

'Coxswain on the lifeboat, ain't I.'

Grant attempted to laugh but started to cough, spilling the water on the bedclothes.

'Lifeboat, eh? What a pillar of the community! So unlike your scallywag of a brother. How proud Mum and Dad must be,' he said with venom.

Jesse couldn't take any more of this bullshit. In a dangerous voice he said, 'Just tell me what the fuck you're doing here.'

'I told you,' Grant smiled. 'I missed my family.' He opened an eye. 'And those lovely boys.' He smiled a smile of pure evil. 'By the way, how is the gorgeous Loveday? Oh, and your uptight wife, Greer? I'd have had a go at Loveday myself, but I don't like taking sloppy seconds, especially from my little brother.'

Jesse lifted his fist and would have smashed it into Grant's face sending him spiralling back to oblivion, if it hadn't been for the door opening and the arrival of Jan and Edward.

Jan ran to Grant's side. 'Son. You're awake. It's OK. You've had a terrible fall but the doctor says you'll be fine. You're safe with your family now. We'll take you home.' She took his hand and, rubbing it, dropped a kiss on his forehead.

'Thanks, Ma,' said Grant. 'Give us a hug.'

Laughing through her tears, she bent and hugged him as best she could.

Over her shoulder Grant looked at Jesse and winked slyly. 'Yeah. I'm home, Ma. With my family. For good.'

26

Normally Jesse took enormous pleasure from arriving at the new offices of Behenna and Clovelly.

He parked his car in his reserved space. He climbed out of the new Jaguar XK V8 and breathed the clean, salty air. His head was aching. He hadn't slept well. Grant's reappearance had left him troubled.

'Morning, Jesse.' Mickey was walking towards him with Loveday. ''Ow's Grant doing?'

'Morning!' Jesse pressed the button on his key fob and the car bleeped and locked itself. 'He's all right. Coming out today. He's going to stay at Mum and Dad's for a bit, but I'm worried for them . . . they could do without a scrounger like him living off them.'

Loveday was concerned. 'Your poor mum. Last thing she needs.' She looked at her watch. 'Give us a kiss, Mick. I'm late for work.' Mickey obliged and both men watched Loveday as she walked into the Behenna and Clovelly offices.

'She loves that job, Jesse,' said Mickey.

'Well, she's very good at it.'

'Yeah. Always good with her head. Better'n me.'

'How are things with the new house?'

'Great. The girls love their room up in the attic and Hal's got space to do his school work in his room rather than on the kitchen table.' Mickey looked at Jesse's car.

'Look at us, Jesse. We ain't done too bad, 'ave we? Remember that old Ford Capri you had?'

'That was a classic.'

''Twas a heap of shit.'

'What about your bike?' said Jesse indignantly. 'That was knackered before you got it.'

'That was class, that was. With Loveday on the back of it, I felt like a king.'

The men smiled. 'Those were the days, Mick,' said Jesse fondly.

'Yeah,' nodded Mick. 'They were shit really, weren't they?' He laughed out loud. 'But look at us. Your'n all prosperous boss an' that. The car, the house, the business.'

'You haven't done so bad! Skipper of the biggest boat in our fleet.'

Mickey looked abashed. 'I wouldn't have any of it if it weren't for you.'

'Nor I if it weren't for you, Mickey.'

'Well, you got your bugger of a brother to deal with now, and I'm glad I ain't got him.'

Jesse sighed. 'I hope he'll just piss off again and never come back.'

*

Having said goodbye to each other, Mickey headed off to his boat and its waiting crew, and Jesse stepped into the air-conditioned luxury of his building. As he glided upstairs in the glass lift, he saw the whole of Trevay spread out below him. Nothing much had changed since he was a boy. The old cottages and houses in the cobbled lanes were looking better kept, though, now, owned as they were by sharp-eyed Londoners who'd bought them as holiday homes. Up on the hill, the housing estate had grown and was sprawling out over what had been farmland, but where else could the locals afford to live? Not in the centre of highly priced Trevay, that was for sure. And they didn't want to. Cramped old houses with wonky floors and no garage? Let the ones from up country have them. Fools and their money, and all that.

The lift stopped with barely a whisper and the door opened, revealing a long, sunny room that had been partitioned into small, private offices or larger open areas, where long couches, glass tables and local art were displayed beautifully. This was Greer's handiwork. Her interiors company was now so busy that she employed three designers and a team of builders and tradesmen. Jesse's office was at the end of the building and took up the entire width of it. His secretary was at her desk, writing something in his diary.

'Morning, Mr Behenna,' she smiled.

'Good morning, Lauren.'

'Coffee? Usual?'

'Yes, please.'

Lauren stood up to go to the canteen. 'By the way, your father's in the office waiting for you. I'll bring you two coffees up.'

Jesse's pleasure at walking into his kingdom, already dissipated, dissolved entirely.

'Dad.' He wrapped a smile on his face. 'Nice surprise. How's Grant?'

Jesse noticed that Edward had aged in the three days since Grant had turned up.

'He's all right. Your mum's fussing at home, making up the bed, writing lists. He's coming out of hospital this afternoon.'

Jesse walked round his big wooden desk and sat down. 'I'd go and collect him for you but . . .' He spread his arms, indicating a day full of work, even though his desktop was clear.

'Your mum and I'll get him. No, it's not what I came to see you about. I want to get things sorted. Legally. Grant's not having what you've got.'

'Dad.' Jesse knew that his father would wash his hands of Grant if he could, but the fact that his father was of the same mind as him regarding the business was music to his ears. However, it was important that his father didn't think Jesse was trying to push Grant out.

'Dad, I'm only number two son.'

'Yeah, but you've worked hard. I am not about to see Grant try to take it from you.'

'Does Mum know about this?'

'She don't need to.'

'Are you sure about that?'

'I won't leave him empty-handed. He'll get what's right, but he ain't getting the business. It's twenty years since Bryn and I agreed that it would be yours and Greer's, and then Freddie's.'

'If he wants it.'

'Why wouldn't he?'

'Because . . . there's a world out there and he wants to see it. Just as I wanted to see it . . .'

Lauren came in, pushing the heavy door with her bottom. 'Two lattes.' She put the two chunky pottery mugs onto the coffee table. 'Anything else I can get you?'

'No, thank you, Lauren.' Jesse smiled impatiently.

Lauren took her cue and left quietly, and Jesse turned

to his father. He didn't want to look this gift horse in the mouth. 'OK. I'll get on to Penrose tomorrow and make sure that the paperwork is watertight, if that's what you want me to do.'

'I do,' his father said firmly. 'And Bryn agrees with me too.'

'So when are you going to tell Grant?' Jesse asked, stirring his coffee. 'Or will you leave it until you're gone and we're at the reading of the will?'

Edward smiled ruefully. 'I'd like to do that, but it's the coward's way out. No, I'll tell him sooner rather than later.' He took a sip of the latte. 'That way, with a bit of luck, he might not be tempted to hang around.'

*

It was a long day, made longer by the nagging thought that Grant was bound to be the bearer of trouble. Jesse was snappy and irritable. Problems heaped up. More than once, Lauren bit her lip and retreated to her desk. The final straw came late in the day when a London chef, not known for his equability, rang complaining about 'this shit you've sent me. I wouldn't give it to me cats. The lobsters aren't big enough, the skate is too expensive, and where's the sodding lemon sole? I'm not paying for this crap . . .' On and on he ranted, in his pseudo-cockney accent. Jesse put the receiver on the desk and rubbed his temples. When the man had calmed down he picked the receiver up and said, with a serenity he did not feel, 'Luigi, I am so sorry. I shall send you up a box of twelve dozen Falmouth oysters on the overnight van, on the house. And, next time you're down here, I'd like you to have dinner here at our expense. What do you say?'

*

An hour later, Jesse climbed back into the dark luxury of the Jaguar. The leather seat gave under his weight and released its hypnotic aroma. Jesse put his head on the steering wheel and closed his eyes. His headache was worse. He gave in to his exhaustion and relaxed the tension in his shoulders. 'What a shit of a day,' he said to himself.

A sharp knock on his window made his heart pound as he jerked upright. His headache shot an arrow of pain through his left eye.

Grant, still wearing his head bandage, was leering through the glass. 'First sign of madness, talking to yourself.'

Jesse turned on the engine and the dashboard glowed sweetly, but even that small pleasure was now spoilt. He opened the electric window. 'Grant. What do you want?' he asked dully.

'A bed for a bit. Ma and Pa's house is too small and Ma's driving me mad. As soon as I got home she was mithering me. I walked out while she was in the kitchen putting the kettle on. She was talking so much she didn't hear me go.'

'What about Dad?' Jesse sighed.

'He'd pissed off to the pub.'

'Why not go with him?'

'Whaaat? When my brother has a fancy new car that needs to be sat in and a beautiful new house that needs to be visited?'

Grant walked round the outside of the car and opened the passenger door. He got in. 'Not bad.' He wiped his none-too-clean hands over the walnut trim.

Jesse was not a happy man. A bad day had just got worse. 'Thank you,' he said flatly.

'Well, come on then!' smiled Grant, rubbing his hands gleefully. 'Show me what this baby can do.'

27

When they had lost Louisa, Greer's father, Bryn, had helped them to move out of Pencil Cottage, with all its sadness, and buy Tide House. Bryn had made enquiries through various solicitors and found that the cove below had passed from the previous owner to distant relatives, who lived in Canada and who had no idea of the beauty – or worth – of it. He had bought it for a song. A wooden gate and a large 'KEEP OUT PRIVATE PROPERTY' sign made sure that no wandering tourist could ever honestly say they didn't know that they were trespassing.

This evening, Freddie was home first for a change; he kicked off his shoes in the hallway. He was starving and headed straight into the kitchen and made a beeline for the fridge. He sighed as he eyed the contents. Six low-fat yogurts, a ready-made couscous salad and a packet of defrosted chicken fillets. If this was the fridge at Hal's house, it would be groaning with Dairylea, mini sausage rolls and thick-cut ham. His stomach groaned loudly as he grabbed one of the yogurts and he pulled a face as he tasted the bland goo.

He heard his mother's car pull up in the drive and made a dash for the stairs and the sanctuary of his room.

His mother's voice drifted up from the hallway. 'Freddie! How many times have I told you not to leave your trainers in the hallway? There is a perfectly good shoe store under the stairs.' He heard her tread on the stairs, heading his way.

She strode proprietorially into his room. 'And how many times have I told you not to eat in bed?'

'They eat wherever they want in Hal's house.'

'Exactly. Point proven.' She picked up the empty yogurt pot and sat on the edge of his bed.

'How was your maths tutorial?'

'Boring. A waste of time.'

'It isn't a waste of time. You've got a good head on your shoulders and all you need to do is apply yourself.'

'No point if I'm going out on the boats.'

Greer frowned. Just because Jesse had left school at 16, it didn't mean that Freddie had to as well. She was determined that Freddie was going to make something of himself. She turned and headed back downstairs towards the kitchen; catching sight of her refection on the staircase, she stopped to appraise herself. Greer now wore her hair in an elegant pixie cut. It accentuated her cheekbones. She was wearing a pair of skinny jeans from All Saints paired with a plain white T-shirt and a navy blazer from Joseph. As usual, she saw herself with a critical eye. It took work to look as good as this and, as well as running a successful interior design business, Greer also saw looking after herself as part of the package. She managed to squeeze in either a Pilates or a yoga class every day, and their basement downstairs was equipped with a state-of-the-art gym, which she made good use of.

'What's for dinner?' Freddie shouted from his room.

'Chicken, new potatoes and salad.'

There was silence above, then, after crashing down

the stairs like a herd of elephants, Freddie made an appearance at the kitchen door.

'Can I go over to Hal's tonight?'

'Freddie, that's the third night this week.'

'Well, if my mates come round here you only complain that they dirty the carpet or leave the toilet seat up. They don't care about any of that at Hal's.'

Greer raised an eyebrow. 'It's "lavatory" – and indeed.'

Freddie persisted. 'I'm doing you a favour. Besides, they're having a barbecue again tonight.'

'You'll have to ask your father. Speaking of which, he sent a text to say he's on his way. Apparently we've got a guest.' She looked out of the kitchen window to see if she could spot his Jaguar. 'I wonder who it is.'

*

It was less than a fifteen-minute drive to get to Jesse's home. At the top of Trevay, he turned right and continued along the cliff road towards the crossroads, where you could go straight on for Truro, left for Pendruggan or right towards Tide Cove. He turned right. The lane was wide enough for two cars at this point, and they were high enough up to see the sun glinting off the Atlantic. Holiday-makers, with sandy bare feet, were struggling up the hill after a long day on the beach. They hauled toddlers and dogs, pushchairs and beach trolleys. Fit young men, in surf suits peeled to their navels, jogged up with surfboards on their backs; gaggles of girls with sea-bleached hair stared after them and giggled. Jesse steered the car care-fully through them all, pulling into impossibly small passing spaces to allow camper vans and Chelsea tractors coming from the beach to get by. About two minutes from the beach itself there was a small left-hand turning, discreetly signed: 'Tide Cove. Private Property'.

Grant was impressed. 'Don't tell me you've got the big house down here?'

Jesse said nothing, but drove the car towards two large metal gates fifty yards ahead. He pulled out a small plastic fob from the ashtray and pointed it through the windscreen.

After a second or two the gates swung cleanly open, revealing a gravelled drive, a landscaped front garden and a beautiful honey-stoned house.

*

'Hello,' called Jesse, unlocking the front door.

'Hi, darling,' called Greer from the rear of the house.

'Hi, Greer,' called Grant gaily. 'Guess who's come for dinner.'

Jesse threw his keys onto the ebony console table under the large Edwardian gilt mirror in the hall. Greer popped out from behind a curved wall holding a gin and tonic and wearing an expression of dread. 'Grant?'

'Aye.' He walked towards her and embraced her. She stood stiffly, still holding her glass. He took it from her. 'Cheers. What's for supper?'

Greer's eyes slid to meet Jesse's, but he was staring resolutely at the floor.

'How's your head?' Greer managed, looking at the bandage.

'Bloody sore.' He took a big mouthful of gin and tonic.

'Should you be drinking with a head trauma?'

'Best thing for it,' said Grant, who was now opening a door to his left. 'What's in here?'

'That's the library,' said Greer automatically.

'Nice.' Grant looked into the room. 'Fancy.' He left the library and, crossing the hall, opened a door on his right. 'And what's in 'ere?'

'The drawing room,' said Greer tightly.

'I'm looking for the bleddy telly,' said Grant in exasperation. 'Don't tell me you ain't got one. Or 'ave you gone so la-di-dah that you listen only to the wireless?'

Jesse pulled himself together. 'The television is in there. In the drawing room.'

Grant looked again round the door. 'I can't bleddy see it.'

'It's behind the bookcase,' said Jesse.

Grant was impressed and then suspicious. 'You'm taking the piss out of me? I've had a bang on the 'ead but I'm still all 'ere.'

Jesse went to the bookcase – actually a fake wall with fake books – and slid it away to reveal an enormous television screen.

Grant gasped. 'Well, fuck me! You'm know how to treat yourselves, don't 'e?' He turned to Greer, who was standing in the doorway looking bewildered, if not horrified. 'Get me another drink, G,' said Grant, holding out his empty glass. 'You're not going to get rid of me now.'

*

Grant was a horrible guest.

''Twas a lovely tea that, Greer.' He belched. Greer closed her eyes. 'My compliments to the cook.' He drained his tin of Skinner's Wink beer and wiped his mouth on the sleeve of his grubby pullover. 'Where's the fridge?

I'll get another one of those. Don't want you waiting on me just because you 'aven't seen me for a long time.'

'It's that cupboard there,' said Freddie, pointing towards the integrated larder fridge/freezer with double doors painted in a colour called Sea Fret.

'Your'n a good lad.' Grant grinned at him. 'That's twice you've saved my life. Once taking me out of the drink, and twice getting the drink into me.'

Freddie was pleased to be a hero, and to have an uncle who was a real-life war veteran. All thoughts of going to Hal's were forgotten. His uncle was like no one else in the family, and the thought that he'd been a commando and had been to prison was very exciting.

'Have you killed anyone face to face?' he asked.

Grant came back with his tin of beer and farted before taking his seat again. Freddie sniggered.

'Several,' said Grant sagely. ''Tis a terrible thing to watch a man die. Even if he is the enemy. But Marines don't shirk their duty.'

Greer stood up quickly and began clearing the table.

'Don't 'e 'ave someone to do that for you?' asked Grant, scratching a scurfy scalp under his head bandage.

'I like to look after my family myself. Without too much help,' said Greer.

'Oh. Very commendable.' He winked at Jesse. 'You got a good 'un there, bro. Cook in the kitchen, angel in the living room. Whore in the bedroom, eh?'

Greer put the plates on the worktop and spun to face Grant. 'That sort of sexist talk is not welcome at our table.'

Grant tilted his chair onto its back legs and laughed. 'Don't tell me you're a feminist lesbo now, G? You weren't so picky about that sort of stuff when you had the hots for Jesse, were you? Used all your girly tricks to trap him then, eh?'

'Watch it Grant,' Jesse warned.

Greer threw her tea towel into the sink and spoke to Jesse. 'Can I speak to you in the library for a moment, please?'

'Of course,' said Jesse, pushing his chair back.

'Uh-oh. Nothing to do with me, I hope?' smirked Grant.

*

In the library, Greer shook with anger and emotion. 'Why the hell didn't you tell me he was coming for supper?'

'I didn't know myself. He's walked out of Mum and Dad's.'

'But he's going back there tonight?'

'I'm not sure.'

'Ask him.'

'It's late. If I throw him out, Mum will be in pieces. She's already a bag of nerves.'

'He's not staying here.' Jesse couldn't look her in the eye. Greer shook her head in disgust. 'I'll tell him then, shall I?' Greer pushed past Jesse and walked out into the hall, where Grant was being helped up the stairs by Freddie. 'Where are you going?' she almost shrieked.

'I'm showing Uncle Grant up to his room,' said Freddie innocently.

'It's so kind of you both to give me a roof over my head,' said Grant. 'I'll be no trouble.'

*

In their perfectly appointed master bedroom, Greer sat at her dressing table, vigorously rubbing cleanser into her face and giving Jesse chapter and verse.

'He looks awful. He drinks too much, he's filthy dirty, he has no manners and he's not staying here more than this one night. Do you understand?'

'I didn't invite him,' groaned Jesse. 'I don't want him here any more than you do.'

'Then send him back to your mother's tomorrow, or . . .' She brightened at the thought. 'Give him a fat cheque and tell him to get lost. That's the only thing he understands.' She plucked three tissues from their box and wiped the cleanser from her face.

'How much?' asked Jesse.

'Five hundred,' asserted Greer.

*

The wad of notes was waiting in a plump envelope on the kitchen table at the breakfast place laid for Grant. 'What's this then?' he asked, picking the envelope up and shaking it.

Neither Jesse nor Greer answered.

''Twouldn't be a little "piss off Grant and don't come back", would it?'

Jesse cleared his throat. 'It's something to tide you over while you find your feet. It should pay for a nice lodging and some food.'

Grant narrowed his eyes thoughtfully. 'I see.' He tapped the envelope on the table, sucking air through his teeth. 'No room at the inn. Is that it?'

They could hear Freddie coming down the stairs.

'Don't say anything to Freddie,' warned Jesse.

'Morning,' said Freddie brightly.

'Morning, boy.' Grant stashed the envelope inside his pullover, much to the relief of Jesse and Greer. 'What you up to today? No school?'

'Another week till we go back.' Freddie stretched across the table and picked up the box of Crunchy Nut Cornflakes. 'Big year this year. GCSEs.'

'GCSEs? There's posh. My education was the university of life, and I'm still learning.' He patted the wad under his jumper and looked slyly at Grant. 'In fact, starting today, your dad's going to teach me all about the family business. I've got a lot of catching up to do.'

*

'This ain't too shabby,' said Grant, as they headed up in the lift towards the top floor. He pulled at the cuffs of his borrowed shirt. ''Ow do I look?'

Jesse, who'd done his best to dissuade Grant from coming to the office with him, said, 'Cleaner.'

'Yeah, well,' said Grant, patting at the fresh jumper Jesse had found for him, 'the life of a gentlemen of the road don't stretch to hot baths and razor blades.'

Jesse looked appalled. 'You were sleeping rough?'

'Yeah. On and off over the last few years. And, after the confines of chokey, I tell 'ee, to sleep under the roof of the heavens was better'n a bed at the Starfish . . . I managed all right, a little bit of this, a little bit of that . . .'

Who knows what he had been up to in the intervening years, if his ravaged features were anything to go by, thought Jesse grimly. Prison, alcohol and those years on the street had all taken their toll.

The lift doors slid open and the scent of opulence surrounded them.

Grant took it all in, a smile of entitlement creeping across his face. He clapped Jesse on the shoulder. 'So, this is what you've been up to. I'll have a slice of this.'

Jesse couldn't bear to look at his brother and strode off towards Lauren and his office, Grant bowling insouciantly beside him.

'Two coffees, Mr Behenna?' asked Lauren, looking at Grant with a questioning arch of one eyebrow.

''Ow do?' said Grant, proffering his hand. 'I'm Grant Behenna. Jesse's older brother. I've been away for a while, but I'm here now, ready to give my all to the family firm.'

Lauren took his hand and felt the calloused, slightly greasy, palm. Grant hung on a little too long and she was afraid he was going to kiss it, but Jesse called him off. 'Grant, if I see you bothering Lauren you'll be out on your ear. Same goes for any woman employed here.'

Grant let go of Lauren's hand and grinned. ''E's jealous. No sugar in me coffee, darlin'.'

Jesse opened his office door and Grant squeezed past him. 'Very nice.' He walked to Jesse's desk and got himself settled behind it. He spun the chair round to take in the view across the estuary. 'When I see Trevay like this, it makes me wonder why I ever left.'

'Get out of my chair,' Jesse ordered. 'And you left Trevay because you went into the Marines, disgraced yourself, and got banged up for eight years for hurting an innocent old man.'

Grant, looking miffed, lifted himself out of the ergonomic chair and grudgingly settled himself in a comfy leather one by the coffee table. 'Just details, old boy.

Details. Now, where are you going to place me and what's the starting salary?'

Jesse had picked up the phone. 'Hi, Johnny? Mr Behenna here. You know that job you've got downstairs? Can I bring a potential candidate down?'

*

Grant looked down at the white overall and white rubber boots he was wearing. 'Here you are.' Johnny, the foreman of the fish market, handed him a white hairnet. 'Put that on and follow me.'

'Of course, I'm just here to learn the business from the bottom. Then I'll be moved around the rest of company to get a taste of all the departments before taking my place on the board,' blagged Grant.

'Sure,' said Johnny. 'That's what they all say.'

Grant caught Johnny's arm and spun him round, pushing him against the brick wall and winding him. 'Listen, you little fucker. I am a Behenna and you will treat me with respect . . . if you want to keep your job.'

'Let go of him immediately.' Edward Behenna, who had been up early, was glad he'd decided to drop in and see how his elder son was doing. Grant let go of Johnny.

'Just playing, Dad. Fooling around. Weren't we, Johnny?'

'Something like that,' said Johnny.

Edward was no fool. 'You have a lot to prove, Grant.'

Grant stood to attention and mock-saluted his father. 'Yessir.' He didn't like playing the lackey one little bit, but to be honest he'd had enough of roaming and he wouldn't mind a bit of what Jesse had managed to secure. Yes indeed, that would do nicely.

Edward ignored his son's sarcasm. 'The tide's running in and there are a lot of boats coming in to unload. I want to see you earning your money.'

*

Edward hadn't been wrong. Several boats chugged in together and tied up on the fish quay, each eager to unload its catch and get the best prices before the next boats came in.

Crates and crates of plastic boxes, full of ice and fish, were unloaded from the bellies of the vessels.

Monkfish, spider crab, mackerel, bass, sole, turbot – you name it, it was there.

Buyers materialised as soon as they heard the catch was in, and it wasn't long before large amounts of money was changing hands. The London chefs had got their orders in already and their boxes were being loaded onto the refrigerated vans immediately.

It was heavy work and Grant, once so fit, had lost his strength. His muscles had turned to fat and his lungs were clogged with nicotine. In a short lull, he sat at the back of the market on a pile of empty boxes, underneath a No Smoking sign. He was desperate for a nicotine hit, but he wanted this job more. Despite all his blustering, even he knew this was last orders in the last-chance saloon.

On the quayside, boats were leaving and more boats were arriving. Johnny spotted Grant. 'Grant, get over here and unload this next boat.' Grant reluctantly did as he was told, as Johnny hailed the skipper of the approaching vessel. 'All right, Mickey boy?'

Mickey threw a rope to Johnny, who tied it onto one of the ancient bollards.

'Bleddy tired,' called back Mickey. 'Good fishin' but no sleep.'

'Hi, Mickey.' Grant had wandered over and said sarcastically, 'My hero.'

Mickey jumped onto the quay. ''Twasn't me 'oo saved you.' Mickey thought that if he'd found Grant he would probably have left him to drown. Definitely would if there was a next time. ''Twas Hal.'

'Hal?' asked Grant innocently. 'Who's Hal?'

'You know – my boy.'

'Your boy? I hear him and Fred are like brothers?'

Mickey smiled fondly. 'Aye. They're like Jesse and I was growing up. 'Tis lovely to see.'

'Like brothers?' Grant feigned amazement. 'Isn't that sweet? Course, I wouldn't know what having a brother to play with was like. Jesse was so much younger – and always ran off with you.'

Mickey was remembering how much he disliked Grant. 'What you doin' here?'

'Learning the business, boy. Learning the business.'

A tall and skinny boy came out of the ship's hold. 'Dad, you ready to unload?'

'Hal, this is Freddie's Uncle Grant.' Mickey nodded towards Grant. 'He'm got something to say to you.'

Grant took his cue and smiled at the boy warmly. 'So you're Hal? I got to thank you for saving my life. You're like a superhero to me.'

Hal blushed. ''Twas nothin'.'

'That's not what I heard. You kept me from going under, didn't you?'

'Yeah.'

'That must have been frightening. Did you think I was dead?'

The memory flashed through Hal's mind and brought the horror back to him. 'Sort of.'

'Takes more'n a dip in the sea to kill off your uncle Grant.' Grant laughed unpleasantly, then said, 'Oh, no, I'm not your uncle, am I? I get mixed up.' He put his hand up to his now bandage-free head. 'I had quite a bang on the old noggin'.'

'Yeah,' said Hal uncertainly, and he turned to Mickey. 'Anyway, Dad. All the boxes are ready . . .'

*

Just as the last boxes were coming off Mickey's boat, Grant heard a familiar female voice call, 'Hiya, Mick. Good trip?' It was Loveday. She was just as sexy as Grant remembered her.

'Well, well, if ain't luscious Loveday Carter,' said Grant, sidling up to her.

She looked at him, recognition dawning. She was shocked at how different he looked. His once muscular frame was now skin and bone. He had never been her cup of tea in the looks department, but he'd always been able to pick up girls. Now his features were gaunt and sallow and he looked ancient. He could only be early forties, by Loveday's calculations.

'Grant. I 'eard you were back.'

Mickey came to join them. 'She's Loveday Chandler now. My missus.' Mickey put his arm protectively around Loveday and squeezed her.

'Oh, yeah,' said Grant, nodding slowly. 'You were up the duff, weren't you?'

Loveday was annoyed. 'Trust you to remember that. Yeah, I was. I was expecting Hal.'

'Oh, that's right.' Grant's voice held a hint of malevolence. 'Trouble with me is, I remember some funny things. I remember the night before Jesse got married. Do you?'

Loveday nervously put a hand to her hair, brushing away an invisible strand. 'Not really.'

'Course you do.' He insisted. 'It was snowing.'

Johnny shouted over to Mickey. 'Mick, come in the office and sign this paperwork, would 'e?'

'Back in a minute, darlin',' said Mick, leaving Grant and Loveday by themselves.

Grant watched Mickey till he was safely out of earshot, then he said slowly and with no small pleasure. 'You went up to the sheds. Why you were there I couldn't say. Maybe you were cold and needed warming up by something . . . or someone?'

Loveday looked at Grant with fear. 'I don't know what you're talking about.'

'I think you do. You see, I was . . .' He stopped and quickly changed the subject as he saw Mickey and Hal coming towards them. 'I was wondering what you do for Jesse now.'

'What?' she said, feeling panicked.

'I was just saying to your missus, Mickey,' Grant raised his voice as Mickey and Hal approached, 'what's she doing here for Jesse?'

Mickey smiled proudly. 'She'm in accounts. Always good with her 'ead.'

Grant suppressed a snigger. 'I'm sure that's true.'

Loveday was desperate to get away from this loathsome man. 'You'm ready to go home, boys?' she asked her son and husband.

'Aye,' they said in unison.

'Then I'll get my things. Hang on a minute.'

As Loveday scurried off, Jesse appeared. 'Had a good day, Grant?'

'Smashing,' said Grant. 'Just catching up with old friends, ain't we, Mickey?'

Loveday came back holding a handbag and a cardigan. 'We're off home now, Jesse,' she said. 'See you tomorrow.'

As the family walked away, Grant couldn't resist sprinkling a little agitant in their brains. 'Cheerio! And thanks again, Hal, for saving my life. Your dad must be so proud of you? Eh, Jesse?'

28

G rant moved out of Tide House with the five hundred pounds in his pocket and the promise of wages, into one of the letting rooms above the Golden Hind. Living in the pub suited him – and Jesse – perfectly.

Grant had settled into his job on the fish market too. He did it well enough, even with a hangover, and over the next few weeks he stopped mithering Jesse about a bigger, better position in the company. At the moment he couldn't really face the extra responsibilities a higher position would entail; he was sure he would take his rightful place at the top of the tree in due course. 'I'm in clover,' he said to himself. 'Living in a pub, all the beer I can drink and a job that I can't be sacked from. Grant, lad, you landed on your arse in butter all right.'

For his part, Jesse was relieved that Grant had apparently settled for his lot. Yes, he drank too much and was sometimes late for work – or didn't turn up at all – but, all in all, it was the best of a bad situation.

*

Greer had been very upset by Grant's reappearance, and Jesse's weakness in dealing with him. She had sanitised the house from top to bottom. 'This room needs fumigating,' she said, stomping around the beautiful *lit bateau* bed in the spare room that Grant had slept in.

'He's only been here a night,' said Jesse testily.

'But where was he the previous nights? Eh?' she'd demanded, snapping on a pair of rubber gloves and stripping the duvet and mattress protector off.

'He was in hospital.'

'Yes, and we all know how filthy hospitals are nowadays, don't we?' She handed Jesse a black bin liner. 'Open that and hold it while I put this bedding in.' Jesse did as he was told. He watched Greer as she moved around the room picking up the towels that Grant had left in a damp heap on the beautiful suede chair by the window; finding three empty tins of Skinner's Wink behind the curtains, and curling her lips as she saw a pair of very dirty, rather stiff socks spread out on the radiator. Greer had been a good wife to him and a great mother to Freddie. When they had lost Louisa, he had made a promise to himself that he would be the best husband and father Greer and Freddie could hope for. And he'd held to that promise.

If there had been any vestige of longing for Loveday, he made sure he'd killed it. Smothering the thoughts till there was no breath left in them. He loved Greer in his own way and he knew she loved him.

'I do love you, Greer,' he said suddenly.

She stopped fussing with the clean sheets and looked at him. 'Don't try to get round me.'

'I'm not.' He put the stuffed bin liner down and came towards her. He put his arms around her waist and pulled her into him. 'I'm sorry about Grant. He won't come back here again.'

She tried to wriggle out of his embrace, saying, 'Too right he won't be coming back here again,' but he held her tighter. He kissed her neck the way she used to like it and he felt her relax just a little.

'What are you doing?' she asked quietly.

'What do you think?' He nibbled her ear.

'I haven't got time for this,' she said after a pause. 'I've got to get this room sorted, then I'm meeting a client over in Liskeard after lunch.'

He persisted with the nibbling. 'We've got plenty of time.'

Greer weighed up all she had to do, versus having sex with her husband. 'OK. But we'll have to be quick.'

*

The summer turned slowly into autumn and Jesse was feeling confident that life was back under his control. Grant was behaving himself. Greer had secured a very lucrative job doing up a huge country house just outside Liskeard. Freddie was back at school and on track to do well in his GCSEs. And the business had just had its best summer profits for three years.

So nothing could have prepared him for the entrance, one afternoon, of Loveday into his office. Her face was blotched and her make-up dislodged by tears.

'What's happened?' he asked, getting up and closing the office door behind her. He glimpsed Lauren looking curiously at him. 'It's OK, Lauren.' He smiled.

'Would you like a tea? Coffee?' Lauren asked, desperate to know what was going on.

'I'll let you know.' He smiled again and closed the door firmly.

He turned to Loveday, his smile replaced with concern. 'What's happened? Is it Mickey? The kids?'

'It's Grant.' She was shaking.

Jesse sat Loveday on one of the comfy chairs by the coffee table. 'What's he done?'

'Nothing . . . n-not yet . . . It's what he's been saying.'

'Tell me.' Jesse was feeling the old dread in his stomach.

'He was overheard in the Hind last night, saying . . .' Loveday's voice broke and she wiped at her tears angrily, '. . . saying that Hal's not Mickey's son. He said that he had a good idea who the father is.'

'Did he give a name?'

Loveday looked at Jesse coldly, 'Of course not. There's no other bloody name but Mickey's.'

Jesse bit his lip. 'Loveday, I don't want to get you cross but . . . are you sure – you know – that Hal is Mickey's?'

She jumped up, looking as if he'd slapped her. 'I've told you. You are nothing to do with Hal.' She was shouting now. 'Get that into your thick bleddy head, will you?'

'All right. All right. Come and sit back down.' He spoke calmly and she returned to her seat. 'So why have you come to tell me this?' he asked gently.

She wiped her eyes and blew her nose. 'Because Grant's your brother and you need to shut him up before Mickey hears anything.'

'OK,' he said slowly. 'Who was he talking to in the pub?'

'Peter the landlord. A few of the boat crews and some of the lads who work downstairs. I heard it from Johnny. He said no one believed a word of it and it was all a load of shit, but he thought I should know.'

'Oh shit,' said Jesse.

'Yeah,' replied a crumpled Loveday.

*

On the upstairs landing of the Hind, Jesse peered at the nameplates on each of the four letting rooms. He walked past Francis Drake, The Armada Room and The Good Queen Bess Suite. When he got to The Pelican he stopped, took a deep breath and knocked with what he hoped was authority.

He heard a shuffling and the creak of a bedspring. He knocked again.

'Piss off,' came Grant's voice.

'It's me. Jesse. Let me in.'

'If it's about me not coming in to work today, I've got the flu. See you tomorrow.'

'It's not that. Let me in.'

Jesse heard a few muttered curses then the sound of approaching feet. The bolt was drawn back and the door opened. Grant looked terrible and smelt as ripe as a whisky distillery.

'I told you. I've got the flu. If I were you I wouldn't come near me.'

Jesse ignored this and pushed his way into the room.

'Good God, Grant. Look at the state of your room. Does no one come in and clean for you?'

Grant looked sheepish. 'I don't like to put the girls to any bother.'

Jesse, with years of the training that Greer had instilled in him, crossed the room and opened the sagging curtains. He pushed at the sash window to let the cool October night air in. It wouldn't budge. Giving up, he picked his way across the floor and its patchwork of beer cans and improvised ashtrays. 'You and I need a little talk.'

'I don't feel very well.'

'Beer and fags tend to make people feel like shit,' glowered Jesse. 'Get downstairs in five minutes.'

Jesse must have looked more threatening than he felt because Grant did appear downstairs without keeping him waiting more than a couple of minutes.

'I'll have a pint, please,' Grant said, walking towards the bar.

'Oh, no.' Jesse pulled his brother towards the door. 'You and I are having a little chat where flapping ears can't hear us.'

*

There was a keen wind whistling over the water as Jesse dragged a reluctant Grant past the public toilets and towards a covered shelter with benches for weary tourists. 'Sit down,' Jesse ordered Grant.

Grant sat and whimpered, 'I ain't done nothing wrong.'

'You shouted your mouth off in the bar last night about Hal Chandler not being Mickey's son.'

Grant looked sly and licked his lips. 'Well, maybe I did and maybe I didn't, and maybe he is and maybe he isn't.'

'You are going to go into the Hind tonight and you'll put the record straight,' said Jesse with impressive menace. 'You will tell them that you are a hopeless piss-head and that you talk all sorts of shit when you've had a drink. What you said was not only untrue, it was hurtful to people who have been good friends to you.'

Grant pulled a wry smile. 'Well, I would say that if it were a lie.'

Jesse looked at his brother coldly. 'It was a lie.'

'I don't think so. The night before you got married to the oh-so-wealthy Greer, I saw you with Loveday. Lying on your old parka on the floor of Dad's old office up at the sheds.'

Jesse pushed his face close to Grant's unshaven, alcohol-ravaged face. 'No you didn't.'

Grant pushed his face into Jesse's and laughed. 'Oh, yes I did. You were giving her a hell of a going-over.'

Jesse could feel something building inside him. Hatred, resentment, anger.

'How dare you? All I've ever done is the right thing, while you . . . you're just a dirty little disappointment who has thrown his life away and broken Mum and Dad's hearts in the process.'

Grant sneered. 'You think you're so much better than me, Daddy's Number One son, but one day we'll be the same. You won't be able to keep me from my rightful inheritance. We'll see who's the "Number One" then.'

Now it was Jesse's turn to laugh. 'You'll never get a penny, Grant. Dad's cut you out and I'll get the business – all of it. We made sure.'

The sneer faded from Grant's face. 'You fucker. I was right about you. Dad would never do this, but you would. You shafted Loveday, you shafted your best friend and now you're going to shaft me.' He pushed his face close to Jesse's and Jesse could smell the sour stench of alcohol, cigarettes and decay on his breath. 'You might fool other people – all respectable with your la-di-dah wife and house – but I know it's just a front. Underneath you're a lying little shit bag – just like me.'

Neither Grant – nor Jesse himself, imprisoned in a red mist – expected the punch that smashed into Grant's jaw, sending teeth and a fine mist of blood in an arc to his left. Jesse, once he'd let loose the first fist, couldn't stop himself. He pummelled his brother until Grant's body slid to the floor, and then didn't stop, kicking him until exhaustion halted him and he stood, dazed and panting, over Grant's prone body.

It was Mickey, on his way for a quick pint, who found them.

'What's happened, Jesse?' he shouted urgently. 'What's happened to Grant?'

Jesse turned his eyes to Mickey and looked at him as if he'd never seen him before.

'Jesse,' said Mickey, reaching out to touch his arm. 'It's me, Mick.'

'Mickey?' Jesse breathed. 'Grant's hurt.'

'Just stay there, Jesse. Don't do anything.' Mickey held his hands out in a pacifying gesture. He pulled his mobile from his pocket. He pressed the 9 button three times. When he'd finished, he put the phone back in his pocket and walked over to Grant, who was lying awkwardly on the cold concrete floor. His breathing didn't sound good. There was a clear greyish-looking liquid coming from his left ear. Mickey took his coat off and rolled it up. He put it under Grant's head.

'Jesse. I want you to take your coat off too and put it over Grant like a blanket. It's got Grant's blood on it anyway.'

Jesse, meek as a child, did as he was told.

'And now, Jesse, you're going to go to the public toilets and wash your face and hands.' Jesse looked at his hands and saw they were stained with blood. 'OK?'

Jesse nodded.

'Good. Be quick because the police and ambulance will be here very soon.'

An efficient constable assessed the situation and, taking his notebook from his top pocket, started to question Jesse and Mickey. 'Do either of you know the injured man?'

'Yes,' said Jesse. 'He's my brother.'

'And can you tell me what happened to him, sir?'

'I . . .' The horror and realisation of what he'd done stole across him. His breathing became shallow and ragged, 'He . . . I . . . we . . .'

Mickey took charge. 'This is Jesse Behenna. My name is Mickey Chandler and he,' he motioned towards Grant who was being loaded onto a stretcher and moaning, 'is Grant Behenna. Jesse's brother.'

Jesse looked helplessly into Mickey's eyes and said, 'It was me, I . . .'

Mickey once more took over. 'That's right, Jesse. You found him.' He turned to the policeman. 'Jesse must have heard something in the shelter. I was walking past, just on my way to the pub and saw him. I saw a man come running out of the shelter as Jesse got there. Must've been the bloke who did it. I called after him but he didn't stop, then I heard Jesse saying Grant's name and I came to see what I could do. I saw Jesse kneeling over Grant and putting his coat over him.'

Jesse grasped Mickey's arm and began to cry with fear and gratitude.

'He's barely recognisable, but we know Grant Behenna. In fact, his name has come up recently in an investigation we're conducting into a drug gang.' The policeman addressed Jesse. 'Is this what happened, sir?' asked the constable.

Jesse nodded; out of the corner of his eye he watched as Grant's battered body was loaded into the ambulance.

'Can I go with Grant to the hospital?' he asked.

'I don't think you're in a fit state, sir. In fact, I recommend you go home and rest. You're in shock. You need a nice cup of tea. We'll drive you home.'

'No,' said Mickey, 'I'll take him home.'

The policeman took down Jesse's address and phone number and also that of Mickey. 'I'll be round to see Mr Behenna tomorrow to complete the paperwork. Get some sleep. Grant Behenna has been in trouble quite a few times and mixes with an unsavoury lot. I'll go down to the hospital now and see if your brother can tell me anything about his assailant, if, I mean – ' he gave an embarrassed cough – '*when* he wakes up.'

29

October 2009

The soft blue of the lights around Grant's intensive care bed threw ghoulish shadows onto his parents' faces. They had come to the hospital as soon as they had heard, which was fourteen hours ago.

Jesse stood back from the scene. He stayed out of the glow around the bed and waited at the dark outer reaches of the room. Through the window he could see that the sun was rising.

The door opened with a slight suction of air and a young female doctor, slender with long dark hair, entered.

'Hello, Mr and Mrs Behenna.' She offered her hand. 'My name is Dr Shawna Dhaliwal. I'm part of the care team for your son.'

'How is he, Doctor?' asked Jan.

'As you know, he has broken ribs, a punctured lung, a broken jaw and a broken nose. But it's the scan we did on his brain that is worrying us.'

Jan closed her eyes and reached out for Edward's hand.

'What do you mean?' asked Edward, his voice cracking.

'We need to get inside and take a look. He hasn't fractured the skull but we believe he may have a substantial bleed and we need to get that fixed as soon as possible. It's imperative we release the pressure on his brain.'

Jan wiped her eyes with the tissue clutched in her shaking hands. 'An operation?'

'Yes,' said Dr Dhaliwal. 'And we need to do it sooner rather than later. Your son is very poorly. Theatre are getting prepared now.'

*

Six hours they waited. Jan trying to keep cheerful. Getting fresh cups of thin milky tea. Edward fretting about the car park ticket. Jesse unable to look either of them in the eye.

Eventually the ward sister came to see them. 'Grant is in recovery. The operation went as well as we could have hoped.'

Jan's hands grasped hers. 'Oh, thank God. He's OK?'

'Dr Dhaliwal is coming to talk to you as soon as she's changed.' The sister wore an unreadable expression. 'Although the operation has gone well, I can't tell you more than that. Would you like some tea?'

At last, Dr Dhaliwal came. 'We found the bleed and we've stopped it, which has released some pressure on Grant's brain. However, his brain is bruised and rather swollen. It has some lacerations which may have been caused when he fell during the attack, or maybe . . . when the attacker had already got him on the floor and had kicked him.'

Edward couldn't contain himself. 'The police had better find this coward before I do.'

Jesse felt sick. 'Dad, the police will do all they can.'

'They'm better 'ad do, or by God I swear I'll kill 'em myself.'

'Edward,' said Jan. 'Let's hear everything the doctor

has to tell us first.' She turned to Dr Dhaliwal. 'What happens next? When can he come home?'

Dr Dhaliwal frowned in a practised, professional and concerned way. 'I'm afraid I can't tell you that. It's a waiting game. We will monitor his progress. It may be a few days or,' she swallowed, 'or maybe weeks, maybe months, before he wakes up.'

Jesse looked at her sharply. 'Will he ever wake up?'

'It's possible that he won't.'

The sound of Jan's anguished wail filled the room.

*

'Live by the sword, die by the sword,' said Greer, handing Jesse a whisky. She settled herself into the depths of their elephant-grey velvet sofa.

Jesse rubbed his forehead. 'Don't say that.'

'I'm just saying he chose to live recklessly and that's what happens.'

'He might never recover.'

'Yes, and that's awful, of course, but it's not your responsibility.'

There was a knock at the front door. 'I'll get it,' said Greer, unfolding her slim legs from underneath her.

Moments later she arrived back in the room with the policeman Jesse remembered from the night before.

The constable stepped awkwardly into the room, his hat under one arm, his radio burbling indecipherable messages. Jesse stood up. 'Hello, I'm sorry, I don't think I got your name last night.'

The policeman held out his hand. 'Constable Steve Durrell. Steve.'

'Sit down, sit down. Would you like a drink?' asked Jesse.

'A soft drink, please.'

Greer disappeared to the kitchen. Steve watched her go.

'I'm afraid I have bad news.'

Jesse felt his stomach twist. 'What?'

'Your brother, Grant . . . He died an hour ago.'

Jesse could hear the rushing of his own blood in his ears. 'He can't have. I've been at the hospital all day. He had his operation. I saw him, on his bed, being wheeled back into his room.'

'I'm sorry.'

Greer came back in with a beautiful tray laid stylishly with a linen napkin, a small jug of orange juice, a glass and a ceramic dish containing olives. 'Here we are,' she said.

*

Grant's body was released after a post mortem. The police investigation had been unable to turn up any leads for the actual attack, but all their enquiries led them to the unsavoury characters and unfortunates with whom he had spent those lost years after he had left prison. Jan was tortured anew as details came out of his years of drug dealing and a drug habit that he had picked up in prison. It seemed that in the last months he had taken up dealing again and his life was starting to spiral out of control. The paraphernalia of a drug habit had been found in his rooms and the general consensus seemed to be that things were heading in only one direction for Grant.

Despite all this, Jesse made sure that the funeral befitted a Behenna. Grant hadn't many friends in Trevay, but the town turned out to honour Edward and Jan. Reverend Rowena gave a suitable tribute to Grant. She didn't go into his army career or his violent and often drunken personality. But she carefully described him as a son of Trevay. One who had had the joy of growing up in a tight community and loving family. 'The choices he made in this life were never the easy ones, but we trust in our heavenly father to take Grant's soul and heal it. We pray too that his murderer will one day be revealed and that the grace of God be with his parents, Edward and Jan, and his brother, Jesse. Let us pray.'

Jesse looked at the hunched figure of his mother, clinging on to her husband like a child as tortured sobs racked her body.

Jesse sat bolt upright in his pew and stared at the stained-glass window of Jesus calling the fishermen to be his disciples. He was glad that no one could hear the conversation in his head. 'Forgive me but I'm glad he's dead,' he said to the sunlit face of Christ. 'I'm glad. He hurt us all. And he's not going to hurt us again. I didn't mean him to die. But he did. Finally he did the right thing.'

The vicar ended her prayer and the congregation intoned 'Amen'.

Greer got up from the embroidered hassock she'd been kneeling on and squeezed Jesse's knee. 'All right?' she whispered.

He nodded.

The organist started to play 'The day Thou gavest, Lord, is ended'. Everyone stood and began to sing. Jesse, Mickey, Hal and Freddie went to the coffin with two of the funeral directors and lifted it onto their shoulders.

Outside the sun shone and a flock of seagulls cast their shadows as they flew over the churchyard cackling into the wind.

The freshly dug grave accepted Grant into its red earth, allowing him to rest on the slate beneath.

Jesse stepped back and bowed his head with a respect he did not feel. Greer slipped her arm through his elbow. 'It's over,' she said to him quietly.

He looked at her sharply. 'What did you say?'

'I said: It's over.'

He looked at her intently to see what, if anything, she knew. He examined the expression in her eyes, the turn of her mouth, the colour of her cheeks, but there was nothing.

'Yes.' He dropped a kiss on her dry lips. 'You're right. It's over.'

30

New Year's Eve 2012

Jesse was woken by the weight of four paws kneading the duvet around his chin.

'Bugger off, Tom.' He pushed the fat rescue cat – which Greer had brought home without asking him – off the bed. Tom sat on the floor twitching his tail and looking astonished, before jumping up again, and this time wiping his wet whiskers across Jesse's lips.

'I said bugger off.' Jesse took his arm from under the covers and caught Tom by the scruff of his neck, throwing him back onto the floor.

The bedroom door opened and Greer came in with a chink of mugs on the morning tea tray.

'Is Tom up here?'

'Yes,' Jesse grunted with his eyes closed and his face pressed into the pillow.

'Did he wake you up?'

'Yes.'

Geer put the tray down and Jesse heard tea being poured. 'Did you wake Daddy up? You naughty puss,' she said to Tom, who was mewing loudly and pushing himself around Greer's legs. 'And did he throw you off the bed?'

'He jumped off of his own accord,' mumbled Jesse.

'I think Daddy's lying,' said Greer, walking round to Jesse's side of the bed and putting his mug of tea on the coaster on the mahogany bedside table. She bent down and kissed his bristly cheek. 'Happy Anniversary, darling.'

He opened his eyes and squinted at her. 'Happy Anniversary.' He sat and yawned, rubbing a hand across his face. 'Twenty years. That's some bleddy time, in't it?' Jesse found it hard to believe that it was twenty years ago that he had walked down the aisle with Greer. Twenty years since he and Loveday . . .

'Yes, it is,' said Greer, getting into her side of the bed and pulling the covers up. She took a sip of tea thoughtfully and said, 'I think we're just about all ready for the party.'

Jesse groaned. 'I 'ate bleddy parties.' He already felt that his house was barely his own. It looked like something from a magazine rather than a real home where a man could be himself. He'd rather be down at the boathouse on the beach at Tide Cove. It was his domain. It housed lobster pots, fishing gear, all the small things that Freddie had made at school, which Greer did not want cluttering her pristine house, but which made Jesse's heart swell with pride and love for his son.

Greer couldn't hide her irritation. 'Well, you only have to come and enjoy it. Everything else has been done for you.'

Tom jumped back onto the bed and nudged Greer's hand. 'Tom, you nearly spilt my tea. Be careful.' She reached out a hand and stroked Tom's ears. He began purring loudly.

'That bleddy animal oughtn't be allowed on the bed. 'Tis unhygienic,' moaned Jesse.

'He's spotless. Besides, he's been out all night in the

cold and needs to warm up.' Tom dribbled with ecstasy and, opening one yellow eye, gave Jesse a look of pure disdain. 'He just wants a little affection.' Greer held Tom to her and nuzzled him against her cheek. 'Don't you, Mr Tom?'

'Mr Jesse could do with a little affection too,' Jesse said, turning to Greer and giving her what he assumed was an alluring look. He put his hand on her thigh and slowly ran it upwards.

Greer was not in the mood. 'Mind Tom. You'll squash him.'

'I don't care.' Jesse began his well-worn foreplay routine and started to nibble Greer's ear. Tom, totally affronted, jumped off the bed and left the room, tail high.

'I've got a mug of hot tea in my hands,' said Greer pathetically, pulling away from her husband.

Jesse stopped the nibbling and took the tea from her. He put it on his side table and turned back to her. 'There. No tea. No Tom. Just you and me.' He restarted his nuzzling.

Greer attempted another diversion. 'The florist is coming at ten. I haven't got time for this.'

'Don't 'ee worry about that. I'll be coming before him.'

'Her. And don't be crude. It puts me off,' she scowled.

'Come on, Greer. It's been a while.' He was on top of her now, whether she liked it or not. 'And it is our anniversary.'

Greer went through the motions. Sex had never really been her thing. Her sex drive had always been at odds with Jesse's. But she'd been dutiful. Nowadays she'd do anything to avoid it. It wasn't that she didn't love Jesse. She did. Very much. But all this physical stuff was, frankly, a bit of a bore. A chore. She'd asked Loveday once when they'd had a couple of glasses of wine on one of their infrequent girls' nights out: 'Do you and Mickey still, you know, fancy each other?'

Loveday had answered with passion. 'Course! It's the glue that keeps a marriage together.'

'Oh. Yes. Absolutely.' Greer had felt a deep sense of inadequacy and a feeling that she really must try harder.

*

'That was lovely, wasn't it?' asked a satisfied Jesse, as he hoicked himself back onto his side of the bed.

'Uha,' Greer replied.

'What's the matter with you? Come, on, give me a cuddle.' He put an arm around her and she was obliged to settle into his shoulder. She waited until his breathing became shallow and even, and then made her escape.

Without disturbing his slumber, she tiptoed to her new pride and joy. The en-suite wet room. This was what turned her on. Her interior design work. Her natural sense of style and feel for colour. The wet room was an oasis of Zen beauty. From the fat alabaster Buddha sitting beneath the waterfall shower, to the underheated Delabole slate on the floor. There was a mirror covering one entire wall and she glanced at herself. The light from the adjacent window, with plantation blinds providing moody shadows, played across her skin. She took off her silk Elle Macpherson chemise and carefully hung it on the padded hanger on the hook on the back of the door.

She looked intently at her still slender body from all angles. The pain she felt at Louisa's death still had the power to take her breath away. It would creep up on her suddenly when she wasn't expecting it. But, looking at her slim outline, she thanked God that she hadn't ended up looking like Loveday. Loveday was fatter than ever and the size of her humungous breasts was just embarrassing. Greer had once asked her if she hadn't thought of a breast reduction. Loveday, hurt and embarrassed, had said something about leaving alone things that God had intended.

Now, Greer switched on the daylight lamp surrounding the circular and magnified mirror above the basin. She checked her wrinkles and the tautness of her neck. She was satisfied. Finally she reached for the tweezers and plucked a couple of stray hairs from her brows and, horror of horrors, a wiry one from her chin.

Job done, she stepped back and took a last pleasing look at herself. Yes, the self-denial over Christmas had paid off. Her Donna Karan evening dress, all four thousand pounds of it, would fit like a glove.

*

The house was busy all day long. The florist, the cleaners and the caterers were finally all done by four o'clock.

At five o'clock, Loveday drove over with the twins, Becca and Bea, who had made the celebration cake as their gift.

'Oh my goodness,' exclaimed Greer, who had to admit that the confection looked rather good. 'When did you girls get so clever?'

'It is good, isn't it!' said Loveday proudly. 'They'm loving their baking. I blame that Mary Berry and Mr Blue Eyes.'

'Paul Hollywood,' sighed the girls in unison. 'We done what you asked for, Auntie Greer. Top tier white chocolate. Bottom tier dark with brandy-soaked cherries.'

'And,' said Loveday, grinning from ear to ear, 'we found you something special to go on the top. Show her, girls.'

From out of one of the many shopping bags they'd brought with them, Becca pulled a smallish cardboard box. She thrust it towards Greer. 'Open it!'

Loveday and her girls stood in harnessed excitement as Greer removed the rubber band then opened the lid, pulling away at some scruffy pink tissue paper. Resting inside were two hideous china figures.

''Tis a bride and a groom,' squealed Bea.

'It's you and Uncle Jesse!' panted Becca. 'We got them in the charity shop over St Mawgan.'

'It's shabby chic. Just your thing!' breathed Bea.

'We washed them in a drop of Milton, so they'm clean,' Loveday told Greer, thrilled with herself and her girls.

Greer didn't know what to say. 'It's . . . the last thing I expected,' she managed to blurt out, and kissed the girls, wondering how she could possibly avoid spoiling the beautiful cake by putting this worst bit of kitsch on the top.

'Right,' said Loveday, gathering up the various bits of baggage that she'd sprawled all over Greer's immaculate kitchen table. 'We'm off home to get ready. Kick-off is at eight o'clock, right?'

'Right,' confirmed Greer. 'Drinks at eight, dinner at nine.'

*

Greer was dressed and looking perfect by seven thirty. She went downstairs to admire her beautiful home. Tide House always scrubbed up well. The candles, the Christmas tree, the flowers. It all looked ravishing. In the library and the drawing room the fires were lit, giving out a subtle and pervasive scent of pine. In the dining room the table, set for twenty friends and immediate family, shimmered with crystal and silver.

One of the four waiting staff stepped into the dining room as Greer was straightening an errant napkin. 'Good evening, Mrs Behenna. You look very nice this evening. Can I get you a drink?'

Greer gave the young man a quick once-over, satisfied to see he was wearing the black linen shirt and trousers with long white apron that she had specified for all the waiting staff. 'Thank you. You look very smart too . . . and yes, please, I'd like a cranberry juice.'

'Of course, Mrs Behenna. Would you like a vodka in that?' He gave her a cheeky glint.

'No, thank you.' She smiled. What a charming young man. 'Too early for me.'

'Not too early for me, though.' Jesse stood in the doorway dressed in black tie. 'Get me a large Scotch, would you, before the hordes arrive?'

'Certainly, Mr Behenna,' said the young man, gliding out of the room.

'He'm bloody gay, ain't 'im?' remarked Jesse.

'You sound just like your father.' Greer tutted. 'Please keep your sexist, racist opinions to yourself.'

Jesse walked into the hall and stood before the large gilt mirror that greeted all guests. He was fiddling with his bow tie. 'Have I tied this thing right? Why you won't let me have one on elastic, I don't know. And this shirt collar is choking me, it's so tight.'

Greer went to him and smoothed his tie and eased his collar. She looked at both their reflections. 'We look OK after twenty years, don't we?'

Freddie came down the stairs in an open-necked white

shirt and tight blue jeans. 'I'd say you look pretty good for a pair of wrinklies.' He kissed Greer and hugged his father.

'How come he got away with jeans and I'm dressed up like next year's turkey?'

'Because he's young and he can get away with anything,' replied Greer, gazing fondly at her son. 'Freddie, would you get my camera for me? It's in the drawing room on the ottoman. I think we need a family photo.'

*

Dinner was delicious. Seared scallops in lemon chilli butter, rib of beef with all the trimmings and a light syllabub with fruit salad and a cheese board to follow.

Greer excused herself from her father-in-law on her right and Mickey on her left and went to the kitchen to congratulate the staff, who were busy stacking the dishwasher.

'Well done, everyone. Superb work.'

'When do you want the cake served?' asked the young chef, Danny.

'Oh, I think mulled wine and cake in the conservatory after the fireworks, don't you?'

'Right-oh, Mrs B.'

'Thank God it's not raining!'

*

At five minutes to midnight, everyone had their coats found for them and they were ushered out, through the conservatory, into the front garden overlooking Tide Cove.

Freddie and Hal found Radio Four on the house sound system and wound up the volume so that everyone in the garden could hear the countdown to Big Ben.

'. . . Three, two, one . . . BONG! Happy New Year!'

Mickey gave his wife a kiss and a cuddle. She still looked beautiful to him and Loveday hugged him back tightly.

'They've put on a good show tonight, don't you think?' He nodded towards Greer and Jesse.

'They always do, don't they? Greer knows how to throw a good party,' Loveday agreed.

'Even Jesse looks like he's enjoying himself.'

Loveday knitted her brow thoughtfully. 'Mmmm.' She hadn't said anything, but she thought Jesse had been drinking a bit more than usual of late. He often worked long hours, but more often than not these days he seemed to have a bottle of whisky to keep him company as he pored over the figures.

'It'll be our anniversary soon,' Mickey said. 'Shall we throw a party?'

Loveday hugged him tighter. 'Let's just do something with the kids, shall we?'

'Whatever you want, darling.'

As the kissing and the singing of 'Auld Lang Syne' gathered strength, a fusillade of rockets went up from the Cove. They were followed by Roman candles, flying lanterns, barrages and brilliant showers of diamond sparks.

*

Greer, tottering slightly after two glasses of very good Pinotage on very high L.K. Bennett heels, slipped her arm through Jesse's. He smelled of whisky and fresh air and she surprised herself by finding him very attractive. More attractive than she had this morning, anyway.

'Do you want to know what your anniversary present is?' she asked him, resting her cheek on his lapel.

'Go on then,' he said. 'I thought you'd forgotten.'

'Well, you've forgotten mine,' she said in a mock huff.

'Ah well. That's where you're wrong. You had so much on today that I thought I'd surprise you tomorrow.'

'Really?' She looked up at him with the excitement of a little girl. 'What have you got me?' she wheedled.

'Not telling.'

'Give me a clue?'

'No. But I'm getting it in the morning.' He kissed the top of her head. 'So, what you got for me?'

'We are going to get on the Whatsit Express and go to . . . Venice!'

'Bloody 'ell, maid. That's some bleddy 'oliday.'

'Yes it is. Romance. Art. Museums. Architecture.'

'Have they got any booze?'

'Plenty.'

'Well, that's all right then.'

'When are we going?'

'The weekend after next.'

Jesse frowned. 'You'll 'ave to put it off until after the end of the financial year. We've got too much on, and I'll have to pull all the stops out if we're to make the numbers.'

'Oh, rubbish,' Greer said. 'You can manage a few days off, surely?'

'I can't. You'll just have to give them a call and re-arrange the dates.'

The drink had made Greer argumentative. 'I will not.

I'm always making sacrifices for you and that company. For once, can't you put me first?'

Jesse felt a dangerous darkness descend. 'Put you first? I've always put you first, Greer. You, your family, the bloody business – and I've never complained.'

'You have no right to complain.' Greer was fired up now. 'My daddy gave you everything you've ever had. If it wasn't for him, you'd be just like any other fisherman down at the harbour: small time. Clovelly Fisheries have given you everything.'

As soon as the words left her mouth, Greer regretted saying them. The look on Jesse's face was like nothing she had seen before.

He regarded her coldly. 'Small time, was I, Greer? Not so small that you didn't follow me around like a dog, grateful for any scraps that I threw in your direction.'

Greer drew a gasp at the words and put her hand to her mouth, but Jesse couldn't stop himself. 'Where would you be if it weren't for me, Greer? Who would have married a stuck-up self-important frigid cow like you – you weren't my first choice, you know that, don't you?'

Greer rallied. 'Oh, that's right, Jesse Behenna, babe magnet. You'd screw any old scrubber down at the sheds. You're lucky to have someone like me. You couldn't even boil an egg without a mother or a wife to do it for you!'

Jesse was just about to let rip in response when Mickey and Loveday came up to say goodbye and thank them for a nice evening. Both Greer and Jesse clammed up immediately and Loveday and Mickey couldn't help but sense the tense atmosphere.

'We're just off now, but wanted to say thanks for a lovely evening.' Loveday gave her friend a huge hug and Greer responded with a tight smile.

'Yeah, thanks, mate – here's to the next twenty years!' laughed Mickey, and drunkenly clapped Jesse on the back.

Jesse shook Mickey's hand as Greer went off to find another drink.

'Bye, Jesse,' said Loveday, and gave him a peck on the cheek.

'Twenty years,' said Jesse, and held onto her for just a moment too long before they departed.

31

A week later

'Oh, Greer, it's lovely.'
Loveday was sitting in the passenger seat of the new 4x4 that Jesse had given Greer as her anniversary present. 'I could've done with one of these when the kids were small.'

Greer was reversing down the steep hill where Loveday and Mickey lived. 'Have I got enough room your side?'

Loveday checked the wing mirror. 'You're fine.'

Greer got to the bottom of the hill without a scrape and put the car into drive. 'Here we go.'

The big car was cumbersome and Greer didn't really like it, but Jesse had meant well when he bought it for her.

The morning after the row, nothing had been said. Jesse was up early and Greer heard him call from the bathroom, 'Where are the paracetamol?'

Smiling to herself she called back, 'On the third shelf of the cabinet.' She paused, then added, 'Would you bring me some, please?'

Greer wasn't much of a drinker, she didn't like losing control, and she and Jesse's argument had left her feeling very churned up and emotionally exhausted, but all of that seemed to be forgotten when Jesse presented her with the 4x4. She'd thanked him and spoken to the travel company, and now she and Jesse would be going to Venice in April. They'd never had such a bad row before, and Greer thought the break would do them both good; they'd had a lot on their plates and tensions were bound to be high.

She had nodded and smiled appreciatively as he had shown off the walnut dashboard and in-car entertainment system. 'Even has a reversing camera, so you can't have any excuses for kerbing the wheels.' She laughed dutifully and spared a thought for Loveday; Mickey would probably take Loveday and the kids to Wetherspoon's for their anniversary. Mind you, Loveday would probably love it, Greer smiled to herself.

Jesse was still talking. 'I thought it would be useful when you're carting all that stuff about to your houses.'

'Carting my stuff?'

'All those fancy cushions and books of wallpaper that your rich people like to look at. And your scrapbooks.'

'Mood albums,' she corrected.

'Whatever. Anyhow, I thought a nice big car would be useful . . . and when you're not using it I can borrow it for fishing or—'

'So you bought it for yourself?' The old resentment started to flourish.

'You didn't buy a trip to Venice solely for me, did you?'

He had her there, and so she kissed him and neutralised the negative turn the conversation had taken and thanked him for such a perfect present.

Today, she and Loveday were making use of the car for a trip to the sales in Bristol.

'I feel so high up,' Loveday said, settling into her leather seat. 'We'll be in Bristol in no time.'

'I'm glad of your company.'

'I like a bargain. The girls have given me a list of stuff they want me to get. As if they didn't have enough already at Christmas!'

'I'm hoping to pick up a lovely little Turkish Kelim for a client and also get some curtain fabric for the Liskeard people.'

'Ain't that job finished yet?'

'I got most of it done in time for Christmas, but now they've decided they want the tall window on the stairs to have curtains. They don't need them. The light it throws onto the panelled walls is a clever piece of design by the architect back in the 1680s, but they think the sun is too bright and, if they want to have curtains, they shall have curtains. At least I talked them out of Venetian blinds.'

'You'm clever, Greer.'

'Well, I can't do what you do.'

'It's only tallying the books,' said Loveday self-deprecatingly.

'Oh, yes, that's easy enough, what I mean is, I couldn't sit in that soulless building that Jesse loves so much, with all those dull people, doing the same thing day in day out.'

Loveday frowned. 'They'm not dull people. They're my friends. And if it wasn't for them you wouldn't have a car like this.'

'I didn't mean it like that,' Greer said. 'I think it's wonderful that some people enjoy mundanity. Whereas I have to be creative.' She glanced at her friend and smiled. 'How are your upholstery classes going?'

Loveday had turned her face to look out of the window so that Greer couldn't see her annoyance. 'OK.'

Greer sensed that she had gone too far. 'Good.'

She drove on for a few minutes, neither speaking. Then, to ease the tension she said, 'Shall I put the radio on?'

*

'What a day.' Greer was in her kitchen and shrugging out of her coat. 'Loveday insisted we went into Ikea. God, what a dreadful place. Nothing in there will stand the test of time. Put the kettle on, would you?'

Jesse did as he was asked. 'How did the car go?'

'Lovely. The boot is full. I bought much too much but some of the fabric was at such a good price, and classic patterns, that I thought it was an investment, really.'

'Where would you like your tea?'

'Shall we sit in the library?'

'You can, I've got to go back to the office. Got some stuff to finish off for the accountants.'

'Will you be home for dinner?'

'Probably not.'

*

The building was warm and silent. He made himself a mug of coffee in the tiny office kitchen and went to his office. Lauren, as always, had prepared his desk for the next day. His bin was empty and his laptop was charging.

He logged on and opened the files he wanted. He read the first page and then the next. He found it brutally boring. He tried again. But again he could not concentrate.

He gave up and spun his chair so that he could look at the view through the glass. Trevay lay peacefully beneath him. His mind wandered as he looked at the familiar streets and buildings. There was his old school, with its memories of Greer, Mickey and Loveday. The church where he'd got married and where Louisa lay next to his grandfather.

The sheds where he and Loveday had made love.

The harbour where his boats were bobbing, tied up against the wall.

The shelter where Grant had died.

No, he mustn't think about Grant. He looked again over the rooftops of Trevay. Now he could see Grant smoking at the school gate.

Grant hiding in the yard outside the sheds watching him and Loveday.

Grant lying in the churchyard.

Grant sitting in this office.

Jesse hated these thoughts. He'd had them on and off since Grant had died. If he was strong enough, he could make them go away. And they would go away, but tonight they were real and sharp. *Why didn't bloody Grant leave him in peace?*

Jesse went to the office kitchen and filled the kettle to make another cup of coffee.

He heard what sounded like the lift, whirring its way up to his floor.

Was that the lift he heard?

He stepped out of the kitchen and listened.

Yes. The lift, definitely.

Who would come into the office at this time?

Had he locked the front door?

He couldn't remember.

He stepped back into the kitchen, turned the light off and stood very still.

The lift stopped.

The doors opened.

He heard the rustle of clothing as someone got out and started walking towards his office.

He could hear his breathing.

He could hear their breathing.

When he judged that they were almost adjacent to the kitchen doorway, he leapt out, shouting a huge roar.

The woman screamed, dropped her bag and ran back to the lift.

'Loveday,' said Jesse, running after her. 'Loveday. 'Tis only me.'

She stopped running and he could see the fear on her face. 'Jesse.' She was breathless. 'What the bleddy 'ell you do that for?'

'I thought you was a burglar.'

'Well, I'm not.' She started to giggle. 'You'm bleddy frightening when you shout like that.'

'I meant to be. Anyhow, serves you right for sneaking up on me.'

'I was not sneaking. I came in to make sure I had all the documents you'll need for the accountant tomorrow and found the front door unlocked. I thought it would be you. I saw your office lights on, so I came up to say hello. Got the bleddy fright of my life instead!'

'Sorry. Want a coffee?'

'I need a bleddy brandy.'

'I've got some whisky?'

'No, you're all right. Give us a coffee, I'll get the papers you need and I'll be off home.'

*

Loveday took her coffee down to her ground-floor office and soon became absorbed in answering emails and checking her diary for the week ahead. The phone on her desk rang, startling her. She looked at her watch and saw that an hour and a half had gone by. It must be Mickey.

'Hi, Mick. Sorry I've been so long. I'm on my way now. Shall I pick up some fish and chips or have you and the kids eaten?'

Jesse's voice replied, 'No, I haven't eaten yet, but I'd love fish and chips with you.'

Loveday laughed. 'Oh, sorry, Jesse. I'm just emailing the stuff up to you now.

'What would I do without you? Did you put the spreadsheets in?'

'Of course.'

'Thank you. The accountants always love a spreadsheet.'

Loveday had the receiver between her shoulder and her chin as she tried to put one arm into the sleeve of her coat. 'Well, I'll be off, if there's nothing else you need.'

'No, that's fine,' said Jesse. 'See you tomorrow.'

'Yeah, see you tomorrow.'

'Oh . . . er, Loveday?'

'Yeah?'

'Fancy that glass of whisky before we shut up shop for the night?'

'Erm . . .' Loveday looked at her watch again. 'As long as I'm home in the next hour.'

'Just ten minutes. Come up to my office.'

*

'What a view you have from up here. Never seen it at night before. You must be almost as high as St Peter's steeple.'

'Not quite.' He handed her a tumbler of Scotch. Loveday noticed that inroads had definitely been made into the bottle, and she thought that Jesse looked a little flushed. 'Sorry, no ice. Cheers.' They clinked glasses.

'Cheers,' said Loveday.

Jesse continued. 'The planners were very strict with us. They made it clear they didn't want us to "impede the view". Which is why we made it pretty much entirely of glass.'

He sat down behind his desk and Loveday sat opposite him. Two old friends comfortable in each other's company.

'I like your Greer's new car.'

'I don't think she does.'

'Yes, she does. She was loving filling it with all her knick-knacks.'

'By knick-knacks do you mean the very latest on the front line of the style war that is raging across the land, in houses that are too big and too expensive, lived in by people who have more money than sense?'

Loveday giggled. It had been a long time since she had had her sushi lunch with Greer and the whisky was leaking warmly into her veins. 'That's very unkind of you.'

'But true.' Jesse motioned at the bottle of Scotch. 'Just a little one for the road?'

'Just a little one.' She watched as Jesse poured. 'But your house is beautiful, ain't it? Greer has done a wonderful job. It's so welcoming and comfortable. I'm not house-proud like that,' said Loveday, taking her shoes off and rubbing one foot against the other. 'With my three and Mickey it'd be like King Canute trying to keep the tide from flooding in.'

Jesse leant forward on the desk. 'How is Mickey?'

'He's great. Loving his job. Loving working with Hal and teaching him the ropes like his dad taught him. I tell you, we Chandlers have got a lot to thank you Behennas for.'

Jesse leant back again and relaxed into his chair. 'Our dads were all mates, weren't they. It's keeping up tradition. Mickey is my best mate. Hal is Freddie's best mate. And so it will go on, as long as Trevay has a fishing industry.'

Loveday nodded her agreement. 'And don't forget the Clovellys. Without Greer's side, neither of us would be sitting in this office drinking whisky.'

Jesse turned his chair to look at Trevay again. 'You're right. Mick and I would be working our arses off up at the sheds.' He sat thinking for a few moments. Loveday shut her eyes, giving in to the whisky, but not to her memory of her and Jesse in the sheds.

Jesse broke the silence. 'I miss those days. Just me and Mickey. You and Greer. No kids. No responsibilities.' She heard the faintest squeak as he spun his chair back to her. Her eyelids were heavy and she didn't have the energy to open them.

'I wish I'd have married you.' He said the words boldly into the still air between them.

She sat still, eyes still shut.

'Did you hear me?'

'Yes.'

'We'd have been happy.'

'Stop it.'

'I know we'd have been happy. That night. In the sheds. When it was snowing. You made me so very happy.'

She opened her eyes and looked at her hand holding the whisky glass. 'Don't talk about it. I don't even think about it.'

'Don't you?' He leant forward again across the desk.

'No.'

'I don't believe you. I was your first and you and I were happy that night.'

'We were pissed. And I think you may be a bit pissed now.' Loveday stood up and put her glass down. 'I'm off home. To Mickey.'

Jesse stood up and walked round the desk, blocking her path. 'I've never stopped loving you, Loveday.'

'You love Greer.' She sidestepped him but he was too quick for her.

'Kiss me,' he begged.

She leant forward and kissed his cheek. 'Night night, Jesse. See you tomorrow.'

She collected up her coat and bag and walked out of the office without a backward glance.

32

Early spring 2014

Lifeboat training was always on a Wednesday night and, on this particular evening, the boat-house was crowded.

The star of the show was, as always, the boat herself. Sitting in the centre of the spotless boat-house, her paint-work gleaming, *The Spirit of Trevay* sat on the runners that sent her through the doors, down the slipway and into the waiting sea. All around her were railings to keep her fans close, but not close enough. Small boys, star-struck mums and men who could only dream of being one of the élite hung over these railings in wonder.

Jesse, in his capacity as coxswain, was speaking from the deck of the boat.

'And so, ladies and gentlemen, it is with great pleasure we welcome our three new crew members to *The Spirit of Trevay*. Would you put your hands together for Miss Katie Farrow! Come up here, Katie.' A pretty blonde girl in her twenties stepped up and faced the crowd, smiling.

'Give us a smile, Katie.' In the middle of the crowd, Katie's mum took a photo of her daughter.

'Muuum,' said Katie, blushing, before trying to melt back into the throng. Jesse stopped her.

'Oh, no you don't. You stay right here, young lady. I

want all three of my new crew to have a picture with the lot of us.' Katie obeyed.

Jesse spoke up again. 'And 'tis with enormous pride I welcome another youngster. His dad, Mickey, has been the *Spirit*'s mechanic for as long as I've been coxswain, and his dad before him the same, so put your hands together for the third generation of Chandlers to serve on the lifeboat: Hal Chandler.' Hal loped up to Jesse. With his height and gangly limbs he towered over everyone. From the back of the room, Loveday gave a whoop and a whistle through her teeth, whilst clinging onto Mickey's arm. Becca and Bea leapt up and down with excitement and chanted Hal's name, falling into giggles when Loveday shushed them.

'And finally,' said Jesse, 'and I don't know 'ow he got on the crew, but I'd like to welcome my own son, Freddie Behenna.'

Freddie bowed his head as he made his way to the front and accepted his father's handshake. Greer, in perfectly tailored navy-blue trousers and an RNLI sweatshirt, smiled tightly but clapped loudly. She had argued with both Jesse and Freddie about joining the crew. Greer desperately wanted Freddie to get good exam results so that he had other options rather than only a life on the boats to look forward to, but because Hal wanted that life, it seemed it was what Freddie wanted too. Greer wondered if perhaps she'd taken her eye off the ball a bit with Freddie. Maybe he'd been spending too much time at the Chandlers' house, as their ways seemed to be rubbing off on him more and more these days. She felt another flutter of fear in her stomach – working on the trawler fleet was dangerous enough. Why did he have to risk his life on the lifeboat too?

'You don't stop me from going out and risking my life,' said Jesse.

'You're different. You know what you're getting your-self into. Freddie is our only child. Why put him in danger?'

But Freddie wanted to do it – and what Freddie wanted, Freddie usually got.

Loveday pushed her way towards Greer. 'Well, that's it. Our precious boys are lifeboatmen.'

'They're only twenty,' said Greer, feeling her throat tighten. 'Boys still, really.'

'But ain't you proud of them?'

Greer pushed her hair behind one ear and tried to be pleased. 'Oh, of course, I'm always proud of them, but . . . they are so young.'

'They'll be fine. They've got Mick and Jesse and the other lads.' Loveday could see that Greer was very upset about the whole thing so she said, 'What you need, Mrs Behenna, is a gin and tonic.'

Greer managed a laugh. 'I probably do, but I'm on coffee duty tonight and then there's the raffle to draw.' As in all lifeboat stations, the opportunities to raise funds were never overlooked. This evening was special because it was an open evening. Lifeboat groupies and RNLI supporters were encouraged to come into the boat-house to look around, ask questions of the crew and, if they had the lucky raffle ticket, even get the chance of going out on the boat that evening.

'Well, I'll sell the tickets, you pour the coffee, and we'll get this show on the road,' said Loveday.

*

A man of maybe sixty was talking very earnestly to Jesse about the merits of the Tamar class of boat as opposed

724

to the Severn class. 'I see that *The Spirit of Trevay* is a Tamar class, but is it as manoeuvrable as the Severn? Although it's a metre longer, it may at first sight appear to be less nimble—' Jesse interrupted the techie flow. 'I'm so sorry, but my wife is wanting me.' He'd never been so grateful to see Greer waving at him.

He shouldered his way over to the other side of the room, to where Greer was anxiously waiting. 'Thanks, darling,' he said when he reached her. 'That bloke's a bleddy fanatic.'

'It's time to make the draw,' Greer told him. 'Loveday's been folding the tickets and putting them in the bucket for the last hour.'

'I hope he doesn't win the trip tonight,' said Jesse, rubbing a hand over his tired face. 'We'm got enough to do without him blethering.'

'Oh, him?' said Greer, spotting the man making his way towards another cup of free coffee. 'He's bought more tickets than anyone else.'

'Shit.'

Mickey reached them. 'Loveday's got the tickets ready for the draw. Who do you want to do it?'

'Get the new kids to do it,' said Jesse. 'Wherever they are.' He scanned the crowd and saw both Hal and Freddie leaning against the crew-room door chatting up Katie. All three of them were dressed in their yellow oilskins and loving it. As Jesse watched, a small boy approached Katie and asked her something. She laughed but took the pen and piece of paper he was holding and signed her name for him. The boy's mother, giggling and emboldened, then asked the lads if she could have a selfie with them.

'Becca, Bea,' called Jesse to the twins, who were just

passing, 'go and get them boys and Katie, would you? I
need them for the raffle.'

*

There was a healthy assortment of raffle prizes on the
table, including a box of chocolates, an RNLI T-shirt,
supper for two at Antonio's Italian pizzeria, a bottle of
whisky and the star prize of a trip on the boat.

The final ticket was drawn by Katie, who rummaged
extravagantly in the bucket before pulling out, 'Green
ticket number four-three-seven.'

A woman's voice yelled loud and clear, 'Here! Yes.'

There were many groans of disappointment from everyone else. Not least the man who'd been interrogating Jesse
about the boat's specifications and performance. He screwed
his tickets up and put them in his pocket, then moved to
position himself in a prime spot to watch the launch.

The crew were on board in their allotted places. The
boat-house doors were open, revealing the slipway and the
smoky sea below. Jesse was on the open bridge.

On Jesse's command, the pin holding the boat on the
slipway was pulled, and she moved swiftly down the rails,
nose-first into the water. Jesse pushed the throttle forward
and the twin engines drove the boat away from the boat-
house and the waving, cheering fans.

'Oooh,' said the woman who'd won the raffle, 'I feel like
Princess Diana on the water ride at Alton Towers!'

*

'Cheers, lads.' Jesse handed out the pints of Skinner's to
Mickey, Hal and Freddie. 'You done a good job tonight.

I don't want you missing any training nights, because we don't know when the real shout will come. I want you ready. It may be tonight. It may be tomorrow or next week. But I want to know that you lads are ready.' He took a satisfying mouthful of beer and wiped his lips. 'By the way, I don't want you thinking that just 'cos Katie's a girl she's a walkover. She's had as much experience at sea as you boys. She's sailed the Atlantic single-handed – you've got to be pretty bleddy tough to do that.'

'She's nice,' said Freddie.

'A bit posh,' said Hal.

'You're punching above your weight with her, boys, so don't even think about it,' laughed Mickey. 'She'd have you for breakfast.'

'How old is she?' asked Freddie.

'Too old for you, son,' said Jesse. 'Besides, you lads need to spread your wild oats.'

'Ha, says you who got married at twenty-one,' joked Freddie.

'Oh, your uncle Mickey and I had our moments, didn't we, Mick?' said Jesse.

'One or two,' nodded Mickey. 'But I knew Loveday was always the one for me.'

'Oh, Dad.' Hal looked embarrassed. 'I don't want to hear.'

Freddie looked at Jesse. 'And was Mum always the only one for you? From school?'

Jesse stuck his chin out and scratched the stubble there. 'You could say that.'

'Granddad Behenna always says he knew he had to get you two together to ensure the future of the company. He said it was like two royal families arranging the marriage of a princess and a prince.'

'Don't pay too much attention to what your granddad says.'

'And he says that Granddad Clovelly was the man who made it all happen.'

Jesse frowned and picked up a beer mat, flipping it over and catching it. Mickey steered the conversation round. 'I was his best man on the day he married your mum, Freddie. And let me tell you, he was as hungover as a highwayman. I could barely get him dressed.' A memory slid into his mind. 'It was Grant who got you drunk, wasn't it?'

Jesse shook his head. 'No. It was me. I went up to the sheds, because I didn't want to go home. I needed to think. 'Tis a big thing getting married. I found my dad's whisky in his desk up at the sheds and . . .' He stopped talking. In the silence the others waited for him to continue. Then he picked up his beer glass and downed the remains. '. . . And I drank it,' he finished abruptly.

'But I thought Grant said he was with you?' Mickey persisted.

Jesse thought for a moment and said, 'Maybe he was. I was so pissed I can't remember.' He stood up. 'Now then, who'd like another?'

*

By the time the pool table came free, the four men were more than merry.

'Right, you lads,' said Jesse, squinting to focus on getting the coins in the slot. 'You whippersnappers against we old Turks. Yes?'

'Fine by us,' said Freddie, passing a cue to Hal and chalking his own. 'What we playing for?'

'Hmm. Let me think,' said Jesse. 'What do you think, Mick?'

'Twenty quid?' ventured Mickey, balancing his cue between his legs as he attempted to tuck his shirt into his jeans.

'Twenty?' shrugged Freddie. 'That's nothing. It's got to be something really worth playing for.'

'Right. If that's what you want,' slurred Jesse, waggling his forefinger. 'How about this. You're both twenty-one later this year, yes?'

'Yes.'

'Well, 'ow about, if you win, I'll buy you a car each for your birthday. But if we win, I don't.'

'Bleddy hell,' blurted Hal.

'We'll hold you to that,' said Freddie. 'Shake on it?'

They shook.

Mickey took Jesse to one side while the boys set the balls up on the table. 'You are joking, aren't you?'

'No. But,' Jesse tapped the side of his nose, 'they'm useless at pool and you and I were bleddy good.'

'That's a long time ago.'

'It's like riding a bike. You and I will pull out the old tricks and they won't know what's hit 'em.'

It didn't take more than seventeen minutes. Hal lined up the black eight ball and hit it cleanly into the pocket.

Jesse chucked his cue onto the baize but he was impressed. 'How the hell did you learn to play like that? You're almost as good as I was at your age. Well. A bet's a bet. You won fair and square.' Jesse walked around the table and clapped Hal on the back.

'Nice one, Dad!' The boys were jubilant. 'Can we choose our own cars?'

'Never on your life.'

Mickey looked worried. 'Boys, don't hold him to it. This was a bit of fun.'

'No it weren't,' stated Jesse firmly. 'My word is my bond, and if I can't treat my son and godson, what kind of a man am I?'

'Just think it over in the morning,' said Mickey. 'I don't want you getting the boys' hopes up.'

Jesse rounded on Mickey. 'I am buying my boys cars for their birthday and that's that.'

'Take it easy, Jesse,' said Mickey, frowning. 'You're perfectly entitled to do what you like for your boy – but me and Loveday will decide what's right for our boy.'

Jesse regarded Mickey. 'My mind's made up, and nothing is going to stop me.'

33

Loveday pushed the door of the office shut with her foot as she dialled Greer's mobile phone number. She'd tried her at Tide House but the answerphone had kicked in and she hadn't dared to leave a message in case Jesse picked it up.

Mickey had come home late last night, annoyed at Jesse's high-handed idea to give Hal and Freddie a car each for their twenty-first birthdays.

'It was the way 'e said it. "I'm buying cars for my boys' birthdays and you're not stopping me". As if we can't afford a car for our own son.'

Loveday had been in bed reading when Mickey had come upstairs and broken this news. She didn't like the sound of it. My boys? What the hell did Jesse mean by that? She put her book aside and wriggled upright. 'Well, he is Hal's godfather and it's very generous but . . . was he pissed?'

'A bit. But that's not the point. It was the way he said it. As if I don't have any say. I'm Freddie's godfather but I can't afford to buy him an expensive present. And what will he get him for a wedding present? A bleddy house?'

As Mickey spoke, he became more and more agitated. He paced the bedroom carpet, sat on the edge of the bed, then sprang up again and paced the carpet once more.

Loveday watched him, her mind trying to second-guess what Jesse was doing.

'Did he say anything else?' she asked.

Mickey stopped pacing and sat down on the bed again. 'I know he's the one with all the money now; he's the boss and all that, whereas I'm just an employee, but I thought he knew us better than this. He knows I've always paid my way, but this time it's like he's trying to get one up on me.'

Loveday got out of bed and took her dressing gown from the hook on the door. 'Want a cup of tea?'

Mickey nodded and took her hand as she opened the door to the landing. 'Thanks, darlin'. Am I overreacting?'

'Let's talk about it.'

Dowstairs, Hal was lolling on the sofa watching a police drama on the television, his long legs spilling over one arm. 'Hey, Mum. Thought you'd be asleep. We had a great night. Fred and I absolutely slaughtered Dad and Uncle Jesse at pool. Did Dad tell you what Uncle Jesse bet us if we beat him?'

'Ah. It was a bet.' Loveday relaxed. A beer-fuelled bet tonight wouldn't be worth the breath it was made with once Jesse sobered up tomorrow and, besides, Mickey and Hal had downed a fair few too by the looks of it. 'I wouldn't get too excited.' She patted Hal's size 12 feet as she went past.

'No, he meant it,' said Hal, grinning with excitement.

'Well, let's just wait and see. I'm not sure your dad and I would be comfortable about him giving you a car, anyway.'

Mickey chipped in, 'Your mum's right.'

Hal reached for the remote control and switched the television off. He stood up and stretched. 'Well, you two can think what you like, but Uncle Jesse has always been decent to me. Treated me the same way he treats Freddie, so why shouldn't I get a car out of him?'

'That's enough,' said Mickey. He took a step towards Hal and jabbed a pointed finger at him. 'Jesse is a friend, not family. If anyone's going to buy you a car, it'll be your mum and me.'

'Really?' Hal's face lit up. 'For my twenty-first?'

Loveday stepped in before Mickey could reply. 'Darlin', this all needs a bit of thinking about. Now go up to bed and don't wake the girls. They'm got their exams in the morning. We'll talk about this when we're all less tired.'

Loveday wondered about what was happening with Jesse. What with that awkward conversation they'd had at the office, plus the drinking . . . what would Greer be making of it all? Loveday tried to crush the creeping sense of anxiety, but it nagged away at her as she returned to bed and tried to get off to sleep.

*

In the morning, Loveday knew she had to speak to Greer. It took a few moments to connect to Greer's mobile, and four or five rings before she picked up.

'Greer, it's Loveday.'

'Morning, Loveday. How are you?'

'Fine. I wanted to talk to you about something.'

'Sorry, you're breaking up. I'm in the lanes on my way to Mevagissey. There's a woman there with the most wonderful antiques. She has a Victorian claw-footed bath, needs restoring and re-enamelling but that's OK, it means it'll be a bargain, and a fabulous, huge oak dresser. She reckons it's seventeenth century, but I need to look at it to be sure—'

Loveday broke into her chatter. 'Can you hear me now?' she asked.

'Sort of, but you're coming and going. Can I ring you back when I'm on my way home later? Is it anything important?'

Loveday took a deep breath and told her. 'Jesse wants to buy Hal a car.'

'What?'

'For his birthday.'

'Sorry, I'm only getting every other word. I'll call you later.'

*

It was just before lunch when the phone on Loveday's desk went.

'Hello, Loveday Chandler.'

'Darling, it's me, Greer. The dresser was a let-down. Early nineteen hundreds and pine, not oak. The bath has a crack through the middle and will leak through an entire house. Total rubbish, and I told her so. Anyway, the upshot is that I'm ten minutes away from Trevay. Shall I swing by for a coffee and you can talk to me about this car business?'

Loveday's stomach was rumbling and she needed more than coffee. 'How hungry are you?'

'Not at all. I never eat lunch nowadays.'

Loveday's heart sank. She had been considering a macaroni cheese. She tried her chances. 'The Fo'c'sle do nice coffee. They've put in a team of baristas and everything.'

'Oh, yes, I'd heard that. OK. See you there.'

*

The new owners had really turned the old place around. Where there had been lines of Formica-topped tables, striplights, and condensation-clouded windows, there were now cosy corner tables, subdued lighting and air conditioning. The hiss and gurgle of the state-of-the-art coffee machine lent the whole place an air of European sophistication. A smart young waitress dressed to look like an early American bartender, with striped waistcoat, white shirt and long apron, welcomed her.

'Where would you like to sit. Inside or out?'

The spring sunshine was bright and the tables outside in the rear courtyard were inviting with their cushioned chairs and jolly parasols. 'Outside would be lovely, thank you.'

'I'll bring you a menu in a moment.' The waitress walked back inside and Loveday perused the menu. The macaroni cheese looked so tempting but, fearful of Greer's disapproval, she settled for a starter-sized portion of smoked salmon.

'Hi, Loveday. What a glorious day.' Greer, wearing sunglasses and carrying an enormous leather handbag, was heading towards her. 'So glad you chose to sit outside. I've been cooped up in that huge tank of a car for hours.' Greer sat elegantly on the chair opposite Loveday and, raising a slender arm in the air, summoned the waitress.

'Yes, Mrs Behenna, what can I get you?'

Greer looked at her over the top of her Fendi shades. 'Miri? How lovely to see you. Home from uni?'

'Yes, just for the Easter holidays.' The young waitress held her notepad in one hand and searched for her pen, stuck into her straggly bun of hair, with the other. 'How's Freddie?'

'He's fine. Working on the fishing fleet – and he's just got on the crew of the lifeboat.'

Miri gave a couple of rapids blinks. 'The lifeboat? Well done him. I bet he looks good in his uniform.'

'He certainly does,' smiled Greer. 'You should give him a bell.'

'Do you think so?'

'Of course. He'd be delighted to hear from you.'

'Well, in that case, I might . . . depends how busy I am . . . Anyway, what can I get you ladies?'

'Loveday, you first, I'm still choosing,' said Greer.

'I'd like the salmon starter and a pot of green tea, please,' Loveday said with an enthusiasm she did not feel.

The waitress wrote the order down. 'And for you, Mrs Behenna?'

'Actually I'm rather hungry. No time for breakfast this morning. I'll have the macaroni cheese, please, and a skinny latte.' Loveday couldn't believe her ears.

'Well, if you're having the macaroni, I'll join you. Thank you.'

'Great. I'll be back with the drinks in a minute.'

When Miri had gone, Loveday asked Greer how she knew her. 'She was at school with the boys. Don't you remember? Miranda? Her mother lives over at Trevone. Was an actress? I did her conservatory for her. She had a splendid divorce and has plenty of cash.'

'The one with the suede fringed jacket, blue sports car and the boob job?'

'That's the one.'

'Miri was sweet on your Freddie, wasn't she?'

'Very. He used to hide upstairs whenever she called

round. Which was frequently.' Greer laughed.

Loveday did too. 'And you've just set him up again.'

'She's turned into an attractive girl. He might thank me.'

Miri arrived with a tray bearing the drinks; as soon as she'd gone again, Greer looked at Loveday. 'I spoke to Jesse after your call and asked him about this business of giving the boys a car each. And he says he's serious. He's always treated them like they're brothers.'

'But they're not brothers,' Loveday said in a low voice. 'Mickey and I want Hal to earn his way in the world and not think that whatever Freddie gets, he'll get too. Life don't work that way.'

Greer thought for a moment. For once she agreed with Loveday. The boys weren't brothers and, fond as she was of Hal, Freddie and he were not equals in her eyes. It was all fine when they were little boys, but now they were growing up and it was time for Freddie to move on to bigger and better things. Of course, Freddie loved the relaxed rules at the Chandlers' house, but it was time that both he and his father thought more ambitiously. If he wanted to buy Hal an old banger, then fair enough, but really his own son deserved something better.

She reached across the table and put her hand on Loveday's. 'Darling, I'm sure he's only going to help Hal out a little bit. It isn't like it's a share in the business.'

'If Hal gets a car, it'll be an old banger. Remember Jesse's old Ford Capri?'

'I do. Filthy smelly thing.'

'Yeah, but he worked for it and he loved it. He had to look after it because no one was going to buy him another one for the hell of it. You give your Freddie anything you like, but let me and Mick do what's right for our son.'

Greer pulled the corners of her mouth down and shrugged. 'Well, in a way I agree with you, but once Jesse has an idea in his head it's very difficult to shake. I have to pick my battles. But I do understand, and I'll talk to him.'

*

Jesse was adamant. 'I want Hal to have the best. He's a good lad. I'm his godfather and I'm going to get him a car. There's no need for him to be a second-class citizen.'

Greer poured them each a glass of wine. 'I don't know why you feel so strongly about him. He's a lovely boy and all that, but when it comes down to it, he's just a godson. You've already done quite enough in your role as his father's best friend. More than enough. He has a good job on the fleet. You've got him on the lifeboat and in the next couple of years you'll give him his own boat to skipper.' Jesse looked up at her sharply. She raised her hand, palm facing him. 'I know you're going to give him his own boat. I do listen to what's happening in the business, you know. I'm not a fool. But where does your generosity stop?' She laughed, a light, scoffing laugh. 'I mean, what are you going to do, give him a share in the company?'

Jesse looked out of the big bay window in the drawing room of Tide House. He could see the cove and the sea beyond. He didn't answer Greer.

'Jesse! Tell me you're not seriously thinking of—'

'All I'm doing is helping a young boy get on in life.'

'As long as that's all?'

Jesse lifted his wine glass and tipped the contents down his throat. 'What's for supper?'

*

Later that night, when Greer had gone to bed, Jesse sat alone in his den. The window was open; on the fresh breeze he could hear the waves as they rolled onto the golden sand below the house. Recently he'd been having bad dreams about Grant. Sometimes Grant accused him of murder. Those dreams were the worst. But Jesse knew he hadn't murdered his own brother. Grant had had a death wish. The injury to his head he'd got when he fell off the cliff into the sea had been what had killed him. Some little weakness in his skull had killed him when they'd scuffled in the bus shelter. I'm not a murderer, Jesse told himself. But, after these dreams, Jesse would feel a tortured sadness. Grant, his own brother, hadn't been able to take his position in the company. It was Grant's own fault, of course. He was a destructive headcase. But Jesse still felt tortured with anguish for a brother who was always going to destroy himself. Dying in the shelter like that was inevitable, and Grant was always going to come to a bad end. It was sad. Tragic. But probably best all round. If only Grant had just kept his mouth shut and not said those terrible things. If he hadn't said anything about Loveday and Hal, he'd still be alive. But he wasn't, and Loveday and Hal needed protection. Hal deserved what was his by rights. Hal and Freddie were brothers, and if Grant couldn't share the company with Jesse, then Jesse would make sure that the next generation would. He'd play it carefully. Not let Mickey guess at anything. He didn't want to break his best mate's heart, after all. He'd talk to Loveday tomorrow. Tell her how he still felt about her. Tell her that he was going to make sure that he did right by Hal.

34

L auren popped her head round Loveday's office door, tying up the soft belt of her lilac mac. 'Boss wants to see you. I'm off up to Tesco to get a sandwich – want anything?'

Loveday was in the middle of collating that month's wages, and wrote a number down on her pad so that she remembered where she was. She looked up. 'Now?'

'Yes.'

Loveday sighed, blowing her cheeks out. 'OK.' She put her hands on her desk and stood up, pushing her chair back at the same time. 'Could you get me a duck wrap and a packet of crisps?'

She knocked on Jesse's door and looked in. Jesse was at his desk, on the phone. He motioned for her to sit down. She waited while he wound the call up.

He smiled at her. 'You look nice, Loveday.'

She gave him a small frown and pulled her chin in with suspicion. 'Uh-oh. What do you want?'

'Nothing.' He gave her an appraising look which made her feel a bit uncomfortable.

'Jesse, if I've done something wrong, just say it.'

'You ain't done nothing wrong. I thank my lucky stars every day that I got you downstairs sorting out the company. Honest as the day is long, aren't you?'

'Yeeees,' she said, cocking her head to one side questioningly. 'So Lauren said you wanted to see me?'

'It's about Hal's present.'

Loveday relaxed. 'Oh, good. Has Greer spoken to you? Only Mickey and I can't accept . . .'

He held his hands up to shush her. 'I understand all your objections, but I can't accept them. I want to buy Freddie a car for his birthday and I can't do that without buying Hal one too.'

Loveday was getting fed up. 'You can and you will. Mickey and I will buy Hal a car. He won't go wanting.'

Jesse leant back in his chair with an air of one who knew he would win out in the end. 'No offence, but the car you and Mickey can afford won't be up to much, will it?'

Loveday had had enough and said so. 'When did you turn into such a pompous prick? His dad and I will buy Hal a car and he'll love it because he's not a spoilt brat.'

Jesse gave a rueful smile. 'I take it from that that you're insinuating Freddie is? I don't think Greer will be too happy to hear her best friend describe her only son like that.'

Loveday stood up, hot with anger. 'I'm not saying that. You've every right to buy your son whatever you want to buy him, but—'

Jesse's face lost its humour and he looked at Loveday with deadly earnest. 'Freddie isn't my only son, is he?'

Loveday's legs gave way and she sat down again. 'Jesse, I've told you time and again. Hal is Mickey's son. Not yours.'

'I don't believe you. I never have. I went along with your little deception for all these years, but now . . . well, Hal's his own person and he has a right to know.'

Loveday's heart was beating fast and her breathing was uneven. She said as clearly as she could: 'Hal is not your son. He is Mickey's.'

Jesse smiled. 'I don't want to upset the apple cart by telling everyone the truth. I just want you to let me help him. A car, a boat – mebbe a house when the time is right. Just the same as I'll do for Freddie. After all, he was conceived before Fred, so Hal is actually my number one son.'

'Shut up.' Loveday stood again.

'I am trying to be reasonable and do the right thing. He deserves what's rightfully his. Just as Grant did. But it was Grant's own fault that I got what should have been his.'

'Shut your mouth. Have you gone mad?' For a moment, Loveday saw something in his face, something that reminded her of Grant with his bullying and threats.

Jesse twisted his leather chair from side to side. His hands folded on his chest. 'What shall we do, then? We could get all Jeremy Kyle about it and I could demand a DNA test, or you could just keep things as they are and let me look after my boys equally.'

Loveday could feel the threat of tears stinging her eyes. She looked at him in anguish. 'Please,' she whispered, 'please don't do this. He's my son. Mickey's son.'

There was a knock on the office door and Lauren came in bearing a Tesco bag. 'There you are – duck wrap and crisps.' She handed the bag to the white-faced Loveday. 'Are you feeling all right? You're awful pale.'

'Bit of a headache,' said Loveday, her hands gripping the bag handles with ferocious tension. 'How much do I owe you?'

'Don't worry about that. My treat. I think you should get on home. Don't you, Mr Behenna?'

*

As Loveday walked home, she had a sense of dread. A feeling that she'd been delivered a fatal wound. One that would go unnoticed for months or maybe years, but that oozed the life force out of her until she became an empty shell. She stopped at a place on the harbour wall where she could lean and look out to the horizon. She wanted to be in a far, faraway place. A town where no one knew her or could judge her. The truth was she didn't know for sure who Hal's father was. With all her heart she wanted it to be Mickey, but she didn't know and she didn't want to know. Hal was theirs – hers and Mickey's – and that was all that mattered.

A local woman she knew a little was walking towards her, a small scruffy dog on a lead by her side. Loveday considered turning round and running, but she held her ground. The woman got closer and said, 'Hello, Loveday. Beautiful day.'

'Yes,' Loveday replied.

'How's your boy and the twins?'

Please go away. 'Fine.'

'I hear your boy's on the lifeboat.'

'Yes.'

'Must be so proud of him.'

'Hmm.'

'What are your twins doing now?'

Please go away. Please. 'They're doing A levels.'

'Is it uni after?'

'Depends on their grades.'

'What they going to do?'

Oh, please God stop talking at me and go away. 'Maybe nursing.'

'Nursing! Well, they need good nurses in the hospitals. My dad had a terrible time when he had his operation. They never fed him nor changed his sheets—'

'I'm so sorry, I'm not feeling very well. I'm on my way home.'

'You should have said.' The woman peered into Loveday's face. 'You'm looking peaky.'

'Yes. Thank you. Well, bye.'

'Bye then.'

The woman finally walked away with her little dog jingling on its lead.

*

Loveday struggled with the key but finally her front door opened. She shut it behind her, leaning on it in relief. After a few moments she headed to the kitchen, taking off her coat and shoes as she went. The Tesco bag, and its contents, she threw into the bin.

The hot cup of tea gave her comfort, as did the familiar surroundings of her home.

Pilot's Cottages stood in a terrace of seventeenth-century dwellings. Mickey and she had bought one cottage in a damp and unmodernised state years ago, and the next-door cottage (in much the same state) a few years later. They'd knocked through and created four bedrooms and a bathroom upstairs, and an open-plan lounge and dining room downstairs, with a good-sized kitchen off it. She loved this house and all that she and

Mickey had done to it. Her favourite thing was the brick archway connecting the kitchen and the lounge. It was like something out of a magazine.

She began to feel a bit better. There was a pile of ironing on the sofa and, as Mickey and Hal were away at sea for a few days, she decided to tackle it later in front of the television. She looked at her watch. Almost time for the girls to come home. There was a half-eaten cottage pie in the fridge. She'd heat it up and that would do for the three of them. They'd eat it on their laps. Loveday took a deep breath. The sky hadn't fallen in. Life was as it always had been. Tomorrow she'd put Jesse straight once and for all.

*

The next morning, as she approached the entrance to Behenna and Clovelly, Jesse's Jaguar slid into its space. He called to her through the open window. 'Loveday. Just the girl. I'm going over to Newlyn at lunchtime. See what the opposition are up to.' He laughed as he got out of the car, still talking. 'I was wondering if you'd come with me. I'd like your professional opinion on their new computer system. See if it would work for us.'

'I don't know anything about IT. You should take Steve.'

Jesse reached into the car and grabbed his fisherman's jumper from the passenger seat. 'Steve can't make it, but he said you'd be the best person. After all, it's you who uses the thing most and knows all the ins and outs.'

'So does Lauren, and every other person who works for you.'

He locked the doors and came towards her. 'Yeah, but I don't owe them an apology, do I?'

'What are you apologising for?' she asked warily.

'Yesterday. I was heavy-handed and put you in an uncomfortable position.'

'Yes. You did.'

'So can I give you a day out in Newlyn, with lunch thrown in?'

'I thought we were going to look at the Newlyn Fish Market, not have a jolly.'

'Yes. We are. But I can throw lunch in too, can't I?'

She eyed him cautiously. 'Promise me you won't say anything more about getting Hal a car?'

'Promise.'

*

They left shortly before eleven and the conversation in the car was work-based and relaxed. Loveday began to think she wasn't going to have to have words with him after all.

The Newlyn operation was interesting, although the computer system wasn't that different from Behenna and Clovelly's. The head of accounts, a woman called April, was friendly, taking Loveday through all the systems she had. Most were familiar to Loveday, but there were one or two short cuts that she'd look into for B&C.

While she was with April, Jesse was in the fish market, looking first at the equipment in there, and later meeting his counterparts in the boardroom, where plans for a new fish-processing plant were discussed. It was clear that the Newlyn company wanted to share the facilities, and the cost, with an injection of cash from – and partnership with – Behenna and Clovelly.

It was four o'clock by the time they left.

'Are you hungry?' Jesse asked Loveday.

'Flipping starving.'

'Sorry about lunch. Fancy an early supper?'

'Sounds good, but I don't want to be home late.'

'Of course not. I know a nice little pub on our way home. We passed it. The Smuggler's Tree?'

'Perfect.'

*

The pub was old but clean. Jesse dodged the low beams as he entered.

'Hello, sir. What can I get you?' asked an elderly barman with thick spectacles and mutton-chop whiskers.

'I'll have a pint of Skinner's, please, and . . .' He turned to Loveday, raising his eyebrows in query.

'Just a lime and soda, please.'

'Coming up,' said the barman. 'Take a seat. I'll bring the drinks over. Will you be eating?'

'Yes, please.'

'I'll bring a menu too. I can recommend the steak.'

*

'That was really nice,' said Loveday, doing up her jacket as they went out into the cool evening. 'Thank you, Jesse.'

'The least I could do.'

They got into the car and Jesse turned on the CD player. Michael Bublé started to sing.

'Oh, I like him,' said Loveday, settling down in her seat. 'I think he's a nice person too.'

'He sings all right,' said Jesse.

The music filled the car and neither Jesse nor Loveday felt the need to talk. Loveday closed her eyes and let the gentle motion of the car and Michael Bublé's voice flood through her.

*

She had lost sense of time but was aware that the car had stopped. She opened her eyes. They weren't in Trevay. Outside it was pitch black. She turned to Jesse, who was looking at her carefully.

'Where are we?' she asked.

'On the moor.'

She looked out of the window again and could just make out some hills against the moonlit skyline. 'Have we run out of petrol? Is there something wrong with the car?'

'I wanted to talk to you.'

She groaned. 'No, Jesse. We've had this conversation.'

'That's not the conversation I'm thinking of.'

She was puzzled. 'What are you talking about?'

'I love you, Loveday. Always have and always will.'

She sat upright in her seat and folded her arms across her body. 'Don't start this again.'

'It's true. I love you.'

'And Mickey and I love you and Greer as friends.'

'You broke my heart. You know that?'

Loveday felt a white-hot rush of anger. 'What the hell are you talking about? I waited for you to come to me on the morning of your wedding. I waited for you, in my bedroom, expecting the knock at the door. Imagining you telling Mr Clovelly that you couldn't marry Greer. But you didn't come and you left me feeling a fool, watching you and Greer get married. It was my heart that was broken.'

He smiled a gentle smile and put his hand to her cheek. 'I knew you still loved me.'

She pulled away from him. 'I did but I don't now. I love Mickey. He's been good and true and he's not a coward, like you were that day.'

He sat back in his seat. 'Well, that's told me, hasn't it?'

'I hope so. Now please take me home.'

He looked regretful. 'I will take you home as soon as we've sorted something out.'

'What?'

'In return for me not telling Mickey about you, me and Hal . . . I want you to be nice to me.'

'Of course. We're friends.'

'Yes, we're friends, but I'd like us to be close friends. I can be your best friend who keeps your deepest, darkest secret in return for, how shall I put this delicately, being my mistress.'

Loveday's slap came hard and fast and stung his cheek. 'You are mad,' she spat. 'I would have done anything for you. But you didn't want that. You wanted your boats, your fancy wife, your fancy life, and now you want my son. Well, it's too late.'

To her horror, Jesse started to cry and began banging his head on the side window. Loveday was filled with disgust. 'You made all the moves and all the decisions and left me feeling a fool. Now you've got the fucking cheek to cry like a baby. Let me tell you, I love my son, I love my husband. My Mickey is worth ten of you.'

Jesse wiped a string of snot from his nose and turned imploring eyes upon her. 'Please, Loveday. You don't know how hard it's been for me, seeing you and Mickey and Hal together. It breaks my heart.'

'You don't know the meaning of heartbreak. Now either get me home or I'll get out and walk.'

He pulled a clean, pressed handkerchief out of his pocket and blew his nose. 'Please don't go.' He grabbed her hand and looked at her in desperation. 'Please. I feel like I'm going mad.' His eyes filled again and he leant towards her and buried his face in her lap. She pushed him away.

'Stop feeling so sorry for yourself and grow up. Like I've had to.'

'But I killed Grant.'

She looked at him in confusion. 'What?'

'I killed Grant. I killed him. He should have had what I've got but I took it from him.'

Loveday was in no mood for this. 'This self-pity is disgusting. You didn't kill Grant. He died because he was an idiot. Like you are being right now.'

He sat up and wiped his eyes. He looked so forlorn that for a moment Loveday pitied him. 'Come on. Let's just go home. Do you want me to drive?'

'No.' He shook himself and rubbed a hand over his face. 'Let's go.'

35

'Happy Father's Day.' Becca and Bea danced into the bedroom brandishing cards and a beautifully wrapped parcel.

'Wake up, Daddy.' Bea stuck a finger in her sleeping father's ear and twisted it.

'Get off me, you stupid maid,' growled Mickey, grabbing her wrist and pushing it away from him.

'Ow-wer. That hurt.' Bea retreated in a sulk. 'I was only playing.'

'Don't be such a wuss,' said Becca, taking her sister's place and putting her hands either side of her father's pillow, squashing it up over his cheeks. 'Get. Up. Dad. We've got cards and a present.'

Loveday lay still, on her side. Her back to Mickey, as she had done for the last couple of days. She'd managed to get home with no more dramas, but today there was no avoiding him.

She felt the mattress move as Mickey sat up against his pillows and the girls settled themselves in any space on the duvet they could find.

'What's this, then?' she heard him say. 'Where are my ugly daughters and what have you two done with them?'

'Just open the cards. Mine's the funniest,' Bea said.

Loveday listened as an envelope was opened and Mickey read out the message. 'Dad, you're like an old fart, you never know when to leave. Happy Father's Day, Love from Bea.' The girls giggled. 'Well, that's charming. Lovely sentiments. Thank you Bea.'

'Open mine now,' said Becca.

There was another rip of an envelope, then, 'To my dear Daddy, you are my star to guide me home, my hug to stop my tears and my fat wallet when I haven't got any money. Love you Daddy, Becca. Well, I must say the quality of greetings cards is going up. Thank you, girls.'

'Now open the present,' the girls chorused.

Loveday opened her eyes and looked at the clock. Just after eight. How was she going to get through today? She turned over and smiled at her family. 'Morning, girls. Happy Father's Day, Mickey.'

'Thank you, darling.' He leant over and kissed her. 'Look what our special little daughters have got for me.' He shook out a T-shirt which had printed on the front the torso of a very muscly man with a six-pack and huge biceps. On the back was written the legend 'Welcome To The Gun Show'.

'It's 'cos your muscles don't show,' explained Becca.

'I'll show you muscles.' The girls shrieked as Mickey grabbed them and began a play-wrestle.

Loveday got out of bed and padded downstairs to the kitchen to make the traditional Father's Day breakfast.

The drive over to Tide House was noisy. The girls and Hal, in the back of the car, were squabbling over some shared earphones. Mickey, wearing his new T-shirt, was driving. The late June sun was warm and the hedges alive with sea pinks and foxgloves. Loveday knew each bend and dip in the lane. Here was Foxy Loxy Corner, named after the night they saw a fox sitting right there in the field. Next came Owl Stone, where most nights a tawny owl would sit, rotating its head with exorcist flexibility. And now, as they breached the hill in the lane and turned right, beneath them appeared Tide Cove. The sea sparkled and flashed in the sun. A small fishing boat with a scarlet wheelhouse was bobbing on a yellow buoy a little way off the beach. Loveday could see two figures on the sand, pushing a rowing boat into the waves. She dropped her sunglasses onto her nose and took slow, deep breaths. She needed to get this day over and done with.

*

'Hello, hello!' said Greer, greeting them at the steps of Tide House. 'The boys are taking provisions from shore to ship as we speak. Hal, would you and the girls like to take a couple more things down to them? Saves your mum and me.'

A box of Coca-Cola tins and some Tupperware containing sandwiches and cake were handed over.

Greer watched as the three trooped off and then turned to Mickey and Loveday. 'Happy Father's Day, Mickey.' She hugged him and then kissed Loveday. 'Aren't we lucky with this weather! Either of you want a cup of coffee and a pee before we set off?'

Loveday tried to pull her mood up to match Greer's relentless cheerfulness. It had been Jesse, of course, who'd suggested that they all get together for a big fishing outing on this Father's Day. The two families had never shared the day before, and Loveday was sick to her toes with anxiety.

'We'll have a coffee with you,' said Mickey, putting his arm around Loveday. 'Won't we, darlin'?'

*

Greer swallowed the last of her coffee and began filling a bag with a camera and a bottle of sunscreen. 'Got everything?'

'I'll just nip to the loo,' said Loveday.

Mickey watched her go then said quietly, 'Does she look all right to you, Greer?'

Greer thought for a moment. 'I think so. Why?'

'I dunno. She's been quiet. Not herself at all.'

Greer searched for and found her sunglasses. 'In what way?'

'Tired. Quiet. D'you think it's the menopause?'

Greer pulled a face. 'She's only in her early forties. I shouldn't think so.' She looked at Mickey more carefully and saw the anxiety in the lines around his eyes and in the slump of his shoulders. 'Maybe get her to see the doctor? She might be anaemic or need a tonic.'

They heard the flush of the downstairs loo and Mickey stood up in readiness. 'Thanks, Greer.'

*

The three of them walked down the lane and through the dappled shade towards Tide Cove. Years ago it had belonged to a syndicate of lobster fishers, long since dead. Ever since, this had been Freddie and Hal's playground. This is where they learnt to fish for bass off the beach, sail a small dinghy, and now put down their own lobster pots from the *Sand Castle*, the little boat with the red wheelhouse that Jesse had bought for family fishing trips.

Loveday saw Jesse and her heart sank. How was she going to get through this day?

'All aboard the *Skylark*,' called Jesse jauntily. Loveday

stared at him with a frown. How was this man able to change from a snivelling wreck to playing happy families? 'Hurry up. The kids will have eaten everything.' He was up to his knees in the waves, his old pink canvas shorts wet on the hem. He was holding the rowing boat for the latecomers. 'Greer, did you bring my specs?' he asked.

'No. Why, haven't you got them?'

'I wouldn't ask you if I had them, would I?'

Greer looked at Loveday and raised her eyebrows in infuriation. 'Men.' Then she called back to Jesse. 'Have you checked the pocket of your smock?'

His smock was tied round his shoulders; as he undid the arms and swung it round to check the pouch, a pair of glasses slid out and splashed gently into the light surf. 'Bugger,' he said and bent to retrieve them.

Loveday was feeling a sense of panic. 'Look, I'm really not feeling too good. Would you mind if I went home, only I think I'll be a terrible hindrance to you all.'

'What's the matter, love?' asked Mickey, all concern.

'Just a headache and a bit of flu maybe.'

Jesse had pulled the boat up and beached it. 'What's this? Not well, Loveday?'

'No. I'm so sorry.'

'You were fine on Friday.'

The memory of Friday and the car stopped on the moor came slicing through her brain.

'Friday?' said Greer.

Loveday answered hurriedly, 'I helped Jesse with that computer thing in Newlyn.'

'Oh, right.' Greer was already uninterested. 'Will you be ok to get yourself home?'

'I'll be fine. So sorry to be a party pooper.' She kissed

Mickey, who held her tight and whispered, 'You sure you're all right? I don't mind coming home with you.'

'No, darlin'. Enjoy the day.'

'Don't I get a hug and a kiss for Father's Day, Loveday?' asked Jesse, smiling innocently, with his arms held wide.

'Yes, of course. ' She stepped forward and he surprised her by picking her up in a bear hug and lifting her off her feet. The smell of him made her want to kill him. He put her down. 'That's better. See you later. You'll be having lobster for your tea if we catch any.'

*

Freddie was already in the wheelhouse when the rest of the party boarded. 'Right little fishes,' he laughed, turning on the engine, 'we'm coming to get you.'

He turned the boat away from Tide Cove and pointed the nose to the horizon. 'Hang onto your hats!' He pushed the throttle forward and the sturdy boat roared through the smooth sea, while Jesse cracked open the beers.

*

Greer was lying in the bow, face in the sunshine, relaxed in the company of her boys, enjoying a rare moment of complete indolence. Jesse and Mickey were fast asleep. Freddie was at the wheel, manoeuvring the boat into a better position from which to drop the lobster pots. The regular chug of the motor was soporific. She thought she might just close her eyes for a moment.

A changed engine note crashed suddenly into her consciousness – a strange and horrible sound that made her stomach lurch with fear. She leapt up, dashing to the stern. Freddie had stopped the boat and joined her; they shared a mutual glance of sick dread before they looked down towards the water.

It was Greer shouting for Jesse that woke Mickey.

'Jesse! Jesse! There's blood. Oh shit. Oh God. Freddie, get in the water, quick; hold his head up!'

Mickey sat up, immediately alert, and saw Greer hanging over the stern, clearly struggling to hold onto something. 'Jesse!' she screamed now in a shrill pitch that finally woke him. He and Mickey got to Greer within seconds of each other. As they too looked over the back of the boat, they saw Freddie, white faced and frightened, hanging onto the unmoving body of Hal.

'Hal!' Mickey was screaming now. 'What the fuck's happened? Hal!' His training on the lifeboat had given him the ability to assess a casualty with speed. Most of Hal's left side was submerged, but Freddie was keeping Hal's head and shoulders out of the water. Mickey could see a deep cut on the left shoulder and similar wounds to the left side of his chest.

'Pull him up!' Jesse somehow managed to lean as far over the boat as he could without falling in and got an arm around Hal's body.

'Push, Freddie,' Mickey ordered.

'I'm trying to,' Freddie sobbed. Slowly Hal's right side was lifted from the water and Freddie, with God-given strength, managed to get him to a height where Jesse and Mickey could take Hal's weight.

Then Mickey saw. 'His arm,' he cried in horror. 'His arm. Where's it gone?'

*

Loveday was waiting at the hospital as the air ambulance landed. Through the glass wall of the A&E department she saw several medics running with a trolley towards it. She turned to the policewoman who was waiting with her. 'Can I go to him?'

The constable took her hand but shook her head. 'He'll be in the building any minute.'

Loveday felt nothing. Her body was standing, but she was floating near the ceiling. She saw herself wide-eyed and numb. No tears. But she was clenching and unclenching her hands. At last the double doors were pushed open and the trolley carrying Hal went past her. She followed and listened. 'Young male. Aged twenty. Left arm severed by a boat propeller. Losing blood.'

'Loveday!' It was Mickey running towards her. 'I'm so sorry.' He was crying. 'I'm so sorry. I was asleep. He was swimming. I don't know how it happened.' He collapsed into her arms and she watched from the ceiling as she comforted him, still following the trolley carrying Hal. 'It's OK, Mickey. He's still with us. He's still with us.'

They were stopped from going into the emergency room. A handsome male nurse said, 'Please take a seat in the relatives' room. The doctor will come and tell you what's happening as soon as she's had a chance to assess your son's injuries.'

Loveday crashed back into her body with a jolt and sat down, but she couldn't stay seated for long. 'I must do something or go mad. Shall I find a cup of tea?'

'I don't want anything,' said Mickey, his head in his hands.

'I'll go,' said the policewoman.

'No,' Loveday insisted. 'I need to do something.'

She left the room, desperate to move around, burn the awful energy flooding her body.

*

In the corridor she met a woman in blue scrubs who asked, 'Mrs Chandler?'

'Yes.'

'I'm looking after Hal. I'm Dr Sutton.'

'Can I see him?'

'He's not looking very good.'

'I want to see him.'

The doctor thought for a moment then relented. 'OK. Just for a few minutes. He's not conscious. He's lost a lot of blood.'

'I just want to see him.'

*

Jesse banged the door of the relatives' room open, making Mickey and the constable jump. 'Mick. How is he?'

'We're just waiting for the doctor,' Mickey said in a quiet, shocked voice. 'Loveday's gone to get tea.' He looked at the clock on the wall. 'She's been gone ages . . .'

'Where's Hal?' Jesse's anguished voice was completely at odds with Mickey's.

'With the doctor.'

'How is he?'

'We're waiting . . .'

'He lost a lot of blood.' Jesse was agitated. 'He'll need a transfusion.'

'Yes. I expect so.'

'I want you to know, Mickey, that I am going to give him my blood.'

'That's kind of you, but if they don't have enough at the hospital, he'll need some from a relative, won't he? Me or Loveday? Or the girls? Where are the girls?'

'With Greer and Freddie at home.'

'Oh, good.'

'But,' Jesse tried to be gentle, 'I might have the right blood.'

'Yes,' Mickey said kindly. 'It might be you. It might be me. It might be lots of people in this hospital, so I'm sure we'll get some.'

The doctor came in. 'Mr Chandler?' She looked from one man to the other. 'Yes,' said Mickey. 'I'm Hal's dad. How is he?'

'He's lost a lot of blood and we're going to start transfusing him before he goes to theatre.'

Jesse leapt to his feet. 'I'll be a donor.'

The doctor looked surprised. 'Are you a relative?'

'I'm his—'

Mickey stepped in. 'He's his godfather.'

The doctor had experience of dealing with shocked and confused relatives, so she smiled and carried on. 'We're always grateful for donors, but there's no need in this instance. Mrs Chandler has offered and she's a perfect match.'

36

There was a police investigation, which found that human error was the strongest factor in what had happened. Freddie hadn't known that Hal was in the water when he nudged the throttle forward to move the boat round slightly.

Mickey and Loveday refused to press charges against him, so he was left with the freedom of liberty but also the imprisonment of guilt. He was filled with remorse and suffering from sleepless nights and panic attacks; the doctor concluded that he was probably suffering from of PTSD. He was suspended from the lifeboat crew on compassionate grounds as he was unable to perform his duties. All talk of a future on the lifeboats was quietly forgotten. For now, he was given shore duties only, at Behenna and Clovelly. The unending kindness and sympathy of Hal, Mickey and Loveday served only to bury him under a dark cloak of depression.

Jesse left Loveday alone after that. In the back of their minds, both Mickey and Jesse blamed themselves for drinking on the boat; both felt that if they had been more alert and professional, the accident might never have happened. But the two sets of friends continued as they always had, albeit with an underlying strain and an overlying brightness, and kept their private thoughts to themselves.

Hal's left arm now finished just above his elbow. The scars on his stump, face and chest began to fade and, incredibly, he bore no resentment. 'I'm alive, aren't I?' he said again and again to the well-wishers who pitied him.

Before his birthday, Loveday had asked Hal what it was he wanted to do.

'Me and Freddie's having a joint party, ain't we?'

'I know that was what you wanted . . . before.' She hesitated. 'But you might feel differently now, what with your arm.'

'No way are we cancelling this party, Mum.'

'I didn't mean cancel . . . just that maybe a joint party with Freddie might be a bit upsetting for both of you,' she said kindly.

'Mum, Freddie's been to hell and back with his guilt and is suffering more than I am. I want Freddie to see that nothing has changed between us. He's my best friend and he always will be.'

Loveday felt tears sting her eyes as she nodded and hugged her brave, loyal son.

*

It was October, and the last Lifeboat Day of the season fell on the Friday Freddie and Hal turned twenty-one. There was no more talk of new cars. Instead, Loveday planned a family lunch, to include the Behennas, at Pilot's Cottages.

It was twelve thirty, and Greer squinted her eyes against the pearly autumn sun that highlighted the peeling paint surrounding the brass Piskey doorknocker and revealed the silvered timbers beneath. She shifted the plastic cake box from her right hand to her left and knocked.

Jesse had parked the car against the low dry-stone wall in front of the cottage's garden, and was walking up the slate path towards her. 'Have you knocked?'

She didn't bother to hide her irritation. 'Of course I have.'

'Try the handle. It won't be locked.'

'I don't like to.'

'Oh, for God's sake.' Jesse pushed his arm in front of her and opened the door. 'Hello!' he called cheerily.

The house released the steam of vegetables boiling on the stove and the smell of a chicken roasting in the oven. They could hear music coming from a radio.

'Mickey boy?' shouted Jesse as he walked into the comfortably loved lounge. 'Where are you, you bugger?'

Greer, standing on the threshold, looked at the surroundings with her usual judgmental eye. If it were stripped back of all the tasteless clutter, it could be so stylish. Thick and wonky stone walls. Flagstoned floor. Original fireplace and stunning views out to the harbour. But Loveday had smothered all that with her Dralon chintz four-piece suite, grim Austrian blinds and, to Greer's mind, pointless gewgaws on every available surface. The room was separated into two areas. The hideous sitting area to the left and a dining area to the right. The table was laid for six and festooned with streamers and birthday cards.

The kitchen was accessed via the worst assault on the concept of design that Greer could remember. A brick arch, a plastic vine nailed to it and raffia-covered bottles of chianti placed at odd angles. Loveday was inordinately proud of it. She had once told Greer, who had never forgotten, that it reminded her of the Greek taverna in *Shirley Valentine*. Greer hadn't the energy to tell Loveday that Greeks drank retsina and not chianti.

The kitchen itself was functional but dull, the walls the same terracotta colour that had once been so desirable in the nineties.

Greer shocked herself with this bitchy inner dialogue. Loveday had been nothing but generous to her after Hal lost his arm. Loveday could – *should* – hate her, but she didn't.

Greer took the cake box into the kitchen and found Loveday standing outside the back door having a cup of coffee.

'Oh,' said Loveday, clutching her chest. 'I didn't hear you, darlin'. I was just thinking about what you and I were doing twenty-one years ago.'

They embraced each other and Greer handed over the cake. 'What a day that was. But we've survived, more or less intact.' Realising what she'd said, she quickly apologised, feeling the heat of horror in her face. 'I'm so sorry, I didn't mean to—'

Loveday was quick with her reassurance. 'No, no, it's fine. Figure of speech. Now then.' She opened the cake box. 'What have you made for us?'

'It's not much. Chocolate sponge, as usual.'

'Tradition, that's what it is,' said Loveday, smiling. 'Imagine if one year you didn't make it? The boys would go mad.'

Greer slipped her coat off and hung it over a kitchen chair. 'How can I help?'

Jesse wandered in. 'Where's that husband of your'n?'

'Upstairs, having a shower.' Loveday handed Greer an apron. 'Can you make some gravy?'

'Yes, of course,' said Greer. 'Did the boys have a good night last night?'

'I didn't hear them come in so it must've been late. I

took them coffee this morning and they don't look too good.'

Greer felt her stomach flip with relief that Freddie was safe. She hated it when she didn't hear from him. She always asked him to text, just to let her know he was OK, but he would forget.

Jesse went to the fridge and found himself a tin of beer. 'Don't mind, do you?'

'Help yourself,' said Loveday, taking the pan of boiled potatoes off the Aga and carrying them to the sink to drain them.

Greer was looking in the larder. 'Do you have any cornflour?'

'What for?' asked Loveday, the steam from the potatoes billowing in her face.

'The gravy.'

Loveday smiled indulgently at her old friend. 'Bless you, Greer. If you look to the right there's a red tub of Bisto granules. They'll do.'

Greer found the tub and felt somehow foolish for asking for the cornflour. She read the instructions with care. 'So all I have to do is boil a kettle?'

'That's all you have to do.'

'Morning, all.' Mickey's lanky frame stood in the archway. His hair was still damp from the shower but combed smooth, and he smelt of Lynx. He spotted Jesse's beer. 'Pass me one of those, Jess.'

'Coming up.' Jesse tossed a tin to Mickey. 'You girls want a drink?'

'Gin and tonic, please,' said Loveday, pouring batter mix into a red-hot roasting tin for Yorkshire pudding.

'Same for me, Jesse, thank you,' said Greer. 'Are the boys up yet, Mickey?'

'Aye, they're showering. Can't believe they're twenty-one. Where's the time gone? Cheers.' He lifted his tin and the girls took their drinks from Jesse. 'Cheers.' They chinked and drank.

*

Greer was mixing the carefully measured gravy granules with the hot water when Freddie appeared and slid an arm round her waist and kissed her. 'All right, Mum?'

He loomed tall above her and she looked up to drink him in. Her one and only precious son. He was in yesterday's jeans and T-shirt and his breath smelt of last night's alcohol, but he looked all right. Her heart beat a little quicker knowing he was safe.

'You should have texted me.'

'Sorry, Mum. Battery went dead.'

'I should have bought you an extra big battery for your birthday.'

'Oh, yes.' He stretched himself tall, grazing his knuckles on the low ceiling. 'It's my birthday. Happy birthday to me!'

'All right, son?' Jesse passed him a tin of beer. 'Need a hair of the dog?'

'Get on then.' He took the can and opened it with a hiss. 'What you got me for my birthday then?'

'You'll have to wait.'

'What about me?' Hal came into the crowded kitchen. His stump was clearly visible under his short-sleeved shirt. He gave his mum and Greer a one-armed hug.

'Happy Birthday, Hal. I hope you had a good night last night?'

'Awesome, weren't it, Fred?'

'Legend,' Freddie agreed. 'Beer, mate?'

'Yes, please.'

'Would you boys please get out of the kitchen and let Greer and I get on?' Loveday shooed them out.

*

'So what's the plan of action today?' Jesse asked, settling himself on the sofa with half an eye on the football that Hal and Freddie had found on the television.

'The Lifeboat Parade starts at two thirty, so if we get down to the harbour around two fifteen we'll have a bit of time to form up with everyone,' said Mickey.

Loveday shouted from the kitchen. 'I've got to get the raffle tickets and collection buckets from the harbour master's office just after two.'

'Well, you can go ahead of us if you want to,' Mickey shouted back.

'I can give you a lift,' said Greer, adding a small knob of butter to the new potatoes in their dish. 'I've got to get the cream teas set up in the hall by three. I was up till one o'clock this morning making the flipping scones. Hundreds of them.' She picked up the bowl of peas and the jug of gravy and walked through to put them on the dining-room table. Loveday surreptitiously added a larger slab of butter to the potatoes. 'Greer,' she called, 'I've got a wine box in the fridge. Specially for you. Chardonnay. I know you like good wine.'

Greer inwardly winced at the notion that any wine in a box could be good, but she thanked Loveday and gamely retrieved the box from the fridge and put it on the table.

'Right,' said Loveday grandly, 'luncheon is served.'

As soon as they sat down, the phone rang. With dramatic huffs and puffs, Loveday pulled herself back out of her chair and answered it. ''Ello? . . . Becca? Hello, darlin'! Is Bea with you? How's uni? . . . yeah . . . yeah . . . sounds brilliant, yeah. Your dad's fine. We're all here having birthday lunch with the boys . . . OK, I'll put you on . . . speak later. Love you. Here's your brother. '

*

Lunch was relaxed and easy. Pudding was Loveday's signature dish: apple crumble and clotted cream. Her crumble topping was always deep and delicious. 'One-third fruit to two-thirds crumble' was her mantra.

'Oh my, look at the time. 'Tis a quarter to two,' Loveday yelped, jumping up. 'We'd better get down to the quay.'

Greer stood too and began to clear the table.

'What are you doing girl?' asked Loveday. 'Get your coat on or we'll be late.'

'I'll just clear these things,' said Greer, who couldn't bear coming home to unwashed dishes.

'No you won't, they'll keep till tomorrow. Come on.'

*

The last Lifeboat Day of the year was always a huge event in the Trevay calendar. There were still quite a few tourists about; they were always keen to watch the parade and throw their spare change into the jingling buckets.

The parade itself was always headed by the Trevay Pipe Band, followed by Trevay's serving lifeboatmen. Behind them came a succession of floats bearing a series of tableaux. This year's theme was 'The Majesty of the

Sea' and entrants included the Trevay Infant School, the WI, the Pavilions Theatre Players, the St Peter's Church Sunday School and, incongruously, a man dressed as a gorilla riding a motorbike.

Trevay quay was awash with revellers, most a little drunk and all enjoying the spectacle, the autumn sun and a day off work.

Loveday walked among them shaking her bucket and doling out sweeties to the children. Greer, having laid out her cream teas and organised the helpers into getting the tea urns on, looked down from the large windows of the Old Hall above the harbour, and watched.

Freddie and Hal were sitting outside the Golden Hind, drinking with a group of mates.

As the lifeboat crew marched past the pub, it was Freddie who saw Jesse touch his trouser pocket and pull out his pager.

Freddie nudged Hal's stump. 'They've got a shout.'

37

David, the divisional launch authority who'd taken the initial message from the coastguards in Falmouth, was waiting in the boat-house crew room.

'What we got?' Jesse asked, as he pulled on his yellow oilskin trousers, boots, jacket and life vest.

'Yacht about seventeen miles out. Broken mast. Falmouth are getting an accurate position for her. Two on board. Father and son. No casualties reported. But weather doesn't look good.'

Jesse looked over the assembled faces of the crew who'd rushed here, ready to put their lives on the line for strangers. He only needed seven of them.

'Mickey, Malcom, Si, Jeff, Kate, Brian and Don. Get your kit on. Everybody else, thanks and stand by launch.'

The chosen ones got into their kit, quietly shitting themselves.

Jesse walked from the crew room to *The Spirit of Trevay* standing shiny on her rails. The doors of the boat-house were opening and the crew boarded the boat and took their positions.

Jesse gave the command. The pin was pulled and she slid with speed down the slip, out of the boat-house and into the open air. The crowd roared its cheer of support as she hit the water and the engines powered her out of the harbour and out to sea.

The radio came to life.

'*Spirit of Trevay*, *Spirit of Trevay*, *Spirit of Trevay*, this is Falmouth Coastguard, Falmouth Coastguard. Over.'

Jesse took up the radio handset. 'Falmouth Coastguard, this is *Spirit of Trevay*. We've launched. Do you have coordinates? Over.'

Jesse made a note as the coastguard reeled them off and made some calculations. 'We should be there in about three and a half hours at our current speed of five knots. Out.'

Malcolm, the helmsman, locked the boat onto auto-pilot. Everything was going by the book. At this rate they'd be home before last orders.

*

Greer was tired as she drove through the electric gates of Tide House. The cream teas had been a huge success and the added excitement of an actual emergency launch had given the visitors a good appetite.

There wasn't a crumb left of the scones or a spoon left of the clotted cream and jam. She hadn't watched the *The Spirit* go out. She'd seen it enough times, as coxswain's wife, to know what it looked like, but she had heard about it via a text from Loveday. She'd sent up a silent prayer of thanks that Freddie was no longer on the crew.

Now, sitting in her huge car parked in front of her beautiful home, she felt drained. She took a few moments and looked up at the house she loved. It was an unusual building for this part of the coast. Not built of granite or brick, but of honey-coloured stone that now glowed in the late sunshine. The glass of the big sash windows was fiery with the first rays of sunset.

Greer opened the heavy car door and felt a breeze coming off the sea below her. It lifted the corners of her grey cashmere cardigan and made her shiver.

She couldn't see the ocean from here. That view was from the house, but she could hear it on the wind. The hiss and suck of the waves as they dragged through the sand and shingle. It was louder than this morning. A sign that the wind was changing. She turned her face to the sky. Clouds were forming on the horizon. She went round to the boot and spent some minutes trundling backwards and forwards with empty cake boxes and bags of bits, until at last she locked the car with the remote key, climbed the steps to her front door and closed it on the early evening chill.

Sanctuary. Her home was welcoming and stylish. Nothing out of place. Peaceful and harmonious. If someone gave her an ornament she disliked she ruthlessly discarded it. The charity shop in Truro, far enough away for the giver of the gift not to find it, always looked forward to her donations. Sentiment had no part to play in her décor.

One of the few rows she'd won with Jesse was that not one of Freddie's school-crafted Christmas decorations or Easter cards were to make their way onto her tree or mantelpiece. That was why Jesse's boat-house on Tide Cove was a shrine to Freddie's schoolboy art. She adored her son, but not to the extent that she was prepared to compromise the look of her home. Thank God there would be no more of it. Now he was twenty-one, he was more interested in boozing and birds than papier-mâché and macramé.

She walked through her dove-grey drawing room, turning on the well-placed lamps that gave the room an ambient glow, through the conservatory with its white orchids and cream cane sofas, and into the kitchen.

She needed a coffee. As she filled the kettle, she heard the cat-flap rattle. Tom danced in with a loud mew. 'Looking for some grub are you, Thomas?' He wound himself through her legs, then sat and curled his tail around his front legs. He gave her a wide-eyed, unblinking, stare. 'OK. OK. What do you want?' She held up two sachets and read from them. 'Prawn in jelly? Or beef casserole?' He yawned when she said casserole. 'Bored with casserole? Prawn in jelly it is, then.'

She prepared his bowl and put it on the floor for him. The kettle boiled and she opened a drawer for a teaspoon, hesitated, then shut it and went to the fridge. She needed a proper drink. She took it to the far end of the kitchen where the plasma television was surrounded by silver-grey striped sofas and a coffee table. The cushions were perfectly plumped. No imprint of previous occupants defiled them. She sat down and closed her eyes. Home. She loved these precious moments when she was alone in the house. Nobody to disturb her with their noise and mess. She opened her eyes and took in the beautiful room. The antique, scrubbed pine kitchen table, big enough to seat twelve, was the perfect foil for the huge bowl of late roses and dogwood stems sitting in the middle of it. The insanely expensive range cooker – she couldn't be doing with the original Aga, which she'd had taken out – was gleaming. She was satisfied. She took a mouthful of her wine and flicked on the TV to watch the news.

Half an hour later she took her second glass of chilled Sancerre up to her bedroom and into the en suite where she ran a deep and bubbly bath. Wallowing, almost floating, in its depths, she heard the first spatter of raindrops on the window, like gravel thrown against it by a lover. The glass of wine, with its beads of condensation, lay cool in her hand. She took another sip and lay her head back on the bath's rim. The rain was sporadic at first but gradually came in drumming gusts. She thought of Jesse and hoped that the weather wouldn't hold him up too much.

*

The heat of the bath and the wine made Greer drowsy. Wrapping a warm bath sheet round her, she lay on her bed, the deeply enveloping duvet closing over her. She hadn't closed her bedroom curtains and she could see that it was almost completely dark outside. The phone rang. She stretched to pick up the receiver. 'Hi. All safe?' she asked, expecting Jesse's voice.

It was Loveday. 'Greer, it's me. I haven't heard anything. Have you?'

'Not yet.' She looked at her clock. 'It's still early, though.'

'Yeah . . .' Loveday hesitated. 'The weather's not too good for them, is it?'

'It might be a bit lumpy out there, but nothing they can't handle.'

'Yeah,' Loveday agreed. 'If I hear anything, I'll give you a shout.'

'Me too.' Greer saw the streaks of rain on her window and heard the wind moan as it pushed itself around the corners of the house. 'Thanks for a lovely lunch, Loveday.'

'My pleasure. I'm stacking the dishwasher now.'

'I should have stayed to help.'

'Absolutely not. Gives me something to do.'

'Right, well, if you hear anything . . .'

'Yeah. Bye.'

'Bye.'

Neither woman would have dreamt of trying the men on their mobiles. It was an unwritten rule. Greer got off the bed and closed the curtains, shutting out the bleakness of the night. She pulled on a pair of soft leggings, cashmere socks and a warm sweatshirt, then padded onto the landing.

At the top of the stairs, a tall, wide window had the clearest view of the sea. On the deep window ledge stood a fat church candle and a box of matches. She shook a match from the box and lit the candle's wick. The flame sputtered before growing tall and unwavering. This was a time-honoured custom. A talisman. A light to guide the lifeboat home. When Freddie was little he was the one who lit it. 'Daddy will see the light and come home to us.'

She walked along the landing and into Freddie's room. God knows when he'd be home. The birthday celebrations could go on for days. He was a different person since the accident and was taking refuge in mates and beer. She drew his curtains and turned his bedside lamp on, just in case. Later she'd turn the corners of his duvet down and pop in a hot-water bottle. She knew he preferred a cold bed, but it was an old habit she enjoyed. He might be glad of it when he came home.

She went downstairs to light the open fire in the library. It was smaller than the formal sitting room and she could feel snug in here with a book. As the fire licked into life she stoked it with coal and a good-sized log, then went to put a chicken casserole in the oven. Something for Jesse when he got back.

*

Loveday put the phone down and spoke to her reflection in the kitchen mirror. 'Come on, girl,' she told it. 'The boys'll be back from the pub and Mickey'll be home and they need food in their bellies.' She threw five jacket potatoes into the Aga and took a packet of sausages out of the fridge. That and a couple of tins of beans would do them just right.

Upstairs she got out of her clothes and had a hot shower, enjoying the warmth on her neck and shoulders. The weather would be hampering *The Spirit* a bit and maybe the yacht was a bit bigger than expected and taking longer to tow in. She dried her hair roughly and sprayed herself with some perfume. She wanted Mickey to hold her and love her when he came home. Since the whole horrible business with Jesse had started, and then stopped so tragically, she'd been unresponsive to Mickey's affections. He'd been kind and patient, he'd even tried to get her to see the doctor, but she couldn't tell anyone about her and Jesse. Well, today was a turning point. Hal was twenty-one and Jesse was history. When Mickey came home tonight she'd show him how much she loved him.

Feeling better, she decided to phone the twins.

''Ello, darling. It's Mum. You all right?'

'Hi, Mum.' Becca pulled a face at her twin sister, Bea, who was listening in. They loved their mum, but why did she have to ring so much? 'How are you? How did the birthday lunch go?'

'Really good, and Lifeboat Day went really well. Gave the grockles something to talk about 'cos the boat went out on a real shout.'

'Oooo, *exciting*,' said Becca, rolling her eyes at her sister.

'How are you doing for money? Not overspending your allowances?'

'No, Mum. We're doing really well.' Becca looked over at the half-drunk litre bottle of vodka and giggled.

'How are your studies going?'

'I was on a geriatric ward this week.'

'Oh, poor old souls. How'd you get on?'

'Good, yeah. I wouldn't mind working in geriatrics.'

Loveday held the phone between her shoulder and her ear and started to open a tin of baked beans.

'And Bea?'

'Ask her yourself. She's right here.'

Bea shook her head wildly but it was too late, Becca had put the phone in her hand.

'Hi, Mum,' she said, balling her fist and miming a punch at her sister, who ducked out of the way, laughing.

'How's your course going?'

'Full on. Lots of work.'

'Well, of course it is, darling. Have you delivered any babies yet?'

'I was at a birth the other night. Little boy, Finlay. Really sweet.'

'Ah. Ain't that lovely? And how are you doing with your allowance? Not overspending?'

'Fine, Mum. I had to get some textbooks the other day, but they were second-hand so not too bad.' Becca heard this and, pulling a shocked face, pointed at the new super-sexy Top Shop dress that her sister was wearing. Bea gave her a playful shove.

'How's Dad?' she managed to say as Becca made her laugh by pointing at her nose and pretending it was growing, Pinocchio style.

''E's out on a shout. Not back yet.'

Bea heard the familiar worry in her mother's voice. 'You OK, Mum?'

'Yeah, I'm fine. It's just that the weather's turned a bit.'

'And where's Hal?'

'In the pub, I think. Celebrating with Freddie.'

'Dad'll be all right, Mum. He always falls on his bum in butter.'

Loveday laughed. 'Well, that's what your grandma always used to say. How's London? Grandma never got there. She'd be so proud of you. Have you seen Buckingham Palace yet?'

'Yes. I'll take you when you come up.' Bea looked over at her sister, who was tapping her watch. They were going out with a gang of mates any minute.

'Mum, I've got to go. Love to Dad and Hal and Fred. Love you.'

'Love you too.'

Loveday smiled, comforting herself with the thought of her clever girls who had chosen such exciting careers. No hanging about in Trevay waiting for life to happen to them. They could travel the world when they were qualified. Loveday felt tears and a tightening in her throat. She missed them so much and worried about them constantly. At least she still had Hal. Hal wouldn't be leaving Trevay. Not now.

She looked at the clock. If he and Mick didn't come home soon, the jacket potatoes would spoil.

38

The sun was setting and the light was dying over the roughening sea. *The Spirit of Trevay*, a sturdy, all-weather, self-righting, Tamar-class boat forged through the waves.

Malcolm, the helmsman, was on the bridge but steering manually now. The sea was getting too big for the autopilot. They'd just gone over the biggest wave of the night. He eased off the throttle as the boat surfed down the other side of it and then pushed the power back on to go up another bigger wave. The splash as he came over the top caught him broadside, filling his ears with water. He pulled the hood of his jacket up. Jesse was standing beside him, eyes scanning the sea.

'All right, Malc?' he asked.

'Yeah.'

The radio came to life. '*Spirit of Trevay*, *Spirit of Trevay*, *Spirit of Trevay*, this is Falmouth Coastguard, Falmouth Coastguard. Over.'

'Falmouth Coastguard, this is *Spirit of Trevay*. Over.'

'Yacht *Ocean Blue* is not responding to radio calls. But we've got the GPS position.'

'Right, give it to me.' Jesse made a note and checked the screen, showing their position and the yacht's last known position. 'That's a long way off the original reference, Falmouth.'

'She's probably drifted. Met Office tells us winds are gusting Force Eight.'

'Shit.' Jesse rubbed a hand over his face. 'Roger that. Setting new course. Out.' Jesse looked up in time to see a huge wave roll past on the portside. 'We need to get below, Malc.'

All crew members came to the main cabin and buckled themselves into their bouncy, shock-absorbent seats. With the hatches tightly shut, it was a bit like sitting in a people carrier, but on a very rough road. There were three seats in front of the dark windscreen. Malc sat on the far left, Jesse was in the middle taking control of the boat, then Si was to his right on radar. Behind Si was the hatch to the survivors' space.

Behind Malc was Mickey and behind him in the doctor's chair was Kate. Opposite Kate, Jeff worked at the chart table. Outside it was definitely getting worse.

Inside, the noise of the engines was deafening. The air was getting uncomfortably hot. Coming off the top of a particularly big wave, the hull dropped through thin air until it smashed onto the trough below, rattling the teeth of everyone. The adrenaline running through the crew was tangible.

Jesse looked over to Si on the radar. 'Doing OK, Si?'

Si was usually the first to get sick. 'Could do with a bucket.'

'Kate?' Jesse called back. 'Pass a bucket to Si.'

After some quiet retching, Si looked a bit better.

Malcolm was next to go. 'Pass the bucket.'

Jesse had never suffered, but he also never underestimated the courage of his crew who felt so ill but still managed to concentrate on the job.

The radio crackled again. 'Trevay, this is Falmouth. How far?'

'We should be there in about ten minutes,' Jesse said.

On the radar, Si picked up an orange blip that looked about the right size for a yacht.

He told Jesse.

Jesse reached for his binoculars. 'Turn the lamps on, Malc.' Immediately the raging sea was illuminated and everyone focused their eyes through the rain-streaked windows.

'There,' said Malcolm as they rose to the top of a wave. 'You'll see it over the top of the next one.'

Jesse saw it. The mast was hanging like a broken limb. The mainsail torn and flapping in the strong wind. He scanned the deck for any sign of the two sailors. He couldn't see them but they were probably, hopefully, tucked below and riding it out.

Jesse steered *The Spirit* towards her, throttling back as he did so. 'Malc, take over,' Jesse barked. 'Open the hatch, Kate.' Opening a locker, he took out a loud-hailer, and climbed through the open hatch.

On deck the wind was strong and he ducked his head as a sheet of water threw itself at him. His eyes stung with the salt. Hanging onto the grab rails, he pulled himself round to starboard deck and raised the loud-hailer to his lips.

'Hello. This is Trevay Lifeboat. We're going to get along-side and give you a tow.'

The wind was ripping the words from his mouth and throwing them backwards, over his shoulder, away from the stricken yacht. He tried again. 'Hello. Is there anybody on board? Can you hear me?'

It was a tiny movement, but he saw a hand raised for a moment from the stern of the vessel.

'Are you OK?' he shouted again. The hand reappeared and gave a limp thumbs-up. Brian and Kate appeared next to him.

He quickly filled them in. 'The cockpit. He must be lying on the bottom. Look. See?'

The hand came up again and gave a painful wave.

Jesse put the loud-hailer to his mouth. 'Can you get a line to us?'

The hand gave a thumbs-down.

Malcolm nudged the lifeboat closer and closer to the damaged yacht. But the waves frustrated him. Eventually he got close enough for Don to leap across a tiny gap before the sea surged them apart again. Don pulled on the lifeboat's line and got it secured to a cleat on the yacht's bow. Now the boats pulled against each other. As one went up, the other came down.

Jesse watched as Don steadied himself and walked with uneven steps to the stern to check on the casualty. He jumped down into the cockpit and knelt so that Jesse could only just see the top of his head. After a few moments, Don stood up and shouted against the wind, miming injuries as he spoke.

Jesse turned to Kate. 'Did you get that?'

'I think he's saying it's a broken arm, shoulder and ankle. Do you want me to go over?'

'Let's get that line attached to the stern first. Brian!' he shouted. 'You and Si, get a line secure on the arse end.'

Mickey appeared on deck. 'Jesse, Falmouth are asking if you need the helicopter?'

'I'll know as soon as we find the second man. Tell them to give me a couple of minutes.'

Brian and Don had at last got the two boats tied together securely. 'Brian,' shouted Jesse, 'do you need Kate to come over?'

'No, let's get him on the lifeboat. Then she can have a look at him.'

'OK. What's happened to the other bloke?'

'His dad thinks the mast hit him.'

Jesse was exasperated. 'Well, have a fucking look then.'

Brian stood up out of the cockpit and stepped onto the deck, steadying himself on the low railing and edging slowly forward. The boat was pitching and yawing and a huge wave crashed over him. He spat out the worst of it and finally got to the torn and flapping sail. The cords attached to it were snapping and flicking with lethal unpredictability. He took an armful of the tough sailcloth and slowly bundled as much as he could into his arms, the wind tugging it all the while. Every armful, he looked underneath for the second man. As he stooped, the boat tipped sharply and he lost his footing. He slid across the deck on his hip, his eyes tight shut, waiting to hit something hard.

'Arrggh.' A cleat caught the hem of his trousers. His leg stopped but the rest of his body spun one hundred and eighty degrees before his head banged something hard. Another wave breached the deck and sea water flooded up his nose and into his mouth.

'Brian!' Jesse was shouting over the loud-hailer. 'Don! Brian's hit his head. Help him.'

Brian was dazed but able enough to board the lifeboat and be sent below to the survivors' space to be seen to by Kate. Getting the injured sailor out of the yacht's cockpit and below deck to join him was harder, but they did it.

'Trevay, this is Falmouth. Will you require the helicopter?'

Jesse, who'd gone to check on Brian, answered: 'Yes. I'm a crew member down. Possible concussion. One casualty taken off yacht with suspected multiple fractures. One person still missing, presumed under the mast and mainsail. Over.'

'Understood. It's on its way. Out.'

Jesse climbed back on deck. The wind had dropped and a small moon gave the scene a silvery shine. 'Don!'

Don was crouching on the deck of the yacht, one arm stuck under the opposite armpit. He looked grey.

'Don,' Jesse said again. 'What is it?'

'I've cut my hand.'

Jesse swore under his breath. 'Badly?' he asked.

Don nodded and brought the wounded hand out from under his arm. Even from where he was standing, Jesse could see the tendons shine white through the neatly sliced flesh.

'How the fuck did you do that?'

Don bent his head towards the flapping cords on the mainsail. 'I tried to catch one.'

'Right, let's get you back over here.'

'Falmouth. This is Trevay. I'm another crew member down. What's the ETA for the chopper?'

Jesse listened as the coastguard spoke to the helicopter. 'Trevay. This is Falmouth. Helicopter is about eighteen minutes away. Over.'

'We're going to find the other casualty. Out.'

Mickey volunteered. 'I'll find him.'

Jesse hesitated. He had three crew members to choose from. Malcolm, who was at the helm; Jeff, who was eager but hadn't been on the boat very long, and Mickey, who was more than capable – but could Jesse spare him?

Jesse looked from one man to the other. He made his decision. 'OK, Mickey, it's you, but be careful.'

Jesse watched as Mickey stepped nimbly from one boat to the other.

'It's a bit calmer. Not so bad,' shouted Mickey. He arrived at the flapping mass of sail and burrowed underneath it. Jesse held his breath, then Mickey popped out.

'Got him. He's unconscious but alive. As far as I can see, the mast is lying at an angle from one hip, across his stomach and up to his shoulder. I'll see if I can get to him.'

As Jesse watched, Mickey took a knife and started to cut the mainsail loose from its rigging. The wind was picking up a little and Jesse felt some rain in his face. The sea beneath his feet started to dance, and from the blackness rolled a wave twice as big as anything they'd seen that night.

'Mickey. Get down!' shouted Jesse, as the wave crashed on top of the yacht and spilled its weight on Mickey's head. It swept Jesse off his feet, but he held a grab rail and jammed his feet against the boat's side. As the water drained away, Jesse yelled, 'Mickey? Mickey?'

'It's OK. I'm OK,' came Mickey's voice.

Jesse saw him hanging over the edge of the yacht. Gripping tight to the railing, his legs in the sea. There was, at most, a metre and a half between both boats. If they were pushed closer together, Mickey would be crushed.

'Oh Jesus,' said Jesse. 'Malc!' he screamed.

Malcolm, at the helm, had seen what had happened and he was doing all he could to keep the boats at a safe distance.

Jesse knew what he had to do. 'I'm coming over, Mickey. I'm coming.'

Mickey, the muscles in his shoulders tearing with the effort of hanging on, shook his head. 'Get Jeff. You're the bleddy coxswain. You can't leave the boat.'

'Watch me.'

Jesse looked at the sea and counted the seconds in between the swell, then jumped, landing safely on the yacht.

'I've got you, Mickey.' He lay on the deck and grabbed Mickey's lifejacket. He got his hands under the shoulders and pulled.

'Thank God you'm a fucking skinny bastard,' he said as he pulled Mickey onto the deck. They lay side by side. Breathless and exhausted.

Mickey spoke first. 'I suppose this makes us even.'

'Even?' Jesse panted.

'Yeah, you saved my life and I saved yours.'

'You've lost me, mate.'

'All those years ago. Remember? The shelter on the harbour where you and Grant had your fight?'

Jesse felt the first stirrings of unease. 'It wasn't me. I found him. You saw the bloke who did it running away.'

Mickey looked at him incredulously. 'No. I didn't see anyone run away, as well you know. But I did see you kicking shit out of your brother. You killed him.'

'No. They never found who killed him.'

'Because I lied for you and saved your life.'

Jesse sat up. 'You've had more of a bang to the head than I thought, boy.'

'I protected you to protect Loveday,' said Mickey, staring at Jesse.

'What?'

Mickey sat up. His breath was ragged and he fought

to get the words out – tears mingled with salty sea water burned his eyes.

'I knew. I always knew I was second best. Grant told me once that you and Loveday had had a fling. The night before you married Greer. He told me that Hal, my Hal, was really your son.' Mickey spoke quietly. 'So you see, I'm as guilty as you. I wanted Grant dead too. To stop him spreading those lies. And when I saw you kicking and kicking and kicking him, I could have stopped you. But I didn't because I wanted him dead so I am as guilty of his murder as you are.'

Jesse edged over to Mickey and clung to him. Shaking him. 'No. No you didn't. I did it. I hated him. I didn't want him in my life.'

Mickey wiped his running nose and looked into Jesse's eyes. 'Tell me the truth. Tell me. Did you sleep with Loveday?'

From the lifeboat, Jeff appeared and shouted: 'The chopper's here.'

Jesse turned and looked into the sky. He saw the searchlight beam coming towards them and heard the thud of the rotor blades.

'Tell me, Jesse,' Mickey pleaded. 'Tell me the truth and we'll never speak of it again.'

The helicopter was directly behind Jesse now. The noise was intense. 'Tell me!' Mickey shouted.

'I'm going to do the right thing, Mickey.' He looked up to the helicopter and gave the thumbs-up to the pilot. The side door of the Sea King opened and the winch man appeared on his wire.

Jesse turned back to his best friend, his silhouette dark against the bright light. 'I love you, Mick.' He moved his hands to his life vest and started to undo its buckles, and then the zip. He took it off and chucked it down on the deck.

'What are you doing?' shouted Mickey, jumping to his feet.

'I'm sorry,' mouthed Jesse over the beat of the thundering rotor blades.

'Jesse, what the fuck are you doing?' screamed Mickey again.

Jesse moved towards Mickey and kissed him on both cheeks.

Then he walked backwards to the edge of the boat and jumped.

39

Greer had woken with a jolt. She looked at her bedside clock. 03.27.

She put a hand out to feel Jesse's side of the bed. Empty.

Turning her sidelight on she got out of bed and went downstairs. Maybe he was in the kitchen.

He wasn't.

She saw her phone and checked for texts from Jesse or Loveday. Nothing. She wondered if she should call Loveday, then decided against it. She'd wait another hour.

She was halfway up the stairs when she realised that the candle in the window had burnt down and extinguished itself. A chill hand gripped her heart.

The buzzer from the electric gates sounded by the front door. She walked calmly back down the stairs and towards the intercom. She lifted the receiver. 'Hello?'

'Mrs Behenna?'

'Yes.'

'Devon and Cornwall police. May we come in, please?'

*

The media arrived like sharks smelling blood. The survival of the two sailors on the yacht was noted, but it was the mystery of the hero coxswain who had taken off his lifejacket and drowned that caught the public's imagination.

Much was written. Little of it was truth.

*

At the inquest Mickey gave his evidence and stuck to the facts. Yes, Jesse was his normal self that day. No, there was nothing to suggest he was suicidal. Yes, he saw Jesse take off his lifejacket. No, he no idea why he had done that.

The coroner recorded an open verdict.

Jesse was never found.

*

A few months after his death, Mickey and Loveday came to see Greer. Jesse's death had hit her hard. Jesse had been everything to her, and her whole life had revolved around him. Her father had been roped in to manage the day-to-day affairs along with Mickey manning the boats. Edward Behenna and his wife were in deep shock at this unexpected blow to their family and it wasn't clear that Jan would ever recover. But both Hal and Freddie were surprising everyone with their handle on the business. Ideas of college had been forgotten for now, but she was glad that she'd encouraged Freddie with his school work. He had a good head for numbers.

Loveday had been a rock for Greer. As well as mucking in alongside everyone with Behenna and Clovelly, she had also helped Greer to keep her interior design business afloat. Greer hadn't taken on any new commissions, but in the back of her mind she hadn't quite given up on it.

Mickey and Greer took a walk down to the beach while Loveday prepared them a light lunch and sat down looking out at the *Sand Castle*, Jesse's cheerful family boat, which still lay moored, waiting for its skipper to take it out.

'Can I ask you something, Mickey?' Greer was still perfectly groomed, but her previously slim frame was now noticeably underweight, and grief and sleepless nights had all aged her in the last few months. Creases now appeared around her eyes and lips.

Mickey put his arms around his old friend. He knew Greer could be a cold fish, but he'd always felt a soft spot for her and wished he could do more to help her through this.

'Of course.'

'Do you think he killed himself?'

Mickey stared out at the big blue sea, calm today, but unpredictable and unknowable. He thought carefully about what to say for a moment. 'His mum always used to say still waters run deep with Jesse.'

'It's just . . .' Greer's voice caught and she struggled to get the words out. 'We had a big row. At our anniversary. I said some awful things that I didn't mean and he said . . . he said I wasn't his first choice.'

Mickey held her closer as sobs escaped her tiny frame.

'The thing is, Mickey . . . I've got this horrible feeling that Jesse wasn't happy. That all of this . . .' She swept her arm backwards to indicate the house and everything that went with it. '. . . Behenna and Clovelly, all of it . . . none of it was what he really wanted. There was something missing. Am I right, Mickey? Please tell me I've got it horribly wrong.'

Mickey thought about his best friend. The Jesse that he knew.

'Jesse did the right thing all his life, Greer, and deep down, I know that he wouldn't have changed a thing. We'll never really know what was in his mind that day, but I do know that he loved you and Freddie.'

Loveday's voice rang out behind them. 'Hey, you two. Lunch is up.' Loveday plonked herself down on the other side of Greer and put her arm around her too.

'I'm starving,' said Mickey. But Greer said nothing and continued to stare at the horizon, ensconced between her two friends but alone with her thoughts.

*

It was a sparkling February day and the clouds were racing across the bright Cornish sky. The small gathering of Trevay folk stood respectfully watching the handsome young man on the dais.

'And so I'd like to thank everyone who helped make this memorial to my father a reality.'

The crowd gave a round of applause and Freddie looked over his shoulder at his mother, who was standing with her hands folded over her neat navy coat. The wind had pulled a whip of hair from her neat bun and her face was expressionless.

'Mum.' Freddie held out his hand to her. 'Would you do the honours?'

She blinked away whatever memories she'd been sorting through and smiled. 'Yes.'

The blue velvet curtains opened smoothly as she pulled the cord, and revealed a simple plaque with Jesse's name and dates on it. There was a short inscription detailing his years with the RNLI and the event that led to his death.

More applause, and a few flashbulb pops as the local paper recorded the moment.

Freddie turned to face the crowd again, now joined by a smiley, petite blonde, who was holding a toddler on her hip.

'The mystery of my father's death may never be solved, but his memory lives on in Trevay. Sadly, we lost my granny, my dad's mum, at Easter, but I like to think she would be very proud of this memorial to her son. In fact, if we don't keep it polished, she'll come and haunt me.'

The crowd laughed.

'But I'm glad to say that my parents' best friends, Mickey and Loveday Chandler, have come all the way back from New Zealand to be with us today.'

The crowd swivelled, hoping to identify them.

'All right!' Mickey raised a hand and beamed at everyone. There were murmurs of recognition as the crowd spotted the tanned and smiling couple standing on the edge of the crowd.

Freddie continued, 'We had supper with Uncle Mickey and Auntie Loveday last night and they've asked me to tell you that anyone going over to New Zealand can have a free holiday with them, stay as long as you like.'

More laughter.

'But seriously . . .' Freddie quietened the crowd. 'They sound as if they're doing all right with their fishing trip business, and as soon as Jesse Junior,' he turned to the toddler on the young woman's hip and chucked him under the chin, 'and Miri and I can, we'll be coming to see you!'

Mickey put his hand up and waved, to another round of applause.

Freddie scanned the crowd. 'Hal? Where are you? Come up here.'

Hal, as tall and lanky as his father, was standing with Loveday and Mickey. He ducked his head when his name was called, hating public attention as much as Freddie loved it.

'Come on, Hal. Don't be shy,' urged Freddie.

Hal made his way through the people and stood next to Freddie, looking as uncomfortable as he felt.

Freddie put an arm round his shoulder. 'Hal Chandler is my best friend. Without him I wouldn't have coped when Dad died, or been able to learn the business without his help. He's got the brains from his mum not his dad!'

Loveday blushed and Mickey squeezed her hand.

Freddie laughed and carried on. 'We share the same birthday, Hal and I, and are brothers in all but name. Even though it's not our birthday till October, I'd like to give him an early birthday present. It's in recognition of all that your dad meant to my dad.' Freddie's voice developed a crack and he swallowed hard before managing to continue. 'Mum and I reckon this is what Dad would have done if he'd been alive, because he always treated us the same. From now on, the company formerly known as Behenna and Clovelly will be called . . .' He paused and looked into Hal's eyes. Loveday held her breath. Mickey clenched his jaw. '. . . Will be called . . . Behenna, Clovelly and Chandler.'

The End